CW01545727

Dog Days

Mavis Cheek was born and grew up in Wimbledon. She began her working life with the contemporary art publishers, Editions Alecto. London was lively and creative in the 'sixties and when Editions Alecto opened a gallery in the West End of London, Mavis worked there with artists such as David Hockney, Allen Jones, Patrick Caulfield, Gillian Ayres, Bridget Riley – from which she learned about modern and contemporary art. After twelve happy years at Editions Alecto, Mavis left to study at Hillcroft College for Women from where she graduated in Arts with distinction. When her daughter Bella was born shortly after graduating she began her writing career in earnest. Journalism and travel writing at first, then short stories, and eventually, in 1988, her novel Pause Between Acts was published by The Bodley Head and won the She/John Menzies First Novel Prize. She has published fifteen novels and her short stories are in various collections.

Mavis has served on both PEN and The Society of Authors committees and was for three years the judge of the McKitterick Prize for Fiction. She is a Fellow of MacDowell Colony, USA and has been the Royal Literature Fund Fellow at both Chichester University and the University of Reading. She is also the Founder and Patron of the Marlborough Literature Festival which aims to put authorship, rather than celebrity, back at the heart of literature festivals. It has proved a resounding success and proves that good writing will always be admired and cherished.

Since 1989 Mavis has run residential courses for the Arvon Foundation; for the Centre for Literature at Ty Newydd in Wales; at Dartington; at Stratford on Avon, Beverley, Charleston Festivals, among others, and at Marlborough College and various other venues and institutions at home and abroad from palaces to prisons. She lives and works in London.

Also By Mavis Cheek

Pause Between Acts
Parlour Games
Dog Days
Janice Gentle Gets Sexy
Aunt Margaret's Lover
Sleeping Beauties
Getting Back Brahms
Three Men on a Plane
Mrs Fytton's *Country Life*
The Sex Life of my Aunt
Patrick Parker's Progress
Yesterday's Houses
Amenable Women
Truth to Tell
The Lovers of Pound Hill

www.mavischeek.co.uk

THE ROBERT LOUIS STEVENSON THRILLER COLLECTION

The Strange Case of Dr. Jekyll & Mr. Hyde, The Master of Ballantrae, The Suicide Club, The Rajah's Diamond, The Bottle Imp, The Story of a Lie, The Body Snatcher

ROBERT LOUIS STEVENSON

This edition contains work that were originally published from 1882 to 1905 and are in the public domain. No claim is made with respect to public domain works.

This edition may reflect minor editorial revisions to the original text.

CONTENTS

THE STRANGE CASE OF DR. JEKYLL AND MR. HYDE

STORY OF THE DOOR

Mr. Utterson the lawyer was a man of a rugged countenance that was never lighted by a smile; cold, scanty and embarrassed in discourse; backward in sentiment; lean, long, dusty, dreary and yet somehow lovable. At friendly meetings, and when the wine was to his taste, something eminently human beaconed from his eye; something indeed which never found its way into his talk, but which spoke not only in these silent symbols of the after-dinner face, but more often and loudly in the acts of his life. He was austere with himself; drank gin when he was alone, to mortify a taste for vintages; and though he enjoyed the theatre, had not crossed the doors of one for twenty years. But he had an approved tolerance for others; sometimes wondering, almost with envy, at the high pressure of spirits involved in their misdeeds; and in any extremity inclined to help rather than to reprove. "I incline to Cain's heresy," he used to say quaintly: "I let my brother go to the devil in his own way." In this character, it was frequently his fortune to be the last reputable acquaintance and the last good influence in the lives of downgoing men. And to such as these, so long as they came about his chambers, he never marked a shade of change in his demeanour.

No doubt the feat was easy to Mr. Utterson; for he was undemonstrative at the best, and even his friendship seemed to be founded in a similar catholicity of good-nature. It is the mark of a modest man to accept his friendly circle ready-made from the hands of opportunity; and that was the lawyer's way. His friends were those of his own blood or those whom he had known the longest; his affections, like ivy, were the growth of time, they implied no aptness in the object. Hence, no doubt the bond that united him to Mr. Richard Enfield, his distant kinsman, the well-known man about town. It was a nut to crack for many, what these two could see in each other, or what subject they could find in common. It was reported by those who encountered them in their Sunday walks, that they said nothing, looked singularly dull and would hail with obvious relief the appearance of a friend. For all that, the two men put the greatest store by these excursions, counted them the chief jewel of each week, and not only set aside occasions of pleasure, but even resisted the calls of business, that they might enjoy them uninterrupted.

It chanced on one of these rambles that their way led them down a by-street in a busy quarter of London. The street was small and what is called quiet, but it drove a thriving trade on the weekdays. The inhabitants were all doing well, it seemed and all emulously hoping to do better still, and laying out the surplus of their grains in coquetry; so that the shop fronts stood along that thoroughfare with an air of invitation, like rows of smiling saleswomen. Even on Sunday, when it veiled its more florid charms and lay comparatively empty of passage, the street shone out in contrast to its dingy neighbourhood, like a fire in a forest; and with its freshly painted shutters, well-polished brasses, and general cleanliness and gaiety of note, instantly caught and pleased the eye of the passenger.

Two doors from one corner, on the left hand going east the line was broken by the entry of a court; and just at that point a certain sinister block of building thrust forward its gable on the street. It was two storeys high; showed no window, nothing but a door on the lower storey and a blind forehead of discoloured wall on the upper; and bore in every feature, the marks of prolonged and sordid negligence. The door, which was equipped with neither bell nor knocker, was blistered and distained. Tramps slouched into the recess and struck matches on the panels; children kept shop upon the steps; the schoolboy had tried his knife on the mouldings; and for close on a generation, no one had appeared to drive away these random visitors or to repair their ravages.

Mr. Enfield and the lawyer were on the other side of the by-street; but when they came abreast of the entry, the former lifted up his cane and pointed.

"Did you ever remark that door?" he asked; and when his companion had replied in the affirmative, "It is connected in my mind," added he, "with a very odd story."

"Indeed?" said Mr. Utterson, with a slight change of voice, "and what was that?"

"Well, it was this way," returned Mr. Enfield: "I was coming home from some place at the end of the world, about three o'clock of a black winter morning, and my way lay through a part of town where there was literally nothing to be seen but lamps. Street after street and all the folks asleep—street after street, all lighted up as if for a procession and all as empty as a church—till at last I got into that state of mind when a man listens and listens and begins to long for the sight of a policeman. All at once, I saw two figures: one a little man who was stumping along eastward at a good walk, and the other a girl of maybe eight or ten who was running as hard as she was able down a cross street. Well, sir, the two ran into one another naturally enough at the corner; and then came the horrible part of the thing; for the man trampled calmly over the child's body and left her screaming on the ground. It sounds nothing to hear, but it was hellish to see. It wasn't like a man; it was like some damned Juggernaut. I gave a few halloa, took to my heels, collared my gentleman, and brought him back to where there was already quite a group about the screaming child. He was perfectly cool and made no resistance, but gave me one look, so ugly that it brought out the sweat on me like running. The people who had turned out were the girl's own family; and pretty soon, the doctor, for whom she had been sent put in his appearance. Well, the child was not much the worse, more frightened, according to the sawbones; and there you might have supposed would be an end to it. But there was one curious circumstance. I had taken a loathing to my gentleman at first sight. So had the child's family, which was only natural. But the doctor's case was what struck me. He was the usual cut and dry apothecary, of no particular age and colour, with a strong Edinburgh accent and about as emotional as a bagpipe. Well, sir, he was like the rest of us; every time he looked at my prisoner, I saw that sawbones turn sick and white with the desire to kill him. I knew what was in his mind, just as he knew what was in mine; and killing being out of the question, we did the next best. We told the man we could and would make such a scandal out of this as should make his name stink from one end of London to the other. If he had any friends or any credit, we undertook that he should lose them. And all the time, as we were pitching it in red hot, we were keeping the women off him as best we could for they were as wild as harpies. I never saw a circle of such hateful faces; and there was the man in the middle, with a kind of black sneering coolness—frightened too, I could see that—but carrying it off, sir, really like Satan. 'If you choose to make capital out of this accident,' said he, 'I am naturally helpless. No gentleman but wishes to avoid a scene,' says he. 'Name your figure.' Well, we screwed him up to a hundred pounds for the child's family; he would have clearly liked to stick out; but there was something about the lot of us that meant mischief, and at last he struck. The next thing was to get the money; and where do you think he carried us but to that place with the door?—whipped out a key, went in, and presently came back with the matter of ten pounds in gold and a cheque for the balance on Coutts's, drawn payable to bearer and signed with a name that I can't mention, though it's one of the points of my story, but it was a name at least very well known and often printed. The figure was stiff; but the signature was good for more than that if it was only genuine. I took the liberty of pointing out to my gentleman that the whole business looked apocryphal, and that a man does not, in real life, walk into a cellar door at four in the morning and come out with another man's cheque for close upon a hundred pounds. But he was quite easy and sneering. 'Set your mind at rest,' says he, 'I will stay with you till the banks open and cash the cheque myself.' So we all set off, the doctor, and the child's father, and our friend and myself, and passed the rest of the night in my chambers; and next day, when we had breakfasted, went in a body to the bank. I gave in the cheque myself, and said I had every reason to believe it was a forgery. Not a bit of it. The cheque was genuine."

"Tut-tut!" said Mr. Utterson.

"I see you feel as I do," said Mr. Enfield. "Yes, it's a bad story. For my man was a fellow that nobody could have to do with, a really damnable man; and the person that drew the cheque is the very pink of the proprieties, celebrated too, and (what makes it worse) one of your fellows who do what they call good. Blackmail, I suppose; an honest man paying through the nose for some of the capers of his youth. Black Mail House is what I call the place with the door, in consequence. Though even that, you know, is far from explaining all," he added, and with the words fell into a vein of musing.

From this he was recalled by Mr. Utterson asking rather suddenly: "And you don't know if the drawer of the cheque lives there?"

"A likely place, isn't it?" returned Mr. Enfield. "But I happen to have noticed his address; he lives in some square or other."

"And you never asked about the—place with the door?" said Mr. Utterson.

"No, sir; I had a delicacy," was the reply. "I feel very strongly about putting questions; it partakes too much of the style of the day of judgment. You start a question, and it's like starting a stone. You sit quietly on the top of a hill; and away the stone goes, starting others; and presently some bland old bird (the last you would have thought of) is knocked on the head in his own back garden and the family have to change their name. No sir, I make it a rule of mine: the more it looks like Queer Street, the less I ask."

"A very good rule, too," said the lawyer.

"But I have studied the place for myself," continued Mr. Enfield. "It seems scarcely a house. There is no other door, and nobody goes in or out of that one but, once in a great while, the gentleman of my adventure. There are three windows looking on the court on the first floor; none below; the windows are always shut but they're clean. And then there is a chimney which is generally smoking; so somebody must live there. And yet it's not so sure; for the buildings are so packed together about the court, that it's hard to say where one ends and another begins."

The pair walked on again for a while in silence; and then "Enfield," said Mr. Utterson, "that's a good rule of yours."

"Yes, I think it is," returned Enfield.

"But for all that," continued the lawyer, "there's one point I want to ask. I want to ask the name of that man who walked over the child."

"Well," said Mr. Enfield, "I can't see what harm it would do. It was a man of the name of Hyde."

"Hm," said Mr. Utterson. "What sort of a man is he to see?"

"He is not easy to describe. There is something wrong with his appearance; something displeasing, something down-right detestable. I never saw a man I so disliked, and yet I scarce know why. He must be deformed somewhere; he gives a strong feeling of deformity, although I couldn't specify the point. He's an extraordinary looking man, and yet I really can name nothing out of the way. No, sir; I can make no hand of it; I can't describe him. And it's not want of memory; for I declare I can see him this moment."

Mr. Utterson again walked some way in silence and obviously under a weight of consideration. "You are sure he used a key?" he inquired at last.

"My dear sir..." began Enfield, surprised out of himself.

"Yes, I know," said Utterson; "I know it must seem strange. The fact is, if I do not ask you the name of the other party, it is because I know it already. You see, Richard, your tale has gone home. If you have been inexact in any point you had better correct it."

"I think you might have warned me," returned the other with a touch of sullenness. "But I have been pedantically exact, as you call it. The fellow had a key; and what's more, he has it still. I saw him use it not a week ago."

Mr. Utterson sighed deeply but said never a word; and the young man presently resumed. "Here is another lesson to say nothing," said he. "I am ashamed of my long tongue. Let us make a bargain never to refer to this again."

"With all my heart," said the lawyer. "I shake hands on that, Richard."

SEARCH FOR MR. HYDE

THAT EVENING MR. UTTERSON came home to his bachelor house in sombre spirits and sat down to dinner without relish. It was his custom of a Sunday, when this meal was over, to sit close by the fire, a volume of some dry divinity on his reading desk, until the clock of the neighbouring church rang out the hour of twelve, when he would go soberly and gratefully to bed. On this night however, as soon as the cloth was taken away, he took up a candle and went into his business room. There he opened his safe, took from the most private part of it a document endorsed on the envelope as Dr. Jekyll's Will and sat down with a clouded brow to study its contents. The will was holograph, for Mr. Utterson though he took charge of it now that it was made, had refused to lend the least assistance in the making of it; it provided not only that, in case of the decease of Henry Jekyll, M.D., D.C.L., L.L.D., F.R.S., etc., all his possessions were to pass into the hands of his "friend and benefactor Edward Hyde," but that in case of Dr. Jekyll's "disappearance or unexplained absence for any period exceeding three calendar months," the said Edward Hyde should step into the said Henry Jekyll's shoes without further delay and free from any burthen or obligation beyond the payment of a few small sums to the members of the doctor's household. This document had long been the lawyer's eyesore. It offended him both as a lawyer and as a lover of the sane and customary sides of life, to whom the fanciful was the immodest. And hitherto it was his ignorance of Mr. Hyde that had swelled his indignation; now, by a sudden turn, it was his knowledge. It was already bad enough when the name was but a name of which he could learn no more. It was worse when it began to be clothed upon with detestable attributes; and out of the shifting, insubstantial mists that had so long baffled his eye, there leaped up the sudden, definite presentment of a fiend.

"I thought it was madness," he said, as he replaced the obnoxious paper in the safe, "and now I begin to fear it is disgrace."

With that he blew out his candle, put on a greatcoat, and set forth in the direction of Cavendish Square, that citadel of medicine, where his friend, the great Dr. Lanyon, had his house and received his crowding patients. "If anyone knows, it will be Lanyon," he had thought.

The solemn butler knew and welcomed him; he was subjected to no stage of delay, but ushered direct from the door to the dining-room where Dr. Lanyon sat alone over his wine. This was a hearty, healthy, dapper, red-faced gentleman, with a shock of hair prematurely white, and a boisterous and decided manner. At sight of Mr. Utterson, he sprang up from his chair and welcomed him with both hands. The geniality, as was the way of the man, was somewhat theatrical to the eye; but it reposed on genuine feeling. For these two were old friends, old mates both at school and college, both thorough respectors of themselves and of each other, and what does not always follow, men who thoroughly enjoyed each other's company.

After a little rambling talk, the lawyer led up to the subject which so disagreeably preoccupied his mind.

"I suppose, Lanyon," said he, "you and I must be the two oldest friends that Henry Jekyll has?"

"I wish the friends were younger," chuckled Dr. Lanyon. "But I suppose we are. And what of that? I see little of him now."

"Indeed?" said Utterson. "I thought you had a bond of common interest."

"We had," was the reply. "But it is more than ten years since Henry Jekyll became too fanciful for me. He began to go wrong, wrong in mind; and though of course I continue to take an interest in him for old sake's sake, as they say, I see and I have seen devilish little of the man. Such unscientific balderdash," added the doctor, flushing suddenly purple, "would have estranged Damon and Pythias."

This little spirit of temper was somewhat of a relief to Mr. Utterson. "They have only differed on some point of science," he thought; and being a man of no scientific passions (except in the matter of conveyancing), he even added: "It is nothing worse than that!" He gave his friend a few seconds to recover his composure, and then approached the question he had come to put. "Did you ever come across a *protégé* of his—one Hyde?" he asked.

"Hyde?" repeated Lanyon. "No. Never heard of him. Since my time."

That was the amount of information that the lawyer carried back with him to the great, dark bed on which he tossed to and fro, until the small hours of the morning began to grow large. It was a night of little ease to his toiling mind, toiling in mere darkness and besieged by questions.

Six o'clock struck on the bells of the church that was so conveniently near to Mr. Utterson's dwelling, and still he was digging at the problem. Hitherto it had touched him on the intellectual side alone; but now his imagination also was engaged, or rather enslaved; and as he lay and tossed in the gross darkness of the night and the curtained room, Mr. Enfield's tale went by before his mind in a scroll of lighted pictures. He would be aware of the great field of lamps of a nocturnal city; then of the figure of a man walking swiftly; then of a child running from the doctor's; and then these met, and that human Juggernaut trod the child down and passed on regardless of her screams. Or else he would see a room in a rich house, where his friend lay asleep, dreaming and smiling at his dreams; and then the door of that room would be opened, the curtains of the bed plucked apart, the sleeper recalled, and lo! there would stand by his side a figure to whom power was given, and even at that dead hour, he must rise and do its bidding. The figure in these two phases haunted the lawyer all night; and if at any time he dozed over, it was but to see it glide more stealthily through sleeping houses, or move the more swiftly and still the more swiftly, even to dizziness, through wider labyrinths of lamplighted city, and at every street corner crush a child and leave her screaming. And still the figure had no face by which he might know it; even in his dreams, it had no face, or one that baffled him and melted before his eyes; and thus it was that there sprang up and grew apace in the lawyer's mind a singularly strong, almost an inordinate, curiosity to behold the features of the real Mr. Hyde. If he could but once set eyes on him, he thought the mystery would lighten and perhaps roll altogether away, as was the habit of mysterious things when well examined. He might see a reason for his friend's strange preference or bondage (call it which you please) and even for the startling clause of the will. At least it would be a face worth seeing: the face of a man who was without bowels of mercy: a face which had but to show itself to raise up, in the mind of the unimpressionable Enfield, a spirit of enduring hatred.

From that time forward, Mr. Utterson began to haunt the door in the by-street of shops. In the morning before office hours, at noon when business was plenty and time scarce, at night under the face of the fogged city moon, by all lights and at all hours of solitude or concourse, the lawyer was to be found on his chosen post.

"If he be Mr. Hyde," he had thought, "I shall be Mr. Seek."

And at last his patience was rewarded. It was a fine dry night; frost in the air; the streets as clean as a ballroom floor; the lamps, unshaken by any wind, drawing a regular pattern of light and shadow. By ten o'clock, when the shops were closed, the by-street was very solitary and, in spite of the low growl of London from all round, very silent. Small sounds carried far; domestic sounds out of the houses were clearly audible on either side of the roadway; and the rumour of the approach of any passenger preceded him by a long time. Mr. Utterson had been some minutes at his post, when he was aware of an odd light footstep drawing near. In the course of his nightly patrols, he had long grown accustomed to the quaint effect with which the footfalls of a single person, while he is still a great way off, suddenly spring out distinct from the vast hum and clatter of the city. Yet his attention had never before been so sharply and decisively arrested; and it was with a strong, superstitious prevision of success that he withdrew into the entry of the court.

The steps drew swiftly nearer, and swelled out suddenly louder as they turned the end of the street. The lawyer, looking forth from the entry, could soon see what manner of man he had to deal with. He was small and very plainly dressed and the look of him, even at that distance, went somehow strongly against the watcher's inclination. But he made straight for the door, crossing the roadway to save time; and as he came, he drew a key from his pocket like one approaching home.

Mr. Utterson stepped out and touched him on the shoulder as he passed. "Mr. Hyde, I think?"

Mr. Hyde shrank back with a hissing intake of the breath. But his fear was only momentary; and though he did not look the lawyer in the face, he answered coolly enough: "That is my name. What do you want?"

"I see you are going in," returned the lawyer. "I am an old friend of Dr. Jekyll's—Mr. Utterson of Gaunt Street—you must have heard of my name; and meeting you so conveniently, I thought you might admit me."

"You will not find Dr. Jekyll; he is from home," replied Mr. Hyde, blowing in the key. And then suddenly, but still without looking up, "How did you know me?" he asked.

"On your side," said Mr. Utterson "will you do me a favour?"

"With pleasure," replied the other. "What shall it be?"

"Will you let me see your face?" asked the lawyer.

Mr. Hyde appeared to hesitate, and then, as if upon some sudden reflection, fronted about with an air of defiance; and the pair stared at each other pretty fixedly for a few seconds. "Now I shall know you again," said Mr. Utterson. "It may be useful."

"Yes," returned Mr. Hyde, "It is as well we have met; and *à propos*, you should have my address." And he gave a number of a street in Soho.

"Good God!" thought Mr. Utterson, "can he, too, have been thinking of the will?" But he kept his feelings to himself and only grunted in acknowledgment of the address.

"And now," said the other, "how did you know me?"

"By description," was the reply.

"Whose description?"

"We have common friends," said Mr. Utterson.

"Common friends," echoed Mr. Hyde, a little hoarsely. "Who are they?"

"Jekyll, for instance," said the lawyer.

"He never told you," cried Mr. Hyde, with a flush of anger. "I did not think you would have lied."

"Come," said Mr. Utterson, "that is not fitting language."

The other snarled aloud into a savage laugh; and the next moment, with extraordinary quickness, he had unlocked the door and disappeared into the house.

The lawyer stood awhile when Mr. Hyde had left him, the picture of disquietude. Then he began slowly to mount the street, pausing every step or two and putting his hand to his brow like a man in mental perplexity. The problem he was thus debating as he walked, was one of a class that is rarely solved. Mr. Hyde was pale and dwarfish, he gave an impression of deformity without any nameable malformation, he had a displeasing smile, he had borne himself to the lawyer with a sort of murderous mixture of timidity and boldness, and he spoke with a husky, whispering and somewhat broken voice; all these were points against him, but not all of these together could explain the hitherto unknown disgust, loathing and fear with which Mr. Utterson regarded him. "There must be something else," said the perplexed gentleman. "There *is* something more, if I could find a name for it. God bless me, the man seems hardly human! Something troglodytic, shall we say? or can it be the old story of Dr. Fell? or is it the mere radiance of a foul soul that thus transpires through, and transfigures, its clay continent? The last, I think; for, O my poor old Harry Jekyll, if ever I read Satan's signature upon a face, it is on that of your new friend."

Round the corner from the by-street, there was a square of ancient, handsome houses, now for the most part decayed from their high estate and let in flats and chambers to all sorts and conditions of men; map-engravers, architects, shady lawyers and the agents of obscure enterprises. One house, however, second from the corner, was still occupied entire; and at the door of this, which wore a great air of wealth and comfort, though it was now plunged in darkness except for the fanlight, Mr. Utterson stopped and knocked. A well-dressed, elderly servant opened the door.

"Is Dr. Jekyll at home, Poole?" asked the lawyer.

"I will see, Mr. Utterson," said Poole, admitting the visitor, as he spoke, into a large, low-roofed, comfortable hall paved with flags, warmed (after the fashion of a country house) by a bright, open fire, and furnished with costly cabinets of oak. "Will you wait here by the fire, sir? or shall I give you a light in the dining-room?"

"Here, thank you," said the lawyer, and he drew near and leaned on the tall fender. This hall, in which he was now left alone, was a pet fancy of his friend the doctor's; and Utterson himself was wont to speak of it as the pleasantest room in London. But tonight there was a shudder in his blood; the face of Hyde sat heavy on his memory; he felt (what was rare with him) a nausea and distaste of life; and in the gloom of his spirits, he seemed to read a menace in the flickering of the firelight on the polished cabinets and the uneasy starting of the shadow on the roof. He was ashamed of his relief, when Poole presently returned to announce that Dr. Jekyll was gone out.

"I saw Mr. Hyde go in by the old dissecting room, Poole," he said. "Is that right, when Dr. Jekyll is from home?"

"Quite right, Mr. Utterson, sir," replied the servant. "Mr. Hyde has a key."

"Your master seems to repose a great deal of trust in that young man, Poole," resumed the other musingly.

"Yes, sir, he does indeed," said Poole. "We have all orders to obey him."

"I do not think I ever met Mr. Hyde?" asked Utterson.

"O, dear no, sir. He never *dines* here," replied the butler. "Indeed we see very little of him on this side of the house; he mostly comes and goes by the laboratory."

"Well, good-night, Poole."

"Good-night, Mr. Utterson."

And the lawyer set out homeward with a very heavy heart. "Poor Harry Jekyll," he thought, "my mind misgives me he is in deep waters! He was wild when he was young; a long while ago to be sure; but in the law of God, there is no statute of limitations. Ay, it must be that; the ghost of some old sin, the cancer of some concealed disgrace: punishment coming, *pede claudo*, years after memory has forgotten and self-love condoned the fault." And the lawyer, scared by the thought, brooded awhile on his own past, groping in all the corners of memory, least by chance some Jack-in-the-Box of an old iniquity should leap to light there. His past was fairly blameless; few men could read the rolls of their life with less apprehension; yet he was humbled to the dust by the many ill things he had done, and raised up again into a sober and fearful gratitude by the many he had come so near to doing yet avoided. And then by a return on his former subject, he conceived a spark of hope. "This Master Hyde, if he were studied," thought he, "must have secrets of his own; black secrets, by the look of him; secrets compared to which poor Jekyll's worst would be like sunshine. Things cannot continue as they are. It turns me cold to think of this creature stealing like a thief to Harry's bedside; poor Harry, what a wakening! And the danger of it; for if this Hyde suspects the existence of the will, he may grow impatient to inherit. Ay, I must put my shoulders to the wheel—if Jekyll will but let me," he added, "if Jekyll will only let me." For once more he saw before his mind's eye, as clear as transparency, the strange clauses of the will.

DR. JEKYLL WAS QUITE AT EASE

A FORTNIGHT LATER, by excellent good fortune, the doctor gave one of his pleasant dinners to some five or six old cronies, all intelligent, reputable men and all judges of good wine; and Mr. Utterson so contrived that he remained behind after the others had departed. This was no new arrangement, but a thing that had befallen many scores of times. Where Utterson was liked, he was liked well. Hosts loved to detain the dry lawyer, when the light-hearted and loose-tongued had already their foot on the threshold; they liked to sit a while in his unobtrusive company, practising for solitude, sobering their minds in the man's rich silence after the expense and strain of gaiety. To this rule, Dr. Jekyll was no exception; and as he now sat on the opposite side of the fire—a large, well-made, smooth-faced man of fifty, with something of a stylish cast perhaps, but every mark of capacity and kindness—you could see by his looks that he cherished for Mr. Utterson a sincere and warm affection.

"I have been wanting to speak to you, Jekyll," began the latter. "You know that will of yours?"

A close observer might have gathered that the topic was distasteful; but the doctor carried it off gaily. "My poor Utterson," said he, "you are unfortunate in such a client. I never saw a man so distressed as you were by my will; unless it were that hide-bound pedant, Lanyon, at what he called my scientific heresies. O, I know he's a good fellow—you needn't frown—an excellent fellow, and I always mean to see more of him; but a hide-bound pedant for all that; an ignorant, blatant pedant. I was never more disappointed in any man than Lanyon."

"You know I never approved of it," pursued Utterson, ruthlessly disregarding the fresh topic.

"My will? Yes, certainly, I know that," said the doctor, a trifle sharply. "You have told me so."

"Well, I tell you so again," continued the lawyer. "I have been learning something of young Hyde."

The large handsome face of Dr. Jekyll grew pale to the very lips, and there came a blackness about his eyes. "I do not care to hear more," said he. "This is a matter I thought we had agreed to drop."

"What I heard was abominable," said Utterson.

"It can make no change. You do not understand my position," returned the doctor, with a certain incoherency of manner. "I am painfully situated, Utterson; my position is a very strange —a very strange one. It is one of those affairs that cannot be mended by talking."

"Jekyll," said Utterson, "you know me: I am a man to be trusted. Make a clean breast of this in confidence; and I make no doubt I can get you out of it."

"My good Utterson," said the doctor, "this is very good of you, this is downright good of you, and I cannot find words to thank you in. I believe you fully; I would trust you before any man alive, ay, before myself, if I could make the choice; but indeed it isn't what you fancy; it is not as bad as that; and just to put your good heart at rest, I will tell you one thing: the moment I choose, I can be rid of Mr. Hyde. I give you my hand upon that; and I thank you again and again; and I will just add one little word, Utterson, that I'm sure you'll take in good part: this is a private matter, and I beg of you to let it sleep."

Utterson reflected a little, looking in the fire.

"I have no doubt you are perfectly right," he said at last, getting to his feet.

"Well, but since we have touched upon this business, and for the last time I hope," continued the doctor, "there is one point I should like you to understand. I have really a very great interest in poor Hyde. I know you have seen him; he told me so; and I fear he was rude. But I do sincerely take a great, a very great interest in that young man; and if I am taken away, Utterson, I wish you to promise me that you will bear with him and get his rights for him. I think you would, if you knew all; and it would be a weight off my mind if you would promise."

"I can't pretend that I shall ever like him," said the lawyer.

"I don't ask that," pleaded Jekyll, laying his hand upon the other's arm; "I only ask for justice; I only ask you to help him for my sake, when I am no longer here."

Utterson heaved an irrepressible sigh. "Well," said he, "I promise."

THE CAREW MURDER CASE

Nearly a year later, in the month of October, 18—, London was startled by a crime of singular ferocity and rendered all the more notable by the high position of the victim. The details were few and startling. A maid servant living alone in a house not far from the river, had gone upstairs to bed about eleven. Although a fog rolled over the city in the small hours, the early part of the night was cloudless, and the lane, which the maid's window overlooked, was brilliantly lit by the full moon. It seems she was romantically given, for she sat down upon her box, which stood immediately under the window, and fell into a dream of musing. Never (she used to say, with streaming tears, when she narrated that experience), never had she felt more at peace with all men or thought more kindly of the world. And as she so sat she became aware of an aged beautiful gentleman with white hair, drawing near along the lane; and advancing to meet him, another and very small gentleman, to whom at first she paid less attention. When they had come within speech (which was just under the maid's eyes) the older man bowed and accosted the other with a very pretty manner of politeness. It did not seem as if the subject of his address were of great importance; indeed, from his pointing, it sometimes appeared as if he were only inquiring his way; but the moon shone on his face as he spoke, and the girl was pleased to watch it, it seemed to breathe such an innocent and old-world kindness of disposition, yet with something high too, as of a well-founded self-content. Presently her eye wandered to the other, and she was surprised to recognise in him a certain Mr. Hyde, who had once visited her master and for whom she had conceived a dislike. He had in his hand a heavy cane, with which he was trifling; but he answered never a word, and seemed to listen with an ill-contained impatience. And then all of a sudden he broke out in a great flame of anger, stamping with his foot, brandishing the cane, and carrying on (as the maid described it) like a madman. The old gentleman took a step back, with the air of one very much surprised and a trifle hurt; and at that Mr. Hyde broke out of all bounds and clubbed him to the earth. And next moment, with ape-like fury, he was trampling his victim under foot and hailing down a storm of blows, under which the bones were audibly shattered and the body jumped upon the roadway. At the horror of these sights and sounds, the maid fainted.

It was two o'clock when she came to herself and called for the police. The murderer was gone long ago; but there lay his victim in the middle of the lane, incredibly mangled. The stick with which the deed had been done, although it was of some rare and very tough and heavy wood, had broken in the middle under the stress of this insensate cruelty; and one splintered half had rolled in the neighbouring gutter—the other, without doubt, had been carried away by the murderer. A purse and gold watch were found upon the victim: but no cards or papers, except a sealed and stamped envelope, which he had been probably carrying to the post, and which bore the name and address of Mr. Utterson.

This was brought to the lawyer the next morning, before he was out of bed; and he had no sooner seen it and been told the circumstances, than he shot out a solemn lip. "I shall say nothing till I have seen the body," said he; "this may be very serious. Have the kindness to wait while I dress." And with the same grave countenance he hurried through his breakfast and drove to the police station, whither the body had been carried. As soon as he came into the cell, he nodded.

"Yes," said he, "I recognise him. I am sorry to say that this is Sir Danvers Carew."

"Good God, sir," exclaimed the officer, "is it possible?" And the next moment his eye lighted up with professional ambition. "This will make a deal of noise," he said. "And perhaps you can help us to the man." And he briefly narrated what the maid had seen, and showed the broken stick.

Mr. Utterson had already quailed at the name of Hyde; but when the stick was laid before him, he could doubt no longer; broken and battered as it was, he recognised it for one that he had himself presented many years before to Henry Jekyll.

"Is this Mr. Hyde a person of small stature?" he inquired.

"Particularly small and particularly wicked-looking, is what the maid calls him," said the officer.

Mr. Utterson reflected; and then, raising his head, "If you will come with me in my cab," he said, "I think I can take you to his house."

It was by this time about nine in the morning, and the first fog of the season. A great chocolate-coloured pall lowered over heaven, but the wind was continually charging and routing these embattled vapours; so that as the cab crawled from street to street, Mr. Utterson beheld a marvelous number of degrees and hues of twilight; for here it would be dark like the back-end of evening; and there would be a glow of a rich, lurid brown, like the light of some strange conflagration; and here, for a moment, the fog would be quite broken up, and a haggard shaft of daylight would glance in between the swirling wreaths. The dismal quarter of Soho seen under these changing glimpses, with its muddy ways, and slatternly passengers, and its lamps, which had never been extinguished or had been kindled afresh to combat this mournful reinvasion of darkness, seemed, in the lawyer's eyes, like a district of some city in a nightmare. The thoughts of his mind, besides, were of the gloomiest dye; and when he glanced at the companion of his drive, he was conscious of some touch of that terror of the law and the law's officers, which may at times assail the most honest.

As the cab drew up before the address indicated, the fog lifted a little and showed him a dingy street, a gin palace, a low French eating house, a shop for the retail of penny numbers and twopenny salads, many ragged children huddled in the doorways, and many women of many different nationalities passing out, key in hand, to have a morning glass; and the next moment the fog settled down again upon that part, as brown as umber, and cut him off from his blackguardly surroundings. This was the home of Henry Jekyll's favourite; of a man who was heir to a quarter of a million sterling.

An ivory-faced and silvery-haired old woman opened the door. She had an evil face, smoothed by hypocrisy: but her manners were excellent. Yes, she said, this was Mr. Hyde's, but he was not at home; he had been in that night very late, but he had gone away again in less than an hour; there was nothing strange in that; his habits were very irregular, and he was often absent; for instance, it was nearly two months since she had seen him till yesterday.

"Very well, then, we wish to see his rooms," said the lawyer; and when the woman began to declare it was impossible, "I had better tell you who this person is," he added. "This is Inspector Newcomen of Scotland Yard."

A flash of odious joy appeared upon the woman's face. "Ah!" said she, "he is in trouble! What has he done?"

Mr. Utterson and the inspector exchanged glances. "He don't seem a very popular character," observed the latter. "And now, my good woman, just let me and this gentleman have a look about us."

In the whole extent of the house, which but for the old woman remained otherwise empty, Mr. Hyde had only used a couple of rooms; but these were furnished with luxury and good taste. A closet was filled with wine; the plate was of silver, the napery elegant; a good picture hung upon the walls, a gift (as Utterson supposed) from Henry Jekyll, who was much of a connoisseur; and the carpets were of many plies and agreeable in colour. At this moment, however, the rooms bore every mark of having been recently and hurriedly ransacked; clothes lay about the floor, with their pockets inside out; lock-fast drawers stood open; and on the hearth there lay a pile of grey ashes, as though many papers had been burned. From these embers the inspector disinterred the butt end of a green cheque book, which had resisted the action of the fire; the other half of the stick was found behind the door; and as this clinched his suspicions, the officer declared himself delighted. A visit to the bank, where several thousand pounds were found to be lying to the murderer's credit, completed his gratification.

"You may depend upon it, sir," he told Mr. Utterson: "I have him in my hand. He must have lost his head, or he never would have left the stick or, above all, burned the cheque book. Why, money's life to the man. We have nothing to do but wait for him at the bank, and get out the handbills."

This last, however, was not so easy of accomplishment; for Mr. Hyde had numbered few familiars—even the master of the servant maid had only seen him twice; his family could nowhere be traced; he had never been photographed; and the few who could describe him differed widely, as common observers will. Only on one point were they agreed; and that was the haunting sense of unexpressed deformity with which the fugitive impressed his beholders.

INCIDENT OF THE LETTER

It was late in the afternoon, when Mr. Utterson found his way to Dr. Jekyll's door, where he was at once admitted by Poole, and carried down by the kitchen offices and across a yard which had once been a garden, to the building which was indifferently known as the laboratory or dissecting rooms. The doctor had bought the house from the heirs of a celebrated surgeon; and his own tastes being rather chemical than anatomical, had changed the destination of the block at the bottom of the garden. It was the first time that the lawyer had been received in that part of his friend's quarters; and he eyed the dingy, windowless structure with curiosity, and gazed round with a distasteful sense of strangeness as he crossed the theatre, once crowded with eager students and now lying gaunt and silent, the tables laden with chemical apparatus, the floor strewn with crates and littered with packing straw, and the light falling dimly through the foggy cupola. At the further end, a flight of stairs mounted to a door covered with red baize; and through this, Mr. Utterson was at last received into the doctor's cabinet. It was a large room fitted round with glass presses, furnished, among other things, with a cheval-glass and a business table, and looking out upon the court by three dusty windows barred with iron. The fire burned in the grate; a lamp was set lighted on the chimney shelf, for even in the houses the fog began to lie thickly; and there, close up to the warmth, sat Dr. Jekyll, looking deathly sick. He did not rise to meet his visitor, but held out a cold hand and bade him welcome in a changed voice.

"And now," said Mr. Utterson, as soon as Poole had left them, "you have heard the news?"

The doctor shuddered. "They were crying it in the square," he said. "I heard them in my dining-room."

"One word," said the lawyer. "Carew was my client, but so are you, and I want to know what I am doing. You have not been mad enough to hide this fellow?"

"Utterson, I swear to God," cried the doctor, "I swear to God I will never set eyes on him again. I bind my honour to you that I am done with him in this world. It is all at an end. And indeed he does not want my help; you do not know him as I do; he is safe, he is quite safe; mark my words, he will never more be heard of."

The lawyer listened gloomily; he did not like his friend's feverish manner. "You seem pretty sure of him," said he; "and for your sake, I hope you may be right. If it came to a trial, your name might appear."

"I am quite sure of him," replied Jekyll; "I have grounds for certainty that I cannot share with any one. But there is one thing on which you may advise me. I have—I have received a letter; and I am at a loss whether I should show it to the police. I should like to leave it in your hands, Utterson; you would judge wisely, I am sure; I have so great a trust in you."

"You fear, I suppose, that it might lead to his detection?" asked the lawyer.

"No," said the other. "I cannot say that I care what becomes of Hyde; I am quite done with him. I was thinking of my own character, which this hateful business has rather exposed."

Utterson ruminated awhile; he was surprised at his friend's selfishness, and yet relieved by it. "Well," said he, at last, "let me see the letter."

The letter was written in an odd, upright hand and signed "Edward Hyde": and it signified, briefly enough, that the writer's benefactor, Dr. Jekyll, whom he had long so unworthily repaid for a thousand generosities, need labour under no alarm for his safety, as he had means of escape on which he placed a sure dependence. The lawyer liked this letter well enough; it put a better colour on the intimacy than he had looked for; and he blamed himself for some of his past suspicions.

"Have you the envelope?" he asked.

"I burned it," replied Jekyll, "before I thought what I was about. But it bore no postmark. The note was handed in."

"Shall I keep this and sleep upon it?" asked Utterson.

"I wish you to judge for me entirely," was the reply. "I have lost confidence in myself."

"Well, I shall consider," returned the lawyer. "And now one word more: it was Hyde who dictated the terms in your will about that disappearance?"

The doctor seemed seized with a qualm of faintness; he shut his mouth tight and nodded.

"I knew it," said Utterson. "He meant to murder you. You had a fine escape."

"I have had what is far more to the purpose," returned the doctor solemnly: "I have had a lesson—O God, Utterson, what a lesson I have had!" And he covered his face for a moment with his hands.

On his way out, the lawyer stopped and had a word or two with Poole. "By the bye," said he, "there was a letter handed in to-day: what was the messenger like?" But Poole was positive nothing had come except by post; "and only circulars by that," he added.

This news sent off the visitor with his fears renewed. Plainly the letter had come by the laboratory door; possibly, indeed, it had been written in the cabinet; and if that were so, it must be differently judged, and handled with the more caution. The newsboys, as he went, were crying themselves hoarse along the footways: "Special edition. Shocking murder of an M.P." That was the funeral oration of one friend and client; and he could not help a certain apprehension lest the good name of another should be sucked down in the eddy of the scandal. It was, at least, a ticklish decision that he had to make; and self-reliant as he was by habit, he began to cherish a longing for advice. It was not to be had directly; but perhaps, he thought, it might be fished for.

Presently after, he sat on one side of his own hearth, with Mr. Guest, his head clerk, upon the other, and midway between, at a nicely calculated distance from the fire, a bottle of a particular old wine that had long dwelt unsunned in the foundations of his house. The fog still slept on the wing above the drowned city, where the lamps glimmered like carbuncles; and through the muffle and smother of these fallen clouds, the procession of the town's life was still rolling in through the great arteries with a sound as of a mighty wind. But the room was gay with firelight. In the bottle the acids were long ago resolved; the imperial dye had softened with time, as the colour grows richer in stained windows; and the glow of hot autumn afternoons on hillside vineyards, was ready to be set free and to disperse the fogs of London. Insensibly the lawyer melted. There was no man from whom he kept fewer secrets than Mr. Guest; and he was not always sure that he kept as many as he meant. Guest had often been on business to the doctor's; he knew Poole; he could scarce have failed to hear of Mr. Hyde's familiarity about the house; he might draw conclusions: was it not as well, then, that he should see a letter which put that mystery to right? and above all since Guest, being a great student and critic of handwriting, would consider the step natural and obliging? The clerk, besides, was a man of counsel; he could scarce read so strange a document without dropping a remark; and by that remark Mr. Utterson might shape his future course.

"This is a sad business about Sir Danvers," he said.

"Yes, sir, indeed. It has elicited a great deal of public feeling," returned Guest. "The man, of course, was mad."

"I should like to hear your views on that," replied Utterson. "I have a document here in his handwriting; it is between ourselves, for I scarce know what to do about it; it is an ugly business at the best. But there it is; quite in your way: a murderer's autograph."

Guest's eyes brightened, and he sat down at once and studied it with passion. "No sir," he said: "not mad; but it is an odd hand."

"And by all accounts a very odd writer," added the lawyer.

Just then the servant entered with a note.

"Is that from Dr. Jekyll, sir?" inquired the clerk. "I thought I knew the writing. Anything private, Mr. Utterson?"

"Only an invitation to dinner. Why? Do you want to see it?"

"One moment. I thank you, sir;" and the clerk laid the two sheets of paper alongside and sedulously compared their contents. "Thank you, sir," he said at last, returning both; "it's a very interesting autograph."

There was a pause, during which Mr. Utterson struggled with himself. "Why did you compare them, Guest?" he inquired suddenly.

"Well, sir," returned the clerk, "there's a rather singular resemblance; the two hands are in many points identical: only differently sloped."

"Rather quaint," said Utterson.

"It is, as you say, rather quaint," returned Guest.

"I wouldn't speak of this note, you know," said the master.

"No, sir," said the clerk. "I understand."

But no sooner was Mr. Utterson alone that night, than he locked the note into his safe, where it reposed from that time forward. "What!" he thought. "Henry Jekyll forge for a murderer!" And his blood ran cold in his veins.

INCIDENT OF DR. LANYON

TIME RAN ON; thousands of pounds were offered in reward, for the death of Sir Danvers was resented as a public injury; but Mr. Hyde had disappeared out of the ken of the police as though he had never existed. Much of his past was unearthed, indeed, and all disreputable: tales came out of the man's cruelty, at once so callous and violent; of his vile life, of his strange associates, of the hatred that seemed to have surrounded his career; but of his present whereabouts, not a whisper. From the time he had left the house in Soho on the morning of the murder, he was simply blotted out; and gradually, as time drew on, Mr. Utterson began to recover from the hotness of his alarm, and to grow more at quiet with himself. The death of Sir Danvers was, to his way of thinking, more than paid for by the disappearance of Mr. Hyde. Now that that evil influence had been withdrawn, a new life began for Dr. Jekyll. He came out of his seclusion, renewed relations with his friends, became once more their familiar guest and entertainer; and whilst he had always been known for charities, he was now no less distinguished for religion. He was busy, he was much in the open air, he did good; his face seemed to open and brighten, as if with an inward consciousness of service; and for more than two months, the doctor was at peace.

On the 8th of January Utterson had dined at the doctor's with a small party; Lanyon had been there; and the face of the host had looked from one to the other as in the old days when the trio were inseparable friends. On the 12th, and again on the 14th, the door was shut against the lawyer. "The doctor was confined to the house," Poole said, "and saw no one." On the 15th, he tried again, and was again refused; and having now been used for the last two months to see his friend almost daily, he found this return of solitude to weigh upon his spirits. The fifth night he had in Guest to dine with him; and the sixth he betook himself to Dr. Lanyon's.

There at least he was not denied admittance; but when he came in, he was shocked at the change which had taken place in the doctor's appearance. He had his death-warrant written legibly upon his face. The rosy man had grown pale; his flesh had fallen away; he was visibly balder and older; and yet it was not so much these tokens of a swift physical decay that arrested the lawyer's notice, as a look in the eye and quality of manner that seemed to testify to some deep-seated terror of the mind. It was unlikely that the doctor should fear death; and yet that was what Utterson was tempted to suspect. "Yes," he thought; "he is a doctor, he must know his own state and that his days are counted; and the knowledge is more than he can bear." And yet when Utterson remarked on his ill looks, it was with an air of great firmness that Lanyon declared himself a doomed man.

"I have had a shock," he said, "and I shall never recover. It is a question of weeks. Well, life has been pleasant; I liked it; yes, sir, I used to like it. I sometimes think if we knew all, we should be more glad to get away."

"Jekyll is ill, too," observed Utterson. "Have you seen him?"

But Lanyon's face changed, and he held up a trembling hand. "I wish to see or hear no more of Dr. Jekyll," he said in a loud, unsteady voice. "I am quite done with that person; and I beg that you will spare me any allusion to one whom I regard as dead."

"Tut, tut!" said Mr. Utterson; and then after a considerable pause, "Can't I do anything?" he inquired. "We are three very old friends, Lanyon; we shall not live to make others."

"Nothing can be done," returned Lanyon; "ask himself."

"He will not see me," said the lawyer.

"I am not surprised at that," was the reply. "Some day, Utterson, after I am dead, you may perhaps come to learn the right and wrong of this. I cannot tell you. And in the meantime, if you can sit and talk with me of other things, for God's sake, stay and do so; but if you cannot keep clear of this accursed topic, then in God's name, go, for I cannot bear it."

As soon as he got home, Utterson sat down and wrote to Jekyll, complaining of his exclusion from the house, and asking the cause of this unhappy break with Lanyon; and the next day brought him a long answer, often very pathetically worded, and sometimes darkly mysterious in drift. The quarrel with Lanyon was incurable. "I do not blame our old friend," Jekyll wrote, "but I share his view that we must never meet. I mean from henceforth to lead a life of extreme seclusion; you must not be surprised, nor must you doubt my friendship, if my door is often shut even to you. You must suffer me to go my own dark way. I have brought on myself a punishment and a danger that I cannot name. If I am the chief of sinners, I am the chief of sufferers also. I could not think that this earth contained a place for sufferings and terrors so unmanning; and you can do but one thing, Utterson, to lighten this destiny, and that is to respect my silence." Utterson was amazed; the dark influence of Hyde had been withdrawn, the doctor had returned to his old tasks and amities; a week ago, the prospect had smiled with every promise of a cheerful and an honoured age; and now in a moment, friendship, and peace of mind, and the whole tenor of his life were wrecked. So great and unprepared a change pointed to madness; but in view of Lanyon's manner and words, there must lie for it some deeper ground.

A week afterwards Dr. Lanyon took to his bed, and in something less than a fortnight he was dead. The night after the funeral, at which he had been sadly affected, Utterson locked the door of his business room, and sitting there by the light of a melancholy candle, drew out and set before him an envelope addressed by the hand and sealed with the seal of his dead friend. "PRIVATE: for the hands of G. J. Utterson ALONE, and in case of his predecease *to be destroyed unread,*" so it was emphatically superscribed; and the lawyer dreaded to behold the contents. "I have buried one friend to-day," he thought: "what if this should cost me another?" And then he condemned the fear as a disloyalty, and broke the seal. Within there was another enclosure, likewise sealed, and marked upon the cover as "not to be opened till the death or disappearance of Dr. Henry Jekyll." Utterson could not trust his eyes. Yes, it was disappearance; here again, as in the mad will which he had long ago restored to its author, here again were the idea of a disappearance and the name of Henry Jekyll bracketted. But in the will, that idea had sprung from the sinister suggestion of the man Hyde; it was set there with a purpose all too plain and horrible. Written by the hand of Lanyon, what should it mean? A great curiosity came on the trustee, to disregard the prohibition and dive at once to the bottom of these mysteries; but professional honour and faith to his dead friend were stringent obligations; and the packet slept in the inmost corner of his private safe.

It is one thing to mortify curiosity, another to conquer it; and it may be doubted if, from that day forth, Utterson desired the society of his surviving friend with the same eagerness. He thought of him kindly; but his thoughts were disquieted and fearful. He went to call indeed; but he was perhaps relieved to be denied admittance; perhaps, in his heart, he preferred to speak with Poole upon the doorstep and surrounded by the air and sounds of the open city, rather than to be admitted into that house of voluntary bondage, and to sit and speak with its inscrutable recluse. Poole had, indeed, no very pleasant news to communicate. The doctor, it appeared, now more than ever confined himself to the cabinet over the laboratory, where he would sometimes even sleep; he was out of spirits, he had grown very silent, he did not read; it seemed as if he had something on his mind. Utterson became so used to the unvarying character of these reports, that he fell off little by little in the frequency of his visits.

INCIDENT AT THE WINDOW

It chanced on Sunday, when Mr. Utterson was on his usual walk with Mr. Enfield, that their way lay once again through the by-street; and that when they came in front of the door, both stopped to gaze on it.

"Well," said Enfield, "that story's at an end at least. We shall never see more of Mr. Hyde."

"I hope not," said Utterson. "Did I ever tell you that I once saw him, and shared your feeling of repulsion?"

"It was impossible to do the one without the other," returned Enfield. "And by the way, what an ass you must have thought me, not to know that this was a back way to Dr. Jekyll's! It was partly your own fault that I found it out, even when I did."

"So you found it out, did you?" said Utterson. "But if that be so, we may step into the court and take a look at the windows. To tell you the truth, I am uneasy about poor Jekyll; and even outside, I feel as if the presence of a friend might do him good."

The court was very cool and a little damp, and full of premature twilight, although the sky, high up overhead, was still bright with sunset. The middle one of the three windows was half-way open; and sitting close beside it, taking the air with an infinite sadness of mien, like some disconsolate prisoner, Utterson saw Dr. Jekyll.

"What! Jekyll!" he cried. "I trust you are better."

"I am very low, Utterson," replied the doctor drearily, "very low. It will not last long, thank God."

"You stay too much indoors," said the lawyer. "You should be out, whipping up the circulation like Mr. Enfield and me. (This is my cousin—Mr. Enfield—Dr. Jekyll.) Come now; get your hat and take a quick turn with us."

"You are very good," sighed the other. "I should like to very much; but no, no, no, it is quite impossible; I dare not. But indeed, Utterson, I am very glad to see you; this is really a great pleasure; I would ask you and Mr. Enfield up, but the place is really not fit."

"Why, then," said the lawyer, good-naturedly, "the best thing we can do is to stay down here and speak with you from where we are."

"That is just what I was about to venture to propose," returned the doctor with a smile. But the words were hardly uttered, before the smile was struck out of his face and succeeded by an expression of such abject terror and despair, as froze the very blood of the two gentlemen below. They saw it but for a glimpse for the window was instantly thrust down; but that glimpse had been sufficient, and they turned and left the court without a word. In silence, too, they traversed the by-street; and it was not until they had come into a neighbouring thoroughfare, where even upon a Sunday there were still some stirrings of life, that Mr. Utterson at last turned and looked at his companion. They were both pale; and there was an answering horror in their eyes.

"God forgive us, God forgive us," said Mr. Utterson.

But Mr. Enfield only nodded his head very seriously, and walked on once more in silence.

THE LAST NIGHT

Mr. Utterson was sitting by his fireside one evening after dinner, when he was surprised to receive a visit from Poole.

"Bless me, Poole, what brings you here?" he cried; and then taking a second look at him, "What ails you?" he added; "is the doctor ill?"

"Mr. Utterson," said the man, "there is something wrong."

"Take a seat, and here is a glass of wine for you," said the lawyer. "Now, take your time, and tell me plainly what you want."

"You know the doctor's ways, sir," replied Poole, "and how he shuts himself up. Well, he's shut up again in the cabinet; and I don't like it, sir—I wish I may die if I like it. Mr. Utterson, sir, I'm afraid."

"Now, my good man," said the lawyer, "be explicit. What are you afraid of?"

"I've been afraid for about a week," returned Poole, doggedly disregarding the question, "and I can bear it no more."

The man's appearance amply bore out his words; his manner was altered for the worse; and except for the moment when he had first announced his terror, he had not once looked the lawyer in the face. Even now, he sat with the glass of wine untasted on his knee, and his eyes directed to a corner of the floor. "I can bear it no more," he repeated.

"Come," said the lawyer, "I see you have some good reason, Poole; I see there is something seriously amiss. Try to tell me what it is."

"I think there's been foul play," said Poole, hoarsely.

"Foul play!" cried the lawyer, a good deal frightened and rather inclined to be irritated in consequence. "What foul play! What does the man mean?"

"I daren't say, sir," was the answer; "but will you come along with me and see for yourself?"

Mr. Utterson's only answer was to rise and get his hat and greatcoat; but he observed with wonder the greatness of the relief that appeared upon the butler's face, and perhaps with no less, that the wine was still untasted when he set it down to follow.

It was a wild, cold, seasonable night of March, with a pale moon, lying on her back as though the wind had tilted her, and flying wrack of the most diaphanous and lawny texture.

The wind made talking difficult, and flecked the blood into the face. It seemed to have swept the streets unusually bare of passengers, besides; for Mr. Utterson thought he had never seen that part of London so deserted. He could have wished it otherwise; never in his life had he been conscious of so sharp a wish to see and touch his fellow-creatures; for struggle as he might, there was borne in upon his mind a crushing anticipation of calamity. The square, when they got there, was full of wind and dust, and the thin trees in the garden were lashing themselves along the railing. Poole, who had kept all the way a pace or two ahead, now pulled up in the middle of the pavement, and in spite of the biting weather, took off his hat and mopped his brow with a red pocket-handkerchief. But for all the hurry of his coming, these were not the dews of exertion that he wiped away, but the moisture of some strangling anguish; for his face was white and his voice, when he spoke, harsh and broken.

"Well, sir," he said, "here we are, and God grant there be nothing wrong."

"Amen, Poole," said the lawyer.

Thereupon the servant knocked in a very guarded manner; the door was opened on the chain; and a voice asked from within, "Is that you, Poole?"

"It's all right," said Poole. "Open the door."

The hall, when they entered it, was brightly lighted up; the fire was built high; and about the hearth the whole of the servants, men and women, stood huddled together like a flock of sheep. At the sight of Mr. Utterson, the housemaid broke into hysterical whimpering; and the cook, crying out "Bless God! it's Mr. Utterson," ran forward as if to take him in her arms.

"What, what? Are you all here?" said the lawyer peevishly. "Very irregular, very unseemly; your master would be far from pleased."

"They're all afraid," said Poole.

Blank silence followed, no one protesting; only the maid lifted her voice and now wept loudly.

"Hold your tongue!" Poole said to her, with a ferocity of accent that testified to his own jangled nerves; and indeed, when the girl had so suddenly raised the note of her lamentation, they had all started and turned towards the inner door with faces of dreadful expectation. "And now," continued the butler, addressing the knife-boy, "reach me a candle, and we'll get this through hands at once." And then he begged Mr. Utterson to follow him, and led the way to the back garden.

"Now, sir," said he, "you come as gently as you can. I want you to hear, and I don't want you to be heard. And see here, sir, if by any chance he was to ask you in, don't go."

Mr. Utterson's nerves, at this unlooked-for termination, gave a jerk that nearly threw him from his balance; but he recollected his courage and followed the butler into the laboratory building through the surgical theatre, with its lumber of crates and bottles, to the foot of the stair. Here Poole motioned him to stand on one side and listen; while he himself, setting down the candle and making a great and obvious call on his resolution, mounted the steps and knocked with a somewhat uncertain hand on the red baize of the cabinet door.

"Mr. Utterson, sir, asking to see you," he called; and even as he did so, once more violently signed to the lawyer to give ear.

A voice answered from within: "Tell him I cannot see anyone," it said complainingly.

"Thank you, sir," said Poole, with a note of something like triumph in his voice; and taking up his candle, he led Mr. Utterson back across the yard and into the great kitchen, where the fire was out and the beetles were leaping on the floor.

"Sir," he said, looking Mr. Utterson in the eyes, "Was that my master's voice?"

"It seems much changed," replied the lawyer, very pale, but giving look for look.

"Changed? Well, yes, I think so," said the butler. "Have I been twenty years in this man's house, to be deceived about his voice? No, sir; master's made away with; he was made away with eight days ago, when we heard him cry out upon the name of God; and *who's* in there instead of him, and *why* it stays there, is a thing that cries to Heaven, Mr. Utterson!"

"This is a very strange tale, Poole; this is rather a wild tale my man," said Mr. Utterson, biting his finger. "Suppose it were as you suppose, supposing Dr. Jekyll to have been—well, murdered what could induce the murderer to stay? That won't hold water; it doesn't commend itself to reason."

"Well, Mr. Utterson, you are a hard man to satisfy, but I'll do it yet," said Poole. "All this last week (you must know) him, or it, whatever it is that lives in that cabinet, has been crying night and day for some sort of medicine and cannot get it to his mind. It was sometimes his way—the master's, that is—to write his orders on a sheet of paper and throw it on the stair. We've had nothing else this week back; nothing but papers, and a closed door, and the very meals left there to be smuggled in when nobody was looking. Well, sir, every day, ay, and twice and thrice in the same day, there have been orders and complaints, and I have been sent flying to all the wholesale chemists in town. Every time I brought the stuff back, there would be another paper telling me to return it, because it was not pure, and another order to a different firm. This drug is wanted bitter bad, sir, whatever for."

"Have you any of these papers?" asked Mr. Utterson.

Poole felt in his pocket and handed out a crumpled note, which the lawyer, bending nearer to the candle, carefully examined. Its contents ran thus: "Dr. Jekyll presents his compliments to Messrs. Maw. He assures them that their last sample is impure and quite useless for his present purpose. In the year 18—, Dr. J. purchased a somewhat large quantity from Messrs. M. He now begs them to search with most sedulous care, and should any of the same quality be left, forward it to him at once. Expense is no consideration. The importance of this to Dr. J. can hardly be exaggerated." So far the letter had run composedly enough, but here with a sudden splutter of the pen, the writer's emotion had broken loose. "For God's sake," he added, "find me some of the old."

"This is a strange note," said Mr. Utterson; and then sharply, "How do you come to have it open?"

"The man at Maw's was main angry, sir, and he threw it back to me like so much dirt," returned Poole.

"This is unquestionably the doctor's hand, do you know?" resumed the lawyer.

"I thought it looked like it," said the servant rather sulkily; and then, with another voice, "But what matters hand of write?" he said. "I've seen him!"

"Seen him?" repeated Mr. Utterson. "Well?"

"That's it!" said Poole. "It was this way. I came suddenly into the theatre from the garden. It seems he had slipped out to look for this drug or whatever it is; for the cabinet door was open, and there he was at the far end of the room digging among the crates. He looked up when I came in, gave a kind of cry, and whipped upstairs into the cabinet. It was but for one minute that I saw him, but the hair stood upon my head like quills. Sir, if that was my master, why had he a mask upon his face? If it was my master, why did he cry out like a rat, and run from me? I have served him long enough. And then..." The man paused and passed his hand over his face.

"These are all very strange circumstances," said Mr. Utterson, "but I think I begin to see daylight. Your master, Poole, is plainly seized with one of those maladies that both torture and deform the sufferer; hence, for aught I know, the alteration of his voice; hence the mask and the avoidance of his friends; hence his eagerness to find this drug, by means of which the poor soul retains some hope of ultimate recovery—God grant that he be not deceived! There is my explanation; it is sad enough, Poole, ay, and appalling to consider; but it is plain and natural, hangs well together, and delivers us from all exorbitant alarms."

"Sir," said the butler, turning to a sort of mottled pallor, "that thing was not my master, and there's the truth. My master"—here he looked round him and began to whisper—"is a tall, fine build of a man, and this was more of a dwarf." Utterson attempted to protest. "O, sir," cried Poole, "do you think I do not know my master after twenty years? Do you think I do not know where his head comes to in the cabinet door, where I saw him every morning of my life? No, sir, that thing in the mask was never Dr. Jekyll—God knows what it was, but it was never Dr. Jekyll; and it is the belief of my heart that there was murder done."

"Poole," replied the lawyer, "if you say that, it will become my duty to make certain. Much as I desire to spare your master's feelings, much as I am puzzled by this note which seems to prove him to be still alive, I shall consider it my duty to break in that door."

"Ah, Mr. Utterson, that's talking!" cried the butler.

"And now comes the second question," resumed Utterson: "Who is going to do it?"

"Why, you and me, sir," was the undaunted reply.

"That's very well said," returned the lawyer; "and whatever comes of it, I shall make it my business to see you are no loser."

"There is an axe in the theatre," continued Poole; "and you might take the kitchen poker for yourself."

The lawyer took that rude but weighty instrument into his hand, and balanced it. "Do you know, Poole," he said, looking up, "that you and I are about to place ourselves in a position of some peril?"

"You may say so, sir, indeed," returned the butler.

"It is well, then that we should be frank," said the other. "We both think more than we have said; let us make a clean breast. This masked figure that you saw, did you recognise it?"

"Well, sir, it went so quick, and the creature was so doubled up, that I could hardly swear to that," was the answer. "But if you mean, was it Mr. Hyde?—why, yes, I think it was! You see, it was much of the same bigness; and it had the same quick, light way with it; and then who else could have got in by the laboratory door? You have not forgot, sir, that at the time of the murder he had still the key with him? But that's not all. I don't know, Mr. Utterson, if you ever met this Mr. Hyde?"

"Yes," said the lawyer, "I once spoke with him."

"Then you must know as well as the rest of us that there was something queer about that gentleman—something that gave a man a turn—I don't know rightly how to say it, sir, beyond this: that you felt in your marrow kind of cold and thin."

"I own I felt something of what you describe," said Mr. Utterson.

"Quite so, sir," returned Poole. "Well, when that masked thing like a monkey jumped from among the chemicals and whipped into the cabinet, it went down my spine like ice. O, I know it's not evidence, Mr. Utterson; I'm book-learned enough for that; but a man has his feelings, and I give you my bible-word it was Mr. Hyde!"

"Ay, ay," said the lawyer. "My fears incline to the same point. Evil, I fear, founded—evil was sure to come—of that connection. Ay truly, I believe you; I believe poor Harry is killed; and I believe his murderer (for what purpose, God alone can tell) is still lurking in his victim's room. Well, let our name be vengeance. Call Bradshaw."

The footman came at the summons, very white and nervous.

"Pull yourself together, Bradshaw," said the lawyer. "This suspense, I know, is telling upon all of you; but it is now our intention to make an end of it. Poole, here, and I are going to force our way into the cabinet. If all is well, my shoulders are broad enough to bear the blame.

Meanwhile, lest anything should really be amiss, or any malefactor seek to escape by the back, you and the boy must go round the corner with a pair of good sticks and take your post at the laboratory door. We give you ten minutes to get to your stations."

As Bradshaw left, the lawyer looked at his watch. "And now, Poole, let us get to ours," he said; and taking the poker under his arm, led the way into the yard. The scud had banked over the moon, and it was now quite dark. The wind, which only broke in puffs and draughts into that deep well of building, tossed the light of the candle to and fro about their steps, until they came into the shelter of the theatre, where they sat down silently to wait. London hummed solemnly all around; but nearer at hand, the stillness was only broken by the sounds of a footfall moving to and fro along the cabinet floor.

"So it will walk all day, sir," whispered Poole; "ay, and the better part of the night. Only when a new sample comes from the chemist, there's a bit of a break. Ah, it's an ill conscience that's such an enemy to rest! Ah, sir, there's blood foully shed in every step of it! But hark again, a little closer—put your heart in your ears, Mr. Utterson, and tell me, is that the doctor's foot?"

The steps fell lightly and oddly, with a certain swing, for all they went so slowly; it was different indeed from the heavy creaking tread of Henry Jekyll. Utterson sighed. "Is there never anything else?" he asked.

Poole nodded. "Once," he said. "Once I heard it weeping!"

"Weeping? how that?" said the lawyer, conscious of a sudden chill of horror.

"Weeping like a woman or a lost soul," said the butler. "I came away with that upon my heart, that I could have wept too."

But now the ten minutes drew to an end. Poole disinterred the axe from under a stack of packing straw; the candle was set upon the nearest table to light them to the attack; and they drew near with bated breath to where that patient foot was still going up and down, up and down, in the quiet of the night.

"Jekyll," cried Utterson, with a loud voice, "I demand to see you." He paused a moment, but there came no reply. "I give you fair warning, our suspicions are aroused, and I must and shall see you," he resumed; "if not by fair means, then by foul—if not of your consent, then by brute force!"

"Utterson," said the voice, "for God's sake, have mercy!"

"Ah, that's not Jekyll's voice—it's Hyde's!" cried Utterson. "Down with the door, Poole!"

Poole swung the axe over his shoulder; the blow shook the building, and the red baize door leaped against the lock and hinges. A dismal screech, as of mere animal terror, rang from the cabinet. Up went the axe again, and again the panels crashed and the frame bounded; four times the blow fell; but the wood was tough and the fittings were of excellent workmanship; and it was not until the fifth, that the lock burst and the wreck of the door fell inwards on the carpet.

The besiegers, appalled by their own riot and the stillness that had succeeded, stood back a little and peered in. There lay the cabinet before their eyes in the quiet lamplight, a good fire glowing and chattering on the hearth, the kettle singing its thin strain, a drawer or two open, papers neatly set forth on the business table, and nearer the fire, the things laid out for tea; the quietest room, you would have said, and, but for the glazed presses full of chemicals, the most commonplace that night in London.

Right in the middle there lay the body of a man sorely contorted and still twitching. They drew near on tiptoe, turned it on its back and beheld the face of Edward Hyde. He was dressed in clothes far too large for him, clothes of the doctor's bigness; the cords of his face still moved with a semblance of life, but life was quite gone; and by the crushed phial in the hand and the strong smell of kernels that hung upon the air, Utterson knew that he was looking on the body of a self-destroyer.

"We have come too late," he said sternly, "whether to save or punish. Hyde is gone to his account; and it only remains for us to find the body of your master."

The far greater proportion of the building was occupied by the theatre, which filled almost the whole ground storey and was lighted from above, and by the cabinet, which formed an upper storey at one end and looked upon the court. A corridor joined the theatre to the door on the by-street; and with this the cabinet communicated separately by a second flight of stairs. There were besides a few dark closets and a spacious cellar. All these they now thoroughly examined. Each closet needed but a glance, for all were empty, and all, by the dust that fell from their doors, had stood long unopened. The cellar, indeed, was filled with crazy lumber, mostly dating from the times of the surgeon who was Jekyll's predecessor; but even as they opened the door they were advertised of the uselessness of further search, by the fall of a perfect mat of cobweb which had for years sealed up the entrance. Nowhere was there any trace of Henry Jekyll, dead or alive.

Poole stamped on the flags of the corridor. "He must be buried here," he said, hearkening to the sound.

"Or he may have fled," said Utterson, and he turned to examine the door in the by-street. It was locked; and lying near by on the flags, they found the key, already stained with rust.

"This does not look like use," observed the lawyer.

"Use!" echoed Poole. "Do you not see, sir, it is broken? much as if a man had stamped on it."

"Ay," continued Utterson, "and the fractures, too, are rusty." The two men looked at each other with a scare. "This is beyond me, Poole," said the lawyer. "Let us go back to the cabinet."

They mounted the stair in silence, and still with an occasional awestruck glance at the dead body, proceeded more thoroughly to examine the contents of the cabinet. At one table, there were traces of chemical work, various measured heaps of some white salt being laid on glass saucers, as though for an experiment in which the unhappy man had been prevented.

"That is the same drug that I was always bringing him," said Poole; and even as he spoke, the kettle with a startling noise boiled over.

This brought them to the fireside, where the easy-chair was drawn cosily up, and the tea things stood ready to the sitter's elbow, the very sugar in the cup. There were several books on a shelf; one lay beside the tea things open, and Utterson was amazed to find it a copy of a pious work, for which Jekyll had several times expressed a great esteem, annotated, in his own hand with startling blasphemies.

Next, in the course of their review of the chamber, the searchers came to the cheval-glass, into whose depths they looked with an involuntary horror. But it was so turned as to show them nothing but the rosy glow playing on the roof, the fire sparkling in a hundred repetitions along the glazed front of the presses, and their own pale and fearful countenances stooping to look in.

"This glass has seen some strange things, sir," whispered Poole.

"And surely none stranger than itself," echoed the lawyer in the same tones. "For what did Jekyll"—he caught himself up at the word with a start, and then conquering the weakness —"what could Jekyll want with it?" he said.

"You may say that!" said Poole.

Next they turned to the business table. On the desk, among the neat array of papers, a large envelope was uppermost, and bore, in the doctor's hand, the name of Mr. Utterson. The lawyer unsealed it, and several enclosures fell to the floor. The first was a will, drawn in the same eccentric terms as the one which he had returned six months before, to serve as a testament in case of death and as a deed of gift in case of disappearance; but in place of the name of Edward Hyde, the lawyer, with indescribable amazement read the name of Gabriel John Utterson. He looked at Poole, and then back at the paper, and last of all at the dead malefactor stretched upon the carpet.

"My head goes round," he said. "He has been all these days in possession; he had no cause to like me; he must have raged to see himself displaced; and he has not destroyed this document."

He caught up the next paper; it was a brief note in the doctor's hand and dated at the top. "O Poole!" the lawyer cried, "he was alive and here this day. He cannot have been disposed of in so short a space; he must be still alive, he must have fled! And then, why fled? and how? and in that case, can we venture to declare this suicide? O, we must be careful. I foresee that we may yet involve your master in some dire catastrophe."

"Why don't you read it, sir?" asked Poole.

"Because I fear," replied the lawyer solemnly. "God grant I have no cause for it!" And with that he brought the paper to his eyes and read as follows:

"My dear Utterson,—When this shall fall into your hands, I shall have disappeared, under what circumstances I have not the penetration to foresee, but my instinct and all the circumstances of my nameless situation tell me that the end is sure and must be early. Go then, and first read the narrative which Lanyon warned me he was to place in your hands; and if you care to hear more, turn to the confession of

"Your unworthy and unhappy friend,

"HENRY JEKYLL."

"There was a third enclosure?" asked Utterson.

"Here, sir," said Poole, and gave into his hands a considerable packet sealed in several places.

The lawyer put it in his pocket. "I would say nothing of this paper. If your master has fled or is dead, we may at least save his credit. It is now ten; I must go home and read these documents in quiet; but I shall be back before midnight, when we shall send for the police."

They went out, locking the door of the theatre behind them; and Utterson, once more leaving the servants gathered about the fire in the hall, trudged back to his office to read the two narratives in which this mystery was now to be explained.

DR. LANYON'S NARRATIVE

On the ninth of January, now four days ago, I received by the evening delivery a registered envelope, addressed in the hand of my colleague and old school companion, Henry Jekyll. I was a good deal surprised by this; for we were by no means in the habit of correspondence; I had seen the man, dined with him, indeed, the night before; and I could imagine nothing in our intercourse that should justify formality of registration. The contents increased my wonder; for this is how the letter ran:

"10*th December*, 18—.

"Dear Lanyon,—You are one of my oldest friends; and although we may have differed at times on scientific questions, I cannot remember, at least on my side, any break in our affection. There was never a day when, if you had said to me, 'Jekyll, my life, my honour, my reason, depend upon you,' I would not have sacrificed my left hand to help you. Lanyon my life, my honour, my reason, are all at your mercy; if you fail me to-night, I am lost. You might suppose, after this preface, that I am going to ask you for something dishonourable to grant. Judge for yourself.

"I want you to postpone all other engagements for to-night—ay, even if you were summoned to the bedside of an emperor; to take a cab, unless your carriage should be actually at the door; and with this letter in your hand for consultation, to drive straight to my house. Poole, my butler, has his orders; you will find him waiting your arrival with a locksmith. The door of my cabinet is then to be forced; and you are to go in alone; to open the glazed press (letter E) on the left hand, breaking the lock if it be shut; and to draw out, *with all its contents as they stand*, the fourth drawer from the top or (which is the same thing) the third from the bottom. In my extreme distress of mind, I have a morbid fear of misdirecting you; but even if I am in error, you may know the right drawer by its contents: some powders, a phial and a paper book. This drawer I beg of you to carry back with you to Cavendish Square exactly as it stands.

"That is the first part of the service: now for the second. You should be back, if you set out at once on the receipt of this, long before midnight; but I will leave you that amount of margin, not only in the fear of one of those obstacles that can neither be prevented nor foreseen, but because an hour when your servants are in bed is to be preferred for what will then remain to do. At midnight, then, I have to ask you to be alone in your consulting room, to admit with your own hand into the house a man who will present himself in my name, and to place in his hands the drawer that you will have brought with you from my cabinet. Then you will have played your part and earned my gratitude completely. Five minutes afterwards, if you insist upon an explanation, you will have understood that these arrangements are of capital importance; and that by the neglect of one of them, fantastic as they must appear, you might have charged your conscience with my death or the shipwreck of my reason.

"Confident as I am that you will not trifle with this appeal, my heart sinks and my hand trembles at the bare thought of such a possibility. Think of me at this hour, in a strange place, labouring under a blackness of distress that no fancy can exaggerate, and yet well aware that, if you will but punctually serve me, my troubles will roll away like a story that is told. Serve me, my dear Lanyon and save

"Your friend,

"H.J.

"P.S.—I had already sealed this up when a fresh terror struck upon my soul. It is possible that the post-office may fail me, and this letter not come into your hands until to-morrow morning. In that case, dear Lanyon, do my errand when it shall be most convenient for you in the course of the day; and once more expect my messenger at midnight. It may then already be too late; and if that night passes without event, you will know that you have seen the last of Henry Jekyll."

Upon the reading of this letter, I made sure my colleague was insane; but till that was proved beyond the possibility of doubt, I felt bound to do as he requested. The less I understood of this farrago, the less I was in a position to judge of its importance; and an appeal so worded could not be set aside without a grave responsibility. I rose accordingly from table, got into a hansom, and drove straight to Jekyll's house. The butler was awaiting my arrival; he had received by the same post as mine a registered letter of instruction, and had sent at once for a locksmith and a carpenter. The tradesmen came while we were yet speaking; and we moved in a body to old Dr. Denman's surgical theatre, from which (as you are doubtless aware) Jekyll's private cabinet is most conveniently entered. The door was very strong, the lock excellent; the carpenter avowed he would have great trouble and have to do much damage, if force were to be used; and the locksmith was near despair. But this last was a handy fellow, and after two hour's work, the door stood open. The press marked E was unlocked; and I took out the drawer, had it filled up with straw and tied in a sheet, and returned with it to Cavendish Square.

Here I proceeded to examine its contents. The powders were neatly enough made up, but not with the nicety of the dispensing chemist; so that it was plain they were of Jekyll's private manufacture; and when I opened one of the wrappers I found what seemed to me a simple crystalline salt of a white colour. The phial, to which I next turned my attention, might have been about half full of a blood-red liquor, which was highly pungent to the sense of smell and seemed to me to contain phosphorus and some volatile ether. At the other ingredients I could make no guess. The book was an ordinary version book and contained little but a series of dates. These covered a period of many years, but I observed that the entries ceased nearly a year ago and quite abruptly. Here and there a brief remark was appended to a date, usually no more than a single word: "double" occurring perhaps six times in a total of several hundred entries; and once very early in the list and followed by several marks of exclamation, "total failure!!!" All this, though it whetted my curiosity, told me little that was definite. Here were a phial of some salt, and the record of a series of experiments that had led (like too many of Jekyll's investigations) to no end of practical usefulness. How could the presence of these articles in my house affect either the honour, the sanity, or the life of my flighty colleague? If his messenger could go to one place, why could he not go to another? And even granting some impediment, why was this gentleman to be received by me in secret? The more I reflected the more convinced I grew that I was dealing with a case of cerebral disease; and though I dismissed my servants to bed, I loaded an old revolver, that I might be found in some posture of self-defence.

Twelve o'clock had scarce rung out over London, ere the knocker sounded very gently on the door. I went myself at the summons, and found a small man crouching against the pillars of the portico.

"Are you come from Dr. Jekyll?" I asked.

He told me "yes" by a constrained gesture; and when I had bidden him enter, he did not obey me without a searching backward glance into the darkness of the square. There was a policeman not far off, advancing with his bull's eye open; and at the sight, I thought my visitor started and made greater haste.

These particulars struck me, I confess, disagreeably; and as I followed him into the bright light of the consulting room, I kept my hand ready on my weapon. Here, at last, I had a chance of clearly seeing him. I had never set eyes on him before, so much was certain. He was small, as I have said; I was struck besides with the shocking expression of his face, with his remarkable combination of great muscular activity and great apparent debility of constitution, and—last but not least—with the odd, subjective disturbance caused by his neighbourhood. This bore some resemblance to incipient rigour, and was accompanied by a marked sinking of the pulse. At the time, I set it down to some idiosyncratic, personal distaste, and merely wondered at the acuteness of the symptoms; but I have since had reason to believe the cause to lie much deeper in the nature of man, and to turn on some nobler hinge than the principle of hatred.

This person (who had thus, from the first moment of his entrance, struck in me what I can only describe as a disgustful curiosity) was dressed in a fashion that would have made an ordinary person laughable; his clothes, that is to say, although they were of rich and sober fabric, were enormously too large for him in every measurement—the trousers hanging on his legs and rolled up to keep them from the ground, the waist of the coat below his haunches, and the collar sprawling wide upon his shoulders. Strange to relate, this ludicrous accoutrement was far from moving me to laughter. Rather, as there was something abnormal and misbegotten in the very essence of the creature that now faced me—something seizing, surprising and revolting—this fresh disparity seemed but to fit in with and to reinforce it; so that to my interest in the man's nature and character, there was added a curiosity as to his origin, his life, his fortune and status in the world.

These observations, though they have taken so great a space to be set down in, were yet the work of a few seconds. My visitor was, indeed, on fire with sombre excitement.

"Have you got it?" he cried. "Have you got it?" And so lively was his impatience that he even laid his hand upon my arm and sought to shake me.

I put him back, conscious at his touch of a certain icy pang along my blood. "Come, sir," said I. "You forget that I have not yet the pleasure of your acquaintance. Be seated, if you please." And I showed him an example, and sat down myself in my customary seat and with as fair an imitation of my ordinary manner to a patient, as the lateness of the hour, the nature of my preoccupations, and the horror I had of my visitor, would suffer me to muster.

"I beg your pardon, Dr. Lanyon," he replied civilly enough. "What you say is very well founded; and my impatience has shown its heels to my politeness. I come here at the instance of your colleague, Dr. Henry Jekyll, on a piece of business of some moment; and I understood..." He paused and put his hand to his throat, and I could see, in spite of his collected manner, that he was wrestling against the approaches of the hysteria—"I understood, a drawer..."

But here I took pity on my visitor's suspense, and some perhaps on my own growing curiosity.

"There it is, sir," said I, pointing to the drawer, where it lay on the floor behind a table and still covered with the sheet.

He sprang to it, and then paused, and laid his hand upon his heart; I could hear his teeth grate with the convulsive action of his jaws; and his face was so ghastly to see that I grew alarmed both for his life and reason.

"Compose yourself," said I.

He turned a dreadful smile to me, and as if with the decision of despair, plucked away the sheet. At sight of the contents, he uttered one loud sob of such immense relief that I sat petrified. And the next moment, in a voice that was already fairly well under control, "Have you a graduated glass?" he asked.

I rose from my place with something of an effort and gave him what he asked.

He thanked me with a smiling nod, measured out a few minims of the red tincture and added one of the powders. The mixture, which was at first of a reddish hue, began, in proportion as the crystals melted, to brighten in colour, to effervesce audibly, and to throw off small fumes of vapour. Suddenly and at the same moment, the ebullition ceased and the compound changed to a dark purple, which faded again more slowly to a watery green. My visitor, who had watched these metamorphoses with a keen eye, smiled, set down the glass upon the table, and then turned and looked upon me with an air of scrutiny.

"And now," said he, "to settle what remains. Will you be wise? will you be guided? will you suffer me to take this glass in my hand and to go forth from your house without further parley? or has the greed of curiosity too much command of you? Think before you answer, for it shall be done as you decide. As you decide, you shall be left as you were before, and neither richer nor wiser, unless the sense of service rendered to a man in mortal distress may be counted as a kind of riches of the soul. Or, if you shall so prefer to choose, a new province of knowledge and new avenues to fame and power shall be laid open to you, here, in this room, upon the instant; and your sight shall be blasted by a prodigy to stagger the unbelief of Satan."

"Sir," said I, affecting a coolness that I was far from truly possessing, "you speak enigmas, and you will perhaps not wonder that I hear you with no very strong impression of belief. But I have gone too far in the way of inexplicable services to pause before I see the end."

"It is well," replied my visitor. "Lanyon, you remember your vows: what follows is under the seal of our profession. And now, you who have so long been bound to the most narrow and material views, you who have denied the virtue of transcendental medicine, you who have derided your superiors—behold!"

He put the glass to his lips and drank at one gulp. A cry followed; he reeled, staggered, clutched at the table and held on, staring with injected eyes, gasping with open mouth; and as I looked there came, I thought, a change—he seemed to swell—his face became suddenly black and the features seemed to melt and alter—and the next moment, I had sprung to my feet and leaped back against the wall, my arms raised to shield me from that prodigy, my mind submerged in terror.

"O God!" I screamed, and "O God!" again and again; for there before my eyes—pale and shaken, and half fainting, and groping before him with his hands, like a man restored from death—there stood Henry Jekyll!

What he told me in the next hour, I cannot bring my mind to set on paper. I saw what I saw, I heard what I heard, and my soul sickened at it; and yet now when that sight has faded from my eyes, I ask myself if I believe it, and I cannot answer. My life is shaken to its roots; sleep has left me; the deadliest terror sits by me at all hours of the day and night; and I feel that my days are numbered, and that I must die; and yet I shall die incredulous. As for the moral turpitude that man unveiled to me, even with tears of penitence, I cannot, even in memory, dwell on it without a start of horror. I will say but one thing, Utterson, and that (if you can bring your mind to credit it) will be more than enough. The creature who crept into my house that night was, on Jekyll's own confession, known by the name of Hyde and hunted for in every corner of the land as the murderer of Carew.

HASTIE LANYON.

HENRY JEKYLL'S FULL STATEMENT OF THE CASE

I WAS BORN in the year 18— to a large fortune, endowed besides with excellent parts, inclined by nature to industry, fond of the respect of the wise and good among my fellowmen, and thus, as might have been supposed, with every guarantee of an honourable and distinguished future. And indeed the worst of my faults was a certain impatient gaiety of disposition, such as has made the happiness of many, but such as I found it hard to reconcile with my imperious desire to carry my head high, and wear a more than commonly grave countenance before the public. Hence it came about that I concealed my pleasures; and that when I reached years of reflection, and began to look round me and take stock of my progress and position in the world, I stood already committed to a profound duplicity of life. Many a man would have even blazoned such irregularities as I was guilty of; but from the high views that I had set before me, I regarded and hid them with an almost morbid sense of shame. It was thus rather the exacting nature of my aspirations than any particular degradation in my faults, that made me what I was, and, with even a deeper trench than in the majority of men, severed in me those provinces of good and ill which divide and compound man's dual nature. In this case, I was driven to reflect deeply and inveterately on that hard law of life, which lies at the root of religion and is one of the most plentiful springs of distress. Though so profound a double-dealer, I was in no sense a hypocrite; both sides of me were in dead earnest; I was no more myself when I laid aside restraint and plunged in shame, than when I laboured, in the eye of day, at the furtherance of knowledge or the relief of sorrow and suffering. And it chanced that the direction of my scientific studies, which led wholly towards the mystic and the transcendental, reacted and shed a strong light on this consciousness of the perennial war among my members. With every day, and from both sides of my intelligence, the moral and the intellectual, I thus drew steadily nearer to that truth, by whose partial discovery I have been doomed to such a dreadful shipwreck: that man is not truly one, but truly two. I say two, because the state of my own knowledge does not pass beyond that point. Others will follow, others will outstrip me on the same lines; and I hazard the guess that man will be ultimately known for a mere polity of multifarious, incongruous and independent denizens. I, for my part, from the nature of my life, advanced infallibly in one direction and in one direction only. It was on the moral side, and in my own person, that I learned to recognise the thorough and primitive duality of man; I saw that, of the two natures that contended in the field of my consciousness, even if I could rightly be said to be either, it was only because I was radically both; and from an early date, even before the course of my scientific discoveries had begun to suggest the most naked possibility of such a miracle, I had learned to dwell with pleasure, as a beloved daydream, on the thought of the separation of these elements. If each, I told myself, could be housed in separate identities, life would be relieved of all that was unbearable; the unjust might go his way, delivered from the aspirations and remorse of his more upright twin; and the just could walk steadfastly and securely on his upward path, doing the good things in which he found his pleasure, and no longer exposed to disgrace and penitence by the hands of this extraneous evil. It was the curse of mankind that these incongruous faggots were thus bound together—that in the agonised womb of consciousness, these polar twins should be continuously struggling. How, then were they dissociated?

I was so far in my reflections when, as I have said, a side light began to shine upon the subject from the laboratory table. I began to perceive more deeply than it has ever yet been stated, the trembling immateriality, the mistlike transience, of this seemingly so solid body in which we walk attired. Certain agents I found to have the power to shake and pluck back that fleshly vestment, even as a wind might toss the curtains of a pavilion. For two good reasons, I will not enter deeply into this scientific branch of my confession. First, because I have been made to learn that the doom and burthen of our life is bound for ever on man's shoulders, and when the attempt is made to cast it off, it but returns upon us with more unfamiliar and more awful pressure. Second, because, as my narrative will make, alas! too evident, my discoveries were incomplete. Enough then, that I not only recognised my natural body from the mere aura and effulgence of certain of the powers that made up my spirit, but managed to compound a drug by which these powers should be dethroned from their supremacy, and a second form and countenance substituted, none the less natural to me because they were the expression, and bore the stamp of lower elements in my soul.

I hesitated long before I put this theory to the test of practice. I knew well that I risked death; for any drug that so potently controlled and shook the very fortress of identity, might, by the least scruple of an overdose or at the least inopportunity in the moment of exhibition, utterly blot out that immaterial tabernacle which I looked to it to change. But the temptation of a discovery so singular and profound at last overcame the suggestions of alarm. I had long since prepared my tincture; I purchased at once, from a firm of wholesale chemists, a large quantity of a particular salt which I knew, from my experiments, to be the last ingredient required; and late one accursed night, I compounded the elements, watched them boil and smoke together in the glass, and when the ebullition had subsided, with a strong glow of courage, drank off the potion.

The most racking pangs succeeded: a grinding in the bones, deadly nausea, and a horror of the spirit that cannot be exceeded at the hour of birth or death. Then these agonies began swiftly to subside, and I came to myself as if out of a great sickness. There was something strange in my sensations, something indescribably new and, from its very novelty, incredibly sweet. I felt younger, lighter, happier in body; within I was conscious of a heady recklessness, a current of disordered sensual images running like a millrace in my fancy, a solution of the bonds of obligation, an unknown but not an innocent freedom of the soul. I knew myself, at the first breath of this new life, to be more wicked, tenfold more wicked, sold a slave to my original evil; and the thought, in that moment, braced and delighted me like wine. I stretched out my hands, exulting in the freshness of these sensations; and in the act, I was suddenly aware that I had lost in stature.

There was no mirror, at that date, in my room; that which stands beside me as I write, was brought there later on and for the very purpose of these transformations. The night however, was far gone into the morning—the morning, black as it was, was nearly ripe for the conception of the day—the inmates of my house were locked in the most rigorous hours of slumber; and I determined, flushed as I was with hope and triumph, to venture in my new shape as far as to my bedroom. I crossed the yard, wherein the constellations looked down upon me, I could have thought, with wonder, the first creature of that sort that their unsleeping vigilance had yet disclosed to them; I stole through the corridors, a stranger in my own house; and coming to my room, I saw for the first time the appearance of Edward Hyde.

I must here speak by theory alone, saying not that which I know, but that which I suppose to be most probable. The evil side of my nature, to which I had now transferred the stamping efficacy, was less robust and less developed than the good which I had just deposed. Again, in the course of my life, which had been, after all, nine tenths a life of effort, virtue and control, it had been much less exercised and much less exhausted. And hence, as I think, it came about that Edward Hyde was so much smaller, slighter and younger than Henry Jekyll. Even as good shone upon the countenance of the one, evil was written broadly and plainly on the face of the other. Evil besides (which I must still believe to be the lethal side of man) had left on that body an imprint of deformity and decay. And yet when I looked upon that ugly idol in the glass, I was conscious of no repugnance, rather of a leap of welcome. This, too, was myself. It seemed natural and human. In my eyes it bore a livelier image of the spirit, it seemed more express and single, than the imperfect and divided countenance I had been hitherto accustomed to call mine. And in so far I was doubtless right. I have observed that when I wore the semblance of Edward Hyde, none could come near to me at first without a visible misgiving of the flesh. This, as I take it, was because all human beings, as we meet them, are commingled out of good and evil: and Edward Hyde, alone in the ranks of mankind, was pure evil.

I lingered but a moment at the mirror: the second and conclusive experiment had yet to be attempted; it yet remained to be seen if I had lost my identity beyond redemption and must flee before daylight from a house that was no longer mine; and hurrying back to my cabinet, I once more prepared and drank the cup, once more suffered the pangs of dissolution, and came to myself once more with the character, the stature and the face of Henry Jekyll.

That night I had come to the fatal cross-roads. Had I approached my discovery in a more noble spirit, had I risked the experiment while under the empire of generous or pious aspirations, all must have been otherwise, and from these agonies of death and birth, I had come forth an angel instead of a fiend. The drug had no discriminating action; it was neither diabolical nor divine; it but shook the doors of the prisonhouse of my disposition; and like the captives of Philippi, that which stood within ran forth. At that time my virtue slumbered; my evil, kept awake by ambition, was alert and swift to seize the occasion; and the thing that was projected was Edward Hyde. Hence, although I had now two characters as well as two appearances, one was wholly evil, and the other was still the old Henry Jekyll, that incongruous compound of whose reformation and improvement I had already learned to despair. The movement was thus wholly toward the worse.

Even at that time, I had not conquered my aversions to the dryness of a life of study. I would still be merrily disposed at times; and as my pleasures were (to say the least) undignified, and I was not only well known and highly considered, but growing towards the elderly man, this incoherency of my life was daily growing more unwelcome. It was on this side that my new power tempted me until I fell in slavery. I had but to drink the cup, to doff at once the body of the noted professor, and to assume, like a thick cloak, that of Edward Hyde. I smiled at the notion; it seemed to me at the time to be humourous; and I made my preparations with the most studious care. I took and furnished that house in Soho, to which Hyde was tracked by the police; and engaged as a housekeeper a creature whom I knew well to be silent and unscrupulous. On the other side, I announced to my servants that a Mr. Hyde (whom I described) was to have full liberty and power about my house in the square; and to parry mishaps, I even called and made myself a familiar object, in my second character. I next drew up that will to which you so much objected; so that if anything befell me in the person of Dr. Jekyll, I could enter on that of Edward Hyde without pecuniary loss. And thus fortified, as I supposed, on every side, I began to profit by the strange immunities of my position.

Men have before hired bravos to transact their crimes, while their own person and reputation sat under shelter. I was the first that ever did so for his pleasures. I was the first that could plod in the public eye with a load of genial respectability, and in a moment, like a schoolboy, strip off these lendings and spring headlong into the sea of liberty. But for me, in my impenetrable mantle, the safety was complete. Think of it—I did not even exist! Let me but escape into my laboratory door, give me but a second or two to mix and swallow the draught that I had always standing ready; and whatever he had done, Edward Hyde would pass away like the stain of breath upon a mirror; and there in his stead, quietly at home, trimming the midnight lamp in his study, a man who could afford to laugh at suspicion, would be Henry Jekyll.

The pleasures which I made haste to seek in my disguise were, as I have said, undignified; I would scarce use a harder term. But in the hands of Edward Hyde, they soon began to turn toward the monstrous. When I would come back from these excursions, I was often plunged into a kind of wonder at my vicarious depravity. This familiar that I called out of my own soul, and sent forth alone to do his good pleasure, was a being inherently malign and villainous; his every act and thought centered on self; drinking pleasure with bestial avidity from any degree of torture to another; relentless like a man of stone. Henry Jekyll stood at times aghast before the acts of Edward Hyde; but the situation was apart from ordinary laws, and insidiously relaxed the grasp of conscience. It was Hyde, after all, and Hyde alone, that was guilty. Jekyll was no worse; he woke again to his good qualities seemingly unimpaired; he would even make haste, where it was possible, to undo the evil done by Hyde. And thus his conscience slumbered.

Into the details of the infamy at which I thus connived (for even now I can scarce grant that I committed it) I have no design of entering; I mean but to point out the warnings and the successive steps with which my chastisement approached. I met with one accident which, as it brought on no consequence, I shall no more than mention. An act of cruelty to a child aroused against me the anger of a passer-by, whom I recognised the other day in the person of your kinsman; the doctor and the child's family joined him; there were moments when I feared for my life; and at last, in order to pacify their too just resentment, Edward Hyde had to bring them to the door, and pay them in a cheque drawn in the name of Henry Jekyll. But this danger was easily eliminated from the future, by opening an account at another bank in the name of Edward Hyde himself; and when, by sloping my own hand backward, I had supplied my double with a signature, I thought I sat beyond the reach of fate.

Some two months before the murder of Sir Danvers, I had been out for one of my adventures, had returned at a late hour, and woke the next day in bed with somewhat odd sensations. It was in vain I looked about me; in vain I saw the decent furniture and tall proportions of my room in the square; in vain that I recognised the pattern of the bed curtains and the design of the mahogany frame; something still kept insisting that I was not where I was, that I had not wakened where I seemed to be, but in the little room in Soho where I was accustomed to sleep in the body of Edward Hyde. I smiled to myself, and in my psychological way, began lazily to inquire into the elements of this illusion, occasionally, even as I did so, dropping back into a comfortable morning doze. I was still so engaged when, in one of my more wakeful moments, my eyes fell upon my hand. Now the hand of Henry Jekyll (as you have often remarked) was professional in shape and size; it was large, firm, white and comely. But the hand which I now saw, clearly enough, in the yellow light of a mid-London morning, lying half shut on the bedclothes, was lean, corded, knuckly, of a dusky pallor and thickly shaded with a swart growth of hair. It was the hand of Edward Hyde.

I must have stared upon it for near half a minute, sunk as I was in the mere stupidity of wonder, before terror woke up in my breast as sudden and startling as the crash of cymbals; and bounding from my bed I rushed to the mirror. At the sight that met my eyes, my blood was changed into something exquisitely thin and icy. Yes, I had gone to bed Henry Jekyll, I had awakened Edward Hyde. How was this to be explained? I asked myself; and then, with another bound of terror—how was it to be remedied? It was well on in the morning; the servants were up; all my drugs were in the cabinet—a long journey down two pairs of stairs, through the back passage, across the open court and through the anatomical theatre, from where I was then standing horror-struck. It might indeed be possible to cover my face; but of what use was that, when I was unable to conceal the alteration in my stature? And then with an overpowering sweetness of relief, it came back upon my mind that the servants were already used to the coming and going of my second self. I had soon dressed, as well as I was able, in clothes of my own size: had soon passed through the house, where Bradshaw stared and drew back at seeing Mr. Hyde at such an hour and in such a strange array; and ten minutes later, Dr. Jekyll had returned to his own shape and was sitting down, with a darkened brow, to make a feint of breakfasting.

Small indeed was my appetite. This inexplicable incident, this reversal of my previous experience, seemed, like the Babylonian finger on the wall, to be spelling out the letters of my judgment; and I began to reflect more seriously than ever before on the issues and possibilities of my double existence. That part of me which I had the power of projecting, had lately been much exercised and nourished; it had seemed to me of late as though the body of Edward Hyde had grown in stature, as though (when I wore that form) I were conscious of a more generous tide of blood; and I began to spy a danger that, if this were much prolonged, the balance of my nature might be permanently overthrown, the power of voluntary change be forfeited, and the character of Edward Hyde become irrevocably mine. The power of the drug had not been always equally displayed. Once, very early in my career, it had totally failed me; since then I had been obliged on more than one occasion to double, and once, with infinite risk of death, to treble the amount; and these rare uncertainties had cast hitherto the sole shadow on my contentment. Now, however, and in the light of that morning's accident, I was led to remark that whereas, in the beginning, the difficulty had been to throw off the body of Jekyll, it had of late gradually but decidedly transferred itself to the other side. All things therefore seemed to point to this; that I was slowly losing hold of my original and better self, and becoming slowly incorporated with my second and worse.

Between these two, I now felt I had to choose. My two natures had memory in common, but all other faculties were most unequally shared between them. Jekyll (who was composite) now with the most sensitive apprehensions, now with a greedy gusto, projected and shared in the pleasures and adventures of Hyde; but Hyde was indifferent to Jekyll, or but remembered him as the mountain bandit remembers the cavern in which he conceals himself from pursuit. Jekyll had more than a father's interest; Hyde had more than a son's indifference. To cast in my lot with Jekyll, was to die to those appetites which I had long secretly indulged and had of late begun to pamper. To cast it in with Hyde, was to die to a thousand interests and aspirations, and to become, at a blow and forever, despised and friendless. The bargain might appear unequal; but there was still another consideration in the scales; for while Jekyll would suffer smartingly in the fires of abstinence, Hyde would be not even conscious of all that he had lost. Strange as my circumstances were, the terms of this debate are as old and commonplace as man; much the same inducements and alarms cast the die for any tempted and trembling sinner; and it fell out with me, as it falls with so vast a majority of my fellows, that I chose the better part and was found wanting in the strength to keep to it.

Yes, I preferred the elderly and discontented doctor, surrounded by friends and cherishing honest hopes; and bade a resolute farewell to the liberty, the comparative youth, the light step, leaping impulses and secret pleasures, that I had enjoyed in the disguise of Hyde. I made this choice perhaps with some unconscious reservation, for I neither gave up the house in Soho, nor destroyed the clothes of Edward Hyde, which still lay ready in my cabinet. For two months, however, I was true to my determination; for two months, I led a life of such severity as I had never before attained to, and enjoyed the compensations of an approving conscience. But time began at last to obliterate the freshness of my alarm; the praises of conscience began to grow into a thing of course; I began to be tortured with throes and longings, as of Hyde struggling after freedom; and at last, in an hour of moral weakness, I once again compounded and swallowed the transforming draught.

I do not suppose that, when a drunkard reasons with himself upon his vice, he is once out of five hundred times affected by the dangers that he runs through his brutish, physical insensibility; neither had I, long as I had considered my position, made enough allowance for the complete moral insensibility and insensate readiness to evil, which were the leading characters of Edward Hyde. Yet it was by these that I was punished. My devil had been long caged, he came out roaring. I was conscious, even when I took the draught, of a more unbridled, a more furious propensity to ill. It must have been this, I suppose, that stirred in my soul that tempest of impatience with which I listened to the civilities of my unhappy victim; I declare, at least, before God, no man morally sane could have been guilty of that crime upon so pitiful a provocation; and that I struck in no more reasonable spirit than that in which a sick child may break a plaything. But I had voluntarily stripped myself of all those balancing instincts by which even the worst of us continues to walk with some degree of steadiness among temptations; and in my case, to be tempted, however slightly, was to fall.

Instantly the spirit of hell awoke in me and raged. With a transport of glee, I mauled the unresisting body, tasting delight from every blow; and it was not till weariness had begun to succeed, that I was suddenly, in the top fit of my delirium, struck through the heart by a cold thrill of terror. A mist dispersed; I saw my life to be forfeit; and fled from the scene of these excesses, at once glorying and trembling, my lust of evil gratified and stimulated, my love of life screwed to the topmost peg. I ran to the house in Soho, and (to make assurance doubly sure) destroyed my papers; thence I set out through the lamplit streets, in the same divided ecstasy of mind, gloating on my crime, light-headedly devising others in the future, and yet still hastening and still hearkening in my wake for the steps of the avenger. Hyde had a song upon his lips as he compounded the draught, and as he drank it, pledged the dead man. The pangs of transformation had not done tearing him, before Henry Jekyll, with streaming tears of gratitude and remorse, had fallen upon his knees and lifted his clasped hands to God. The veil of self-indulgence was rent from head to foot. I saw my life as a whole: I followed it up from the days of childhood, when I had walked with my father's hand, and through the self-denying toils of my professional life, to arrive again and again, with the same sense of unreality, at the damned horrors of the evening. I could have screamed aloud; I sought with tears and prayers to smother down the crowd of hideous images and sounds with which my memory swarmed against me;

and still, between the petitions, the ugly face of my iniquity stared into my soul. As the acuteness of this remorse began to die away, it was succeeded by a sense of joy. The problem of my conduct was solved. Hyde was thenceforth impossible; whether I would or not, I was now confined to the better part of my existence; and O, how I rejoiced to think of it! with what willing humility I embraced anew the restrictions of natural life! with what sincere renunciation I locked the door by which I had so often gone and come, and ground the key under my heel!

The next day, came the news that the murder had not been overlooked, that the guilt of Hyde was patent to the world, and that the victim was a man high in public estimation. It was not only a crime, it had been a tragic folly. I think I was glad to know it; I think I was glad to have my better impulses thus buttressed and guarded by the terrors of the scaffold. Jekyll was now my city of refuge; let but Hyde peep out an instant, and the hands of all men would be raised to take and slay him.

I resolved in my future conduct to redeem the past; and I can say with honesty that my resolve was fruitful of some good. You know yourself how earnestly, in the last months of the last year, I laboured to relieve suffering; you know that much was done for others, and that the days passed quietly, almost happily for myself. Nor can I truly say that I wearied of this beneficent and innocent life; I think instead that I daily enjoyed it more completely; but I was still cursed with my duality of purpose; and as the first edge of my penitence wore off, the lower side of me, so long indulged, so recently chained down, began to growl for licence. Not that I dreamed of resuscitating Hyde; the bare idea of that would startle me to frenzy: no, it was in my own person that I was once more tempted to trifle with my conscience; and it was as an ordinary secret sinner that I at last fell before the assaults of temptation.

There comes an end to all things; the most capacious measure is filled at last; and this brief condescension to my evil finally destroyed the balance of my soul. And yet I was not alarmed; the fall seemed natural, like a return to the old days before I had made my discovery. It was a fine, clear, January day, wet under foot where the frost had melted, but cloudless overhead; and the Regent's Park was full of winter chirrupings and sweet with spring odours. I sat in the sun on a bench; the animal within me licking the chops of memory; the spiritual side a little drowsed, promising subsequent penitence, but not yet moved to begin. After all, I reflected, I was like my neighbours; and then I smiled, comparing myself with other men, comparing my active good-will with the lazy cruelty of their neglect. And at the very moment of that vainglorious thought, a qualm came over me, a horrid nausea and the most deadly shuddering. These passed away, and left me faint; and then as in its turn faintness subsided, I began to be aware of a change in the temper of my thoughts, a greater boldness, a contempt of danger, a solution of the bonds of obligation. I looked down; my clothes hung formlessly on my shrunken limbs; the hand that lay on my knee was corded and hairy. I was once more Edward Hyde. A moment before I had been safe of all men's respect, wealthy, beloved—the cloth laying for me in the dining-room at home; and now I was the common quarry of mankind, hunted, houseless, a known murderer, thrall to the gallows.

My reason wavered, but it did not fail me utterly. I have more than once observed that in my second character, my faculties seemed sharpened to a point and my spirits more tensely elastic; thus it came about that, where Jekyll perhaps might have succumbed, Hyde rose to the importance of the moment. My drugs were in one of the presses of my cabinet; how was I to reach them? That was the problem that (crushing my temples in my hands) I set myself to solve. The laboratory door I had closed. If I sought to enter by the house, my own servants would consign me to the gallows. I saw I must employ another hand, and thought of Lanyon. How was he to be reached? how persuaded? Supposing that I escaped capture in the streets, how was I to make my way into his presence? and how should I, an unknown and displeasing visitor, prevail on the famous physician to rifle the study of his colleague, Dr. Jekyll? Then I remembered that of my original character, one part remained to me: I could write my own hand; and once I had conceived that kindling spark, the way that I must follow became lighted up from end to end.

Thereupon, I arranged my clothes as best I could, and summoning a passing hansom, drove to an hotel in Portland Street, the name of which I chanced to remember. At my appearance (which was indeed comical enough, however tragic a fate these garments covered) the driver could not conceal his mirth. I gnashed my teeth upon him with a gust of devilish fury; and the smile withered from his face—happily for him—yet more happily for myself, for in another instant I had certainly dragged him from his perch. At the inn, as I entered, I looked about me with so black a countenance as made the attendants tremble; not a look did they exchange in my presence; but obsequiously took my orders, led me to a private room, and brought me wherewithal to write. Hyde in danger of his life was a creature new to me; shaken with inordinate anger, strung to the pitch of murder, lusting to inflict pain. Yet the creature was astute; mastered his fury with a great effort of the will; composed his two important letters, one to Lanyon and one to Poole; and that he might receive actual evidence of their being posted, sent them out with directions that they should be registered. Thenceforward, he sat all day over the fire in the private room, gnawing his nails; there he dined, sitting alone with his fears, the waiter visibly quailing before his eye; and thence, when the night was fully come, he set forth in the corner of a closed cab, and was driven to and fro about the streets of the city. He, I say—I cannot say, I. That child of Hell had nothing human; nothing lived in him but fear and hatred. And when at last, thinking the driver had begun to grow suspicious, he discharged the cab and ventured on foot, attired in his misfitting clothes, an object marked out for observation, into the midst of the nocturnal passengers, these two base passions raged within him like a tempest. He walked fast, hunted by his fears, chattering to himself, skulking through the less frequented thoroughfares, counting the minutes that still divided him from midnight. Once a woman spoke to him, offering, I think, a box of lights. He smote her in the face, and she fled.

When I came to myself at Lanyon's, the horror of my old friend perhaps affected me somewhat: I do not know; it was at least but a drop in the sea to the abhorrence with which I looked back upon these hours. A change had come over me. It was no longer the fear of the gallows, it was the horror of being Hyde that racked me. I received Lanyon's condemnation partly in a dream; it was partly in a dream that I came home to my own house and got into bed. I slept after the prostration of the day, with a stringent and profound slumber which not even the nightmares that wrung me could avail to break. I awoke in the morning shaken, weakened, but refreshed. I still hated and feared the thought of the brute that slept within me, and I had not of course forgotten the appalling dangers of the day before; but I was once more at home, in my own house and close to my drugs; and gratitude for my escape shone so strong in my soul that it almost rivalled the brightness of hope.

I was stepping leisurely across the court after breakfast, drinking the chill of the air with pleasure, when I was seized again with those indescribable sensations that heralded the change; and I had but the time to gain the shelter of my cabinet, before I was once again raging and freezing with the passions of Hyde. It took on this occasion a double dose to recall me to myself; and alas! six hours after, as I sat looking sadly in the fire, the pangs returned, and the drug had to be re-administered. In short, from that day forth it seemed only by a great effort as of gymnastics, and only under the immediate stimulation of the drug, that I was able to wear the countenance of Jekyll. At all hours of the day and night, I would be taken with the premonitory shudder; above all, if I slept, or even dozed for a moment in my chair, it was always as Hyde that I awakened. Under the strain of this continually impending doom and by the sleeplessness to which I now condemned myself, ay, even beyond what I had thought possible to man, I became, in my own person, a creature eaten up and emptied by fever, languidly weak both in body and mind, and solely occupied by one thought: the horror of my other self. But when I slept, or when the virtue of the medicine wore off, I would leap almost without transition (for the pangs of transformation grew daily less marked) into the possession of a fancy brimming with images of terror, a soul boiling with causeless hatreds, and a body that seemed not strong enough to contain the raging energies of life. The powers of Hyde seemed to have grown with the sickliness of Jekyll. And certainly the hate that now divided them was equal on each side. With Jekyll, it was a thing of vital instinct. He had now seen the full deformity of that creature that shared with him some of the phenomena of consciousness, and was co-heir with him to death: and beyond these links of community, which in themselves made the most poignant part of his distress, he thought of Hyde, for all his energy of life, as of something not only hellish but inorganic. This was the shocking thing; that the slime of the pit seemed to utter cries and voices; that the amorphous dust gesticulated and sinned; that what was dead, and had no shape, should usurp the offices of life. And this again, that that insurgent horror was knit to him closer than a wife, closer than an eye; lay caged in his flesh, where he heard it mutter and felt it struggle to be born; and at every hour of weakness, and in the confidence of slumber, prevailed against him, and deposed him out of life. The hatred of Hyde for Jekyll was of a different order. His terror of the gallows drove him continually to commit temporary suicide, and return to his subordinate station of a part instead of a person; but he loathed the necessity, he loathed the despondency into which Jekyll was now fallen, and he resented the dislike with which he was himself regarded. Hence the ape-like tricks that he would play me, scrawling in my own hand blasphemies on the pages of my books, burning the letters and destroying the portrait of my father; and indeed, had it not been for his fear of death, he would long ago have ruined himself in order to involve me in the ruin. But his love of me is wonderful; I go further: I, who sicken and freeze at the mere thought of him, when I recall the abjection and passion of this attachment, and when I know how he fears my power to cut him off by suicide, I find it in my heart to pity him.

It is useless, and the time awfully fails me, to prolong this description; no one has ever suffered such torments, let that suffice; and yet even to these, habit brought—no, not alleviation—but a certain callousness of soul, a certain acquiescence of despair; and my punishment might have gone on for years, but for the last calamity which has now fallen, and which has finally severed me from my own face and nature. My provision of the salt, which had never been renewed since the date of the first experiment, began to run low. I sent out for a fresh supply and mixed the draught; the ebullition followed, and the first change of colour, not the second; I drank it and it was without efficiency. You will learn from Poole how I have had London ransacked; it was in vain; and I am now persuaded that my first supply was impure, and that it was that unknown impurity which lent efficacy to the draught.

About a week has passed, and I am now finishing this statement under the influence of the last of the old powders. This, then, is the last time, short of a miracle, that Henry Jekyll can think his own thoughts or see his own face (now how sadly altered!) in the glass. Nor must I delay too long to bring my writing to an end; for if my narrative has hitherto escaped destruction, it has been by a combination of great prudence and great good luck. Should the throes of change take me in the act of writing it, Hyde will tear it in pieces; but if some time shall have elapsed after I have laid it by, his wonderful selfishness and circumscription to the moment will probably save it once again from the action of his ape-like spite. And indeed the doom that is closing on us both has already changed and crushed him. Half an hour from now, when I shall again and forever reindue that hated personality, I know how I shall sit shuddering and weeping in my chair, or continue, with the most strained and fearstruck ecstasy of listening, to pace up and down this room (my last earthly refuge) and give ear to every sound of menace. Will Hyde die upon the scaffold? or will he find courage to release himself at the last moment? God knows; I am careless; this is my true hour of death, and what is to follow concerns another than myself. Here then, as I lay down the pen and proceed to seal up my confession, I bring the life of that unhappy Henry Jekyll to an end.

THE MASTER OF BALLANTRAE

PREFACE

Although an old, consistent exile, the editor of the following pages revisits now and again the city of which he exults to be a native; and there are few things more strange, more painful, or more salutary, than such revisitations. Outside, in foreign spots, he comes by surprise and awakens more attention than he had expected; in his own city, the relation is reversed, and he stands amazed to be so little recollected. Elsewhere he is refreshed to see attractive faces, to remark possible friends; there he scouts the long streets, with a pang at heart, for the faces and friends that are no more. Elsewhere he is delighted with the presence of what is new, there tormented by the absence of what is old. Elsewhere he is content to be his present self; there he is smitten with an equal regret for what he once was and for what he once hoped to be.

He was feeling all this dimly, as he drove from the station, on his last visit; he was feeling it still as he alighted at the door of his friend Mr. Johnstone Thomson, W.S., with whom he was to stay. A hearty welcome, a face not altogether changed, a few words that sounded of old days, a laugh provoked and shared, a glimpse in passing of the snowy cloth and bright decanters and the Piranesis on the dining-room wall, brought him to his bed-room with a somewhat lightened cheer, and when he and Mr. Thomson sat down a few minutes later, cheek by jowl, and pledged the past in a preliminary bumper, he was already almost consoled, he had already almost forgiven himself his two unpardonable errors, that he should ever have left his native city, or ever returned to it.

"I have something quite in your way," said Mr. Thomson. "I wished to do honour to your arrival; because, my dear fellow, it is my own youth that comes back along with you; in a very tattered and withered state, to be sure, but—well!—all that's left of it."

"A great deal better than nothing," said the editor. "But what is this which is quite in my way?"

"I was coming to that," said Mr. Thomson: "Fate has put it in my power to honour your arrival with something really original by way of dessert. A mystery."

"A mystery?" I repeated.

"Yes," said his friend, "a mystery. It may prove to be nothing, and it may prove to be a great deal. But in the meanwhile it is truly mysterious, no eye having looked on it for near a hundred years; it is highly genteel, for it treats of a titled family; and it ought to be melodramatic, for (according to the superscription) it is concerned with death."

"I think I rarely heard a more obscure or a more promising annunciation," the other remarked. "But what is It?"

"You remember my predecessor's, old Peter M'Brair's business?"

"I remember him acutely; he could not look at me without a pang of reprobation, and he could not feel the pang without betraying it. He was to me a man of a great historical interest, but the interest was not returned."

"Ah well, we go beyond him," said Mr. Thomson. "I daresay old Peter knew as little about this as I do. You see, I succeeded to a prodigious accumulation of old law-papers and old tin boxes, some of them of Peter's hoarding, some of his father's, John, first of the dynasty, a great man in his day. Among other collections, were all the papers of the Durrisdeers."

"The Durrisdeers!" cried I. "My dear fellow, these may be of the greatest interest. One of them was out in the '45; one had some strange passages with the devil—you will find a note of it in Law's *Memorials*, I think; and there was an unexplained tragedy, I know not what, much later, about a hundred years ago—"

"More than a hundred years ago," said Mr. Thomson. "In 1783."

"How do you know that? I mean some death."

"Yes, the lamentable deaths of my Lord Durrisdeer and his brother, the Master of Ballantrae (attainted in the troubles)," said Mr. Thomson with something the tone of a man quoting. "Is that it?"

"To say truth," said I, "I have only seen some dim reference to the things in memoirs; and heard some traditions dimmer still, through my uncle (whom I think you knew). My uncle lived when he was a boy in the neighbourhood of St. Bride's; he has often told me of the avenue closed up and grown over with grass, the great gates never opened, the last lord and his old maid sister who lived in the back parts of the house, a quiet, plain, poor, hum-drum couple it would seem—but pathetic too, as the last of that stirring and brave house—and, to the country folk, faintly terrible from some deformed traditions."

"Yes," said Mr. Thomson. "Henry Graeme Durie, the last lord, died in 1820; his sister, the honourable Miss Katherine Durie, in '27; so much I know; and by what I have been going over the last few days, they were what you say, decent, quiet people and not rich. To say truth, it was a letter of my lord's that put me on the search for the packet we are going to open this evening. Some papers could not be found; and he wrote to Jack M'Brair suggesting they might be among those sealed up by a Mr. Mackellar. M'Brair answered, that the papers in question were all in Mackellar's own hand, all (as the writer understood) of a purely narrative character; and besides, said he, 'I am bound not to open them before the year 1889.' You may fancy if these words struck me: I instituted a hunt through all the M'Brair repositories; and at last hit upon that packet which (if you have had enough wine) I propose to show you at once."

In the smoking-room, to which my host now led me, was a packet, fastened with many seals and enclosed in a single sheet of strong paper thus endorsed:

> Papers relating to the lives and lamentable deaths of the late Lord Durisdeer, and his elder brother James, commonly called Master of Ballantrae, attainted in the troubles: entrusted into the hands of John M'Brair in the Lawnmarket of Edinburgh, W.S.; this 20th day of September Anno Domini 1789; by him to be kept secret until the revolution of one hundred years complete, or until the 20th day of September 1889: the same compiled and written by me, Ephraim Mackellar,
>
> For near forty years Land Steward on the estates of his Lordship.

PREFACE

As Mr. Thomson is a married man, I will not say what hour had struck when we laid down the last of the following pages; but I will give a few words of what ensued.

"Here," said Mr. Thomson, "is a novel ready to your hand: all you have to do is to work up the scenery, develop the characters, and improve the style."

"My dear fellow," said I, "they are just the three things that I would rather die than set my hand to. It shall be published as it stands."

"But it's so bald," objected Mr. Thomson.

"I believe there is nothing so noble as baldness," replied I, "and I am sure there in nothing so interesting. I would have all literature bald, and all authors (if you like) but one."

"Well, well," add Mr. Thomson, "we shall see."

I

SUMMARY OF EVENTS DURING THIS MASTER'S WANDERINGS

THE FULL TRUTH of this odd matter is what the world has long been looking for, and public curiosity is sure to welcome. It so befell that I was intimately mingled with the last years and history of the house; and there does not live one man so able as myself to make these matters plain, or so desirous to narrate them faithfully. I knew the Master; on many secret steps of his career I have an authentic memoir in my hand; I sailed with him on his last voyage almost alone; I made one upon that winter's journey of which so many tales have gone abroad; and I was there at the man's death. As for my late Lord Durrisdeer, I served him and loved him near twenty years; and thought more of him the more I knew of him. Altogether, I think it not fit that so much evidence should perish; the truth is a debt I owe my lord's memory; and I think my old years will flow more smoothly, and my white hair lie quieter on the pillow, when the debt is paid.

The Duries of Durrisdeer and Ballantrae were a strong family in the south-west from the days of David First. A rhyme still current in the countryside—

Kittle folk are the Durrisdeers,
They ride wi' over mony spears—

bears the mark of its antiquity; and the name appears in another, which common report attributes to Thomas of Ercildoune himself—I cannot say how truly, and which some have applied—I dare not say with how much justice—to the events of this narration:

Twa Duries in Durrisdeer,
Ane to tie and ane to ride,
An ill day for the groom
And a waur day for the bride.

Authentic history besides is filled with their exploits which (to our modern eyes) seem not very commendable: and the family suffered its full share of those ups and downs to which the great houses of Scotland have been ever liable. But all these I pass over, to come to that memorable year 1745, when the foundations of this tragedy were laid.

At that time there dwelt a family of four persons in the house of Durrisdeer, near St. Bride's, on the Solway shore; a chief hold of their race since the Reformation. My old lord, eighth of the name, was not old in years, but he suffered prematurely from the disabilities of age; his place was at the chimney side; there he sat reading, in a lined gown, with few words for any man, and wry words for none: the model of an old retired housekeeper; and yet his mind very well nourished with study, and reputed in the country to be more cunning than he seemed. The master of Ballantrae, James in baptism, took from his father the love of serious reading; some of his tact perhaps as well, but that which was only policy in the father became black dissimulation in the son. The face of his behaviour was merely popular and wild: he sat late at wine, later at the cards; had the name in the country of "an unco man for the lasses;" and was ever in the front of broils. But for all he was the first to go in, yet it was observed he was invariably the best to come off; and his partners in mischief were usually alone to pay the piper. This luck or dexterity got him several ill-wishers, but with the rest of the country, enhanced his reputation; so that great things were looked for in his future, when he should have gained more gravity. One very black mark he had to his name; but the matter was hushed up at the time, and so defaced by legends before I came into those parts, that I scruple to set it down. If it was true, it was a horrid fact in one so young; and if false, it was a horrid calumny. I think it notable that he had always vaunted himself quite implacable, and was taken at his word; so that he had the addition among his neighbours of "an ill man to cross." Here was altogether a young nobleman (not yet twenty-four in the year '45) who had made a figure in the country beyond his time of life. The less marvel if there were little heard of the second son, Mr. Henry (my late Lord Durrisdeer), who was neither very bad nor yet very able, but an honest, solid sort of lad like many of his neighbours. Little heard, I say; but indeed it was a case of little spoken. He was known among the salmon fishers in the firth, for that was a sport that he assiduously followed; he was an excellent good horse-doctor besides; and took a chief hand, almost from a boy, in the management of the estates. How hard a part that was, in the situation of that family, none knows better than myself; nor yet with how little colour of justice a man may there acquire the reputation of a tyrant and a miser. The fourth person in the house was Miss Alison Graeme, a near kinswoman, an orphan, and the heir to a considerable fortune which her father had acquired in trade. This money was loudly called for by my lord's necessities; indeed the land was deeply mortgaged; and Miss Alison was designed accordingly to be the Master's wife, gladly enough on her side; with how much good-will on his, is another matter. She was a comely girl, and in those days very spirited and self-willed; for the old lord having no daughter of his own, and my lady being long dead, she had grown up as best she might.

To these four came the news of Prince Charlie's landing, and set them presently by the ears. My lord, like the chimney-keeper that he was, was all for temporising. Miss Alison held the other side, because it appeared romantical; and the Master (though I have heard they did not agree often) was for this once of her opinion. The adventure tempted him, as I conceive; he was tempted by the opportunity to raise the fortunes of the house, and not less by the hope of paying off his private liabilities, which were heavy beyond all opinion. As for Mr. Henry, it appears he said little enough at first; his part came later on. It took the three a whole day's disputation, before they agreed to steer a middle course, one son going forth to strike a blow for King James, my lord and the other staying at home to keep in favour with King George. Doubtless this was my lord's decision; and, as is well known, it was the part played by many considerable families. But the one dispute settled, another opened. For my lord, Miss Alison, and Mr. Henry all held the one view: that it was the cadet's part to go out; and the Master, what with restlessness and vanity, would at no rate consent to stay at home. My lord pleaded, Miss Alison wept, Mr. Henry was very plain spoken: all was of no avail.

"It is the direct heir of Durrisdeer that should ride by his King's bridle," says the Master.

"If we were playing a manly part," says Mr. Henry, "there might be sense in such talk. But what are we doing? Cheating at cards!"

"We are saving the house of Durrisdeer, Henry," his father said.

"And see, James," said Mr. Henry, "if I go, and the Prince has the upper hand, it will be easy to make your peace with King James. But if you go, and the expedition fails, we divide the right and the title. And what shall I be then?"

"You will be Lord Durrisdeer," said the Master. "I put all I have upon the table."

"I play at no such game," cries Mr. Henry. "I shall be left in such a situation as no man of sense and honour could endure. I shall be neither fish nor flesh!" he cried. And a little after he had another expression, plainer perhaps than he intended. "It is your duty to be here with my father," said he. "You know well enough you are the favourite."

"Ay?" said the Master. "And there spoke Envy! Would you trip up my heels—Jacob?" said he, and dwelled upon the name maliciously.

Mr. Henry went and walked at the low end of the hall without reply; for he had an excellent gift of silence. Presently he came back.

"I am the cadet and I *should* go," said he. "And my lord here in the master, and he says I *shall* go. What say ye to that, my brother?"

"I say this, Harry," returned the Master, "that when very obstinate folk are met, there are only two ways out: Blows—and I think none of us could care to go so far; or the arbitrament of chance—and here is a guinea piece. Will you stand by the toss of the coin?"

"I will stand and fall by it," said Mr. Henry. "Heads, I go; shield, I stay."

The coin was spun, and it fell shield. "So there is a lesson for Jacob," says the Master.

"We shall live to repent of this," says Mr. Henry, and flung out of the hall.

As for Miss Alison, she caught up that piece of gold which had just sent her lover to the wars, and flung it clean through the family shield in the great painted window.

"If you loved me as well as I love you, you would have stayed," cried she.

"'I could not love you, dear, so well, loved I not honour more,'" sang the Master.

"Oh!" she cried, "you have no heart—I hope you may be killed!" and she ran from the room, and in tears, to her own chamber.

It seems the Master turned to my lord with his most comical manner, and says he, "This looks like a devil of a wife."

"I think you are a devil of a son to me," cried his father, "you that have always been the favourite, to my shame be it spoken. Never a good hour have I gotten of you, since you were born; no, never one good hour," and repeated it again the third time. Whether it was the Master's levity, or his insubordination, or Mr. Henry's word about the favourite son, that had so much disturbed my lord, I do not know; but I incline to think it was the last, for I have it by all accounts that Mr. Henry was more made up to from that hour.

Altogether it was in pretty ill blood with his family that the Master rode to the North; which was the more sorrowful for others to remember when it seemed too late. By fear and favour he had scraped together near upon a dozen men, principally tenants' sons; they were all pretty full when they set forth, and rode up the hill by the old abbey, roaring and singing, the white cockade in every hat. It was a desperate venture for so small a company to cross the most of Scotland unsupported; and (what made folk think so the more) even as that poor dozen was clattering up the hill, a great ship of the king's navy, that could have brought them under with a single boat, lay with her broad ensign streaming in the bay. The next afternoon, having given the Master a fair start, it was Mr. Henry's turn; and he rode off, all by himself, to offer his sword and carry letters from his father to King George's Government. Miss Alison was shut in her room, and did little but weep, till both were gone; only she stitched the cockade upon the Master's hat, and (as John Paul told me) it was wetted with tears when he carried it down to him.

In all that followed, Mr. Henry and my old lord were true to their bargain. That ever they accomplished anything is more than I could learn; and that they were anyway strong on the king's side, more than believe. But they kept the letter of loyalty, corresponded with my Lord President, sat still at home, and had little or no commerce with the Master while that business lasted. Nor was he, on his side, more communicative. Miss Alison, indeed, was always sending him expresses, but I do not know if she had many answers. Macconochie rode for her once, and found the highlanders before Carlisle, and the Master riding by the Prince's side in high favour; he took the letter (so Macconochie tells), opened it, glanced it through with a mouth like a man whistling, and stuck it in his belt, whence, on his horse passageing, it fell unregarded to the ground. It was Macconochie who picked it up; and he still kept it, and indeed I have seen it in his hands. News came to Durrisdeer of course, by the common report, as it goes travelling through a country, a thing always wonderful to me. By that means the family learned more of the Master's favour with the Prince, and the ground it was said to stand on: for by a strange condescension in a man so proud—only that he was a man still more ambitious—he was said to have crept into notability by truckling to the Irish. Sir Thomas Sullivan, Colonel Burke and the rest, were his daily comrades, by which course he withdrew himself from his own country-folk. All the small intrigues he had a hand in fomenting; thwarted my Lord George upon a thousand points; was always for the advice that seemed palatable to the Prince, no matter if it was good or bad; and seems upon the whole (like the gambler he was all through life) to have had less regard to the chances of the campaign than to the greatness of favour he might aspire to, if, by any luck, it should succeed. For the rest, he did very well in the field; no one questioned that; for he was no coward.

The next was the news of Culloden, which was brought to Durrisdeer by one of the tenants' sons—the only survivor, he declared, of all those that had gone singing up the hill. By an unfortunate chance John Paul and Macconochie had that very morning found the guinea piece —which was the root of all the evil—sticking in a holly bush; they had been "up the gait," as the servants say at Durrisdeer, to the change-house; and if they had little left of the guinea, they had less of their wits. What must John Paul do but burst into the hall where the family sat at dinner, and cry the news to them that "Tam Macmorland was but new lichtit at the door, and—wirra, wirra—there were nane to come behind him"?

They took the word in silence like folk condemned; only Mr. Henry carrying his palm to his face, and Miss Alison laying her head outright upon her hands. As for my lord, he was like ashes.

"I have still one son," says he. "And, Henry, I will do you this justice—it is the kinder that is left."

It was a strange thing to say in such a moment; but my lord had never forgotten Mr. Henry's speech, and he had years of injustice on his conscience. Still it was a strange thing, and more than Miss Alison could let pass. She broke out and blamed my lord for his unnatural words, and Mr. Henry because he was sitting there in safety when his brother lay dead, and herself because she had given her sweetheart ill words at his departure, calling him the flower of the flock, wringing her hands, protesting her love, and crying on him by his name—so that the servants stood astonished.

Mr. Henry got to his feet, and stood holding his chair. It was he that was like ashes now.

"Oh!" he burst out suddenly, "I know you loved him."

"The world knows that, glory be to God!" cries she; and then to Mr. Henry: "There is none but me to know one thing—that you were a traitor to him in your heart."

"God knows," groans he, "it was lost love on both sides."

Time went by in the house after that without much change; only they were now three instead of four, which was a perpetual reminder of their loss. Miss Alison's money, you are to bear in mind, wag highly needful for the estates; and the one brother being dead, my old lord soon set his heart upon her marrying the other. Day in, day out, he would work upon her, sitting by the chimney-side with his finger in his Latin book, and his eyes set upon her face with a kind of pleasant intentness that became the old gentleman very well. If she wept, he would condole with her like an ancient man that has seen worse times and begins to think lightly even of sorrow; if she raged, he would fall to reading again in his Latin book, but always with some civil excuse; if she offered, as she often did, to let them have her money in a gift, he would show her how little it consisted with his honour, and remind her, even if he should consent, that Mr. Henry would certainly refuse. *Non vi sed saepe cadendo* was a favourite word of his; and no doubt this quiet persecution wore away much of her resolve; no doubt, besides, he had a great influence on the girl, having stood in the place of both her parents; and, for that matter, she was herself filled with the spirit of the Duries, and would have gone a great way for the glory of Durrisdeer; but not so far, I think, as to marry my poor patron, had it not been—strangely enough—for the circumstance of his extreme unpopularity.

This was the work of Tam Macmorland. There was not much harm in Tam; but he had that grievous weakness, a long tongue; and as the only man in that country who had been out—or, rather, who had come in again—he was sure of listeners. Those that have the underhand in any fighting, I have observed, are ever anxious to persuade themselves they were betrayed. By Tam's account of it, the rebels had been betrayed at every turn and by every officer they had; they had been betrayed at Derby, and betrayed at Falkirk; the night march was a step of treachery of my Lord George's; and Culloden was lost by the treachery of the Macdonalds. This habit of imputing treason grew upon the fool, till at last he must have in Mr. Henry also. Mr. Henry (by his account) had betrayed the lads of Durrisdeer; he had promised to follow with more men, and instead of that he had ridden to King George. "Ay, and the next day!" Tam would cry. "The puir bonnie Master, and the puir, kind lads that rade wi' him, were hardly ower the scaur, or he was aff—the Judis! Ay, weel—he has his way o't: he's to be my lord, nae less, and there's mony a cold corp amang the Hieland heather!" And at this, if Tam had been drinking, he would begin to weep.

Let anyone speak long enough, he will get believers. This view of Mr. Henry's behaviour crept about the country by little and little; it was talked upon by folk that knew the contrary, but were short of topics; and it was heard and believed and given out for gospel by the ignorant and the ill-willing. Mr. Henry began to be shunned; yet awhile, and the commons began to murmur as he went by, and the women (who are always the most bold because they are the most safe) to cry out their reproaches to his face. The Master was cried up for a saint. It was remembered how he had never any hand in pressing the tenants; as, indeed, no more he had, except to spend the money. He was a little wild perhaps, the folk said; but how much better was a natural, wild lad that would soon have settled down, than a skinflint and a sneckdraw, sitting, with his nose in an account book, to persecute poor tenants! One trollop, who had had a child to the Master, and by all accounts been very badly used, yet made herself a kind of champion of his memory. She flung a stone one day at Mr. Henry.

"Whaur's the bonnie lad that trustit ye?" she cried.

Mr. Henry reined in his horse and looked upon her, the blood flowing from his lip. "Ay, Jess?" says he. "You too? And yet ye should ken me better." For it was he who had helped her with money.

The woman had another stone ready, which she made as if she would cast; and he, to ward himself, threw up the hand that held his riding-rod.

"What, would ye beat a lassie, ye ugly—?" cries she, and ran away screaming as though he had struck her.

Next day word went about the country like wildfire that Mr. Henry had beaten Jessie Broun within an inch of her life. I give it as one instance of how this snowball grew, and one calumny brought another; until my poor patron was so perished in reputation that he began to keep the house like my lord. All this while, you may be very sure, he uttered no complaints at home; the very ground of the scandal was too sore a matter to be handled; and Mr. Henry was very proud and strangely obstinate in silence. My old lord must have heard of it, by John Paul, if by no one else; and he must at least have remarked the altered habits of his son. Yet even he, it is probable, knew not how high the feeling ran; and as for Miss Alison, she was ever the last person to hear news, and the least interested when she heard them.

In the height of the ill-feeling (for it died away as it came, no man could say why) there was an election forward in the town of St. Bride's, which is the next to Durrisdeer, standing on the Water of Swift; some grievance was fermenting, I forget what, if ever I heard; and it was currently said there would be broken heads ere night, and that the sheriff had sent as far as Dumfries for soldiers. My lord moved that Mr. Henry should be present, assuring him it was necessary to appear, for the credit of the house. "It will soon be reported," said he, "that we do not take the lead in our own country."

"It is a strange lead that I can take," said Mr. Henry; and when they had pushed him further, "I tell you the plain truth," he said, "I dare not show my face."

"You are the first of the house that ever said so," cries Miss Alison.

"We will go all three," said my lord; and sure enough he got into his boots (the first time in four years—a sore business John Paul had to get them on), and Miss Alison into her riding-coat, and all three rode together to St. Bride's.

The streets were full of the rift-raff of all the countryside, who had no sooner clapped eyes on Mr. Henry than the hissing began, and the hooting, and the cries of "Judas!" and "Where was the Master?" and "Where were the poor lads that rode with him?" Even a stone was cast; but the more part cried shame at that, for my old lord's sake, and Miss Alison's. It took not ten minutes to persuade my lord that Mr. Henry had been right. He said never a word, but turned his horse about, and home again, with his chin upon his bosom. Never a word said Miss Alison; no doubt she thought the more; no doubt her pride was stung, for she was a bone-bred Durie; and no doubt her heart was touched to see her cousin so unjustly used. That night she was never in bed; I have often blamed my lady—when I call to mind that night, I readily forgive her all; and the first thing in the morning she came to the old lord in his usual seat.

"If Henry still wants me," said she, "he can have me now." To himself she had a different speech: "I bring you no love, Henry; but God knows, all the pity in the world."

June the 1st, 1748, was the day of their marriage. It was December of the same year that first saw me alighting at the doors of the great house; and from there I take up the history of events as they befell under my own observation, like a witness in a court.

2
SUMMARY OF EVENTS (CONTINUED)

I MADE the last of my journey in the cold end of December, in a mighty dry day of frost, and who should be my guide but Patey Macmorland, brother of Tam! For a tow-headed, bare-legged brat of ten, he had more ill tales upon his tongue than ever I heard the match of; having drunken betimes in his brother's cup. I was still not so old myself; pride had not yet the upper hand of curiosity; and indeed it would have taken any man, that cold morning, to hear all the old clashes of the country, and be shown all the places by the way where strange things had fallen out. I had tales of Claverhouse as we came through the bogs, and tales of the devil, as we came over the top of the scaur. As we came in by the abbey I heard somewhat of the old monks, and more of the freetraders, who use its ruins for a magazine, landing for that cause within a cannon-shot of Durrisdeer; and along all the road the Duries and poor Mr. Henry were in the first rank of slander. My mind was thus highly prejudiced against the family I was about to serve, so that I was half surprised when I beheld Durrisdeer itself, lying in a pretty, sheltered bay, under the Abbey Hill; the house most commodiously built in the French fashion, or perhaps Italianate, for I have no skill in these arts; and the place the most beautified with gardens, lawns, shrubberies, and trees I had ever seen. The money sunk here unproductively would have quite restored the family; but as it was, it cost a revenue to keep it up.

Mr. Henry came himself to the door to welcome me: a tall dark young gentleman (the Duries are all black men) of a plain and not cheerful face, very strong in body, but not so strong in health: taking me by the hand without any pride, and putting me at home with plain kind speeches. He led me into the hall, booted as I was, to present me to my lord. It was still daylight; and the first thing I observed was a lozenge of clear glass in the midst of the shield in the painted window, which I remember thinking a blemish on a room otherwise so handsome, with its family portraits, and the pargeted ceiling with pendants, and the carved chimney, in one corner of which my old lord sat reading in his Livy. He was like Mr. Henry, with much the same plain countenance, only more subtle and pleasant, and his talk a thousand times more entertaining. He had many questions to ask me, I remember, of Edinburgh College, where I had just received my mastership of arts, and of the various professors, with whom and their proficiency he seemed well acquainted; and thus, talking of things that I knew, I soon got liberty of speech in my new home.

In the midst of this came Mrs. Henry into the room; she was very far gone, Miss Katharine being due in about six weeks, which made me think less of her beauty at the first sight; and she used me with more of condescension than the rest; so that, upon all accounts, I kept her in the third place of my esteem.

It did not take long before all Patey Macmorland's tales were blotted out of my belief, and I was become, what I have ever since remained, a loving servant of the house of Durrisdeer. Mr. Henry had the chief part of my affection. It was with him I worked; and I found him an exacting master, keeping all his kindness for those hours in which we were unemployed, and in the steward's office not only loading me with work, but viewing me with a shrewd supervision. At length one day he looked up from his paper with a kind of timidness, and says he, "Mr. Mackellar, I think I ought to tell you that you do very well." That was my first word of commendation; and from that day his jealousy of my performance was relaxed; soon it was "Mr. Mackellar" here, and "Mr. Mackellar" there, with the whole family; and for much of my service at Durrisdeer, I have transacted everything at my own time, and to my own fancy, and never a farthing challenged. Even while he was driving me, I had begun to find my heart go out to Mr. Henry; no doubt, partly in pity, he was a man so palpably unhappy. He would fall into a deep muse over our accounts, staring at the page or out of the window; and at those times the look of his face, and the sigh that would break from him, awoke in me strong feelings of curiosity and commiseration. One day, I remember, we were late upon some business in the steward's room.

This room is in the top of the house, and has a view upon the bay, and over a little wooded cape, on the long sands; and there, right over against the sun, which was then dipping, we saw the freetraders, with a great force of men and horses, scouring on the beach. Mr. Henry had been staring straight west, so that I marvelled he was not blinded by the sun; suddenly he frowns, rubs his hand upon his brow, and turns to me with a smile.

"You would not guess what I was thinking," says he. "I was thinking I would be a happier man if I could ride and run the danger of my life, with these lawless companions."

I told him I had observed he did not enjoy good spirits; and that it was a common fancy to envy others and think we should be the better of some change; quoting Horace to the point, like a young man fresh from college.

"Why, just so," said he. "And with that we may get back to our accounts."

It was not long before I began to get wind of the causes that so much depressed him. Indeed a blind man must have soon discovered there was a shadow on that house, the shadow of the Master of Ballantrae. Dead or alive (and he was then supposed to be dead) that man was his brother's rival: his rival abroad, where there was never a good word for Mr. Henry, and nothing but regret and praise for the Master; and his rival at home, not only with his father and his wife, but with the very servants.

They were two old serving-men that were the leaders. John Paul, a little, bald, solemn, stomachy man, a great professor of piety and (take him for all in all) a pretty faithful servant, was the chief of the Master's faction. None durst go so far as John. He took a pleasure in disregarding Mr. Henry publicly, often with a slighting comparison. My lord and Mrs. Henry took him up, to be sure, but never so resolutely as they should; and he had only to pull his weeping face and begin his lamentations for the Master—"his laddie," as he called him—to have the whole condoned. As for Henry, he let these things pass in silence, sometimes with a sad and sometimes with a black look. There was no rivalling the dead, he knew that; and how to censure an old serving-man for a fault of loyalty, was more than he could see. His was not the tongue to do it.

Macconochie was chief upon the other side; an old, ill-spoken, swearing, ranting, drunken dog; and I have often thought it an odd circumstance in human nature that these two serving-men should each have been the champion of his contrary, and blackened their own faults and made light of their own virtues when they beheld them in a master. Macconochie had soon smelled out my secret inclination, took me much into his confidence, and would rant against the Master by the hour, so that even my work suffered. "They're a' daft here," he would cry, "and be damned to them! The Master—the deil's in their thrapples that should call him sae! it's Mr. Henry should be master now! They were nane sae fond o' the Master when they had him, I'll can tell ye that. Sorrow on his name! Never a guid word did I hear on his lips, nor naebody else, but just fleering and flyting and profane cursing—deil hae him! There's nane kent his wickedness: him a gentleman! Did ever ye hear tell, Mr. Mackellar, o' Wully White the wabster? No? Aweel, Wully was an unco praying kind o' man; a dreigh body, nane o' my kind, I never could abide the sight o' him; onyway he was a great hand by his way of it, and he up and rebukit the Master for some of his on-goings. It was a grand thing for the Master o' Ball'ntrae to tak up a feud wi' a' wabster, wasnae't?" Macconochie would sneer; indeed, he never took the full name upon his lips but with a sort of a whine of hatred. "But he did! A fine employ it was: chapping at the man's door, and crying 'boo' in his lum, and puttin' poother in his fire, and pee-oys[1] in his window; till the man thocht it was auld Hornie was come seekin' him. Weel, to mak a lang story short, Wully gaed gyte. At the hinder end, they couldnae get him frae his knees, but he just roared and prayed and grat straucht on, till he got his release. It was fair murder, a'body said that. Ask John Paul—he was brawly ashamed o' that game, him that's sic a Christian man! Grand doin's for the Master o' Ball'ntrae!" I asked him what the Master had thought of it himself. "How would I ken?" says he. "He never said naething." And on again in his usual manner of banning and swearing, with every now and again a "Master of Ballantrae" sneered through his nose. It was in one of these confidences that he showed me the Carlisle letter, the print of the horse-shoe still stamped in the paper. Indeed, that was our last confidence; for he then expressed himself so ill-naturedly of Mrs. Henry that I had to reprimand him sharply, and must thenceforth hold him at a distance.

My old lord was uniformly kind to Mr. Henry; he had even pretty ways of gratitude, and would sometimes clap him on the shoulder and say, as if to the world at large: "This is a very good son to me." And grateful he was, no doubt, being a man of sense and justice. But I think that was all, and I am sure Mr. Henry thought so. The love was all for the dead son. Not that this was often given breath to; indeed, with me but once. My lord had asked me one day how I got on with Mr. Henry, and I had told him the truth.

"Ay," said he, looking sideways on the burning fire, "Henry is a good lad, a very good lad," said he. "You have heard, Mr. Mackellar, that I had another son? I am afraid he was not so virtuous a lad as Mr. Henry; but dear me, he's dead, Mr. Mackellar! and while he lived we were all very proud of him, all very proud. If he was not all he should have been in some ways, well, perhaps we loved him better!" This last he said looking musingly in the fire; and then to me, with a great deal of briskness, "But I am rejoiced you do so well with Mr. Henry. You will find him a good master." And with that he opened his book, which was the customary signal of dismission. But it would be little that he read, and less that he understood; Culloden field and the Master, these would be the burthen of his thought; and the burthen of mine was an unnatural jealousy of the dead man for Mr. Henry's sake, that had even then begun to grow on me.

I am keeping Mrs. Henry for the last, so that this expression of my sentiment may seem unwarrantably strong: the reader shall judge for himself when I have done. But I must first tell of another matter, which was the means of bringing me more intimate. I had not yet been six months at Durrisdeer when it chanced that John Paul fell sick and must keep his bed; drink was the root of his malady, in my poor thought; but he was tended, and indeed carried himself, like an afflicted saint; and the very minister, who came to visit him, professed himself edified when he went away. The third morning of his sickness, Mr. Henry comes to me with something of a hang-dog look.

"Mackellar," says he, "I wish I could trouble you upon a little service. There is a pension we pay; it is John's part to carry it, and now that he is sick I know not to whom I should look unless it was yourself. The matter is very delicate; I could not carry it with my own hand for a sufficient reason; I dare not send Macconochie, who is a talker, and I am—I have—I am desirous this should not come to Mrs. Henry's ears," says he, and flushed to his neck as he said it.

To say truth, when I found I was to carry money to one Jessie Broun, who was no better than she should be, I supposed it was some trip of his own that Mr. Henry was dissembling. I was the more impressed when the truth came out.

It was up a wynd off a side street in St. Bride's that Jessie had her lodging. The place was very ill inhabited, mostly by the freetrading sort. There was a man with a broken head at the entry; half-way up, in a tavern, fellows were roaring and singing, though it was not yet nine in the day. Altogether, I had never seen a worse neighbourhood, even in the great city of Edinburgh, and I was in two minds to go back. Jessie's room was of a piece with her surroundings, and herself no better. She would not give me the receipt (which Mr. Henry had told me to demand, for he was very methodical) until she had sent out for spirits, and I had pledged her in a glass; and all the time she carried on in a light-headed, reckless way—now aping the manners of a lady, now breaking into unseemly mirth, now making coquettish advances that oppressed me to the ground. Of the money she spoke more tragically.

"It's blood money!" said she; "I take it for that: blood money for the betrayed! See what I'm brought down to! Ah, if the bonnie lad were back again, it would be changed days. But he's deid—he's lyin' deid amang the Hieland hills—the bonnie lad, the bonnie lad!"

She had a rapt manner of crying on the bonnie lad, clasping her hands and casting up her eyes, that I think she must have learned of strolling players; and I thought her sorrow very much of an affectation, and that she dwelled upon the business because her shame was now all she had to be proud of. I will not say I did not pity her, but it was a loathing pity at the best; and her last change of manner wiped it out. This was when she had had enough of me for an audience, and had set her name at last to the receipt. "There!" says she, and taking the most unwomanly oaths upon her tongue, bade me begone and carry it to the Judas who had sent me. It was the first time I had heard the name applied to Mr. Henry; I was staggered besides at her sudden vehemence of word and manner, and got forth from the room, under this shower of curses, like a beaten dog. But even then I was not quit, for the vixen threw up her window, and, leaning forth, continued to revile me as I went up the wynd; the freetraders, coming to the tavern door, joined in the mockery, and one had even the inhumanity to set upon me a very savage small dog, which bit me in the ankle. This was a strong lesson, had I required one, to avoid ill company; and I rode home in much pain from the bite and considerable indignation of mind.

Mr. Henry was in the steward's room, affecting employment, but I could see he was only impatient to hear of my errand.

"Well?" says he, as soon as I came in; and when I had told him something of what passed, and that Jessie seemed an undeserving woman and far from grateful: "She is no friend to me," said he; "but, indeed, Mackellar, I have few friends to boast of, and Jessie has some cause to be unjust. I need not dissemble what all the country knows: she was not very well used by one of our family." This was the first time I had heard him refer to the Master even distantly; and I think he found his tongue rebellious even for that much, but presently he resumed—"This is why I would have nothing said. It would give pain to Mrs. Henry . . . and to my father," he added, with another flush.

"Mr. Henry," said I, "if you will take a freedom at my hands, I would tell you to let that woman be. What service is your money to the like of her? She has no sobriety and no economy—as for gratitude, you will as soon get milk from a whinstone; and if you will pretermit your bounty, it will make no change at all but just to save the ankles of your messengers."

Mr. Henry smiled. "But I am grieved about your ankle," said he, the next moment, with a proper gravity.

"And observe," I continued, "I give you this advice upon consideration; and yet my heart was touched for the woman in the beginning."

"Why, there it is, you see!" said Mr. Henry. "And you are to remember that I knew her once a very decent lass. Besides which, although I speak little of my family, I think much of its repute."

And with that he broke up the talk, which was the first we had together in such confidence. But the same afternoon I had the proof that his father was perfectly acquainted with the business, and that it was only from his wife that Mr. Henry kept it secret.

"I fear you had a painful errand to-day," says my lord to me, "for which, as it enters in no way among your duties, I wish to thank you, and to remind you at the same time (in case Mr. Henry should have neglected) how very desirable it is that no word of it should reach my daughter. Reflections on the dead, Mr. Mackellar, are doubly painful."

Anger glowed in my heart; and I could have told my lord to his face how little he had to do, bolstering up the image of the dead in Mrs. Henry's heart, and how much better he were employed to shatter that false idol; for by this time I saw very well how the land lay between my patron and his wife.

My pen is clear enough to tell a plain tale; but to render the effect of an infinity of small things, not one great enough in itself to be narrated; and to translate the story of looks, and the message of voices when they are saying no great matter; and to put in half a page the essence of near eighteen months—this is what I despair to accomplish. The fault, to be very blunt, lay all in Mrs. Henry. She felt it a merit to have consented to the marriage, and she took it like a martyrdom; in which my old lord, whether he knew it or not, fomented her. She made a merit, besides, of her constancy to the dead, though its name, to a nicer conscience, should have seemed rather disloyalty to the living; and here also my lord gave her his countenance. I suppose he was glad to talk of his loss, and ashamed to dwell on it with Mr. Henry. Certainly, at least, he made a little coterie apart in that family of three, and it was the husband who was shut out. It seems it was an old custom when the family were alone in Durrisdeer, that my lord should take his wine to the chimney-side, and Miss Alison, instead of withdrawing, should bring a stool to his knee, and chatter to him privately; and after she had become my patron's wife the same manner of doing was continued. It should have been pleasant to behold this ancient gentleman so loving with his daughter, but I was too much a partisan of Mr. Henry's to be anything but wroth at his exclusion. Many's the time I have seen him make an obvious resolve, quit the table, and go and join himself to his wife and my Lord Durrisdeer; and on their part, they were never backward to make him welcome, turned to him smilingly as to an intruding child, and took him into their talk with an effort so ill-concealed that he was soon back again beside me at the table, whence (so great is the hall of Durrisdeer) we could but hear the murmur of voices at the chimney. There he would sit and watch, and I along with him; and sometimes by my lord's head sorrowfully shaken, or his hand laid on Mrs. Henry's head, or hers upon his knee as if in consolation, or sometimes by an exchange of tearful looks, we would draw our conclusion that the talk had gone to the old subject and the shadow of the dead was in the hall.

I have hours when I blame Mr. Henry for taking all too patiently; yet we are to remember he was married in pity, and accepted his wife upon that term. And, indeed, he had small encouragement to make a stand. Once, I remember, he announced he had found a man to replace the pane of the stained window, which, as it was he that managed all the business, was a thing clearly within his attributions. But to the Master's fancies, that pane was like a relic; and on the first word of any change, the blood flew to Mrs. Henry's face.

"I wonder at you!" she cried.

"I wonder at myself," says Mr. Henry, with more of bitterness than I had ever heard him to express.

Thereupon my old lord stepped in with his smooth talk, so that before the meal was at an end all seemed forgotten; only that, after dinner, when the pair had withdrawn as usual to the chimney-side, we could see her weeping with her head upon his knee. Mr. Henry kept up the talk with me upon some topic of the estates—he could speak of little else but business, and was never the best of company; but he kept it up that day with more continuity, his eye straying ever and again to the chimney, and his voice changing to another key, but without check of delivery. The pane, however, was not replaced; and I believe he counted it a great defeat.

Whether he was stout enough or no, God knows he was kind enough. Mrs. Henry had a manner of condescension with him, such as (in a wife) would have pricked my vanity into an ulcer; he took it like a favour. She held him at the staff's end; forgot and then remembered and unbent to him, as we do to children; burthened him with cold kindness; reproved him with a change of colour and a bitten lip, like one shamed by his disgrace: ordered him with a look of the eye, when she was off her guard; when she was on the watch, pleaded with him for the most natural attentions, as though they were unheard-of favours. And to all this he replied with the most unwearied service, loving, as folk say, the very ground she trod on, and carrying that love in his eyes as bright as a lamp. When Miss Katharine was to be born, nothing would serve but he must stay in the room behind the head of the bed. There he sat, as white (they tell me) as a sheet, and the sweat dropping from his brow; and the handkerchief he had in his hand was crushed into a little ball no bigger than a musket-bullet. Nor could he bear the sight of Miss Katharine for many a day; indeed, I doubt if he was ever what he should have been to my young lady; for the which want of natural feeling he was loudly blamed.

Such was the state of this family down to the 7th April, 1749, when there befell the first of that series of events which were to break so many hearts and lose so many lives.

On that day I was sitting in my room a little before supper, when John Paul burst open the door with no civility of knocking, and told me there was one below that wished to speak with the steward; sneering at the name of my office.

I asked what manner of man, and what his name was; and this disclosed the cause of John's ill-humour; for it appeared the visitor refused to name himself except to me, a sore affront to the major-domo's consequence.

"Well," said I, smiling a little, "I will see what he wants."

I found in the entrance hall a big man, very plainly habited, and wrapped in a sea-cloak, like one new landed, as indeed he was. Not, far off Macconochie was standing, with his tongue out of his mouth and his hand upon his chin, like a dull fellow thinking hard; and the stranger, who had brought his cloak about his face, appeared uneasy. He had no sooner seen me coming than he went to meet me with an effusive manner.

"My dear man," said he, "a thousand apologies for disturbing you, but I'm in the most awkward position. And there's a son of a ramrod there that I should know the looks of, and more betoken I believe that he knows mine. Being in this family, sir, and in a place of some responsibility (which was the cause I took the liberty to send for you), you are doubtless of the honest party?"

"You may be sure at least," says I, "that all of that party are quite safe in Durrisdeer."

"My dear man, it is my very thought," says he. "You see, I have just been set on shore here by a very honest man, whose name I cannot remember, and who is to stand off and on for me till morning, at some danger to himself; and, to be clear with you, I am a little concerned lest it should be at some to me. I have saved my life so often, Mr. —, I forget your name, which is a very good one—that, faith, I would be very loath to lose it after all. And the son of a ramrod, whom I believe I saw before Carlisle . . . "

"Oh, sir," said I, "you can trust Macconochie until to-morrow."

"Well, and it's a delight to hear you say so," says the stranger. "The truth is that my name is not a very suitable one in this country of Scotland. With a gentleman like you, my dear man, I would have no concealments of course; and by your leave I'll just breathe it in your ear. They call me Francis Burke—Colonel Francis Burke; and I am here, at a most damnable risk to myself, to see your masters—if you'll excuse me, my good man, for giving them the name, for I'm sure it's a circumstance I would never have guessed from your appearance. And if you would just be so very obliging as to take my name to them, you might say that I come bearing letters which I am sure they will be very rejoiced to have the reading of."

Colonel Francis Burke was one of the Prince's Irishmen, that did his cause such an infinity of hurt, and were so much distasted of the Scots at the time of the rebellion; and it came at once into my mind, how the Master of Ballantrae had astonished all men by going with that party. In the same moment a strong foreboding of the truth possessed my soul.

"If you will step in here," said I, opening a chamber door, "I will let my lord know."

"And I am sure it's very good of you, Mr. What-is-your-name," says the Colonel.

Up to the hall I went, slow-footed. There they were, all three—my old lord in his place, Mrs. Henry at work by the window, Mr. Henry (as was much his custom) pacing the low end. In the midst was the table laid for supper. I told them briefly what I had to say. My old lord lay back in his seat. Mrs. Henry sprang up standing with a mechanical motion, and she and her husband stared at each other's eyes across the room; it was the strangest, challenging look these two exchanged, and as they looked, the colour faded in their faces. Then Mr. Henry turned to me; not to speak, only to sign with his finger; but that was enough, and I went down again for the Colonel.

When we returned, these three were in much the same position I same left them in; I believe no word had passed.

"My Lord Durrisdeer, no doubt?" says the Colonel, bowing, and my lord bowed in answer. "And this," continues the Colonel, "should be the Master of Ballantrae?"

"I have never taken that name," said Mr. Henry; "but I am Henry Durie, at your service."

Then the Colonel turns to Mrs. Henry, bowing with his hat upon his heart and the most killing airs of gallantry. "There can be no mistake about so fine a figure of a lady," says he. "I address the seductive Miss Alison, of whom I have so often heard?"

Once more husband and wife exchanged a look.

"I am Mrs. Henry Durie," said she; "but before my marriage my name was Alison Graeme."

Then my lord spoke up. "I am an old man, Colonel Burke," said he, "and a frail one. It will be mercy on your part to be expeditious. Do you bring me news of—" he hesitated, and then the words broke from him with a singular change of voice—"my son?"

"My dear lord, I will be round with you like a soldier," said the Colonel. "I do."

My lord held out a wavering hand; he seemed to wave a signal, but whether it was to give him time or to speak on, was more than we could guess. At length he got out the one word, "Good?"

"Why, the very best in the creation!" cries the Colonel. "For my good friend and admired comrade is at this hour in the fine city of Paris, and as like as not, if I know anything of his habits, he will be drawing in his chair to a piece of dinner.—Bedad, I believe the lady's fainting."

Mrs. Henry was indeed the colour of death, and drooped against the window-frame. But when Mr. Henry made a movement as if to run to her, she straightened with a sort of shiver. "I am well," she said, with her white lips.

Mr. Henry stopped, and his face had a strong twitch of anger. The next moment he had turned to the Colonel. "You must not blame yourself," says he, "for this effect on Mrs. Durie. It is only natural; we were all brought up like brother and sister."

Mrs. Henry looked at her husband with something like relief or even gratitude. In my way of thinking, that speech was the first step he made in her good graces.

"You must try to forgive me, Mrs. Durie, for indeed and I am just an Irish savage," said the Colonel; "and I deserve to be shot for not breaking the matter more artistically to a lady. But here are the Master's own letters; one for each of the three of you; and to be sure (if I know anything of my friend's genius) he will tell his own story with a better grace."

He brought the three letters forth as he spoke, arranged them by their superscriptions, presented the first to my lord, who took it greedily, and advanced towards Mrs. Henry holding out the second.

But the lady waved it back. "To my husband," says she, with a choked voice.

The Colonel was a quick man, but at this he was somewhat nonplussed. "To be sure!" says he; "how very dull of me! To be sure!" But he still held the letter.

At last Mr. Henry reached forth his hand, and there was nothing to be done but give it up. Mr. Henry took the letters (both hers and his own), and looked upon their outside, with his brows knit hard, as if he were thinking. He had surprised me all through by his excellent behaviour; but he was to excel himself now.

"Let me give you a hand to your room," said he to his wife. "This has come something of the suddenest; and, at any rate, you will wish to read your letter by yourself."

Again she looked upon him with the same thought of wonder; but he gave her no time, coming straight to where she stood. "It will be better so, believe me," said he; "and Colonel Burke is too considerate not to excuse you." And with that he took her hand by the fingers, and led her from the hall.

Mrs. Henry returned no more that night; and when Mr. Henry went to visit her next morning, as I heard long afterwards, she gave him the letter again, still unopened.

"Oh, read it and be done!" he had cried.

"Spare me that," said she.

And by these two speeches, to my way of thinking, each undid a great part of what they had previously done well. But the letter, sure enough, came into my hands, and by me was burned, unopened.

To be very exact as to the adventures of the Master after Culloden, I wrote not long ago to Colonel Burke, now a Chevalier of the Order of St. Louis, begging him for some notes in writing, since I could scarce depend upon my memory at so great an interval. To confess the truth, I have been somewhat embarrassed by his response; for he sent me the complete memoirs of his life, touching only in places on the Master; running to a much greater length than my whole story, and not everywhere (as it seems to me) designed for edification. He begged in his letter, dated from Ettenheim, that I would find a publisher for the whole, after I had made what use of it I required; and I think I shall best answer my own purpose and fulfil his wishes by printing certain parts of it in full. In this way my readers will have a detailed, and, I believe, a very genuine account of some essential matters; and if any publisher should take a fancy to the Chevalier's manner of narration, he knows where to apply for the rest, of which there is plenty at his service. I put in my first extract here, so that it may stand in the place of what the Chevalier told us over our wine in the hall of Durrisdeer; but you are to suppose it was not the brutal fact, but a very varnished version that he offered to my lord.

---

1. A kind of firework made with damp powder.

3

THE MASTER'S WANDERINGS

FROM THE MEMOIRS OF THE CHEVALIER DE BURKE.

. . . I left Ruthven (it's hardly necessary to remark) with much greater satisfaction than I had come to it; but whether I missed my way in the deserts, or whether my companions failed me, I soon found myself alone. This was a predicament very disagreeable; for I never understood this horrid country or savage people, and the last stroke of the Prince's withdrawal had made us of the Irish more unpopular than ever. I was reflecting on my poor chances, when I saw another horseman on the hill, whom I supposed at first to have been a phantom, the news of his death in the very front at Culloden being current in the army generally. This was the Master of Ballantrae, my Lord Durrisdeer's son, a young nobleman of the rarest gallantry and parts, and equally designed by nature to adorn a Court and to reap laurels in the field. Our meeting was the more welcome to both, as he was one of the few Scots who had used the Irish with consideration, and as he might now be of very high utility in aiding my escape. Yet what founded our particular friendship was a circumstance, by itself as romantic as any fable of King Arthur.

This was on the second day of our flight, after we had slept one night in the rain upon the inclination of a mountain. There was an Appin man, Alan Black Stewart (or some such name,[1] but I have seen him since in France) who chanced to be passing the same way, and had a jealousy of my companion. Very uncivil expressions were exchanged; and Stewart calls upon the Master to alight and have it out.

"Why, Mr. Stewart," says the Master, "I think at the present time I would prefer to run a race with you." And with the word claps spurs to his horse.

Stewart ran after us, a childish thing to do, for more than a mile; and I could not help laughing, as I looked back at last and saw him on a hill, holding his hand to his side, and nearly burst with running.

"But, all the same," I could not help saying to my companion, "I would let no man run after me for any such proper purpose, and not give him his desire. It was a good jest, but it smells a trifle cowardly."

He bent his brows at me. "I do pretty well," says he, "when I saddle myself with the most unpopular man in Scotland, and let that suffice for courage."

"O, bedad," says I, "I could show you a more unpopular with the naked eye. And if you like not my company, you can 'saddle' yourself on some one else."

"Colonel Burke," says he, "do not let us quarrel; and, to that effect, let me assure you I am the least patient man in the world."

"I am as little patient as yourself," said I. "I care not who knows that."

"At this rate," says he, reining in, "we shall not go very far. And I propose we do one of two things upon the instant: either quarrel and be done; or make a sure bargain to bear everything at each other's hands."

"Like a pair of brothers?" said I.

"I said no such foolishness," he replied. "I have a brother of my own, and I think no more of him than of a colewort. But if we are to have our noses rubbed together in this course of flight, let us each dare to be ourselves like savages, and each swear that he will neither resent nor deprecate the other. I am a pretty bad fellow at bottom, and I find the pretence of virtues very irksome."

"O, I am as bad as yourself," said I. "There is no skim milk in Francis Burke. But which is it to be? Fight or make friends?"

"Why," says he, "I think it will be the best manner to spin a coin for it."

This proposition was too highly chivalrous not to take my fancy; and, strange as it may seem of two well-born gentlemen of to-day, we span a half-crown (like a pair of ancient paladins) whether we were to cut each other's throats or be sworn friends. A more romantic circumstance can rarely have occurred; and it is one of those points in my memoirs, by which we may see the old tales of Homer and the poets are equally true to-day—at least, of the noble and genteel. The coin fell for peace, and we shook hands upon our bargain. And then it was that my companion explained to me his thought in running away from Mr. Stewart, which was certainly worthy of his political intellect. The report of his death, he said, was a great guard to him; Mr. Stewart having recognised him, had become a danger; and he had taken the briefest road to that gentleman's silence. "For," says he, "Alan Black is too vain a man to narrate any such story of himself."

Towards afternoon we came down to the shores of that loch for which we were heading; and there was the ship, but newly come to anchor. She was the *Sainte-Marie-des-Anges*, out of the port of Havre-de-Grace. The Master, after we had signalled for a boat, asked me if I knew the captain. I told him he was a countryman of mine, of the most unblemished integrity, but, I was afraid, a rather timorous man.

"No matter," says he. "For all that, he should certainly hear the truth."

I asked him if he meant about the battle? for if the captain once knew the standard was down, he would certainly put to sea again at once.

"And even then!" said he; "the arms are now of no sort of utility."

"My dear man," said I, "who thinks of the arms? But, to be sure, we must remember our friends. They will be close upon our heels, perhaps the Prince himself, and if the ship be gone, a great number of valuable lives may be imperilled."

"The captain and the crew have lives also, if you come to that," says Ballantrae.

This I declared was but a quibble, and that I would not hear of the captain being told; and then it was that Ballantrae made me a witty answer, for the sake of which (and also because I have been blamed myself in this business of the *Sainte-Marie-des-Anges*) I have related the whole conversation as it passed.

"Frank," says he, "remember our bargain. I must not object to your holding your tongue, which I hereby even encourage you to do; but, by the same terms, you are not to resent my telling."

I could not help laughing at this; though I still forewarned him what would come of it.

"The devil may come of it for what I care," says the reckless fellow. "I have always done exactly as I felt inclined."

As is well known, my prediction came true. The captain had no sooner heard the news than he cut his cable and to sea again; and before morning broke, we were in the Great Minch.

The ship was very old; and the skipper, although the most honest of men (and Irish too), was one of the least capable. The wind blew very boisterous, and the sea raged extremely. All that day we had little heart whether to eat or drink; went early to rest in some concern of mind; and (as if to give us a lesson) in the night the wind chopped suddenly into the north-east, and blew a hurricane. We were awaked by the dreadful thunder of the tempest and the stamping of the mariners on deck; so that I supposed our last hour was certainly come; and the terror of my mind was increased out of all measure by Ballantrae, who mocked at my devotions. It is in hours like these that a man of any piety appears in his true light, and we find (what we are taught as babes) the small trust that can be set in worldly friends. I would be unworthy of my religion if I let this pass without particular remark. For three days we lay in the dark in the cabin, and had but a biscuit to nibble. On the fourth the wind fell, leaving the ship dismasted and heaving on vast billows. The captain had not a guess of whither we were blown; he was stark ignorant of his trade, and could do naught but bless the Holy Virgin; a very good thing, too, but scarce the whole of seamanship. It seemed, our one hope was to be picked up by another vessel; and if that should prove to be an English ship, it might be no great blessing to the Master and myself.

The fifth and sixth days we tossed there helpless. The seventh some sail was got on her, but she was an unwieldy vessel at the best, and we made little but leeway. All the time, indeed, we had been drifting to the south and west, and during the tempest must have driven in that direction with unheard-of violence. The ninth dawn was cold and black, with a great sea running, and every mark of foul weather. In this situation we were overjoyed to sight a small ship on the horizon, and to perceive her go about and head for the *Sainte-Marie*. But our gratification did not very long endure; for when she had laid to and lowered a boat, it was immediately filled with disorderly fellows, who sang and shouted as they pulled across to us, and swarmed in on our deck with bare cutlasses, cursing loudly. Their leader was a horrible villain, with his face blacked and his whiskers curled in ringlets; Teach, his name; a most notorious pirate. He stamped about the deck, raving and crying out that his name was Satan, and his ship was called Hell. There was something about him like a wicked child or a half-witted person, that daunted me beyond expression. I whispered in the ear of Ballantrae that I would not be the last to volunteer, and only prayed God they might be short of hands; he approved my purpose with a nod.

"Bedad," said I to Master Teach, "if you are Satan, here is a devil for ye."

The word pleased him; and (not to dwell upon these shocking incidents) Ballantrae and I and two others were taken for recruits, while the skipper and all the rest were cast into the sea by the method of walking the plank. It was the first time I had seen this done; my heart died within me at the spectacle; and Master Teach or one of his acolytes (for my head was too much lost to be precise) remarked upon my pale face in a very alarming manner. I had the strength to cut a step or two of a jig, and cry out some ribaldry, which saved me for that time; but my legs were like water when I must get down into the skiff among these miscreants; and what with my horror of my company and fear of the monstrous billows, it was all I could do to keep an Irish tongue and break a jest or two as we were pulled aboard. By the blessing of God, there was a fiddle in the pirate ship, which I had no sooner seen than I fell upon; and in my quality of crowder I had the heavenly good luck to get favour in their eyes. *Crowding Pat* was the name they dubbed me with; and it was little I cared for a name so long as my skin was whole.

What kind of a pandemonium that vessel was, I cannot describe, but she was commanded by a lunatic, and might be called a floating Bedlam. Drinking, roaring, singing, quarrelling, dancing, they were never all sober at one time; and there were days together when, if a squall had supervened, it must have sent us to the bottom; or if a king's ship had come along, it would have found us quite helpless for defence. Once or twice we sighted a sail, and, if we were sober enough, overhauled it, God forgive us! and if we were all too drunk, she got away, and I would bless the saints under my breath. Teach ruled, if you can call that rule which brought no order, by the terror he created; and I observed the man was very vain of his position. I have known marshals of France—ay, and even Highland chieftains—that were less openly puffed up; which throws a singular light on the pursuit of honour and glory. Indeed, the longer we live, the more we perceive the sagacity of Aristotle and the other old philosophers; and though I have all my life been eager for legitimate distinctions, I can lay my hand upon my heart, at the end of my career, and declare there is not one—no, nor yet life itself—which is worth acquiring or preserving at the slightest cost of dignity.

It was long before I got private speech of Ballantrae; but at length one night we crept out upon the boltsprit, when the rest were better employed, and commiserated our position.

"None can deliver us but the saints," said I.

"My mind is very different," said Ballantrae; "for I am going to deliver myself. This Teach is the poorest creature possible; we make no profit of him, and lie continually open to capture; and," says he, "I am not going to be a tarry pirate for nothing, nor yet to hang in chains if I can help it." And he told me what was in his mind to better the state of the ship in the way of discipline, which would give us safety for the present, and a sooner hope of deliverance when they should have gained enough and should break up their company.

I confessed to him ingenuously that my nerve was quite shook amid these horrible surroundings, and I durst scarce tell him to count upon me.

"I am not very easy frightened," said he, "nor very easy beat."

A few days after, there befell an accident which had nearly hanged us all; and offers the most extraordinary picture of the folly that ruled in our concerns. We were all pretty drunk: and some bedlamite spying a sail, Teach put the ship about in chase without a glance, and we began to bustle up the arms and boast of the horrors that should follow. I observed Ballantrae stood quiet in the bows, looking under the shade of his hand; but for my part, true to my policy among these savages, I was at work with the busiest and passing Irish jests for their diversion.

"Run up the colours," cries Teach. "Show the —s the Jolly Roger!"

It was the merest drunken braggadocio at such a stage, and might have lost us a valuable prize; but I thought it no part of mine to reason, and I ran up the black flag with my own hand.

Ballantrae steps presently aft with a smile upon his face.

"You may perhaps like to know, you drunken dog," says he, "that you are chasing a king's ship."

Teach roared him the lie; but he ran at the same time to the bulwarks, and so did they all. I have never seen so many drunken men struck suddenly sober. The cruiser had gone about, upon our impudent display of colours; she was just then filling on the new tack; her ensign blew out quite plain to see; and even as we stared, there came a puff of smoke, and then a report, and a shot plunged in the waves a good way short of us. Some ran to the ropes, and got the *Sarah* round with an incredible swiftness. One fellow fell on the rum barrel, which stood broached upon the deck, and rolled it promptly overboard. On my part, I made for the Jolly Roger, struck it, tossed it in the sea; and could have flung myself after, so vexed was I with our mismanagement. As for Teach, he grew as pale as death, and incontinently went down to his cabin. Only twice he came on deck that afternoon; went to the taffrail; took a long look at the king's ship, which was still on the horizon heading after us; and then, without speech, back to his cabin. You may say he deserted us; and if it had not been for one very capable sailor we had on board, and for the lightness of the airs that blew all day, we must certainly have gone to the yard-arm.

It is to be supposed Teach was humiliated, and perhaps alarmed for his position with the crew; and the way in which he set about regaining what he had lost, was highly characteristic of the man. Early next day we smelled him burning sulphur in his cabin and crying out of "Hell, hell!" which was well understood among the crew, and filled their minds with apprehension. Presently he comes on deck, a perfect figure of fun, his face blacked, his hair and whiskers curled, his belt stuck full of pistols; chewing bits of glass so that the blood ran down his chin, and brandishing a dirk. I do not know if he had taken these manners from the Indians of America, where he was a native; but such was his way, and he would always thus announce that he was wound up to horrid deeds. The first that came near him was the fellow who had sent the rum overboard the day before; him he stabbed to the heart, damning him for a mutineer; and then capered about the body, raving and swearing and daring us to come on. It was the silliest exhibition; and yet dangerous too, for the cowardly fellow was plainly working himself up to another murder.

All of a sudden Ballantrae stepped forth. "Have done with this play-acting," says he. "Do you think to frighten us with making faces? We saw nothing of you yesterday, when you were wanted; and we did well without you, let me tell you that."

There was a murmur and a movement in the crew, of pleasure and alarm, I thought, in nearly equal parts. As for Teach, he gave a barbarous howl, and swung his dirk to fling it, an art in which (like many seamen) he was very expert.

"Knock that out of his hand!" says Ballantrae, so sudden and sharp that my arm obeyed him before my mind had understood.

Teach stood like one stupid, never thinking on his pistols.

"Go down to your cabin," cries Ballantrae, "and come on deck again when you are sober. Do you think we are going to hang for you, you black-faced, half-witted, drunken brute and butcher? Go down!" And he stamped his foot at him with such a sudden smartness that Teach fairly ran for it to the companion.

"And now, mates," says Ballantrae, "a word with you. I don't know if you are gentlemen of fortune for the fun of the thing, but I am not. I want to make money, and get ashore again, and spend it like a man. And on one thing my mind is made up: I will not hang if I can help it. Come: give me a hint; I'm only a beginner! Is there no way to get a little discipline and common sense about this business?"

One of the men spoke up: he said by rights they should have a quartermaster; and no sooner was the word out of his mouth than they were all of that opinion. The thing went by acclamation, Ballantrae was made quartermaster, the rum was put in his charge, laws were passed in imitation of those of a pirate by the name of Roberts, and the last proposal was to make an end of Teach. But Ballantrae was afraid of a more efficient captain, who might be a counterweight to himself, and he opposed this stoutly. Teach, he said, was good enough to board ships and frighten fools with his blacked face and swearing; we could scarce get a better man than Teach for that; and besides, as the man was now disconsidered and as good as deposed, we might reduce his proportion of the plunder. This carried it; Teach's share was cut down to a mere derision, being actually less than mine; and there remained only two points: whether he would consent, and who was to announce to him this resolution.

"Do not let that stick you," says Ballantrae, "I will do that."

And he stepped to the companion and down alone into the cabin to face that drunken savage.

"This is the man for us," cries one of the hands. "Three cheers for the quartermaster!" which were given with a will, my own voice among the loudest, and I dare say these plaudits had their effect on Master Teach in the cabin, as we have seen of late days how shouting in the streets may trouble even the minds of legislators.

What passed precisely was never known, though some of the heads of it came to the surface later on; and we were all amazed, as well as gratified, when Ballantrae came on deck with Teach upon his arm, and announced that all had been consented.

I pass swiftly over those twelve or fifteen months in which we continued to keep the sea in the North Atlantic, getting our food and water from the ships we over-hauled, and doing on the whole a pretty fortunate business. Sure, no one could wish to read anything so ungenteel as the memoirs of a pirate, even an unwilling one like me! Things went extremely better with our designs, and Ballantrae kept his lead, to my admiration, from that day forth. I would be tempted to suppose that a gentleman must everywhere be first, even aboard a rover: but my birth is every whit as good as any Scottish lord's, and I am not ashamed to confess that I stayed Crowding Pat until the end, and was not much better than the crew's buffoon. Indeed, it was no scene to bring out my merits. My health suffered from a variety of reasons; I was more at home to the last on a horse's back than a ship's deck; and, to be ingenuous, the fear of the sea was constantly in my mind, battling with the fear of my companions. I need not cry myself up for courage; I have done well on many fields under the eyes of famous generals, and earned my late advancement by an act of the most distinguished valour before many witnesses. But when we must proceed on one of our abordages, the heart of Francis Burke was in his boots; the little eggshell skiff in which we must set forth, the horrible heaving of the vast billows, the height of the ship that we must scale, the thought of how many might be there in garrison upon their legitimate defence, the scowling heavens which (in that climate) so often looked darkly down upon our exploits, and the mere crying of the wind in my ears, were all considerations most unpalatable to my valour. Besides which, as I was always a creature of the nicest sensibility, the scenes that must follow on our success tempted me as little as the chances of defeat. Twice we found women on board; and though I have seen towns sacked, and of late days in France some very horrid public tumults, there was something in the smallness of the numbers engaged, and the bleak dangerous sea-surroundings, that made these acts of piracy far the most revolting. I confess ingenuously I could never proceed unless I was three parts drunk; it was the same even with the crew; Teach himself was fit for no enterprise till he was full of rum; and it was one of the most difficult parts of Ballantrae's performance, to serve us with liquor in the proper quantities. Even this he did to admiration; being upon the whole the most capable man I ever met with, and the one of the most natural genius. He did not even scrape favour with the crew, as I did, by continual buffoonery made upon a very anxious heart; but preserved on most occasions a great deal of gravity and distance; so that he was like a parent among a family of young children, or a schoolmaster with his boys. What made his part the harder to perform, the men were most inveterate grumblers; Ballantrae's discipline, little as it was, was yet irksome to their love of licence; and what was worse, being kept sober they had time to think. Some of them accordingly would fall to repenting their abominable crimes; one in particular, who was a good Catholic, and with whom I would sometimes steal apart for prayer; above all in bad weather, fogs, lashing rain and the like, when we would be the less observed; and I am sure no two criminals in the cart have ever performed their devotions with more anxious sincerity. But the rest, having no such grounds of hope, fell to another pastime, that of computation. All day long they would he telling up their shares or grooming over the result. I have said we were pretty fortunate. But an observation fails to be made: that in this world, in no business that I have tried, do the profits rise to a man's expectations. We found many ships and took many; yet few of them contained much money, their goods were usually nothing to our purpose—what did we want with a cargo of ploughs, or even of tobacco?—and it is quite a painful reflection how many whole crews we have made to walk the plank for no more than a stock of biscuit or an anker or two of spirit.

In the meanwhile our ship was growing very foul, and it was high time we should make for our *port de carrénage,* which was in the estuary of a river among swamps. It was openly understood that we should then break up and go and squander our proportions of the spoil; and this made every man greedy of a little more, so that our decision was delayed from day to day. What finally decided matters, was a trifling accident, such as an ignorant person might suppose incidental to our way of life. But here I must explain: on only one of all the ships we boarded, the first on which we found women, did we meet with any genuine resistance. On that occasion we had two men killed and several injured, and if it had not been for the gallantry of Ballantrae we had surely been beat back at last. Everywhere else the defence (where there was any at all) was what the worst troops in Europe would have laughed at; so that the most dangerous part of our employment was to clamber up the side of the ship; and I have even known the poor souls on board to cast us a line, so eager were they to volunteer instead of walking the plank. This constant immunity had made our fellows very soft, so that I understood how Teach had made so deep a mark upon their minds; for indeed the company of that lunatic was the chief danger in our way of life. The accident to which I have referred was this:—We had sighted a little full-rigged ship very close under our board in a haze; she sailed near as well as we did—I should be nearer truth if I said, near as ill; and we cleared the bow-chaser to see if we could bring a spar or two about their ears. The swell was exceeding great; the motion of the ship beyond description; it was little wonder if our gunners should fire thrice and be still quite broad of what they aimed at. But in the meanwhile the chase had cleared a stern gun, the thickness of the air concealing them; and being better marksmen, their first shot struck us in the bows, knocked our two gunners into mince-meat, so that we were all sprinkled with the blood, and plunged through the deck into the forecastle, where we slept. Ballantrae would have held on; indeed, there was nothing in this *contretemps*to affect the mind of any soldier; but he had a quick perception of the men's wishes, and it was plain this lucky shot had given them a sickener of their trade. In a moment they were all of one mind: the chase was drawing away from us, it was needless to hold on, the *Sarah* was too foul to overhaul a bottle, it was mere foolery to keep the sea with her; and on these pretended grounds her head was incontinently put about and the course laid for the river. It was strange to see what merriment fell on that ship's company, and how they stamped about the deck jesting, and each computing what increase had come to his share by the death of the two gunners.

We were nine days making our port, so light were the airs we had to sail on, so foul the ship's bottom; but early on the tenth, before dawn, and in a light lifting haze, we passed the head. A little after, the haze lifted, and fell again, showing us a cruiser very close. This was a sore blow, happening so near our refuge. There was a great debate of whether she had seen us, and if so whether it was likely they had recognised the *Sarah.* We were very careful, by destroying every member of those crews we overhauled, to leave no evidence as to our own persons; but the appearance of the *Sarah* herself we could not keep so private; and above all of late, since she had been foul, and we had pursued many ships without success, it was plain that her description had been often published. I supposed this alert would have made us separate upon the instant. But here again that original genius of Ballantrae's had a surprise in store for me. He and Teach (and it was the most remarkable step of his success) had gone hand in hand since the first day of his appointment. I often questioned him upon the fact, and never got an answer but once, when he told me he and Teach had an understanding "which would very much surprise the crew if they should hear of it, and would surprise himself a good deal if it was carried out." Well, here again he and Teach were of a mind; and by their joint procurement the anchor was no sooner down than the whole crew went off upon a scene of drunkenness indescribable. By afternoon we were a mere shipful of lunatical persons, throwing of things overboard, howling of different songs at the same time, quarrelling and falling together, and then forgetting our quarrels to embrace. Ballantrae had bidden me drink nothing, and feign drunkenness, as I valued my life; and I have never passed a day so wearisomely, lying the best part of the time upon the forecastle and watching the swamps and thickets by which our little basin was entirely surrounded for the eye. A little after dusk Ballantrae stumbled up to my side, feigned to fall, with a drunken laugh, and before he got his feet again, whispered me to "reel down into the cabin and seem to fall asleep upon a locker, for there would be need of me soon." I did as I was told, and coming into the cabin, where it was quite dark, let myself fall on the first locker. There was a man there already; by the way he stirred and threw me off, I could not think he was much in liquor; and yet when I had found another place, he seemed to continue to sleep on. My heart now beat very hard, for I saw some desperate matter was in act. Presently down came Ballantrae, lit the lamp, looked about the cabin, nodded as if pleased, and on deck again without a word. I peered out from between my fingers, and saw there were three of us slumbering, or feigning to slumber, on the lockers: myself, one Dutton and one Grady, both resolute men. On deck the rest were got to a pitch of revelry quite beyond the bounds of what is human; so that no reasonable name can describe the sounds they were now making. I have heard many a drunken bout in my time, many on board that very*Sarah,* but never anything the least like this, which made me early suppose the liquor had been tampered with. It was a long while before these yells and howls died out into a sort of miserable moaning, and then to silence; and it seemed a long while after that before Ballantrae came down again, this time with Teach upon his heels. The latter cursed at the sight of us three upon the lockers.

"Tut," says Ballantrae, "you might fire a pistol at their ears. You know what stuff they have been swallowing."

There was a hatch in the cabin floor, and under that the richest part of the booty was stored against the day of division. It fastened with a ring and three padlocks, the keys (for greater security) being divided; one to Teach, one to Ballantrae, and one to the mate, a man called Hammond. Yet I was amazed to see they were now all in the one hand; and yet more amazed (still looking through my fingers) to observe Ballantrae and Teach bring up several packets, four of them in all, very carefully made up and with a loop for carriage.

"And now," says Teach, "let us be going."

"One word," says Ballantrae. "I have discovered there is another man besides yourself who knows a private path across the swamp; and it seems it is shorter than yours."

Teach cried out, in that case, they were undone.

"I do not know for that," says Ballantrae. "For there are several other circumstances with which I must acquaint you. First of all, there is no bullet in your pistols, which (if you remember) I was kind enough to load for both of us this morning. Secondly, as there is someone else who knows a passage, you must think it highly improbable I should saddle myself with a lunatic like you. Thirdly, these gentlemen (who need no longer pretend to be asleep) are those of my party, and will now proceed to gag and bind you to the mast; and when your men awaken (if they ever do awake after the drugs we have mingled in their liquor), I am sure they will be so obliging as to deliver you, and you will have no difficulty, I daresay, to explain the business of the keys."

Not a word said Teach, but looked at us like a frightened baby as we gagged and bound him.

"Now you see, you moon-calf," says Ballantrae, "why we made four packets. Heretofore you have been called Captain Teach, but I think you are now rather Captain Learn."

That was our last word on board the *Sarah*. We four, with our four packets, lowered ourselves softly into a skiff, and left that ship behind us as silent as the grave, only for the moaning of some of the drunkards. There was a fog about breast-high on the waters; so that Dutton, who knew the passage, must stand on his feet to direct our rowing; and this, as it forced us to row gently, was the means of our deliverance. We were yet but a little way from the ship, when it began to come grey, and the birds to fly abroad upon the water. All of a sudden Dutton clapped down upon his hams, and whispered us to be silent for our lives, and hearken. Sure enough, we heard a little faint creak of oars upon one hand, and then again, and further off, a creak of oars upon the other. It was clear we had been sighted yesterday in the morning; here were the cruiser's boats to cut us out; here were we defenceless in their very midst. Sure, never were poor souls more perilously placed; and as we lay there on our oars, praying God the mist might hold, the sweat poured from my brow. Presently we heard one of the boats where we might have thrown a biscuit in her. "Softly, men," we heard an officer whisper; and I marvelled they could not hear the drumming of my heart.

"Never mind the path," says Ballantrae; "we must get shelter anyhow; let us pull straight ahead for the sides of the basin."

This we did with the most anxious precaution, rowing, as best we could, upon our hands, and steering at a venture in the fog, which was (for all that) our only safety. But Heaven guided us; we touched ground at a thicket; scrambled ashore with our treasure; and having no other way of concealment, and the mist beginning already to lighten, hove down the skiff and let her sink. We were still but new under cover when the sun rose; and at the same time, from the midst of the basin, a great shouting of seamen sprang up, and we knew the *Sarah* was being boarded. I heard afterwards the officer that took her got great honour; and it's true the approach was creditably managed, but I think he had an easy capture when he came to board.[2]

I was still blessing the saints for my escape, when I became aware we were in trouble of another kind. We were here landed at random in a vast and dangerous swamp; and how to come at the path was a concern of doubt, fatigue, and peril. Dutton, indeed, was of opinion we should wait until the ship was gone, and fish up the skiff; for any delay would be more wise than to go blindly ahead in that morass. One went back accordingly to the basin-side and (peering through the thicket) saw the fog already quite drunk up, and English colours flying on the *Sarah*, but no movement made to get her under way. Our situation was now very doubtful. The swamp was an unhealthful place to linger in; we had been so greedy to bring treasures that we had brought but little food; it was highly desirable, besides, that we should get clear of the neighbourhood and into the settlements before the news of the capture went abroad; and against all these considerations, there was only the peril of the passage on the other side. I think it not wonderful we decided on the active part.

It was already blistering hot when we set forth to pass the marsh, or rather to strike the path, by compass. Dutton took the compass, and one or other of us three carried his proportion of the treasure. I promise you he kept a sharp eye to his rear, for it was like the man's soul that he must trust us with. The thicket was as close as a bush; the ground very treacherous, so that we often sank in the most terrifying manner, and must go round about; the heat, besides, was stifling, the air singularly heavy, and the stinging insects abounded in such myriads that each of us walked under his own cloud. It has often been commented on, how much better gentlemen of birth endure fatigue than persons of the rabble; so that walking officers who must tramp in the dirt beside their men, shame them by their constancy. This was well to be observed in the present instance; for here were Ballantrae and I, two gentlemen of the highest breeding, on the one hand; and on the other, Grady, a common mariner, and a man nearly a giant in physical strength. The case of Dutton is not in point, for I confess he did as well as any of us. [3] But as for Grady, he began early to lament his case, tailed in the rear, refused to carry Dutton's packet when it came his turn, clamoured continually for rum (of which we had too little), and at last even threatened us from behind with a cooked pistol, unless we should allow him rest. Ballantrae would have fought it out, I believe; but I prevailed with him the other way; and we made a stop and ate a meal. It seemed to benefit Grady little; he was in the rear again at once, growling and bemoaning his lot; and at last, by some carelessness, not having followed properly in our tracks, stumbled into a deep part of the slough where it was mostly water, gave some very dreadful screams, and before we could come to his aid had sunk along with his booty. His fate, and above all these screams of his, appalled us to the soul; yet it was on the whole a fortunate circumstance and the means of our deliverance, for it moved Dutton to mount into a tree, whence he was able to perceive and to show me, who had climbed after him, a high piece of the wood, which was a landmark for the path. He went forward the more carelessly, I must suppose; for presently we saw him sink a little down, draw up his feet and sink again, and so twice. Then he turned his face to us, pretty white.

"Lend a hand," said he, "I am in a bad place."

"I don't know about that," says Ballantrae, standing still.

Dutton broke out into the most violent oaths, sinking a little lower as he did, so that the mud was nearly to his waist, and plucking a pistol from his belt, "Help me," he cries, "or die and be damned to you!"

"Nay," says Ballantrae, "I did but jest. I am coming." And he set down his own packet and Dutton's, which he was then carrying. "Do not venture near till we see if you are needed," said he to me, and went forward alone to where the man was bogged. He was quiet now, though he still held the pistol; and the marks of terror in his countenance were very moving to behold.

"For the Lord's sake," says he, "look sharp."

Ballantrae was now got close up. "Keep still," says he, and seemed to consider; and then, "Reach out both your hands!"

Dutton laid down his pistol, and so watery was the top surface that it went clear out of sight; with an oath he stooped to snatch it; and as he did so, Ballantrae leaned forth and stabbed him between the shoulders. Up went his hands over his head—I know not whether with the pain or to ward himself; and the next moment he doubled forward in the mud.

Ballantrae was already over the ankles; but he plucked himself out, and came back to me, where I stood with my knees smiting one another. "The devil take you, Francis!" says he. "I believe you are a half-hearted fellow, after all. I have only done justice on a pirate. And here we are quite clear of the *Sarah*! Who shall now say that we have dipped our hands in any irregularities?"

I assured him he did me injustice; but my sense of humanity was so much affected by the horridness of the fact that I could scarce find breath to answer with.

"Come," said he, "you must be more resolved. The need for this fellow ceased when he had shown you where the path ran; and you cannot deny I would have been daft to let slip so fair an opportunity."

I could not deny but he was right in principle; nor yet could I refrain from shedding tears, of which I think no man of valour need have been ashamed; and it was not until I had a share of the rum that I was able to proceed. I repeat, I am far from ashamed of my generous emotion; mercy is honourable in the warrior; and yet I cannot altogether censure Ballantrae, whose step was really fortunate, as we struck the path without further misadventure, and the same night, about sundown, came to the edge of the morass.

We were too weary to seek far; on some dry sands, still warm with the day's sun, and close under a wood of pines, we lay down and were instantly plunged in sleep.

We awaked the next morning very early, and began with a sullen spirit a conversation that came near to end in blows. We were now cast on shore in the southern provinces, thousands of miles from any French settlement; a dreadful journey and a thousand perils lay in front of us; and sure, if there was ever need for amity, it was in such an hour. I must suppose that Ballantrae had suffered in his sense of what is truly polite; indeed, and there is nothing strange in the idea, after the sea-wolves we had consorted with so long; and as for myself, he fubbed me off unhandsomely, and any gentleman would have resented his behaviour.

I told him in what light I saw his conduct; he walked a little off, I following to upbraid him; and at last he stopped me with his hand.

"Frank," says he, "you know what we swore; and yet there is no oath invented would induce me to swallow such expressions, if I did not regard you with sincere affection. It is impossible you should doubt me there: I have given proofs. Dutton I had to take, because he knew the pass, and Grady because Dutton would not move without him; but what call was there to carry you along? You are a perpetual danger to me with your cursed Irish tongue. By rights you should now be in irons in the cruiser. And you quarrel with me like a baby for some trinkets!"

I considered this one of the most unhandsome speeches ever made; and indeed to this day I can scarce reconcile it to my notion of a gentleman that was my friend. I retorted upon him with his Scotch accent, of which he had not so much as some, but enough to be very barbarous and disgusting, as I told him plainly; and the affair would have gone to a great length, but for an alarming intervention.

We had got some way off upon the sand. The place where we had slept, with the packets lying undone and the money scattered openly, was now between us and the pines; and it was out of these the stranger must have come. There he was at least, a great hulking fellow of the country, with a broad axe on his shoulder, looking open-mouthed, now at the treasure, which was just at his feet, and now at our disputation, in which we had gone far enough to have weapons in our hands. We had no sooner observed him than he found his legs and made off again among the pines.

This was no scene to put our minds at rest: a couple of armed men in sea-clothes found quarrelling over a treasure, not many miles from where a pirate had been captured—here was enough to bring the whole country about our ears. The quarrel was not even made up; it was blotted from our minds; and we got our packets together in the twinkling of an eye, and made off, running with the best will in the world. But the trouble was, we did not know in what direction, and must continually return upon our steps. Ballantrae had indeed collected what he could from Dutton; but it's hard to travel upon hearsay; and the estuary, which spreads into a vast irregular harbour, turned us off upon every side with a new stretch of water.

We were near beside ourselves, and already quite spent with running, when, coming to the top of a dune, we saw we were again cut off by another ramification of the bay. This was a creek, however, very different from those that had arrested us before; being set in rocks, and so precipitously deep that a small vessel was able to lie alongside, made fast with a hawser; and her crew had laid a plank to the shore. Here they had lighted a fire, and were sitting at their meal. As for the vessel herself, she was one of those they build in the Bermudas.

The love of gold and the great hatred that everybody has to pirates were motives of the most influential, and would certainly raise the country in our pursuit. Besides, it was now plain we were on some sort of straggling peninsula, like the fingers of a hand; and the wrist, or passage to the mainland, which we should have taken at the first, was by this time not improbably secured. These considerations put us on a bolder counsel. For as long as we dared, looking every moment to hear sounds of the chase, we lay among some bushes on the top of the dune; and having by this means secured a little breath and recomposed our appearance, we strolled down at last, with a great affectation of carelessness, to the party by the fire.

It was a trader and his negroes, belonging to Albany, in the province of New York, and now on the way home from the Indies with a cargo; his name I cannot recall. We were amazed to learn he had put in here from terror of the *Sarah*; for we had no thought our exploits had been so notorious. As soon as the Albanian heard she had been taken the day before, he jumped to his feet, gave us a cup of spirits for our good news, and sent big negroes to get sail on the Bermudan. On our side, we profited by the dram to become more confidential, and at last offered ourselves as passengers. He looked askance at our tarry clothes and pistols, and replied civilly enough that he had scarce accommodation for himself; nor could either our prayers or our offers of money, in which we advanced pretty far, avail to shake him.

"I see, you think ill of us," says Ballantrae, "but I will show you how well we think of you by telling you the truth. We are Jacobite fugitives, and there is a price upon our heads."

At this, the Albanian was plainly moved a little. He asked us many questions as to the Scotch war, which Ballantrae very patiently answered. And then, with a wink, in a vulgar manner, "I guess you and your Prince Charlie got more than you cared about," said he.

"Bedad, and that we did," said I. "And, my dear man, I wish you would set a new example and give us just that much."

This I said in the Irish way, about which there is allowed to be something very engaging. It's a remarkable thing, and a testimony to the love with which our nation is regarded, that this address scarce ever fails in a handsome fellow. I cannot tell how often I have seen a private soldier escape the horse, or a beggar wheedle out a good alms by a touch of the brogue. And, indeed, as soon as the Albanian had laughed at me I was pretty much at rest. Even then, however, he made many conditions, and—for one thing—took away our arms, before he suffered us aboard; which was the signal to cast off; so that in a moment after, we were gliding down the bay with a good breeze, and blessing the name of God for our deliverance. Almost in the mouth of the estuary, we passed the cruiser, and a little after the poor *Sarah* with her prize crew; and these were both sights to make us tremble. The Bermudan seemed a very safe place to be in, and our bold stroke to have been fortunately played, when we were thus reminded of the case of our companions. For all that, we had only exchanged traps, jumped out of the frying-pan into the fire, ran from the yard-arm to the block, and escaped the open hostility of the man-of-war to lie at the mercy of the doubtful faith of our Albanian merchant.

From many circumstances, it chanced we were safer than we could have dared to hope. The town of Albany was at that time much concerned in contraband trade across the desert with the Indians and the French. This, as it was highly illegal, relaxed their loyalty, and as it brought them in relation with the politest people on the earth, divided even their sympathies. In short, they were like all the smugglers in the world, spies and agents ready-made for either party. Our Albanian, besides, was a very honest man indeed, and very greedy; and, to crown our luck, he conceived a great delight in our society. Before we had reached the town of New York we had come to a full agreement, that he should carry us as far as Albany upon his ship, and thence put us on a way to pass the boundaries and join the French. For all this we were to pay at a high rate; but beggars cannot be choosers, nor outlaws bargainers.

We sailed, then, up the Hudson River, which, I protest, is a very fine stream, and put up at the "King's Arms" in Albany. The town was full of the militia of the province, breathing slaughter against the French. Governor Clinton was there himself, a very busy man, and, by what I could learn, very near distracted by the factiousness of his Assembly. The Indians on both sides were on the war-path; we saw parties of them bringing in prisoners and (what was much worse) scalps, both male and female, for which they were paid at a fixed rate; and I assure you the sight was not encouraging. Altogether, we could scarce have come at a period more unsuitable for our designs; our position in the chief inn was dreadfully conspicuous; our Albanian fubbed us off with a thousand delays, and seemed upon the point of a retreat from his engagements; nothing but peril appeared to environ the poor fugitives, and for some time we drowned our concern in a very irregular course of living.

This, too, proved to be fortunate; and it's one of the remarks that fall to be made upon our escape, how providentially our steps were conducted to the very end. What a humiliation to the dignity of man! My philosophy, the extraordinary genius of Ballantrae, our valour, in which I grant that we were equal—all these might have proved insufficient without the Divine blessing on our efforts. And how true it is, as the Church tells us, that the Truths of Religion are, after all, quite applicable even to daily affairs! At least, it was in the course of our revelry that we made the acquaintance of a spirited youth by the name of Chew. He was one of the most daring of the Indian traders, very well acquainted with the secret paths of the wilderness, needy, dissolute, and, by a last good fortune, in some disgrace with his family. Him we persuaded to come to our relief; he privately provided what was needful for our flight, and one day we slipped out of Albany, without a word to our former friend, and embarked, a little above, in a canoe.

To the toils and perils of this journey, it would require a pen more elegant than mine to do full justice. The reader must conceive for himself the dreadful wilderness which we had now to thread; its thickets, swamps, precipitous rocks, impetuous rivers, and amazing waterfalls. Among these barbarous scenes we must toil all day, now paddling, now carrying our canoe upon our shoulders; and at night we slept about a fire, surrounded by the howling of wolves and other savage animals. It was our design to mount the headwaters of the Hudson, to the neighbourhood of Crown Point, where the French had a strong place in the woods, upon Lake Champlain. But to have done this directly were too perilous; and it was accordingly gone upon by such a labyrinth of rivers, lakes, and portages as makes my head giddy to remember. These paths were in ordinary times entirely desert; but the country was now up, the tribes on the war-path, the woods full of Indian scouts. Again and again we came upon these parties when we least expected, them; and one day, in particular, I shall never forget, how, as dawn was coming in, we were suddenly surrounded by five or six of these painted devils, uttering a very dreary sort of cry, and brandishing their hatchets. It passed off harmlessly, indeed, as did the rest of our encounters; for Chew was well known and highly valued among the different tribes. Indeed, he was a very gallant, respectable young man; but even with the advantage of his companionship, you must not think these meetings were without sensible peril. To prove friendship on our part, it was needful to draw upon our stock of rum—indeed, under whatever disguise, that is the true business of the Indian trader, to keep a travelling public-house in the forest; and when once the braves had got their bottle of *scaura* (as they call this beastly liquor), it behoved us to set forth and paddle for our scalps. Once they were a little drunk, goodbye to any sense or decency; they had but the one thought, to get more *scaura*. They might easily take it in their heads to give us chase, and had we been overtaken, I had never written these memoirs.

We were come to the most critical portion of our course, where we might equally expect to fall into the hands of French or English, when a terrible calamity befell us. Chew was taken suddenly sick with symptoms like those of poison, and in the course of a few hours expired in the bottom of the canoe. We thus lost at once our guide, our interpreter, our boatman, and our passport, for he was all these in one; and found ourselves reduced, at a blow, to the most desperate and irremediable distress. Chew, who took a great pride in his knowledge, had indeed often lectured us on the geography; and Ballantrae, I believe, would listen. But for my part I have always found such information highly tedious; and beyond the fact that we were now in the country of the Adirondack Indians, and not so distant from our destination, could we but have found the way, I was entirely ignorant. The wisdom of my course was soon the more apparent; for with all his pains, Ballantrae was no further advanced than myself. He knew we must continue to go up one stream; then, by way of a portage, down another; and then up a third. But you are to consider, in a mountain country, how many streams come rolling in from every hand. And how is a gentleman, who is a perfect stranger in that part of the world, to tell any one of them from any other? Nor was this our only trouble. We were great novices, besides, in handling a canoe; the portages were almost beyond our strength, so that I have seen us sit down in despair for half an hour at a time without one word; and the appearance of a single Indian, since we had now no means of speaking to them, would have been in all probability the means of our destruction. There is altogether some excuse if Ballantrae showed something of a grooming disposition; his habit of imputing blame to others, quite as capable as himself, was less tolerable, and his language it was not always easy to accept. Indeed, he had contracted on board the pirate ship a manner of address which was in a high degree unusual between gentlemen; and now, when you might say he was in a fever, it increased upon him hugely.

The third day of these wanderings, as we were carrying the canoe upon a rocky portage, she fell, and was entirely bilged. The portage was between two lakes, both pretty extensive; the track, such as it was, opened at both ends upon the water, and on both hands was enclosed by the unbroken woods; and the sides of the lakes were quite impassable with bog: so that we beheld ourselves not only condemned to go without our boat and the greater part of our provisions, but to plunge at once into impenetrable thickets and to desert what little guidance we still had—the course of the river. Each stuck his pistols in his belt, shouldered an axe, made a pack of his treasure and as much food as he could stagger under; and deserting the rest of our possessions, even to our swords, which would have much embarrassed us among the woods, we set forth on this deplorable adventure. The labours of Hercules, so finely described by Homer, were a trifle to what we now underwent. Some parts of the forest were perfectly dense down to the ground, so that we must cut our way like mites in a cheese. In some the bottom was full of deep swamp, and the whole wood entirely rotten. I have leaped on a great fallen log and sunk to the knees in touchwood; I have sought to stay myself, in falling, against what looked to be a solid trunk, and the whole thing has whiffed away at my touch like a sheet of paper. Stumbling, falling, bogging to the knees, hewing our way, our eyes almost put out with twigs and branches, our clothes plucked from our bodies, we laboured all day, and it is doubtful if we made two miles. What was worse, as we could rarely get a view of the country, and were perpetually justled from our path by obstacles, it was impossible even to have a guess in what direction we were moving.

A little before sundown, in an open place with a stream, and set about with barbarous mountains, Ballantrae threw down his pack. "I will go no further," said he, and bade me light the fire, damning my blood in terms not proper for a chairman.

I told him to try to forget he had ever been a pirate, and to remember he had been a gentleman.

"Are you mad?" he cried. "Don't cross me here!" And then, shaking his fist at the hills, "To think," cries he, "that I must leave my bones in this miserable wilderness! Would God I had died upon the scaffold like a gentleman!" This he said ranting like an actor; and then sat biting his fingers and staring on the ground, a most unchristian object.

I took a certain horror of the man, for I thought a soldier and a gentleman should confront his end with more philosophy. I made him no reply, therefore, in words; and presently the evening fell so chill that I was glad, for my own sake, to kindle a fire. And yet God knows, in such an open spot, and the country alive with savages, the act was little short of lunacy. Ballantrae seemed never to observe me; but at last, as I was about parching a little corn, he looked up.

"Have you ever a brother?" said be.

"By the blessing of Heaven," said I, "not less than five."

"I have the one," said he, with a strange voice; and then presently, "He shall pay me for all this," he added. And when I asked him what was his brother's part in our distress, "What!" he cried, "he sits in my place, he bears my name, he courts my wife; and I am here alone with a damned Irishman in this tooth-chattering desert! Oh, I have been a common gull!" he cried.

The explosion was in all ways so foreign to my friend's nature that I was daunted out of all my just susceptibility. Sure, an offensive expression, however vivacious, appears a wonderfully small affair in circumstances so extreme! But here there is a strange thing to be noted. He had only once before referred to the lady with whom he was contracted. That was when we came in view of the town of New York, when he had told me, if all had their rights, he was now in sight of his own property, for Miss Graeme enjoyed a large estate in the province. And this was certainly a natural occasion; but now here she was named a second time; and what is surely fit to be observed, in this very month, which was November, '47, and *I believe upon that very day as we sat among these barbarous mountains*, his brother and Miss Graeme were married. I am the least superstitious of men; but the hand of Providence is here displayed too openly not to be remarked.[4]

The next day, and the next, were passed in similar labours; Ballantrae often deciding on our course by the spinning of a coin; and once, when I expostulated on this childishness, he had an odd remark that I have never forgotten. "I know no better way," said he, "to express my scorn of human reason." I think it was the third day that we found the body of a Christian, scalped and most abominably mangled, and lying in a pudder of his blood; the birds of the desert screaming over him, as thick as flies. I cannot describe how dreadfully this sight affected us; but it robbed me of all strength and all hope for this world. The same day, and only a little after, we were scrambling over a part of the forest that had been burned, when Ballantrae, who was a little ahead, ducked suddenly behind a fallen trunk. I joined him in this shelter, whence we could look abroad without being seen ourselves; and in the bottom of the next vale, beheld a large war party of the savages going by across our line. There might be the value of a weak battalion present; all naked to the waist, blacked with grease and soot, and painted with white lead and vermilion, according to their beastly habits. They went one behind another like a string of geese, and at a quickish trot; so that they took but a little while to rattle by, and disappear again among the woods. Yet I suppose we endured a greater agony of hesitation and suspense in these few minutes than goes usually to a man's whole life. Whether they were French or English Indians, whether they desired scalps or prisoners, whether we should declare ourselves upon the chance, or lie quiet and continue the heart-breaking business of our journey: sure, I think these were questions to have puzzled the brains of Aristotle himself. Ballantrae turned to me with a face all wrinkled up and his teeth showing in his mouth, like what I have read of people starving; he said no word, but his whole appearance was a kind of dreadful question.

"They may be of the English side," I whispered; "and think! the best we could then hope, is to begin this over again."

"I know—I know," he said. "Yet it must come to a plunge at last." And he suddenly plucked out his coin, shook it in his closed hands, looked at it, and then lay down with his face in the dust.

Addition by Mr. Mackellar.—I drop the Chevalier's narration at this point because the couple quarrelled and separated the same day; and the Chevalier's account of the quarrel seems to me (I must confess) quite incompatible with the nature of either of the men. Henceforth they wandered alone, undergoing extraordinary sufferings; until first one and then the other was picked up by a party from Fort St. Frederick. Only two things are to be noted. And first (as most important for my purpose) that the Master, in the course of his miseries buried his treasure, at a point never since discovered, but of which he took a drawing in his own blood on the lining of his hat. And second, that on his coming thus penniless to the Fort, he was welcomed like a brother by the Chevalier, who thence paid his way to France. The simplicity of Mr. Burke's character leads him at this point to praise the Master exceedingly; to an eye more worldly wise, it would seem it was the Chevalier alone that was to be commended. I have the more pleasure in pointing to this really very noble trait of my esteemed correspondent, as I fear I may have wounded him immediately before. I have refrained from comments on any of his extraordinary and (in my eyes) immoral opinions, for I know him to be jealous of respect. But his version of the quarrel is really more than I can reproduce; for I knew the Master myself, and a man more insusceptible of fear is not conceivable. I regret this oversight of the Chevalier's, and all the more because the tenor of his narrative (set aside a few flourishes) strikes me as highly ingenuous.

---

1. *Note by Mr. Mackellar.* Should not this be Alan *Breck* Stewart, afterwards notorious as the Appin murderer? The Chevalier is sometimes very weak on names.
2. *Note by Mr. Mackellar.* This Teach of the *Sarah* must not be confused with the celebrated Blackbeard. The dates and facts by no means tally. It is possible the second Teach may have at once borrowed the name and imitated the more excessive part of his manners from the first. Even the Master of Ballantrae could make admirers.
3. *Note by Mr. Mackellar.* And is not this the whole explanation? since this Dutton, exactly like the officers, enjoyed the stimulus of some responsibility.
4. *Note by Mr. Mackellar*: A complete blunder: there was at this date no word of the marriage: see above in my own narration.

4
PERSECUTIONS ENDURED BY MR. HENRY

You can guess on what part of his adventures the Colonel principally dwelled. Indeed, if we had heard it all, it is to be thought the current of this business had been wholly altered; but the pirate ship was very gently touched upon. Nor did I hear the Colonel to an end even of that which he was willing to disclose; for Mr. Henry, having for some while been plunged in a brown study, rose at last from his seat and (reminding the Colonel there were matters that he must attend to) bade me follow him immediately to the office.

Once there, he sought no longer to dissemble his concern, walking to and fro in the room with a contorted face, and passing his hand repeatedly upon his brow.

"We have some business," he began at last; and there broke off, declared we must have wine, and sent for a magnum of the best. This was extremely foreign to his habitudes; and what was still more so, when the wine had come, he gulped down one glass upon another like a man careless of appearances. But the drink steadied him.

"You will scarce be surprised, Mackellar," says he, "when I tell you that my brother—whose safety we are all rejoiced to learn—stands in some need of money."

I told him I had misdoubted as much; but the time was not very fortunate, as the stock was low.

"Not mine," said he. "There is the money for the mortgage."

I reminded him it was Mrs. Henry's.

"I will be answerable to my wife," he cried violently.

"And then," said I, "there is the mortgage."

"I know," said he; "it is on that I would consult you."

I showed him how unfortunate a time it was to divert this money from its destination; and how, by so doing, we must lose the profit of our past economies, and plunge back the estate into the mire. I even took the liberty to plead with him; and when he still opposed me with a shake of the head and a bitter dogged smile, my zeal quite carried me beyond my place. "This is midsummer madness," cried I; "and I for one will be no party to it."

"You speak as though I did it for my pleasure," says he. "But I have a child now; and, besides, I love order; and to say the honest truth, Mackellar, I had begun to take a pride in the estates." He gloomed for a moment. "But what would you have?" he went on. "Nothing is mine, nothing. This day's news has knocked the bottom out of my life. I have only the name and the shadow of things—only the shadow; there is no substance in my rights."

"They will prove substantial enough before a court," said I.

He looked at me with a burning eye, and seemed to repress the word upon his lips; and I repented what I had said, for I saw that while he spoke of the estate he had still a side-thought to his marriage. And then, of a sudden, he twitched the letter from his pocket, where it lay all crumpled, smoothed it violently on the table, and read these words to me with a trembling tongue: "'My dear Jacob'—This is how he begins!" cries he—"'My dear Jacob, I once called you so, you may remember; and you have now done the business, and flung my heels as high as Criffel.' What do you think of that, Mackellar," says he, "from an only brother? I declare to God I liked him very well; I was always staunch to him; and this is how he writes! But I will not sit down under the imputation"—walking to and fro—"I am as good as he; I am a better man than he, I call on God to prove it! I cannot give him all the monstrous sum he asks; he knows the estate to be incompetent; but I will give him what I have, and it in more than he expects. I have borne all this too long. See what he writes further on; read it for yourself: 'I know you are a niggardly dog.' A niggardly dog! I niggardly? Is that true, Mackellar? You think it is?" I really thought he would have struck me at that. "Oh, you all think so! Well, you shall see, and he shall see, and God shall see. If I ruin the estate and go barefoot, I shall stuff this bloodsucker. Let him ask all—all, and he shall have it! It is all his by rights. Ah!" he cried, "and I foresaw all this, and worse, when he would not let me go." He poured out another glass of wine, and was about to carry it to his lips, when I made so bold as to lay a finger on his arm. He stopped a moment. "You are right," said he, and flung glass and all in the fireplace. "Come, let us count the money."

I durst no longer oppose him; indeed, I was very much affected by the sight of so much disorder in a man usually so controlled; and we sat down together, counted the money, and made it up in packets for the greater ease of Colonel Burke, who was to be the bearer. This done, Mr. Henry returned to the hall, where he and my old lord sat all night through with their guest.

A little before dawn I was called and set out with the Colonel. He would scarce have liked a less responsible convoy, for he was a man who valued himself; nor could we afford him one more dignified, for Mr. Henry must not appear with the freetraders. It was a very bitter morning of wind, and as we went down through the long shrubbery the Colonel held himself muffled in his cloak.

"Sir," said I, "this is a great sum of money that your friend requires. I must suppose his necessities to be very great."

"We must suppose so," says he, I thought drily; but perhaps it was the cloak about his mouth.

"I am only a servant of the family," said I. "You may deal openly with me. I think we are likely to get little good by him?"

"My dear man," said the Colonel, "Ballantrae is a gentleman of the most eminent natural abilities, and a man that I admire, and that I revere, to the very ground he treads on." And then he seemed to me to pause like one in a difficulty.

"But for all that," said I, "we are likely to get little good by him?"

"Sure, and you can have it your own way, my dear man," says the Colonel.

By this time we had come to the side of the creek, where the boat awaited him. "Well," said be, "I am sure I am very much your debtor for all your civility, Mr. Whatever-your-name-is; and just as a last word, and since you show so much intelligent interest, I will mention a small circumstance that may be of use to the family. For I believe my friend omitted to mention that he has the largest pension on the Scots Fund of any refugee in Paris; and it's the more disgraceful, sir," cries the Colonel, warming, "because there's not one dirty penny for myself."

He cocked his hat at me, as if I had been to blame for this partiality; then changed again into his usual swaggering civility, shook me by the hand, and set off down to the boat, with the money under his arms, and whistling as he went the pathetic air of *Shule Aroon*. It was the first time I had heard that tune; I was to hear it again, words and all, as you shall learn, but I remember how that little stave of it ran in my head after the freetraders had bade him "Wheesht, in the deil's name," and the grating of the oars had taken its place, and I stood and watched the dawn creeping on the sea, and the boat drawing away, and the lugger lying with her foresail backed awaiting it.

The gap made in our money was a sore embarrassment, and, among other consequences, it had this: that I must ride to Edinburgh, and there raise a new loan on very questionable terms to keep the old afloat; and was thus, for close upon three weeks, absent from the house of Durrisdeer.

What passed in the interval I had none to tell me, but I found Mrs. Henry, upon my return, much changed in her demeanour. The old talks with my lord for the most part pretermitted; a certain deprecation visible towards her husband, to whom I thought she addressed herself more often; and, for one thing, she was now greatly wrapped up in Miss Katharine. You would think the change was agreeable to Mr. Henry; no such matter! To the contrary, every circumstance of alteration was a stab to him; he read in each the avowal of her truant fancies. That constancy to the Master of which she was proud while she supposed him dead, she had to blush for now she knew he was alive, and these blushes were the hated spring of her new conduct. I am to conceal no truth; and I will here say plainly, I think this was the period in which Mr. Henry showed the worst. He contained himself, indeed, in public; but there was a deep-seated irritation visible underneath. With me, from whom he had less concealment, he was often grossly unjust, and even for his wife he would sometimes have a sharp retort: perhaps when she had ruffled him with some unwonted kindness; perhaps upon no tangible occasion, the mere habitual tenor of the man's annoyance bursting spontaneously forth. When he would thus forget himself (a thing so strangely out of keeping with the terms of their relation), there went a shook through the whole company, and the pair would look upon each other in a kind of pained amazement.

All the time, too, while he was injuring himself by this defect of temper, he was hurting his position by a silence, of which I scarce know whether to say it was the child of generosity or pride. The freetraders came again and again, bringing messengers from the Master, and none departed empty-handed. I never durst reason with Mr. Henry; he gave what was asked of him in a kind of noble rage. Perhaps because he knew he was by nature inclining to the parsimonious, he took a backforemost pleasure in the recklessness with which he supplied his brother's exigence. Perhaps the falsity of the position would have spurred a humbler man into the same excess. But the estate (if I may say so) groaned under it; our daily expenses were shorn lower and lower; the stables were emptied, all but four roadsters; servants were discharged, which raised a dreadful murmuring in the country, and heated up the old disfavour upon Mr. Henry; and at last the yearly visit to Edinburgh must be discontinued.

This was in 1756. You are to suppose that for seven years this bloodsucker had been drawing the life's blood from Durrisdeer, and that all this time my patron had held his peace. It was an effect of devilish malice in the Master that he addressed Mr. Henry alone upon the matter of his demands, and there was never a word to my lord. The family had looked on, wondering at our economies. They had lamented, I have no doubt, that my patron had become so great a miser—a fault always despicable, but in the young abhorrent, and Mr. Henry was not yet thirty years of age. Still, he had managed the business of Durrisdeer almost from a boy; and they bore with these changes in a silence as proud and bitter as his own, until the coping-stone of the Edinburgh visit.

At this time I believe my patron and his wife were rarely together, save at meals. Immediately on the back of Colonel Burke's announcement Mrs. Henry made palpable advances; you might say she had laid a sort of timid court to her husband, different, indeed, from her former manner of unconcern and distance. I never had the heart to blame Mr. Henry because he recoiled from these advances; nor yet to censure the wife, when she was cut to the quick by their rejection. But the result was an entire estrangement, so that (as I say) they rarely spoke, except at meals. Even the matter of the Edinburgh visit was first broached at table, and it chanced that Mrs. Henry was that day ailing and querulous. She had no sooner understood her husband's meaning than the red flew in her face.

"At last," she cried, "this is too much! Heaven knows what pleasure I have in my life, that I should be denied my only consolation. These shameful proclivities must be trod down; we are already a mark and an eyesore in the neighbourhood. I will not endure this fresh insanity."

"I cannot afford it," says Mr. Henry.

"Afford?" she cried. "For shame! But I have money of my own."

"That is all mine, madam, by marriage," he snarled, and instantly left the room.

My old lord threw up his hands to Heaven, and he and his daughter, withdrawing to the chimney, gave me a broad hint to be gone. I found Mr. Henry in his usual retreat, the steward's room, perched on the end of the table, and plunging his penknife in it with a very ugly countenance.

"Mr. Henry," said I, "you do yourself too much injustice, and it is time this should cease."

"Oh!" cries he, "nobody minds here. They think it only natural. I have shameful proclivities. I am a niggardly dog," and he drove his knife up to the hilt. "But I will show that fellow," he cried with an oath, "I will show him which is the more generous."

"This is no generosity," said I; "this is only pride."

"Do you think I want morality?" he asked.

I thought he wanted help, and I should give it him, willy-nilly; and no sooner was Mrs. Henry gone to her room than I presented myself at her door and sought admittance.

She openly showed her wonder. "What do you want with me, Mr. Mackellar?" said she.

"The Lord knows, madam," says I, "I have never troubled you before with any freedoms; but this thing lies too hard upon my conscience, and it will out. Is it possible that two people can be so blind as you and my lord? and have lived all these years with a noble gentleman like Mr. Henry, and understand so little of his nature?"

"What does this mean?" she cried.

"Do you not know where his money goes to? his—and yours—and the money for the very wine he does not drink at table?" I went on. "To Paris—to that man! Eight thousand pounds has he had of us in seven years, and my patron fool enough to keep it secret!"

"Eight thousand pounds!" she repeated. "It in impossible; the estate is not sufficient."

"God knows how we have sweated farthings to produce it," said I. "But eight thousand and sixty is the sum, beside odd shillings. And if you can think my patron miserly after that, this shall be my last interference."

"You need say no more, Mr. Mackellar," said she. "You have done most properly in what you too modestly call your interference. I am much to blame; you must think me indeed a very unobservant wife" (looking upon me with a strange smile), "but I shall put this right at once.

The Master was always of a very thoughtless nature; but his heart is excellent; he is the soul of generosity. I shall write to him myself. You cannot think how you have pained me by this communication."

"Indeed, madam, I had hoped to have pleased you," said I, for I raged to see her still thinking of the Master.

"And pleased," said she, "and pleased me of course."

That same day (I will not say but what I watched) I had the satisfaction to see Mr. Henry come from his wife's room in a state most unlike himself; for his face was all bloated with weeping, and yet he seemed to me to walk upon the air. By this, I was sure his wife had made him full amends for once. "Ah," thought I to myself, "I have done a brave stroke this day."

On the morrow, as I was seated at my books, Mr. Henry came in softly behind me, took me by the shoulders, and shook me in a manner of playfulness. "I find you are a faithless fellow after all," says he, which was his only reference to my part; but the tone he spoke in was more to me than any eloquence of protestation. Nor was this all I had effected; for when the next messenger came (as he did not long afterwards) from the Master, he got nothing away with him but a letter. For some while back it had been I myself who had conducted these affairs; Mr. Henry not setting pen to paper, and I only in the dryest and most formal terms. But this letter I did not even see; it would scarce be pleasant reading, for Mr. Henry felt he had his wife behind him for once, and I observed, on the day it was despatched, he had a very gratified expression.

Things went better now in the family, though it could scarce be pretended they went well. There was now at least no misconception; there was kindness upon all sides; and I believe my patron and his wife might again have drawn together if he could but have pocketed his pride, and she forgot (what was the ground of all) her brooding on another man. It is wonderful how a private thought leaks out; it is wonderful to me now how we should all have followed the current of her sentiments; and though she bore herself quietly, and had a very even disposition, yet we should have known whenever her fancy ran to Paris. And would not any one have thought that my disclosure must have rooted up that idol? I think there is the devil in women: all these years passed, never a sight of the man, little enough kindness to remember (by all accounts) even while she had him, the notion of his death intervening, his heartless rapacity laid bare to her; that all should not do, and she must still keep the best place in her heart for this accursed fellow, is a thing to make a plain man rage. I had never much natural sympathy for the passion of love; but this unreason in my patron's wife disgusted me outright with the whole matter. I remember checking a maid because she sang some bairnly kickshaw while my mind was thus engaged; and my asperity brought about my ears the enmity of all the petticoats about the house; of which I reeked very little, but it amused Mr. Henry, who rallied me much upon our joint unpopularity. It is strange enough (for my own mother was certainly one of the salt of the earth, and my Aunt Dickson, who paid my fees at the University, a very notable woman), but I have never had much toleration for the female sex, possibly not much understanding; and being far from a bold man, I have ever shunned their company. Not only do I see no cause to regret this diffidence in myself, but have invariably remarked the most unhappy consequences follow those who were less wise. So much I thought proper to set down, lest I show myself unjust to Mrs. Henry. And, besides, the remark arose naturally, on a re-perusal of the letter which was the next step in these affairs, and reached me, to my sincere astonishment, by a private hand, some week or so after the departure of the last messenger.

Letter from Colonel Burke (*afterwards Chevalier*) *to* Mr. Mackellar.

Troyes in Champagne,

July 12, 1756

My Dear Sir,—You will doubtless be surprised to receive a communication from one so little known to you; but on the occasion I had the good fortune to rencounter you at Durrisdeer, I remarked you for a young man of a solid gravity of character: a qualification which I profess I admire and revere next to natural genius or the bold chivalrous spirit of the soldier. I was, besides, interested in the noble family which you have the honour to serve, or (to speak more by the book) to be the humble and respected friend of; and a conversation I had the pleasure to have with you very early in the morning has remained much upon my mind.

Being the other day in Paris, on a visit from this famous city, where I am in garrison, I took occasion to inquire your name (which I profess I had forgot) at my friend, the Master of B.; and a fair opportunity occurring, I write to inform you of what's new.

The Master of B. (when we had last some talk of him together) was in receipt, as I think I then told you, of a highly advantageous pension on the Scots Fund. He next received a company, and was soon after advanced to a regiment of his own. My dear sir, I do not offer to explain this circumstance; any more than why I myself, who have rid at the right hand of Princes, should be fubbed off with a pair of colours and sent to rot in a hole at the bottom of the province. Accustomed as I am to Courts, I cannot but feel it is no atmosphere for a plain soldier; and I could never hope to advance by similar means, even could I stoop to the endeavour. But our friend has a particular aptitude to succeed by the means of ladies; and if all be true that I have heard, he enjoyed a remarkable protection. It is like this turned against him; for when I had the honour to shake him by the hand, he was but newly released from the Bastille, where he had been cast on a sealed letter; and, though now released, has both lost his regiment and his pension. My dear sir, the loyalty of a plain Irishman will ultimately succeed in the place of craft; as I am sure a gentleman of your probity will agree.

Now, sir, the Master is a man whose genius I admire beyond expression, and, besides, he is my friend; but I thought a little word of this revolution in his fortunes would not come amiss, for, in my opinion, the man's desperate. He spoke, when I saw him, of a trip to India (whither I am myself in some hope of accompanying my illustrious countryman, Mr. Lally); but for this he would require (as I understood) more money than was readily at his command. You may have heard a military proverb: that it is a good thing to make a bridge of gold to a flying enemy? I trust you will take my meaning and I subscribe myself, with proper respects to my Lord Durrisdeer, to his son, and to the beauteous Mrs. Durie,

My dear Sir,
Your obedient humble servant,
Francis Burke.

This missive I carried at once to Mr. Henry; and I think there was but the one thought between the two of us: that it had come a week too late. I made haste to send an answer to Colonel Burke, in which I begged him, if he should see the Master, to assure him his next messenger would be attended to. But with all my haste I was not in time to avert what was impending; the arrow had been drawn, it must now fly. I could almost doubt the power of Providence (and certainly His will) to stay the issue of events; and it is a strange thought, how many of us had been storing up the elements of this catastrophe, for how long a time, and with how blind an ignorance of what we did.

From the coming of the Colonel's letter, I had a spyglass in my room, began to drop questions to the tenant folk, and as there was no great secrecy observed, and the freetrade (in our part) went by force as much as stealth, I had soon got together a knowledge of the signals in use, and knew pretty well to an hour when any messenger might be expected. I say, I questioned the tenants; for with the traders themselves, desperate blades that went habitually armed, I could never bring myself to meddle willingly. Indeed, by what proved in the sequel an unhappy chance, I was an object of scorn to some of these braggadocios; who had not only gratified me with a nickname, but catching me one night upon a by-path, and being all (as they would have said) somewhat merry, had caused me to dance for their diversion. The method employed was that of cruelly chipping at my toes with naked cutlasses, shouting at the same time "Square-Toes"; and though they did me no bodily mischief, I was none the less deplorably affected, and was indeed for several days confined to my bed: a scandal on the state of Scotland on which no comment is required.

It happened on the afternoon of November 7th, in this same unfortunate year, that I espied, during my walk, the smoke of a beacon fire upon the Muckleross. It was drawing near time for my return; but the uneasiness upon my spirits was that day so great that I must burst through the thickets to the edge of what they call the Craig Head. The sun was already down, but there was still a broad light in the west, which showed me some of the smugglers treading out their signal fire upon the Ross, and in the bay the lugger lying with her sails brailed up. She was plainly but new come to anchor, and yet the skiff was already lowered and pulling for the landing-place at the end of the long shrubbery. And this I knew could signify but one thing, the coming of a messenger for Durrisdeer.

I laid aside the remainder of my terrors, clambered down the brae—a place I had never ventured through before, and was hid among the shore-side thickets in time to see the boat touch. Captain Crail himself was steering, a thing not usual; by his side there sat a passenger; and the men gave way with difficulty, being hampered with near upon half a dozen portmanteaus, great and small. But the business of landing was briskly carried through; and presently the baggage was all tumbled on shore, the boat on its return voyage to the lugger, and the passenger standing alone upon the point of rock, a tall slender figure of a gentleman, habited in black, with a sword by his side and a walking-cane upon his wrist. As he so stood, he waved the cane to Captain Crail by way of salutation, with something both of grace and mockery that wrote the gesture deeply on my mind.

No sooner was the boat away with my sworn enemies than I took a sort of half courage, came forth to the margin of the thicket, and there halted again, my mind being greatly pulled about between natural diffidence and a dark foreboding of the truth. Indeed, I might have stood there swithering all night, had not the stranger turned, spied me through the mists, which were beginning to fall, and waved and cried on me to draw near. I did so with a heart like lead.

"Here, my good man," said he, in the English accent, "there are some things for Durrisdeer."

I was now near enough to see him, a very handsome figure and countenance, swarthy, lean, long, with a quick, alert, black look, as of one who was a fighter, and accustomed to command; upon one cheek he had a mole, not unbecoming; a large diamond sparkled on his hand; his clothes, although of the one hue, were of a French and foppish design; his ruffles, which he wore longer than common, of exquisite lace; and I wondered the more to see him in such a guise when he was but newly landed from a dirty smuggling lugger. At the same time he had a better look at me, toised me a second time sharply, and then smiled.

"I wager, my friend," says he, "that I know both your name and your nickname. I divined these very clothes upon your hand of writing, Mr. Mackellar."

At these words I fell to shaking.

"Oh," says he, "you need not be afraid of me. I bear no malice for your tedious letters; and it is my purpose to employ you a good deal. You may call me Mr. Bally: it is the name I have assumed; or rather (since I am addressing so great a precision) it is so I have curtailed my own. Come now, pick up that and that"—indicating two of the portmanteaus. "That will be as much as you are fit to bear, and the rest can very well wait. Come, lose no more time, if you please."

His tone was so cutting that I managed to do as he bid by a sort of instinct, my mind being all the time quite lost. No sooner had I picked up the portmanteaus than he turned his back and marched off through the long shrubbery, where it began already to be dusk, for the wood is thick and evergreen. I followed behind, loaded almost to the dust, though I profess I was not conscious of the burthen; being swallowed up in the monstrosity of this return, and my mind flying like a weaver's shuttle.

On a sudden I set the portmanteaus to the ground and halted. He turned and looked back at me.

"Well?" said he.

"You are the Master of Ballantrae?"

"You will do me the justice to observe," says he, "I have made no secret with the astute Mackellar."

"And in the name of God," cries I, "what brings you here? Go back, while it is yet time."

"I thank you," said he. "Your master has chosen this way, and not I; but since he has made the choice, he (and you also) must abide by the result. And now pick up these things of mine, which you have set down in a very boggy place, and attend to that which I have made your business."

But I had no thought now of obedience; I came straight up to him. "If nothing will move you to go back," said I; "though, sure, under all the circumstances, any Christian or even any gentleman would scruple to go forward . . . "

"These are gratifying expressions," he threw in.

"If nothing will move you to go back," I continued, "there are still some decencies to be observed. Wait here with your baggage, and I will go forward and prepare your family. Your father is an old man; and . . . " I stumbled . . . "there are decencies to be observed."

"Truly," said he, "this Mackellar improves upon acquaintance. But look you here, my man, and understand it once for all—you waste your breath upon me, and I go my own way with inevitable motion."

"Ah!" says I. "Is that so? We shall see then!"

And I turned and took to my heels for Durrisdeer. He clutched at me and cried out angrily, and then I believe I heard him laugh, and then I am certain he pursued me for a step or two, and (I suppose) desisted. One thing at least is sure, that I came but a few minutes later to the door of the great house, nearly strangled for the lack of breath, but quite alone. Straight up the stair I ran, and burst into the hall, and stopped before the family without the power of speech; but I must have carried my story in my looks, for they rose out of their places and stared on me like changelings.

"He has come," I panted out at last.

"He?" said Mr. Henry.

"Himself," said I.

"My son?" cried my lord. "Imprudent, imprudent boy! Oh, could he not stay where he was safe!"

Never a word says Mrs. Henry; nor did I look at her, I scarce knew why.

"Well," said Mr. Henry, with a very deep breath, "and where is he?"

"I left him in the long shrubbery," said I.

"Take me to him," said he.

So we went out together, he and I, without another word from any one; and in the midst of the gravelled plot encountered the Master strolling up, whistling as he came, and beating the air with his cane. There was still light enough overhead to recognise, though not to read, a countenance.

"Ah! Jacob," says the Master. "So here is Esau back."

"James," says Mr. Henry, "for God's sake, call me by my name. I will not pretend that I am glad to see you; but I would fain make you as welcome as I can in the house of our fathers."

"Or in *my* house? or *yours*?" says the Master. "Which were you about to say? But this is an old sore, and we need not rub it. If you would not share with me in Paris, I hope you will yet scarce deny your elder brother a corner of the fire at Durrisdeer?"

"That is very idle speech," replied Mr. Henry. "And you understand the power of your position excellently well."

"Why, I believe I do," said the other with a little laugh. And this, though they had never touched hands, was (as we may say) the end of the brothers' meeting; for at this the Master turned to me and bade me fetch his baggage.

I, on my side, turned to Mr. Henry for a confirmation; perhaps with some defiance.

"As long as the Master is here, Mr. Mackellar, you will very much oblige me by regarding his wishes as you would my own," says Mr. Henry. "We are constantly troubling you: will you be so good as send one of the servants?"—with an accent on the word.

If this speech were anything at all, it was surely a well-deserved reproof upon the stranger; and yet, so devilish was his impudence, he twisted it the other way.

"And shall we be common enough to say 'Sneck up'?" inquires he softly, looking upon me sideways.

Had a kingdom depended on the act, I could not have trusted myself in words; even to call a servant was beyond me; I had rather serve the man myself than speak; and I turned away in silence and went into the long shrubbery, with a heart full of anger and despair. It was dark under the trees, and I walked before me and forgot what business I was come upon, till I near broke my shin on the portmanteaus. Then it was that I remarked a strange particular; for whereas I had before carried both and scarce observed it, it was now as much as I could do to manage one. And this, as it forced me to make two journeys, kept me the longer from the hall.

When I got there, the business of welcome was over long ago; the company was already at supper; and by an oversight that cut me to the quick, my place had been forgotten. I had seen one side of the Master's return; now I was to see the other. It was he who first remarked my coming in and standing back (as I did) in some annoyance. He jumped from his seat.

"And if I have not got the good Mackellar's place!" cries he. "John, lay another for Mr. Bally; I protest he will disturb no one, and your table is big enough for all."

I could scarce credit my ears, nor yet my senses, when he took me by the shoulders and thrust me, laughing, into my own place—such an affectionate playfulness was in his voice. And while John laid the fresh place for him (a thing on which he still insisted), he went and leaned on his father's chair and looked down upon him, and the old man turned about and looked upwards on his son, with such a pleasant mutual tenderness that I could have carried my hand to my head in mere amazement.

Yet all was of a piece. Never a harsh word fell from him, never a sneer showed upon his lip. He had laid aside even his cutting English accent, and spoke with the kindly Scots' tongue, that set a value on affectionate words; and though his manners had a graceful elegance mighty foreign to our ways in Durrisdeer, it was still a homely courtliness, that did not shame but flattered us. All that, he did throughout the meal, indeed, drinking wine with me with a notable respect, turning about for a pleasant word with John, fondling his father's hand, breaking into little merry tales of his adventures, calling up the past with happy reference—all he did was so becoming, and himself so handsome, that I could scarce wonder if my lord and Mrs. Henry sat about the board with radiant faces, or if John waited behind with dropping tears.

As soon as supper was over, Mrs. Henry rose to withdraw.

"This was never your way, Alison," said he.

"It is my way now," she replied: which was notoriously false, "and I will give you a good-night, James, and a welcome—from the dead," said she, and her voice dropped and trembled.

Poor Mr. Henry, who had made rather a heavy figure through the meal, was more concerned than ever; pleased to see his wife withdraw, and yet half displeased, as he thought upon the cause of it; and the next moment altogether dashed by the fervour of her speech.

On my part, I thought I was now one too many; and was stealing after Mrs. Henry, when the Master saw me.

"Now, Mr. Mackellar," says he, "I take this near on an unfriendliness. I cannot have you go: this is to make a stranger of the prodigal son; and let me remind you where—in his own father's house! Come, sit ye down, and drink another glass with Mr. Bally."

"Ay, ay, Mr. Mackellar," says my lord, "we must not make a stranger either of him or you. I have been telling my son," he added, his voice brightening as usual on the word, "how much we valued all your friendly service."

So I sat there, silent, till my usual hour; and might have been almost deceived in the man's nature but for one passage, in which his perfidy appeared too plain. Here was the passage; of which, after what he knows of the brothers' meeting, the reader shall consider for himself. Mr. Henry sitting somewhat dully, in spite of his best endeavours to carry things before my lord, up jumps the Master, passes about the board, and claps his brother on the shoulder.

"Come, come, *Hairry lad,*" says he, with a broad accent such as they must have used together when they were boys, "you must not be downcast because your brother has come home. All's yours, that's sure enough, and little I grudge it you. Neither must you grudge me my place beside my father's fire."

"And that is too true, Henry," says my old lord with a little frown, a thing rare with him. "You have been the elder brother of the parable in the good sense; you must be careful of the other."

"I am easily put in the wrong," said Mr. Henry.

"Who puts you in the wrong?" cried my lord, I thought very tartly for so mild a man. "You have earned my gratitude and your brother's many thousand times: you may count on its endurance; and let that suffice."

"Ay, Harry, that you may," said the Master; and I thought Mr. Henry looked at him with a kind of wildness in his eye.

On all the miserable business that now followed, I have four questions that I asked myself often at the time and ask myself still:—Was the man moved by a particular sentiment against Mr. Henry? or by what he thought to be his interest? or by a mere delight in cruelty such as cats display and theologians tell us of the devil? or by what he would have called love? My common opinion halts among the three first; but perhaps there lay at the spring of his behaviour an element of all. As thus:—Animosity to Mr. Henry would explain his hateful usage of him when they were alone; the interests he came to serve would explain his very different attitude before my lord; that and some spice of a design of gallantry, his care to stand well with Mrs. Henry; and the pleasure of malice for itself, the pains he was continually at to mingle and oppose these lines of conduct.

Partly because I was a very open friend to my patron, partly because in my letters to Paris I had often given myself some freedom of remonstrance, I was included in his diabolical amusement. When I was alone with him, he pursued me with sneers; before the family he used me with the extreme of friendly condescension. This was not only painful in itself; not only did it put me continually in the wrong; but there was in it an element of insult indescribable. That he should thus leave me out in his dissimulation, as though even my testimony were too despicable to be considered, galled me to the blood. But what it was to me is not worth notice. I make but memorandum of it here; and chiefly for this reason, that it had one good result, and gave me the quicker sense of Mr. Henry's martyrdom.

It was on him the burthen fell. How was he to respond to the public advances of one who never lost a chance of gibing him in private? How was he to smile back on the deceiver and the insulter? He was condemned to seem ungracious. He was condemned to silence. Had he been less proud, had he spoken, who would have credited the truth? The acted calumny had done its work; my lord and Mrs. Henry were the daily witnesses of what went on; they could have sworn in court that the Master was a model of long-suffering good-nature, and Mr. Henry a pattern of jealousy and thanklessness. And ugly enough as these must have appeared in any one, they seemed tenfold uglier in Mr. Henry; for who could forget that the Master lay in peril of his life, and that he had already lost his mistress, his title, and his fortune?

"Henry, will you ride with me?" asks the Master one day.

And Mr. Henry, who had been goaded by the man all morning, raps out: "I will not."

"I sometimes wish you would be kinder, Henry," says the other, wistfully.

I give this for a specimen; but such scenes befell continually. Small wonder if Mr. Henry was blamed; small wonder if I fretted myself into something near upon a bilious fever; nay, and at the mere recollection feel a bitterness in my blood.

Sure, never in this world was a more diabolical contrivance: so perfidious, so simple, so impossible to combat. And yet I think again, and I think always, Mrs. Henry might have road between the lines; she might have had more knowledge of her husband's nature; after all these years of marriage she might have commanded or captured his confidence. And my old lord, too—that very watchful gentleman—where was all his observation? But, for one thing, the deceit was practised by a master hand, and might have gulled an angel. For another (in the case of Mrs. Henry), I have observed there are no persons so far away as those who are both married and estranged, so that they seem out of ear-shot or to have no common tongue. For a third (in the case of both of these spectators), they were blinded by old ingrained predilection. And for a fourth, the risk the Master was supposed to stand in (supposed, I say—you will soon hear why) made it seem the more ungenerous to criticise; and, keeping them in a perpetual tender solicitude about his life, blinded them the more effectually to his faults.

It was during this time that I perceived most clearly the effect of manner, and was led to lament most deeply the plainness of my own. Mr. Henry had the essence of a gentleman; when he was moved, when there was any call of circumstance, he could play his part with dignity and spirit; but in the day's commerce (it is idle to deny it) he fell short of the ornamental. The Master (on the other hand) had never a movement but it commanded him. So it befell that when the one appeared gracious and the other ungracious, every trick of their bodies seemed to call out confirmation. Not that alone: but the more deeply Mr. Henry floundered in his brother's toils, the more clownish he grew; and the more the Master enjoyed his spiteful entertainment, the more engagingly, the more smilingly, he went! So that the plot, by its own scope and progress, furthered and confirmed itself.

It was one of the man's arts to use the peril in which (as I say) he was supposed to stand. He spoke of it to those who loved him with a gentle pleasantry, which made it the more touching. To Mr. Henry he used it as a cruel weapon of offence. I remember his laying his finger on the clean lozenge of the painted window one day when we three were alone together in the hall. "Here went your lucky guinea, Jacob," said he. And when Mr. Henry only looked upon him darkly, "Oh!" he added, "you need not look such impotent malice, my good fly. You can be rid of your spider when you please. How long, O Lord? When are you to be wrought to the point of a denunciation, scrupulous brother? It is one of my interests in this dreary hole. I ever loved experiment." Still Mr. Henry only stared upon him with a grooming brow, and a changed colour; and at last the Master broke out in a laugh and clapped him on the shoulder, calling him a sulky dog. At this my patron leaped back with a gesture I thought very dangerous; and I must suppose the Master thought so too, for he looked the least in the world discountenance, and I do not remember him again to have laid hands on Mr. Henry.

But though he had his peril always on his lips in the one way or the other, I thought his conduct strangely incautious, and began to fancy the Government—who had set a price upon his head—was gone sound asleep. I will not deny I was tempted with the wish to denounce him; but two thoughts withheld me: one, that if he were thus to end his life upon an honourable scaffold, the man would be canonised for good in the minds of his father and my patron's wife; the other, that if I was anyway mingled in the matter, Mr. Henry himself would scarce escape some glancings of suspicion. And in the meanwhile our enemy went in and out more than I could have thought possible, the fact that he was home again was buzzed about all the country-side, and yet he was never stirred. Of all these so-many and so-different persons who were acquainted with his presence, none had the least greed—as I used to say in my annoyance—or the least loyalty; and the man rode here and there—fully more welcome, considering the lees of old unpopularity, than Mr. Henry—and considering the freetraders, far safer than myself.

Not but what he had a trouble of his own; and this, as it brought about the gravest consequences, I must now relate. The reader will scarce have forgotten Jessie Broun; her way of life was much among the smuggling party; Captain Crail himself was of her intimates; and she had early word of Mr. Bally's presence at the house. In my opinion, she had long ceased to care two straws for the Master's person; but it was become her habit to connect herself continually with the Master's name; that was the ground of all her play-acting; and so now, when he was back, she thought she owed it to herself to grow a haunter of the neighbourhood of Durrisdeer. The Master could scarce go abroad but she was there in wait for him; a scandalous figure of a woman, not often sober; hailing him wildly as "her bonny laddie," quoting pedlar's poetry, and, as I receive the story, even seeking to weep upon his neck. I own I rubbed my hands over this persecution; but the Master, who laid so much upon others, was himself the least patient of men. There were strange scenes enacted in the policies. Some say he took his cane to her, and Jessie fell back upon her former weapons—stones. It is certain at least that he made a motion to Captain Crail to have the woman trepanned, and that the Captain refused the proposition with uncommon vehemence. And the end of the matter was victory for Jessie. Money was got together; an interview took place, in which my proud gentleman must consent to be kissed and wept upon; and the woman was set up in a public of her own, somewhere on Solway side (but I forget where), and, by the only news I ever had of it, extremely ill-frequented.

This is to look forward. After Jessie had been but a little while upon his heels, the Master comes to me one day in the steward's office, and with more civility than usual, "Mackellar," says he, "there is a damned crazy wench comes about here. I cannot well move in the matter myself, which brings me to you. Be so good as to see to it: the men must have a strict injunction to drive the wench away."

"Sir," said I, trembling a little, "you can do your own dirty errands for yourself."

He said not a word to that, and left the room.

Presently came Mr. Henry. "Here is news!" cried he. "It seems all is not enough, and you must add to my wretchedness. It seems you have insulted Mr. Bally."

"Under your kind favour, Mr. Henry," said I, "it was he that insulted me, and, as I think, grossly. But I may have been careless of your position when I spoke; and if you think so when you know all, my dear patron, you have but to say the word. For you I would obey in any point whatever, even to sin, God pardon me!" And thereupon I told him what had passed.

Mr. Henry smiled to himself; a grimmer smile I never witnessed. "You did exactly well," said he. "He shall drink his Jessie Broun to the dregs." And then, spying the Master outside, he opened the window, and crying to him by the name of Mr. Bally, asked him to step up and have a word.

"James," said he, when our persecutor had come in and closed the door behind him, looking at me with a smile, as if he thought I was to be humbled, "you brought me a complaint against Mr. Mackellar, into which I have inquired. I need not tell you I would always take his word against yours; for we are alone, and I am going to use something of your own freedom. Mr. Mackellar is a gentleman I value; and you must contrive, so long as you are under this roof, to bring yourself into no more collisions with one whom I will support at any possible cost to me or mine. As for the errand upon which you came to him, you must deliver yourself from the consequences of your own cruelty, and, none of my servants shall be at all employed in such a case."

"My father's servants, I believe," says the Master.

"Go to him with this tale," said Mr. Henry.

The Master grew very white. He pointed at me with his finger. "I want that man discharged," he said.

"He shall not be," said Mr. Henry.

"You shall pay pretty dear for this," says the Master.

"I have paid so dear already for a wicked brother," said Mr. Henry, "that I am bankrupt even of fears. You have no place left where you can strike me."

"I will show you about that," says the Master, and went softly away.

"What will he do next, Mackellar?" cries Mr. Henry.

"Let me go away," said I. "My dear patron, let me go away; I am but the beginning of fresh sorrows."

"Would you leave me quite alone?" said he.

We were not long in suspense as to the nature of the new assault. Up to that hour the Master had played a very close game with Mrs. Henry; avoiding pointedly to be alone with her, which I took at the time for an effect of decency, but now think to be a most insidious art; meeting her, you may say, at meal-time only; and behaving, when he did so, like an affectionate brother. Up to that hour, you may say he had scarce directly interfered between Mr. Henry and his wife; except in so far as he had manoeuvred the one quite forth from the good graces of the other. Now all that was to be changed; but whether really in revenge, or because he was wearying of Durrisdeer and looked about for some diversion, who but the devil shall decide?

From that hour, at least, began the siege of Mrs. Henry; a thing so deftly carried on that I scarce know if she was aware of it herself, and that her husband must look on in silence. The first parallel was opened (as was made to appear) by accident. The talk fell, as it did often, on the exiles in France; so it glided to the matter of their songs.

"There is one," says the Master, "if you are curious in these matters, that has always seemed to me very moving. The poetry is harsh; and yet, perhaps because of my situation, it has always found the way to my heart. It is supposed to be sung, I should tell you, by an exile's sweetheart; and represents perhaps, not so much the truth of what she is thinking, as the truth of what he hopes of her, poor soul! in these far lands." And here the Master sighed, "I protest it is a pathetic sight when a score of rough Irish, all common sentinels, get to this song; and you may see, by their falling tears, how it strikes home to them. It goes thus, father," says he, very adroitly taking my lord for his listener, "and if I cannot get to the end of it, you must think it is a common case with us exiles." And thereupon he struck up the same air as I had heard the Colonel whistle; but now to words, rustic indeed, yet most pathetically setting forth a poor girl's aspirations for an exiled lover; of which one verse indeed (or something like it) still sticks by me:—

O, I will dye my petticoat red,
With my dear boy I'll beg my bread,
Though all my friends should wish me dead,
For Willie among the rushes, O!

He sang it well, even as a song; but he did better yet a performer. I have heard famous actors, when there was not a dry eye in the Edinburgh theatre; a great wonder to behold; but no more wonderful than how the Master played upon that little ballad, and on those who heard him, like an instrument, and seemed now upon the point of failing, and now to conquer his distress, so that words and music seemed to pour out of his own heart and his own past, and to be aimed directly at Mrs. Henry. And his art went further yet; for all was so delicately touched, it seemed impossible to suspect him of the least design; and so far from making a parade of emotion, you would have sworn he was striving to be calm. When it came to an end, we all sat silent for a time; he had chosen the dusk of the afternoon, so that none could see his neighbour's face; but it seemed as if we held our breathing; only my old lord cleared his throat. The first to move was the singer, who got to his feet suddenly and softly, and went and walked softly to and fro in the low end of the hall, Mr. Henry's customary place. We were to suppose that he there struggled down the last of his emotion; for he presently returned and launched into a disquisition on the nature of the Irish (always so much miscalled, and whom he defended) in his natural voice; so that, before the lights were brought, we were in the usual course of talk. But even then, methought Mrs. Henry's face was a shade pale; and, for another thing, she withdrew almost at once.

The next sign was a friendship this insidious devil struck up with innocent Miss Katharine; so that they were always together, hand in hand, or she climbing on his knee, like a pair of children. Like all his diabolical acts, this cut in several ways. It was the last stroke to Mr. Henry, to see his own babe debauched against him; it made him harsh with the poor innocent, which brought him still a peg lower in his wife's esteem; and (to conclude) it was a bond of union between the lady and the Master. Under this influence, their old reserve melted by daily stages. Presently there came walks in the long shrubbery, talks in the Belvedere, and I know not what tender familiarity. I am sure Mrs. Henry was like many a good woman; she had a whole conscience but perhaps by the means of a little winking. For even to so dull an observer as myself, it was plain her kindness was of a more moving nature than the sisterly. The tones of her voice appeared more numerous; she had a light and softness in her eye; she was more gentle with all of us, even with Mr. Henry, even with myself; methought she breathed of some quiet melancholy happiness.

To look on at this, what a torment it was for Mr. Henry! And yet it brought our ultimate deliverance, as I am soon to tell.

The purport of the Master's stay was no more noble (gild it as they might) than to wring money out. He had some design of a fortune in the French Indies, as the Chevalier wrote me; and it was the sum required for this that he came seeking. For the rest of the family it spelled ruin; but my lord, in his incredible partiality, pushed ever for the granting. The family was now so narrowed down (indeed, there were no more of them than just the father and the two sons) that it was possible to break the entail and alienate a piece of land. And to this, at first by hints, and then by open pressure, Mr. Henry was brought to consent. He never would have done so, I am very well assured, but for the weight of the distress under which he laboured. But for his passionate eagerness to see his brother gone, he would not thus have broken with his own sentiment and the traditions of his house. And even so, he sold them his consent at a dear rate, speaking for once openly, and holding the business up in its own shameful colours.

"You will observe," he said, "this is an injustice to my son, if ever I have one."

"But that you are not likely to have," said my lord.

"God knows!" says Mr. Henry. "And considering the cruel falseness of the position in which I stand to my brother, and that you, my lord, are my father, and have the right to command me, I set my hand to this paper. But one thing I will say first: I have been ungenerously pushed, and when next, my lord, you are tempted to compare your sons, I call on you to remember what I have done and what he has done. Acts are the fair test."

My lord was the most uneasy man I ever saw; even in his old face the blood came up. "I think this is not a very wisely chosen moment, Henry, for complaints," said he. "This takes away from the merit of your generosity."

"Do not deceive yourself, my lord," said Mr. Henry. "This injustice is not done from generosity to him, but in obedience to yourself."

"Before strangers . . . " begins my lord, still more unhappily affected.

"There is no one but Mackellar here," said Mr. Henry; "he is my friend. And, my lord, as you make him no stranger to your frequent blame, it were hard if I must keep him one to a thing so rare as my defence."

Almost I believe my lord would have rescinded his decision; but the Master was on the watch.

"Ah! Henry, Henry," says he, "you are the best of us still. Rugged and true! Ah! man, I wish I was as good."

And at that instance of his favourite's generosity my lord desisted from his hesitation, and the deed was signed.

As soon as it could he brought about, the land of Ochterhall was sold for much below its value, and the money paid over to our leech and sent by some private carriage into France. Or so he said; though I have suspected since it did not go so far. And now here was all the man's business brought to a successful head, and his pockets once more bulging with our gold; and yet the point for which we had consented to this sacrifice was still denied us, and the visitor still lingered on at Durrisdeer. Whether in malice, or because the time was not yet come for his adventure to the Indies, or because he had hopes of his design on Mrs. Henry, or from the orders of the Government, who shall say? but linger he did, and that for weeks.

You will observe I say: from the orders of Government; for about this time the man's disreputable secret trickled out.

The first hint I had was from a tenant, who commented on the Master's stay, and yet more on his security; for this tenant was a Jacobitish sympathiser, and had lost a son at Culloden, which gave him the more critical eye. "There is one thing," said he, "that I cannot but think strange; and that is how he got to Cockermouth."

"To Cockermouth?" said I, with a sudden memory of my first wonder on beholding the man disembark so point-de-vice after so long a voyage.

"Why, yes," says the tenant, "it was there he was picked up by Captain Crail. You thought he had come from France by sea? And so we all did."

I turned this news a little in my head, and then carried it to Mr. Henry. "Here is an odd circumstance," said I, and told him.

"What matters how he came, Mackellar, so long as he is here?" groans Mr. Henry.

"No, sir," said I, "but think again! Does not this smack a little of some Government connivance? You know how much we have wondered already at the man's security."

"Stop," said Mr. Henry. "Let me think of this." And as he thought, there came that grim smile upon his face that was a little like the Master's. "Give me paper," said he. And he sat without another word and wrote to a gentleman of his acquaintance—I will name no unnecessary names, but he was one in a high place. This letter I despatched by the only hand I could depend upon in such a case—Macconochie's; and the old man rode hard, for he was back with the reply before even my eagerness had ventured to expect him. Again, as he read it, Mr. Henry had the same grim smile.

"This is the best you have done for me yet, Mackellar," says he. "With this in my hand I will give him a shog. Watch for us at dinner."

At dinner accordingly Mr. Henry proposed some very public appearance for the Master; and my lord, as he had hoped, objected to the danger of the course.

"Oh!" says Mr. Henry, very easily, "you need no longer keep this up with me. I am as much in the secret as yourself."

"In the secret?" says my lord. "What do you mean, Henry? I give you my word, I am in no secret from which you are excluded."

The Master had changed countenance, and I saw he was struck in a joint of his harness.

"How?" says Mr. Henry, turning to him with a huge appearance of surprise. "I see you serve your masters very faithfully; but I had thought you would have been humane enough to set your father's mind at rest."

"What are you talking of? I refuse to have my business publicly discussed. I order this to cease," cries the Master very foolishly and passionately, and indeed more like a child than a man.

"So much discretion was not looked for at your hands, I can assure you," continued Mr. Henry. "For see what my correspondent writes"—unfolding the paper—"'It is, of course, in the interests both of the Government and the gentleman whom we may perhaps best continue to call Mr. Bally, to keep this understanding secret; but it was never meant his own family should continue to endure the suspense you paint so feelingly; and I am pleased mine should be the hand to set these fears at rest. Mr. Bally is as safe in Great Britain as yourself.'"

"Is this possible?" cries my lord, looking at his son, with a great deal of wonder and still more of suspicion in his face.

"My dear father," says the Master, already much recovered. "I am overjoyed that this may be disclosed. My own instructions, direct from London, bore a very contrary sense, and I was charged to keep the indulgence secret from every one, yourself not excepted, and indeed yourself expressly named—as I can show in black and white unless I have destroyed the letter. They must have changed their mind very swiftly, for the whole matter is still quite fresh; or rather, Henry's correspondent must have misconceived that part, as he seems to have misconceived the rest. To tell you the truth, sir," he continued, getting visibly more easy, "I had supposed this unexplained favour to a rebel was the effect of some application from yourself; and the injunction to secrecy among my family the result of a desire on your part to conceal your kindness. Hence I was the more careful to obey orders. It remains now to guess by what other channel indulgence can have flowed on so notorious an offender as myself; for I do not think your son need defend himself from what seems hinted at in Henry's letter. I have never yet heard of a Durrisdeer who was a turncoat or a spy," says he, proudly.

And so it seemed he had swum out of this danger unharmed; but this was to reckon without a blunder he had made, and without the pertinacity of Mr. Henry, who was now to show he had something of his brother's spirit.

"You say the matter is still fresh," says Mr. Henry.

"It is recent," says the Master, with a fair show of stoutness and yet not without a quaver.

"Is it so recent as that?" asks Mr. Henry, like a man a little puzzled, and spreading his letter forth again.

In all the letter there was no word as to the date; but how was the Master to know that?

"It seemed to come late enough for me," says he, with a laugh. And at the sound of that laugh, which rang false, like a cracked bell, my lord looked at him again across the table, and I saw his old lips draw together close.

"No," said Mr. Henry, still glancing on his letter, "but I remember your expression. You said it was very fresh."

And here we had a proof of our victory, and the strongest instance yet of my lord's incredible indulgence; for what must he do but interfere to save his favourite from exposure!

"I think, Henry," says he, with a kind of pitiful eagerness, "I think we need dispute no more. We are all rejoiced at last to find your brother safe; we are all at one on that; and, as grateful subjects, we can do no less than drink to the king's health and bounty."

Thus was the Master extricated; but at least he had been put to his defence, he had come lamely out, and the attraction of his personal danger was now publicly plucked away from him. My lord, in his heart of hearts, now knew his favourite to be a Government spy; and Mrs. Henry (however she explained the tale) was notably cold in her behaviour to the discredited hero of romance. Thus in the best fabric of duplicity, there is some weak point, if you can strike it, which will loosen all; and if, by this fortunate stroke, we had not shaken the idol, who can say how it might have gone with us at the catastrophe?

And yet at the time we seemed to have accomplished nothing. Before a day or two he had wiped off the ill-results of his discomfiture, and, to all appearance, stood as high as ever. As for my Lord Durrisdeer, he was sunk in parental partiality; it was not so much love, which should be an active quality, as an apathy and torpor of his other powers; and forgiveness (so to misapply a noble word) flowed from him in sheer weakness, like the tears of senility. Mrs. Henry's was a different case; and Heaven alone knows what he found to say to her, or how he persuaded her from her contempt. It is one of the worst things of sentiment, that the voice grows to be more important than the words, and the speaker than that which is spoken. But some excuse the Master must have found, or perhaps he had even struck upon some art to wrest this exposure to his own advantage; for after a time of coldness, it seemed as if things went worse than ever between him and Mrs. Henry. They were then constantly together. I would not be thought to cut one shadow of blame, beyond what is due to a half-wilful blindness, on that unfortunate lady; but I do think, in these last days, she was playing very near the fire; and whether I be wrong or not in that, one thing is sure and quite sufficient: Mr. Henry thought so. The poor gentleman sat for days in my room, so great a picture of distress that I could never venture to address him; yet it is to be thought he found some comfort even in my presence and the knowledge of my sympathy. There were times, too, when we talked, and a strange manner of talk it was; there was never a person named, nor an individual circumstance referred to; yet we had the same matter in our minds, and we were each aware of it. It is a strange art that can thus be practised; to talk for hours of a thing, and never name nor yet so much as hint at it. And I remember I wondered if it was by some such natural skill that the Master made love to Mrs. Henry all day long (as he manifestly did), yet never startled her into reserve.

To show how far affairs had gone with Mr. Henry, I will give some words of his, uttered (as I have cause not to forget) upon the 26th of February, 1757. It was unseasonable weather, a cast back into Winter: windless, bitter cold, the world all white with rime, the sky low and gray: the sea black and silent like a quarry-hole. Mr. Henry sat close by the fire, and debated (as was now common with him) whether "a man" should "do things," whether "interference was wise," and the like general propositions, which each of us particularly applied. I was by the window, looking out, when there passed below me the Master, Mrs. Henry, and Miss Katharine, that now constant trio. The child was running to and fro, delighted with the frost; the Master spoke close in the lady's ear with what seemed (even from so far) a devilish grace of insinuation; and she on her part looked on the ground like a person lost in listening. I broke out of my reserve.

"If I were you, Mr. Henry," said I, "I would deal openly with my lord."

"Mackellar, Mackellar," said he, "you do not see the weakness of my ground. I can carry no such base thoughts to any one—to my father least of all; that would be to fall into the bottom of his scorn. The weakness of my ground," he continued, "lies in myself, that I am not one who engages love. I have their gratitude, they all tell me that; I have a rich estate of it! But I am not present in their minds; they are moved neither to think with me nor to think for me. There is my loss!" He got to his feet, and trod down the fire. "But some method must be found, Mackellar," said he, looking at me suddenly over his shoulder; "some way must be found. I am a man of a great deal of patience—far too much—far too much. I begin to despise myself. And yet, sure, never was a man involved in such a toil!" He fell back to his brooding.

"Cheer up," said I. "It will burst of itself."

"I am far past anger now," says he, which had so little coherency with my own observation that I let both fall.

5

ACCOUNT OF ALL THAT PASSED ON THE NIGHT ON FEBRUARY 27TH, 1757

On the evening of the interview referred to, the Master went abroad; he was abroad a great deal of the next day also, that fatal 27th; but where he went, or what he did, we never concerned ourselves to ask until next day. If we had done so, and by any chance found out, it might have changed all. But as all we did was done in ignorance, and should be so judged, I shall so narrate these passages as they appeared to us in the moment of their birth, and reserve all that I since discovered for the time of its discovery. For I have now come to one of the dark parts of my narrative, and must engage the reader's indulgence for my patron.

All the 27th that rigorous weather endured: a stifling cold; the folk passing about like smoking chimneys; the wide hearth in the hall piled high with fuel; some of the spring birds that had already blundered north into our neighbourhood, besieging the windows of the house or trotting on the frozen turf like things distracted. About noon there came a blink of sunshine, showing a very pretty, wintry, frosty landscape of white hills and woods, with Crail's lugger waiting for a wind under the Craig Head, and the smoke mounting straight into the air from every farm and cottage. With the coming of night, the haze closed in overhead; it fell dark and still and starless, and exceeding cold: a night the most unseasonable, fit for strange events.

Mrs. Henry withdrew, as was now her custom, very early. We had set ourselves of late to pass the evening with a game of cards; another mark that our visitor was wearying mightily of the life at Durrisdeer; and we had not been long at this when my old lord slipped from his place beside the fire, and was off without a word to seek the warmth of bed. The three thus left together had neither love nor courtesy to share; not one of us would have sat up one instant to oblige another; yet from the influence of custom, and as the cards had just been dealt, we continued the form of playing out the round. I should say we were late sitters; and though my lord had departed earlier than was his custom, twelve was already gone some time upon the clock, and the servants long ago in bed. Another thing I should say, that although I never saw the Master anyway affected with liquor, he had been drinking freely, and was perhaps (although he showed it not) a trifle heated.

Anyway, he now practised one of his transitions; and so soon as the door closed behind my lord, and without the smallest change of voice, shifted from ordinary civil talk into a stream of insult.

"My dear Henry, it is yours to play," he had been saying, and now continued: "It is a very strange thing how, even in so small a matter as a game of cards, you display your rusticity. You play, Jacob, like a bonnet laird, or a sailor in a tavern. The same dulness, the same petty greed, *cette lenteur d'hebété qui me fait rager*; it is strange I should have such a brother. Even Square-toes has a certain vivacity when his stake is imperilled; but the dreariness of a game with you I positively lack language to depict."

Mr. Henry continued to look at his cards, as though very maturely considering some play; but his mind was elsewhere.

"Dear God, will this never be done?" cries the Master. "*Quel lourdeau*! But why do I trouble you with French expressions, which are lost on such an ignoramus? A *lourdeau*, my dear brother, is as we might say a bumpkin, a clown, a clodpole: a fellow without grace, lightness, quickness; any gift of pleasing, any natural brilliancy: such a one as you shall see, when you desire, by looking in the mirror. I tell you these things for your good, I assure you; and besides, Square-toes" (looking at me and stifling a yawn), "it is one of my diversions in this very dreary spot to toast you and your master at the fire like chestnuts. I have great pleasure in your case, for I observe the nickname (rustic as it is) has always the power to make you writhe. But sometimes I have more trouble with this dear fellow here, who seems to have gone to sleep upon his cards. Do you not see the applicability of the epithet I have just explained, dear Henry? Let me show you. For instance, with all those solid qualities which I delight to recognise in you, I never knew a woman who did not prefer me—nor, I think," he continued, with the most silken deliberation, "I think—who did not continue to prefer me."

Mr. Henry laid down his cards. He rose to his feet very softly, and seemed all the while like a person in deep thought. "You coward!" he said gently, as if to himself. And then, with neither hurry nor any particular violence, he struck the Master in the mouth.

The Master sprang to his feet like one transfigured; I had never seen the man so beautiful. "A blow!" he cried. "I would not take a blow from God Almighty!"

"Lower your voice," said Mr. Henry. "Do you wish my father to interfere for you again?"

"Gentlemen, gentlemen," I cried, and sought to come between them.

The Master caught me by the shoulder, held me at arm's length, and still addressing his brother: "Do you know what this means?" said he.

"It was the most deliberate act of my life," says Mr. Henry.

"I must have blood, I must have blood for this," says the Master.

"Please God it shall be yours," said Mr. Henry; and he went to the wall and took down a pair of swords that hung there with others, naked. These he presented to the Master by the points. "Mackellar shall see us play fair," said Mr. Henry. "I think it very needful."

"You need insult me no more," said the Master, taking one of the swords at random. "I have hated you all my life."

"My father is but newly gone to bed," said Mr. Henry. "We must go somewhere forth of the house."

"There is an excellent place in the long shrubbery," said the Master.

"Gentlemen," said I, "shame upon you both! Sons of the same mother, would you turn against the life she gave you?"

"Even so, Mackellar," said Mr. Henry, with the same perfect quietude of manner he had shown throughout.

"It is what I will prevent," said I.

And now here is a blot upon my life. At these words of mine the Master turned his blade against my bosom; I saw the light run along the steel; and I threw up my arms and fell to my knees before him on the floor. "No, no," I cried, like a baby.

"We shall have no more trouble with him," said the Master. "It is a good thing to have a coward in the house."

"We must have light," said Mr. Henry, as though there had been no interruption.

"This trembler can bring a pair of candles," said the Master.

To my shame be it said, I was still so blinded with the flashing of that bare sword that I volunteered to bring a lantern.

"We do not need a l-l-lantern," says the Master, mocking me. "There is no breath of air. Come, get to your feet, take a pair of lights, and go before. I am close behind with this—" making. the blade glitter as he spoke.

I took up the candlesticks and went before them, steps that I would give my hand to recall; but a coward is a slave at the best; and even as I went, my teeth smote each other in my mouth. It was as he had said: there was no breath stirring; a windless stricture of frost had bound the air; and as we went forth in the shine of the candles, the blackness was like a roof over our heads. Never a word was said; there was never a sound but the creaking of our steps along the frozen path. The cold of the night fell about me like a bucket of water; I shook as I went with more than terror; but my companions, bare-headed like myself, and fresh from the warm ball, appeared not even conscious of the change.

"Here is the place," said the Master. "Set down the candles."

I did as he bid me, and presently the flames went up, as steady as in a chamber, in the midst of the frosted trees, and I beheld these two brothers take their places.

"The light is something in my eyes," said the Master.

"I will give you every advantage," replied Mr. Henry, shifting his ground, "for I think you are about to die." He spoke rather sadly than otherwise, yet there was a ring in his voice.

"Henry Durie," said the Master, "two words before I begin. You are a fencer, you can hold a foil; you little know what a change it makes to hold a sword! And by that I know you are to fall. But see how strong is my situation! If you fall, I shift out of this country to where my money is before me. If I fall, where are you? My father, your wife—who is in love with me, as you very well know—your child even, who prefers me to yourself:—how will these avenge me! Had you thought of that, dear Henry?" He looked at his brother with a smile; then made a fencing-room salute.

Never a word said Mr. Henry, but saluted too, and the swords rang together.

I am no judge of the play; my head, besides, was gone with cold and fear and horror; but it seems that Mr. Henry took and kept the upper hand from the engagement, crowding in upon his foe with a contained and glowing fury. Nearer and nearer he crept upon the man, till of a sudden the Master leaped back with a little sobbing oath; and I believe the movement brought the light once more against his eyes. To it they went again, on the fresh ground; but now methought closer, Mr. Henry pressing more outrageously, the Master beyond doubt with shaken confidence. For it is beyond doubt he now recognised himself for lost, and had some taste of the cold agony of fear; or he had never attempted the foul stroke. I cannot say I followed it, my untrained eye was never quick enough to seize details, but it appears he caught his brother's blade with his left hand, a practice not permitted. Certainly Mr. Henry only saved himself by leaping on one side; as certainly the Master, lunging in the air, stumbled on his knee, and before he could move the sword was through his body.

I cried out with a stifled scream, and ran in; but the body was already fallen to the ground, where it writhed a moment like a trodden worm, and then lay motionless.

"Look at his left hand," said Mr. Henry.

"It is all bloody," said I.

"On the inside?" said he.

"It is cut on the inside," said I.

"I thought so," said he, and turned his back.

I opened the man's clothes; the heart was quite still, it gave not a flutter.

"God forgive us, Mr. Henry!" said I. "He is dead."

"Dead?" he repeated, a little stupidly; and then with a rising tone, "Dead? dead?" says he, and suddenly cast his bloody sword upon the ground.

"What must we do?" said I. "Be yourself, sir. It is too late now: you must be yourself."

He turned and stared at me. "Oh, Mackellar!" says he, and put his face in his hands.

I plucked him by the coat. "For God's sake, for all our sakes, be more courageous!" said I. "What must we do?"

He showed me his face with the same stupid stare.

"Do?" says he. And with that his eye fell on the body, and "Oh!" he cries out, with his hand to his brow, as if he had never remembered; and, turning from me, made off towards the house of Durrisdeer at a strange stumbling run.

I stood a moment mused; then it seemed to me my duty lay most plain on the side of the living; and I ran after him, leaving the candles on the frosty ground and the body lying in their light under the trees. But run as I pleased, he had the start of me, and was got into the house, and up to the hall, where I found him standing before the fire with his face once more in his hands, and as he so stood he visibly shuddered.

"Mr. Henry, Mr. Henry," I said, "this will be the ruin of us all."

"What is this that I have done?" cries he, and then looking upon me with a countenance that I shall never forget, "Who is to tell the old man?" he said.

The word knocked at my heart; but it was no time for weakness. I went and poured him out a glass of brandy. "Drink that," said I, "drink it down." I forced him to swallow it like a child; and, being still perished with the cold of the night, I followed his example.

"It has to be told, Mackellar," said he. "It must be told." And he fell suddenly in a seat—my old lord's seat by the chimney-side—and was shaken with dry sobs.

Dismay came upon my soul; it was plain there was no help in Mr. Henry. "Well," said I, "sit there, and leave all to me." And taking a candle in my hand, I set forth out of the room in the dark house. There was no movement; I must suppose that all had gone unobserved; and I was now to consider how to smuggle through the rest with the like secrecy. It was no hour for scruples; and I opened my lady's door without so much as a knock, and passed boldly in.

"There is some calamity happened," she cried, sitting up in bed.

"Madam," said I, "I will go forth again into the passage; and do you get as quickly as you can into your clothes. There is much to be done."

She troubled me with no questions, nor did she keep me waiting. Ere I had time to prepare a word of that which I must say to her, she was on the threshold signing me to enter.

"Madam," said I, "if you cannot be very brave, I must go elsewhere; for if no one helps me to-night, there is an end of the house of Durrisdeer."

"I am very courageous," said she; and she looked at me with a sort of smile, very painful to see, but very brave too.

"It has come to a duel," said I.

"A duel?" she repeated. "A duel! Henry and—"

"And the Master," said I. "Things have been borne so long, things of which you know nothing, which you would not believe if I should tell. But to-night it went too far, and when he insulted you—"

"Stop," said she. "He? Who?"

"Oh! madam," cried I, my bitterness breaking forth, "do you ask me such a question? Indeed, then, I may go elsewhere for help; there is none here!"

"I do not know in what I have offended you," said she. "Forgive me; put me out of this suspense."

But I dared not tell her yet; I felt not sure of her; and at the doubt, and under the sense of impotence it brought with it, I turned on the poor woman with something near to anger.

"Madam," said I, "we are speaking of two men: one of them insulted you, and you ask me which. I will help you to the answer. With one of these men you have spent all your hours: has the other reproached you? To one you have been always kind; to the other, as God sees me and judges between us two, I think not always: has his love ever failed you? To-night one of these two men told the other, in my hearing—the hearing of a hired stranger,—that you were in love with him. Before I say one word, you shall answer your own question: Which was it? Nay, madam, you shall answer me another: If it has come to this dreadful end, whose fault is it?"

She stared at me like one dazzled. "Good God!" she said once, in a kind of bursting exclamation; and then a second time in a whisper to herself: "Great God!—In the name of mercy, Mackellar, what is wrong?" she cried. "I am made up; I can hear all."

"You are not fit to hear," said I. "Whatever it was, you shall say first it was your fault."

"Oh!" she cried, with a gesture of wringing her hands, "this man will drive me mad! Can you not put me out of your thoughts?"

"I think not once of you," I cried. "I think of none but my dear unhappy master."

"Ah!" she cried, with her hand to her heart, "is Henry dead?"

"Lower your voice," said I. "The other."

I saw her sway like something stricken by the wind; and I know not whether in cowardice or misery, turned aside and looked upon the floor. "These are dreadful tidings," said I at length, when her silence began to put me in some fear; "and you and I behove to be the more bold if the house is to be saved." Still she answered nothing. "There is Miss Katharine, besides," I added: "unless we bring this matter through, her inheritance is like to be of shame."

I do not know if it was the thought of her child or the naked word shame, that gave her deliverance; at least, I had no sooner spoken than a sound passed her lips, the like of it I never heard; it was as though she had lain buried under a hill and sought to move that burthen. And the next moment she had found a sort of voice.

"It was a fight," she whispered. "It was not—" and she paused upon the word.

"It was a fair fight on my dear master's part," said I. "As for the other, he was slain in the very act of a foul stroke."

"Not now!" she cried.

"Madam," said I, "hatred of that man glows in my bosom like a burning fire; ay, even now he is dead. God knows, I would have stopped the fighting, had I dared. It is my shame I did not. But when I saw him fall, if I could have spared one thought from pitying of my master, it had been to exult in that deliverance."

I do not know if she marked; but her next words were, "My lord?"

"That shall be my part," said I.

"You will not speak to him as you have to me?" she asked.

"Madam," said I, "have you not some one else to think of? Leave my lord to me."

"Some one else?" she repeated.

"Your husband," said I. She looked at me with a countenance illegible. "Are you going to turn your back on him?" I asked.

Still she looked at me; then her hand went to her heart again. "No," said she.

"God bless you for that word!" I said. "Go to him now, where he sits in the hall; speak to him—it matters not what you say; give him your hand; say, 'I know all;'—if God gives you grace enough, say, 'Forgive me.'"

"God strengthen you, and make you merciful," said she. "I will go to my husband."

"Let me light you there," said I, taking up the candle.

"I will find my way in the dark," she said, with a shudder, and I think the shudder was at me.

So we separated—she down stairs to where a little light glimmered in the hall-door, I along the passage to my lord's room. It seems hard to say why, but I could not burst in on the old man as I could on the young woman; with whatever reluctance, I must knock. But his old slumbers were light, or perhaps he slept not; and at the first summons I was bidden enter.

He, too, sat up in bed; very aged and bloodless he looked; and whereas he had a certain largeness of appearance when dressed for daylight, he now seemed frail and little, and his face (the wig being laid aside) not bigger than a child's. This daunted me; nor less, the haggard surmise of misfortune in his eye. Yet his voice was even peaceful as he inquired my errand. I set my candle down upon a chair, leaned on the bed-foot, and looked at him.

"Lord Durrisdeer," said I, "it is very well known to you that I am a partisan in your family."

"I hope we are none of us partisans," said he. "That you love my son sincerely, I have always been glad to recognise."

"Oh! my lord, we are past the hour of these civilities," I replied. "If we are to save anything out of the fire, we must look the fact in its bare countenance. A partisan I am; partisans we have all been; it is as a partisan that I am here in the middle of the night to plead before you. Hear me; before I go, I will tell you why."

"I would always hear you, Mr. Mackellar," said he, "and that at any hour, whether of the day or night, for I would be always sure you had a reason. You spoke once before to very proper purpose; I have not forgotten that."

"I am here to plead the cause of my master," I said. "I need not tell you how he acts. You know how he is placed. You know with what generosity, he has always met your other—met your wishes," I corrected myself, stumbling at that name of son. "You know—you must know—what he has suffered—what he has suffered about his wife."

"Mr. Mackellar!" cried my lord, rising in bed like a bearded lion.

"You said you would hear me," I continued. "What you do not know, what you should know, one of the things I am here to speak of, is the persecution he must bear in private. Your back is not turned before one whom I dare not name to you falls upon him with the most unfeeling taunts; twits him—pardon me, my lord—twits him with your partiality, calls him Jacob, calls him clown, pursues him with ungenerous raillery, not to be borne by man. And let but one of you appear, instantly he changes; and my master must smile and courtesy to the man who has been feeding him with insults; I know, for I have shared in some of it, and I tell you the life is insupportable. All these months it has endured; it began with the man's landing; it was by the name of Jacob that my master was greeted the first night."

My lord made a movement as if to throw aside the clothes and rise. "If there be any truth in this—" said he.

"Do I look like a man lying?" I interrupted, checking him with my hand.

"You should have told me at first," he odd.

"Ah, my lord! indeed I should, and you may well hate the face of this unfaithful servant!" I cried.

"I will take order," said he, "at once." And again made the movement to rise.

Again I checked him. "I have not done," said I. "Would God I had! All this my dear, unfortunate patron has endured without help or countenance. Your own best word, my lord, was only gratitude. Oh, but he was your son, too! He had no other father. He was hated in the country, God knows how unjustly. He had a loveless marriage. He stood on all hands without affection or support—dear, generous, ill-fated, noble heart!"

"Your tears do you much honour and me much shame," says my lord, with a palsied trembling. "But you do me some injustice. Henry has been ever dear to me, very dear. James (I do not deny it, Mr. Mackellar), James is perhaps dearer; you have not seen my James in quite a favourable light; he has suffered under his misfortunes; and we can only remember how great and how unmerited these were. And even now his is the more affectionate nature. But I will not speak of him. All that you say of Henry is most true; I do not wonder, I know him to be very magnanimous; you will say I trade upon the knowledge? It is possible; there are dangerous virtues: virtues that tempt the encroacher. Mr. Mackellar, I will make it up to him; I will take order with all this. I have been weak; and, what is worse, I have been dull!"

"I must not hear you blame yourself, my lord, with that which I have yet to tell upon my conscience," I replied. "You have not been weak; you have been abused by a devilish dissembler. You saw yourself how he had deceived you in the matter of his danger; he has deceived you throughout in every step of his career. I wish to pluck him from your heart; I wish to force your eyes upon your other son; ah, you have a son there!"

"No, no," said he, "two sons—I have two sons."

I made some gesture of despair that struck him; he looked at me with a changed face. "There is much worse behind?" he asked, his voice dying as it rose upon the question.

"Much worse," I answered. "This night he said these words to Mr. Henry: 'I have never known a woman who did not prefer me to you, and I think who did not continue to prefer me.'"

"I will hear nothing against my daughter," he cried; and from his readiness to stop me in this direction, I conclude his eyes were not so dull as I had fancied, and he had looked not without anxiety upon the siege of Mrs. Henry.

"I think not of blaming her," cried I. "It is not that. These words were said in my hearing to Mr. Henry; and if you find them not yet plain enough, these others but a little after: Your wife, who is in love with me!'"

"They have quarrelled?" he said.

I nodded.

"I must fly to them," he said, beginning once again to leave his bed.

"No, no!" I cried, holding forth my hands.

"You do not know," said he. "These are dangerous words."

"Will nothing make you understand, my lord?" said I.

His eyes besought me for the truth.

I flung myself on my knees by the bedside. "Oh, my lord," cried I, "think on him you have left; think of this poor sinner whom you begot, whom your wife bore to you, whom we have none of us strengthened as we could; think of him, not of yourself; he is the other sufferer—think of him! That is the door for sorrow—Christ's door, God's door: oh! it stands open. Think of him, even as he thought of you. *'Who is to tell the old man?'*—these were his words. It was for that I came; that is why I am here pleading at your feet."

"Let me get up," he cried, thrusting me aside, and was on his feet before myself. His voice shook like a sail in the wind, yet he spoke with a good loudness; his face was like the snow, but his eyes were steady and dry.

"Here is too much speech," said he. "Where was it?"

"In the shrubbery," said I.

"And Mr. Henry?" he asked. And when I had told him he knotted his old face in thought.

"And Mr. James?" says he.

"I have left him lying," said I, "beside the candles."

"Candles?" he cried. And with that he ran to the window, opened it, and looked abroad. "It might be spied from the road."

"Where none goes by at such an hour," I objected.

"It makes no matter," he said. "One might. Hark!" cries he. "What is that?"

It was the sound of men very guardedly rowing in the bay; and I told him so.

"The freetraders," said my lord. "Run at once, Mackellar; put these candles out. I will dress in the meanwhile; and when you return we can debate on what is wisest."

I groped my way downstairs, and out at the door. From quite a far way off a sheen was visible, making points of brightness in the shrubbery; in so black a night it might have been remarked for miles; and I blamed myself bitterly for my incaution. How much more sharply when I reached the place! One of the candlesticks was overthrown, and that taper quenched. The other burned steadily by itself, and made a broad space of light upon the frosted ground. All within that circle seemed, by the force of contrast and the overhanging blackness, brighter than by day. And there was the bloodstain in the midst; and a little farther off Mr. Henry's sword, the pommel of which was of silver; but of the body, not a trace. My heart thumped upon my ribs, the hair stirred upon my scalp, as I stood there staring—so strange was the sight, so dire the fears it wakened. I looked right and left; the ground was so hard, it told no story. I stood and listened till my ears ached, but the night was hollow about me like an empty church; not even a ripple stirred upon the shore; it seemed you might have heard a pin drop in the county.

I put the candle out, and the blackness fell about me groping dark; it was like a crowd surrounding me; and I went back to the house of Durrisdeer, with my chin upon my shoulder, startling, as I went, with craven suppositions. In the door a figure moved to meet me, and I had near screamed with terror ere I recognised Mrs. Henry.

"Have you told him?" says she.

"It was he who sent me," said I. "It is gone. But why are you here?"

"It is gone!" she repeated. "What is gone?"

"The body," said I. "Why are you not with your husband?"

"Gone!" said she. "You cannot have looked. Come back."

"There is no light now," said I. "I dare not."

"I can see in the dark. I have been standing here so long—so long," said she. "Come, give me your hand."

We returned to the shrubbery hand in hand, and to the fatal place.

"Take care of the blood," said I.

"Blood?" she cried, and started violently back.

"I suppose it will be," said I. "I am like a blind man."

"No!" said she, "nothing! Have you not dreamed?"

"Ah, would to God we had!" cried I.

She spied the sword, picked it up, and seeing the blood, let it fall again with her hands thrown wide. "Ah!" she cried. And then, with an instant courage, handled it the second time, and thrust it to the hilt into the frozen ground. "I will take it back and clean it properly," says she, and again looked about her on all sides. "It cannot be that he was dead?" she added.

"There was no flutter of his heart," said I, and then remembering: "Why are you not with your husband?"

"It is no use," said she; "he will not speak to me."

"Not speak to you?" I repeated. "Oh! you have not tried."

"You have a right to doubt me," she replied, with a gentle dignity.

At this, for the first time, I was seized with sorrow for her. "God knows, madam," I cried, "God knows I am not so hard as I appear; on this dreadful night who can veneer his words? But I am a friend to all who are not Henry Durie's enemies."

"It is hard, then, you should hesitate about his wife," said she.

I saw all at once, like the rending of a veil, how nobly she had borne this unnatural calamity, and how generously my reproaches.

"We must go back and tell this to my lord," said I.

"Him I cannot face," she cried.

"You will find him the least moved of all of us," said I.

"And yet I cannot face him," said she.

"Well," said I, "you can return to Mr. Henry; I will see my lord."

As we walked back, I bearing the candlesticks, she the sword—a strange burthen for that woman—she had another thought. "Should we tell Henry?" she asked.

"Let my lord decide," said I.

My lord was nearly dressed when I came to his chamber. He heard me with a frown. "The freetraders," said he. "But whether dead or alive?"

"I thought him—" said I, and paused, ashamed of the word.

"I know; but you may very well have been in error. Why should they remove him if not living?" he asked. "Oh! here is a great door of hope. It must be given out that he departed—as he came—without any note of preparation. We must save all scandal."

I saw he had fallen, like the rest of us, to think mainly of the house. Now that all the living members of the family were plunged in irremediable sorrow, it was strange how we turned to that conjoint abstraction of the family itself, and sought to bolster up the airy nothing of its reputation: not the Duries only, but the hired steward himself.

"Are we to tell Mr. Henry?" I asked him.

"I will see," said he. "I am going first to visit him; then I go forth with you to view the shrubbery and consider."

We went downstairs into the hall. Mr. Henry sat by the table with his head upon his hand, like a man of stone. His wife stood a little back from him, her hand at her mouth; it was plain she could not move him. My old lord walked very steadily to where his son was sitting; he had a steady countenance, too, but methought a little cold. When he was come quite up, he held out both his hands and said, "My son!"

With a broken, strangled cry, Mr. Henry leaped up and fell on his father's neck, crying and weeping, the most pitiful sight that ever a man witnessed. "Oh! father," he cried, "you know I loved him; you know I loved him in the beginning; I could have died for him—you know that! I would have given my life for him and you. Oh! say you know that. Oh! say you can forgive me. O father, father, what have I done—what have I done? And we used to be bairns together!" and wept and sobbed, and fondled the old man, and clutched him about the neck, with the passion of a child in terror.

And then he caught sight of his wife (you would have thought for the first time), where she stood weeping to hear him, and in a moment had fallen at her knees. "And O my lass," he cried, "you must forgive me, too! Not your husband—I have only been the ruin of your life. But you knew me when I was a lad; there was no harm in Henry Durie then; he meant aye to be a friend to you. It's him—it's the old bairn that played with you—oh, can ye never, never forgive him?"

Throughout all this my lord was like a cold, kind spectator with his wits about him. At the first cry, which was indeed enough to call the house about us, he had said to me over his shoulder, "Close the door." And now he nodded to himself.

"We may leave him to his wife now," says he. "Bring a light, Mr. Mackellar."

Upon my going forth again with my lord, I was aware of a strange phenomenon; for though it was quite dark, and the night not yet old, methought I smelt the morning. At the same time there went a tossing through the branches of the evergreens, so that they sounded like a quiet sea, and the air pulled at times against our faces, and the flame of the candle shook. We made the more speed, I believe, being surrounded by this bustle; visited the scene of the duel, where my lord looked upon the blood with stoicism; and passing farther on toward the landing-place, came at last upon some evidences of the truth. For, first of all, where there was a pool across the path, the ice had been trodden in, plainly by more than one man's weight; next, and but a little farther, a young tree was broken, and down by the landing-place, where the traders' boats were usually beached, another stain of blood marked where the body must have been infallibly set down to rest the bearers.

This stain we set ourselves to wash away with the sea-water, carrying it in my lord's hat; and as we were thus engaged there came up a sudden moaning gust and left us instantly benighted.

"It will come to snow," says my lord; "and the best thing that we could hope. Let us go back now; we can do nothing in the dark."

As we went houseward, the wind being again subsided, we were aware of a strong pattering noise about us in the night; and when we issued from the shelter of the trees, we found it raining smartly.

Throughout the whole of this, my lord's clearness of mind, no less than his activity of body, had not ceased to minister to my amazement. He set the crown upon it in the council we held on our return. The freetraders had certainly secured the Master, though whether dead or alive we were still left to our conjectures; the rain would, long before day, wipe out all marks of the transaction; by this we must profit. The Master had unexpectedly come after the fall of night; it must now he given out he had as suddenly departed before the break of day; and, to make all this plausible, it now only remained for me to mount into the man's chamber, and pack and conceal his baggage. True, we still lay at the discretion of the traders; but that was the incurable weakness of our guilt.

I heard him, as I said, with wonder, and hastened to obey. Mr. and Mrs. Henry were gone from the hall; my lord, for warmth's sake, hurried to his bed; there was still no sign of stir among the servants, and as I went up the tower stair, and entered the dead man's room, a horror of solitude weighed upon my mind. To my extreme surprise, it was all in the disorder of departure. Of his three portmanteaux, two were already locked; the third lay open and near full. At once there flashed upon me some suspicion of the truth. The man had been going, after all; he had but waited upon Crail, as Crail waited upon the wind; early in the night the seamen had perceived the weather changing; the boat had come to give notice of the change and call the passenger aboard, and the boat's crew had stumbled on him dying in his blood. Nay, and there was more behind. This pre-arranged departure shed some light upon his inconceivable insult of the night before; it was a parting shot, hatred being no longer checked by policy. And, for another thing, the nature of that insult, and the conduct of Mrs. Henry, pointed to one conclusion, which I have never verified, and can now never verify until the great assize—the conclusion that he had at last forgotten himself, had gone too far in his advances, and had been rebuffed. It can never be verified, as I say; but as I thought of it that morning among his baggage, the thought was sweet to me like honey.

Into the open portmanteau I dipped a little ere I closed it. The most beautiful lace and linen, many suits of those fine plain clothes in which he loved to appear; a book or two, and those of the best, Cæsar's "Commentaries," a volume of Mr. Hobbes, the "Henriade" of M. de Voltaire, a book upon the Indies, one on the mathematics, far beyond where I have studied: these were what I observed with very mingled feelings. But in the open portmanteau, no papers of any description. This set me musing. It was possible the man was dead; but, since the traders had carried him away, not likely. It was possible he might still die of his wound; but it was also possible he might not. And in this latter case I was determined to have the means of some defence.

One after another I carried his portmanteaux to a loft in the top of the house which we kept locked; went to my own room for my keys, and, returning to the loft, had the gratification to find two that fitted pretty well. In one of the portmanteaux there was a shagreen letter-case, which I cut open with my knife; and thenceforth (so far as any credit went) the man was at my mercy. Here was a vast deal of gallant correspondence, chiefly of his Paris days; and, what was more to the purpose, here were the copies of his own reports to the English Secretary, and the originals of the Secretary's answers: a most damning series: such as to publish would be to wreck the Master's honour and to set a price upon his life. I chuckled to myself as I ran through the documents; I rubbed my hands, I sang aloud in my glee. Day found me at the pleasing task; nor did I then remit my diligence, except in so far as I went to the window—looked out for a moment, to see the frost quite gone, the world turned black again, and the rain and the wind driving in the bay—and to assure myself that the lugger was gone from its anchorage, and the Master (whether dead or alive) now tumbling on the Irish Sea.

It is proper I should add in this place the very little I have subsequently angled out upon the doings of that night. It took me a long while to gather it; for we dared not openly ask, and the freetraders regarded me with enmity, if not with scorn. It was near six months before we even knew for certain that the man survived; and it was years before I learned from one of Crail's men, turned publican on his ill-gotten gain, some particulars which smack to me of truth. It seems the traders found the Master struggled on one elbow, and now staring round him, and now gazing at the candle or at his hand which was all bloodied, like a man stupid. Upon their coming, he would seem to have found his mind, bade them carry him aboard, and hold their tongues; and on the captain asking how he had come in such a pickle, replied with a burst of passionate swearing, and incontinently fainted. They held some debate, but they were momently looking for a wind, they were highly paid to smuggle him to France, and did not care to delay. Besides which, he was well enough liked by these abominable wretches: they supposed him under capital sentence, knew not in what mischief he might have got his wound, and judged it a piece of good nature to remove him out of the way of danger. So he was taken aboard, recovered on the passage over, and was set ashore a convalescent at the Havre de Grace. What is truly notable: he said not a word to anyone of the duel, and not a trader knows to this day in what quarrel, or by the hand of what adversary, he fell. With any other man I should have set this down to natural decency; with him, to pride. He could not bear to avow, perhaps even to himself, that he had been vanquished by one whom he had so much insulted whom he so cruelly despised.

6

SUMMARY OF EVENTS DURING THE MASTER'S SECOND ABSENCE

Of the heavy sickness which declared itself next morning I can think with equanimity, as of the last unmingled trouble that befell my master; and even that was perhaps a mercy in disguise; for what pains of the body could equal the miseries of his mind? Mrs. Henry and I had the watching by the bed. My old lord called from time to time to take the news, but would not usually pass the door. Once, I remember, when hope was nigh gone, he stepped to the bedside, looked awhile in his son's face, and turned away with a gesture of the head and hand thrown up, that remains upon my mind as something tragic; such grief and such a scorn of sublunary things were there expressed. But the most of the time Mrs. Henry and I had the room to ourselves, taking turns by night, and bearing each other company by day, for it was dreary watching. Mr. Henry, his shaven head bound in a napkin, tossed fro without remission, beating the bed with his hands. His tongue never lay; his voice ran continuously like a river, so that my heart was weary with the sound of it. It was notable, and to me inexpressibly mortifying, that he spoke all the while on matters of no import: comings and goings, horses—which he was ever calling to have saddled, thinking perhaps (the poor soul!) that he might ride away from his discomfort—matters of the garden, the salmon nets, and (what I particularly raged to hear) continually of his affairs, cyphering figures and holding disputation with the tenantry. Never a word of his father or his wife, nor of the Master, save only for a day or two, when his mind dwelled entirely in the past, and he supposed himself a boy again and upon some innocent child's play with his brother. What made this the more affecting: it appeared the Master had then run some peril of his life, for there was a cry—"Oh! Jamie will be drowned—Oh, save Jamie!" which he came over and over with a great deal of passion.

This, I say, was affecting, both to Mrs. Henry and myself; but the balance of my master's wanderings did him little justice. It seemed he had set out to justify his brother's calumnies; as though he was bent to prove himself a man of a dry nature, immersed in money-getting. Had I been there alone, I would not have troubled my thumb; but all the while, as I listened, I was estimating the effect on the man's wife, and telling myself that he fell lower every day. I was the one person on the surface of the globe that comprehended him, and I was bound there should be yet another. Whether he was to die there and his virtues perish: or whether he should save his days and come back to that inheritance of sorrows, his right memory: I was bound he should be heartily lamented in the one case, and unaffectedly welcomed in the other, by the person he loved the most, his wife.

Finding no occasion of free speech, I bethought me at last of a kind of documentary disclosure; and for some nights, when I was off duty and should have been asleep, I gave my time to the preparation of that which I may call my budget. But this I found to be the easiest portion of my task, and that which remained—namely, the presentation to my lady—almost more than I had fortitude to overtake. Several days I went about with my papers under my arm, spying for some juncture of talk to serve as introduction. I will not deny but that some offered; only when they did my tongue clove to the roof of my mouth; and I think I might have been carrying about my packet till this day, had not a fortunate accident delivered me from all my hesitations. This was at night, when I was once more leaving the room, the thing not yet done, and myself in despair at my own cowardice.

"What do you carry about with you, Mr. Mackellar?" she asked. "These last days, I see you always coming in and out with the same armful."

I returned upon my steps without a word, laid the papers before her on the table, and left her to her reading. Of what that was, I am now to give you some idea; and the best will be to reproduce a letter of my own which came first in the budget and of which (according to an excellent habitude) I have preserved the scroll. It will show, too, the moderation of my part in these affairs, a thing which some have called recklessly in question.

"Durrisdeer.
"1757.

"Honoured Madam,

"I trust I would not step out of my place without occasion; but I see how much evil has flowed in the past to all of your noble house from that unhappy and secretive fault of reticency, and the papers on which I venture to call your attention are family papers, and all highly worthy your acquaintance.

"I append a schedule with some necessary observations,

"And am,
"Honoured Madam,
"Your ladyship's obliged, obedient servant,
"Ephraim Mackellar.

"Schedule of Papers.

"A. Scroll of ten letters from Ephraim Mackellar to the Hon. James Durie, Esq., by courtesy Master of Ballantrae during the latter's residence in Paris: under dates . . . " (follow the dates) . . . "Nota: to be read in connection with B. and C.

"B. Seven original letters from the said Mr of Ballantrae to the said E. Mackellar, under dates . . . " (follow the dates.)

"C. Three original letters from the Mr of Ballantrae to the Hon. Henry Durie, Esq., under dates . . . " (follow the dates) . . . "Nota: given me by Mr. Henry to answer: copies of my answers A 4, A 5, and A 9 of these productions. The purport of Mr. Henry's communications, of which I can find no scroll, may be gathered from those of his unnatural brother.

"D. A correspondence, original and scroll, extending over a period of three years till January of the current year, between the said Mr of Ballantrae and — —, Under Secretary of State; twenty-seven in all. Nota: found among the Master's papers."

Weary as I was with watching and distress of mind, it was impossible for me to sleep. All night long I walked in my chamber, revolving what should be the issue, and sometimes repenting the temerity of my immixture in affairs so private; and with the first peep of the morning I was at the sick-room door. Mrs. Henry had thrown open the shutters and even the window, for the temperature was mild. She looked steadfastly before her; where was nothing to see, or only the blue of the morning creeping among woods. Upon the stir of my entrance she did not so much as turn about her face: a circumstance from which I augured very ill.

"Madam," I began; and then again, "Madam;" but could make no more of it. Nor yet did Mrs. Henry come to my assistance with a word. In this pass I began gathering up the papers where they lay scattered on the table; and the first thing that struck me, their bulk appeared to have diminished. Once I ran them through, and twice; but the correspondence with the Secretary of State, on which I had reckoned so much against the future, was nowhere to be found. I looked in the chimney; amid the smouldering embers, black ashes of paper fluttered in the draught; and at that my timidity vanished.

"Good God, madam," cried I, in a voice not fitting for a sick-room, "Good God, madam, what have you done with my papers?"

"I have burned them," said Mrs. Henry, turning about. "It is enough, it is too much, that you and I have seen them."

"This is a fine night's work that you have done!" cried I. "And all to save the reputation of a man that ate bread by the shedding of his comrades' blood, as I do by the shedding of ink."

"To save the reputation of that family in which you are a servant, Mr. Mackellar," she returned, "and for which you have already done so much."

"It is a family I will not serve much longer," I cried, "for I am driven desperate. You have stricken the sword out of my hands; you have left us all defenceless. I had always these letters I could shake over his head; and now—What is to do? We are so falsely situate we dare not show the man the door; the country would fly on fire against us; and I had this one hold upon him—and now it is gone—now he may come back to-morrow, and we must all sit down with him to dinner, go for a stroll with him on the terrace, or take a hand at cards, of all things, to divert his leisure! No, madam! God forgive you, if He can find it in His heart; for I cannot find it in mine."

"I wonder to find you so simple, Mr. Mackellar," said Mrs. Henry. "What does this man value reputation? But he knows how high we prize it; he knows we would rather die than make these letters public; and do you suppose he would not trade upon the knowledge? What you call your sword, Mr. Mackellar, and which had been one indeed against a man of any remnant of propriety, would have been but a sword of paper against him. He would smile in your face at such a threat. He stands upon his degradation, he makes that his strength; it is in vain to struggle with such characters." She cried out this last a little desperately, and then with more quiet: "No, Mr. Mackellar; I have thought upon this matter all night, and there is no way out of it. Papers or no papers, the door of this house stands open for him; he is the rightful heir, forsooth! If we sought to exclude him, all would redound against poor Henry, and I should see him stoned again upon the streets. Ah! if Henry dies, it is a different matter! They have broke the entail for their own good purposes; the estate goes to my daughter; and I shall see who sets a foot upon it. But if Henry lives, my poor Mr. Mackellar, and that man returns, we must suffer: only this time it will be together."

On the whole I was well pleased with Mrs. Henry's attitude of mind; nor could I even deny there was some cogency in that which she advanced about the papers.

"Let us say no more about it," said I. "I can only be sorry I trusted a lady with the originals, which was an unbusinesslike proceeding at the best. As for what I said of leaving the service of the family, it was spoken with the tongue only; and you may set your mind at rest. I belong to Durrisdeer, Mrs. Henry, as if I had been born there."

I must do her the justice to say she seemed perfectly relieved; so that we began this morning, as we were to continue for so many years, on a proper ground of mutual indulgence and respect.

The same day, which was certainly prededicate to joy, we observed the first signal of recovery in Mr. Henry; and about three of the following afternoon he found his mind again, recognising me by name with the strongest evidences of affection. Mrs. Henry was also in the room, at the bedfoot; but it did not appear that he observed her. And indeed (the fever being gone) he was so weak that he made but the one effort and sank again into lethargy. The course of his restoration was now slow but equal; every day his appetite improved; every week we were able to remark an increase both of strength and flesh; and before the end of the month he was out of bed and had even begun to be carried in his chair upon the terrace.

It was perhaps at this time that Mrs. Henry and I were the most uneasy in mind. Apprehension for his days was at an end; and a worse fear succeeded. Every day we drew consciously nearer to a day of reckoning; and the days passed on, and still there was nothing. Mr. Henry bettered in strength, he held long talks with us on a great diversity of subjects, his father came and sat with him and went again; and still there was no reference to the late tragedy or to the former troubles which had brought it on. Did he remember, and conceal his dreadful knowledge? or was the whole blotted from his mind? This was the problem that kept us watching and trembling all day when we were in his company and held us awake at night when we were in our lonely beds. We knew not even which alternative to hope for, both appearing so unnatural and pointing so directly to an unsound brain. Once this fear offered, I observed his conduct with sedulous particularity. Something of the child he exhibited: a cheerfulness quite foreign to his previous character, an interest readily aroused, and then very tenacious, in small matters which he had heretofore despised. When he was stricken down, I was his only confidant, and I may say his only friend, and he was on terms of division with his wife; upon his recovery, all was changed, the past forgotten, the wife first and even single in his thoughts. He turned to her with all his emotions, like a child to its mother, and seemed secure of sympathy; called her in all his needs with something of that querulous familiarity that marks a certainty of indulgence; and I must say, in justice to the woman, he was never disappointed. To her, indeed, this changed behaviour was inexpressibly affecting; and I think she felt it secretly as a reproach; so that I have seen her, in early days, escape out of the room that she might indulge herself in weeping. But to me the change appeared not natural; and viewing it along with all the rest, I began to wonder, with many head-shakings, whether his reason were perfectly erect.

As this doubt stretched over many years, endured indeed until my master's death, and clouded all our subsequent relations, I may well consider of it more at large. When he was able to resume some charge of his affairs, I had many opportunities to try him with precision. There was no lack of understanding, nor yet of authority; but the old continuous interest had quite departed; he grew readily fatigued, and fell to yawning; and he carried into money relations, where it is certainly out of place, a facility that bordered upon slackness. True, since we had no longer the exactions of the Master to contend against, there was the less occasion to raise strictness into principle or do battle for a farthing. True, again, there was nothing excessive in these relaxations, or I would have been no party to them. But the whole thing marked a change, very slight yet very perceptible; and though no man could say my master had gone at all out of his mind, no man could deny that he had drifted from his character. It was the same to the end, with his manner and appearance. Some of the heat of the fever lingered in his veins: his movements a little hurried, his speech notably more voluble, yet neither truly amiss. His whole mind stood open to happy impressions, welcoming these and making much of them; but the smallest suggestion of trouble or sorrow he received with visible impatience and dismissed again with immediate relief. It was to this temper that he owed the felicity of his later days; and yet here it was, if anywhere, that you could call the man insane. A great part of this life consists in contemplating what we cannot cure; but Mr. Henry, if he could not dismiss solicitude by an effort of the mind, must instantly and at whatever cost annihilate the cause of it; so that he played alternately the ostrich and the bull. It is to this strenuous cowardice of pain that I have to set down all the unfortunate and excessive steps of his subsequent career. Certainly this was the reason of his beating McManus, the groom, a thing so much out of all his former practice, and which awakened so much comment at the time. It is to this, again, that I must lay the total lose of near upon two hundred pounds, more than the half of which I could have saved if his impatience would have suffered me. But he preferred loss or any desperate extreme to a continuance of mental suffering.

All this has led me far from our immediate trouble: whether he remembered or had forgotten his late dreadful act; and if he remembered, in what light he viewed it. The truth burst upon us suddenly, and was indeed one of the chief surprises of my life. He had been several times abroad, and was now beginning to walk a little with an arm, when it chanced I should be left alone with him upon the terrace. He turned to me with a singular furtive smile, such as schoolboys use when in fault; and says he, in a private whisper and without the least preface: "Where have you buried him?"

I could not make one sound in answer.

"Where have you buried him?" he repeated. "I want to see his grave."

I conceived I had best take the bull by the horns. "Mr. Henry," said I, "I have news to give that will rejoice you exceedingly. In all human likelihood, your hands are clear of blood. I reason from certain indices; and by these it should appear your brother was not dead, but was carried in a swound on board the lugger. But now he may be perfectly recovered."

What there was in his countenance I could not read. "James?" he asked.

"Your brother James," I answered. "I would not raise a hope that may be found deceptive, but in my heart I think it very probable he is alive."

"Ah!" says Mr. Henry; and suddenly rising from his seat with more alacrity than he had yet discovered, set one finger on my breast, and cried at me in a kind of screaming whisper, "Mackellar"—these were his words—"nothing can kill that man. He is not mortal. He is bound upon my back to all eternity—to all eternity!" says he, and, sitting down again, fell upon a stubborn silence.

A day or two after, with the same secret smile, and first looking about as if to be sure we were alone, "Mackellar," said he, "when you have any intelligence, be sure and let me know. We must keep an eye upon him, or he will take us when we least expect."

"He will not show face here again," said I.

"Oh yes he will," said Mr. Henry. "Wherever I am, there will he be." And again he looked all about him.

"You must not dwell upon this thought, Mr. Henry," said I.

"No," said he, "that is a very good advice. We will never think of it, except when you have news. And we do not know yet," he added; "he may be dead."

The manner of his saying this convinced me thoroughly of what I had scarce ventured to suspect: that, so far from suffering any penitence for the attempt, he did but lament his failure. This was a discovery I kept to myself, fearing it might do him a prejudice with his wife. But I might have saved myself the trouble; she had divined it for herself, and found the sentiment quite natural. Indeed, I could not but say that there were three of us, all of the same mind; nor could any news have reached Durrisdeer more generally welcome than tidings of the Master's death.

This brings me to speak of the exception, my old lord. As soon as my anxiety for my own master began to be relaxed, I was aware of a change in the old gentleman, his father, that seemed to threaten mortal consequences.

His face was pale and swollen; as he sat in the chimney-side with his Latin, he would drop off sleeping and the book roll in the ashes; some days he would drag his foot, others stumble in speaking. The amenity of his behaviour appeared more extreme; full of excuses for the least trouble, very thoughtful for all; to myself, of a most flattering civility. One day, that he had sent for his lawyer and remained a long while private, he met me as he was crossing the hall with painful footsteps, and took me kindly by the hand. "Mr. Mackellar," said he, "I have had many occasions to set a proper value on your services; and to-day, when I re-cast my will, I have taken the freedom to name you for one of my executors. I believe you bear love enough to our house to render me this service." At that very time he passed the greater portion of his days in clamber, from which it was often difficult to rouse him; seemed to have losst all count of years, and had several times (particularly on waking) called for his wife and for an old servant whose very gravestone was now green with moss. If I had been put to my oath, I must have declared he was incapable of testing; and yet there was never a will drawn more sensible in every trait, or showing a more excellent judgment both of persons and affairs.

His dissolution, though it took not very long, proceeded by infinitesimal gradations. His faculties decayed together steadily; the power of his limbs was almost gone, he was extremely deaf, his speech had sunk into mere mumblings; and yet to the end he managed to discover something of his former courtesy and kindness, pressing the hand of any that helped him, presenting me with one of his Latin books, in which he had laboriously traced my name, and in a thousand ways reminding us of the greatness of that loss which it might almost be said we had already suffered. To the end, the power of articulation returned to him in flashes; it seemed he had only forgotten the art of speech as a child forgets his lesson, and at times he would call some part of it to mind. On the last night of his life he suddenly broke silence with these words from Virgil: "Gnatique pratisque, alma, precor, miserere," perfectly uttered, and with a fitting accent. At the sudden clear sound of it we started from our several occupations; but it was in vain we turned to him; he sat there silent, and, to all appearance, fatuous. A little later he was had to bed with more difficulty than ever before; and some time in the night, without any more violence, his spirit fled.

At a far later period I chanced to speak of these particulars with a doctor of medicine, a man of so high a reputation that I scruple to adduce his name. By his view of it father and son both suffered from the affection: the father from the strain of his unnatural sorrows—the son perhaps in the excitation of the fever; each had ruptured a vessel on the brain, and there was probably (my doctor added) some predisposition in the family to accidents of that description. The father sank, the son recovered all the externals of a healthy man; but it is like there was some destruction in those delicate tissues where the soul resides and does her earthly business; her heavenly, I would fain hope, cannot be thus obstructed by material accidents. And yet, upon a more mature opinion, it matters not one jot; for He who shall pass judgment on the records of our life is the same that formed us in frailty.

The death of my old lord was the occasion of a fresh surprise to us who watched the behaviour of his successor. To any considering mind, the two sons had between them slain their father, and he who took the sword might be even said to have slain him with his hand, but no such thought appeared to trouble my new lord. He was becomingly grave; I could scarce say sorrowful, or only with a pleasant sorrow; talking of the dead with a regretful cheerfulness, relating old examples of his character, smiling at them with a good conscience; and when the day of the funeral came round, doing the honours with exact propriety. I could perceive, besides, that he found a solid gratification in his accession to the title; the which he was punctilious in exacting.

And now there came upon the scene a new character, and one that played his part, too, in the story; I mean the present lord, Alexander, whose birth (17th July, 1757) filled the cup of my poor master's happiness. There was nothing then left him to wish for; nor yet leisure to wish for it. Indeed, there never was a parent so fond and doting as he showed himself. He was continually uneasy in his son's absence. Was the child abroad? the father would be watching the clouds in case it rained. Was it night? he would rise out of his bed to observe its slumbers. His conversation grew even wearyful to strangers, since he talked of little but his son. In matters relating to the estate, all was designed with a particular eye to Alexander; and it would be:—"Let us put it in hand at once, that the wood may be grown against Alexander's majority;" or, "This will fall in again handsomely for Alexander's marriage." Every day this absorption of the man's nature became more observable, with many touching and some very blameworthy particulars. Soon the child could walk abroad with him, at first on the terrace, hand in hand, and afterward at large about the policies; and this grew to be my lord's chief occupation. The sound of their two voices (audible a great way off, for they spoke loud) became familiar in the neighbourhood; and for my part I found it more agreeable than the sound of birds. It was pretty to see the pair returning, full of briars, and the father as flushed and sometimes as bemuddied as the child, for they were equal sharers in all sorts of boyish entertainment, digging in the beach, damming of streams, and what not; and I have seen them gaze through a fence at cattle with the same childish contemplation.

The mention of these rambles brings me to a strange scene of which I was a witness. There was one walk I never followed myself without emotion, so often had I gone there upon miserable errands, so much had there befallen against the house of Durrisdeer. But the path lay handy from all points beyond the Muckle Ross; and I was driven, although much against my will, to take my use of it perhaps once in the two months. It befell when Mr. Alexander was of the age of seven or eight, I had some business on the far side in the morning, and entered the shrubbery, on my homeward way, about nine of a bright forenoon. It was that time of year when the woods are all in their spring colours, the thorns all in flower, and the birds in the high season of their singing. In contrast to this merriment, the shrubbery was only the more sad, and I the more oppressed by its associations. In this situation of spirit it struck me disagreeably to hear voices a little way in front, and to recognise the tones of my lord and Mr. Alexander. I pushed ahead, and came presently into their view. They stood together in the open space where the duel was, my lord with his hand on his son's shoulder, and speaking with some gravity. At least, as he raised his head upon my coming, I thought I could perceive his countenance to lighten.

"Ah!" says he, "here comes the good Mackellar. I have just been telling Sandie the story of this place, and how there was a man whom the devil tried to kill, and how near he came to kill the devil instead."

I had thought it strange enough he should bring the child into that scene; that he should actually be discoursing of his act, passed measure. But the worst was yet to come; for he added, turning to his son—"You can ask Mackellar; he was here and saw it."

"Is it true, Mr. Mackellar?" asked the child. "And did you really see the devil?"

"I have not heard the tale," I replied; "and I am in a press of business." So far I said a little sourly, fencing with the embarrassment of the position; and suddenly the bitterness of the past, and the terror of that scene by candle-light, rushed in upon my mind. I bethought me that, for a difference of a second's quickness in parade, the child before me might have never seen the day; and the emotion that always fluttered round my heart in that dark shrubbery burst forth in words. "But so much is true," I cried, "that I have met the devil in these woods, and seen him foiled here. Blessed be God that we escaped with life—blessed be God that one stone yet stands upon another in the walls of Durrisdeer! And, oh! Mr. Alexander, if ever you come by this spot, though it was a hundred years hence, and you came with the gayest and the highest in the land, I would step aside and remember a bit prayer."

My lord bowed his head gravely. "Ah!" says he, "Mackellar is always in the right. Come, Alexander, take your bonnet off." And with that he uncovered, and held out his hand. "O Lord," said he, "I thank Thee, and my son thanks Thee, for Thy manifold great mercies. Let us have peace for a little; defend us from the evil man. Smite him, O Lord, upon the lying mouth!" The last broke out of him like a cry; and at that, whether remembered anger choked his utterance, or whether he perceived this was a singular sort of prayer, at least he suddenly came to a full stop; and, after a moment, set back his hat upon his head.

"I think you have forgot a word, my lord," said I. "'Forgive us our trespasses, as we forgive them that trespass against us. For Thine is the kingdom, and the power, and the glory, for ever and ever. Amen.'"

"Ah! that is easy saying," said my lord. "That is very easy saying, Mackellar. But for me to forgive!—I think I would cut a very silly figure if I had the affectation to pretend it."

"The bairn, my lord!" said I, with some severity, for I thought his expressions little fitted for the care of children.

"Why, very true," said he. "This is dull work for a bairn. Let's go nesting."

I forget if it was the same day, but it was soon after, my lord, finding me alone, opened himself a little more on the same head.

"Mackellar," he said, "I am now a very happy man."

"I think so indeed, my lord," said I, "and the sight of it gives me a light heart."

"There is an obligation in happiness—do you not think so?" says he, musingly.

"I think so indeed," says I, "and one in sorrow, too. If we are not here to try to do the best, in my humble opinion the sooner we are away the better for all parties."

"Ay, but if you were in my shoes, would you forgive him?" asks my lord.

The suddenness of the attack a little gravelled me.

"It is a duty laid upon us strictly," said I.

"Hut!" said he. "These are expressions! Do you forgive the man yourself?"

"Well—no!" said I. "God forgive me, I do not."

"Shake hands upon that!" cries my lord, with a kind of joviality.

"It is an ill sentiment to shake hands upon," said I, "for Christian people. I think I will give you mine on some more evangelical occasion."

This I said, smiling a little; but as for my lord, he went from the room laughing aloud.

For my lord's slavery to the child, I can find no expression adequate. He lost himself in that continual thought: business, friends, and wife being all alike forgotten, or only remembered with a painful effort, like that of one struggling with a posset. It was most notable in the matter of his wife. Since I had known Durrisdeer, she had been the burthen of his thought and the loadstone of his eyes; and now she was quite cast out. I have seen him come to the door of a room, look round, and pass my lady over as though she were a dog before the fire. It would be Alexander he was seeking, and my lady knew it well. I have heard him speak to her so ruggedly that I nearly found it in my heart to intervene: the cause would still be the same, that she had in some way thwarted Alexander. Without doubt this was in the nature of a judgment on my lady. Without doubt she had the tables turned upon her, as only Providence can do it; she who had been cold so many years to every mark of tenderness, it was her part now to be neglected: the more praise to her that she played it well.

An odd situation resulted: that we had once more two parties in the house, and that now I was of my lady's. Not that ever I lost the love I bore my master. But, for one thing, he had the less use for my society. For another, I could not but compare the case of Mr. Alexander with that of Miss Katharine; for whom my lord had never found the least attention. And for a third, I was wounded by the change he discovered to his wife, which struck me in the nature of an infidelity. I could not but admire, besides, the constancy and kindness she displayed. Perhaps her sentiment to my lord, as it had been founded from the first in pity, was that rather of a mother than a wife; perhaps it pleased her—if I may so say—to behold her two children so happy in each other; the more as one had suffered so unjustly in the past. But, for all that, and though I could never trace in her one spark of jealousy, she must fall back for society on poor neglected Miss Katharine; and I, on my part, came to pass my spare hours more and more with the mother and daughter. It would be easy to make too much of this division, for it was a pleasant family, as families go; still the thing existed; whether my lord knew it or not, I am in doubt. I do not think he did; he was bound up so entirely in his son; but the rest of us knew it, and in a manner suffered from the knowledge.

What troubled us most, however, was the great and growing danger to the child. My lord was his father over again; it was to be feared the son would prove a second Master. Time has proved these fears to have been quite exaggerate. Certainly there is no more worthy gentleman to-day in Scotland than the seventh Lord Durrisdeer. Of my own exodus from his employment it does not become me to speak, above all in a memorandum written only to justify his father. . . .

[*Editor's Note. Five pages of Mr. Mackellar's MS. are here omitted. I have gathered from their perusal an impression that Mr. Mackellar, in his old age, was rather an exacting servant. Against the seventh Lord Durrisdeer (with whom, at any rate, we have no concern) nothing material is alleged.*—R. L. S.]

. . . But our fear at the time was lest he should turn out, in the person of his son, a second edition of his brother. My lady had tried to interject some wholesome discipline; she had been glad to give that up, and now looked on with secret dismay; sometimes she even spoke of it by hints; and sometimes, when there was brought to her knowledge some monstrous instance of my lord's indulgence, she would betray herself in a gesture or perhaps an exclamation. As for myself, I was haunted by the thought both day and night: not so much for the child's sake as for the father's. The man had gone to sleep, he was dreaming a dream, and any rough wakening must infallibly prove mortal. That he should survive its death was inconceivable; and the fear of its dishonour made me cover my face.

It was this continual preoccupation that screwed me up at last to a remonstrance: a matter worthy to be narrated in detail. My lord and I sat one day at the same table upon some tedious business of detail; I have said that he had lost his former interest in such occupations; he was plainly itching to be gone, and he looked fretful, weary, and methought older than I had ever previously observed. I suppose it was the haggard face that put me suddenly upon my enterprise.

"My lord," said I, with my head down, and feigning to continue my occupation—"or, rather, let me call you again by the name of Mr. Henry, for I fear your anger and want you to think upon old times—"

"My good Mackellar!" said he; and that in tones so kindly that I had near forsook my purpose. But I called to mind that I was speaking for his good, and stuck to my colours.

"Has it never come in upon your mind what you are doing?" I asked.

"What I am doing?" he repeated; "I was never good at guessing riddles."

"What you are doing with your son?" said I.

"Well," said he, with some defiance in his tone, "and what am I doing with my son?"

"Your father was a very good man," says I, straying from the direct path. "But do you think he was a wise father?"

There was a pause before he spoke, and then: "I say nothing against him," he replied. "I had the most cause perhaps; but I say nothing."

"Why, there it is," said I. "You had the cause at least. And yet your father was a good man; I never knew a better, save on the one point, nor yet a wiser. Where he stumbled, it is highly possible another man should fail. He had the two sons—"

My lord rapped suddenly and violently on the table.

"What is this?" cried he. "Speak out!"

"I will, then," said I, my voice almost strangled with the thumping of my heart. "If you continue to indulge Mr. Alexander, you are following in your father's footsteps. Beware, my lord, lest (when he grows up) your son should follow in the Master's."

I had never meant to put the thing so crudely; but in the extreme of fear, there comes a brutal kind of courage, the most brutal indeed of all; and I burnt my ships with that plain word. I never had the answer. When I lifted my head, my lord had risen to his feet, and the next moment he fell heavily on the floor. The fit or seizure endured not very long; he came to himself vacantly, put his hand to his head, which I was then supporting, and says he, in a broken voice: "I have been ill," and a little after: "Help me." I got him to his feet, and he stood pretty well, though he kept hold of the table. "I have been ill, Mackellar," he said again. "Something broke, Mackellar—or was going to break, and then all swam away. I think I was very angry. Never you mind, Mackellar; never you mind, my man. I wouldnae hurt a hair upon your head. Too much has come and gone. It's a certain thing between us two. But I think, Mackellar, I will go to Mrs. Henry—I think I will go to Mrs. Henry," said he, and got pretty steadily from the room, leaving me overcome with penitence.

Presently the door flew open, and my lady swept in with flashing eyes. "What is all this?" she cried. "What have you done to my husband? Will nothing teach you your position in this house? Will you never cease from making and meddling?"

"My lady," said I, "since I have been in this house I have had plenty of hard words. For a while they were my daily diet, and I swallowed them all. As for to-day, you may call me what you please; you will never find the name hard enough for such a blunder. And yet I meant it for the best."

I told her all with ingenuity, even as it is written here; and when she had heard me out, she pondered, and I could see her animosity fall. "Yes," she said, "you meant well indeed. I have had the same thought myself, or the same temptation rather, which makes me pardon you. But, dear God, can you not understand that he can bear no more? He can bear no more!" she cried. "The cord is stretched to snapping. What matters the future if he have one or two good days?"

"Amen," said I. "I will meddle no more. I am pleased enough that you should recognise the kindness of my meaning."

"Yes," said my lady; "but when it came to the point, I have to suppose your courage failed you; for what you said was said cruelly." She paused, looking at me; then suddenly smiled a little, and said a singular thing: "Do you know what you are, Mr. Mackellar? You are an old maid."

No more incident of any note occurred in the family until the return of that ill-starred man the Master. But I have to place here a second extract from the memoirs of Chevalier Burke, interesting in itself, and highly necessary for my purpose. It is our only sight of the Master on his Indian travels; and the first word in these pages of Secundra Dass. One fact, it is to observe, appears here very clearly, which if we had known some twenty years ago, how many calamities and sorrows had been spared!—that Secundra Dass spoke English.

7

ADVENTURE OF CHEVALIER BURKE IN INDIA

EXTRACTED FROM HIS MEMOIRS.

. . . Here was I, therefore, on the streets of that city, the name of which I cannot call to mind, while even then I was so ill-acquainted with its situation that I knew not whether to go south or north. The alert being sudden, I had run forth without shoes or stockings; my hat had been struck from my head in the mellay; my kit was in the hands of the English; I had no companion but the cipaye, no weapon but my sword, and the devil a coin in my pocket. In short, I was for all the world like one of those calendars with whom Mr. Galland has made us acquainted in his elegant tales. These gentlemen, you will remember, were for ever falling in with extraordinary incidents; and I was myself upon the brink of one so astonishing that I protest I cannot explain it to this day.

The cipaye was a very honest man; he had served many years with the French colours, and would have let himself be cut to pieces for any of the brave countrymen of Mr. Lally. It is the same fellow (his name has quite escaped me) of whom I have narrated already a surprising instance of generosity of mind—when he found Mr. de Fessac and myself upon the ramparts, entirely overcome with liquor, and covered us with straw while the commandant was passing by. I consulted him, therefore, with perfect freedom. It was a fine question what to do; but we decided at last to escalade a garden wall, where we could certainly sleep in the shadow of the trees, and might perhaps find an occasion to get hold of a pair of slippers and a turban. In that part of the city we had only the difficulty of the choice, for it was a quarter consisting entirely of walled gardens, and the lanes which divided them were at that hour of the night deserted. I gave the cipaye a back, and we had soon dropped into a large enclosure full of trees. The place was soaking with the dew, which, in that country, is exceedingly unwholesome, above all to whites; yet my fatigue was so extreme that I was already half asleep, when the cipaye recalled me to my senses. In the far end of the enclosure a bright light had suddenly shone out, and continued to burn steadily among the leaves. It was a circumstance highly unusual in such a place and hour; and, in our situation, it behoved us to proceed with some timidity. The cipaye was sent to reconnoitre, and pretty soon returned with the intelligence that we had fallen extremely amiss, for the house belonged to a white man, who was in all likelihood English.

"Faith," says I, "if there is a white man to be seen, I will have a look at him; for, the Lord be praised! there are more sorts than the one!"

The cipaye led me forward accordingly to a place from which I had a clear view upon the house. It was surrounded with a wide verandah; a lamp, very well trimmed, stood upon the floor of it, and on either side of the lamp there sat a man, cross-legged, after the Oriental manner. Both, besides, were bundled up in muslin like two natives; and yet one of them was not only a white man, but a man very well known to me and the reader, being indeed that very Master of Ballantrae of whose gallantry and genius I have had to speak so often. Word had reached me that he was come to the Indies, though we had never met at least, and I heard little of his occupations. But, sure, I had no sooner recognised him, and found myself in the arms of so old a comrade, than I supposed my tribulations were quite done. I stepped plainly forth into the light of the moon, which shone exceeding strong, and hailing Ballantrae by name, made him in a few words master of my grievous situation. He turned, started the least thing in the world, looked me fair in the face while I was speaking, and when I had done addressed himself to his companion in the barbarous native dialect. The second person, who was of an extraordinary delicate appearance, with legs like walking canes and fingers like the stalk of a tobacco pipe,[1] now rose to his feet.

"The Sahib," says he, "understands no English language. I understand it myself, and I see you make some small mistake—oh! which may happen very often. But the Sahib would be glad to know how you come in a garden."

"Ballantrae!" I cried, "have you the damned impudence to deny me to my face?"

Ballantrae never moved a muscle, staring at me like an image in a pagoda.

"The Sahib understands no English language," says the native, as glib as before. "He be glad to know how you come in a garden."

"Oh! the divil fetch him," says I. "He would be glad to know how I come in a garden, would he? Well, now, my dear man, just have the civility to tell the Sahib, with my kind love, that we are two soldiers here whom he never met and never heard of, but the cipaye is a broth of a boy, and I am a broth of a boy myself; and if we don't get a full meal of meat, and a turban, and slippers, and the value of a gold mohur in small change as a matter of convenience, bedad, my friend, I could lay my finger on a garden where there is going to be trouble."

They carried their comedy so far as to converse awhile in Hindustanee; and then says the Hindu, with the same smile, but sighing as if he were tired of the repetition, "The Sahib would be glad to know how you come in a garden."

"Is that the way of it?" says I, and laying my hand on my sword-hilt I bade the cipaye draw.

Ballantrae's Hindu, still smiling, pulled out a pistol from his bosom, and though Ballantrae himself never moved a muscle I knew him well enough to be sure he was prepared.

"The Sahib thinks you better go away," says the Hindu.

Well, to be plain, it was what I was thinking myself; for the report of a pistol would have been, under Providence, the means of hanging the pair of us.

"Tell the Sahib I consider him no gentleman," says I, and turned away with a gesture of contempt.

I was not gone three steps when the voice of the Hindu called me back. "The Sahib would be glad to know if you are a dam low Irishman," says he; and at the words Ballantrae smiled and bowed very low.

"What is that?" says I.

"The Sahib say you ask your friend Mackellar," says the Hindu. "The Sahib he cry quits."

"Tell the Sahib I will give him a cure for the Scots fiddle when next we meet," cried I.

The pair were still smiling as I left.

There is little doubt some flaws may be picked in my own behaviour; and when a man, however gallant, appeals to posterity with an account of his exploits, he must almost certainly expect to share the fate of Cæsar and Alexander, and to meet with some detractors. But there is one thing that can never be laid at the door of Francis Burke: he never turned his back on a friend. . . .

(Here follows a passage which the Chevalier Burke has been at the pains to delete before sending me his manuscript. Doubtless it was some very natural complaint of what he supposed to be an indiscretion on my part; though, indeed, I can call none to mind. Perhaps Mr. Henry was less guarded; or it is just possible the Master found the means to examine my correspondence, and himself read the letter from Troyes: in revenge for which this cruel jest was perpetrated on Mr. Burke in his extreme necessity. The Master, for all his wickedness, was not without some natural affection; I believe he was sincerely attached to Mr. Burke in the beginning; but the thought of treachery dried up the springs of his very shallow friendship, and his detestable nature appeared naked.—E. McK.)

---

1. Note by Mr. Mackellar.—Plainly Secundra Dass.—E. McK.

8

THE ENEMY IN THE HOUSE

It is a strange thing that I should be at a stick for a date—the date, besides, of an incident that changed the very nature of my life, and sent us all into foreign lands. But the truth is, I was stricken out of all my habitudes, and find my journals very ill redd-up,[1] the day not indicated sometimes for a week or two together, and the whole fashion of the thing like that of a man near desperate. It was late in March at least, or early in April, 1764. I had slept heavily, and wakened with a premonition of some evil to befall. So strong was this upon my spirit that I hurried downstairs in my shirt and breeches, and my hand (I remember) shook upon the rail. It was a cold, sunny morning, with a thick white frost; the blackbirds sang exceeding sweet and loud about the house of Durrisdeer, and there was a noise of the sea in all the chambers. As I came by the doors of the hall, another sound arrested me—of voices talking. I drew nearer, and stood like a man dreaming. Here was certainly a human voice, and that in my own master's house, and yet I knew it not; certainly human speech, and that in my native land; and yet, listen as I pleased, I could not catch one syllable. An old tale started up in my mind of a fairy wife (or perhaps only a wandering stranger), that came to the place of my fathers some generations back, and stayed the matter of a week, talking often in a tongue that signified nothing to the hearers; and went again, as she had come, under cloud of night, leaving not so much as a name behind her. A little fear I had, but more curiosity; and I opened the hall-door, and entered.

The supper-things still lay upon the table; the shutters were still closed, although day peeped in the divisions; and the great room was lighted only with a single taper and some lurching reverberation of the fire. Close in the chimney sat two men. The one that was wrapped in a cloak and wore boots, I knew at once: it was the bird of ill omen back again. Of the other, who was set close to the red embers, and made up into a bundle like a mummy, I could but see that he was an alien, of a darker hue than any man of Europe, very frailly built, with a singular tall forehead, and a secret eye. Several bundles and a small valise were on the floor; and to judge by the smallness of this luggage, and by the condition of the Master's boots, grossly patched by some unscrupulous country cobbler, evil had not prospered.

He rose upon my entrance; our eyes crossed; and I know not why it should have been, but my courage rose like a lark on a May morning.

"Ha!" said I, "is this you?"—and I was pleased with the unconcern of my own voice.

"It is even myself, worthy Mackellar," says the Master.

"This time you have brought the black dog visibly upon your back," I continued.

"Referring to Secundra Dass?" asked the Master. "Let me present you. He is a native gentleman of India."

"Hum!" said I. "I am no great lover either of you or your friends, Mr. Bally. But I will let a little daylight in, and have a look at you." And so saying, I undid the shutters of the eastern window.

By the light of the morning I could perceive the man was changed. Later, when we were all together, I was more struck to see how lightly time had dealt with him; but the first glance was otherwise.

"You are getting an old man," said I.

A shade came upon his face. "If you could see yourself," said he, "you would perhaps not dwell upon the topic."

"Hut!" I returned, "old age is nothing to me. I think I have been always old; and I am now, I thank God, better known and more respected. It is not every one that can say that, Mr. Bally! The lines in your brow are calamities; your life begins to close in upon you like a prison; death will soon be rapping at the door; and I see not from what source you are to draw your consolations."

Here the Master addressed himself to Secundra Dass in Hindustanee, from which I gathered (I freely confess, with a high degree of pleasure) that my remarks annoyed him. All this while, you may be sure, my mind had been busy upon other matters, even while I rallied my enemy; and chiefly as to how I should communicate secretly and quickly with my lord. To this, in the breathing-space now given me, I turned all the forces of my mind; when, suddenly shifting my eyes, I was aware of the man himself standing in the doorway, and, to all appearance, quite composed. He had no sooner met my looks than he stepped across the threshold. The Master heard him coming, and advanced upon the other side; about four feet apart, these brothers came to a full pause, and stood exchanging steady looks, and then my lord smiled, bowed a little forward, and turned briskly away.

"Mackellar," says he, "we must see to breakfast for these travellers."

It was plain the Master was a trifle disconcerted; but he assumed the more impudence of speech and manner. "I am as hungry as a hawk," says he. "Let it be something good, Henry."

My lord turned to him with the same hard smile.

"Lord Durrisdeer," says he.

"Oh! never in the family," returned the Master.

"Every one in this house renders me my proper title," says my lord. "If it please you to make an exception, I will leave you to consider what appearance it will bear to strangers, and whether it may not be translated as an effect of impotent jealousy."

I could have clapped my hands together with delight: the more so as my lord left no time for any answer, but, bidding me with a sign to follow him, went straight out of the hall.

"Come quick," says he; "we have to sweep vermin from the house." And he sped through the passages, with so swift a step that I could scarce keep up with him, straight to the door of John Paul, the which he opened without summons and walked in. John was, to all appearance, sound asleep, but my lord made no pretence of waking him.

"John Paul," said he, speaking as quietly as ever I heard him, "you served my father long, or I would pack you from the house like a dog. If in half an hour's time I find you gone, you shall continue to receive your wages in Edinburgh. If you linger here or in St. Bride's—old man, old servant, and altogether—I shall find some very astonishing way to make you smart for your disloyalty. Up and begone. The door you let them in by will serve for your departure. I do not choose my son shall see your face again."

"I am rejoiced to find you bear the thing so quietly," said I, when we were forth again by ourselves.

"Quietly!" cries he, and put my hand suddenly against his heart, which struck upon his bosom like a sledge.

At this revelation I was filled with wonder and fear. There was no constitution could bear so violent a strain—his least of all, that was unhinged already; and I decided in my mind that we must bring this monstrous situation to an end.

"It would be well, I think, if I took word to my lady," said I. Indeed, he should have gone himself, but I counted—not in vain—on his indifference.

"Aye," says he, "do. I will hurry breakfast: we must all appear at the table, even Alexander; it must appear we are untroubled."

I ran to my lady's room, and with no preparatory cruelty disclosed my news.

"My mind was long ago made up," said she. "We must make our packets secretly to-day, and leave secretly to-night. Thank Heaven, we have another house! The first ship that sails shall bear us to New York."

"And what of him?" I asked.

"We leave him Durrisdeer," she cried. "Let him work his pleasure upon that."

"Not so, by your leave," said I. "There shall be a dog at his heels that can hold fast. Bed he shall have, and board, and a horse to ride upon, if he behave himself; but the keys—if you think well of it, my lady—shall be left in the hands of one Mackellar. There will be good care taken; trust him for that."

"Mr. Mackellar," she cried, "I thank you for that thought. All shall be left in your hands. If we must go into a savage country, I bequeath it to you to take our vengeance. Send Macconochie to St. Bride's, to arrange privately for horses and to call the lawyer. My lord must leave procuration."

At that moment my lord came to the door, and we opened our plan to him.

"I will never hear of it," he cried; "he would think I feared him. I will stay in my own house, please God, until I die. There lives not the man can beard me out of it. Once and for all, here I am, and here I stay in spite of all the devils in hell." I can give no idea of the vehemency of his words and utterance; but we both stood aghast, and I in particular, who had been a witness of his former self-restraint.

My lady looked at me with an appeal that went to my heart and recalled me to my wits. I made her a private sign to go, and when my lord and I were alone, went up to him where he was racing to and fro in one end of the room like a half-lunatic, and set my hand firmly on his shoulder.

"My lord," says I, "I am going to be the plain-dealer once more; if for the last time, so much the better, for I am grown weary of the part."

"Nothing will change me," he answered. "God forbid I should refuse to hear you; but nothing will change me." This he said firmly, with no signal of the former violence, which already raised my hopes.

"Very well," said I "I can afford to waste my breath." I pointed to a chair, and he sat down and looked at me. "I can remember a time when my lady very much neglected you," said I.

"I never spoke of it while it lasted," returned my lord, with a high flush of colour; "and it is all changed now."

"Do you know how much?" I said. "Do you know how much it is all changed? The tables are turned, my lord! It is my lady that now courts you for a word, a look—ay, and courts you in vain. Do you know with whom she passes her days while you are out gallivanting in the policies? My lord, she is glad to pass them with a certain dry old grieve[2] of the name of Ephraim Mackellar; and I think you may be able to remember what that means, for I am the more in a mistake or you were once driven to the same company yourself."

"Mackellar!" cries my lord, getting to his feet. "O my God, Mackellar!"

"It is neither the name of Mackellar nor the name of God that can change the truth," said I; "and I am telling you the fact. Now for you, that suffered so much, to deal out the same suffering to another, is that the part of any Christian? But you are so swallowed up in your new friend that the old are all forgotten. They are all clean vanished from your memory. And yet they stood by you at the darkest; my lady not the least. And does my lady ever cross your mind? Does it ever cross your mind what she went through that night?—or what manner of a wife she has been to you thenceforward?—or in what kind of a position she finds herself to-day? Never. It is your pride to stay and face him out, and she must stay along with you. Oh! my lord's pride—that's the great affair! And yet she is the woman, and you are a great hulking man! She is the woman that you swore to protect; and, more betoken, the own mother of that son of yours!"

"You are speaking very bitterly, Mackellar," said he; "but, the Lord knows, I fear you are speaking very true. I have not proved worthy of my happiness. Bring my lady back."

My lady was waiting near at hand to learn the issue. When I brought her in, my lord took a hand of each of us, and laid them both upon his bosom. "I have had two friends in my life," said he. "All the comfort ever I had, it came from one or other. When you two are in a mind, I think I would be an ungrateful dog—" He shut his mouth very hard, and looked on us with swimming eyes. "Do what ye like with me," says he, "only don't think—" He stopped again. "Do what ye please with me: God knows I love and honour you." And dropping our two hands, he turned his back and went and gazed out of the window. But my lady ran after, calling his name, and threw herself upon his neck in a passion of weeping.

I went out and shut the door behind me, and stood and thanked God from the bottom of my heart.

At the breakfast board, according to my lord's design, we were all met. The Master had by that time plucked off his patched boots and made a toilet suitable to the hour; Secundra Dass was no longer bundled up in wrappers, but wore a decent plain black suit, which misbecame him strangely; and the pair were at the great window, looking forth, when the family entered. They turned; and the black man (as they had already named him in the house) bowed almost to his knees, but the Master was for running forward like one of the family. My lady stopped him, curtseying low from the far end of the hall, and keeping her children at her back. My lord was a little in front: so there were the three cousins of Durrisdeer face to face. The hand of time was very legible on all; I seemed to read in their changed faces a *memento mori*; and what affected me still more, it was the wicked man that bore his years the handsomest. My lady was quite transfigured into the matron, a becoming woman for the head of a great tableful of children and dependents. My lord was grown slack in his limbs; he stooped; he walked with a running motion, as though he had learned again from Mr. Alexander; his face was drawn; it seemed a trifle longer than of old; and it wore at times a smile very singularly mingled, and which (in my eyes) appeared both bitter and pathetic. But the Master still bore himself erect, although perhaps with effort; his brow barred about the centre with imperious lines, his mouth set as for command. He had all the gravity and something of the splendour of Satan in the "Paradise Lost." I could not help but see the man with admiration, and was only surprised that I saw him with so little fear.

But indeed (as long as we were at the table) it seemed as if his authority were quite vanished and his teeth all drawn. We had known him a magician that controlled the elements; and here he was, transformed into an ordinary gentleman, chatting like his neighbours at the breakfast-board. For now the father was dead, and my lord and lady reconciled, in what ear was he to pour his calumnies? It came upon me in a kind of vision how hugely I had overrated the man's subtlety. He had his malice still; he was false as ever; and, the occasion being gone that made his strength, he sat there impotent; he was still the viper, but now spent his venom on a file. Two more thoughts occurred to me while yet we sat at breakfast: the first, that he was abashed —I had almost said, distressed—to find his wickedness quite unavailing; the second, that perhaps my lord was in the right, and we did amiss to fly from our dismasted enemy. But my poor man's leaping heart came in my mind, and I remembered it was for his life we played the coward.

When the meal was over, the Master followed me to my room, and, taking a chair (which I had never offered him), asked me what was to be done with him.

"Why, Mr. Bally," said I, "the house will still be open to you for a time."

"For a time?" says he. "I do not know if I quite take your meaning."

"It is plain enough," said I. "We keep you for our reputation; as soon as you shall have publicly disgraced yourself by some of your misconduct, we shall pack you forth again."

"You are become an impudent rogue," said the Master, bending his brows at me dangerously.

"I learned in a good school," I returned. "And you must have perceived yourself that with my old lord's death your power is quite departed. I do not fear you now, Mr. Bally; I think even—God forgive me—that I take a certain pleasure in your company."

He broke out in a burst of laughter, which I clearly saw to be assumed.

"I have come with empty pockets," says he, after a pause.

"I do not think there will be any money going," I replied. "I would advise you not to build on that."

"I shall have something to say on the point," he returned.

"Indeed?" said I. "I have not a guess what it will be, then."

"Oh! you affect confidence," said the Master. "I have still one strong position—that you people fear a scandal, and I enjoy it."

"Pardon me, Mr. Bally," says I. "We do not in the least fear a scandal against you."

He laughed again. "You have been studying repartee," he said. "But speech is very easy, and sometimes very deceptive. I warn you fairly: you will find me vitriol in the house. You would do wiser to pay money down and see my back." And with that he waved his hand to me and left the room.

A little after, my lord came with the lawyer, Mr. Carlyle; a bottle of old wine was brought, and we all had a glass before we fell to business. The necessary deeds were then prepared and executed, and the Scotch estates made over in trust to Mr. Carlyle and myself.

"There is one point, Mr. Carlyle," said my lord, when these affairs had been adjusted, "on which I wish that you would do us justice. This sudden departure coinciding with my brother's return will be certainly commented on. I wish you would discourage any conjunction of the two."

"I will make a point of it, my lord," said Mr. Carlyle. "The Mas— Bally does not, then, accompany you?"

"It is a point I must approach," said my lord. "Mr. Bally remains at Durrisdeer, under the care of Mr. Mackellar; and I do not mean that he shall even know our destination."

"Common report, however—" began the lawyer.

"Ah! but, Mr. Carlyle, this is to be a secret quite among ourselves," interrupted my lord. "None but you and Mackellar are to be made acquainted with my movements."

"And Mr. Bally stays here? Quite so," said Mr. Carlyle. "The powers you leave—" Then he broke off again. "Mr. Mackellar, we have a rather heavy weight upon us."

"No doubt," said I.

"No doubt," said he. "Mr. Bally will have no voice?"

"He will have no voice," said my lord; "and, I hope, no influence. Mr. Bally is not a good adviser."

"I see," said the lawyer. "By the way, has Mr. Bally means?"

"I understand him to have nothing," replied my lord. "I give him table, fire, and candle in this house."

"And in the matter of an allowance? If I am to share the responsibility, you will see how highly desirable it is that I should understand your views," said the lawyer. "On the question of an allowance?"

"There will be no allowance," said my lord. "I wish Mr. Bally to live very private. We have not always been gratified with his behaviour."

"And in the matter of money," I added, "he has shown himself an infamous bad husband. Glance your eye upon that docket, Mr. Carlyle, where I have brought together the different sums the man has drawn from the estate in the last fifteen or twenty years. The total is pretty."

Mr. Carlyle made the motion of whistling. "I had no guess of this," said he. "Excuse me once more, my lord, if I appear to push you; but it is really desirable I should penetrate your intentions. Mr. Mackellar might die, when I should find myself alone upon this trust. Would it not be rather your lordship's preference that Mr. Bally should—ahem—should leave the country?"

My lord looked at Mr. Carlyle. "Why do you ask that?" said he.

"I gather, my lord, that Mr. Bally is not a comfort to his family," says the lawyer with a smile.

My lord's face became suddenly knotted. "I wish he was in hell!" cried he, and filled himself a glass of wine, but with a hand so tottering that he spilled the half into his bosom. This was the second time that, in the midst of the most regular and wise behaviour, his animosity had spirted out. It startled Mr. Carlyle, who observed my lord thenceforth with covert curiosity; and to me it restored the certainty that we were acting for the best in view of my lord's health and reason.

Except for this explosion the interview was very successfully conducted. No doubt Mr. Carlyle would talk, as lawyers do, little by little. We could thus feel we had laid the foundations of a better feeling in the country, and the man's own misconduct would certainly complete what we had begun. Indeed, before his departure, the lawyer showed us there had already gone abroad some glimmerings of the truth.

"I should perhaps explain to you, my lord," said he, pausing, with his hat in his hand, "that I have not been altogether surprised with your lordship's dispositions in the case of Mr. Bally. Something of this nature oozed out when he was last in Durrisdeer. There was some talk of a woman at St. Bride's, to whom you had behaved extremely handsome, and Mr. Bally with no small degree of cruelty. There was the entail, again, which was much controverted. In short, there was no want of talk, back and forward; and some of our wise-acres took up a strong opinion. I remained in suspense, as became one of my cloth; but Mr. Mackellar's docket here has finally opened my eyes. I do not think, Mr. Mackellar, that you and I will give him that much rope."

The rest of that important day passed prosperously through. It was our policy to keep the enemy in view, and I took my turn to be his watchman with the rest. I think his spirits rose as he perceived us to be so attentive, and I know that mine insensibly declined. What chiefly daunted me was the man's singular dexterity to worm himself into our troubles. You may have felt (after a horse accident) the hand of a bone-setter artfully divide and interrogate the muscles, and settle strongly on the injured place? It was so with the Master's tongue, that was so cunning to question; and his eyes, that were so quick to observe. I seemed to have said nothing, and yet to have let all out. Before I knew where I was the man was condoling with me on my lord's neglect of my lady and myself, and his hurtful indulgence to his son. On this last point I perceived him (with panic fear) to return repeatedly. The boy had displayed a certain shrinking from his uncle; it was strong in my mind his father had been fool enough to indoctrinate the same, which was no wise beginning: and when I looked upon the man before me, still so handsome, so apt a speaker, with so great a variety of fortunes to relate, I saw he was the very personage to captivate a boyish fancy. John Paul had left only that morning; it was not to be supposed he had been altogether dumb upon his favourite subject: so that here would be Mr. Alexander in the part of Dido, with a curiosity inflamed to hear; and there would be the Master, like a diabolical Æneas, full of matter the most pleasing in the world to any youthful ear, such as battles, sea-disasters, flights, the forests of the West, and (since his later voyage) the ancient cities of the Indies. How cunningly these baits might be employed, and what an empire might be so founded, little by little, in the mind of any boy, stood obviously clear to me. There was no inhibition, so long as the man was in the house, that would be strong enough to hold these two apart; for if it be hard to charm serpents, it is no very difficult thing to cast a glamour on a little chip of manhood not very long in breeches. I recalled an ancient sailor-man who dwelt in a lone house beyond the Figgate Whins (I believe, he called it after Portobello), and how the boys would troop out of Leith on a Saturday, and sit and listen to his swearing tales, as thick as crows about a carrion: a thing I often remarked as I went by, a young student, on my own more meditative holiday diversion. Many of these boys went, no doubt, in the face of an express command; many feared and even hated the old brute of whom they made their hero; and I have seen them flee from him when he was tipsy, and stone him when he was drunk. And yet there they came each Saturday! How much more easily would a boy like Mr. Alexander fall under the influence of a high-looking, high-spoken gentleman-adventurer, who should conceive the fancy to entrap him; and, the influence gained, how easy to employ it for the child's perversion!

I doubt if our enemy had named Mr. Alexander three times before I perceived which way his mind was aiming—all this train of thought and memory passed in one pulsation through my own—and you may say I started back as though an open hole had gaped across a pathway. Mr. Alexander: there was the weak point, there was the Eve in our perishable paradise; and the serpent was already hissing on the trail.

I promise you, I went the more heartily about the preparations; my last scruple gone, the danger of delay written before me in huge characters. From that moment forth I seem not to have sat down or breathed. Now I would be at my post with the Master and his Indian; now in the garret, buckling a valise; now sending forth Macconochie by the side postern and the wood-path to bear it to the trysting-place; and, again, snatching some words of counsel with my lady. This was the *verso* of our life in Durrisdeer that day; but on the *recto* all appeared quite settled, as of a family at home in its paternal seat; and what perturbation may have been observable, the Master would set down to the blow of his unlooked-for coming, and the fear he was accustomed to inspire.

Supper went creditably off, cold salutations passed and the company trooped to their respective chambers. I attended the Master to the last. We had put him next door to his Indian, in the north wing; because that was the most distant and could be severed from the body of the house with doors. I saw he was a kind friend or a good master (whichever it was) to his Secundra Dass—seeing to his comfort; mending the fire with his own hand, for the Indian complained of cold; inquiring as to the rice on which the stranger made his diet; talking with him pleasantly in the Hindustanee, while I stood by, my candle in my hand, and affected to be overcome with slumber. At length the Master observed my signals of distress. "I perceive," says he, "that you have all your ancient habits: early to bed and early to rise. Yawn yourself away!"

Once in my own room, I made the customary motions of undressing, so that I might time myself; and when the cycle was complete, set my tinder-box ready, and blew out my taper. The matter of an hour afterward I made a light again, put on my shoes of list that I had worn by my lord's sick-bed, and set forth into the house to call the voyagers. All were dressed and waiting —my lord, my lady, Miss Katharine, Mr. Alexander, my lady's woman Christie; and I observed the effect of secrecy even upon quite innocent persons, that one after another showed in the chink of the door a face as white as paper. We slipped out of the side postern into a night of darkness, scarce broken by a star or two; so that at first we groped and stumbled and fell among the bushes. A few hundred yards up the wood-path Macconochie was waiting us with a great lantern; so the rest of the way we went easy enough, but still in a kind of guilty silence. A little beyond the abbey the path debauched on the main road and some quarter of a mile farther, at the place called Eagles, where the moors begin, we saw the lights of the two carriages stand shining by the wayside. Scarce a word or two was uttered at our parting, and these regarded business: a silent grasping of hands, a turning of faces aside, and the thing was over; the horses broke into a trot, the lamplight sped like Will-o'-the-Wisp upon the broken moorland, it dipped beyond Stony Brae; and there were Macconochie and I alone with our lantern on the road. There was one thing more to wait for, and that was the reappearance of the coach upon Cartmore. It seems they must have pulled up upon the summit, looked back for a last time, and seen our lantern not yet moved away from the place of separation. For a lamp was taken from a carriage, and waved three times up and down by way of a farewell. And then they were gone indeed, having looked their last on the kind roof of Durrisdeer, their faces toward a barbarous country. I never knew before, the greatness of that vault of night in which we two poor serving-men—the one old, and the one elderly—stood for the first time deserted; I had never felt before my own dependency upon the countenance of others. The sense of isolation burned in my bowels like a fire. It seemed that we who remained at home were the true exiles, and that Durrisdeer and Solwayside, and all that made my country native, its air good to me, and its language welcome, had gone forth and was far over the sea with my old masters.

The remainder of that night I paced to and fro on the smooth highway, reflecting on the future and the past. My thoughts, which at first dwelled tenderly on those who were just gone, took a more manly temper as I considered what remained for me to do. Day came upon the inland mountain-tops, and the fowls began to cry, and the smoke of homesteads to arise in the brown bosom of the moors, before I turned my face homeward, and went down the path to where the roof of Durrisdeer shone in the morning by the sea.

At the customary hour I had the Master called, and awaited his coming in the hall with a quiet mind. He looked about him at the empty room and the three covers set.

"We are a small party," said he. "How comes?"

"This is the party to which we must grow accustomed," I replied.

He looked at me with a sudden sharpness. "What is all this?" said he.

"You and I and your friend Mr. Dass are now all the company," I replied. "My lord, my lady, and the children, are gone upon a voyage."

"Upon my word!" said he. "Can this be possible? I have indeed fluttered your Volscians in Corioli! But this is no reason why our breakfast should go cold. Sit down, Mr. Mackellar, if you please"—taking, as he spoke, the head of the table, which I had designed to occupy myself—"and as we eat, you can give me the details of this evasion."

I could see he was more affected than his language carried, and I determined to equal him in coolness. "I was about to ask you to take the head of the table," said I; "for though I am now thrust into the position of your host, I could never forget that you were, after all, a member of the family."

For a while he played the part of entertainer, giving directions to Macconochie, who received them with an evil grace, and attending specially upon Secundra. "And where has my good family withdrawn to?" he asked carelessly.

"Ah! Mr. Bally, that is another point," said I. "I have no orders to communicate their destination."

"To me," he corrected.

"To any one," said I.

"It is the less pointed," said the master; *"c'est de bon ton*: my brother improves as he continues. And I, dear Mr. Mackellar?"

"You will have bed and board, Mr. Bally," said I. "I am permitted to give you the run of the cellar, which is pretty reasonably stocked. You have only to keep well with me, which is no very difficult matter, and you shall want neither for wine nor a saddle-horse."

He made an excuse to send Macconochie from the room.

"And for money?" he inquired. "Have I to keep well with my good friend Mackellar for my pocket-money also? This is a pleasing return to the principles of boyhood."

"There was no allowance made," said I; "but I will take it on myself to see you are supplied in moderation."

"In moderation?" he repeated. "And you will take it on yourself?" He drew himself up, and looked about the hall at the dark rows of portraits. "In the name of my ancestors, I thank you," says he; and then, with a return to irony, "But there must certainly be an allowance for Secundra Dass?" he said. "It in not possible they have omitted that?"

"I will make a note of it, and ask instructions when I write," said I.

And he, with a sudden change of manner, and leaning forward with an elbow on the table—"Do you think this entirely wise?"

"I execute my orders, Mr. Bally," said I.

"Profoundly modest," said the Master; "perhaps not equally ingenuous. You told me yesterday my power was fallen with my father's death. How comes it, then, that a peer of the realm flees under cloud of night out of a house in which his fathers have stood several sieges? that he conceals his address, which must be a matter of concern to his Gracious Majesty and to the whole republic? and that he should leave me in possession, and under the paternal charge of his invaluable Mackellar? This smacks to me of a very considerable and genuine apprehension."

I sought to interrupt him with some not very truthful denegation; but he waved me down, and pursued his speech.

"I say, it smacks of it," he said; "but I will go beyond that, for I think the apprehension grounded. I came to this house with some reluctancy. In view of the manner of my last departure, nothing but necessity could have induced me to return. Money, however, is that which I must have. You will not give with a good grace; well, I have the power to force it from you. Inside of a week, without leaving Durrisdeer, I will find out where these fools are fled to. I will follow; and when I have run my quarry down, I will drive a wedge into that family that shall once more burst it into shivers. I shall see then whether my Lord Durrisdeer" (said with indescribable scorn and rage) "will choose to buy my absence; and you will all see whether, by that time, I decide for profit or revenge."

I was amazed to hear the man so open. The truth is, he was consumed with anger at my lord's successful flight, felt himself to figure as a dupe, and was in no humour to weigh language.

"Do you consider *this* entirely wise?" said I, copying his words.

"These twenty years I have lived by my poor wisdom," he answered with a smile that seemed almost foolish in its vanity.

"And come out a beggar in the end," said I, "if beggar be a strong enough word for it."

"I would have you to observe, Mr. Mackellar," cried he, with a sudden imperious heat, in which I could not but admire him, "that I am scrupulously civil: copy me in that, and we shall be the better friends."

Throughout this dialogue I had been incommoded by the observation of Secundra Dass. Not one of us, since the first word, had made a feint of eating: our eyes were in each other's faces—you might say, in each other's bosoms; and those of the Indian troubled me with a certain changing brightness, as of comprehension. But I brushed the fancy aside, telling myself once more he understood no English; only, from the gravity of both voices, and the occasional scorn and anger in the Master's, smelled out there was something of import in the wind.

For the matter of three weeks we continued to live together in the house of Durrisdeer: the beginning of that most singular chapter of my life—what I must call my intimacy with the Master. At first he was somewhat changeable in his behaviour: now civil, now returning to his old manner of flouting me to my face; and in both I met him half-way. Thanks be to Providence, I had now no measure to keep with the man; and I was never afraid of black brows, only of naked swords. So that I found a certain entertainment in these bouts of incivility, and was not always ill-inspired in my rejoinders. At last (it was at supper) I had a droll expression that entirely vanquished him. He laughed again and again; and "Who would have guessed," he cried, "that this old wife had any wit under his petticoats?"

"It is no wit, Mr. Bally," said I: "a dry Scot's humour, and something of the driest." And, indeed, I never had the least pretension to be thought a wit.

From that hour he was never rude with me, but all passed between us in a manner of pleasantry. One of our chief times of daffing[3] was when he required a horse, another bottle, or some money. He would approach me then after the manner of a schoolboy, and I would carry it on by way of being his father: on both sides, with an infinity of mirth. I could not but perceive that he thought more of me, which tickled that poor part of mankind, the vanity. He dropped, besides (I must suppose unconsciously), into a manner that was not only familiar, but even friendly; and this, on the part of one who had so long detested me, I found the more insidious. He went little abroad; sometimes even refusing invitations. "No," he would say, "what do I care for these thick-headed bonnet-lairds? I will stay at home, Mackellar; and we shall share a bottle quietly, and have one of our good talks." And, indeed, meal-time at Durrisdeer must have been a delight to any one, by reason of the brilliancy of the discourse. He would often express wonder at his former indifference to my society. "But, you see," he would add, "we were upon opposite sides. And so we are to-day; but let us never speak of that. I would think much less of you if you were not staunch to your employer." You are to consider he seemed to me quite impotent for any evil; and how it is a most engaging form of flattery when (after many years) tardy justice is done to a man's character and parts. But I have no thought to excuse myself. I was to blame; I let him cajole me, and, in short, I think the watch-dog was going sound asleep, when he was suddenly aroused.

I should say the Indian was continually travelling to and fro in the house. He never spoke, save in his own dialect and with the Master; walked without sound; and was always turning up where you would least expect him, fallen into a deep abstraction, from which he would start (upon your coming) to mock you with one of his grovelling obeisances. He seemed so quiet, so frail, and so wrapped in his own fancies, that I came to pass him over without much regard, or even to pity him for a harmless exile from his country. And yet without doubt the creature was still eavesdropping; and without doubt it was through his stealth and my security that our secret reached the Master.

It was one very wild night, after supper, and when we had been making more than usually merry, that the blow fell on me.

"This is all very fine," says the Master, "but we should do better to be buckling our valise."

"Why so?" I cried. "Are you leaving?"

"We are all leaving to-morrow in the morning," said he. "For the port of Glascow first, thence for the province of New York."

I suppose I must have groaned aloud.

"Yes," he continued, "I boasted; I said a week, and it has taken me near twenty days. But never mind; I shall make it up; I will go the faster."

"Have you the money for this voyage?" I asked.

"Dear and ingenuous personage, I have," said he. "Blame me, if you choose, for my duplicity; but while I have been wringing shillings from my daddy, I had a stock of my own put by against a rainy day. You will pay for your own passage, if you choose to accompany us on our flank march; I have enough for Secundra and myself, but not more—enough to be dangerous, not enough to be generous. There is, however, an outside seat upon the chaise which I will let you have upon a moderate commutation; so that the whole menagerie can go together—the house-dog, the monkey, and the tiger."

"I go with you," said I.

"I count upon it," said the Master. "You have seen me foiled; I mean you shall see me victorious. To gain that I will risk wetting you like a sop in this wild weather."

"And at least," I added, "you know very well you could not throw me off."

"Not easily," said he. "You put your finger on the point with your usual excellent good sense. I never fight with the inevitable."

"I suppose it is useless to appeal to you?" said I.

"Believe me, perfectly," said he.

"And yet, if you would give me time, I could write—" I began.

"And what would be my Lord Durrisdeer's answer?" asks he.

"Aye," said I, "that is the rub."

"And, at any rate, how much more expeditions that I should go myself!" says he. "But all this is quite a waste of breath. At seven to-morrow the chaise will be at the door. For I start from the door, Mackellar; I do not skulk through woods and take my chaise upon the wayside—shall we say, at Eagles?"

My mind was now thoroughly made up. "Can you spare me quarter of an hour at St. Bride's?" said I. "I have a little necessary business with Carlyle."

"An hour, if you prefer," said he. "I do not seek to deny that the money for your seat is an object to me; and you could always get the first to Glascow with saddle-horses."

"Well," said I, "I never thought to leave old Scotland."

"It will brisken you up," says he.

"This will be an ill journey for some one," I said. "I think, sir, for you. Something speaks in my bosom; and so much it says plain—that this is an ill-omened journey."

"If you take to prophecy," says he, "listen to that."

There came up a violent squall off the open Solway, and the rain was dashed on the great windows.

"Do ye ken what that bodes, warlock?" said he, in a broad accent: "that there'll be a man Mackellar unco' sick at sea."

When I got to my chamber, I sat there under a painful excitation, hearkening to the turmoil of the gale, which struck full upon that gable of the house. What with the pressure on my spirits, the eldritch cries of the wind among the turret-tops, and the perpetual trepidation of the masoned house, sleep fled my eyelids utterly. I sat by my taper, looking on the black panes of the window, where the storm appeared continually on the point of bursting in its entrance; and upon that empty field I beheld a perspective of consequences that made the hair to rise upon my scalp. The child corrupted, the home broken up, my master dead or worse than dead, my mistress plunged in desolation—all these I saw before me painted brightly on the darkness; and the outcry of the wind appeared to mock at my inaction.

---

1. Ordered.
2. Land steward.
3. Fooling.

9

MR. MACKELLAR'S JOURNEY WITH THE MASTER

THE CHAISE CAME to the door in a strong drenching mist. We took our leave in silence: the house of Durrisdeer standing with dropping gutters and windows closed, like a place dedicate to melancholy. I observed the Master kept his head out, looking back on these splashed walls and glimmering roofs, till they were suddenly swallowed in the mist; and I must suppose some natural sadness fell upon the man at this departure; or was it some provision of the end? At least, upon our mounting the long brae from Durrisdeer, as we walked side by side in the wet, he began first to whistle and then to sing the saddest of our country tunes, which sets folk weeping in a tavern, *Wandering Willie.* The set of words he used with it I have not heard elsewhere, and could never come by any copy; but some of them which were the most appropriate to our departure linger in my memory. One verse began—

Home was home then, my dear, full of kindly faces,
Home was home then, my dear, happy for the child.

And ended somewhat thus—

Now, when day dawns on the brow of the moorland,
Lone stands the house, and the chimney-stone is cold.
Lone let it stand, now the folks are all departed,
The kind hearts, the true hearts, that loved the place of old.

I could never be a judge of the merit of these verses; they were so hallowed by the melancholy of the air, and were sung (or rather "soothed") to me by a master-singer at a time so fitting. He looked in my face when he had done, and saw that my eyes watered.

"Ah! Mackellar," said he, "do you think I have never a regret?"

"I do not think you could be so bad a man," said I, "if you had not all the machinery to be a good one."

"No, not all," says he: "not all. You are there in error. The malady of not wanting, my evangelist." But methought he sighed as he mounted again into the chaise.

All day long we journeyed in the same miserable weather: the mist besetting us closely, the heavens incessantly weeping on my head. The road lay over moorish hills, where was no sound but the crying of moor-fowl in the wet heather and the pouring of the swollen burns. Sometimes I would doze off in slumber, when I would find myself plunged at once in some foul and ominous nightmare, from the which I would awake strangling. Sometimes, if the way was steep and the wheels turning slowly, I would overhear the voices from within, talking in that tropical tongue which was to me as inarticulate as the piping of the fowls. Sometimes, at a longer ascent, the Master would set foot to ground and walk by my side, mostly without speech. And all the time, sleeping or waking, I beheld the same black perspective of approaching ruin; and the same pictures rose in my view, only they were now painted upon hillside mist. One, I remember, stood before me with the colours of a true illusion. It showed me my lord seated at a table in a small room; his head, which was at first buried in his hands, he slowly raised, and turned upon me a countenance from which hope had fled. I saw it first on the black window-panes, my last night in Durrisdeer; it haunted and returned upon me half the voyage through; and yet it was no effect of lunacy, for I have come to a ripe old age with no decay of my intelligence; nor yet (as I was then tempted to suppose) a heaven-sent warning of the future, for all manner of calamities befell, not that calamity—and I saw many pitiful sights, but never that one.

It was decided we should travel on all night; and it was singular, once the dusk had fallen, my spirits somewhat rose. The bright lamps, shining forth into the mist and on the smoking horses and the hodding post-boy, gave me perhaps an outlook intrinsically more cheerful than what day had shown; or perhaps my mind had become wearied of its melancholy. At least, I spent some waking hours, not without satisfaction in my thoughts, although wet and weary in my body; and fell at last into a natural slumber without dreams. Yet I must have been at work even in the deepest of my sleep; and at work with at least a measure of intelligence. For I started broad awake, in the very act of crying out to myself

Home was home then, my dear, happy for the child,

stricken to find in it an appropriateness, which I had not yesterday observed, to the Master's detestable purpose in the present journey.

We were then close upon the city of Glascow, where we were soon breakfasting together at an inn, and where (as the devil would have it) we found a ship in the very article of sailing. We took our places in the cabin; and, two days after, carried our effects on board. Her name was the *Nonesuch,* a very ancient ship and very happily named. By all accounts this should be her last voyage; people shook their heads upon the quays, and I had several warnings offered me by strangers in the street to the effect that she was rotten as a cheese, too deeply loaden, and must infallibly founder if we met a gale. From this it fell out we were the only passengers; the Captain, McMurtrie, was a silent, absorbed man, with the Glascow or Gaelic accent; the mates ignorant rough seafarers, come in through the hawsehole; and the Master and I were cast upon each other's company.

The Nonesuch carried a fair wind out of the Clyde, and for near upon a week we enjoyed bright weather and a sense of progress. I found myself (to my wonder) a born seaman, in so far at least as I was never sick; yet I was far from tasting the usual serenity of my health. Whether it was the motion of the ship on the billows, the confinement, the salted food, or all of these together, I suffered from a blackness of spirit and a painful strain upon my temper. The nature of my errand on that ship perhaps contributed; I think it did no more; the malady (whatever it was) sprang from my environment; and if the ship were not to blame, then it was the Master. Hatred and fear are ill bedfellows; but (to my shame be it spoken) I have tasted those in other places, lain down and got up with them, and eaten and drunk with them, and yet never before, nor after, have I been so poisoned through and through, in soul and body, as I was on board the *Nonesuch*. I freely confess my enemy set me a fair example of forbearance; in our worst days displayed the most patient geniality, holding me in conversation as long as I would suffer, and when I had rebuffed his civility, stretching himself on deck to read. The book he had on board with him was Mr. Richardson's famous *Clarissa*! and among other small attentions he would read me passages aloud; nor could any elocutionist have given with greater potency the pathetic portions of that work. I would retort upon him with passages out of the Bible, which was all my library—and very fresh to me, my religious duties (I grieve to say it) being always and even to this day extremely neglected. He tasted the merits of the word like the connoisseur he was; and would sometimes take it from my hand, turn the leaves over like a man that knew his way, and give me, with his fine declamation, a Roland for my Oliver. But it was singular how little he applied his reading to himself; it passed high above his head like summer thunder: Lovelace and Clarissa, the tales of David's generosity, the psalms of his penitence, the solemn questions of the book of Job, the touching poetry of Isaiah—they were to him a source of entertainment only, like the scraping of a fiddle in a change-house. This outer sensibility and inner toughness set me against him; it seemed of a piece with that impudent grossness which I knew to underlie the veneer of his fine manners; and sometimes my gorge rose against him as though he were deformed—and sometimes I would draw away as though from something partly spectral. I had moments when I thought of him as of a man of pasteboard—as though, if one should strike smartly through the buckram of his countenance, there would be found a mere vacuity within. This horror (not merely fanciful, I think) vastly increased my detestation of his neighbourhood; I began to feel something shiver within me on his drawing near; I had at times a longing to cry out; there were days when I thought I could have struck him. This frame of mind was doubtless helped by shame, because I had dropped during our last days at Durrisdeer into a certain toleration of the man; and if any one had then told me I should drop into it again, I must have laughed in his face. It is possible he remained unconscious of this extreme fever of my resentment; yet I think he was too quick; and rather that he had fallen, in a long life of idleness, into a positive need of company, which obliged him to confront and tolerate my unconcealed aversion. Certain, at least, that he loved the note of his own tongue, as, indeed, he entirely loved all the parts and properties of himself; a sort of imbecility which almost necessarily attends on wickedness. I have seen him driven, when I proved recalcitrant, to long discourses with the skipper; and this, although the man plainly testified his weariness, fiddling miserably with both hand and foot, and replying only with a grunt.

After the first week out we fell in with foul winds and heavy weather. The sea was high. The *Nonesuch*, being an old-fashioned ship and badly loaden, rolled beyond belief; so that the skipper trembled for his masts, and I for my life. We made no progress on our course. An unbearable ill-humour settled on the ship: men, mates, and master, girding at one another all day long. A saucy word on the one hand, and a blow on the other, made a daily incident. There were times when the whole crew refused their duty; and we of the afterguard were twice got under arms—being the first time that ever I bore weapons—in the fear of mutiny.

In the midst of our evil season sprang up a hurricane of wind; so that all supposed she must go down. I was shut in the cabin from noon of one day till sundown of the next; the Master was somewhere lashed on deck. Secundra had eaten of some drug and lay insensible; so you may say I passed these hours in an unbroken solitude. At first I was terrified beyond motion, and almost beyond thought, my mind appearing to be frozen. Presently there stole in on me a ray of comfort. If the *Nonesuch* foundered, she would carry down with her into the deeps of that unsounded sea the creature whom we all so feared and hated; there would be no more Master of Ballantrae, the fish would sport among his ribs; his schemes all brought to nothing, his harmless enemies at peace. At first, I have said, it was but a ray of comfort; but it had soon grown to be broad sunshine. The thought of the man's death, of his deletion from this world, which he embittered for so many, took possession of my mind. I hugged it, I found it sweet in my belly. I conceived the ship's last plunge, the sea bursting upon all sides into the cabin, the brief mortal conflict there, all by myself, in that closed place; I numbered the horrors, I had almost said with satisfaction; I felt I could bear all and more, if the *Nonesuch* carried down with her, overtook by the same ruin, the enemy of my poor master's house. Towards noon of the second day the screaming of the wind abated; the ship lay not so perilously over, and it began to be clear to me that we were past the height of the tempest. As I hope for mercy, I was singly disappointed. In the selfishness of that vile, absorbing passion of hatred, I forgot the case of our innocent shipmates, and thought but of myself and my enemy. For myself, I was already old; I had never been young, I was not formed for the world's pleasures, I had few affections; it mattered not the toss of a silver tester whether I was drowned there and then in the Atlantic, or dribbled out a few more years, to die, perhaps no less terribly, in a deserted sick-bed. Down I went upon my knees—holding on by the locker, or else I had been instantly dashed across the tossing cabin—and, lifting up my voice in the midst of that clamour of the abating hurricane, impiously prayed for my own death. "O God!" I cried, "I would be liker a man if I rose and struck this creature down; but Thou madest me a coward from my mother's womb. O Lord, Thou madest me so, Thou knowest my weakness, Thou knowest that any face of death will set me shaking in my shoes. But, lo! here is Thy servant ready, his mortal weakness laid aside. Let me give my life for this creature's; take the two of them, Lord! take the two, and have mercy on the innocent!" In some such words as these, only yet more irreverent and with more sacred adjurations, I continued to pour forth my spirit. God heard me not, I must suppose in mercy; and I was still absorbed in my agony of supplication when some one, removing the tarpaulin cover, let the light of the sunset pour into the cabin. I stumbled to my feet ashamed, and was seized with surprise to find myself totter and ache like one that had been stretched upon the rack. Secundra Dass, who had slept off the effects of his drug, stood in a corner not far off, gazing at me with wild eyes; and from the open skylight the captain thanked me for my supplications.

"It's you that saved the ship, Mr. Mackellar," says he. "There is no craft of seamanship that could have kept her floating: well may we say, 'Except the Lord the city keep, the watchmen watch in vain!'"

I was abashed by the captain's error; abashed, also, by the surprise and fear with which the Indian regarded me at first, and the obsequious civilities with which he soon began to cumber me. I know now that he must have overheard and comprehended the peculiar nature of my prayers. It is certain, of course, that he at once disclosed the matter to his patron; and looking back with greater knowledge, I can now understand what so much puzzled me at the moment, those singular and (so to speak) approving smiles with which the Master honoured me. Similarly, I can understand a word that I remember to have fallen from him in conversation that same night; when, holding up his hand and smiling, "Ah! Mackellar," said he, "not every man is so great a coward as he thinks he is—nor yet so good a Christian." He did not guess how true he spoke! For the fact is, the thoughts which had come to me in the violence of the storm retained their hold upon my spirit; and the words that rose to my lips unbidden in the instancy of prayer continued to sound in my ears: with what shameful consequences, it is fitting I should honestly relate; for I could not support a part of such disloyalty as to describe the sins of others and conceal my own.

The wind fell, but the sea hove ever the higher. All night the *Nonesuch* rolled outrageously; the next day dawned, and the next, and brought no change. To cross the cabin was scarce possible; old experienced seamen were cast down upon the deck, and one cruelly mauled in the concussion; every board and block in the old ship cried out aloud; and the great bell by the anchor-bitts continually and dolefully rang. One of these days the Master and I sate alone together at the break of the poop. I should say the *Nonesuch* carried a high, raised poop. About the top of it ran considerable bulwarks, which made the ship unweatherly; and these, as they approached the front on each side, ran down in a fine, old-fashioned, carven scroll to join the bulwarks of the waist. From this disposition, which seems designed rather for ornament than use, it followed there was a discontinuance of protection: and that, besides, at the very margin of the elevated part where (in certain movements of the ship) it might be the most needful. It was here we were sitting: our feet hanging down, the Master betwixt me and the side, and I holding on with both hands to the grating of the cabin skylight; for it struck me it was a dangerous position, the more so as I had continually before my eyes a measure of our evolutions in the person of the Master, which stood out in the break of the bulwarks against the sun. Now his head would be in the zenith and his shadow fall quite beyond the *Nonesuch* on the farther side; and now he would swing down till he was underneath my feet, and the line of the sea leaped high above him like the ceiling of a room. I looked on upon this with a growing fascination, as birds are said to look on snakes. My mind, besides, was troubled with an astonishing diversity of noises; for now that we had all sails spread in the vain hope to bring her to the sea, the ship sounded like a factory with their reverberations. We spoke first of the mutiny with which we had been threatened; this led us on to the topic of assassination; and that offered a temptation to the Master more strong than he was able to resist. He must tell me a tale, and show me at the same time how clever he was and how wicked. It was a thing he did always with affectation and display; generally with a good effect. But this tale, told in a high key in the midst of so great a tumult, and by a narrator who was one moment looking down at me from the skies and the next up from under the soles of my feet—this particular tale, I say, took hold upon me in a degree quite singular.

"My friend the count," it was thus that he began his story, "had for an enemy a certain German baron, a stranger in Rome. It matters not what was the ground of the count's enmity; but as he had a firm design to be revenged, and that with safety to himself, he kept it secret even from the baron. Indeed, that is the first principle of vengeance; and hatred betrayed is hatred impotent. The count was a man of a curious, searching mind; he had something of the artist; if anything fell for him to do, it must always be done with an exact perfection, not only as to the result, but in the very means and instruments, or he thought the thing miscarried. It chanced he was one day riding in the outer suburbs, when he came to a disused by-road branching off into the moor which lies about Rome. On the one hand was an ancient Roman tomb; on the other a deserted house in a garden of evergreen trees. This road brought him presently into a field of ruins, in the midst of which, in the side of a hill, he saw an open door, and, not far off, a single stunted pine no greater than a currant-bush. The place was desert and very secret; a voice spoke in the count's bosom that there was something here to his advantage. He tied his horse to the pine-tree, took his flint and steel in his hand to make a light, and entered into the hill. The doorway opened on a passage of old Roman masonry, which shortly after branched in two. The count took the turning to the right, and followed it, groping forward in the dark, till he was brought up by a kind of fence, about elbow-high, which extended quite across the passage. Sounding forward with his foot, he found an edge of polished stone, and then vacancy. All his curiosity was now awakened, and, getting some rotten sticks that lay about the floor, he made a fire. In front of him was a profound well; doubtless some neighbouring peasant had once used it for his water, and it was he that had set up the fence. A long while the count stood leaning on the rail and looking down into the pit. It was of Roman foundation, and, like all that nation set their hands to, built as for eternity; the sides were still straight, and the joints smooth; to a man who should fall in, no escape was possible. 'Now,' the count was thinking, 'a strong impulsion brought me to this place. What for? what have I gained? why should I be sent to gaze into this well?' when the rail of the fence gave suddenly under his weight, and he came within an ace of falling headlong in. Leaping back to save himself, he trod out the last flicker of his fire, which gave him thenceforward no more light, only an incommoding smoke. 'Was I sent here to my death?' says he, and shook from head to foot. And then a thought flashed in his mind. He crept forth on hands and knees to the brink of the pit, and felt above him in the air. The rail had been fast to a pair of uprights; it had only broken from the one, and still depended from the other. The count set it back again as he had found it, so that the place meant death to the first comer, and groped out of the catacomb like a sick man. The next day, riding in the Corso with the baron, he purposely betrayed a strong preoccupation. The other (as he had designed) inquired into the cause; and he, after some fencing, admitted that his spirits had been dashed by an unusual dream. This was calculated to draw on the baron—a superstitious man, who affected the scorn of superstition. Some rallying followed, and then the count, as if suddenly carried away, called on his friend to beware, for it was of him that he had dreamed. You know enough of human nature, my excellent Mackellar, to be certain of one thing: I mean that the baron did not rest till he had heard the dream. The count, sure that he would never desist, kept him in play till his curiosity was highly inflamed, and then suffered himself, with seeming reluctance, to be overborne. 'I warn you,' says he, 'evil will come of it; something tells me so. But since there is to be no peace either for you or me except on this condition, the blame be on your own head! This was the dream:—I beheld you riding, I know not where, yet I think it must have been near Rome, for on your one hand was an ancient tomb, and on the other a garden of evergreen trees. Methought I cried and cried upon you to come back in a very agony of terror; whether you heard me I know not, but you went doggedly on. The road brought you to a desert place among ruins, where was a door in a hillside, and hard by the door a misbegotten pine. Here you dismounted (I still crying on you to beware), tied your horse to the pine-tree, and entered resolutely in by the door. Within, it was dark; but in my dream I could still see you, and still besought you to hold back. You felt your way along the right-hand wall, took a branching passage to the right, and came to a little chamber, where was a well with a railing. At this—I know not why—my alarm for you increased a thousandfold, so that I seemed to scream myself hoarse with warnings, crying it was still time, and bidding you begone at once from that vestibule. Such was the word I used in my dream, and it seemed then to have a clear significancy; but to-day, and awake, I profess I know not what it means. To all my outcry you rendered not the least attention, leaning the while upon the rail and looking down intently in the water. And then there was made to you a communication; I do not think I even gathered what it was, but the fear of it plucked me clean out of my slumber, and I awoke shaking and sobbing. And now,' continues the count, 'I thank you from my heart for your insistency. This dream lay on me like a load; and now I have told it in plain words and in the broad daylight, it seems no great matter.'—'I do not know,' says the baron. 'It is in some points strange. A communication, did you say? Oh! it is an odd dream. It will make a story to amuse our friends.'—'I am not so sure,' says the count. 'I am sensible of some reluctancy. Let us rather forget it.'—'By all means,' says the baron. And (in fact) the dream was not again referred to. Some days after, the count proposed a ride in the fields, which the baron (since they were daily growing faster friends) very readily accepted. On the way back to Rome, the count led them insensibly by a particular route. Presently he reined in his horse, clapped his hand before his eyes, and cried out aloud. Then he showed his face again (which was now quite white, for he was a consummate actor), and stared upon the baron. 'What ails you?' cries the baron. 'What is wrong with you?'—'Nothing,' cries the count. 'It is nothing. A seizure, I know not what. Let us hurry back to Rome.' But in the meanwhile the baron had looked about him; and there, on the left-hand side of the way as they went back to Rome, he saw a dusty by-road with a tomb upon the one hand and a garden of evergreen trees upon the other.—'Yes,' says he, with a changed voice. 'Let us by all means hurry back to Rome. I fear you are not well in health.'—'Oh, for God's sake!' cries the count, shuddering, 'back to Rome and let me get to bed.' They made their return with scarce a word; and the count, who should by rights have gone into society, took to his bed and gave out he had a touch of country fever. The next day the baron's horse was found tied to the pine, but himself was never heard of from that hour.—And, now, was that a murder?" says the Master, breaking sharply off.

"Are you sure he was a count?" I asked.

"I am not certain of the title," said he, "but he was a gentleman of family: and the Lord deliver you, Mackellar, from an enemy so subtile!"

These last words he spoke down at me, smiling, from high above; the next, he was under my feet. I continued to follow his evolutions with a childish fixity; they made me giddy and vacant, and I spoke as in a dream.

"He hated the baron with a great hatred?" I asked.

"His belly moved when the man came near him," said the Master.

"I have felt that same," said I.

"Verily!" cries the Master. "Here is news indeed! I wonder—do I flatter myself? or am I the cause of these ventral perturbations?"

He was quite capable of choosing out a graceful posture, even with no one to behold him but myself, and all the more if there were any element of peril. He sat now with one knee flung across the other, his arms on his bosom, fitting the swing of the ship with an exquisite balance, such as a featherweight might overthrow. All at once I had the vision of my lord at the table, with his head upon his hands; only now, when he showed me his countenance, it was heavy with reproach. The words of my own prayer—*I were liker a man if I struck this creature down*—shot at the same time into my memory. I called my energies together, and (the ship then heeling downward toward my enemy) thrust at him swiftly with my foot. It was written I should have the guilt of this attempt without the profit. Whether from my own uncertainty or his incredible quickness, he escaped the thrust, leaping to his feet and catching hold at the same moment of a stay.

I do not know how long a time passed by. I lying where I was upon the deck, overcome with terror and remorse and shame: he standing with the stay in his hand, backed against the bulwarks, and regarding me with an expression singularly mingled. At last he spoke.

"Mackellar," said he, "I make no reproaches, but I offer you a bargain. On your side, I do not suppose you desire to have this exploit made public; on mine, I own to you freely I do not care to draw my breath in a perpetual terror of assassination by the man I sit at meat with. Promise me—but no," says he, breaking off, "you are not yet in the quiet possession of your mind; you might think I had extorted the promise from your weakness; and I would leave no door open for casuistry to come in—that dishonesty of the conscientious. Take time to meditate."

With that he made off up the sliding deck like a squirrel, and plunged into the cabin. About half an hour later he returned—I still lying as he had left me.

"Now," says he, "will you give me your troth as a Christian, and a faithful servant of my brother's, that I shall have no more to fear from your attempts?"

"I give it you," said I.

"I shall require your hand upon it," says he.

"You have the right to make conditions," I replied, and we shook hands.

He sat down at once in the same place and the old perilous attitude.

"Hold on!" cried I, covering my eyes. "I cannot bear to see you in that posture. The least irregularity of the sea might plunge you overboard."

"You are highly inconsistent," he replied, smiling, but doing as I asked. "For all that, Mackellar, I would have you to know you have risen forty feet in my esteem. You think I cannot set a price upon fidelity? But why do you suppose I carry that Secundra Dass about the world with me? Because he would die or do murder for me to-morrow; and I love him for it. Well, you may think it odd, but I like you the better for this afternoon's performance. I thought you were magnetised with the Ten Commandments; but no—God damn my soul!"—he cries, "the old wife has blood in his body after all! Which does not change the fact," he continued, smiling again, "that you have done well to give your promise; for I doubt if you would ever shine in your new trade."

"I suppose," said I, "I should ask your pardon and God's for my attempt. At any rate, I have passed my word, which I will keep faithfully. But when I think of those you persecute—" I paused.

"Life is a singular thing," said he, "and mankind a very singular people. You suppose yourself to love my brother. I assure you, it is merely custom. Interrogate your memory; and when first you came to Durrisdeer, you will find you considered him a dull, ordinary youth. He is as dull and ordinary now, though not so young. Had you instead fallen in with me, you would to-day be as strong upon my side."

"I would never say you were ordinary, Mr. Bally," I returned; "but here you prove yourself dull. You have just shown your reliance on my word. In other terms, that is my conscience—the same which starts instinctively back from you, like the eye from a strong light."

"Ah!" says he, "but I mean otherwise. I mean, had I met you in my youth. You are to consider I was not always as I am to-day; nor (had I met in with a friend of your description) should I have ever been so."

"Hut, Mr. Bally," says I, "you would have made a mock of me; you would never have spent ten civil words on such a Square-toes."

But he was now fairly started on his new course of justification, with which he wearied me throughout the remainder of the passage. No doubt in the past he had taken pleasure to paint himself unnecessarily black, and made a vaunt of his wickedness, bearing it for a coat-of-arms. Nor was he so illogical as to abate one item of his old confessions. "But now that I know you are a human being," he would say, "I can take the trouble to explain myself. For I assure you I am human, too, and have my virtues, like my neighbours." I say, he wearied me, for I had only the one word to say in answer: twenty times I must have said it: "Give up your present purpose and return with me to Durrisdeer; then I will believe you."

Thereupon he would shake his head at me. "Ah! Mackellar, you might live a thousand years and never understand my nature," he would say. "This battle is now committed, the hour of reflection quite past, the hour for mercy not yet come. It began between us when we span a coin in the hall of Durrisdeer, now twenty years ago; we have had our ups and downs, but never either of us dreamed of giving in; and as for me, when my glove is cast, life and honour go with it."

"A fig for your honour!" I would say. "And by your leave, these warlike similitudes are something too high-sounding for the matter in hand. You want some dirty money; there is the bottom of your contention; and as for your means, what are they? to stir up sorrow in a family that never harmed you, to debauch (if you can) your own nephew, and to wring the heart of your born brother! A footpad that kills an old granny in a woollen mutch with a dirty bludgeon, and that for a shilling-piece and a paper of snuff—there is all the warrior that you are."

When I would attack him thus (or somewhat thus) he would smile, and sigh like a man misunderstood. Once, I remember, he defended himself more at large, and had some curious sophistries, worth repeating, for a light upon his character.

"You are very like a civilian to think war consists in drums and banners," said he. "War (as the ancients said very wisely) is *ultima ratio*. When we take our advantage unrelentingly, then we make war. Ah! Mackellar, you are a devil of a soldier in the steward's room at Durrisdeer, or the tenants do you sad injustice!"

"I think little of what war is or is not," I replied. "But you weary me with claiming my respect. Your brother is a good man, and you are a bad one—neither more nor less."

"Had I been Alexander—" he began.

"It is so we all dupe ourselves," I cried. "Had I been St. Paul, it would have been all one; I would have made the same hash of that career that you now see me making of my own."

"I tell you," he cried, bearing down my interruption, "had I been the least petty chieftain in the Highlands, had I been the least king of naked negroes in the African desert, my people would have adored me. A bad man, am I? Ah! but I was born for a good tyrant! Ask Secundra Dass; he will tell you I treat him like a son. Cast in your lot with me to-morrow, become my slave, my chattel, a thing I can command as I command the powers of my own limbs and spirit—you will see no more that dark side that I turn upon the world in anger. I must have all or none. But where all is given, I give it back with usury. I have a kingly nature: there is my loss!"

"It has been hitherto rather the loss of others," I remarked, "which seems a little on the hither side of royalty."

"Tilly-vally!" cried he. "Even now, I tell you, I would spare that family in which you take so great an interest: yes, even now—to-morrow I would leave them to their petty welfare, and disappear in that forest of cut-throats and thimble-riggers that we call the world. I would do it to-morrow!" says he. "Only—only—"

"Only what?" I asked.

"Only they must beg it on their bended knees. I think in public, too," he added, smiling. "Indeed, Mackellar, I doubt if there be a hall big enough to serve my purpose for that act of reparation."

"Vanity, vanity!" I moralised. "To think that this great force for evil should be swayed by the same sentiment that sets a lassie mincing to her glass!"

"Oh! there are double words for everything: the word that swells, the word that belittles; you cannot fight me with a word!" said he. "You said the other day that I relied on your conscience: were I in your humour of detraction, I might say I built upon your vanity. It is your pretension to be *un homme de parole*; 'tis mine not to accept defeat. Call it vanity, call it virtue, call it greatness of soul—what signifies the expression? But recognise in each of us a common strain: that we both live for an idea."

It will be gathered from so much familiar talk, and so much patience on both sides, that we now lived together upon excellent terms. Such was again the fact, and this time more seriously than before. Apart from disputations such as that which I have tried to reproduce, not only consideration reigned, but, I am tempted to say, even kindness. When I fell sick (as I did shortly after our great storm), he sat by my berth to entertain me with his conversation, and treated me with excellent remedies, which I accepted with security. Himself commented on the circumstance. "You see," says he, "you begin to know me better. A very little while ago, upon this lonely ship, where no one but myself has any smattering of science, you would have made sure I had designs upon your life. And, observe, it is since I found you had designs upon my own, that I have shown you most respect. You will tell me if this speaks of a small mind." I found little to reply. In so far as regarded myself, I believed him to mean well; I am, perhaps, the more a dupe of his dissimulation, but I believed (and I still believe) that he regarded me with genuine kindness. Singular and sad fact! so soon as this change began, my animosity abated, and these haunting visions of my master passed utterly away. So that, perhaps, there was truth in the man's last vaunting word to me, uttered on the second day of July, when our long voyage was at last brought almost to an end, and we lay becalmed at the sea end of the vast harbour of New York, in a gasping heat, which was presently exchanged for a surprising waterfall of rain. I stood on the poop, regarding the green shores near at hand, and now and then the light smoke of the little town, our destination. And as I was even then devising how to steal a march on my familiar enemy, I was conscious of a shade of embarrassment when he approached me with his hand extended.

"I am now to bid you farewell," said he, "and that for ever. For now you go among my enemies, where all your former prejudices will revive. I never yet failed to charm a person when I wanted; even you, my good friend—to call you so for once—even you have now a very different portrait of me in your memory, and one that you will never quite forget. The voyage has not lasted long enough, or I should have wrote the impression deeper. But now all is at an end, and we are again at war. Judge by this little interlude how dangerous I am; and tell those fools"—pointing with his finger to the town—"to think twice and thrice before they set me at defiance."

10

PASSAGES AT NEW YORK

I HAVE MENTIONED I was resolved to steal a march upon the Master; and this, with the complicity of Captain McMurtrie, was mighty easily effected: a boat being partly loaded on the one side of our ship and the Master placed on board of it, the while a skiff put off from the other, carrying me alone. I had no more trouble in finding a direction to my lord's house, whither I went at top speed, and which I found to be on the outskirts of the place, a very suitable mansion, in a fine garden, with an extraordinary large barn, byre, and stable, all in one. It was here my lord was walking when I arrived; indeed, it had become his chief place of frequentation, and his mind was now filled with farming. I burst in upon him breathless, and gave him my news: which was indeed no news at all, several ships having outsailed the *Nonesuch* in the interval.

"We have been expecting you long," said my lord; "and indeed, of late days, ceased to expect you any more. I am glad to take your hand again, Mackellar. I thought you had been at the bottom of the sea."

"Ah! my lord, would God I had!" cried I. "Things would have been better for yourself."

"Not in the least," says he, grimly. "I could not ask better. There is a long score to pay, and now—at last—I can begin to pay it."

I cried out against his security.

"Oh!" says he, "this is not Durrisdeer, and I have taken my precautions. His reputation awaits him; I have prepared a welcome for my brother. Indeed, fortune has served me; for I found here a merchant of Albany who knew him after the '45 and had mighty convenient suspicions of a murder: some one of the name of Chew it was, another Albanian. No one here will be surprised if I deny him my door; he will not be suffered to address my children, nor even to salute my wife: as for myself, I make so much exception for a brother that he may speak to me. I should lose my pleasure else," says my lord, rubbing his palms.

Presently he bethought himself, and set men off running, with billets, to summon the magnates of the province. I cannot recall what pretext he employed; at least, it was successful; and when our ancient enemy appeared upon the scene, he found my lord pacing in front of his house under some trees of shade, with the Governor upon one hand and various notables upon the other. My lady, who was seated in the verandah, rose with a very pinched expression and carried her children into the house.

The Master, well dressed and with an elegant walking-sword, bowed to the company in a handsome manner and nodded to my lord with familiarity. My lord did not accept the salutation, but looked upon his brother with bended brows.

"Well, sir," says he, at last, "what ill wind brings you hither of all places, where (to our common disgrace) your reputation has preceded you?"

"Your lordship is pleased to be civil," said the Master, with a fine start.

"I am pleased to be very plain," returned my lord; "because it is needful you should clearly understand your situation. At home, where you were so little known, it was still possible to keep appearances; that would be quite vain in this province; and I have to tell you that I am quite resolved to wash my hands of you. You have already ruined me almost to the door, as you ruined my father before me;—whose heart you also broke. Your crimes escape the law; but my friend the Governor has promised protection to my family. Have a care, sir!" cries my lord, shaking his cane at him: "if you are observed to utter two words to any of my innocent household, the law shall be stretched to make you smart for it."

"Ah!" says the Master, very slowly. "And so this is the advantage of a foreign land! These gentlemen are unacquainted with our story, I perceive. They do not know that I am the Lord Durrisdeer; they do not know you are my younger brother, sitting in my place under a sworn family compact; they do not know (or they would not be seen with you in familiar correspondence) that every acre is mine before God Almighty—and every doit of the money you withhold from me, you do it as a thief, a perjurer, and a disloyal brother!"

"General Clinton," I cried, "do not listen to his lies. I am the steward of the estate, and there is not one word of truth in it. The man is a forfeited rebel turned into a hired spy: there is his story in two words."

It was thus that (in the heat of the moment) I let slip his infamy.

"Fellow," said the Governor, turning his face sternly on the Master, "I know more of you than you think for. We have some broken ends of your adventures in the provinces, which you will do very well not to drive me to investigate. There is the disappearance of Mr. Jacob Chew with all his merchandise; there is the matter of where you came ashore from with so much money and jewels, when you were picked up by a Bermudan out of Albany. Believe me, if I let these matters lie, it is in commiseration for your family and out of respect for my valued friend, Lord Durrisdeer."

There was a murmur of applause from the provincials.

"I should have remembered how a title would shine out in such a hole as this," says the Master, white as a sheet: "no matter how unjustly come by. It remains for me, then, to die at my lord's door, where my dead body will form a very cheerful ornament."

"Away with your affectations!" cries my lord. "You know very well I have no such meaning; only to protect myself from calumny, and my home from your intrusion. I offer you a choice. Either I shall pay your passage home on the first ship, when you may perhaps be able to resume your occupations under Government, although God knows I would rather see you on the highway! Or, if that likes you not, stay here and welcome! I have inquired the least sum on which body and soul can be decently kept together in New York; so much you shall have, paid weekly; and if you cannot labour with your hands to better it, high time you should betake yourself to learn. The condition is—that you speak with no member of my family except myself," he added.

I do not think I have ever seen any man so pale as was the Master; but he was erect and his mouth firm.

"I have been met here with some very unmerited insults," said he, "from which I have certainly no idea to take refuge by flight. Give me your pittance; I take it without shame, for it is mine already—like the shirt upon your back; and I choose to stay until these gentlemen shall understand me better. Already they must spy the cloven hoof, since with all your pretended eagerness for the family honour, you take a pleasure to degrade it in my person."

"This is all very fine," says my lord; "but to us who know you of old, you must be sure it signifies nothing. You take that alternative out of which you think that you can make the most. Take it, if you can, in silence; it will serve you better in the long run, you may believe me, than this ostentation of ingratitude."

"Oh, gratitude, my lord!" cries the Master, with a mounting intonation and his forefinger very conspicuously lifted up. "Be at rest: it will not fail you. It now remains that I should salute these gentlemen whom we have wearied with our family affairs."

And he bowed to each in succession, settled his walking-sword, and took himself off, leaving every one amazed at his behaviour, and me not less so at my lord's.

We were now to enter on a changed phase of this family division. The Master was by no manner of means so helpless as my lord supposed, having at his hand, and entirely devoted to his service, an excellent artist in all sorts of goldsmith work. With my lord's allowance, which was not so scanty as he had described it, the pair could support life; and all the earnings of Secundra Dass might be laid upon one side for any future purpose. That this was done, I have no doubt. It was in all likelihood the Master's design to gather a sufficiency, and then proceed in quest of that treasure which he had buried long before among the mountains; to which, if he had confined himself, he would have been more happily inspired. But unfortunately for himself and all of us, he took counsel of his anger. The public disgrace of his arrival—which I sometimes wonder he could manage to survive—rankled in his bones; he was in that humour when a man—in the words of the old adage—will cut off his nose to spite his face; and he must make himself a public spectacle in the hopes that some of the disgrace might spatter on my lord.

He chose, in a poor quarter of the town, a lonely, small house of boards, overhung with some acacias. It was furnished in front with a sort of hutch opening, like that of a dog's kennel, but about as high as a table from the ground, in which the poor man that built it had formerly displayed some wares; and it was this which took the Master's fancy and possibly suggested his proceedings. It appears, on board the pirate ship he had acquired some quickness with the needle—enough, at least, to play the part of tailor in the public eye; which was all that was required by the nature of his vengeance. A placard was hung above the hutch, bearing these words in something of the following disposition:

James Durie,
formerly MASTER of BALLANTRAE.
Clothes Neatly Clouted.

SECUNDRA DASS,
Decayed Gentleman of India.
Fine Goldsmith Work.

Underneath this, when he had a job, my gentleman sat withinside tailor-wise and busily stitching. I say, when he had a job; but such customers as came were rather for Secundra, and the Master's sewing would be more in the manner of Penelope's. He could never have designed to gain even butter to his bread by such a means of livelihood: enough for him that there was the name of Durie dragged in the dirt on the placard, and the sometime heir of that proud family set up cross-legged in public for a reproach upon his brother's meanness. And in so far his device succeeded that there was murmuring in the town and a party formed highly inimical to my lord. My lord's favour with the Governor laid him more open on the other side; my lady (who was never so well received in the colony) met with painful innuendoes; in a party of women, where it would be the topic most natural to introduce, she was almost debarred from the naming of needle-work; and I have seen her return with a flushed countenance and vow that she would go abroad no more.

In the meanwhile my lord dwelled in his decent mansion, immersed in farming; a popular man with his intimates, and careless or unconscious of the rest. He laid on flesh; had a bright, busy face; even the heat seemed to prosper with him; and my lady—in despite of her own annoyances—daily blessed Heaven her father should have left her such a paradise. She had looked on from a window upon the Master's humiliation; and from that hour appeared to feel at ease. I was not so sure myself; as time went on, there seemed to me a something not quite wholesome in my lord's condition. Happy he was, beyond a doubt, but the grounds of this felicity were wont; even in the bosom of his family he brooded with manifest delight upon some private thought; and I conceived at last the suspicion (quite unworthy of us both) that he kept a mistress somewhere in the town. Yet he went little abroad, and his day was very fully occupied; indeed, there was but a single period, and that pretty early in the morning, while Mr. Alexander was at his lesson-book, of which I was not certain of the disposition. It should be borne in mind, in the defence of that which I now did, that I was always in some fear my lord was not quite justly in his reason; and with our enemy sitting so still in the same town with us, I did well to be upon my guard. Accordingly I made a pretext, had the hour changed at which I taught Mr. Alexander the foundation of cyphering and the mathematic, and set myself instead to dog my master's footsteps.

Every morning, fair or foul, he took his gold-headed cane, set his hat on the back of his head —a recent habitude, which I thought to indicate a burning brow—and betook himself to make a certain circuit. At the first his way was among pleasant trees and beside a graveyard, where he would sit awhile, if the day were fine, in meditation. Presently the path turned down to the waterside, and came back along the harbour-front and past the Master's booth. As he approached this second part of his circuit, my Lord Durrisdeer began to pace more leisurely, like a man delighted with the air and scene; and before the booth, half-way between that and the water's edge, would pause a little, leaning on his staff. It was the hour when the Master sate within upon his board and plied his needle. So these two brothers would gaze upon each other with hard faces; and then my lord move on again, smiling to himself.

It was but twice that I must stoop to that ungrateful necessity of playing spy. I was then certain of my lord's purpose in his rambles and of the secret source of his delight. Here was his mistress: it was hatred and not love that gave him healthful colours. Some moralists might have been relieved by the discovery; I confess that I was dismayed. I found this situation of two brethren not only odious in itself, but big with possibilities of further evil; and I made it my practice, in so far as many occupations would allow, to go by a shorter path and be secretly present at their meeting. Coming down one day a little late, after I had been near a week prevented, I was struck with surprise to find a new development. I should say there was a bench against the Master's house, where customers might sit to parley with the shopman; and here I found my lord seated, nursing his cane and looking pleasantly forth upon the bay. Not three feet from him sate the Master, stitching. Neither spoke; nor (in this new situation) did my lord so much as cut a glance upon his enemy. He tasted his neighbourhood, I must suppose, less indirectly in the bare proximity of person; and, without doubt, drank deep of hateful pleasures.

He had no sooner come away than I openly joined him. "My lord, my lord," said I, "this is no manner of behaviour."

"I grow fat upon it," he replied; and not merely the words, which were strange enough, but the whole character of his expression, shocked me.

"I warn you, my lord, against this indulgency of evil feeling," said I. "I know not to which it is more perilous, the soul or the reason; but you go the way to murder both."

"You cannot understand," said he. "You had never such mountains of bitterness upon your heart."

"And if it were no more," I added, "you will surely goad the man to some extremity."

"To the contrary; I am breaking his spirit," says my lord.

Every morning for hard upon a week my lord took his same place upon the bench. It was a pleasant place, under the green acacias, with a sight upon the bay and shipping, and a sound (from some way off) of marines singing at their employ. Here the two sate without speech or any external movement, beyond that of the needle or the Master biting off a thread, for he still clung to his pretence of industry; and here I made a point to join them, wondering at myself and my companions. If any of my lord's friends went by, he would hail them cheerfully, and cry out he was there to give some good advice to his brother, who was now (to his delight) grown quite industrious. And even this the Master accepted with a steady countenance; what was in his mind, God knows, or perhaps Satan only.

All of a sudden, on a still day of what they call the Indian Summer, when the woods were changed into gold and pink and scarlet, the Master laid down his needle and burst into a fit of merriment. I think he must have been preparing it a long while in silence, for the note in itself was pretty naturally pitched; but breaking suddenly from so extreme a silence, and in circumstances so averse from mirth, it sounded ominously on my ear.

"Henry," said he, "I have for once made a false step, and for once you have had the wit to profit by it. The farce of the cobbler ends to-day; and I confess to you (with my compliments) that you have had the best of it. Blood will out; and you have certainly a choice idea of how to make yourself unpleasant."

Never a word said my lord; it was just as though the Master had not broken silence.

"Come," resumed the Master, "do not be sulky; it will spoil your attitude. You can now afford (believe me) to be a little gracious; for I have not merely a defeat to accept. I had meant to continue this performance till I had gathered enough money for a certain purpose; I confess ingenuously, I have not the courage. You naturally desire my absence from this town; I have come round by another way to the same idea. And I have a proposition to make; or, if your lordship prefers, a favour to ask."

"Ask it," says my lord.

"You may have heard that I had once in this country a considerable treasure," returned the Master; "it matters not whether or no—such is the fact; and I was obliged to bury it in a spot of which I have sufficient indications. To the recovery of this, has my ambition now come down; and, as it is my own, you will not grudge it me."

"Go and get it," says my lord. "I make no opposition."

"Yes," said the Master; "but to do so, I must find men and carriage. The way is long and rough, and the country infested with wild Indians. Advance me only so much as shall be needful: either as a lump sum, in lieu of my allowance; or, if you prefer it, as a loan, which I shall repay on my return. And then, if you so decide, you may have seen the last of me."

My lord stared him steadily in the eyes; there was a hard smile upon his face, but he uttered nothing.

"Henry," said the Master, with a formidable quietness, and drawing at the same time somewhat back—"Henry, I had the honour to address you."

"Let us be stepping homeward," says my lord to me, who was plucking at his sleeve; and with that he rose, stretched himself, settled his hat, and still without a syllable of response, began to walk steadily along the shore.

I hesitated awhile between the two brothers, so serious a climax did we seem to have reached. But the Master had resumed his occupation, his eyes lowered, his hand seemingly as deft as ever; and I decided to pursue my lord.

"Are you mad?" I cried, so soon as I had overtook him. "Would you cast away so fair an opportunity?"

"Is it possible you should still believe in him?" inquired my lord, almost with a sneer.

"I wish him forth of this town!" I cried. "I wish him anywhere and anyhow but as he is."

"I have said my say," returned my lord, "and you have said yours. There let it rest."

But I was bent on dislodging the Master. That sight of him patiently returning to his needlework was more than my imagination could digest. There was never a man made, and the Master the least of any, that could accept so long a series of insults. The air smelt blood to me. And I vowed there should be no neglect of mine if, through any chink of possibility, crime could be yet turned aside. That same day, therefore, I came to my lord in his business room, where he sat upon some trivial occupation.

"My lord," said I, "I have found a suitable investment for my small economies. But these are unhappily in Scotland; it will take some time to lift them, and the affair presses. Could your lordship see his way to advance me the amount against my note?"

He read me awhile with keen eyes. "I have never inquired into the state of your affairs, Mackellar," says he. "Beyond the amount of your caution, you may not be worth a farthing, for what I know."

"I have been a long while in your service, and never told a lie, nor yet asked a favour for myself," said I, "until to-day."

"A favour for the Master," he returned, quietly. "Do you take me for a fool, Mackellar? Understand it once and for all, I treat this beast in my own way; fear nor favour shall not move me; and before I am hoodwinked, it will require a trickster less transparent than yourself. I ask service, loyal service; not that you should make and mar behind my back, and steal my own money to defeat me."

"My lord," said I, "these are very unpardonable expressions."

"Think once more, Mackellar," he replied; "and you will see they fit the fact. It is your own subterfuge that is unpardonable. Deny (if you can) that you designed this money to evade my orders with, and I will ask your pardon freely. If you cannot, you must have the resolution to hear your conduct go by its own name."

"If you think I had any design but to save you—" I began.

"Oh! my old friend," said he, "you know very well what I think! Here is my hand to you with all my heart; but of money, not one rap."

Defeated upon this side, I went straight to my room, wrote a letter, ran with it to the harbour, for I knew a ship was on the point of sailing; and came to the Master's door a little before dusk. Entering without the form of any knock, I found him sitting with his Indian at a simple meal of maize porridge with some milk. The house within was clean and poor; only a few books upon a shelf distinguished it, and (in one corner) Secundra's little bench.

"Mr. Bally," said I, "I have near five hundred pounds laid by in Scotland, the economies of a hard life. A letter goes by yon ship to have it lifted. Have so much patience till the return ship comes in, and it is all yours, upon the same condition you offered to my lord this morning."

He rose from the table, came forward, took me by the shoulders, and looked me in the face, smiling.

"And yet you are very fond of money!" said he. "And yet you love money beyond all things else, except my brother!"

"I fear old age and poverty," said I, "which is another matter."

"I will never quarrel for a name. Call it so," he replied. "Ah! Mackellar, Mackellar, if this were done from any love to me, how gladly would I close upon your offer!"

"And yet," I eagerly answered—"I say it to my shame, but I cannot see you in this poor place without compunction. It is not my single thought, nor my first; and yet it's there! I would gladly see you delivered. I do not offer it in love, and far from that; but, as God judges me—and I wonder at it too!—quite without enmity."

"Ah!" says he, still holding my shoulders, and now gently shaking me, "you think of me more than you suppose. 'And I wonder at it too,'" he added, repeating my expression and, I suppose, something of my voice. "You are an honest man, and for that cause I spare you."

"Spare me?" I cried.

"Spare you," he repeated, letting me go and turning away. And then, fronting me once more. "You little know what I would do with it, Mackellar! Did you think I had swallowed my defeat indeed? Listen: my life has been a series of unmerited cast-backs. That fool, Prince Charlie, mismanaged a most promising affair: there fell my first fortune. In Paris I had my foot once more high upon the ladder: that time it was an accident; a letter came to the wrong hand, and I was bare again. A third time, I found my opportunity; I built up a place for myself in India with an infinite patience; and then Clive came, my rajah was swallowed up, and I escaped out of the convulsion, like another Æneas, with Secundra Dass upon my back. Three times I have had my hand upon the highest station: and I am not yet three-and-forty. I know the world as few men know it when they come to die—Court and camp, the East and the West; I know where to go, I see a thousand openings. I am now at the height of my resources, sound of health, of inordinate ambition. Well, all this I resign; I care not if I die, and the world never hear of me; I care only for one thing, and that I will have. Mind yourself; lest, when the roof falls, you, too, should be crushed under the ruins."

As I came out of his house, all hope of intervention quite destroyed, I was aware of a stir on the harbour-side, and, raising my eyes, there was a great ship newly come to anchor. It seems strange I could have looked upon her with so much indifference, for she brought death to the brothers of Durrisdeer. After all the desperate episodes of this contention, the insults, the opposing interests, the fraternal duel in the shrubbery, it was reserved for some poor devil in Grub Street, scribbling for his dinner, and not caring what he scribbled, to cast a spell across four thousand miles of the salt sea, and send forth both these brothers into savage and wintry deserts, there to die. But such a thought was distant from my mind; and while all the provincials were fluttered about me by the unusual animation of their port, I passed throughout their midst on my return homeward, quite absorbed in the recollection of my visit and the Master's speech.

The same night there was brought to us from the ship a little packet of pamphlets. The next day my lord was under engagement to go with the Governor upon some party of pleasure; the time was nearly due, and I left him for a moment alone in his room and skimming through the pamphlets. When I returned, his head had fallen upon the table, his arms lying abroad amongst the crumpled papers.

"My lord, my lord!" I cried as I ran forward, for I supposed he was in some fit.

He sprang up like a figure upon wires, his countenance deformed with fury, so that in a strange place I should scarce have known him. His hand at the same time flew above his head, as though to strike me down. "Leave me alone!" he screeched, and I fled, as fast as my shaking legs would bear me, for my lady. She, too, lost no time; but when we returned, he had the door locked within, and only cried to us from the other side to leave him be. We looked in each other's faces, very white—each supposing the blow had come at last.

"I will write to the Governor to excuse him," says she. "We must keep our strong friends." But when she took up the pen, it flew out of her fingers. "I cannot write," said she. "Can you?"

"I will make a shift, my lady," said I.

She looked over me as I wrote. "That will do," she said, when I had done. "Thank God, Mackellar, I have you to lean upon! But what can it be now? What, what can it be?"

In my own mind, I believed there was no explanation possible, and none required; it was my fear that the man's madness had now simply burst forth its way, like the long-smothered flames of a volcano; but to this (in mere mercy to my lady) I durst not give expression.

"It is more to the purpose to consider our own behaviour," said I. "Must we leave him there alone?"

"I do not dare disturb him," she replied. "Nature may know best; it may be Nature that cries to be alone; and we grope in the dark. Oh yes, I would leave him as he is."

"I will, then, despatch this letter, my lady, and return here, if you please, to sit with you," said I.

"Pray do," cries my lady.

All afternoon we sat together, mostly in silence, watching my lord's door. My own mind was busy with the scene that had just passed, and its singular resemblance to my vision. I must say a word upon this, for the story has gone abroad with great exaggeration, and I have even seen it printed, and my own name referred to for particulars. So much was the same: here was my lord in a room, with his head upon the table, and when he raised his face, it wore such an expression as distressed me to the soul. But the room was different, my lord's attitude at the table not at all the same, and his face, when he disclosed it, expressed a painful degree of fury instead of that haunting despair which had always (except once, already referred to) characterised it in the vision. There is the whole truth at last before the public; and if the differences be great, the coincidence was yet enough to fill me with uneasiness. All afternoon, as I say, I sat and pondered upon this quite to myself; for my lady had trouble of her own, and it was my last thought to vex her with fancies. About the midst of our time of waiting, she conceived an ingenious scheme, had Mr. Alexander fetched, and bid him knock at his father's door. My lord sent the boy about his business, but without the least violence, whether of manner or expression; so that I began to entertain a hope the fit was over.

At last, as the night fell and I was lighting a lamp that stood there trimmed, the door opened and my lord stood within upon the threshold. The light was not so strong that we could read his countenance; when he spoke, methought his voice a little altered but yet perfectly steady.

"Mackellar," said he, "carry this note to its destination with your own hand. It is highly private. Find the person alone when you deliver it."

"Henry," says my lady, "you are not ill?"

"No, no," says he, querulously, "I am occupied. Not at all; I am only occupied. It is a singular thing a man must be supposed to be ill when he has any business! Send me supper to this room, and a basket of wine: I expect the visit of a friend. Otherwise I am not to be disturbed."

And with that he once more shut himself in.

The note was addressed to one Captain Harris, at a tavern on the portside. I knew Harris (by reputation) for a dangerous adventurer, highly suspected of piracy in the past, and now following the rude business of an Indian trader. What my lord should have to say to him, or he to my lord, it passed my imagination to conceive: or yet how my lord had heard of him, unless by a disgraceful trial from which the man was recently escaped. Altogether I went upon the errand with reluctance, and from the little I saw of the captain, returned from it with sorrow. I found him in a foul-smelling chamber, sitting by a guttering candle and an empty bottle; he had the remains of a military carriage, or rather perhaps it was an affectation, for his manners were low.

"Tell my lord, with my service, that I will wait upon his lordship in the inside of half an hour," says he, when he had read the note; and then had the servility, pointing to his empty bottle, to propose that I should buy him liquor.

Although I returned with my best speed, the Captain followed close upon my heels, and he stayed late into the night. The cock was crowing a second time when I saw (from my chamber window) my lord lighting him to the gate, both men very much affected with their potations, and sometimes leaning one upon the other to confabulate. Yet the next morning my lord was abroad again early with a hundred pounds of money in his pocket. I never supposed that he returned with it; and yet I was quite sure it did not find its way to the Master, for I lingered all morning within view of the booth. That was the last time my Lord Durrisdeer passed his own enclosure till we left New York; he walked in his barn, or sat and talked with his family, all much as usual; but the town saw nothing of him, and his daily visits to the Master seemed forgotten. Nor yet did Harris reappear; or not until the end.

I was now much oppressed with a sense of the mysteries in which we had begun to move. It was plain, if only from his change of habitude, my lord had something on his mind of a grave nature; but what it was, whence it sprang, or why he should now keep the house and garden, I could make no guess at. It was clear, even to probation, the pamphlets had some share in this revolution; I read all I could find, and they were all extremely insignificant, and of the usual kind of party scurrility; even to a high politician, I could spy out no particular matter of offence, and my lord was a man rather indifferent on public questions. The truth is, the pamphlet which was the spring of this affair, lay all the time on my lord's bosom. There it was that I found it at last, after he was dead, in the midst of the north wilderness: in such a place, in such dismal circumstances, I was to read for the first time these idle, lying words of a Whig pamphleteer declaiming against indulgency to Jacobites:—"Another notorious Rebel, the M—r of B—e, is to have his Title restored," the passage ran. "This Business has been long in hand, since he rendered some very disgraceful Services in Scotland and France. His Brother, *L—d D—r*, is known to be no better than himself in Inclination; and the supposed Heir, who is now to be set aside, was bred up in the most detestable Principles. In the old Phrase, it is *six of the one and half a dozen of the other*; but the Favour of such a Reposition is too extreme to be passed over." A man in his right wits could not have cared two straws for a tale so manifestly false; that Government should ever entertain the notion, was inconceivable to any reasoning creature, unless possibly the fool that penned it; and my lord, though never brilliant, was ever remarkable for sense. That he should credit such a rodomontade, and carry the pamphlet on his bosom and the words in his heart, is the clear proof of the man's lunacy. Doubtless the mere mention of Mr. Alexander, and the threat directly held out against the child's succession, precipitated that which had so long impended. Or else my master had been truly mad for a long time, and we were too dull or too much used to him, and did not perceive the extent of his infirmity.

About a week after the day of the pamphlets I was late upon the harbour-side, and took a turn towards the Master's, as I often did. The door opened, a flood of light came forth upon the road, and I beheld a man taking his departure with friendly salutations. I cannot say how singularly I was shaken to recognise the adventurer Harris. I could not but conclude it was the hand of my lord that had brought him there; and prolonged my walk in very serious and apprehensive thought. It was late when I came home, and there was my lord making up his portmanteau for a voyage.

"Why do you come so late?" he cried. "We leave to-morrow for Albany, you and I together; and it is high time you were about your preparations."

"For Albany, my lord?" I cried. "And for what earthly purpose?"

"Change of scene," said he.

And my lady, who appeared to have been weeping, gave me the signal to obey without more parley. She told me a little later (when we found occasion to exchange some words) that he had suddenly announced his intention after a visit from Captain Harris, and her best endeavours, whether to dissuade him from the journey, or to elicit some explanation of its purpose, had alike proved unavailing.

II

THE JOURNEY IN THE WILDERNESS

We made a prosperous voyage up that fine river of the Hudson, the weather grateful, the hills singularly beautified with the colours of the autumn. At Albany we had our residence at an inn, where I was not so blind and my lord not so cunning but what I could see he had some design to hold me prisoner. The work he found for me to do was not so pressing that we should transact it apart from necessary papers in the chamber of an inn; nor was it of such importance that I should be set upon as many as four or five scrolls of the same document. I submitted in appearance; but I took private measures on my own side, and had the news of the town communicated to me daily by the politeness of our host. In this way I received at last a piece of intelligence for which, I may say, I had been waiting. Captain Harris (I was told) with "Mr. Mountain, the trader," had gone by up the river in a boat. I would have feared the landlord's eye, so strong the sense of some complicity upon my master's part oppressed me. But I made out to say I had some knowledge of the Captain, although none of Mr. Mountain, and to inquire who else was of the party. My informant knew not; Mr. Mountain had come ashore upon some needful purchases; had gone round the town buying, drinking, and prating; and it seemed the party went upon some likely venture, for he had spoken much of great things he would do when he returned. No more was known, for none of the rest had come ashore, and it seemed they were pressed for time to reach a certain spot before the snow should fall.

And sure enough, the next day, there fell a sprinkle even in Albany; but it passed as it came, and was but a reminder of what lay before us. I thought of it lightly then, knowing so little as I did of that inclement province: the retrospect is different; and I wonder at times if some of the horror of there events which I must now rehearse flowed not from the foul skies and savage winds to which we were exposed, and the agony of cold that we must suffer.

The boat having passed by, I thought at first we should have left the town. But no such matter. My lord continued his stay in Albany where he had no ostensible affairs, and kept me by him, far from my due employment, and making a pretence of occupation. It is upon this passage I expect, and perhaps deserve, censure. I was not so dull but what I had my own thoughts. I could not see the Master entrust himself into the hands of Harris, and not suspect some underhand contrivance. Harris bore a villainous reputation, and he had been tampered with in private by my lord; Mountain, the trader, proved, upon inquiry, to be another of the same kidney; the errand they were all gone upon being the recovery of ill-gotten treasures, offered in itself a very strong incentive to foul play; and the character of the country where they journeyed promised impunity to deeds of blood. Well: it is true I had all these thoughts and fears, and guesses of the Master's fate. But you are to consider I was the same man that sought to dash him from the bulwarks of a ship in the mid-sea; the same that, a little before, very impiously but sincerely offered God a bargain, seeking to hire God to be my bravo. It is true again that I had a good deal melted towards our enemy. But this I always thought of as a weakness of the flesh and even culpable; my mind remaining steady and quite bent against him. True, yet again, that it was one thing to assume on my own shoulders the guilt and danger of a criminal attempt, and another to stand by and see my lord imperil and besmirch himself. But this was the very ground of my inaction. For (should I anyway stir in the business) I might fail indeed to save the Master, but I could not miss to make a byword of my lord.

Thus it was that I did nothing; and upon the same reasons, I am still strong to justify my course. We lived meanwhile in Albany, but though alone together in a strange place, had little traffic beyond formal salutations. My lord had carried with him several introductions to chief people of the town and neighbourhood; others he had before encountered in New York: with this consequence, that he went much abroad, and I am sorry to say was altogether too convivial in his habits. I was often in bed, but never asleep, when he returned; and there was scarce a night when he did not betray the influence of liquor. By day he would still lay upon me endless tasks, which he showed considerable ingenuity to fish up and renew, in the manner of Penelope's web. I never refused, as I say, for I was hired to do his bidding; but I took no pains to keep my penetration under a bushel, and would sometimes smile in his face.

"I think I must be the devil and you Michael Scott," I said to him one day. "I have bridged Tweed and split the Eildons; and now you set me to the rope of sand."

He looked at me with shining eyes, and looked away again, his jaw chewing, but without words.

"Well, well, my lord," said I, "your will is my pleasure. I will do this thing for the fourth time; but I would beg of you to invent another task against to-morrow, for by my troth, I am weary of this one."

"You do not know what you are saying," returned my lord, putting on his hat and turning his back to me. "It is a strange thing you should take a pleasure to annoy me. A friend—but that is a different affair. It is a strange thing. I am a man that has had ill-fortune all my life through. I am still surrounded by contrivances. I am always treading in plots," he burst out. "The whole world is banded against me."

"I would not talk wicked nonsense if I were you," said I; "but I will tell you what I *would* do —I would put my head in cold water, for you had more last night than you could carry."

"Do ye think that?" said he, with a manner of interest highly awakened. "Would that be good for me? It's a thing I never tried."

"I mind the days when you had no call to try, and I wish, my lord, that they were back again," said I. "But the plain truth is, if you continue to exceed, you will do yourself a mischief."

"I don't appear to carry drink the way I used to," said my lord. "I get overtaken, Mackellar. But I will be more upon my guard."

"That is what I would ask of you," I replied. "You are to bear in mind that you are Mr. Alexander's father: give the bairn a chance to carry his name with some responsibility."

"Ay, ay," said he. "Ye're a very sensible man, Mackellar, and have been long in my employ.

But I think, if you have nothing more to say to me I will be stepping. If you have nothing more to say?" he added, with that burning, childish eagerness that was now so common with the man.

"No, my lord, I have nothing more," said I, dryly enough.

"Then I think I will be stepping," says my lord, and stood and looked at me fidgeting with his hat, which he had taken off again. "I suppose you will have no errands? No? I am to meet Sir William Johnson, but I will be more upon my guard." He was silent for a time, and then, smiling: "Do you call to mind a place, Mackellar—it's a little below Engles—where the burn runs very deep under a wood of rowans. I mind being there when I was a lad—dear, it comes over me like an old song!—I was after the fishing, and I made a bonny cast. Eh, but I was happy. I wonder, Mackellar, why I am never happy now?"

"My lord," said I, "if you would drink with more moderation you would have the better chance. It is an old byword that the bottle is a false consoler."

"No doubt," said he, "no doubt. Well, I think I will be going."

"Good-morning, my lord," said I.

"Good-morning, good-morning," said he, and so got himself at last from the apartment.

I give that for a fair specimen of my lord in the morning; and I must have described my patron very ill if the reader does not perceive a notable falling off. To behold the man thus fallen: to know him accepted among his companions for a poor, muddled toper, welcome (if he were welcome at all) for the bare consideration of his title; and to recall the virtues he had once displayed against such odds of fortune; was not this a thing at once to rage and to be humbled at?

In his cups, he was more expensive. I will give but the one scene, close upon the end, which is strongly marked upon my memory to this day, and at the time affected me almost with horror.

I was in bed, lying there awake, when I heard him stumbling on the stair and singing. My lord had no gift of music, his brother had all the graces of the family, so that when I say singing, you are to understand a manner of high, carolling utterance, which was truly neither speech nor song. Something not unlike is to be heard upon the lips of children, ere they learn shame; from those of a man grown elderly, it had a strange effect. He opened the door with noisy precaution; peered in, shading his candle; conceived me to slumber; entered, set his light upon the table, and took off his hat. I saw him very plain; a high, feverish exultation appeared to boil in his veins, and he stood and smiled and smirked upon the candle. Presently he lifted up his arm, snapped his fingers, and fell to undress. As he did so, having once more forgot my presence, he took back to his singing; and now I could hear the words, which were those from the old song of the *Twa Corbies* endlessly repeated:

> *"And over his banes when they are bare*
> *The wind sall blaw for evermair!"*

I have said there was no music in the man. His strains had no logical succession except in so far as they inclined a little to the minor mode; but they exercised a rude potency upon the feelings, and followed the words, and signified the feelings of the singer with barbaric fitness. He took it first in the time and manner of a rant; presently this ill-favoured gleefulness abated, he began to dwell upon the notes more feelingly, and sank at last into a degree of maudlin pathos that was to me scarce bearable. By equal steps, the original briskness of his acts declined; and when he was stripped to his breeches, he sat on the bedside and fell to whimpering. I know nothing less respectable than the tears of drunkenness, and turned my back impatiently on this poor sight.

But he had started himself (I am to suppose) on that slippery descent of self-pity; on the which, to a man unstrung by old sorrows and recent potations there is no arrest except exhaustion. His tears continued to flow, and the man to sit there, three parts naked, in the cold air of the chamber. I twitted myself alternately with inhumanity and sentimental weakness, now half rising in my bed to interfere, now reading myself lessons of indifference and courting slumber, until, upon a sudden, the *quantum mutatus ab illo* shot into my mind; and calling to remembrance his old wisdom, constancy, and patience, I was overborne with a pity almost approaching the passionate, not for my master alone but for the sons of man.

At this I leaped from my place, went over to his side and laid a hand on his bare shoulder, which was cold as stone. He uncovered his face and showed it me all swollen and begrutten[1] like a child's; and at the sight my impatience partially revived.

"Think shame to yourself," said I. "This is bairnly conduct. I might have been snivelling myself, if I had cared to swill my belly with wine. But I went to my bed sober like a man. Come: get into yours, and have done with this pitiable exhibition."

"Oh, Mackellar," said he, "my heart is wae!"

"Wae?" cried I. "For a good cause, I think. What words were these you sang as you came in? Show pity to others, we then can talk of pity to yourself. You can be the one thing or the other, but I will be no party to half-way houses. If you're a striker, strike, and if you're a bleater, bleat!"

"Cry!" cries he, with a burst, "that's it—strike! that's talking! Man, I've stood it all too long. But when they laid a hand upon the child, when the child's threatened"—his momentary vigour whimpering off—"my child, my Alexander!"—and he was at his tears again.

I took him by the shoulders and shook him. "Alexander!" said I. "Do you even think of him? Not you! Look yourself in the face like a brave man, and you'll find you're but a self-deceiver. The wife, the friend, the child, they're all equally forgot, and you sunk in a mere log of selfishness."

"Mackellar," said he, with a wonderful return to his old manner and appearance, "you may say what you will of me, but one thing I never was—I was never selfish."

"I will open your eyes in your despite," said I. "How long have we been here? and how often have you written to your family? I think this is the first time you were ever separate: have you written at all? Do they know if you are dead or living?"

I had caught him here too openly; it braced his better nature; there was no more weeping, he thanked me very penitently, got to bed and was soon fast asleep; and the first thing he did the next morning was to sit down and begin a letter to my lady: a very tender letter it was too, though it was never finished. Indeed all communication with New York was transacted by myself; and it will be judged I had a thankless task of it. What to tell my lady and in what words, and how far to be false and how far cruel, was a thing that kept me often from my slumber.

All this while, no doubt, my lord waited with growing impatiency for news of his accomplices. Harris, it is to be thought, had promised a high degree of expedition; the time was already overpast when word was to be looked for; and suspense was a very evil counsellor to a man of an impaired intelligence. My lord's mind throughout this interval dwelled almost wholly in the Wilderness, following that party with whose deeds he had so much concern. He continually conjured up their camps and progresses, the fashion of the country, the perpetration in a thousand different manners of the same horrid fact, and that consequent spectacle of the Master's bones lying scattered in the wind. These private, guilty considerations I would continually observe to peep forth in the man's talk, like rabbits from a hill. And it is the less wonder if the scene of his meditations began to draw him bodily.

It is well known what pretext he took. Sir William Johnson had a diplomatic errand in these parts; and my lord and I (from curiosity, as was given out) went in his company. Sir William was well attended and liberally supplied. Hunters brought us venison, fish was taken for us daily in the streams, and brandy ran like water. We proceeded by day and encamped by night in the military style; sentinels were set and changed; every man had his named duty; and Sir William was the spring of all. There was much in this that might at times have entertained me; but for our misfortune, the weather was extremely harsh, the days were in the beginning open, but the nights frosty from the first. A painful keen wind blew most of the time, so that we sat in the boat with blue fingers, and at night, as we scorched our faces at the fire, the clothes upon our back appeared to be of paper. A dreadful solitude surrounded our steps; the land was quite dispeopled, there was no smoke of fires, and save for a single boat of merchants on the second day, we met no travellers. The season was indeed late, but this desertion of the waterways impressed Sir William himself; and I have heard him more than once express a sense of intimidation. "I have come too late, I fear; they must have dug up the hatchet;" he said; and the future proved how justly he had reasoned.

I could never depict the blackness of my soul upon this journey. I have none of those minds that are in love with the unusual: to see the winter coming and to lie in the field so far from any house, oppressed me like a nightmare; it seemed, indeed, a kind of awful braving of God's power; and this thought, which I daresay only writes me down a coward, was greatly exaggerated by my private knowledge of the errand we were come upon. I was besides encumbered by my duties to Sir William, whom it fell upon me to entertain; for my lord was quite sunk into a state bordering on *pervigilium*, watching the woods with a rapt eye, sleeping scarce at all, and speaking sometimes not twenty words in a whole day. That which he said was still coherent; but it turned almost invariably upon the party for whom he kept his crazy lookout. He would tell Sir William often, and always as if it were a new communication, that he had "a brother somewhere in the woods," and beg that the sentinels should be directed "to inquire for him." "I am anxious for news of my brother," he would say. And sometimes, when we were under way, he would fancy he spied a canoe far off upon the water or a camp on the shore, and exhibit painful agitation. It was impossible but Sir William should be struck with these singularities; and at last he led me aside, and hinted his uneasiness. I touched my head and shook it; quite rejoiced to prepare a little testimony against possible disclosures.

"But in that case," cries Sir William, "is it wise to let him go at large?"

"Those that know him best," said I, "are persuaded that he should be humoured."

"Well, well," replied Sir William, "it is none of my affairs. But if I had understood, you would never have been here."

Our advance into this savage country had thus uneventfully proceeded for about a week, when we encamped for a night at a place where the river ran among considerable mountains clothed in wood. The fires were lighted on a level space at the water's edge; and we supped and lay down to sleep in the customary fashion. It chanced the night fell murderously cold; the stringency of the frost seized and bit me through my coverings so that pain kept me wakeful; and I was afoot again before the peep of day, crouching by the fires or trotting to and for at the stream's edge, to combat the aching of my limbs. At last dawn began to break upon hoar woods and mountains, the sleepers rolled in their robes, and the boisterous river dashing among spears of ice. I stood looking about me, swaddled in my stiff coat of a bull's fur, and the breath smoking from my scorched nostrils, when, upon a sudden, a singular, eager cry rang from the borders of the wood. The sentries answered it, the sleepers sprang to their feet; one pointed, the rest followed his direction with their eyes, and there, upon the edge of the forest and betwixt two trees, we beheld the figure of a man reaching forth his hands like one in ecstasy. The next moment he ran forward, fell on his knees at the side of the camp, and burst in tears.

This was John Mountain, the trader, escaped from the most horrid perils; and his fist word, when he got speech, was to ask if we had seen Secundra Dass.

"Seen what?" cries Sir William.

"No," said I, "we have seen nothing of him. Why?"

"Nothing?" says Mountain. "Then I was right after all." With that he struck his palm upon his brow. "But what takes him back?" he cried. "What takes the man back among dead bodies. There is some damned mystery here."

This was a word which highly aroused our curiosity, but I shall be more perspicacious, if I narrate these incidents in their true order. Here follows a narrative which I have compiled out of three sources, not very consistent in all points:

First, a written statement by Mountain, in which everything criminal is cleverly smuggled out of view;

Second, two conversations with Secundra Dass; and

Third, many conversations with Mountain himself, in which he was pleased to be entirely plain; for the truth is he regarded me as an accomplice.

NARRATIVE OF THE TRADER, MOUNTAIN.

The crew that went up the river under the joint command of Captain Harris and the Master numbered in all nine persons, of whom (if I except Secundra Dass) there was not one that had not merited the gallows. From Harris downward the voyagers were notorious in that colony for desperate, bloody-minded miscreants; some were reputed pirates, the most hawkers of rum; all ranters and drinkers; all fit associates, embarking together without remorse, upon this treacherous and murderous design. I could not hear there was much discipline or any set captain in the gang; but Harris and four others, Mountain himself, two Scotchmen—Pinkerton and Hastie—and a man of the name of Hicks, a drunken shoemaker, put their heads together and agreed upon the course. In a material sense, they were well enough provided; and the Master in particular brought with him a tent where he might enjoy some privacy and shelter.

Even this small indulgence told against him in the minds of his companions. But indeed he was in a position so entirely false (and even ridiculous) that all his habit of command and arts of pleasing were here thrown away. In the eyes of all, except Secundra Dass, he figured as a common gull and designated victim; going unconsciously to death; yet he could not but suppose himself the contriver and the leader of the expedition; he could scarce help but so conduct himself and at the least hint of authority or condescension, his deceivers would be laughing in their sleeves. I was so used to see and to conceive him in a high, authoritative attitude, that when I had conceived his position on this journey, I was pained and could have blushed. How soon he may have entertained a first surmise, we cannot know; but it was long, and the party had advanced into the Wilderness beyond the reach of any help, ere he was fully awakened to the truth.

It fell thus. Harris and some others had drawn apart into the woods for consultation, when they were startled by a rustling in the brush. They were all accustomed to the arts of Indian warfare, and Mountain had not only lived and hunted, but fought and earned some reputation, with the savages. He could move in the woods without noise, and follow a trail like a hound;

and upon the emergence of this alert, he was deputed by the rest to plunge into the thicket for intelligence. He was soon convinced there was a man in his close neighbourhood, moving with precaution but without art among the leaves and branches; and coming shortly to a place of advantage, he was able to observe Secundra Dass crawling briskly off with many backward glances. At this he knew not whether to laugh or cry; and his accomplices, when he had returned and reported, were in much the same dubiety. There was now no danger of an Indian onslaught; but on the other hand, since Secundra Dass was at the pains to spy upon them, it was highly probable he knew English, and if he knew English it was certain the whole of their design was in the Master's knowledge. There was one singularity in the position. If Secundra Dass knew and concealed his knowledge of English, Harris was a proficient in several of the tongues of India, and as his career in that part of the world had been a great deal worse than profligate, he had not thought proper to remark upon the circumstance. Each side had thus a spy-hole on the counsels of the other. The plotters, so soon as this advantage was explained, returned to camp; Harris, hearing the Hindustani was once more closeted with his master, crept to the side of the tent; and the rest, sitting about the fire with their tobacco, awaited his report with impatience. When he came at last, his face was very black. He had overheard enough to confirm the worst of his suspicions. Secundra Dass was a good English scholar; he had been some days creeping and listening, the Master was now fully informed of the conspiracy, and the pair proposed on the morrow to fall out of line at a carrying place and plunge at a venture in the woods: preferring the full risk of famine, savage beasts, and savage men to their position in the midst of traitors.

What, then, was to be done? Some were for killing the Master on the spot; but Harris assured them that would be a crime without profit, since the secret of the treasure must die along with him that buried it. Others were for desisting at once from the whole enterprise and making for New York; but the appetising name of treasure, and the thought of the long way they had already travelled dissuaded the majority. I imagine they were dull fellows for the most part. Harris, indeed, had some acquirements, Mountain was no fool, Hastie was an educated man; but even these had manifestly failed in life, and the rest were the dregs of colonial rascality. The conclusion they reached, at least, was more the offspring of greed and hope, than reason. It was to temporise, to be wary and watch the Master, to be silent and supply no further aliment to his suspicions, and to depend entirely (as well as I make out) on the chance that their victim was as greedy, hopeful, and irrational as themselves, and might, after all, betray his life and treasure.

Twice in the course of the next day Secundra and the Master must have appeared to themselves to have escaped; and twice they were circumvented. The Master, save that the second time he grew a little pale, displayed no sign of disappointment, apologised for the stupidity with which he had fallen aside, thanked his recapturers as for a service, and rejoined the caravan with all his usual gallantry and cheerfulness of mien and bearing. But it is certain he had smelled a rat; for from thenceforth he and Secundra spoke only in each other's ear, and Harris listened and shivered by the tent in vain. The same night it was announced they were to leave the boats and proceed by foot, a circumstance which (as it put an end to the confusion of the portages) greatly lessened the chances of escape.

And now there began between the two sides a silent contest, for life on the one hand, for riches on the other. They were now near that quarter of the desert in which the Master himself must begin to play the part of guide; and using this for a pretext of persecution, Harris and his men sat with him every night about the fire, and laboured to entrap him into some admission. If he let slip his secret, he knew well it was the warrant for his death; on the other hand, he durst not refuse their questions, and must appear to help them to the best of his capacity, or he practically published his mistrust. And yet Mountain assures me the man's brow was never ruffled. He sat in the midst of these jackals, his life depending by a thread, like some easy, witty householder at home by his own fire; an answer he had for everything—as often as not, a jesting answer; avoided threats, evaded insults; talked, laughed, and listened with an open countenance; and, in short, conducted himself in such a manner as must have disarmed suspicion, and went near to stagger knowledge. Indeed, Mountain confessed to me they would soon have disbelieved the Captain's story, and supposed their designated victim still quite innocent of their designs; but for the fact that he continued (however ingeniously) to give the slip to questions, and the yet stronger confirmation of his repeated efforts to escape. The last of these, which brought things to a head, I am now to relate. And first I should say that by this time the temper of Harris's companions was utterly worn out; civility was scarce pretended; and for one very significant circumstance, the Master and Secundra had been (on some pretext) deprived of weapons. On their side, however, the threatened pair kept up the parade of friendship handsomely; Secundra was all bows, the Master all smiles; and on the last night of the truce he had even gone so far as to sing for the diversion of the company. It was observed that he had also eaten with unusual heartiness, and drank deep, doubtless from design.

At least, about three in the morning, he came out of the tent into the open air, audibly mourning and complaining, with all the manner of a sufferer from surfeit. For some while, Secundra publicly attended on his patron, who at last became more easy, and fell asleep on the frosty ground behind the tent, the Indian returning within. Some time after, the sentry was changed; had the Master pointed out to him, where he lay in what is called a robe of buffalo: and thenceforth kept an eye upon him (he declared) without remission. With the first of the dawn, a draught of wind came suddenly and blew open one side the corner of the robe; and with the same puff, the Master's hat whirled in the air and fell some yards away. The sentry thinking it remarkable the sleeper should not awaken, thereupon drew near; and the next moment, with a great shout, informed the camp their prisoner was escaped. He had left behind his Indian, who (in the first vivacity of the surprise) came near to pay the forfeit of his life, and was, in fact, inhumanly mishandled; but Secundra, in the midst of threats and cruelties, stuck to it with extraordinary loyalty, that he was quite ignorant of his master's plans, which might indeed be true, and of the manner of his escape, which was demonstrably false. Nothing was therefore left to the conspirators but to rely entirely on the skill of Mountain. The night had been frosty, the ground quite hard; and the sun was no sooner up than a strong thaw set in. It was Mountain's boast that few men could have followed that trail, and still fewer (even of the native Indians) found it. The Master had thus a long start before his pursuers had the scent, and he must have travelled with surprising energy for a pedestrian so unused, since it was near noon before Mountain had a view of him. At this conjuncture the trader was alone, all his companions following, at his own request, several hundred yards in the rear; he knew the Master was unarmed; his heart was besides heated with the exercise and lust of hunting; and seeing the quarry so close, so defenceless, and seeming so fatigued, he vain-gloriously determined to effect the capture with his single hand. A step or two farther brought him to one margin of a little clearing; on the other, with his arms folded and his back to a huge stone, the Master sat. It is possible Mountain may have made a rustle, it is certain, at least, the Master raised his head and gazed directly at that quarter of the thicket where his hunter lay; "I could not be sure he saw me," Mountain said; "he just looked my way like a man with his mind made up, and all the courage ran out of me like rum out of a bottle." And presently, when the Master looked away again, and appeared to resume those meditations in which he had sat immersed before the trader's coming, Mountain slunk stealthily back and returned to seek the help of his companions.

And now began the chapter of surprises, for the scout had scarce informed the others of his discovery, and they were yet preparing their weapons for a rush upon the fugitive, when the man himself appeared in their midst, walking openly and quietly, with his hands behind his back.

"Ah, men!" says he, on his beholding them. "Here is a fortunate encounter. Let us get back to camp."

Mountain had not mentioned his own weakness or the Master's disconcerting gaze upon the thicket, so that (with all the rest) his return appeared spontaneous. For all that, a hubbub arose; oaths flew, fists were shaken, and guns pointed.

"Let us get back to camp," said the Master. "I have an explanation to make, but it must be laid before you all. And in the meanwhile I would put up these weapons, one of which might very easily go off and blow away your hopes of treasure. I would not kill," says he, smiling, "the goose with the golden eggs."

The charm of his superiority once more triumphed; and the party, in no particular order, set off on their return. By the way, he found occasion to get a word or two apart with Mountain.

"You are a clever fellow and a bold," says he, "but I am not so sure that you are doing yourself justice. I would have you to consider whether you would not do better, ay, and safer, to serve me instead of serving so commonplace a rascal as Mr. Harris. Consider of it," he concluded, dealing the man a gentle tap upon the shoulder, "and don't be in haste. Dead or alive, you will find me an ill man to quarrel with."

When they were come back to the camp, where Harris and Pinkerton stood guard over Secundra, these two ran upon the Master like viragoes, and were amazed out of measure when they were bidden by their comrades to "stand back and hear what the gentleman had to say." The Master had not flinched before their onslaught; nor, at this proof of the ground he had gained, did he betray the least sufficiency.

"Do not let us be in haste," says he. "Meat first and public speaking after."

With that they made a hasty meal: and as soon as it was done, the Master, leaning on one elbow, began his speech. He spoke long, addressing himself to each except Harris, finding for each (with the same exception) some particular flattery. He called them "bold, honest blades," declared he had never seen a more jovial company, work better done, or pains more merrily supported. "Well, then," says he, "some one asks me, Why the devil I ran away? But that is scarce worth answer, for I think you all know pretty well. But you know only pretty well: that is a point I shall arrive at presently, and be you ready to remark it when it comes. There is a traitor here: a double traitor: I will give you his name before I am done; and let that suffice for now. But here comes some other gentleman and asks me, 'Why, in the devil, I came back?' Well, before I answer that question, I have one to put to you. It was this cur here, this Harris, that speaks Hindustani?" cries he, rising on one knee and pointing fair at the man's face, with a gesture indescribably menacing; and when he had been answered in the affirmative, "Ah!" says he, "then are all my suspicions verified, and I did rightly to come back. Now, men, hear the truth for the first time." Thereupon he launched forth in a long story, told with extraordinary skill, how he had all along suspected Harris, how he had found the confirmation of his fears, and how Harris must have misrepresented what passed between Secundra and himself. At this point he made a bold stroke with excellent effect. "I suppose," says he, "you think you are going shares with Harris; I suppose you think you will see to that yourselves; you would naturally not think so flat a rogue could cozen you. But have a care! These half idiots have a sort of cunning, as the skunk has its stench; and it may be news to you that Harris has taken care of himself already. Yes, for him the treasure is all money in the bargain. You must find it or go starve. But he has been paid beforehand; my brother paid him to destroy me; look at him, if you doubt—look at him, grinning and gulping, a detected thief!" Thence, having made this happy impression, he explained how he had escaped, and thought better of it, and at last concluded to come back, lay the truth before the company, and take his chance with them once more: persuaded as he was, they would instantly depose Harris and elect some other leader. "There is the whole truth," said he: "and with one exception, I put myself entirely in your hands. What is the exception? There he sits," he cried, pointing once more to Harris; "a man that has to die! Weapons and conditions are all one to me; put me face to face with him, and if you give me nothing but a stick, in five minutes I will show you a sop of broken carrion, fit for dogs to roll in."

It was dark night when he made an end; they had listened in almost perfect silence; but the firelight scarce permitted any one to judge, from the look of his neighbours, with what result of persuasion or conviction. Indeed, the Master had set himself in the brightest place, and kept his face there, to be the centre of men's eyes: doubtless on a profound calculation. Silence followed for awhile, and presently the whole party became involved in disputation: the Master lying on his back, with his hands knit under his head and one knee flung across the other, like a person unconcerned in the result. And here, I daresay, his bravado carried him too far and prejudiced his case. At least, after a cast or two back and forward, opinion settled finally against him. It's possible he hoped to repeat the business of the pirate ship, and be himself, perhaps, on hard enough conditions, elected leader; and things went so far that way, that Mountain actually threw out the proposition. But the rock he split upon was Hastie. This fellow was not well liked, being sour and slow, with an ugly, glowering disposition, but he had studied some time for the church at Edinburgh College, before ill conduct had destroyed his prospects, and he now remembered and applied what he had learned. Indeed he had not proceeded very far, when the Master rolled carelessly upon one side, which was done (in Mountain's opinion) to conceal the beginnings of despair upon his countenance. Hastie dismissed the most of what they had heard as nothing to the matter: what they wanted was the treasure. All that was said of Harris might be true, and they would have to see to that in time. But what had that to do with the treasure? They had heard a vast of words; but the truth was just this, that Mr. Durie was damnably frightened and had several times run off. Here he was—whether caught or come back was all one to Hastie: the point was to make an end of the business. As for the talk of deposing and electing captains, he hoped they were all free men and could attend their own affairs. That was dust flung in their eyes, and so was the proposal to fight Harris. "He shall fight no one in this camp, I can tell him that," said Hastie. "We had trouble enough to get his arms away from him, and we should look pretty fools to give them back again. But if it's excitement the gentleman is after, I can supply him with more than perhaps he cares about. For I have no intention to spend the remainder of my life in these mountains; already I have been too long; and I propose that he should immediately tell us where that treasure is, or else immediately be shot. And there," says he, producing his weapon, "there is the pistol that I mean to use."

"Come, I call you a man," cries the Master, sitting up and looking at the speaker with an air of admiration.

"I didn't ask you to call me anything," returned Hastie; "which is it to be?"

"That's an idle question," said the Master. "Needs must when the devil drives. The truth is we are within easy walk of the place, and I will show it you to-morrow."

With that, as if all were quite settled, and settled exactly to his mind, he walked off to his tent, whither Secundra had preceded him.

I cannot think of these last turns and wriggles of my old enemy except with admiration; scarce even pity is mingled with the sentiment, so strongly the man supported, so boldly resisted his misfortunes. Even at that hour, when he perceived himself quite lost, when he saw he had but effected an exchange of enemies, and overthrown Harris to set Hastie up, no sign of weakness appeared in his behaviour, and he withdrew to his tent, already determined (I must suppose) upon affronting the incredible hazard of his last expedient, with the same easy, assured, genteel expression and demeanour as he might have left a theatre withal to join a supper of the wits. But doubtless within, if we could see there, his soul trembled.

Early in the night, word went about the camp that he was sick; and the first thing the next morning he called Hastie to his side, and inquired most anxiously if he had any skill in medicine. As a matter of fact, this was a vanity of that fallen divinity student's, to which he had cunningly addressed himself. Hastie examined him; and being flattered, ignorant, and highly auspicious, knew not in the least whether the man was sick or malingering. In this state he went forth again to his companions; and (as the thing which would give himself most consequence either way) announced that the patient was in a fair way to die.

"For all that," he added with an oath, "and if he bursts by the wayside, he must bring us this morning to the treasure."

But there were several in the camp (Mountain among the number) whom this brutality revolted. They would have seen the Master pistolled, or pistolled him themselves, without the smallest sentiment of pity; but they seemed to have been touched by his gallant fight and unequivocal defeat the night before; perhaps, too, they were even already beginning to oppose themselves to their new leader: at least, they now declared that (if the man was sick) he should have a day's rest in spite of Hastie's teeth.

The next morning he was manifestly worse, and Hastie himself began to display something of humane concern, so easily does even the pretence of doctoring awaken sympathy. The third the Master called Mountain and Hastie to the tent, announced himself to be dying, gave them full particulars as to the position of the cache, and begged them to set out incontinently on the quest, so that they might see if he deceived them, and (if they were at first unsuccessful) he should be able to correct their error.

But here arose a difficulty on which he doubtless counted. None of these men would trust another, none would consent to stay behind. On the other hand, although the Master seemed extremely low, spoke scarce above a whisper, and lay much of the time insensible, it was still possible it was a fraudulent sickness; and if all went treasure-hunting, it might prove they had gone upon a wild-goose chase, and return to find their prisoner flown. They concluded, therefore, to hang idling round the camp, alleging sympathy to their reason; and certainly, so mingled are our dispositions, several were sincerely (if not very deeply) affected by the natural peril of the man whom they callously designed to murder. In the afternoon, Hastie was called to the bedside to pray: the which (incredible as it must appear) he did with unction; about eight at night, the wailing of Secundra announced that all was over; and before ten, the Indian, with a link stuck in the ground, was toiling at the grave. Sunrise of next day beheld the Master's burial, all hands attending with great decency of demeanour; and the body was laid in the earth, wrapped in a fur robe, with only the face uncovered; which last was of a waxy whiteness, and had the nostrils plugged according to some Oriental habit of Secundra's. No sooner was the grave filled than the lamentations of the Indian once more struck concern to every heart; and it appears this gang of murderers, so far from resenting his outcries, although both distressful and (in such a country) perilous to their own safety, roughly but kindly endeavoured to console him.

But if human nature is even in the worst of men occasionally kind, it is still, and before all things, greedy; and they soon turned from the mourner to their own concerns. The cache of the treasure being hard by, although yet unidentified, it was concluded not to break camp; and the day passed, on the part of the voyagers, in unavailing exploration of the woods, Secundra the while lying on his master's grave. That night they placed no sentinel, but lay altogether about the fire, in the customary woodman fashion, the heads outward, like the spokes of a wheel. Morning found them in the same disposition; only Pinkerton, who lay on Mountain's right, between him and Hastie, had (in the hours of darkness) been secretly butchered, and there lay, still wrapped as to his body in his mantle, but offering above that ungodly and horrific spectacle of the scalped head. The gang were that morning as pale as a company of phantoms, for the pertinacity of Indian war (or to speak more correctly, Indian murder) was well known to all. But they laid the chief blame on their unsentinelled posture; and fired with the neighbourhood of the treasure, determined to continue where they were. Pinkerton was buried hard by the Master; the survivors again passed the day in exploration, and returned in a mingled humour of anxiety and hope, being partly certain they were now close on the discovery of what they sought, and on the other hand (with the return of darkness) were infected with the fear of Indians. Mountain was the first sentry; he declares he neither slept nor yet sat down, but kept his watch with a perpetual and straining vigilance, and it was even with unconcern that (when he saw by the stars his time was up) he drew near the fire to awaken his successor. This man (it was Hicks the shoemaker) slept on the lee side of the circle, something farther off in consequence than those to windward, and in a place darkened by the blowing smoke. Mountain stooped and took him by the shoulder; his hand was at once smeared by some adhesive wetness; and (the wind at the moment veering) the firelight shone upon the sleeper, and showed him, like Pinkerton, dead and scalped.

It was clear they had fallen in the hands of one of those matchless Indian bravos, that will sometimes follow a party for days, and in spite of indefatigable travel, and unsleeping watch, continue to keep up with their advance, and steal a scalp at every resting-place. Upon this discovery, the treasure-seekers, already reduced to a poor half dozen, fell into mere dismay, seized a few necessaries, and deserting the remainder of their goods, fled outright into the forest. Their fire they left still burning, and their dead comrade unburied. All day they ceased not to flee, eating by the way, from hand to mouth; and since they feared to sleep, continued to advance at random even in the hours of darkness. But the limit of man's endurance is soon reached; when they rested at last it was to sleep profoundly; and when they woke, it was to find that the enemy was still upon their heels, and death and mutilation had once more lessened and deformed their company.

By this they had become light-headed, they had quite missed their path in the wilderness, their stores were already running low. With the further horrors, it is superfluous that I should swell this narrative, already too prolonged. Suffice it to say that when at length a night passed by innocuous, and they might breathe again in the hope that the murderer had at last desisted from pursuit, Mountain and Secundra were alone. The trader is firmly persuaded their unseen enemy was some warrior of his own acquaintance, and that he himself was spared by favour. The mercy extended to Secundra he explains on the ground that the East Indian was thought to be insane; partly from the fact that, through all the horrors of the flight and while others were casting away their very food and weapons, Secundra continued to stagger forward with a mattock on his shoulder, and partly because, in the last days and with a great degree of heat and fluency, he perpetually spoke with himself in his own language. But he was sane enough when it came to English.

"You think he will be gone quite away?" he asked, upon their blest awakening in safety.

"I pray God so, I believe so, I dare to believe so," Mountain had replied almost with incoherence, as he described the scene to me.

And indeed he was so much distempered that until he met us, the next morning, he could scarce be certain whether he had dreamed, or whether it was a fact, that Secundra had thereupon turned directly about and returned without a word upon their footprints, setting his face for these wintry and hungry solitudes, along a path whose every stage was mile-stoned with a mutilated corpse.

1. Tear-marked.

⸙ 12 ⸙

THE JOURNEY IN THE WILDERNESS (CONTINUED)

MOUNTAIN'S STORY, as it was laid before Sir William Johnson and my lord, was shorn, of course, of all the earlier particulars, and the expedition described to have proceeded uneventfully, until the Master sickened. But the latter part was very forcibly related, the speaker visibly thrilling to his recollections; and our then situation, on the fringe of the same desert, and the private interests of each, gave him an audience prepared to share in his emotions. For Mountain's intelligence not only changed the world for my Lord Durrisdeer, but materially affected the designs of Sir William Johnson.

These I find I must lay more at length before the reader. Word had reached Albany of dubious import; it had been rumoured some hostility was to be put in act; and the Indian diplomatist had, thereupon, sped into the wilderness, even at the approach of winter, to nip that mischief in the bud. Here, on the borders, he learned that he was come too late; and a difficult choice was thus presented to a man (upon the whole) not any more bold than prudent. His standing with the painted braves may be compared to that of my Lord President Culloden among the chiefs of our own Highlanders at the 'forty-five; that is as much as to say, he was, to these men, reason's only speaking trumpet, and counsels of peace and moderation, if they were to prevail at all, must prevail singly through his influence. If, then, he should return, the province must lie open to all the abominable tragedies of Indian war—the houses blaze, the wayfarer be cut off, and the men of the woods collect their usual disgusting spoil of human scalps. On the other side, to go farther forth, to risk so small a party deeper in the desert, to carry words of peace among warlike savages already rejoicing to return to war: here was an extremity from which it was easy to perceive his mind revolted.

"I have come too late," he said more than once, and would fall into a deep consideration, his head bowed in his hands, his foot patting the ground.

At length he raised his face and looked upon us, that is to say upon my lord, Mountain, and myself, sitting close round a small fire, which had been made for privacy in one corner of the camp.

"My lord, to be quite frank with you, I find myself in two minds," said he. "I think it very needful I should go on, but not at all proper I should any longer enjoy the pleasure of your company. We are here still upon the water side; and I think the risk to southward no great matter. Will not yourself and Mr. Mackellar take a single boat's crew and return to Albany?"

My lord, I should say, had listened to Mountain's narrative, regarding him throughout with a painful intensity of gaze; and since the tale concluded, had sat as in a dream. There was something very daunting in his look; something to my eyes not rightly human; the face, lean, and dark, and aged, the mouth painful, the teeth disclosed in a perpetual rictus; the eyeball swimming clear of the lids upon a field of blood-shot white. I could not behold him myself without a jarring irritation, such as, I believe, is too frequently the uppermost feeling on the sickness of those dear to us. Others, I could not but remark. were scarce able to support his neighbourhood—Sir William eviting to be near him, Mountain dodging his eye, and, when he met it, blenching and halting in his story. At this appeal, however, my lord appeared to recover his command upon himself.

"To Albany?" said he, with a good voice.

"Not short of it, at least," replied Sir William. "There is no safety nearer hand."

"I would be very sweir[1] to return," says my lord. "I am not afraid—of Indians," he added, with a jerk.

"I wish that I could say so much," returned Sir William, smiling; "although, if any man durst say it, it should be myself. But you are to keep in view my responsibility, and that as the voyage has now become highly dangerous, and your business—if you ever had any," says he, "brought quite to a conclusion by the distressing family intelligence you have received, I should be hardly justified if I even suffered you to proceed, and run the risk of some obloquy if anything regrettable should follow."

My lord turned to Mountain. "What did he pretend he died of?" he asked.

"I don't think I understand your honour," said the trader, pausing like a man very much affected, in the dressing of some cruel frost-bites.

For a moment my lord seemed at a full stop; and then, with some irritation, "I ask you what he died of. Surely that's a plain question," said he.

"Oh! I don't know," said Mountain. "Hastie even never knew. He seemed to sicken natural, and just pass away."

"There it is, you see!" concluded my lord, turning to Sir William.

"Your lordship is too deep for me," replied Sir William.

"Why," says my lord, "this in a matter of succession; my son's title may be called in doubt; and the man being supposed to be dead of nobody can tell what, a great deal of suspicion would be naturally roused."

"But, God damn me, the man's buried!" cried Sir William.

"I will never believe that," returned my lord, painfully trembling. "I'll never believe it!" he cried again, and jumped to his feet. "Did he *look* dead?" he asked of Mountain.

"Look dead?" repeated the trader. "He looked white. Why, what would he be at? I tell you, I put the sods upon him."

My lord caught Sir William by the coat with a hooked hand. "This man has the name of my brother," says he, "but it's well understood that he was never canny."

"Canny?" says Sir William. "What is that?"

"He's not of this world," whispered my lord, "neither him nor the black deil that serves him. I have struck my sword throughout his vitals," he cried; "I have felt the hilt dirl[2] on his breastbone, and the hot blood spirt in my very face, time and again, time and again!" he repeated, with a gesture indescribable. "But he was never dead for that," said he, and I sighed aloud. "Why should I think he was dead now? No, not till I see him rotting," says he.

Sir William looked across at me with a long face. Mountain forgot his wounds, staring and gaping.

"My lord," said I, "I wish you would collect your spirits." But my throat was so dry, and my own wits so scattered, I could add no more.

"No," says my lord, "it's not to be supposed that he would understand me. Mackellar does, for he kens all, and has seen him buried before now. This is a very good servant to me, Sir William, this man Mackellar; he buried him with his own hands—he and my father—by the light of two siller candlesticks. The other man is a familiar spirit; he brought him from Coromandel. I would have told ye this long syne, Sir William, only it was in the family." These last remarks he made with a kind of a melancholy composure, and his time of aberration seemed to pass away. "You can ask yourself what it all means," he proceeded. "My brother falls sick, and dies, and is buried, as so they say; and all seems very plain. But why did the familiar go back? I think ye must see for yourself it's a point that wants some clearing."

"I will be at your service, my lord, in half a minute," said Sir William, rising. "Mr. Mackellar, two words with you;" and he led me without the camp, the frost crunching in our steps, the trees standing at our elbow, hoar with frost, even as on that night in the Long Shrubbery. "Of course, this is midsummer madness," said Sir William, as soon as we were gotten out of bearing.

"Why, certainly," said I. "The man is mad. I think that manifest."

"Shall I seize and bind him?" asked Sir William. "I will upon your authority. If these are all ravings, that should certainly be done."

I looked down upon the ground, back at the camp, with its bright fires and the folk watching us, and about me on the woods and mountains; there was just the one way that I could not look, and that was in Sir William's face.

"Sir William," said I at last, "I think my lord not sane, and have long thought him so. But there are degrees in madness; and whether he should be brought under restraint—Sir William, I am no fit judge," I concluded.

"I will be the judge," said he. "I ask for facts. Was there, in all that jargon, any word of truth or sanity? Do you hesitate?" he asked. "Am I to understand you have buried this gentleman before?"

"Not buried," said I; and then, taking up courage at last, "Sir William," said I, "unless I were to tell you a long story, which much concerns a noble family (and myself not in the least), it would be impossible to make this matter clear to you. Say the word, and I will do it, right or wrong. And, at any rate, I will say so much, that my lord is not so crazy as he seems. This is a strange matter, into the tail of which you are unhappily drifted."

"I desire none of your secrets," replied Sir William; "but I will be plain, at the risk of incivility, and confess that I take little pleasure in my present company."

"I would be the last to blame you," said I, "for that."

"I have not asked either for your censure or your praise, sir," returned Sir William. "I desire simply to be quit of you; and to that effect, I put a boat and complement of men at your disposal."

"This is fairly offered," said I, after reflection. "But you must suffer me to say a word upon the other side. We have a natural curiosity to learn the truth of this affair; I have some of it myself; my lord (it is very plain) has but too much. The matter of the Indian's return is enigmatical."

"I think so myself," Sir William interrupted, "and I propose (since I go in that direction) to probe it to the bottom. Whether or not the man has gone like a dog to die upon his master's grave, his life, at least, is in great danger, and I propose, if I can, to save it. There is nothing against his character?"

"Nothing, Sir William," I replied.

"And the other?" he said. "I have heard my lord, of course; but, from the circumstances of his servant's loyalty, I must suppose he had some noble qualities."

"You must not ask me that!" I cried. "Hell may have noble flames. I have known him a score of years, and always hated, and always admired, and always slavishly feared him."

"I appear to intrude again upon your secrets," said Sir William, "believe me, inadvertently. Enough that I will see the grave, and (if possible) rescue the Indian. Upon these terms, can you persuade your master to return to Albany?"

"Sir William," said I, "I will tell you how it is. You do not see my lord to advantage; it will seem even strange to you that I should love him; but I do, and I am not alone. If he goes back to Albany, it must be by force, and it will be the death-warrant of his reason, and perhaps his life. That is my sincere belief; but I am in your hands, and ready to obey, if you will assume so much responsibility as to command."

"I will have no shred of responsibility; it is my single endeavour to avoid the same," cried Sir William. "You insist upon following this journey up; and be it so! I wash my hands of the whole matter."

With which word, he turned upon his heel and gave the order to break camp; and my lord, who had been hovering near by, came instantly to my side.

"Which is it to be?" said he.

"You are to have your way," I answered. "You shall see the grave."

The situation of the Master's grave was, between guides, easily described; it lay, indeed, beside a chief landmark of the wilderness, a certain range of peaks, conspicuous by their design and altitude, and the source of many brawling tributaries to that inland sea, Lake Champlain. It was therefore possible to strike for it direct, instead of following back the blood-stained trail of the fugitives, and to cover, in some sixteen hours of march, a distance which their perturbed wanderings had extended over more than sixty. Our boats we left under a guard upon the river; it was, indeed, probable we should return to find them frozen fast; and the small equipment with which we set forth upon the expedition, included not only an infinity of furs to protect us from the cold, but an arsenal of snow-shoes to render travel possible, when the inevitable snow should fall. Considerable alarm was manifested at our departure; the march was conducted with soldierly precaution, the camp at night sedulously chosen and patrolled; and it was a consideration of this sort that arrested us, the second day, within not many hundred yards of our destination—the night being already imminent, the spot in which we stood well qualified to be a strong camp for a party of our numbers; and Sir William, therefore, on a sudden thought, arresting our advance.

Before us was the high range of mountains toward which we had been all day deviously drawing near. From the first light of the dawn, their silver peaks had been the goal of our advance across a tumbled lowland forest, thrid with rough streams, and strewn with monstrous boulders; the peaks (as I say) silver, for already at the higher altitudes the snow fell nightly; but the woods and the low ground only breathed upon with frost. All day heaven had been charged with ugly vapours, in the which the sun swam and glimmered like a shilling piece; all day the wind blew on our left cheek barbarous cold, but very pure to breathe. With the end of the afternoon, however, the wind fell; the clouds, being no longer reinforced, were scattered or drunk up; the sun set behind us with some wintry splendour, and the white brow of the mountains shared its dying glow.

It was dark ere we had supper; we ate in silence, and the meal was scarce despatched before my lord slunk from the fireside to the margin of the camp; whither I made haste to follow him. The camp was on high ground, overlooking a frozen lake, perhaps a mile in its longest measurement; all about us, the forest lay in heights and hollows; above rose the white mountains; and higher yet, the moon rode in a fair sky. There was no breath of air; nowhere a twig creaked; and the sounds of our own camp were hushed and swallowed up in the surrounding stillness. Now that the sun and the wind were both gone down, it appeared almost warm, like a night of July: a singular illusion of the sense, when earth, air, and water were strained to bursting with the extremity of frost.

My lord (or what I still continued to call by his loved name) stood with his elbow in one hand, and his chin sunk in the other, gazing before him on the surface of the wood. My eyes followed his, and rested almost pleasantly upon the frosted contexture of the pines, rising in moonlit hillocks, or sinking in the shadow of small glens. Hard by, I told myself, was the grave of our enemy, now gone where the wicked cease from troubling, the earth heaped for ever on his once so active limbs. I could not but think of him as somehow fortunate to be thus done with man's anxiety and weariness, the daily expense of spirit, and that daily river of circumstance to be swum through, at any hazard, under the penalty of shame or death. I could not but think how good was the end of that long travel; and with that, my mind swung at a tangent to my lord. For was not my lord dead also? a maimed soldier, looking vainly for discharge, lingering derided in the line of battle? A kind man, I remembered him; wise, with a decent pride, a son perhaps too dutiful, a husband only too loving, one that could suffer and be silent, one whose hand I loved to press. Of a sudden, pity caught in my windpipe with a sob; I could have wept aloud to remember and behold him; and standing thus by his elbow, under the broad moon, I prayed fervently either that he should be released, or I strengthened to persist in my affection.

"Oh God," said I, "this was the best man to me and to himself, and now I shrink from him. He did no wrong, or not till he was broke with sorrows; these are but his honourable wounds that we begin to shrink from. Oh, cover them up, oh, take him away, before we hate him!"

I was still so engaged in my own bosom, when a sound broke suddenly upon the night. It was neither very loud, nor very near; yet, bursting as it did from so profound and so prolonged a silence, it startled the camp like an alarm of trumpets. Ere I had taken breath, Sir William was beside me, the main part of the voyagers clustered at his back, intently giving ear. Methought, as I glanced at them across my shoulder, there was a whiteness, other than moonlight, on their cheeks; and the rays of the moon reflected with a sparkle on the eyes of some, and the shadows lying black under the brows of others (according as they raised or bowed the head to listen) gave to the group a strange air of animation and anxiety. My lord was to the front, crouching a little forth, his hand raised as for silence: a man turned to stone. And still the sounds continued, breathlessly renewed with a precipitate rhythm.

Suddenly Mountain spoke in a loud, broken whisper, as of a man relieved. "I have it now," he said; and, as we all turned to hear him, "the Indian must have known the cache," he added. "That is he—he is digging out the treasure."

"Why, to be sure!" exclaimed Sir William. "We were geese not to have supposed so much."

"The only thing is," Mountain resumed, "the sound is very close to our old camp. And, again, I do not see how he is there before us, unless the man had wings!"

"Greed and fear are wings," remarked Sir William. "But this rogue has given us an alert, and I have a notion to return the compliment. What say you, gentlemen, shall we have a moonlight hunt?"

It was so agreed; dispositions were made to surround Secundra at his task; some of Sir

William's Indians hastened in advance; and a strong guard being left at our headquarters, we set forth along the uneven bottom of the forest; frost crackling, ice sometimes loudly splitting under foot; and overhead the blackness of pine-woods, and the broken brightness of the moon. Our way led down into a hollow of the land; and as we descended, the sounds diminished and had almost died away. Upon the other slope it was more open, only dotted with a few pines, and several vast and scattered rocks that made inky shadows in the moonlight. Here the sounds began to reach us more distinctly; we could now perceive the ring of iron, and more exactly estimate the furious degree of haste with which the digger plied his instrument. As we neared the top of the ascent, a bird or two winged aloft and hovered darkly in the moonlight; and the next moment we were gazing through a fringe of trees upon a singular picture.

A narrow plateau, overlooked by the white mountains, and encompassed nearer hand by woods, lay bare to the strong radiance of the moon. Rough goods, such as make the wealth of foresters, were sprinkled here and there upon the ground in meaningless disarray. About the midst, a tent stood, silvered with frost: the door open, gaping on the black interior. At the one end of this small stage lay what seemed the tattered remnants of a man. Without doubt we had arrived upon the scene of Harris's encampment; there were the goods scattered in the panic of flight; it was in yon tent the Master breathed his last; and the frozen carrion that lay before us was the body of the drunken shoemaker. It was always moving to come upon the theatre of any tragic incident; to come upon it after so many days, and to find it (in the seclusion of a desert) still unchanged, must have impressed the mind of the most careless. And yet it was not that which struck us into pillars of stone; but the sight (which yet we had been half expecting) of Secundra ankle deep in the grave of his late master. He had cast the main part of his raiment by, yet his frail arms and shoulders glistered in the moonlight with a copious sweat; his face was contracted with anxiety and expectation; his blows resounded on the grave, as thick as sobs; and behind him, strangely deformed and ink-black upon the frosty ground, the creature's shadow repeated and parodied his swift gesticulations. Some night birds arose from the boughs upon our coming, and then settled back; but Secundra, absorbed in his toil; heard or heeded not at all.

I heard Mountain whisper to Sir William, "Good God! it's the grave! He's digging him up!" It was what we had all guessed, and yet to hear it put in language thrilled me. Sir William violently started.

"You damned sacrilegious hound!" he cried. "What's this?"

Secundra leaped in the air, a little breathless cry escaped him, the tool flew from his grasp, and he stood one instant staring at the speaker. The next, swift as an arrow, he sped for the woods upon the farther side; and the next again, throwing up his hands with a violent gesture of resolution, he had begun already to retrace his steps.

"Well, then, you come, you help—" he was saying. But by now my lord had stepped beside Sir William; the moon shone fair upon his face, and the words were still upon Secundra's lips, when he beheld and recognised his master's enemy. "Him!" he screamed, clasping his hands, and shrinking on himself.

"Come, come!" said Sir William. "There is none here to do you harm, if you be innocent; and if you be guilty, your escape is quite cut off. Speak, what do you here among the graves of the dead and the remains of the unburied?"

"You no murderer?" inquired Secundra. "You true man? you see me safe?"

"I will see you safe, if you be innocent," returned Sir William. "I have said the thing, and I see not wherefore you should doubt it."

"There all murderers," cried Secundra, "that is why! He kill—murderer," pointing to Mountain; "there two hire-murderers," pointing to my lord and myself—"all gallows—

murderers! Ah! I see you all swing in a rope. Now I go save the sahib; he see you swing in a rope. The sahib," he continued, pointing to the grave, "he not dead. He bury, he not dead."

My lord uttered a little noise, moved nearer to the grave, and stood and stared in it.

"Buried and not dead?" exclaimed Sir William. "What kind of rant is this?"

"See, sahib," said Secundra. "The sahib and I alone with murderers; try all way to escape, no way good. Then try this way: good way in warm climate, good way in India; here, in this dam cold place, who can tell? I tell you pretty good hurry: you help, you light a fire, help rub."

"What is the creature talking of?" cried Sir William. "My head goes round."

"I tell you I bury him alive," said Secundra. "I teach him swallow his tongue. Now dig him up pretty good hurry, and he not much worse. You light a fire."

Sir William turned to the nearest of his men. "Light a fire," said he. "My lot seems to be cast with the insane."

"You good man," returned Secundra. "Now I go dig the sahib up."

He returned as he spoke to the grave, and resumed his former toil. My lord stood rooted, and I at my lord's side, fearing I knew not what.

The frost was not yet very deep, and presently the Indian threw aside his tool, and began to scoop the dirt by handfuls. Then he disengaged a corner of a buffalo robe; and then I saw hair catch among his fingers: yet, a moment more, and the moon shone on something white. Awhile Secundra crouched upon his knees, scraping with delicate fingers, breathing with puffed lips; and when he moved aside, I beheld the face of the Master wholly disengaged. It was deadly white, the eyes closed, the ears and nostrils plugged, the cheeks fallen, the nose sharp as if in death; but for all he had lain so many days under the sod, corruption had not approached him, and (what strangely affected all of us) his lips and chin were mantled with a swarthy beard.

"My God!" cried Mountain, "he was as smooth as a baby when we laid him there!"

"They say hair grows upon the dead," observed Sir William; but his voice was thick and weak.

Secundra paid no heed to our remarks, digging swift as a terrier in the loose earth. Every moment the form of the Master, swathed in his buffalo robe, grew more distinct in the bottom of that shallow trough; the moon shining strong, and the shadows of the standers-by, as they drew forward and back, falling and flitting over his emergent countenance. The sight held us with a horror not before experienced. I dared not look my lord in the face; but for as long as it lasted, I never observed him to draw breath; and a little in the background one of the men (I know not whom) burst into a kind of sobbing.

"Now," said Secundra, "you help me lift him out."

Of the flight of time, I have no idea; it may have been three hours, and it may have been five, that the Indian laboured to reanimate his master's body. One thing only I know, that it was still night, and the moon was not yet set, although it had sunk low, and now barred the plateau with long shadows, when Secundra uttered a small cry of satisfaction; and, leaning swiftly forth, I thought I could myself perceive a change upon that icy countenance of the unburied. The next moment I beheld his eyelids flutter; the next they rose entirely, and the week-old corpse looked me for a moment in the face.

So much display of life I can myself swear to. I have heard from others that he visibly strove to speak, that his teeth showed in his beard, and that his brow was contorted as with an agony of pain and effort. And this may have been; I know not, I was otherwise engaged. For at that first disclosure of the dead man's eyes, my Lord Durrisdeer fell to the ground, and when I raised him up, he was a corpse.

Day came, and still Secundra could not be persuaded to desist from his unavailing efforts.

Sir William, leaving a small party under my command, proceeded on his embassy with the first light; and still the Indian rubbed the limbs and breathed in the mouth of the dead body. You would think such labours might have vitalised a stone; but, except for that one moment (which was my lord's death), the black spirit of the Master held aloof from its discarded clay; and by about the hour of noon, even the faithful servant was at length convinced. He took it with unshaken quietude.

"Too cold," said he, "good way in India, no good here." And, asking for some food, which he ravenously devoured as soon as it was set before him, he drew near to the fire and took his place at my elbow. In the same spot, as soon as he had eaten, he stretched himself out, and fell into a childlike slumber, from which I must arouse him, some hours afterwards, to take his part as one of the mourners at the double funeral. It was the same throughout; he seemed to have outlived at once and with the same effort, his grief for his master and his terror of myself and Mountain.

One of the men left with me was skilled in stone-cutting; and before Sir William returned to pick us up, I had chiselled on a boulder this inscription, with a copy of which I may fitly bring my narrative to a close:

J. D.,
HEIR TO A SCOTTISH TITLE,
A MASTER OF THE ARTS AND GRACES,
ADMIRED IN EUROPE, ASIA, AMERICA,
IN WAR AND PEACE,
IN THE TENTS OF SAVAGE HUNTERS AND THE
CITADELS OF KINGS, AFTER SO MUCH
ACQUIRED, ACCOMPLISHED, AND
ENDURED, LIES HERE FORGOTTEN.

H. D.,
HIS BROTHER,
AFTER A LIFE OF UNMERITED DISTRESS,
BRAVELY SUPPORTED,
DIED ALMOST IN THE SAME HOUR,
AND SLEEPS IN THE SAME GRAVE
WITH HIS FRATERNAL ENEMY.

THE PIETY OF HIS WIFE AND ONE OLD
SERVANT RAISED THIS STONE
TO BOTH.

---

1. Unwilling.
2. Ring.

THE SUICIDE CLUB

I

STORY OF THE YOUNG MAN WITH THE CREAM TARTS

During his residence in London, the accomplished Prince Florizel of Bohemia gained the affection of all classes by the seduction of his manner and by a well-considered generosity. He was a remarkable man even by what was known of him; and that was but a small part of what he actually did. Although of a placid temper in ordinary circumstances, and accustomed to take the world with as much philosophy as any ploughman, the Prince of Bohemia was not without a taste for ways of life more adventurous and eccentric than that to which he was destined by his birth. Now and then, when he fell into a low humour, when there was no laughable play to witness in any of the London theatres, and when the season of the year was unsuitable to those field sports in which he excelled all competitors, he would summon his confidant and Master of the Horse, Colonel Geraldine, and bid him prepare himself against an evening ramble. The Master of the Horse was a young officer of a brave and even temerarious disposition. He greeted the news with delight, and hastened to make ready. Long practice and a varied acquaintance of life had given him a singular facility in disguise; he could adapt not only his face and bearing, but his voice and almost his thoughts, to those of any rank, character, or nation; and in this way he diverted attention from the Prince, and sometimes gained admission for the pair into strange societies. The civil authorities were never taken into the secret of these adventures; the imperturbable courage of the one and the ready invention and chivalrous devotion of the other had brought them through a score of dangerous passes; and they grew in confidence as time went on.

One evening in March they were driven by a sharp fall of sleet into an Oyster Bar in the immediate neighbourhood of Leicester Square. Colonel Geraldine was dressed and painted to represent a person connected with the Press in reduced circumstances; while the Prince had, as usual, travestied his appearance by the addition of false whiskers and a pair of large adhesive eyebrows. These lent him a shaggy and weather-beaten air, which, for one of his urbanity, formed the most impenetrable disguise. Thus equipped, the commander and his satellite sipped their brandy and soda in security.

The bar was full of guests, male and female; but though more than one of these offered to fall into talk with our adventurers, none of them promised to grow interesting upon a nearer acquaintance. There was nothing present but the lees of London and the commonplace of disrespectability; and the Prince had already fallen to yawning, and was beginning to grow weary of the whole excursion, when the swing doors were pushed violently open, and a young man, followed by a couple of commissionaires, entered the bar. Each of the commissionaires carried a large dish of cream tarts under a cover, which they at once removed; and the young man made the round of the company, and pressed these confections upon every one's acceptance with an exaggerated courtesy. Sometimes his offer was laughingly accepted; sometimes it was firmly, or even harshly, rejected. In these latter cases the new-comer always ate the tart himself, with some more or less humorous commentary.

At last he accosted Prince Florizel.

"Sir," said he, with a profound obeisance, proffering the tart at the same time between his thumb and forefinger, "will you so far honour an entire stranger? I can answer for the quality of the pastry, having eaten two dozen and three of them myself since five o'clock."

"I am in the habit," replied the Prince, "of looking not so much to the nature of a gift as to the spirit in which it is offered."

"The spirit, sir," returned the young man, with another bow, "is one of mockery."

"Mockery?" repeated Florizel. "And whom do you propose to mock?"

"I am not here to expound my philosophy," replied the other, "but to distribute these cream tarts. If I mention that I heartily include myself in the ridicule of the transaction, I hope you will consider honour satisfied and condescend. If not, you will constrain me to eat my twenty-eighth, and I own to being weary of the exercise."

"You touch me," said the Prince, "and I have all the will in the world to rescue you from this dilemma, but upon one condition. If my friend and I eat your cakes—for which we have neither of us any natural inclination—we shall expect you to join us at supper by way of recompense."

The young man seemed to reflect.

"I have still several dozen upon hand," he said at last; "and that will make it necessary for me to visit several more bars before my great affair is concluded. This will take some time; and if you are hungry—"

The Prince interrupted him with a polite gesture.

"My friend and I will accompany you," he said; "for we have already a deep interest in your very agreeable mode of passing an evening. And now that the preliminaries of peace are settled, allow me to sign the treaty for both."

And the Prince swallowed the tart with the best grace imaginable.

"It is delicious," said he.

"I perceive you are a connoisseur," replied the young man.

Colonel Geraldine likewise did honour to the pastry; and every one in that bar having now either accepted or refused his delicacies, the young man with the cream tarts led the way to another and similar establishment. The two commissionaires, who seemed to have grown accustomed to their absurd employment, followed immediately after; and the Prince and the Colonel brought up the rear, arm in arm, and smiling to each other as they went. In this order the company visited two other taverns, where scenes were enacted of a like nature to that already described—some refusing, some accepting, the favours of this vagabond hospitality, and the young man himself eating each rejected tart.

On leaving the third saloon the young man counted his store. There were but nine remaining, three in one tray and six in the other.

"Gentlemen," said he, addressing himself to his two new followers, "I am unwilling to delay your supper. I am positively sure you must be hungry. I feel that I owe you a special consideration. And on this great day for me, when I am closing a career of folly by my most conspicuously silly action, I wish to behave handsomely to all who give me countenance. Gentlemen, you shall wait no longer. Although my constitution is shattered by previous excesses, at the risk of my life I liquidate the suspensory condition."

With these words he crushed the nine remaining tarts into his mouth, and swallowed them at a single movement each. Then, turning to the commissionaires, he gave them a couple of sovereigns.

"I have to thank you," said be, "for your extraordinary patience."

And he dismissed them with a bow apiece. For some seconds he stood looking at the purse from which he had just paid his assistants, then, with a laugh, he tossed it into the middle of the street, and signified his readiness for supper.

In a small French restaurant in Soho, which had enjoyed an exaggerated reputation for some little while, but had already begun to be forgotten, and in a private room up two pair of stairs, the three companions made a very elegant supper, and drank three or four bottles of champagne, talking the while upon indifferent subjects. The young man was fluent and gay, but he laughed louder than was natural in a person of polite breeding; his hands trembled violently, and his voice took sudden and surprising inflections, which seemed to be independent of his will. The dessert had been cleared away, and all three had lighted their cigars, when the Prince addressed him in these words:—

"You will, I am sure, pardon my curiosity. What I have seen of you has greatly pleased but even more puzzled me. And though I should be loth to seem indiscreet, I must tell you that my friend and I are persons very well worthy to be entrusted with a secret. We have many of our own, which we are continually revealing to improper ears. And if, as I suppose, your story is a silly one, you need have no delicacy with us, who are two of the silliest men in England. My name is Godall, Theophilus Godall; my friend is Major Alfred Hammersmith—or at least, such is the name by which he chooses to be known. We pass our lives entirely in the search for extravagant adventures; and there is no extravagance with which we are not capable of sympathy."

"I like you, Mr. Godall," returned the young man; "you inspire me with a natural confidence; and I have not the slightest objection to your friend the Major, whom I take to be a nobleman in masquerade. At least, I am sure he is no soldier."

The Colonel smiled at this compliment to the perfection of his art; and the young man went on in a more animated manner.

"There is every reason why I should not tell you my story. Perhaps that is just the reason why I am going to do so. At least, you seem so well prepared to hear a tale of silliness that I cannot find it in my heart to disappoint you. My name, in spite of your example, I shall keep to myself. My age is not essential to the narrative. I am descended from my ancestors by ordinary generation, and from them I inherited the very eligible human tenement which I still occupy and a fortune of three hundred pounds a year. I suppose they also handed on to me a hare-brain humour, which it has been my chief delight to indulge. I received a good education. I can play the violin nearly well enough to earn money in the orchestra of a penny gaff, but not quite. The same remark applies to the flute and the French horn. I learned enough of whist to lose about a hundred a year at that scientific game. My acquaintance with French was sufficient to enable me to squander money in Paris with almost the same facility as in London. In short, I am a person full of manly accomplishments. I have had every sort of adventure, including a duel about nothing. Only two months ago I met a young lady exactly suited to my taste in mind and body; I found my heart melt; I saw that I had come upon my fate at last, and was in the way to fall in love. But when I came to reckon up what remained to me of my capital, I found it amounted to something less than four hundred pounds! I ask you fairly—can a man who respects himself fall in love on four hundred pounds? I concluded, certainly not; left the presence of my charmer, and slightly accelerating my usual rate of expenditure, came this morning to my last eighty pounds. This I divided into two equal parts; forty I reserved for a particular purpose; the remaining forty I was to dissipate before the night. I have passed a very entertaining day, and played many farces besides that of the cream tarts which procured me the advantage of your acquaintance; for I was determined, as I told you, to bring a foolish career to a still more foolish conclusion; and when you saw me throw my purse into the street, the forty pounds were at an end. Now you know me as well as I know myself: a fool, but consistent in his folly; and, as I will ask you to believe, neither a whimperer nor a coward."

From the whole tone of the young man's statement it was plain that he harboured very bitter and contemptuous thoughts about himself. His auditors were led to imagine that his love affair was nearer his heart than he admitted, and that he had a design on his own life. The farce of the cream tarts began to have very much the air of a tragedy in disguise.

"Why, is this not odd," broke out Geraldine, giving a look to Prince Florizel, "that we three fellows should have met by the merest accident in so large a wilderness as London, and should be so nearly in the same condition?"

"How?" cried the young man. "Are you, too, ruined? Is this supper a folly like my cream tarts? Has the devil brought three of his own together for a last carouse?"

"The devil, depend upon it, can sometimes do a very gentlemanly thing," returned Prince Florizel; "and I am so much touched by this coincidence, that, although we are not entirely in the same case, I am going to put an end to the disparity. Let your heroic treatment of the last cream tarts be my example."

So saying, the Prince drew out his purse and took from it a small bundle of bank-notes.

"You see, I was a week or so behind you, but I mean to catch you up and come neck and neck into the winning-post," he continued. "This," laying one of the notes upon the table, "will suffice for the bill. As for the rest—"

He tossed them into the fire, and they went up the chimney in a single blaze.

The young man tried to catch his arm, but as the table was between them his interference came too late.

"Unhappy man," he cried, "you should not have burned them all! You should have kept forty pounds."

"Forty pounds!" repeated the Prince. "Why, in heaven's name, forty pounds?"

"Why not eighty?" cried the Colonel; "for to my certain knowledge there must have been a hundred in the bundle."

"It was only forty pounds he needed," said the young man gloomily. "But without them there is no admission. The rule is strict. Forty pounds for each. Accursed life, where a man cannot even die without money!"

The Prince and the Colonel exchanged glances. "Explain yourself," said the latter. "I have still a pocket-book tolerably well lined, and I need not say how readily I should share my wealth with Godall. But I must know to what end: you must certainly tell us what you mean."

The young man seemed to awaken; he looked uneasily from one to the other, and his face flushed deeply.

"You are not fooling me?" he asked. "You are indeed ruined men like me?"

"Indeed, I am for my part," replied the Colonel.

"And for mine," said the Prince, "I have given you proof. Who but a ruined man would throw his notes into the fire? The action speaks for itself."

"A ruined man—yes," returned the other suspiciously, "or else a millionaire."

"Enough, sir," said the Prince; "I have said so, and I am not accustomed to have my word remain in doubt."

"Ruined?" said the young man. "Are you ruined, like me? Are you, after a life of indulgence, come to such a pass that you can only indulge yourself in one thing more? Are you"—he kept lowering his voice as he went on—"are you going to give yourselves that last indulgence? Are you going to avoid the consequences of your folly by the one infallible and easy path? Are you going to give the slip to the sheriff's officers of conscience by the one open door?"

Suddenly he broke off and attempted to laugh.

"Here is your health!" he cried, emptying his glass, "and good night to you, my merry ruined men."

Colonel Geraldine caught him by the arm as he was about to rise.

"You lack confidence in us," he said, "and you are wrong. To all your questions I make answer in the affirmative. But I am not so timid, and can speak the Queen's English plainly. We too, like yourself, have had enough of life, and are determined to die. Sooner or later, alone or together, we meant to seek out death and beard him where he lies ready. Since we have met you, and your case is more pressing, let it be to-night—and at once—and, if you will, all three together. Such a penniless trio," he cried, "should go arm in arm into the halls of Pluto, and give each other some countenance among the shades!"

Geraldine had hit exactly on the manners and intonations that became the part he was playing. The Prince himself was disturbed, and looked over at his confidant with a shade of doubt. As for the young man, the flush came back darkly into his cheek, and his eyes threw out a spark of light.

"You are the men for me!" he cried, with an almost terrible gaiety. "Shake hands upon the bargain!" (his hand was cold and wet). "You little know in what a company you will begin the march! You little know in what a happy moment for yourselves you partook of my cream tarts! I am only a unit, but I am a unit in an army. I know Death's private door. I am one of his familiars, and can show you into eternity without ceremony and yet without scandal."

They called upon him eagerly to explain his meaning.

"Can you muster eighty pounds between you?" he demanded.

Geraldine ostentatiously consulted his pocket-book, and replied in the affirmative.

"Fortunate beings!" cried the young man. "Forty pounds is the entry money of the Suicide Club."

"The Suicide Club," said the Prince, "why, what the devil is that?"

"Listen," said the young man; "this is the age of conveniences, and I have to tell you of the last perfection of the sort. We have affairs in different places; and hence railways were invented. Railways separated us infallibly from our friends; and so telegraphs were made that we might communicate speedier at great distances. Even in hotels we have lifts to spare us a climb of some hundred steps. Now, we know that life is only a stage to play the fool upon as long as the part amuses us. There was one more convenience lacking to modern comfort; a decent, easy way to quit that stage; the back stairs to liberty; or, as I said this moment, Death's private door. This, my two fellow-rebels, is supplied by the Suicide Club. Do not suppose that you and I are alone, or even exceptional in the highly reasonable desire that we profess. A large number of our fellowmen, who have grown heartily sick of the performance in which they are expected to join daily and all their lives long, are only kept from flight by one or two considerations. Some have families who would be shocked, or even blamed, if the matter became public; others have a weakness at heart and recoil from the circumstances of death. That is, to some extent, my own experience. I cannot put a pistol to my head and draw the trigger; for something stronger than myself withholds the act; and although I loathe life, I have not strength enough in my body to take hold of death and be done with it. For such as I, and for all who desire to be out of the coil without posthumous scandal, the Suicide Club has been inaugurated. How this has been managed, what is its history, or what may be its ramifications in other lands, I am myself uninformed; and what I know of its constitution, I am not at liberty to communicate to you. To this extent, however, I am at your service. If you are truly tired of life, I will introduce you to-night to a meeting; and if not to-night, at least some time within the week, you will be easily relieved of your existences. It is now (consulting his watch) eleven; by half-past, at latest, we must leave this place; so that you have half-an-hour before you to consider my proposal. It is more serious than a cream tart," he added, with a smile; "and I suspect more palatable."

"More serious, certainly," returned Colonel Geraldine; "and as it is so much more so, will you allow me five minutes' speech in private with my friend, Mr. Godall?"

"It is only fair," answered the young man. "If you will permit, I will retire."

"You will be very obliging," said the Colonel.

As soon as the two were alone—"What," said Prince Florizel, "is the use of this confabulation, Geraldine? I see you are flurried, whereas my mind is very tranquilly made up. I will see the end of this."

"Your Highness," said the Colonel, turning pale; "let me ask you to consider the importance of your life, not only to your friends, but to the public interest. 'If not to-night,' said this madman; but supposing that to-night some irreparable disaster were to overtake your Highness's person, what, let me ask you, what would be my despair, and what the concern and disaster of a great nation?"

"I will see the end of this," repeated the Prince in his most deliberate tones; "and have the kindness, Colonel Geraldine, to remember and respect your word of honour as a gentleman. Under no circumstances, recollect, nor without my special authority, are you to betray the incognito under which I choose to go abroad. These were my commands, which I now reiterate. And now," he added, "let me ask you to call for the bill."

Colonel Geraldine bowed in submission; but he had a very white face as he summoned the young man of the cream tarts, and issued his directions to the waiter. The Prince preserved his undisturbed demeanour, and described a Palais Royal farce to the young suicide with great humour and gusto. He avoided the Colonel's appealing looks without ostentation, and selected another cheroot with more than usual care. Indeed, he was now the only man of the party who kept any command over his nerves.

The bill was discharged, the Prince giving the whole change of the note to the astonished waiter; and the three drove off in a four-wheeler. They were not long upon the way before the cab stopped at the entrance to a rather dark court. Here all descended.

After Geraldine had paid the fare, the young man turned, and addressed Prince Florizel as follows:—

"It is still time, Mr. Godall, to make good your escape into thraldom. And for you too, Major Hammersmith. Reflect well before you take another step; and if your hearts say no—here are the cross-roads."

"Lead on, sir," said the Prince. "I am not the man to go back from a thing once said."

"Your coolness does me good," replied their guide. "I have never seen any one so unmoved at this conjuncture; and yet you are not the first whom I have escorted to this door. More than one of my friends has preceded me, where I knew I must shortly follow. But this is of no interest to you. Wait me here for only a few moments; I shall return as soon as I have arranged the preliminaries of your introduction."

And with that the young man, waving his hand to his companions, turned into the court, entered a doorway and disappeared.

"Of all our follies," said Colonel Geraldine in a low voice, "this is the wildest and most dangerous."

"I perfectly believe so," returned the Prince.

"We have still," pursued the Colonel, "a moment to ourselves. Let me beseech your Highness to profit by the opportunity and retire. The consequences of this step are so dark, and may be so grave, that I feel myself justified in pushing a little farther than usual the liberty which your Highness is so condescending as to allow me in private."

"Am I to understand that Colonel Geraldine is afraid?" asked his Highness, taking his cheroot from his lips, and looking keenly into the other's face.

"My fear is certainly not personal," replied the other proudly; "of that your Highness may rest well assured."

"I had supposed as much," returned the Prince, with undisturbed good humour; "but I was unwilling to remind you of the difference in our stations. No more—no more," he added, seeing Geraldine about to apologise, "you stand excused."

And he smoked placidly, leaning against a railing, until the young man returned.

"Well," he asked, "has our reception been arranged?"

"Follow me," was the reply. "The President will see you in the cabinet. And let me warn you to be frank in your answers. I have stood your guarantee; but the club requires a searching inquiry before admission; for the indiscretion of a single member would lead to the dispersion of the whole society for ever."

The Prince and Geraldine put their heads together for a moment. "Bear me out in this," said the one; and "bear me out in that," said the other; and by boldly taking up the characters of men with whom both were acquainted, they had come to an agreement in a twinkling, and were ready to follow their guide into the President's cabinet.

There were no formidable obstacles to pass. The outer door stood open; the door of the cabinet was ajar; and there, in a small but very high apartment, the young man left them once more.

"He will be here immediately," he said, with a nod, as he disappeared.

Voices were audible in the cabinet through the folding doors which formed one end; and now and then the noise of a champagne cork, followed by a burst of laughter, intervened among the sounds of conversation. A single tall window looked out upon the river and the embankment; and by the disposition of the lights they judged themselves not far from Charing Cross station. The furniture was scanty, and the coverings worn to the thread; and there was nothing movable except a hand-bell in the centre of a round table, and the hats and coats of a considerable party hung round the wall on pegs.

"What sort of a den is this?" said Geraldine.

"That is what I have come to see," replied the Prince. "If they keep live devils on the premises, the thing may grow amusing."

Just then the folding door was opened no more than was necessary for the passage of a human body; and there entered at the same moment a louder buzz of talk, and the redoubtable President of the Suicide Club. The President was a man of fifty or upwards; large and rambling in his gait, with shaggy side whiskers, a bald top to his head, and a veiled grey eye, which now and then emitted a twinkle. His mouth, which embraced a large cigar, he kept continually screwing round and round and from side to side, as he looked sagaciously and coldly at the strangers. He was dressed in light tweeds, with his neck very open in a striped shirt collar; and carried a minute book under one arm.

"Good evening," said he, after he had closed the door behind him. "I am told you wish to speak with me."

"We have a desire, sir, to join the Suicide Club," replied the Colonel.

The President rolled his cigar about in his mouth. "What is that?" he said abruptly.

"Pardon me," returned the Colonel, "but I believe you are the person best qualified to give us information on that point."

"I?" cried the President. "A Suicide Club? Come, come! this is a frolic for All Fools' Day. I can make allowances for gentlemen who get merry in their liquor; but let there be an end to this."

"Call your Club what you will," said the Colonel, "you have some company behind these doors, and we insist on joining it."

"Sir," returned the President curtly, "you have made a mistake. This is a private house, and you must leave it instantly."

The Prince had remained quietly in his seat throughout this little colloquy; but now, when the Colonel looked over to him, as much as to say, "Take your answer and come away, for God's sake!" he drew his cheroot from his mouth, and spoke—

"I have come here," said he, "upon the invitation of a friend of yours. He has doubtless informed you of my intention in thus intruding on your party. Let me remind you that a person in my circumstances has exceedingly little to bind him, and is not at all likely to tolerate much rudeness. I am a very quiet man, as a usual thing; but, my dear sir, you are either going to oblige me in the little matter of which you are aware, or you shall very bitterly repent that you ever admitted me to your ante-chamber."

The President laughed aloud.

"That is the way to speak," said he. "You are a man who is a man. You know the way to my heart, and can do what you like with me. Will you," he continued, addressing Geraldine, "will you step aside for a few minutes? I shall finish first with your companion, and some of the club's formalities require to be fulfilled in private."

With these words he opened the door of a small closet, into which he shut the Colonel.

"I believe in you," he said to Florizel, as soon as they were alone; "but are you sure of your friend?"

"Not so sure as I am of myself, though he has more cogent reasons," answered Florizel, "but sure enough to bring him here without alarm. He has had enough to cure the most tenacious man of life. He was cashiered the other day for cheating at cards."

"A good reason, I daresay," replied the President; "at least, we have another in the same case, and I feel sure of him. Have you also been in the Service, may I ask?"

"I have," was the reply; "but I was too lazy, I left it early."

"What is your reason for being tired of life?" pursued the President.

"The same, as near as I can make out," answered the Prince; "unadulterated laziness."

The President started. "D—n it," said he, "you must have something better than that."

"I have no more money," added Florizel. "That is also a vexation, without doubt. It brings my sense of idleness to an acute point."

The President rolled his cigar round in his mouth for some seconds, directing his gaze straight into the eyes of this unusual neophyte; but the Prince supported his scrutiny with unabashed good temper.

"If I had not a deal of experience," said the President at last, "I should turn you off. But I know the world; and this much any way, that the most frivolous excuses for a suicide are often the toughest to stand by. And when I downright like a man, as I do you, sir, I would rather strain the regulation than deny him."

The Prince and the Colonel, one after the other, were subjected to a long and particular interrogatory: the Prince alone; but Geraldine in the presence of the Prince, so that the President might observe the countenance of the one while the other was being warmly cross-examined. The result was satisfactory; and the President, after having booked a few details of each case, produced a form of oath to be accepted. Nothing could be conceived more passive than the obedience promised, or more stringent than the terms by which the juror bound himself. The man who forfeited a pledge so awful could scarcely have a rag of honour or any of the consolations of religion left to him. Florizel signed the document, but not without a shudder; the Colonel followed his example with an air of great depression. Then the President received the entry money; and without more ado, introduced the two friends into the smoking-room of the Suicide Club.

The smoking-room of the Suicide Club was the same height as the cabinet into which it opened, but much larger, and papered from top to bottom with an imitation of oak wainscot. A large and cheerful fire and a number of gas-jets illuminated the company. The Prince and his follower made the number up to eighteen. Most of the party were smoking, and drinking champagne; a feverish hilarity reigned, with sudden and rather ghastly pauses.

"Is this a full meeting?" asked the Prince.

"Middling," said the President. "By the way," he added, "if you have any money, it is usual to offer some champagne. It keeps up a good spirit, and is one of my own little perquisites."

"Hammersmith," said Florizel, "I may leave the champagne to you."

And with that he turned away and began to go round among the guests. Accustomed to play the host in the highest circles, he charmed and dominated all whom he approached; there was something at once winning and authoritative in his address; and his extraordinary coolness gave him yet another distinction in this half maniacal society. As he went from one to another he kept both his eyes and ears open, and soon began to gain a general idea of the people among whom he found himself. As in all other places of resort, one type predominated: people in the prime of youth, with every show of intelligence and sensibility in their appearance, but with little promise of strength or the quality that makes success. Few were much above thirty, and not a few were still in their teens. They stood, leaning on tables and shifting on their feet; sometimes they smoked extraordinarily fast, and sometimes they let their cigars go out; some talked well, but the conversation of others was plainly the result of nervous tension, and was equally without wit or purport. As each new bottle of champagne was opened, there was a manifest improvement in gaiety. Only two were seated—one in a chair in the recess of the window, with his head hanging and his hands plunged deep into his trouser pockets, pale, visibly moist with perspiration, saying never a word, a very wreck of soul and body; the other sat on the divan close by the chimney, and attracted notice by a trenchant dissimilarity from all the rest. He was probably upwards of forty, but he looked fully ten years older; and Florizel thought he had never seen a man more naturally hideous, nor one more ravaged by disease and ruinous excitements. He was no more than skin and bone, was partly paralysed, and wore spectacles of such unusual power, that his eyes appeared through the glasses greatly magnified and distorted in shape. Except the Prince and the President, he was the only person in the room who preserved the composure of ordinary life.

There was little decency among the members of the club. Some boasted of the disgraceful actions, the consequences of which had reduced them to seek refuge in death; and the others listened without disapproval. There was a tacit understanding against moral judgments; and whoever passed the club doors enjoyed already some of the immunities of the tomb. They drank to each other's memories, and to those of notable suicides in the past. They compared and developed their different views of death—some declaring that it was no more than blackness and cessation; others full of a hope that that very night they should be scaling the stars and commencing with the mighty dead.

"To the eternal memory of Baron Trenck, the type of suicides!" cried one. "He went out of a small cell into a smaller, that he might come forth again to freedom."

"For my part," said a second, "I wish no more than a bandage for my eyes and cotton for my ears. Only they have no cotton thick enough in this world."

A third was for reading the mysteries of life in a future state; and a fourth professed that he would never have joined the club, if he had not been induced to believe in Mr. Darwin.

"I could not bear," said this remarkable suicide, "to be descended from an ape."

Altogether, the Prince was disappointed by the bearing and conversation of the members.

"It does not seem to me," he thought, "a matter for so much disturbance. If a man has made up his mind to kill himself, let him do it, in God's name, like a gentleman. This flutter and big talk is out of place."

In the meanwhile Colonel Geraldine was a prey to the blackest apprehensions; the club and its rules were still a mystery, and he looked round the room for some one who should be able to set his mind at rest. In this survey his eye lighted on the paralytic person with the strong spectacles; and seeing him so exceedingly tranquil, he besought the President, who was going in and out of the room under a pressure of business, to present him to the gentleman on the divan.

The functionary explained the needlessness of all such formalities within the club, but nevertheless presented Mr. Hammersmith to Mr. Malthus.

Mr. Malthus looked at the Colonel curiously, and then requested him to take a seat upon his right.

"You are a new-comer," he said, "and wish information? You have come to the proper source. It is two years since I first visited this charming club."

The Colonel breathed again. If Mr. Malthus had frequented the place for two years there could be little danger for the Prince in a single evening. But Geraldine was none the less astonished, and began to suspect a mystification.

"What!" cried he, "two years! I thought—but indeed I see I have been made the subject of a pleasantry."

"By no means," replied Mr. Malthus mildly. "My case is peculiar. I am not, properly speaking, a suicide at all; but, as it were, an honorary member. I rarely visit the club twice in two months. My infirmity and the kindness of the President have procured me these little immunities, for which besides I pay at an advanced rate. Even as it is my luck has been extraordinary."

"I am afraid," said the Colonel, "that I must ask you to be more explicit. You must remember that I am still most imperfectly acquainted with the rules of the club."

"An ordinary member who comes here in search of death like yourself," replied the paralytic, "returns every evening until fortune favours him. He can even, if he is penniless, get board and lodging from the President: very fair, I believe, and clean, although, of course, not luxurious; that could hardly be, considering the exiguity (if I may so express myself) of the subscription. And then the President's company is a delicacy in itself."

"Indeed!" cried Geraldine, "he had not greatly prepossessed me."

"Ah!" said Mr. Malthus, "you do not know the man: the drollest fellow! What stories! What cynicism! He knows life to admiration and, between ourselves, is probably the most corrupt rogue in Christendom."

"And he also," asked the Colonel, "is a permanency—like yourself, if I may say so without offence?"

"Indeed, he is a permanency in a very different sense from me," replied Mr. Malthus. "I have hem graciously spared, but I must go at last. Now he never plays. He shuffles and deals for the club, and makes the necessary arrangements. That man, my dear Mr. Hammersmith, is the very soul of ingenuity. For three years he has pursued in London his useful and, I think I may add, his artistic calling; and not so much as a whisper of suspicion has been once aroused. I believe him myself to be inspired. You doubtless remember the celebrated case, six months ago, of the gentleman who was accidentally poisoned in a chemists shop? That was one of the least rich, one of the least racy, of his notions; but then, how simple! and how safe!"

"You astound me," said the Colonel. "Was that unfortunate gentleman one of the—" He was about to say "victims"; but bethinking himself in time, he substituted—"members of the club?"

In the same flash of thought, it occurred to him that Mr. Malthus himself had not at all spoken in the tone of one who is in love with death; and he added hurriedly:

"But I perceive I am still in the dark. You speak of shuffling and dealing; pray for what end? And since you seem rather unwilling to die than otherwise, I must own that I cannot conceive what brings you here at all."

"You say truly that you are in the dark," replied Mr. Malthus with more animation. "Why, my dear sir, this club is the temple of intoxication. If my enfeebled health could support the excitement more often, you may depend upon it I should be more often here. It requires all the sense of duty engendered by a long habit of ill-health and careful regimen, to keep me from excess in this, which is, I may say, my last dissipation. I have tried them all, sir," he went on, laying his hand on Geraldine's arm, "all without exception, and I declare to you, upon my honour, there is not one of them that has not been grossly and untruthfully overrated. People trifle with love. Now, I deny that love is a strong passion. Fear is the strong passion; it is with fear that you must trifle, if you wish to taste the intensest joys of living. Envy me—envy me, sir," he added with a chuckle, "I am a coward!"

Geraldine could scarcely repress a movement of repulsion for this deplorable wretch; but he commanded himself with an effort, and continued his inquiries.

"How, sir," he asked, "is the excitement so artfully prolonged? and where is there any element of uncertainty?"

"I must tell you how the victim for every evening is selected," returned Mr. Malthus; "and not only the victim, but another member, who is to be the instrument in the club's hands, and death's high priest for that occasion."

"Good God!" said the Colonel, "do they then kill each other?"

"The trouble of suicide is removed in that way," returned Malthus with a nod.

"Merciful heavens!" ejaculated the Colonel, "and may you—may I—may the—my friend I mean—may any of us be pitched upon this evening as the slayer of another man's body and immortal spirit? Can such things be possible among men born of women? Oh! infamy of infamies!"

He was about to rise in his horror, when he caught the Prince's eye. It was fixed upon him from across the room with a frowning and angry stare. And in a moment Geraldine recovered his composure.

"After all," he added, "why not? And since you say the game is interesting, *vogue la galère*—I follow the club!"

Mr. Malthus had keenly enjoyed the Colonel's amazement and disgust. He had the vanity of wickedness; and it pleased him to see another man give way to a generous movement, while he felt himself, in his entire corruption, superior to such emotions.

"You now, after your first moment of surprise," said he, "are in a position to appreciate the delights of our society. You can see how it combines the excitement of a gaming-table, a duel, and a Roman amphitheatre. The Pagans did well enough; I cordially admire the refinement of their minds; but it has been reserved for a Christian country to attain this extreme, this quintessence, this absolute of poignancy. You will understand how vapid are all amusements to a man who has acquired a taste for this one. The game we play," he continued, "is one of extreme simplicity. A full pack—but I perceive you are about to see the thing in progress. Will you lend me the help of your arm? I am unfortunately paralysed."

Indeed, just as Mr. Malthus was beginning his description, another pair of folding-doors was thrown open, and the whole club began to pass, not without some hurry, into the adjoining room. It was similar in every respect to the one from which it was entered, but somewhat differently furnished. The centre was occupied by a long green table, at which the President sat shuffling a pack of cards with great particularity. Even with the stick and the Colonel's arm, Mr. Malthus walked with so much difficulty that every one was seated before this pair and the Prince, who had waited for them, entered the apartment; and, in consequence, the three took seats close together at the lower end of the board.

"It is a pack of fifty-two," whispered Mr. Malthus. "Watch for the ace of spades, which is the sign of death, and the ace of clubs, which designates the official of the night. Happy, happy young men!" he added. "You have good eyes, and can follow the game. Alas! I cannot tell an ace from a deuce across the table."

And he proceeded to equip himself with a second pair of spectacles.

"I must at least watch the faces," he explained.

The Colonel rapidly informed his friend of all that he had learned from the honorary member, and of the horrible alternative that lay before them. The Prince was conscious of a deadly chill and a contraction about his heart; he swallowed with difficulty, and looked from side to side like a man in a maze.

"One bold stroke," whispered the Colonel, "and we may still escape."

But the suggestion recalled the Prince's spirits.

"Silence!" said be. "Let me see that you can play like a gentleman for any stake, however serious."

And he looked about him, once more to all appearance at his ease, although his heart beat thickly, and he was conscious of an unpleasant heat in his bosom. The members were all very quiet and intent; every one was pale, but none so pale as Mr. Malthus. His eyes protruded; his head kept nodding involuntarily upon his spine; his hands found their way, one after the other, to his mouth, where they made clutches at his tremulous and ashen lips. It was plain that the honorary member enjoyed his membership on very startling terms.

"Attention, gentlemen!" said the President.

And he began slowly dealing the cards about the table in the reverse direction, pausing until each man had shown his card. Nearly every one hesitated; and sometimes you would see a player's fingers stumble more than once before he could turn over the momentous slip of pasteboard. As the Prince's turn drew nearer, he was conscious of a growing and almost suffocating excitement; but he had somewhat of the gambler's nature, and recognised almost with astonishment, that there was a degree of pleasure in his sensations. The nine of clubs fell to his lot; the three of spades was dealt to Geraldine; and the queen of hearts to Mr. Malthus, who was unable to suppress a sob of relief. The young man of the cream tarts almost immediately afterwards turned over the ace of clubs, and remained frozen with horror, the card still resting on his finger; he had not come there to kill, but to be killed; and the Prince in his generous sympathy with his position almost forgot the peril that still hung over himself and his friend.

The deal was coming round again, and still Death's card had not come out. The players held their respiration, and only breathed by gasps. The Prince received another club; Geraldine had a diamond; but when Mr. Malthus turned up his card a horrible noise, like that of something breaking, issued from his mouth; and he rose from his seat and sat down again, with no sign of his paralysis. It was the ace of spades. The honorary member had trifled once too often with his terrors.

Conversation broke out again almost at once. The players relaxed their rigid attitudes, and began to rise from the table and stroll back by twos and threes into the smoking-room. The President stretched his arms and yawned, like a man who has finished his day's work. But Mr. Malthus sat in his place, with his head in his hands, and his hands upon the table, drunk and motionless—a thing stricken down.

The Prince and Geraldine made their escape at once. In the cold night air their horror of what they had witnessed was redoubled.

"Alas!" cried the Prince, "to be bound by an oath in such a matter! to allow this wholesale trade in murder to be continued with profit and impunity! If I but dared to forfeit my pledge!"

"That is impossible for your Highness," replied the Colonel, "whose honour is the honour of Bohemia. But I dare, and may with propriety, forfeit mine."

"Geraldine," said the Prince, "if your honour suffers in any of the adventures into which you follow me, not only will I never pardon you, but—what I believe will much more sensibly affect you—I should never forgive myself."

"I receive your Highness's commands," replied the Colonel. "Shall we go from this accursed spot?"

"Yes," said the Prince. "Call a cab in Heaven's name, and let me try to forget in slumber the memory of this night's disgrace."

But it was notable that he carefully read the name of the court before he left it.

The next morning, as soon as the Prince was stirring, Colonel Geraldine brought him a daily newspaper, with the following paragraph marked:—

"Melancholy Accident.—This morning, about two o'clock, Mr. Bartholomew Malthus, of 16 Chepstow Place, Westbourne Grove, on his way home from a party at a friend's house, fell over the upper parapet in Trafalgar Square, fracturing his skull and breaking a leg and an arm. Death was instantaneous. Mr. Malthus, accompanied by a friend, was engaged in looking for a cab at the time of the unfortunate occurrence. As Mr. Malthus was paralytic, it is thought that his fall may have been occasioned by another seizure. The unhappy gentleman was well known in the most respectable circles, and his loss will be widely and deeply deplored."

"If ever a soul went straight to Hell," said Geraldine solemnly, "it was that paralytic man's."

The Prince buried his face in his hands, and remained silent.

"I am almost rejoiced," continued the Colonel, "to know that he is dead. But for our young man of the cream tarts I confess my heart bleeds."

"Geraldine," said the Prince, raising his face, "that unhappy lad was last night as innocent as you and I; and this morning the guilt of blood is on his soul. When I think of the President, my heart grows sick within me. I do not know how it shall be done, but I shall have that scoundrel at my mercy as there is a God in heaven. What an experience, what a lesson, was that game of cards!"

"One," said the Colonel, "never to be repeated."

The Prince remained so long without replying, that Geraldine grew alarmed.

"You cannot mean to return," he said. "You have suffered too much and seen too much horror already. The duties of your high position forbid the repetition of the hazard."

"There is much in what you say," replied Prince Florizel, "and I am not altogether pleased with my own determination. Alas! in the clothes of the greatest potentate, what is there but a man? I never felt my weakness more acutely than now, Geraldine, but it is stronger than I. Can I cease to interest myself in the fortunes of the unhappy young man who supped with us some hours ago? Can I leave the President to follow his nefarious career unwatched? Can I begin an adventure so entrancing, and not follow it to an end? No, Geraldine: you ask of the Prince more than the man is able to perform. To-night, once more, we take our places at the table of the Suicide Club."

Colonel Geraldine fell upon his knees.

"Will your Highness take my life?" he cried. "It is his—his freely; but do not, O do not! let him ask me to countenance so terrible a risk."

"Colonel Geraldine," replied the Prince, with some haughtiness of manner, "your life is absolutely your own. I only looked for obedience; and when that is unwillingly rendered, I shall look for that no longer. I add one word your: importunity in this affair has been sufficient."

The Master of the Horse regained his feet at once.

"Your Highness," he said, "may I be excused in my attendance this afternoon? I dare not, as an honourable man, venture a second time into that fatal house until I have perfectly ordered my affairs. Your Highness shall meet, I promise him, with no more opposition from the most devoted and grateful of his servants."

"My dear Geraldine," returned Prince Florizel, "I always regret when you oblige me to remember my rank. Dispose of your day as you think fit, but be here before eleven in the same disguise."

The club, on this second evening, was not so fully attended; and when Geraldine and the Prince arrived, there were not above half-a-dozen persons in the smoking-room. His Highness took the President aside and congratulated him warmly on the demise of Mr. Malthus.

"I like," he said, "to meet with capacity, and certainly find much of it in you. Your profession is of a very delicate nature, but I see you are well qualified to conduct it with success and secrecy."

The President was somewhat affected by these compliments from one of his Highness's superior bearing. He acknowledged them almost with humility.

"Poor Malthy!" he added, "I shall hardly know the club without him. The most of my patrons are boys, sir, and poetical boys, who are not much company for me. Not but what Malthy had some poetry, too; but it was of a kind that I could understand."

"I can readily imagine you should find yourself in sympathy with Mr. Malthus," returned the Prince. "He struck me as a man of a very original disposition."

The young man of the cream tarts was in the room, but painfully depressed and silent. His late companions sought in vain to lead him into conversation.

"How bitterly I wish," he cried, "that I had never brought you to this infamous abode! Begone, while you are clean-handed. If you could have heard the old man scream as he fell, and the noise of his bones upon the pavement! Wish me, if you have any kindness to so fallen a being—wish the ace of spades for me to-night!"

A few more members dropped in as the evening went on, but the club did not muster more than the devil's dozen when they took their places at the table. The Prince was again conscious of a certain joy in his alarms; but he was astonished to see Geraldine so much more self-possessed than on the night before.

"It is extraordinary," thought the Prince, "that a will, made or unmade, should so greatly influence a young man's spirit."

"Attention, gentlemen!" said the President, and he began to deal.

Three times the cards went all round the table, and neither of the marked cards had yet fallen from his hand. The excitement as he began the fourth distribution was overwhelming. There were just cards enough to go once more entirely round. The Prince, who sat second from the dealer's left, would receive, in the reverse mode of dealing practised at the club, the second last card. The third player turned up a black ace—it was the ace of clubs. The next received a diamond, the next a heart, and so on; but the ace of spades was still undelivered. At last, Geraldine, who sat upon the Prince's left, turned his card; it was an ace, but the ace of hearts.

When Prince Florizel saw his fate upon the table in front of him, his heart stood still. He was a brave man, but the sweat poured off his face. There were exactly fifty chances out of a hundred that he was doomed. He reversed the card; it was the ace of spades. A loud roaring filled his brain, and the table swam before his eyes. He heard the player on his right break into a fit of laughter that sounded between mirth and disappointment; he saw the company rapidly dispersing, but his mind was full of other thoughts. He recognised how foolish, how criminal, had been his conduct. In perfect health, in the prime of his years, the heir to a throne, he had gambled away his future and that of a brave and loyal country. "God," he cried, "God forgive me!" And with that, the confusion of his senses passed away, and he regained his self-possession in a moment.

To his surprise Geraldine had disappeared. There was no one in the card-room but his destined butcher consulting with the President, and the young man of the cream tarts, who slipped up to the Prince, and whispered in his ear:—

"I would give a million, if I had it, for your luck."

His Highness could not help reflecting, as the young man departed, that he would have sold his opportunity for a much more moderate sum.

The whispered conference now came to an end. The holder of the ace of clubs left the room with a look of intelligence, and the President, approaching the unfortunate Prince, proffered him his hand.

"I am pleased to have met you, sir," said he, "and pleased to have been in a position to do you this trifling service. At least, you cannot complain of delay. On the second evening—what a stroke of luck!"

The Prince endeavoured in vain to articulate something in response, but his mouth was dry and his tongue seemed paralysed.

"You feel a little sickish?" asked the President, with some show of solicitude. "Most gentlemen do. Will you take a little brandy?"

The Prince signified in the affirmative, and the other immediately filled some of the spirit into a tumbler.

"Poor old Malthy!" ejaculated the President, as the Prince drained the glass. "He drank near upon a pint, and little enough good it seemed to do him!"

"I am more amenable to treatment," said the Prince, a good deal revived. "I am my own man again at once, as you perceive. And so, let me ask you, what are my directions?"

"You will proceed along the Strand in the direction of the City, and on the left-hand pavement, until you meet the gentleman who has just left the room. He will continue your instructions, and him you will have the kindness to obey; the authority of the club is vested in his person for the night. And now," added the President, "I wish you a pleasant walk."

Florizel acknowledged the salutation rather awkwardly, and took his leave. He passed through the smoking-room, where the bulk of the players were still consuming champagne, some of which he had himself ordered and paid for; and he was surprised to find himself cursing them in his heart. He put on his hat and greatcoat in the cabinet, and selected his umbrella from a corner. The familiarity of these acts, and the thought that he was about them for the last time, betrayed him into a fit of laughter which sounded unpleasantly in his own ears. He conceived a reluctance to leave the cabinet, and turned instead to the window. The sight of the lamps and the darkness recalled him to himself.

"Come, come, I must be a man," he thought, "and tear myself away."

At the corner of Box Court three men fell upon Prince Florizel and he was unceremoniously thrust into a carriage, which at once drove rapidly away. There was already an occupant.

"Will your Highness pardon my zeal?" said a well known voice.

The Prince threw himself upon the Colonel's neck in a passion of relief.

"How can I ever thank you?" he cried. "And how was this effected?"

Although he had been willing to march upon his doom, he was overjoyed to yield to friendly violence, and return once more to life and hope.

"You can thank me effectually enough," replied the Colonel, "by avoiding all such dangers in the future. And as for your second question, all has been managed by the simplest means. I arranged this afternoon with a celebrated detective. Secrecy has been promised and paid for. Your own servants have been principally engaged in the affair. The house in Box Court has been surrounded since nightfall, and this, which is one of your own carriages, has been awaiting you for nearly an hour."

"And the miserable creature who was to have slain me—what of him?" inquired the Prince.

"He was pinioned as he left the club," replied the Colonel, "and now awaits your sentence at the Palace, where he will soon be joined by his accomplices."

"Geraldine," said the Prince, "you have saved me against my explicit orders, and you have done well. I owe you not only my life, but a lesson; and I should be unworthy of my rank if I did not show myself grateful to my teacher. Let it be yours to choose the manner."

There was a pause, during which the carriage continued to speed through the streets, and the two men were each buried in his own reflections. The silence was broken by Colonel Geraldine.

"Your Highness," said he, "has by this time a considerable body of prisoners. There is at least one criminal among the number to whom justice should be dealt. Our oath forbids us all recourse to law; and discretion would forbid it equally if the oath were loosened. May I inquire your Highness's intention?"

"It is decided," answered Florizel; "the President must fall in duel. It only remains to choose his adversary."

"Your Highness has permitted me to name my own recompense," said the Colonel. "Will he permit me to ask the appointment of my brother? It is an honourable post, but I dare assure your Highness that the lad will acquit himself with credit."

"You ask me an ungracious favour," said the Prince, "but I must refuse you nothing."

The Colonel kissed his hand with the greatest affection; and at that moment the carriage rolled under the archway of the Prince's splendid residence.

An hour after, Florizel in his official robes, and covered with all the orders of Bohemia, received the members of the Suicide Club.

"Foolish and wicked men," said he, "as many of you as have been driven into this strait by the lack of fortune shall receive employment and remuneration from my officers. Those who suffer under a sense of guilt must have recourse to a higher and more generous Potentate than I. I feel pity for all of you, deeper than you can imagine; to-morrow you shall tell me your stories; and as you answer more frankly, I shall be the more able to remedy your misfortunes. As for you," he added, turning to the President, "I should only offend a person of your parts by any offer of assistance; but I have instead a piece of diversion to propose to you. Here," laying his hand on the shoulder of Colonel Geraldine's young brother, "is an officer of mine who desires to make a little tour upon the Continent; and I ask you, as a favour, to accompany him on this excursion. Do you," he went on, changing his tone, "do you shoot well with the pistol? Because you may have need of that accomplishment. When two men go travelling together, it is best to be prepared for all. Let me add that, if by any chance you should lose young Mr. Geraldine upon the way, I shall always have another member of my household to place at your disposal; and I am known, Mr. President, to have long eyesight, and as long an arm."

With these words, said with much sternness, the Prince concluded his address. Next morning the members of the club were suitably provided for by his munificence, and the President set forth upon his travels, under the supervision of Mr. Geraldine, and a pair of faithful and adroit lackeys, well trained in the Prince's household. Not content with this, discreet agents were put in possession of the house in Box Court, and all letters or visitors for the Suicide Club or its officials were to be examined by Prince Florizel in person.

2

STORY OF THE PHYSICIAN AND THE SARATOGA TRUNK

MR. SILAS Q. SCUDDAMORE was a young American of a simple and harmless disposition, which was the more to his credit as he came from New England—a quarter of the New World not precisely famous for those qualities. Although he was exceedingly rich, he kept a note of all his expenses in a little paper pocket-book; and he had chosen to study the attractions of Paris from the seventh story of what is called a furnished hotel, in the Latin Quarter. There was a great deal of habit in his penuriousness; and his virtue, which was very remarkable among his associates, was principally founded upon diffidence and youth.

The next room to his was inhabited by a lady, very attractive in her air and very elegant in toilette, whom, on his first arrival, he had taken for a Countess. In course of time he had learned that she was known by the name of Madame Zéphyrine, and that whatever station she occupied in life it was not that of a person of title. Madame Zéphyrine, probably in the hope of enchanting the young American, used to flaunt by him on the stairs with a civil inclination, a word of course, and a knock-down look out of her black eyes, and disappear in a rustle of silk, and with the revelation of an admirable foot and ankle. But these advances, so far from encouraging Mr. Scuddamore, plunged him into the depths of depression and bashfulness. She had come to him several times for a light, or to apologise for the imaginary depredations of her poodle; but his mouth was closed in the presence of so superior a being, his French promptly left him, and he could only stare and stammer until she was gone. The slenderness of their intercourse did not prevent him from throwing out insinuations of a very glorious order when he was safely alone with a few males.

The room on the other side of the American's—for there were three rooms on a floor in the hotel—was tenanted by an old English physician of rather doubtful reputation. Dr. Noel, for that was his name, had been forced to leave London, where he enjoyed a large and increasing practice; and it was hinted that the police had been the instigators of this change of scene. At least he, who had made something of a figure in earlier life, now dwelt in the Latin Quarter in great simplicity and solitude, and devoted much of his time to study. Mr. Scuddamore had made his acquaintance, and the pair would now and then dine together frugally in a restaurant across the street.

Silas Q. Scuddamore had many little vices of the more respectable order, and was not restrained by delicacy from indulging them in many rather doubtful ways. Chief among his foibles stood curiosity. He was a born gossip; and life, and especially those parts of it in which he had no experience, interested him to the degree of passion. He was a pert, invincible questioner, pushing his inquiries with equal pertinacity and indiscretion; he had been observed, when he took a letter to the post, to weigh it in his hand, to turn it over and over, and to study the address with care; and when he found a flaw in the partition between his room and Madame Zéphyrine's, instead of filling it up, he enlarged and improved the opening, and made use of it as a spy-hole on his neighbour's affairs.

One day, in the end of March, his curiosity growing as it was indulged, he enlarged the hole a little further, so that he might command another corner of the room. That evening, when he went as usual to inspect Madame Zéphyrine's movements, he was astonished to find the aperture obscured in an odd manner on the other side, and still more abashed when the obstacle was suddenly withdrawn and a titter of laughter reached his ears. Some of the plaster had evidently betrayed the secret of his spy-hole, and his neighbour had been returning the compliment in kind. Mr. Scuddamore was moved to a very acute feeling of annoyance; he condemned Madame Zéphyrine unmercifully; he even blamed himself; but when he found, next day, that she had taken no means to baulk him of his favourite pastime, he continued to profit by her carelessness, and gratify his idle curiosity.

That next day Madame Zéphyrine received a long visit from a tall, loosely-built man of fifty or upwards, whom Silas had not hitherto seen. His tweed suit and coloured shirt, no less than his shaggy side-whiskers, identified him as a Britisher, and his dull grey eye affected Silas with a sense of cold. He kept screwing his mouth from side to side and round and round during the whole colloquy, which was carried on in whispers. More than once it seemed to the young New Englander as if their gestures indicated his own apartment; but the only thing definite he could gather by the most scrupulous attention was this remark made by the Englishman in a somewhat higher key, as if in answer to some reluctance or opposition.

"I have studied his taste to a nicety, and I tell you again and again you are the only woman of the sort that I can lay my hands on."

In answer to this, Madame Zéphyrine sighed, and appeared by a gesture to resign herself, like one yielding to unqualified authority.

That afternoon the observatory was finally blinded, a wardrobe having been drawn in front of it upon the other side; and while Silas was still lamenting over this misfortune, which he attributed to the Britisher's malign suggestion, the concierge brought him up a letter in a female handwriting. It was conceived in French of no very rigorous orthography, bore no signature, and in the most encouraging terms invited the young American to be present in a certain part of the Bullier Ball at eleven o'clock that night. Curiosity and timidity fought a long battle in his heart; sometimes he was all virtue, sometimes all fire and daring; and the result of it was that, long before ten, Mr. Silas Q. Scuddamore presented himself in unimpeachable attire at the door of the Bullier Ball Rooms, and paid his entry money with a sense of reckless devilry that was not without its charm.

It was Carnival time, and the Ball was very full and noisy. The lights and the crowd at first rather abashed our young adventurer, and then, mounting to his brain with a sort of intoxication, put him in possession of more than his own share of manhood. He felt ready to face the devil, and strutted in the ballroom with the swagger of a cavalier. While he was thus parading, he became aware of Madame Zéphyrine and her Britisher in conference behind a pillar. The cat-like spirit of eaves-dropping overcame him at once. He stole nearer and nearer on the couple from behind, until he was within earshot.

"That is the man," the Britisher was saying; "there—with the long blond hair—speaking to a girl in green."

Silas identified a very handsome young fellow of small stature, who was plainly the object of this designation.

"It is well," said Madame Zéphyrine. "I shall do my utmost. But, remember, the best of us may fail in such a matter."

"Tut!" returned her companion; "I answer for the result. Have I not chosen you from thirty? Go; but be wary of the Prince. I cannot think what cursed accident has brought him here to-night. As if there were not a dozen balls in Paris better worth his notice than this riot of students and counter-jumpers! See him where he sits, more like a reigning Emperor at home than a Prince upon his holidays!"

Silas was again lucky. He observed a person of rather a full build, strikingly handsome, and of a very stately and courteous demeanour, seated at table with another handsome young man, several years his junior, who addressed him with conspicuous deference. The name of Prince struck gratefully on Silas's Republican hearing, and the aspect of the person to whom that name was applied exercised its usual charm upon his mind. He left Madame Zéphyrine and her Englishman to take care of each other, and threading his way through the assembly, approached the table which the Prince and his confidant had honoured with their choice.

"I tell you, Geraldine," the former was saying, "the action is madness. Yourself (I am glad to remember it) chose your brother for this perilous service, and you are bound in duty to have a guard upon his conduct. He has consented to delay so many days in Paris; that was already an imprudence, considering the character of the man he has to deal with; but now, when he is within eight-and-forty hours of his departure, when he is within two or three days of the decisive trial, I ask you, is this a place for him to spend his time? He should be in a gallery at practice; he should be sleeping long hours and taking moderate exercise on foot; he should be on a rigorous diet, without white wines or brandy. Does the dog imagine we are all playing comedy? The thing is deadly earnest, Geraldine."

"I know the lad too well to interfere," replied Colonel Geraldine, "and well enough not to be alarmed. He is more cautious than you fancy, and of an indomitable spirit. If it had been a woman I should not say so much, but I trust the President to him and the two valets without an instant's apprehension."

"I am gratified to hear you say so," replied the Prince; "but my mind is not at rest. These servants are well-trained spies, and already has not this miscreant succeeded three times in eluding their observation and spending several hours on end in private, and most likely dangerous, affairs? An amateur might have lost him by accident, but if Rudolph and Jérome were thrown off the scent, it must have been done on purpose, and by a man who had a cogent reason and exceptional resources."

"I believe the question is now one between my brother and myself," replied Geraldine, with a shade of offence in his tone.

"I permit it to be so, Colonel Geraldine," returned Prince Florizel. "Perhaps, for that very reason, you should be all the more ready to accept my counsels. But enough. That girl in yellow dances well."

And the talk veered into the ordinary topics of a Paris ballroom in the Carnival.

Silas remembered where he was, and that the hour was already near at hand when he ought to be upon the scene of his assignation. The more he reflected the less he liked the prospect, and as at that moment an eddy in the crowd began to draw him in the direction of the door, he suffered it to carry him away without resistance. The eddy stranded him in a corner under the gallery, where his ear was immediately struck with the voice of Madame Zéphyrine. She was speaking in French with the young man of the blond locks who had been pointed out by the strange Britisher not half-an-hour before.

"I have a character at stake," she said, "or I would put no other condition than my heart recommends. But you have only to say so much to the porter, and he will let you go by without a word."

"But why this talk of debt?" objected her companion.

"Heavens!" said she, "do you think I do not understand my own hotel?"

And she went by, clinging affectionately to her companion's arm.

This put Silas in mind of his billet.

"Ten minutes hence," thought he, "and I may be walking with as beautiful a woman as that, and even better dressed—perhaps a real lady, possibly a woman or title."

And then he remembered the spelling, and was a little downcast.

"But it may have been written by her maid," he imagined.

The clock was only a few minutes from the hour, and this immediate proximity set his heart beating at a curious and rather disagreeable speed. He reflected with relief that he was in no way bound to put in an appearance. Virtue and cowardice were together, and he made once more for the door, but this time of his own accord, and battling against the stream of people which was now moving in a contrary direction. Perhaps this prolonged resistance wearied him, or perhaps he was in that frame of mind when merely to continue in the same determination for a certain number of minutes produces a reaction and a different purpose. Certainly, at least, he wheeled about for a third time, and did not stop until he had found a place of concealment within a few yards of the appointed place.

Here he went through an agony of spirit, in which he several times prayed to God for help, for Silas had been devoutly educated. He had now not the least inclination for the meeting; nothing kept him from flight but a silly fear lest he should be thought unmanly; but this was so powerful that it kept head against all other motives; and although it could not decide him to advance, prevented him from definitely running away. At last the clock indicated ten minutes past the hour. Young Scuddamore's spirit began to rise; he peered round the corner and saw no one at the place of meeting; doubtless his unknown correspondent had wearied and gone away. He became as bold as he had formerly been timid. It seemed to him that if he came at all to the appointment, however late, he was clear from the charge of cowardice. Nay, now he began to suspect a hoax, and actually complimented himself on his shrewdness in having suspected and outmanoeuvred his mystifiers. So very idle a thing is a boy's mind!

Armed with these reflections, he advanced boldly from his corner; but he had not taken above a couple of steps before a hand was laid upon his arm. He turned and beheld a lady cast in a very large mould and with somewhat stately features, but bearing no mark of severity in her looks.

"I see that you are a very self-confident lady-killer," said she; "for you make yourself expected. But I was determined to meet you. When a woman has once so far forgotten herself as to make the first advance, she has long ago left behind her all considerations of petty pride."

Silas was overwhelmed by the size and attractions of his correspondent and the suddenness with which she had fallen upon him. But she soon set him at his ease. She was very towardly and lenient in her behaviour; she led him on to make pleasantries, and then applauded him to the echo; and in a very short time, between blandishments and a liberal exhibition of warm brandy, she had not only induced him to fancy himself in love, but to declare his passion with the greatest vehemence.

"Alas!" she said; "I do not know whether I ought not to deplore this moment, great as is the pleasure you give me by your words. Hitherto I was alone to suffer; now, poor boy, there will be two. I am not my own mistress. I dare not ask you to visit me at my own house, for I am watched by jealous eyes. Let me see," she added; "I am older than you, although so much weaker; and while I trust in your courage and determination, I must employ my own knowledge of the world for our mutual benefit. Where do you live?"

He told her that he lodged in a furnished hotel, and named the street and number.

She seemed to reflect for some minutes, with an effort of mind.

"I see," she said at last. "You will be faithful and obedient, will you not?"

Silas assured her eagerly of his fidelity.

"To-morrow night, then," she continued, with an encouraging smile, "you must remain at home all the evening; and if any friends should visit you, dismiss them at once on any pretext that most readily presents itself. Your door is probably shut by ten?" she asked.

"By eleven," answered Silas.

"At a quarter past eleven," pursued the lady, "leave the house. Merely cry for the door to be opened, and be sure you fall into no talk with the porter, as that might ruin everything. Go straight to the corner where the Luxembourg Gardens join the Boulevard; there you will find me waiting you. I trust you to follow my advice from point to point: and remember, if you fail me in only one particular, you will bring the sharpest trouble on a woman whose only fault is to have seen and loved you."

"I cannot see the use of all these instructions," said Silas.

"I believe you are already beginning to treat me as a master," she cried, tapping him with her fan upon the arm. "Patience, patience! that should come in time. A woman loves to be obeyed at first, although afterwards she finds her pleasure in obeying. Do as I ask you, for Heaven's sake, or I will answer for nothing. Indeed, now I think of it," she added, with the manner of one who has just seen further into a difficulty, "I find a better plan of keeping importunate visitors away. Tell the porter to admit no one for you, except a person who may come that night to claim a debt; and speak with some feeling, as though you feared the interview, so that he may take your words in earnest."

"I think you may trust me to protect myself against intruders," he said, not without a little pique.

"That is how I should prefer the thing arranged," she answered coldly. "I know you men; you think nothing of a woman's reputation."

Silas blushed and somewhat hung his head; for the scheme he had in view had involved a little vain-glorying before his acquaintances.

"Above all," she added, "do not speak to the porter as you come out."

"And why?" said he. "Of all your instructions, that seems to me the least important."

"You at first doubted the wisdom of some of the others, which you now see to be very necessary," she replied. "Believe me, this also has its uses; in time you will see them; and what am I to think of your affection, if you refuse me such trifles at our first interview?"

Silas confounded himself in explanations and apologies; in the middle of these she looked up at the clock and clapped her hands together with a suppressed scream.

"Heavens!" she cried, "is it so late? I have not an instant to lose. Alas, we poor women, what slaves we are! What have I not risked for you already?"

And after repeating her directions, which she artfully combined with caresses and the most abandoned looks, she bade him farewell and disappeared among the crowd.

The whole of the next day Silas was filled with a sense of great importance; he was now sure she was a countess; and when evening came he minutely obeyed her orders and was at the corner of the Luxembourg Gardens by the hour appointed. No one was there. He waited nearly half-an-hour, looking in the face of every one who passed or loitered near the spot; he even visited the neighbouring corners of the Boulevard and made a complete circuit of the garden railings; but there was no beautiful countess to throw herself into his arms. At last, and most reluctantly, he began to retrace his steps towards his hotel. On the way he remembered the words he had heard pass between Madame Zéphyrine and the blond young man, and they gave him an indefinite uneasiness.

"It appears," he reflected, "that every one has to tell lies to our porter."

He rang the bell, the door opened before him, and the porter in his bed-clothes came to offer him a light.

"Has he gone?" inquired the porter.

"He? Whom do you mean?" asked Silas, somewhat sharply, for he was irritated by his disappointment.

"I did not notice him go out," continued the porter, "but I trust you paid him. We do not care, in this house, to have lodgers who cannot meet their liabilities."

"What the devil do you mean?" demanded Silas rudely. "I cannot understand a word of this farrago."

"The short blond young man who came for his debt," returned the other. "Him it is I mean. Who else should it be, when I had your orders to admit no one else?"

"Why, good God, of course he never came," retorted Silas.

"I believe what I believe," returned the porter, putting his tongue into his cheek with a most roguish air.

"You are an insolent scoundrel," cried Silas, and, feeling that he had made a ridiculous exhibition of asperity, and at the same time bewildered by a dozen alarms, he turned and began to run upstairs.

"Do you not want a light then?" cried the porter.

But Silas only hurried the faster, and did not pause until he had reached the seventh landing and stood in front of his own door. There he waited a moment to recover his breath, assailed by the worst forebodings and almost dreading to enter the room.

When at last he did so he was relieved to find it dark, and to all appearance, untenanted. He drew a long breath. Here he was, home again in safety, and this should be his last folly as certainly as it had been his first. The matches stood on a little table by the bed, and he began to grope his way in that direction. As he moved, his apprehensions grew upon him once more, and he was pleased, when his foot encountered an obstacle, to find it nothing more alarming than a chair. At last he touched curtains. From the position of the window, which was faintly visible, he knew he must be at the foot of the bed, and had only to feel his way along it in order to reach the table in question.

He lowered his hand, but what it touched was not simply a counterpane—it was a counterpane with something underneath it like the outline of a human leg. Silas withdrew his arm and stood a moment petrified.

"What, what," he thought, "can this betoken?"

He listened intently, but there was no sound of breathing. Once more, with a great effort, he reached out the end of his finger to the spot he had already touched; but this time he leaped back half a yard, and stood shivering and fixed with terror. There was something in his bed. What it was he knew not, but there was something there.

It was some seconds before he could move. Then, guided by an instinct, he fell straight upon the matches, and keeping his back towards the bed lighted a candle. As soon as the flame had kindled, he turned slowly round and looked for what he feared to see. Sure enough, there was the worst of his imaginations realised. The coverlid was drawn carefully up over the pillow, but it moulded the outline of a human body lying motionless; and when he dashed forward and flung aside the sheets, he beheld the blond young man whom he had seen in the Bullier Ball the night before, his eyes open and without speculation, his face swollen and blackened, and a thin stream of blood trickling from his nostrils.

Silas uttered a long, tremulous wail, dropped the candle, and fell on his knees beside the bed.

Silas was awakened from the stupor into which his terrible discovery had plunged him by a prolonged but discreet tapping at the door. It took him some seconds to remember his position; and when he hastened to prevent anyone from entering it was already too late. Dr. Noel, in a tall night-cap, carrying a lamp which lighted up his long white countenance, sidling in his gait, and peering and cocking his head like some sort of bird, pushed the door slowly open, and advanced into the middle of the room.

"I thought I heard a cry," began the Doctor, "and fearing you might be unwell I did not hesitate to offer this intrusion."

Silas, with a flushed face and a fearful beating heart, kept between the Doctor and the bed; but he found no voice to answer.

"You are in the dark," pursued the Doctor; "and yet you have not even begun to prepare for rest. You will not easily persuade me against my own eyesight; and your face declares most eloquently that you require either a friend or a physician—which is it to be? Let me feel your pulse, for that is often a just reporter of the heart."

He advanced to Silas, who still retreated before him backwards, and sought to take him by the wrist; but the strain on the young American's nerves had become too great for endurance. He avoided the Doctor with a febrile movement, and, throwing himself upon the floor, burst into a flood of weeping.

As soon as Dr. Noel perceived the dead man in the bed his face darkened; and hurrying back to the door which he had left ajar, he hastily closed and double-locked it.

"Up!" he cried, addressing Silas in strident tones; "this is no time for weeping. What have you done? How came this body in your room? Speak freely to one who may be helpful. Do you imagine I would ruin you? Do you think this piece of dead flesh on your pillow can alter in any degree the sympathy with which you have inspired me? Credulous youth, the horror with which blind and unjust law regards an action never attaches to the doer in the eyes of those who love him; and if I saw the friend of my heart return to me out of seas of blood he would be in no way changed in my affection. Raise yourself," he said; "good and ill are a chimera; there is nought in life except destiny, and however you may be circumstanced there is one at your side who will help you to the last."

Thus encouraged, Silas gathered himself together, and in a broken voice, and helped out by the Doctor's interrogations, contrived at last to put him in possession of the facts. But the conversation between the Prince and Geraldine he altogether omitted, as he had understood little of its purport, and had no idea that it was in any way related to his own misadventure.

"Alas!" cried Dr. Noel, "I am much abused, or you have fallen innocently into the most dangerous hands in Europe. Poor boy, what a pit has been dug for your simplicity! into what a deadly peril have your unwary feet been conducted! This man," he said, "this Englishman, whom you twice saw, and whom I suspect to be the soul of the contrivance, can you describe him? Was he young or old? tall or short?"

But Silas, who, for all his curiosity, had not a seeing eye in his head, was able to supply nothing but meagre generalities, which it was impossible to recognise.

"I would have it a piece of education in all schools!" cried the Doctor angrily. "Where is the use of eyesight and articulate speech if a man cannot observe and recollect the features of his enemy? I, who know all the gangs of Europe, might have identified him, and gained new weapons for your defence. Cultivate this art in future, my poor boy; you may find it of momentous service."

"The future!" repeated Silas. "What future is there left for me except the gallows?"

"Youth is but a cowardly season," returned the Doctor; "and a man's own troubles look blacker than they are. I am old, and yet I never despair."

"Can I tell such a story to the police?" demanded Silas.

"Assuredly not," replied the Doctor. "From what I see already of the machination in which you have been involved, your case is desperate upon that side; and for the narrow eye of the authorities you are infallibly the guilty person. And remember that we only know a portion of the plot; and the same infamous contrivers have doubtless arranged many other circumstances which would be elicited by a police inquiry, and help to fix the guilt more certainly upon your innocence."

"I am then lost, indeed!" cried Silas.

"I have not said so," answered Dr. Noel "for I am a cautious man."

"But look at this!" objected Silas, pointing to the body. "Here is this object in my bed; not to be explained, not to be disposed of, not to be regarded without horror."

"Horror?" replied the Doctor. "No. When this sort of clock has run down, it is no more to me than an ingenious piece of mechanism, to be investigated with the bistoury. When blood is once cold and stagnant, it is no longer human blood; when flesh is once dead, it is no longer that flesh which we desire in our lovers and respect in our friends. The grace, the attraction, the terror, have all gone from it with the animating spirit. Accustom yourself to look upon it with composure; for if my scheme is practicable you will have to live some days in constant proximity to that which now so greatly horrifies you."

"Your scheme?" cried Silas. "What is that? Tell me speedily, Doctor; for I have scarcely courage enough to continue to exist."

Without replying, Doctor Noel turned towards the bed, and proceeded to examine the corpse.

"Quite dead," he murmured. "Yes, as I had supposed, the pockets empty. Yes, and the name cut off the shirt. Their work has been done thoroughly and well. Fortunately, he is of small stature."

Silas followed these words with an extreme anxiety. At last the Doctor, his autopsy completed, took a chair and addressed the young American with a smile.

"Since I came into your room," said he, "although my ears and my tongue have been so busy, I have not suffered my eyes to remain idle. I noted a little while ago that you have there, in the corner, one of those monstrous constructions which your fellow-countrymen carry with them into all quarters of the globe—in a word, a Saratoga trunk. Until this moment I have never been able to conceive the utility of these erections; but then I began to have a glimmer. Whether it was for convenience in the slave trade, or to obviate the results of too ready an employment of the bowie-knife, I cannot bring myself to decide. But one thing I see plainly—the object of such a box is to contain a human body.

"Surely," cried Silas, "surely this is not a time for jesting."

"Although I may express myself with some degree of pleasantry," replied the Doctor, "the purport of my words is entirely serious. And the first thing we have to do, my young friend, is to empty your coffer of all that it contains."

Silas, obeying the authority of Doctor Noel, put himself at his disposition. The Saratoga trunk was soon gutted of its contents, which made a considerable litter on the floor; and then—Silas taking the heels and the Doctor supporting the shoulders—the body of the murdered man was carried from the bed, and, after some difficulty, doubled up and inserted whole into the empty box. With an effort on the part of both, the lid was forced down upon this unusual baggage, and the trunk was locked and corded by the Doctor's own hand, while Silas disposed of what had been taken out between the closet and a chest of drawers.

"Now," said the Doctor, "the first step has been taken on the way to your deliverance. To-morrow, or rather to-day, it must be your task to allay the suspicions of your porter, paying him all that you owe; while you may trust me to make the arrangements necessary to a safe conclusion. Meantime, follow me to my room, where I shall give you a safe and powerful opiate; for, whatever you do, you must have rest."

The next day was the longest in Silas's memory; it seemed as if it would never be done. He denied himself to his friends, and sat in a corner with his eyes fixed upon the Saratoga trunk in dismal contemplation. His own former indiscretions were now returned upon him in kind; for the observatory had been once more opened, and he was conscious of an almost continual study from Madame Zéphyrine's apartment. So distressing did this become, that he was at last obliged to block up the spy-hole from his own side; and when he was thus secured from observation he spent a considerable portion of his time in contrite tears and prayer.

Late in the evening Dr. Noel entered the room carrying in his hand a pair of sealed envelopes without address, one somewhat bulky, and the other so slim as to seem without enclosure.

"Silas," he said, seating himself at the table, "the time has now come for me to explain my plan for your salvation. To-morrow morning, at an early hour, Prince Florizel of Bohemia returns to London, after having diverted himself for a few days with the Parisian Carnival. It was my fortune, a good while ago, to do Colonel Geraldine, his Master of the Horse, one of those services, so common in my profession, which are never forgotten upon either side. I have no need to explain to you the nature of the obligation under which he was laid; suffice it to say that I knew him ready to serve me in any practicable manner. Now, it was necessary for you to gain London with your trunk unopened. To this the Custom House seemed to oppose a fatal difficulty; but I bethought me that the baggage of so considerable a person as the Prince, is, as a matter of courtesy, passed without examination by the officers of Custom. I applied to Colonel Geraldine, and succeeded in obtaining a favourable answer. To-morrow, if you go before six to the hotel where the Prince lodges, your baggage will be passed over as a part of his, and you yourself will make the journey as a member of his suite."

"It seems to me, as you speak, that I have already seen both the Prince and Colonel Geraldine; I even overheard some of their conversation the other evening at the Bullier Ball."

"It is probable enough; for the Prince loves to mix with all societies," replied the Doctor. "Once arrived in London," he pursued, "your task is nearly ended. In this more bulky envelope I have given you a letter which I dare not address; but in the other you will find the designation of the house to which you must carry it along with your box, which will there be taken from you and not trouble you any more."

"Alas!" said Silas, "I have every wish to believe you; but how is it possible? You open up to me a bright prospect, but, I ask you, is my mind capable of receiving so unlikely a solution? Be more generous, and let me further understand your meaning."

The Doctor seemed painfully impressed.

"Boy," he answered, "you do not know how hard a thing you ask of me. But be it so. I am now inured to humiliation; and it would be strange if I refused you this, after having granted you so much. Know, then, that although I now make so quiet an appearance—frugal, solitary, addicted to study—when I was younger, my name was once a rallying-cry among the most astute and dangerous spirits of London; and while I was outwardly an object for respect and consideration, my true power resided in the most secret, terrible, and criminal relations. It is to one of the persons who then obeyed me that I now address myself to deliver you from your burden. They were men of many different nations and dexterities, all bound together by a formidable oath, and working to the same purposes; the trade of the association was in murder; and I who speak to you, innocent as I appear, was the chieftain of this redoubtable crew."

"What?" cried Silas. "A murderer? And one with whom murder was a trade? Can I take your hand? Ought I so much as to accept your services? Dark and criminal old man, would you make an accomplice of my youth and my distress?"

The Doctor bitterly laughed.

"You are difficult to please, Mr. Scuddamore," said he; "but I now offer you your choice of company between the murdered man and the murderer. If your conscience is too nice to accept my aid, say so, and I will immediately leave you. Thenceforward you can deal with your trunk and its belongings as best suits your upright conscience."

"I own myself wrong," replied Silas. "I should have remembered how generously you offered to shield me, even before I had convinced you of my innocence, and I continue to listen to your counsels with gratitude."

"That is well," returned the Doctor; "and I perceive you are beginning to learn some of the lessons of experience."

"At the same time," resumed the New-Englander, "as you confess yourself accustomed to this tragical business, and the people to whom you recommend me are your own former associates and friends, could you not yourself undertake the transport of the box, and rid me at once of its detested presence?"

"Upon my word," replied the Doctor, "I admire you cordially. If you do not think I have already meddled sufficiently in your concerns, believe me, from my heart I think the contrary. Take or leave my services as I offer them; and trouble me with no more words of gratitude, for I value your consideration even more lightly than I do your intellect. A time will come, if you should be spared to see a number of years in health of mind, when you will think differently of all this, and blush for your to-night's behaviour."

So saying, the Doctor arose from his chair, repeated his directions briefly and clearly, and departed from the room without permitting Silas any time to answer.

The next morning Silas presented himself at the hotel, where he was politely received by Colonel Geraldine, and relieved, from that moment, of all immediate alarm about his trunk and its grisly contents. The journey passed over without much incident, although the young man was horrified to overhear the sailors and railway porters complaining among themselves about the unusual weight of the Prince's baggage. Silas travelled in a carriage with the valets, for Prince Florizel chose to be alone with his Master of the Horse. On board the steamer, however, Silas attracted his Highness's attention by the melancholy of his air and attitude as he stood gazing at the pile of baggage; for he was still full of disquietude about the future.

"There is a young man," observed the Prince, "who must have some cause for sorrow."

"That," replied Geraldine, "is the American for whom I obtained permission to travel with your suite."

"You remind me that I have been remiss in courtesy," said Prince Florizel, and advancing to Silas, he addressed him with the most exquisite condescension in these words:—"I was charmed, young sir, to be able to gratify the desire you made known to me through Colonel Geraldine. Remember, if you please, that I shall be glad at any future time to lay you under a more serious obligation."

And he then put some questions as to the political condition of America, which Silas answered with sense and propriety.

"You are still a young man," said the Prince; "but I observe you to be very serious for your years. Perhaps you allow your attention to be too much occupied with grave studies. But, perhaps, on the other hand, I am myself indiscreet and touch upon a painful subject."

"I have certainly cause to be the most miserable of men," said Silas; "never has a more innocent person been more dismally abused."

"I will not ask you for your confidence," returned Prince Florizel. "But do not forget that Colonel Geraldine's recommendation is an unfailing passport; and that I am not only willing, but possibly more able than many others, to do you a service."

Silas was delighted with the amiability of this great personage; but his mind soon returned upon its gloomy preoccupations; for not even the favour of a Prince to a Republican can discharge a brooding spirit of its cares.

The train arrived at Charing Cross, where the officers of the Revenue respected the baggage of Prince Florizel in the usual manner. The most elegant equipages were in waiting; and Silas was driven, along with the rest, to the Prince's residence. There Colonel Geraldine sought him out, and expressed himself pleased to have been of any service to a friend of the physician's, for whom he professed a great consideration.

"I hope," he added, "that you will find none of your porcelain injured. Special orders were given along the line to deal tenderly with the Prince's effects."

And then, directing the servants to place one of the carriages at the young gentleman's disposal, and at once to charge the Saratoga trunk upon the dickey, the Colonel shook hands and excused himself on account of his occupations in the princely household.

Silas now broke the seal of the envelope containing the address, and directed the stately footman to drive him to Box Court, opening off the Strand. It seemed as if the place were not at all unknown to the man, for he looked startled and begged a repetition of the order. It was with a heart full of alarms, that Silas mounted into the luxurious vehicle, and was driven to his destination. The entrance to Box Court was too narrow for the passage of a coach; it was a mere footway between railings, with a post at either end. On one of these posts was seated a man, who at once jumped down and exchanged a friendly sign with the driver, while the footman opened the door and inquired of Silas whether he should take down the Saratoga trunk, and to what number it should be carried.

"If you please," said Silas. "To number three."

The footman and the man who had been sitting on the post, even with the aid of Silas himself, had hard work to carry in the trunk; and before it was deposited at the door of the house in question, the young American was horrified to find a score of loiterers looking on. But he knocked with as good a countenance as he could muster up, and presented the other envelope to him who opened.

"He is not at home," said he, "but if you will leave your letter and return to-morrow early, I shall be able to inform you whether and when he can receive your visit. Would you like to leave your box?" he added.

"Dearly," cried Silas; and the next moment he repented his precipitation, and declared, with equal emphasis, that he would rather carry the box along with him to the hotel.

The crowd jeered at his indecision and followed him to the carriage with insulting remarks; and Silas, covered with shame and terror, implored the servants to conduct him to some quiet and comfortable house of entertainment in the immediate neighbourhood.

The Prince's equipage deposited Silas at the Craven Hotel in Craven Street, and immediately drove away, leaving him alone with the servants of the inn. The only vacant room, it appeared, was a little den up four pairs of stairs, and looking towards the back. To this hermitage, with infinite trouble and complaint, a pair of stout porters carried the Saratoga trunk. It is needless to mention that Silas kept closely at their heels throughout the ascent, and had his heart in his mouth at every corner. A single false step, he reflected, and the box might go over the banisters and land its fatal contents, plainly discovered, on the pavement of the hall.

Arrived in the room, he sat down on the edge of his bed to recover from the agony that he had just endured; but he had hardly taken his position when he was recalled to a sense of his peril by the action of the boots, who had knelt beside the trunk, and was proceeding officiously to undo its elaborate fastenings.

"Let it be!" cried Silas. "I shall want nothing from it while I stay here."

"You might have let it lie in the hall, then," growled the man; "a thing as big and heavy as a church. What you have inside I cannot fancy. If it is all money, you are a richer man than me."

"Money?" repeated Silas, in a sudden perturbation. "What do you mean by money? I have no money, and you are speaking like a fool."

"All right, captain," retorted the boots with a wink. "There's nobody will touch your lordship's money. I'm as safe as the bank," he added; "but as the box is heavy, I shouldn't mind drinking something to your lordship's health."

Silas pressed two Napoleons upon his acceptance, apologising, at the same time, for being obliged to trouble him with foreign money, and pleading his recent arrival for excuse. And the man, grumbling with even greater fervour, and looking contemptuously from the money in his hand to the Saratoga trunk and back again from the one to the other, at last consented to withdraw.

For nearly two days the dead body had been packed into Silas's box; and as soon as he was alone the unfortunate New-Englander nosed all the cracks and openings with the most passionate attention. But the weather was cool, and the trunk still managed to contain his shocking secret.

He took a chair beside it, and buried his face in his hands, and his mind in the most profound reflection. If he were not speedily relieved, no question but he must be speedily discovered. Alone in a strange city, without friends or accomplices, if the Doctor's introduction failed him, he was indubitably a lost New-Englander. He reflected pathetically over his ambitious designs for the future; he should not now become the hero and spokesman of his native place of Bangor, Maine; he should not, as he had fondly anticipated, move on from office to office, from honour to honour; he might as well divest himself at once of all hope of being acclaimed President of the United States, and leaving behind him a statue, in the worst possible style of art, to adorn the Capitol at Washington. Here he was, chained to a dead Englishman doubled up inside a Saratoga trunk; whom he must get rid of, or perish from the rolls of national glory!

I should be afraid to chronicle the language employed by this young man to the Doctor, to the murdered man, to Madame Zéphyrine, to the boots of the hotel, to the Prince's servants, and, in a word, to all who had been ever so remotely connected with his horrible misfortune.

He slunk down to dinner about seven at night; but the yellow coffee-room appalled him, the eyes of the other diners seemed to rest on his with suspicion, and his mind remained upstairs with the Saratoga trunk. When the waiter came to offer him cheese, his nerves were already so much on edge that he leaped half-way out of his chair and upset the remainder of a pint of ale upon the table-cloth.

The fellow offered to show him to the smoking-room when he had done; and although he would have much preferred to return at once to his perilous treasure, he had not the courage to refuse, and was shown downstairs to the black, gas-lit cellar, which formed, and possibly still forms, the divan of the Craven Hotel.

Two very sad betting men were playing billiards, attended by a moist, consumptive marker;

and for the moment Silas imagined that these were the only occupants of the apartment. But at the next glance his eye fell upon a person smoking in the farthest corner, with lowered eyes and a most respectable and modest aspect. He knew at once that he had seen the face before; and, in spite of the entire change of clothes, recognised the man whom he had found seated on a post at the entrance to Box Court, and who had helped him to carry the trunk to and from the carriage. The New-Englander simply turned and ran, nor did he pause until he had locked and bolted himself into his bedroom.

There, all night long, a prey to the most terrible imaginations, he watched beside the fatal boxful of dead flesh. The suggestion of the boots that his trunk was full of gold inspired him with all manner of new terrors, if he so much as dared to close an eye; and the presence in the smoking-room, and under an obvious disguise, of the loiterer from Box Court convinced him that he was once more the centre of obscure machinations.

Midnight had sounded some time, when, impelled by uneasy suspicions, Silas opened his bedroom door and peered into the passage. It was dimly illuminated by a single jet of gas; and some distance off he perceived a man sleeping on the floor in the costume of an hotel under-servant. Silas drew near the man on tiptoe. He lay partly on his back, partly on his side, and his right forearm concealed his face from recognition. Suddenly, while the American was still bending over him, the sleeper removed his arm and opened his eyes, and Silas found himself once more face to face with the loiterer of Box Court.

"Good-night, sir," said the man, pleasantly.

But Silas was too profoundly moved to find an answer, and regained his room in silence.

Towards morning, worn out by apprehension, he fell asleep on his chair, with his head forward on the trunk. In spite of so constrained an attitude and such a grisly pillow, his slumber was sound and prolonged, and he was only awakened at a late hour and by a sharp tapping at the door.

He hurried to open, and found the boots without.

"You are the gentleman who called yesterday at Box Court?" he asked.

Silas, with a quaver, admitted that he had done so.

"Then this note is for you," added the servant, proffering a sealed envelope.

Silas tore it open, and found inside the words: "Twelve o'clock."

He was punctual to the hour; the trunk was carried before him by several stout servants; and he was himself ushered into a room, where a man sat warming himself before the fire with his back towards the door. The sound of so many persons entering and leaving, and the scraping of the trunk as it was deposited upon the bare boards, were alike unable to attract the notice of the occupant; and Silas stood waiting, in an agony of fear, until he should deign to recognise his presence.

Perhaps five minutes had elapsed before the man turned leisurely about, and disclosed the features of Prince Florizel of Bohemia.

"So, sir," he said, with great severity, "this is the manner in which you abuse my politeness. You join yourselves to persons of condition, I perceive, for no other purpose than to escape the consequences of your crimes; and I can readily understand your embarrassment when I addressed myself to you yesterday."

"Indeed," cried Silas, "I am innocent of everything except misfortune."

And in a hurried voice, and with the greatest ingenuousness, he recounted to the Prince the whole history of his calamity.

"I see I have been mistaken," said his Highness, when he had heard him to an end. "You are no other than a victim, and since I am not to punish you may be sure I shall do my utmost to help. And now," he continued, "to business. Open your box at once, and let me see what it contains."

Silas changed colour.

"I almost fear to look upon it," he exclaimed.

"Nay," replied the Prince, "have you not looked at it already? This is a form of sentimentality to be resisted. The sight of a sick man, whom we can still help, should appeal more directly to the feelings than that of a dead man who is equally beyond help or harm, love or hatred. Nerve yourself, Mr. Scuddamore," and then, seeing that Silas still hesitated, "I do not desire to give another name to my request," he added.

The young American awoke as if out of a dream, and with a shiver of repugnance addressed himself to loose the straps and open the lock of the Saratoga trunk. The Prince stood by, watching with a composed countenance and his hands behind his back. The body was quite stiff, and it cost Silas a great effort, both moral and physical, to dislodge it from its position, and discover the face.

Prince Florizel started back with an exclamation of painful surprise.

"Alas!" he cried, "you little know, Mr. Scuddamore, what a cruel gift you have brought me. This is a young man of my own suite, the brother of my trusted friend; and it was upon matters of my own service that he has thus perished at the hands of violent and treacherous men. Poor Geraldine," he went on, as if to himself, "in what words am I to tell you of your brother's fate? How can I excuse myself in your eyes, or in the eyes of God, for the presumptuous schemes that led him to this bloody and unnatural death? Ah, Florizel! Florizel! when will you learn the discretion that suits mortal life, and be no longer dazzled with the image of power at your disposal? Power!" he cried; "who is more powerless? I look upon this young man whom I have sacrificed, Mr. Scuddamore, and feel how small a thing it is to be a Prince."

Silas was moved at the sight of his emotion. He tried to murmur some consolatory words, and burst into tears.

The Prince, touched by his obvious intention, came up to him and took him by the hand.

"Command yourself," said he. "We have both much to learn, and we shall both be better men for to-day's meeting."

Silas thanked him in silence with an affectionate look.

"Write me the address of Doctor Noel on this piece of paper," continued the Prince, leading him towards the table; "and let me recommend you, when you are again in Paris, to avoid the society of that dangerous man. He has acted in this matter on a generous inspiration; that I must believe; had he been privy to young Geraldine's death he would never have despatched the body to the care of the actual criminal."

"The actual criminal!" repeated Silas in astonishment.

"Even so," returned the Prince. "This letter, which the disposition of Almighty Providence has so strangely delivered into my hands, was addressed to no less a person than the criminal himself, the infamous President of the Suicide Club. Seek to pry no further in these perilous affairs, but content yourself with your own miraculous escape, and leave this house at once. I have pressing affairs, and must arrange at once about this poor clay, which was so lately a gallant and handsome youth."

Silas took a grateful and submissive leave of Prince Florizel, but he lingered in Box Court until he saw him depart in a splendid carriage on a visit to Colonel Henderson of the police. Republican as he was, the young American took off his hat with almost a sentiment of devotion to the retreating carriage. And the same night he started by rail on his return to Paris.

3

THE ADVENTURE OF THE HANSOM CABS

LIEUTENANT BRACKENBURY RICH had greatly distinguished himself in one of the lesser Indian hill wars. He it was who took the chieftain prisoner with his own hand; his gallantry was universally applauded; and when he came home, prostrated by an ugly sabre cut and a protracted jungle fever, society was prepared to welcome the Lieutenant as a celebrity of minor lustre. But his was a character remarkable for unaffected modesty; adventure was dear to his heart, but he cared little for adulation; and he waited at foreign watering-places and in Algiers until the fame of his exploits had run through its nine days' vitality and begun to be forgotten. He arrived in London at last, in the early season, with as little observation as he could desire; and as he was an orphan and had none but distant relatives who lived in the provinces, it was almost as a foreigner that he installed himself in the capital of the country for which he had shed his blood.

On the day following his arrival he dined alone at a military club. He shook hands with a few old comrades, and received their warm congratulations; but as one and all had some engagement for the evening, he found himself left entirely to his own resources. He was in dress, for he had entertained the notion of visiting a theatre. But the great city was new to him; he had gone from a provincial school to a military college, and thence direct to the Eastern Empire; and he promised himself a variety of delights in this world for exploration. Swinging his cane, he took his way westward. It was a mild evening, already dark, and now and then threatening rain. The succession of faces in the lamplight stirred the Lieutenant's imagination; and it seemed to him as if he could walk for ever in that stimulating city atmosphere and surrounded by the mystery of four million private lives. He glanced at the houses, and marvelled what was passing behind those warmly-lighted windows; he looked into face after face, and saw them each intent upon some unknown interest, criminal or kindly.

"They talk of war," he thought, "but this is the great battlefield of mankind."

And then he began to wonder that he should walk so long in this complicated scene, and not chance upon so much as the shadow of an adventure for himself.

"All in good time," he reflected. "I am still a stranger, and perhaps wear a strange air. But I must be drawn into the eddy before long."

The night was already well advanced when a plump of cold rain fell suddenly out of the darkness. Brackenbury paused under some trees, and as he did so he caught sight of a hansom cabman making him a sign that he was disengaged. The circumstance fell in so happily to the occasion that he at once raised his cane in answer, and had soon ensconced himself in the London gondola.

"Where to, sir?" asked the driver.

"Where you please," said Brackenbury.

And immediately, at a pace of surprising swiftness, the hansom drove off through the rain into a maze of villas. One villa was so like another, each with its front garden, and there was so little to distinguish the deserted lamp-lit streets and crescents through which the flying hansom took its way, that Brackenbury soon lost all idea of direction.

He would have been tempted to believe that the cabman was amusing himself by driving him round and round and in and out about a small quarter, but there was something business-like in the speed which convinced him of the contrary. The man had an object in view, he was hastening towards a definite end; and Brackenbury was at once astonished at the fellow's skill in picking a way through such a labyrinth, and a little concerned to imagine what was the occasion of his hurry. He had heard tales of strangers falling ill in London. Did the driver belong to some bloody and treacherous association? and was he himself being whirled to a murderous death?

The thought had scarcely presented itself, when the cab swung sharply round a corner and pulled up before the garden gate of a villa in a long and wide road. The house was brilliantly lighted up. Another hansom had just driven away, and Brackenbury could see a gentleman being admitted at the front door and received by several liveried servants. He was surprised that the cabman should have stopped so immediately in front of a house where a reception was being held; but he did not doubt it was the result of accident, and sat placidly smoking where he was, until he heard the trap thrown open over his head.

"Here we are, sir," said the driver.

"Here!" repeated Brackenbury. "Where?"

"You told me to take you where I pleased, sir," returned the man with a chuckle, "and here we are."

It struck Brackenbury that the voice was wonderfully smooth and courteous for a man in so inferior a position; he remembered the speed at which he had been driven; and now it occurred to him that the hansom was more luxuriously appointed than the common run of public conveyances.

"I must ask you to explain," said he. "Do you mean to turn me out into the rain? My good man, I suspect the choice is mine."

"The choice is certainly yours," replied the driver; "but when I tell you all, I believe I know how a gentleman of your figure will decide. There is a gentlemen's party in this house. I do not know whether the master be a stranger to London and without acquaintances of his own; or whether he is a man of odd notions. But certainly I was hired to kidnap single gentlemen in evening dress, as many as I pleased, but military officers by preference. You have simply to go in and say that Mr. Morris invited you."

"Are you Mr. Morris?" inquired the Lieutenant.

"Oh, no," replied the cabman. "Mr. Morris is the person of the house."

"It is not a common way of collecting guests," said Brackenbury: "but an eccentric man might very well indulge the whim without any intention to offend. And suppose that I refuse Mr. Morris's invitation," he went on, "what then?"

"My orders are to drive you back where I took you from," replied the man, "and set out to look for others up to midnight. Those who have no fancy for such an adventure, Mr. Morris said, were not the guests for him."

These words decided the Lieutenant on the spot.

"After all," he reflected, as he descended from the hansom, "I have not had long to wait for my adventure."

He had hardly found footing on the side-walk, and was still feeling in his pocket for the fare, when the cab swung about and drove off by the way it came at the former break-neck velocity. Brackenbury shouted after the man, who paid no heed, and continued to drive away; but the sound of his voice was overheard in the house, the door was again thrown open, emitting a flood of light upon the garden, and a servant ran down to meet him holding an umbrella.

"The cabman has been paid," observed the servant in a very civil tone; and he proceeded to escort Brackenbury along the path and up the steps. In the hall several other attendants relieved him of his hat, cane, and paletot, gave him a ticket with a number in return, and politely hurried him up a stair adorned with tropical flowers, to the door of an apartment on the first storey. Here a grave butler inquired his name, and announcing "Lieutenant Brackenbury Rich," ushered him into the drawing-room of the house.

A young man, slender and singularly handsome, came forward and greeted him with an air at once courtly and affectionate. Hundreds of candles, of the finest wax, lit up a room that was perfumed, like the staircase, with a profusion of rare and beautiful flowering shrubs. A side-table was loaded with tempting viands. Several servants went to and fro with fruits and goblets of champagne. The company was perhaps sixteen in number, all men, few beyond the prime of life, and with hardly an exception, of a dashing and capable exterior. They were divided into two groups, one about a roulette board, and the other surrounding a table at which one of their number held a bank of baccarat.

"I see," thought Brackenbury, "I am in a private gambling saloon, and the cabman was a tout."

His eye had embraced the details, and his mind formed the conclusion, while his host was still holding him by the hand; and to him his looks returned from this rapid survey. At a second view Mr. Morris surprised him still more than on the first. The easy elegance of his manners, the distinction, amiability, and courage that appeared upon his features, fitted very ill with the Lieutenant's preconceptions on the subject of the proprietor of a hell; and the tone of his conversation seemed to mark him out for a man of position and merit. Brackenbury found he had an instinctive liking for his entertainer; and though he chid himself for the weakness, he was unable to resist a sort of friendly attraction for Mr. Morris's person and character.

"I have heard of you, Lieutenant Rich," said Mr. Morris, lowering his tone; "and believe me I am gratified to make your acquaintance. Your looks accord with the reputation that has preceded you from India. And if you will forget for a while the irregularity of your presentation in my house, I shall feel it not only an honour, but a genuine pleasure besides. A man who makes a mouthful of barbarian cavaliers," he added with a laugh, "should not be appalled by a breach of etiquette, however serious."

And he led him towards the sideboard and pressed him to partake of some refreshment.

"Upon my word," the Lieutenant reflected, "this is one of the pleasantest fellows and, I do not doubt, one of the most agreeable societies in London."

He partook of some champagne, which he found excellent; and observing that many of the company were already smoking, he lit one of his own Manillas, and strolled up to the roulette board, where he sometimes made a stake and sometimes looked on smilingly on the fortune of others. It was while he was thus idling that he became aware of a sharp scrutiny to which the whole of the guests were subjected. Mr. Morris went here and there, ostensibly busied on hospitable concerns; but he had ever a shrewd glance at disposal; not a man of the party escaped his sudden, searching looks; he took stock of the bearing of heavy losers, he valued the amount of the stakes, he paused behind couples who were deep in conversation; and, in a word, there was hardly a characteristic of any one present but he seemed to catch and make a note of it. Brackenbury began to wonder if this were indeed a gambling hell: it had so much the air of a private inquisition. He followed Mr. Morris in all his movements; and although the man had a ready smile, he seemed to perceive, as it were under a mask, a haggard, careworn, and preoccupied spirit. The fellows around him laughed and made their game; but Brackenbury had lost interest in the guests.

"This Morris," thought he, "is no idler in the room. Some deep purpose inspires him; let it be mine to fathom it."

Now and then Mr. Morris would call one of his visitors aside; and after a brief colloquy in an ante-room, he would return alone, and the visitors in question reappeared no more. After a certain number of repetitions, this performance excited Brackenbury's curiosity to a high degree. He determined to be at the bottom of this minor mystery at once; and strolling into the ante-room, found a deep window recess concealed by curtains of the fashionable green. Here he hurriedly ensconced himself; nor had he to wait long before the sound of steps and voices drew near him from the principal apartment. Peering through the division, he saw Mr. Morris escorting a fat and ruddy personage, with somewhat the look of a commercial traveller, whom Brackenbury had already remarked for his coarse laugh and under-bred behaviour at the table. The pair halted immediately before the window, so that Brackenbury lost not a word of the following discourse:—

"I beg you a thousand pardons!" began Mr. Morris, with the most conciliatory manner; "and, if I appear rude, I am sure you will readily forgive me. In a place so great as London accidents must continually happen; and the best that we can hope is to remedy them with as small delay as possible. I will not deny that I fear you have made a mistake and honoured my poor house by inadvertence; for, to speak openly, I cannot at all remember your appearance. Let me put the question without unnecessary circumlocution—between gentlemen of honour a word will suffice—Under whose roof do you suppose yourself to be?"

"That of Mr. Morris," replied the other, with a prodigious display of confusion, which had been visibly growing upon him throughout the last few words.

"Mr. John or Mr. James Morris?" inquired the host.

"I really cannot tell you," returned the unfortunate guest. "I am not personally acquainted with the gentleman, any more than I am with yourself."

"I see," said Mr. Morris. "There is another person of the same name farther down the street; and I have no doubt the policeman will be able to supply you with his number. Believe me, I felicitate myself on the misunderstanding which has procured me the pleasure of your company for so long; and let me express a hope that we may meet again upon a more regular footing. Meantime, I would not for the world detain you longer from your friends. John," he added, raising his voice, "will you see that this gentleman finds his great-coat?"

And with the most agreeable air Mr. Morris escorted his visitor as far as the ante-room door, where he left him under conduct of the butler. As he passed the window, on his return to the drawing-room, Brackenbury could hear him utter a profound sigh, as though his mind was loaded with a great anxiety, and his nerves already fatigued with the task on which he was engaged.

For perhaps an hour the hansoms kept arriving with such frequency, that Mr. Morris had to receive a new guest for every old one that he sent away, and the company preserved its number undiminished. But towards the end of that time the arrivals grew few and far between, and at length ceased entirely, while the process of elimination was continued with unimpaired activity. The drawing-room began to look empty: the baccarat was discontinued for lack of a banker; more than one person said good-night of his own accord, and was suffered to depart without expostulation; and in the meanwhile Mr. Morris redoubled in agreeable attentions to those who stayed behind. He went from group to group and from person to person with looks of the readiest sympathy and the most pertinent and pleasing talk; he was not so much like a host as like a hostess, and there was a feminine coquetry and condescension in his manner which charmed the hearts of all.

As the guests grew thinner, Lieutenant Rich strolled for a moment out of the drawing-room into the hall in quest of fresher air. But he had no sooner passed the threshold of the ante-chamber than he was brought to a dead halt by a discovery of the most surprising nature. The flowering shrubs had disappeared from the staircase; three large furniture waggons stood before the garden gate; the servants were busy dismantling the house upon all sides; and some of them had already donned their great-coats and were preparing to depart. It was like the end of a country ball, where everything has been supplied by contract. Brackenbury had indeed some matter for reflection. First, the guests, who were no real guests after all, had been dismissed; and now the servants, who could hardly be genuine servants, were actively dispersing.

'"Was the whole establishment a sham?" he asked himself. "The mushroom of a single night which should disappear before morning?"

Watching a favourable opportunity, Brackenbury dashed upstairs to the highest regions of the house. It was as he had expected. He ran from room to room, and saw not a stick of furniture nor so much as a picture on the walls. Although the house had been painted and papered, it was not only uninhabited at present, but plainly had never been inhabited at all. The young officer remembered with astonishment its specious, settled, and hospitable air on his arrival. It was only at a prodigious cost that the imposture could have been carried out upon so great a scale.

Who, then, was Mr. Morris? What was his intention in thus playing the householder for a single night in the remote west of London? And why did he collect his visitors at hazard from the streets?

Brackenbury remembered that he had already delayed too long, and hastened to join the company. Many had left during his absence; and counting the Lieutenant and his host, there were not more than five persons in the drawing-room—recently so thronged. Mr. Morris greeted him, as he re-entered the apartment, with a smile, and immediately rose to his feet.

"It is now time, gentlemen," said he, "to explain my purpose in decoying you from your amusements. I trust you did not find the evening hang very dully on your hands; but my object, I will confess it, was not to entertain your leisure, but to help myself in an unfortunate necessity. You are all gentlemen," he continued, "your appearance does you that much justice, and I ask for no better security. Hence, I speak it without concealment, I ask you to render me a dangerous and delicate service; dangerous because you may run the hazard of your lives, and delicate because I must ask an absolute discretion upon all that you shall see or hear. From an utter stranger the request is almost comically extravagant; I am well aware of this; and I would add at once, if there be any one present who has heard enough, if there be one among the party who recoils from a dangerous confidence and a piece of Quixotic devotion to he knows not whom—here is my hand ready, and I shall wish him good-night and God-speed with all the sincerity in the world."

A very tall, black man, with a heavy stoop, immediately responded to this appeal.

"I commend your frankness, Sir," said he; "and, for my part, I go. I make no reflections; but I cannot deny that you fill me with suspicious thoughts. I go myself, as I say; and perhaps you will think I have no right to add words to my example."

"On the contrary," replied Mr. Morris, "I am obliged to you for all you say. It would be impossible to exaggerate the gravity of my proposal."

"Well, gentlemen, what do you say?" said the tall man, addressing the others. "We have had our evening's frolic; shall we all go homeward peaceably in a body? You will think well of my suggestion in the morning, when you see the sun again in innocence and safety."

The speaker pronounced the last words with an intonation which added to their force; and his face wore a singular expression, full of gravity and significance. Another of the company rose hastily, and, with some appearance of alarm, prepared to take his leave. There were only two who held their ground, Brackenbury and an old red-nosed cavalry Major; but these two preserved a nonchalant demeanour, and, beyond a look of intelligence which they rapidly exchanged, appeared entirely foreign to the discussion that had just been terminated.

Mr. Morris conducted the deserters as far as the door, which he closed upon their heels; then he turned round, disclosing a countenance of mingled relief and animation, and addressed the two officers as follows.

"I have chosen my men like Joshua in the Bible," said Mr. Morris, "and I now believe I have the pick of London. Your appearance pleased my hansom cabmen; then it delighted me; I have watched your behaviour in a strange company, and under the most unusual circumstances: I have studied how you played and how you bore your losses; lastly, I have put you to the test of a staggering announcement, and you received it like an invitation to dinner. It is not for nothing," he cried, "that I have been for years the companion and the pupil of the bravest and wisest potentate in Europe."

"At the affair of Bunderchang," observed the Major, "I asked for twelve volunteers, and every trooper in the ranks replied to my appeal. But a gaming party is not the same thing as a regiment under fire. You may be pleased, I suppose, to have found two, and two who will not fail you at a push. As for the pair who ran away, I count them among the most pitiful hounds I ever met with. Lieutenant Rich," he added, addressing Brackenbury, "I have heard much of you of late; and I cannot doubt but you have also heard of me. I am Major O'Rooke."

And the veteran tendered his hand, which was red and tremulous, to the young Lieutenant.

"Who has not?" answered Brackenbury.

"When this little matter is settled," said Mr. Morris, "you will think I have sufficiently rewarded you; for I could offer neither a more valuable service than to make him acquainted with the other."

"And now," said Major O'Rooke, "is it a duel?"

"A duel after a fashion," replied Mr. Morris, "a duel with unknown and dangerous enemies, and, as I gravely fear, a duel to the death. I must ask you," he continued, "to call me Morris no longer; call me, if you please, Hammersmith; my real name, as well as that of another person to whom I hope to present you before long, you will gratify me by not asking and not seeking to discover for yourselves. Three days ago the person of whom I speak disappeared suddenly from home; and, until this morning, I received no hint of his situation. You will fancy my alarm when I tell you that he is engaged upon a work of private justice. Bound by an unhappy oath, too lightly sworn, he finds it necessary, without the help of law, to rid the earth of an insidious and bloody villain. Already two of our friends, and one of them my own born brother, have perished in the enterprise. He himself, or I am much deceived, is taken in the same fatal toils. But at least he still lives and still hopes, as this billet sufficiently proves."

And the speaker, no other than Colonel Geraldine, proffered a letter, thus conceived:—

"Major Hammersmith,—On Wednesday, at 3 A.M., you will be admitted by the small door to the gardens of Rochester House, Regent's Park, by a man who is entirely in my interest. I must request you not to fail me by a second. Pray bring my case of swords, and, if you can find them, one or two gentlemen of conduct and discretion to whom my person is unknown. My name must not be used in this affair.

T. Godall."

"From his wisdom alone, if he had no other title," pursued Colonel Geraldine, when the others had each satisfied his curiosity, "my friend is a man whose directions should implicitly be followed. I need not tell you, therefore, that I have not so much as visited the neighbourhood of Rochester House; and that I am still as wholly in the dark as either of yourselves as to the nature of my friend's dilemma. I betook myself, as soon as I had received this order, to a furnishing contractor, and, in a few hours, the house in which we now are had assumed its late air of festival. My scheme was at least original; and I am far from regretting an action which has procured me the services of Major O'Rooke and Lieutenant Brackenbury Rich. But the servants in the street will have a strange awakening. The house which this evening was full of lights and visitors they will find uninhabited and for sale to-morrow morning. Thus even the most serious concerns," added the Colonel, "have a merry side."

"And let us add a merry ending," said Brackenbury.

The Colonel consulted his watch.

"It is now hard on two," he said. "We have an hour before us, and a swift cab is at the door. Tell me if I may count upon your help."

"During a long life," replied Major O'Rooke, "I never took back my hand from anything, nor so much as hedged a bet."

Brackenbury signified his readiness in the most becoming terms; and after they had drunk a glass or two of wine, the Colonel gave each of them a loaded revolver, and the three mounted into the cab and drove off for the address in question.

Rochester House was a magnificent residence on the banks of the canal. The large extent of the garden isolated it in an unusual degree from the annoyances of neighbourhood. It seemed the *parc aux cerfs* of some great nobleman or millionaire. As far as could be seen from the street, there was not a glimmer of light in any of the numerous windows of the mansion; and the place had a look of neglect, as though the master had been long from home.

The cab was discharged, and the three gentlemen were not long in discovering the small door, which was a sort of postern in a lane between two garden walls. It still wanted ten or fifteen minutes of the appointed time; the rain fell heavily, and the adventurers sheltered themselves below some pendant ivy, and spoke in low tones of the approaching trial.

Suddenly Geraldine raised his finger to command silence, and all three bent their hearing to the utmost. Through the continuous noise of the rain, the steps and voices of two men became audible from the other side of the wall; and, as they drew nearer, Brackenbury, whose sense of hearing was remarkably acute, could even distinguish some fragments of their talk.

"Is the grave dug?" asked one.

"It is," replied the other; "behind the laurel hedge. When the job is done, we can cover it with a pile of stakes."

The first speaker laughed, and the sound of his merriment was shocking to the listeners on the other side.

"In an hour from now," he said.

And by the sound of the steps it was obvious that the pair had separated, and were proceeding in contrary directions.

Almost immediately after the postern door was cautiously opened, a white face was protruded into the lane, and a hand was seen beckoning to the watchers. In dead silence the three passed the door, which was immediately locked behind them, and followed their guide through several garden alleys to the kitchen entrance of the house. A single candle burned in the great paved kitchen, which was destitute of the customary furniture; and as the party proceeded to ascend from thence by a flight of winding stairs, a prodigious noise of rats testified still more plainly to the dilapidation of the house.

Their conductor preceded them, carrying the candle. He was a lean man, much bent, but still agile; and he turned from time to time and admonished silence and caution by his gestures. Colonel Geraldine followed on his heels, the case of swords under one arm, and a pistol ready in the other. Brackenbury's heart beat thickly. He perceived that they were still in time; but he judged from the alacrity of the old man that the hour of action must be near at hand; and the circumstances of this adventure were so obscure and menacing, the place seemed so well chosen for the darkest acts, that an older man than Brackenbury might have been pardoned a measure of emotion as he closed the procession up the winding stair.

At the top the guide threw open a door and ushered the three officers before him into a small apartment, lighted by a smoky lamp and the glow of a modest fire. At the chimney corner sat a man in the early prime of life, and of a stout but courtly and commanding appearance. His attitude and expression were those of the most unmoved composure; he was smoking a cheroot with much enjoyment and deliberation, and on a table by his elbow stood a long glass of some effervescing beverage which diffused an agreeable odour through the room.

"Welcome," said he, extending his hand to Colonel Geraldine. "I knew I might count on your exactitude."

"On my devotion," replied the Colonel, with a bow.

"Present me to your friends," continued the first; and, when that ceremony had been performed, "I wish, gentlemen," he added, with the most exquisite affability, "that I could offer you a more cheerful programme; it is ungracious to inaugurate an acquaintance upon serious affairs; but the compulsion of events is stronger than the obligations of good-fellowship. I hope and believe you will be able to forgive me this unpleasant evening; and for men of your stamp it will be enough to know that you are conferring a considerable favour."

"Your Highness," said the Major, "must pardon my bluntness. I am unable to hide what I know. For some time back I have suspected Major Hammersmith, but Mr. Godall is unmistakable. To seek two men in London unacquainted with Prince Florizel of Bohemia was to ask too much at Fortune's hands."

"Prince Florizel!" cried Brackenbury in amazement.

And he gazed with the deepest interest on the features of the celebrated personage before him.

"I shall not lament the loss of my incognito," remarked the Prince, "for it enables me to thank you with the more authority. You would have done as much for Mr. Godall, I feel sure, as for the Prince of Bohemia; but the latter can perhaps do more for you. The gain is mine," he added, with a courteous gesture.

And the next moment he was conversing with the two officers about the Indian army and the native troops, a subject on which, as on all others, he had a remarkable fund of information and the soundest views.

There was something so striking in this man's attitude at a moment of deadly peril that Brackenbury was overcome with respectful admiration; nor was he less sensible to the charm of his conversation or the surprising amenity of his address. Every gesture, every intonation, was not only noble in itself, but seemed to ennoble the fortunate mortal for whom it was intended; and Brackenbury confessed to himself with enthusiasm that this was a sovereign for whom a brave man might thankfully lay down his life.

Many minutes had thus passed, when the person who had introduced them into the house, and who had sat ever since in a corner, and with his watch in his hand, arose and whispered a word into the Prince's ear.

"It is well, Dr. Noel," replied Florizel, aloud; and then addressing the others, "You will excuse me, gentlemen," he added, "if I have to leave you in the dark. The moment now approaches."

Dr. Noel extinguished the lamp. A faint, grey light, premonitory of the dawn, illuminated the window, but was not sufficient to illuminate the room; and when the Prince rose to his feet, it was impossible to distinguish his features or to make a guess at the nature of the emotion which obviously affected him as he spoke. He moved towards the door, and placed himself at one side of it in an attitude of the wariest attention.

"You will have the kindness," he said, "to maintain the strictest silence, and to conceal yourselves in the densest of the shadow."

The three officers and the physician hastened to obey, and for nearly ten minutes the only sound in Rochester House was occasioned by the excursions of the rats behind the woodwork. At the end of that period, a loud creak of a hinge broke in with surprising distinctness on the silence; and shortly after, the watchers could distinguish a slow and cautious tread approaching up the kitchen stair. At every second step the intruder seemed to pause and lend an ear, and during these intervals, which seemed of an incalculable duration, a profound disquiet possessed the spirit of the listeners. Dr. Noel, accustomed as he was to dangerous emotions, suffered an almost pitiful physical prostration; his breath whistled in his lungs, his teeth grated one upon another, and his joints cracked aloud as he nervously shifted his position.

At last a hand was laid upon the door, and the bolt shot back with a slight report. There followed another pause, during which Brackenbury could see the Prince draw himself together noiselessly as if for some unusual exertion. Then the door opened, letting in a little more of the light of the morning; and the figure of a man appeared upon the threshold and stood motionless. He was tall, and carried a knife in his hand. Even in the twilight they could see his upper teeth bare and glistening, for his mouth was open like that of a hound about to leap. The man had evidently been over the head in water but a minute or two before; and even while he stood there the drops kept falling from his wet clothes and pattered on the floor.

The next moment he crossed the threshold. There was a leap, a stifled cry, an instantaneous struggle; and before Colonel Geraldine could spring to his aid, the Prince held the man disarmed and helpless, by the shoulders.

"Dr. Noel," he said, "you will be so good as to re-light the lamp."

And relinquishing the charge of his prisoner to Geraldine and Brackenbury, he crossed the room and set his back against the chimney-piece. As soon as the lamp had kindled, the party beheld an unaccustomed sternness on the Prince's features. It was no longer Florizel, the careless gentleman; it was the Prince of Bohemia, justly incensed and full of deadly purpose, who now raised his head and addressed the captive President of the Suicide Club.

"President," he said, "you have laid your last snare, and your own feet are taken in it. The day is beginning; it is your last morning. You have just swum the Regent's Canal; it is your last bathe in this world. Your old accomplice, Dr. Noel, so far from betraying me, has delivered you into my hands for judgment. And the grave you had dug for me this afternoon shall serve, in God's almighty providence, to hide your own just doom from the curiosity of mankind. Kneel and pray, sir, if you have a mind that way; for your time is short, and God is weary of your iniquities."

The President made no answer either by word or sign; but continued to hang his head and gaze sullenly on the floor, as though he were conscious of the Prince's prolonged and unsparing regard.

"Gentlemen," continued Florizel, resuming the ordinary tone of his conversation, "this is a fellow who has long eluded me, but whom, thanks to Dr. Noel, I now have tightly by the heels. To tell the story of his misdeeds would occupy more time than we can now afford; but if the canal had contained nothing but the blood of his victims, I believe the wretch would have been no drier than you see him. Even in an affair of this sort I desire to preserve the forms of honour. But I make you the judges, gentlemen—this is more an execution than a duel and to give the rogue his choice of weapons would be to push too far a point of etiquette. I cannot afford to lose my life in such a business," he continued, unlocking the case of swords; "and as a pistol-bullet travels so often on the wings of chance, and skill and courage may fall by the most trembling marksman, I have decided, and I feel sure you will approve my determination, to put this question to the touch of swords."

When Brackenbury and Major O'Rooke, to whom these remarks were particularly addressed, had each intimated his approval, "Quick, sir," added Prince Florizel to the President, "choose a blade and do not keep me waiting; I have an impatience to be done with you for ever."

For the first time since he was captured and disarmed the President raised his head, and it was plain that he began instantly to pluck up courage.

"Is it to be stand up?" he asked eagerly, "and between you and me?"

"I mean so far to honour you," replied the Prince.

"Oh, come!" cried the President. "With a fair field, who knows how things may happen? I must add that I consider it handsome behaviour on your Highness's part; and if the worst comes to the worst I shall die by one of the most gallant gentlemen in Europe."

And the President, liberated by those who had detained him, stepped up to the table and began, with minute attention, to select a sword. He was highly elated, and seemed to feel no doubt that he should issue victorious from the contest. The spectators grew alarmed in the face of so entire a confidence, and adjured Prince Florizel to reconsider his intention.

"It is but a farce," he answered; "and I think I can promise you, gentlemen, that it will not be long a-playing."

"Your Highness will be careful not to over-reach," said Colonel Geraldine.

"Geraldine," returned the Prince, "did you ever know me fail in a debt of honour? I owe you this man's death, and you shall have it."

The President at last satisfied himself with one of the rapiers, and signified his readiness by a gesture that was not devoid of a rude nobility. The nearness of peril, and the sense of courage, even to this obnoxious villain, lent an air of manhood and a certain grace.

The Prince helped himself at random to a sword.

"Colonel Geraldine and Doctor Noel," he said, "will have the goodness to await me in this room. I wish no personal friend of mine to be involved in this transaction. Major O'Rooke, you are a man of some years and a settled reputation—let me recommend the President to your good graces. Lieutenant Rich will be so good as lend me his attentions: a young man cannot have too much experience in such affairs."

"Your Highness," replied Brackenbury, "it is an honour I shall prize extremely."

"It is well," returned Prince Florizel; "I shall hope to stand your friend in more important circumstances."

And so saying he led the way out of the apartment and down the kitchen stairs.

The two men who were thus left alone threw open the window and leaned out, straining every sense to catch an indication of the tragical events that were about to follow. The rain was now over; day had almost come, and the birds were piping in the shrubbery and on the forest trees of the garden. The Prince and his companions were visible for a moment as they followed an alley between two flowering thickets; but at the first corner a clump of foliage intervened, and they were again concealed from view. This was all that the Colonel and the Physician had an opportunity to see, and the garden was so vast, and the place of combat evidently so remote from the house, that not even the noise of sword-play reached their ears.

"He has taken him towards the grave," said Dr. Noel, with a shudder.

"God," cried the Colonel, "God defend the right!"

And they awaited the event in silence, the Doctor shaking with fear, the Colonel in an agony of sweat. Many minutes must have elapsed, the day was sensibly broader, and the birds were singing more heartily in the garden before a sound of returning footsteps recalled their glances towards the door. It was the Prince and the two Indian officers who entered. God had defended the right.

"I am ashamed of my emotion," said Prince Florizel; "I feel it is a weakness unworthy of my station, but the continued existence of that hound of hell had begun to prey upon me like a disease, and his death has more refreshed me than a night of slumber. Look, Geraldine," he continued, throwing his sword upon the floor, "there is the blood of the man who killed your brother. It should be a welcome sight. And yet," he added, "see how strangely we men are made! my revenge is not yet five minutes old, and already I am beginning to ask myself if even revenge be attainable on this precarious stage of life. The ill he did, who can undo it? The career in which he amassed a huge fortune (for the house itself in which we stand belonged to him)—that career is now a part of the destiny of mankind for ever; and I might weary myself making thrusts in carte until the crack of judgment, and Geraldine's brother would be none the less dead, and a thousand other innocent persons would be none the less dishonoured and debauched! The existence of a man is so small a thing to take, so mighty a thing to employ! Alas!" he cried, "is there anything in life so disenchanting as attainment?"

"God's justice has been done," replied the Doctor. "So much I behold. The lesson, your Highness, has been a cruel one for me; and I await my own turn with deadly apprehension."

"What was I saying?" cried the Prince. "I have punished, and here is the man beside us who can help me to undo. Ah, Dr. Noel! you and I have before us many a day of hard and honourable toil; and perhaps, before we have none, you may have more than redeemed your early errors."

"And in the meantime," said the Doctor, "let me go and bury my oldest friend."

THE RAJAH'S DIAMOND

I

STORY OF THE BANDBOX

UP to the age of sixteen, at a private school and afterwards at one of those great institutions for which England is justly famous, Mr. Harry Hartley had received the ordinary education of a gentleman. At that period, he manifested a remarkable distaste for study; and his only surviving parent being both weak and ignorant, he was permitted thenceforward to spend his time in the attainment of petty and purely elegant accomplishments. Two years later, he was left an orphan and almost a beggar. For all active and industrious pursuits, Harry was unfitted alike by nature and training. He could sing romantic ditties, and accompany himself with discretion on the piano; he was a graceful although a timid cavalier; he had a pronounced taste for chess; and nature had sent him into the world with one of the most engaging exteriors that can well be fancied. Blond and pink, with dove's eyes and a gentle smile, he had an air of agreeable tenderness and melancholy, and the most submissive and caressing manners. But when all is said, he was not the man to lead armaments of war, or direct the councils of a State.

A fortunate chance and some influence obtained for Harry, at the time of his bereavement, the position of private secretary to Major-General Sir Thomas Vandeleur, C.B. Sir Thomas was a man of sixty, loud-spoken, boisterous, and domineering. For some reason, some service the nature of which had been often whispered and repeatedly denied, the Rajah of Kashgar had presented this officer with the sixth known diamond of the world. The gift transformed General Vandeleur from a poor into a wealthy man, from an obscure and unpopular soldier into one of the lions of London society; the possessor of the Rajah's Diamond was welcome in the most exclusive circles; and he had found a lady, young, beautiful, and well-born, who was willing to call the diamond hers even at the price of marriage with Sir Thomas Vandeleur. It was commonly said at the time that, as like draws to like, one jewel had attracted another; certainly Lady Vandeleur was not only a gem of the finest water in her own person, but she showed herself to the world in a very costly setting; and she was considered by many respectable authorities, as one among the three or four best dressed women in England.

Harry's duty as secretary was not particularly onerous; but he had a dislike for all prolonged work; it gave him pain to ink his fingers; and the charms of Lady Vandeleur and her toilettes drew him often from the library to the boudoir. He had the prettiest ways among women, could talk fashions with enjoyment, and was never more happy than when criticising a shade of ribbon, or running on an errand to the milliner's. In short, Sir Thomas's correspondence fell into pitiful arrears, and my Lady had another lady's maid.

At last the General, who was one of the least patient of military commanders, arose from his place in a violent access of passion, and indicated to his secretary that he had no further need for his services, with one of those explanatory gestures which are most rarely employed between gentlemen. The door being unfortunately open, Mr. Hartley fell downstairs head foremost.

He arose somewhat hurt and very deeply aggrieved. The life in the General's house precisely suited him; he moved, on a more or less doubtful footing, in very genteel company, he did little, he ate of the best, and he had a lukewarm satisfaction in the presence of Lady Vandeleur, which, in his own heart, he dubbed by a more emphatic name.

Immediately after he had been outraged by the military foot, he hurried to the boudoir and recounted his sorrows.

"You know very well, my dear Harry," replied Lady Vandeleur, for she called him by name like a child or a domestic servant, "that you never by any chance do what the General tells you. No more do I, you may say. But that is different. A woman can earn her pardon for a good year of disobedience by a single adroit submission; and, besides, no one is married to his private secretary. I shall be sorry to lose you; but since you cannot stay longer in a house where you have been insulted, I shall wish you good-bye, and I promise you to make the General smart for his behaviour."

Harry's countenance fell; tears came into his eyes, and he gazed on Lady Vandeleur with a tender reproach.

"My Lady," said he, "what is an insult? I should think little indeed of any one who could not forgive them by the score. But to leave one's friends; to tear up the bonds of affection—"

He was unable to continue, for his emotion choked him, and he began to weep.

Lady Vandeleur looked at him with a curious expression. "This little fool," she thought, "imagines himself to be in love with me. Why should he not become my servant instead of the General's? He is good-natured, obliging, and understands dress; and besides it will keep him out of mischief. He is positively too pretty to be unattached." That night she talked over the General, who was already somewhat ashamed of his vivacity; and Harry was transferred to the feminine department, where his life was little short of heavenly. He was always dressed with uncommon nicety, wore delicate flowers in his button-hole, and could entertain a visitor with tact and pleasantry. He took a pride in servility to a beautiful woman; received Lady Vandeleur's commands as so many marks of favour; and was pleased to exhibit himself before other men, who derided and despised him, in his character of male lady's-maid and man milliner. Nor could he think enough of his existence from a moral point of view. Wickedness seemed to him an essentially male attribute, and to pass one's days with a delicate woman, and principally occupied about trimmings, was to inhabit an enchanted isle among the storms of life.

One fine morning he came into the drawing-room and began to arrange some music on the top of the piano. Lady Vandeleur, at the other end of the apartment, was speaking somewhat eagerly with her brother, Charlie Pendragon, an elderly young man, much broken with dissipation, and very lame of one foot. The private secretary, to whose entrance they paid no regard, could not avoid overhearing a part of their conversation.

"To-day or never," said the lady. "Once and for all, it shall be done to-day."

"To-day, if it must be," replied the brother, with a sigh. "But it is a false step, a ruinous step, Clara; and we shall live to repent it dismally."

Lady Vandeleur looked her brother steadily and somewhat strangely in the face.

"You forget," she said; "the man must die at last."

"Upon my word, Clara," said Pendragon, "I believe you are the most heartless rascal in England."

"You men," she returned, "are so coarsely built, that you can never appreciate a shade of meaning. You are yourselves rapacious, violent, immodest, careless of distinction; and yet the least thought for the future shocks you in a woman. I have no patience with such stuff. You would despise in a common banker the imbecility that you expect to find in us."

"You are very likely right," replied her brother; "you were always cleverer than I. And, anyway, you know my motto: The family before all."

"Yes, Charlie," she returned, taking his hand in hers, "I know your motto better than you know it yourself. 'And Clara before the family!' Is not that the second part of it? Indeed, you are the best of brothers, and I love you dearly."

Mr. Pendragon got up, looking a little confused by these family endearments.

"I had better not be seen," said he. "I understand my part to a miracle, and I'll keep an eye on the Tame Cat."

"Do," she replied. "He is an abject creature, and might ruin all."

She kissed the tips of her fingers to him daintily; and the brother withdrew by the boudoir and the back stair.

"Harry," said Lady Vandeleur, turning towards the secretary as soon as they were alone, "I have a commission for you this morning. But you shall take a cab; I cannot have my secretary freckled."

She spoke the last words with emphasis and a look of half-motherly pride that caused great contentment to poor Harry; and he professed himself charmed to find an opportunity of serving her.

"It is another of our great secrets," she went on archly, "and no one must know of it but my secretary and me. Sir Thomas would make the saddest disturbance; and if you only knew how weary I am of these scenes! Oh, Harry, Harry, can you explain to me what makes you men so violent and unjust? But, indeed, I know you cannot; you are the only man in the world who knows nothing of these shameful passions; you are so good, Harry, and so kind; you, at least, can be a woman's friend; and, do you know? I think you make the others more ugly by comparison."

"It is you," said Harry gallantly, "who are so kind to me. You treat me like—"

"Like a mother," interposed Lady Vandeleur; "I try to be a mother to you. Or, at least," she corrected herself with a smile, "almost a mother. I am afraid I am too young to be your mother really. Let us say a friend—a dear friend."

She paused long enough to let her words take effect in Harry's sentimental quarters, but not long enough to allow him a reply.

"But all this is beside our purpose," she resumed. "You will find a bandbox in the left-hand side of the oak wardrobe; it is underneath the pink slip that I wore on Wednesday with my Mechlin. You will take it immediately to this address," and she gave him a paper, "but do not, on any account, let it out of your hands until you have received a receipt written by myself. Do you understand? Answer, if you please—answer! This is extremely important, and I must ask you to pay some attention."

Harry pacified her by repeating her instructions perfectly; and she was just going to tell him more when General Vandeleur flung into the apartment, scarlet with anger, and holding a long and elaborate milliner's bill in his hand.

"Will you look at this, madam?" cried he. "Will you have the goodness to look at this document? I know well enough you married me for my money, and I hope I can make as great allowances as any other man in the service; but, as sure as God made me, I mean to put a period to this disreputable prodigality."

"Mr. Hartley," said Lady Vandeleur, "I think you understand what you have to do. May I ask you to see to it at once?"

"Stop," said the General, addressing Harry, "one word before you go." And then, turning again to Lady Vandeleur, "What is this precious fellow's errand?" he demanded. "I trust him no further than I do yourself, let me tell you. If he had as much as the rudiments of honesty, he would scorn to stay in this house; and what he does for his wages is a mystery to all the world. What is his errand, madam? and why are you hurrying him away?"

"I supposed you had something to say to me in private," replied the lady.

"You spoke about an errand," insisted the General. "Do not attempt to deceive me in my present state of temper. You certainly spoke about an errand."

"If you insist on making your servants privy to our humiliating dissensions," replied Lady Vandeleur, "perhaps I had better ask Mr. Hartley to sit down. No?" she continued; "then you may go, Mr. Hartley. I trust you may remember all that you have heard in this room; it may be useful to you."

Harry at once made his escape from the drawing-room; and as he ran upstairs he could hear the General's voice upraised in declamation, and the thin tones of Lady Vandeleur planting icy repartees at every opening. How cordially he admired the wife! How skilfully she could evade an awkward question! with what secure effrontery she repeated her instructions under the very guns of the enemy! and on the other hand, how he detested the husband!

There had been nothing unfamiliar in the morning's events, for he was continually in the habit of serving Lady Vandeleur on secret missions, principally connected with millinery. There was a skeleton in the house, as he well knew. The bottomless extravagance and the unknown liabilities of the wife had long since swallowed her own fortune, and threatened day by day to engulph that of the husband. Once or twice in every year exposure and ruin seemed imminent, and Harry kept trotting round to all sorts of furnishers' shops, telling small fibs, and paying small advances on the gross amount, until another term was tided over, and the lady and her faithful secretary breathed again. For Harry, in a double capacity, was heart and soul upon that side of the war: not only did he adore Lady Vandeleur and fear and dislike her husband, but he naturally sympathised with the love of finery, and his own single extravagance was at the tailor's.

He found the bandbox where it had been described, arranged his toilette with care, and left the house. The sun shone brightly; the distance he had to travel was considerable, and he remembered with dismay that the General's sudden irruption had prevented Lady Vandeleur from giving him money for a cab. On this sultry day there was every chance that his complexion would suffer severely; and to walk through so much of London with a bandbox on his arm was a humiliation almost insupportable to a youth of his character. He paused, and took counsel with himself. The Vandeleurs lived in Eaton Place; his destination was near Notting Hill; plainly, he might cross the Park by keeping well in the open and avoiding populous alleys; and he thanked his stars when he reflected that it was still comparatively early in the day.

Anxious to be rid of his incubus, he walked somewhat faster than his ordinary, and he was already some way through Kensington Gardens when, in a solitary spot among trees, he found himself confronted by the General.

"I beg your pardon, Sir Thomas," observed Harry, politely falling on one side; for the other stood directly in his path.

"Where are you going, sir?" asked the General.

"I am taking a little walk among the trees," replied the lad.

The General struck the bandbox with his cane.

"With that thing?" he cried; "you lie, sir, and you know you lie!"

"Indeed, Sir Thomas," returned Harry, "I am not accustomed to be questioned in so high a key."

"You do not understand your position," said the General. "You are my servant, and a servant of whom I have conceived the most serious suspicions. How do I know but that your box is full of teaspoons?"

"It contains a silk hat belonging to a friend," said Harry.

"Very well," replied General Vandeleur. "Then I want to see your friend's silk hat. I have," he added grimly, "a singular curiosity for hats; and I believe you know me to be somewhat positive."

"I beg your pardon, Sir Thomas, I am exceedingly grieved," Harry apologised; "but indeed this is a private affair."

The General caught him roughly by the shoulder with one hand, while he raised his cane in the most menacing manner with the other. Harry gave himself up for lost; but at the same moment Heaven vouchsafed him an unexpected defender in the person of Charlie Pendragon, who now strode forward from behind the trees.

"Come, come, General, hold your hand," said he, "this is neither courteous nor manly."

"Aha!" cried the General, wheeling round upon his new antagonist, "Mr. Pendragon! And do you suppose, Mr. Pendragon, that because I have had the misfortune to marry your sister, I shall suffer myself to be dogged and thwarted by a discredited and bankrupt libertine like you? My acquaintance with Lady Vandeleur, sir, has taken away all my appetite for the other members of her family."

"And do you fancy, General Vandeleur," retorted Charlie, "that because my sister has had the misfortune to marry you, she there and then forfeited her rights and privileges as a lady? I own, sir, that by that action she did as much as anybody could to derogate from her position; but to me she is still a Pendragon. I make it my business to protect her from ungentlemanly outrage, and if you were ten times her husband I would not permit her liberty to be restrained, nor her private messengers to be violently arrested."

"How is that, Mr. Hartley?" interrogated the General. "Mr. Pendragon is of my opinion, it appears. He too suspects that Lady Vandeleur has something to do with your friend's silk hat."

Charlie saw that he had committed an unpardonable blunder, which he hastened to repair.

"How, sir?" he cried; "I suspect, do you say? I suspect nothing. Only where I find strength abused and a man brutalising his inferiors, I take the liberty to interfere."

As he said these words he made a sign to Harry, which the latter was too dull or too much troubled to understand.

"In what way am I to construe your attitude, sir?" demanded Vandeleur.

"Why, sir, as you please," returned Pendragon.

The General once more raised his cane, and made a cut for Charlie's head; but the latter, lame foot and all, evaded the blow with his umbrella, ran in, and immediately closed with his formidable adversary.

"Run, Harry, run!" he cried; "run, you dolt!"

Harry stood petrified for a moment, watching the two men sway together in this fierce embrace; then he turned and took to his heels. When he cast a glance over his shoulder he saw the General prostrate under Charlie's knee, but still making desperate efforts to reverse the situation; and the Gardens seemed to have filled with people, who were running from all directions towards the scene of fight. This spectacle lent the secretary wings; and he did not relax his pace until he had gained the Bayswater road, and plunged at random into an unfrequented by-street.

To see two gentlemen of his acquaintance thus brutally mauling each other was deeply shocking to Harry. He desired to forget the sight; he desired, above all, to put as great a distance as possible between himself and General Vandeleur; and in his eagerness for this he forgot everything about his destination, and hurried before him headlong and trembling. When he remembered that Lady Vandeleur was the wife of one and the sister of the other of these gladiators, his heart was touched with sympathy for a woman so distressingly misplaced in life. Even his own situation in the General's household looked hardly so pleasing as usual in the light of these violent transactions.

He had walked some little distance, busied with these meditations, before a slight collision with another passenger reminded him of the bandbox on his arm.

"Heavens!" cried he, "where was my head? and whither have I wandered?"

Thereupon he consulted the envelope which Lady Vandeleur had given him. The address was there, but without a name. Harry was simply directed to ask for "the gentleman who expected a parcel from Lady Vandeleur," and if he were not at home to await his return. The gentleman, added the note, should present a receipt in the handwriting of the lady herself. All this seemed mightily mysterious, and Harry was above all astonished at the omission of the name and the formality of the receipt. He had thought little of this last when he heard it dropped in conversation; but reading it in cold blood, and taking it in connection with the other strange particulars, he became convinced that he was engaged in perilous affairs. For half a moment he had a doubt of Lady Vandeleur herself; for he found these obscure proceedings somewhat unworthy of so high a lady, and became more critical when her secrets were preserved against himself. But her empire over his spirit was too complete, he dismissed his suspicions, and blamed himself roundly for having so much as entertained them.

In one thing, however, his duty and interest, his generosity and his terrors, coincided—to get rid of the bandbox with the greatest possible despatch.

He accosted the first policeman and courteously inquired his way. It turned out that he was already not far from his destination, and a walk of a few minutes brought him to a small house in a lane, freshly painted, and kept with the most scrupulous attention. The knocker and bell-pull were highly polished; flowering pot-herbs garnished the sills of the different windows; and curtains of some rich material concealed the interior from the eyes of curious passengers. The place had an air of repose and secrecy; and Harry was so far caught with this spirit that he knocked with more than usual discretion, and was more than usually careful to remove all impurity from his boots.

A servant-maid of some personal attractions immediately opened the door, and seemed to regard the secretary with no unkind eyes.

"This is the parcel from Lady Vandeleur," said Harry.

"I know," replied the maid, with a nod. "But the gentleman is from home. Will you leave it with me?"

"I cannot," answered Harry. "I am directed not to part with it but upon a certain condition, and I must ask you, I am afraid, to let me wait."

"Well," said she, "I suppose I may let you wait. I am lonely enough, I can tell you, and you do not look as though you would eat a girl. But be sure and do not ask the gentleman's name, for that I am not to tell you."

"Do you say so?" cried Harry. "Why, how strange! But indeed for some time back I walk among surprises. One question I think I may surely ask without indiscretion: Is he the master of this house?"

"He is a lodger, and not eight days old at that," returned the maid. "And now a question for a question: Do you know lady Vandeleur?"

"I am her private secretary," replied Harry with a glow of modest pride.

"She is pretty, is she not?" pursued the servant.

"Oh, beautiful!" cried Harry; "wonderfully lovely, and not less good and kind!"

"You look kind enough yourself," she retorted; "and I wager you are worth a dozen Lady Vandeleurs."

Harry was properly scandalised.

"I!" he cried. "I am only a secretary!"

"Do you mean that for me?" said the girl. "Because I am only a housemaid, if you please." And then, relenting at the sight of Harry's obvious confusion, "I know you mean nothing of the sort," she added; "and I like your looks; but I think nothing of your Lady Vandeleur. Oh, these mistresses!" she cried. "To send out a real gentleman like you—with a bandbox—in broad day!"

During this talk they had remained in their original positions—she on the doorstep, he on the side-walk, bareheaded for the sake of coolness, and with the bandbox on his arm. But upon this last speech Harry, who was unable to support such point-blank compliments to his appearance, nor the encouraging look with which they were accompanied, began to change his attitude, and glance from left to right in perturbation. In so doing he turned his face towards the lower end of the lane, and there, to his indescribable dismay, his eyes encountered those of General Vandeleur. The General, in a prodigious fluster of heat, hurry, and indignation, had been scouring the streets in chase of his brother-in-law; but so soon as he caught a glimpse of the delinquent secretary, his purpose changed, his anger flowed into a new channel, and he turned on his heel and came tearing up the lane with truculent gestures and vociferations.

Harry made but one bolt of it into the house, driving the maid before him; and the door was slammed in his pursuer's countenance.

"Is there a bar? Will it lock?" asked Harry, while a salvo on the knocker made the house echo from wall to wall.

"Why, what is wrong with you?" asked the maid. "Is it this old gentleman?"

"If he gets hold of me," whispered Harry, "I am as good as dead. He has been pursuing me all day, carries a sword-stick, and is an Indian military officer."

"These are fine manners," cried the maid. "And what, if you please, may be his name?"

"It is the General, my master," answered Harry. "He is after this bandbox."

"Did not I tell you?" cried the maid in triumph. "I told you I thought worse than nothing of your Lady Vandeleur; and if you had an eye in your head you might see what she is for yourself. An ungrateful minx, I will be bound for that!"

The General renewed his attack upon the knocker, and his passion growing with delay, began to kick and beat upon the panels of the door.

"It is lucky," observed the girl, "that I am alone in the house; your General may hammer until he is weary, and there is none to open for him. Follow me!"

So saying she led Harry into the kitchen, where she made him sit down, and stood by him herself in an affectionate attitude, with a hand upon his shoulder. The din at the door, so far from abating, continued to increase in volume, and at each blow the unhappy secretary was shaken to the heart.

"What is your name?" asked the girl.

"Harry Hartley," he replied.

"Mine," she went on, "is Prudence. Do you like it?"

"Very much," said Harry. "But hear for a moment how the General beats upon the door. He will certainly break it in, and then, in heaven's name, what have I to look for but death?"

"You put yourself very much about with no occasion," answered Prudence. "Let your General knock, he will do no more than blister his hands. Do you think I would keep you here if I were not sure to save you? Oh, no, I am a good friend to those that please me! and we have a back door upon another lane. But," she added, checking him, for he had got upon his feet immediately on this welcome news, "but I will not show where it is unless you kiss me. Will you, Harry?"

"That I will," he cried, remembering his gallantry, "not for your back door, but because you are good and pretty."

And he administered two or three cordial salutes, which were returned to him in kind.

Then Prudence led him to the back gate, and put her hand upon the key.

"Will you come and see me?" she asked.

"I will indeed," said Harry. "Do not I owe you my life?"

"And now," she added, opening the door, "run as hard as you can, for I shall let in the General."

Harry scarcely required this advice; fear had him by the forelock; and he addressed himself diligently to flight. A few steps, and he believed he would escape from his trials, and return to Lady Vandeleur in honour and safety. But these few steps had not been taken before he heard a man's voice hailing him by name with many execrations, and, looking over his shoulder, he beheld Charlie Pendragon waving him with both arms to return. The shock of this new incident was so sudden and profound, and Harry was already worked into so high a state of nervous tension, that he could think of nothing better than to accelerate his pace, and continue running. He should certainly have remembered the scene in Kensington Gardens; he should certainly have concluded that, where the General was his enemy, Charlie Pendragon could be no other than a friend. But such was the fever and perturbation of his mind that he was struck by none of these considerations, and only continued to run the faster up the lane.

Charlie, by the sound of his voice and the vile terms that he hurled after the secretary, was obviously beside himself with rage. He, too, ran his very best; but, try as he might, the physical advantages were not upon his side, and his outcries and the fall of his lame foot on the macadam began to fall farther and farther into the wake.

Harry's hopes began once more to arise. The lane was both steep and narrow, but it was exceedingly solitary, bordered on either hand by garden walls, overhung with foliage; and, for as far as the fugitive could see in front of him, there was neither a creature moving nor an open door. Providence, weary of persecution, was now offering him an open field for his escape.

Alas! as he came abreast of a garden door under a tuft of chestnuts, it was suddenly drawn back, and he could see inside, upon a garden path, the figure of a butcher's boy with his tray upon his arm. He had hardly recognised the fact before he was some steps beyond upon the other side. But the fellow had had time to observe him; he was evidently much surprised to see a gentleman go by at so unusual a pace; and he came out into the lane and began to call after Harry with shouts of ironical encouragement.

His appearance gave a new idea to Charlie Pendragon, who, although he was now sadly out of breath, once more upraised his voice.

"Stop, thief!" he cried.

And immediately the butcher's boy had taken up the cry and joined in the pursuit.

This was a bitter moment for the hunted secretary. It is true that his terror enabled him once more to improve his pace, and gain with every step on his pursuers; but he was well aware that he was near the end of his resources, and should he meet any one coming the other way, his predicament in the narrow lane would be desperate indeed.

"I must find a place of concealment," he thought, "and that within the next few seconds, or all is over with me in this world."

Scarcely had the thought crossed his mind than the lane took a sudden turning; and he found himself hidden from his enemies. There are circumstances in which even the least energetic of mankind learn to behave with vigour and decision; and the most cautious forget their prudence and embrace foolhardy resolutions. This was one of those occasions for Harry Hartley; and those who knew him best would have been the most astonished at the lad's audacity. He stopped dead, flung the bandbox over a garden wall, and leaping upward with incredible agility and seizing the copestone with his hands, he tumbled headlong after it into the garden.

He came to himself a moment afterwards, seated in a border of small rosebushes. His hands and knees were cut and bleeding, for the wall had been protected against such an escalade by a liberal provision of old bottles; and he was conscious of a general dislocation and a painful swimming in the head. Facing him across the garden, which was in admirable order, and set with flowers of the most delicious perfume, he beheld the back of a house. It was of considerable extent, and plainly habitable; but, in odd contrast to the grounds, it was crazy, ill-kept, and of a mean appearance. On all other sides the circuit of the garden wall appeared unbroken.

He took in these features of the scene with mechanical glances, but his mind was still unable to piece together or draw a rational conclusion from what he saw. And when he heard footsteps advancing on the gravel, although he turned his eyes in that direction, it was with no thought either for defence or flight.

The new-comer was a large, coarse, and very sordid personage, in gardening clothes, and with a watering-pot in his left hand. One less confused would have been affected with some alarm at the sight of this man's huge proportions and black and lowering eyes. But Harry was too gravely shaken by his fall to be so much as terrified; and if he was unable to divert his glances from the gardener, he remained absolutely passive, and suffered him to draw near, to take him by the shoulder, and to plant him roughly on his feet, without a motion of resistance.

For a moment the two stared into each other's eyes, Harry fascinated, the man filled with wrath and a cruel, sneering humour.

"Who are you?" he demanded at last. "Who are you to come flying over my wall and break my *Gloire de Dijons*! What is your name?" he added, shaking him; "and what may be your business here?"

Harry could not as much as proffer a word in explanation.

But just at that moment Pendragon and the butcher's boy went clumping past, and the sound of their feet and their hoarse cries echoed loudly in the narrow lane. The gardener had received his answer; and he looked down into Harry's face with an obnoxious smile.

"A thief!" he said. "Upon my word, and a very good thing you must make of it; for I see you dressed like a gentleman from top to toe. Are you not ashamed to go about the world in such a trim, with honest folk, I dare say, glad to buy your cast-off finery second hand? Speak up, you dog," the man went on; "you can understand English, I suppose; and I mean to have a bit of talk with you before I march you to the station."

"Indeed, sir," said Harry, "this is all a dreadful misconception; and if you will go with me to Sir Thomas Vandeleur's in Eaton Place, I can promise that all will be made plain. The most upright person, as I now perceive, can be led into suspicious positions."

"My little man," replied the gardener, "I will go with you no farther than the station-house in the next street. The inspector, no doubt, will be glad to take a stroll with you as far as Eaton Place, and have a bit of afternoon tea with your great acquaintances. Or would you prefer to go direct to the Home Secretary? Sir Thomas Vandeleur, indeed! Perhaps you think I don't know a gentleman when I see one, from a common run-the-hedge like you? Clothes or no clothes, I can read you like a book. Here is a shirt that maybe cost as much as my Sunday hat; and that coat, I take it, has never seen the inside of Rag-fair, and then your boots—"

The man, whose eyes had fallen upon the ground, stopped short in his insulting commentary, and remained for a moment looking intently upon something at his feet. When he spoke his voice was strangely altered.

"What, in God's name," said he, "is all this?"

Harry, following the direction of the man's eyes, beheld a spectacle that struck him dumb with terror and amazement. In his fall he had descended vertically upon the bandbox and burst it open from end to end; thence a great treasure of diamonds had poured forth, and now lay abroad, part trodden in the soil, part scattered on the surface in regal and glittering profusion. There was a magnificent coronet which he had often admired on Lady Vandeleur; there were rings and brooches, ear-drops and bracelets, and even unset brilliants rolling here and there among the rosebushes like drops of morning dew. A princely fortune lay between the two men upon the ground—a fortune in the most inviting, solid, and durable form, capable of being carried in an apron, beautiful in itself, and scattering the sunlight in a million rainbow flashes.

"Good God!" said Harry, "I am lost!"

His mind raced backwards into the past with the incalculable velocity of thought, and he began to comprehend his day's adventures, to conceive them as a whole, and to recognise the sad imbroglio in which his own character and fortunes had become involved. He looked round him as if for help, but he was alone in the garden, with his scattered diamonds and his redoubtable interlocutor; and when he gave ear, there was no sound but the rustle of the leaves and the hurried pulsation of his heart. It was little wonder if the young man felt himself deserted by his spirits, and with a broken voice repeated his last ejaculation—"I am lost!"

The gardener peered in all directions with an air of guilt; but there was no face at any of the windows, and he seemed to breathe again.

"Pick up a heart," he said, "you fool! The worst of it is done. Why could you not say at first there was enough for two? Two?" he repeated, "aye, and for two hundred! But come away from here, where we may be observed; and, for the love of wisdom, straighten out your hat and brush your clothes. You could not travel two steps the figure of fun you look just now."

While Harry mechanically adopted these suggestions, the gardener, getting upon his knees, hastily drew together the scattered jewels and returned them to the bandbox. The touch of these costly crystals sent a shiver of emotion through the man's stalwart frame; his face was transfigured, and his eyes shone with concupiscence; indeed it seemed as if he luxuriously prolonged his occupation, and dallied with every diamond that he handled. At last, however, it was done; and, concealing the bandbox in his smock, the gardener beckoned to Harry and preceded him in the direction of the house.

Near the door they were met by a young man evidently in holy orders, dark and strikingly handsome, with a look of mingled weakness and resolution, and very neatly attired after the manner of his caste. The gardener was plainly annoyed by this encounter; but he put as good a face upon it as he could, and accosted the clergyman with an obsequious and smiling air.

"Here is a fine afternoon, Mr. Rolles," said he: "a fine afternoon, as sure as God made it! And here is a young friend of mine who had a fancy to look at my roses. I took the liberty to bring him in, for I thought none of the lodgers would object."

"Speaking for myself," replied the Reverend Mr. Rolles, "I do not; nor do I fancy any of the rest of us would be more difficult upon so small a matter. The garden is your own, Mr. Raeburn; we must none of us forget that; and because you give us liberty to walk there we should be indeed ungracious if we so far presumed upon your politeness as to interfere with the convenience of your friends. But, on second thoughts," he added, "I believe that this gentleman and I have met before. Mr. Hartley, I think. I regret to observe that you have had a fall."

And he offered his hand.

A sort of maiden dignity and a desire to delay as long as possible the necessity for explanation moved Harry to refuse this chance of help, and to deny his own identity. He chose the tender mercies of the gardener, who was at least unknown to him, rather than the curiosity and perhaps the doubts of an acquaintance.

"I fear there is some mistake," said he. "My name is Thomlinson and I am a friend of Mr. Raeburn's."

"Indeed?" said Mr. Rolles. "The likeness is amazing."

Mr. Raeburn, who had been upon thorns throughout this colloquy, now felt it high time to bring it to a period.

"I wish you a pleasant saunter, sir," said he.

And with that he dragged Harry after him into the house, and then into a chamber on the garden. His first care was to draw down the blind, for Mr. Rolles still remained where they had left him, in an attitude of perplexity and thought. Then he emptied the broken bandbox on the table, and stood before the treasure, thus fully displayed, with an expression of rapturous greed, and rubbing his hands upon his thighs. For Harry, the sight of the man's face under the influence of this base emotion, added another pang to those he was already suffering. It seemed incredible that, from his life of pure and delicate trifling, he should be plunged in a breath among sordid and criminal relations. He could reproach his conscience with no sinful act; and yet he was now suffering the punishment of sin in its most acute and cruel forms—the dread of punishment, the suspicions of the good, and the companionship and contamination of vile and brutal natures. He felt he could lay his life down with gladness to escape from the room and the society of Mr. Raeburn.

"And now," said the latter, after he had separated the jewels into two nearly equal parts, and drawn one of them nearer to himself; "and now," said he, "everything in this world has to be paid for, and some things sweetly. You must know, Mr. Hartley, if such be your name, that I am a man of a very easy temper, and good nature has been my stumbling-block from first to last. I could pocket the whole of these pretty pebbles, if I chose, and I should like to see you dare to say a word; but I think I must have taken a liking to you; for I declare I have not the heart to shave you so close. So, do you see, in pure kind feeling, I propose that we divide; and these," indicating the two heaps, "are the proportions that seem to me just and friendly. Do you see any objection, Mr. Hartley, may I ask? I am not the man to stick upon a brooch."

"But, sir," cried Harry, "what you propose to me is impossible. The jewels are not mine, and I cannot share what is another's, no matter with whom, nor in what proportions."

"They are not yours, are they not?" returned Raeburn. "And you could not share them with anybody, couldn't you? Well now, that is what I call a pity; for here am I obliged to take you to the station. The police—think of that," he continued; "think of the disgrace for your respectable parents; think," he went on, taking Harry by the wrist; "think of the Colonies and the Day of Judgment."

"I cannot help it," wailed Harry. "It is not my fault. You will not come with me to Eaton Place?"

"No," replied the man, "I will not, that is certain. And I mean to divide these playthings with you here."

And so saying he applied a sudden and severe torsion to the lad's wrist.

Harry could not suppress a scream, and the perspiration burst forth upon his face. Perhaps pain and terror quickened his intelligence, but certainly at that moment the whole business flashed across him in another light; and he saw that there was nothing for it but to accede to the ruffian's proposal, and trust to find the house and force him to disgorge, under more favourable circumstances, and when he himself was clear from all suspicion.

"I agree," he said.

"There is a lamb," sneered the gardener. "I thought you would recognise your interests at last. This bandbox," he continued, "I shall burn with my rubbish; it is a thing that curious folk might recognise; and as for you, scrape up your gaieties and put them in your pocket."

Harry proceeded to obey, Raeburn watching him, and every now and again his greed rekindled by some bright scintillation, abstracting another jewel from the secretary's share, and adding it to his own.

When this was finished, both proceeded to the front door, which Raeburn cautiously opened to observe the street. This was apparently clear of passengers; for he suddenly seized Harry by the nape of the neck, and holding his face downward so that he could see nothing but the roadway and the doorsteps of the houses, pushed him violently before him down one street and up another for the space of perhaps a minute and a half. Harry had counted three corners before the bully relaxed his grasp, and crying, "Now be off with you!" sent the lad flying head foremost with a well-directed and athletic kick.

When Harry gathered himself up, half-stunned and bleeding freely at the nose, Mr. Raeburn had entirely disappeared. For the first time, anger and pain so completely overcame the lad's spirits that he burst into a fit of tears and remained sobbing in the middle of the road.

After he had thus somewhat assuaged his emotion, he began to look about him and read the names of the streets at whose intersection he had been deserted by the gardener. He was still in an unfrequented portion of West London, among villas and large gardens; but he could see some persons at a window who had evidently witnessed his misfortune; and almost immediately after a servant came running from the house and offered him a glass of water. At the same time, a dirty rogue, who had been slouching somewhere in the neighbourhood, drew near him from the other side.

"Poor fellow," said the maid, "how vilely you have been handled, to be sure! Why, your knees are all cut, and your clothes ruined! Do you know the wretch who used you so?"

"That I do!" cried Harry, who was somewhat refreshed by the water; "and shall run him home in spite of his precautions. He shall pay dearly for this day's work, I promise you."

"You had better come into the house and have yourself washed and brushed," continued the maid. "My mistress will make you welcome, never fear. And see, I will pick up your hat. Why, love of mercy!" she screamed, "if you have not dropped diamonds all over the street!"

Such was the case; a good half of what remained to him after the depredations of Mr. Raeburn, had been shaken out of his pockets by the summersault and once more lay glittering on the ground. He blessed his fortune that the maid had been so quick of eye; "there is nothing so bad but it might be worse," thought he; and the recovery of these few seemed to him almost as great an affair as the loss of all the rest. But, alas! as he stooped to pick up his treasures, the loiterer made a rapid onslaught, overset both Harry and the maid with a movement of his arms, swept up a double handful of the diamonds, and made off along the street with an amazing swiftness.

Harry, as soon as he could get upon his feet, gave chase to the miscreant with many cries, but the latter was too fleet of foot, and probably too well acquainted with the locality; for turn where the pursuer would he could find no traces of the fugitive.

In the deepest despondency, Harry revisited the scene of his mishap, where the maid, who was still waiting, very honestly returned him his hat and the remainder of the fallen diamonds. Harry thanked her from his heart, and being now in no humour for economy, made his way to the nearest cab-stand and set off for Eaton Place by coach.

The house, on his arrival, seemed in some confusion, as if a catastrophe had happened in the family; and the servants clustered together in the hall, and were unable, or perhaps not altogether anxious, to suppress their merriment at the tatterdemalion figure of the secretary. He passed them with as good an air of dignity as he could assume, and made directly for the boudoir. When he opened the door an astonishing and even menacing spectacle presented itself to his eyes; for he beheld the General and his wife and, of all people, Charlie Pendragon, closeted together and speaking with earnestness and gravity on some important subject. Harry saw at once that there was little left for him to explain—plenary confession had plainly been made to the General of the intended fraud upon his pocket, and the unfortunate miscarriage of the scheme; and they had all made common cause against a common danger.

"Thank Heaven!" cried Lady Vandeleur, "here he is! The bandbox, Harry—the bandbox!"

But Harry stood before them silent and downcast.

"Speak!" she cried. "Speak! Where is the bandbox?"

And the men, with threatening gestures, repeated the demand.

Harry drew a handful of jewels from his pocket. He was very white.

"This is all that remains," said he. "I declare before Heaven it was through no fault of mine; and if you will have patience, although some are lost, I am afraid, for ever, others, I am sure, may be still recovered."

"Alas!" cried Lady Vandeleur, "all our diamonds are gone, and I owe ninety thousand pounds for dress!"

"Madam," said the General, "you might have paved the gutter with your own trash; you might have made debts to fifty times the sum you mention; you might have robbed me of my mother's coronet and ring; and Nature might have still so far prevailed that I could have forgiven you at last. But, madam, you have taken the Rajah's Diamond—the Eye of Light, as the Orientals poetically termed it—the Pride of Kashgar! You have taken from me the Rajah's Diamond," he cried, raising his hands, "and all, madam, all is at an end between us!"

"Believe me, General Vandeleur," she replied, "that is one of the most agreeable speeches that ever I heard from your lips; and since we are to be ruined, I could almost welcome the change, if it delivers me from you. You have told me often enough that I married you for your money; let me tell you now that I always bitterly repented the bargain; and if you were still marriageable, and had a diamond bigger than your head, I should counsel even my maid against a union so uninviting and disastrous. As for you, Mr. Hartley," she continued, turning on the secretary, "you have sufficiently exhibited your valuable qualities in this house; we are now persuaded that you equally lack manhood, sense, and self-respect; and I can see only one course open for you—to withdraw instanter, and, if possible, return no more. For your wages you may rank as a creditor in my late husband's bankruptcy."

Harry had scarcely comprehended this insulting address before the General was down upon him with another.

"And in the meantime," said that personage, "follow me before the nearest Inspector of Police. You may impose upon a simple-minded soldier, sir, but the eye of the law will read your disreputable secret. If I must spend my old age in poverty through your underhand intriguing with my wife, I mean at least that you shall not remain unpunished for your pains; and God, sir, will deny me a very considerable satisfaction if you do not pick oakum from now until your dying day."

With that, the General dragged Harry from the apartment, and hurried him downstairs and along the street to the police-station of the district.

2

STORY OF THE YOUNG MAN IN HOLY ORDERS

THE REVEREND MR. SIMON ROLLES had distinguished himself in the Moral Sciences, and was more than usually proficient in the study of Divinity. His essay "On the Christian Doctrine of the Social Obligations" obtained for him, at the moment of its production, a certain celebrity in the University of Oxford; and it was understood in clerical and learned circles that young Mr. Rolles had in contemplation a considerable work—a folio, it was said—on the authority of the Fathers of the Church. These attainments, these ambitious designs, however, were far from helping him to any preferment; and he was still in quest of his first curacy when a chance ramble in that part of London, the peaceful and rich aspect of the garden, a desire for solitude and study, and the cheapness of the lodging, led him to take up his abode with Mr. Raeburn, the nurseryman of Stockdove Lane.

It was his habit every afternoon, after he had worked seven or eight hours on St. Ambrose or St. Chrysostom, to walk for a while in meditation among the roses. And this was usually one of the most productive moments of his day. But even a sincere appetite for thought, and the excitement of grave problems awaiting solution, are not always sufficient to preserve the mind of the philosopher against the petty shocks and contacts of the world. And when Mr. Rolles found General Vandeleur's secretary, ragged and bleeding, in the company of his landlord; when he saw both change colour and seek to avoid his questions; and, above all, when the former denied his own identity with the most unmoved assurance, he speedily forgot the Saints and Fathers in the vulgar interest of curiosity.

"I cannot be mistaken," thought he. "That is Mr. Hartley beyond a doubt. How comes he in such a pickle? why does he deny his name? and what can be his business with that black-looking ruffian, my landlord?"

As he was thus reflecting, another peculiar circumstance attracted his attention. The face of Mr. Raeburn appeared at a low window next the door; and, as chance directed, his eyes met those of Mr. Rolles. The nurseryman seemed disconcerted, and even alarmed; and immediately after the blind of the apartment was pulled sharply down.

"This may all be very well," reflected Mr. Rolles; "it may be all excellently well; but I confess freely that I do not think so. Suspicious, underhand, untruthful, fearful of observation—I believe upon my soul," he thought, "the pair are plotting some disgraceful action."

The detective that there is in all of us awoke and became clamant in the bosom of Mr. Rolles; and with a brisk, eager step, that bore no resemblance to his usual gait, he proceeded to make the circuit of the garden. When he came to the scene of Harry's escalade, his eye was at once arrested by a broken rosebush and marks of trampling on the mould. He looked up, and saw scratches on the brick, and a rag of trouser floating from a broken bottle. This, then, was the mode of entrance chosen by Mr. Raeburn's particular friend! It was thus that General Vandeleur's secretary came to admire a flower-garden! The young clergyman whistled softly to himself as he stooped to examine the ground. He could make out where Harry had landed from his perilous leap; he recognised the flat foot of Mr. Raeburn where it had sunk deeply in the soil as he pulled up the Secretary by the collar; nay, on a closer inspection, he seemed to distinguish the marks of groping fingers, as though something had been spilt abroad and eagerly collected.

"Upon my word," he thought, "the thing grows vastly interesting."

And just then he caught sight of something almost entirely buried in the earth. In an instant he had disinterred a dainty morocco case, ornamented and clasped in gilt. It had been trodden heavily underfoot, and thus escaped the hurried search of Mr. Raeburn. Mr. Rolles opened the case, and drew a long breath of almost horrified astonishment; for there lay before him, in a cradle of green velvet, a diamond of prodigious magnitude and of the finest water. It was of the bigness of a duck's egg; beautifully shaped, and without a flaw; and as the sun shone upon it, it gave forth a lustre like that of electricity, and seemed to burn in his hand with a thousand internal fires.

He knew little of precious stones; but the Rajah's Diamond was a wonder that explained itself; a village child, if he found it, would run screaming for the nearest cottage; and a savage would prostrate himself in adoration before so imposing a fetish. The beauty of the stone flattered the young clergyman's eyes; the thought of its incalculable value overpowered his intellect. He knew that what he held in his hand was worth more than many years' purchase of an archiepiscopal see; that it would build cathedrals more stately than Ely or Cologne; that he who possessed it was set free for ever from the primal curse, and might follow his own inclinations without concern or hurry, without let or hindrance. And as he suddenly turned it, the rays leaped forth again with renewed brilliancy, and seemed to pierce his very heart.

Decisive actions are often taken in a moment and without any conscious deliverance from the rational parts of man. So it was now with Mr. Rolles. He glanced hurriedly round; beheld, like Mr. Raeburn before him, nothing but the sunlit flower-garden, the tall tree-tops, and the house with blinded windows; and in a trice he had shut the case, thrust it into his pocket, and was hastening to his study with the speed of guilt.

The Reverend Simon Rolles had stolen the Rajah's Diamond.

Early in the afternoon the police arrived with Harry Hartley. The nurseryman, who was beside himself with terror, readily discovered his hoard; and the jewels were identified and inventoried in the presence of the Secretary. As for Mr. Rolles, he showed himself in a most obliging temper, communicated what he knew with freedom, and professed regret that he could do no more to help the officers in their duty.

"Still," he added, "I suppose your business is nearly at an end."

"By no means," replied the man from Scotland Yard; and he narrated the second robbery of which Harry had been the immediate victim, and gave the young clergyman a description of the more important jewels that were still not found, dilating particularly on the Rajah's Diamond.

"It must be worth a fortune," observed Mr. Rolles.

"Ten fortunes—twenty fortunes," cried the officer.

"The more it is worth," remarked Simon shrewdly, "the more difficult it must be to sell. Such a thing has a physiognomy not to be disguised, and I should fancy a man might as easily negotiate St. Paul's Cathedral."

"Oh, truly!" said the officer; "but if the thief be a man of any intelligence, he will cut it into three or four, and there will be still enough to make him rich."

"Thank you," said the clergyman. "You cannot imagine how much your conversation interests me."

Whereupon the functionary admitted that they knew many strange things in his profession, and immediately after took his leave.

Mr. Rolles regained his apartment. It seemed smaller and barer than usual; the materials for his great work had never presented so little interest; and he looked upon his library with the eye of scorn. He took down, volume by volume, several Fathers of the Church, and glanced them through; but they contained nothing to his purpose.

"These old gentlemen," thought he, "are no doubt very valuable writers, but they seem to me conspicuously ignorant of life. Here am I, with learning enough to be a Bishop, and I positively do not know how to dispose of a stolen diamond. I glean a hint from a common policeman, and, with all my folios, I cannot so much as put it into execution. This inspires me with very low ideas of University training."

Herewith he kicked over his book-shelf and, putting on his hat, hastened from the house to the club of which he was a member. In such a place of mundane resort he hoped to find some man of good counsel and a shrewd experience in life. In the reading-room he saw many of the country clergy and an Archdeacon; there were three journalists and a writer upon the Higher Metaphysic, playing pool; and at dinner only the raff of ordinary club frequenters showed their commonplace and obliterated countenances. None of these, thought Mr. Rolles, would know more on dangerous topics than he knew himself; none of them were fit to give him guidance in his present strait. At length in the smoking-room, up many weary stairs, he hit upon a gentleman of somewhat portly build and dressed with conspicuous plainness. He was smoking a cigar and reading the *Fortnightly Review*; his face was singularly free from all sign of preoccupation or fatigue; and there was something in his air which seemed to invite confidence and to expect submission. The more the young clergyman scrutinised his features, the more he was convinced that he had fallen on one capable of giving pertinent advice.

"Sir," said he, "you will excuse my abruptness; but I judge you from your appearance to be pre-eminently a man of the world."

"I have indeed considerable claims to that distinction," replied the stranger, laying aside his magazine with a look of mingled amusement and surprise.

"I, sir," continued the Curate, "am a recluse, a student, a creature of ink-bottles and patristic folios. A recent event has brought my folly vividly before my eyes, and I desire to instruct myself in life. By life," he added, "I do not mean Thackeray's novels; but the crimes and secret possibilities of our society, and the principles of wise conduct among exceptional events. I am a patient reader; can the thing be learnt in books?"

"You put me in a difficulty," said the stranger. "I confess I have no great notion of the use of books, except to amuse a railway journey; although, I believe, there are some very exact treatises on astronomy, the use of the globes, agriculture, and the art of making paper flowers. Upon the less apparent provinces of life I fear you will find nothing truthful. Yet stay," he added, "have you read Gaboriau?"

Mr. Rolles admitted he had never even heard the name.

"You may gather some notions from Gaboriau," resumed the stranger. "He is at least suggestive; and as he is an author much studied by Prince Bismarck, you will, at the worst, lose your time in good society."

"Sir," said the Curate, "I am infinitely obliged by your politeness."

"You have already more than repaid me," returned the other.

"How?" inquired Simon.

"By the novelty of your request," replied the gentleman; and with a polite gesture, as though to ask permission, he resumed the study of the *Fortnightly Review*.

On his way home Mr. Rolles purchased a work on precious stones and several of Gaboriau's novels. These last he eagerly skimmed until an advanced hour in the morning; but although they introduced him to many new ideas, he could nowhere discover what to do with a stolen diamond. He was annoyed, moreover, to find the information scattered amongst romantic story-telling, instead of soberly set forth after the manner of a manual; and he concluded that, even if the writer had thought much upon these subjects, he was totally lacking in educational method. For the character and attainments of Lecoq, however, he was unable to contain his admiration.

"He was truly a great creature," ruminated Mr. Rolles. "He knew the world as I know Paley's Evidences. There was nothing that he could not carry to a termination with his own hand, and against the largest odds. Heavens!" he broke out suddenly, "is not this the lesson? Must I not learn to cut diamonds for myself?"

It seemed to him as if he had sailed at once out of his perplexities; he remembered that he knew a jeweller, one B. Macculloch, in Edinburgh, who would be glad to put him in the way of the necessary training; a few months, perhaps a few years, of sordid toil, and he would be sufficiently expert to divide and sufficiently cunning to dispose with advantage of the Rajah's Diamond. That done, he might return to pursue his researches at leisure, a wealthy and luxurious student, envied and respected by all. Golden visions attended him through his slumber, and he awoke refreshed and light-hearted with the morning sun.

Mr. Raeburn's house was on that day to be closed by the police, and this afforded a pretext for his departure. He cheerfully prepared his baggage, transported it to King's Cross, where he left it in the cloak-room, and returned to the club to while away the afternoon and dine.

"If you dine here to-day, Rolles," observed an acquaintance, "you may see two of the most remarkable men in England—Prince Florizel of Bohemia, and old Jack Vandeleur."

"I have heard of the Prince," replied Mr. Rolles; "and General Vandeleur I have even met in society."

"General Vandeleur is an ass!" returned the other. "This is his brother John, the biggest adventurer, the best judge of precious stones, and one of the most acute diplomatists in Europe. Have you never heard of his duel with the Duc de Val d'Orge? of his exploits and atrocities when he was Dictator of Paraguay? of his dexterity in recovering Sir Samuel Levi's jewellery? nor of his services in the Indian Mutiny—services by which the Government profited, but which the Government dared not recognise? You make me wonder what we mean by fame, or even by infamy; for Jack Vandeleur has prodigious claims to both. Run downstairs," he continued, "take a table near them, and keep your ears open. You will hear some strange talk, or I am much misled."

"But how shall I know them?" inquired the clergyman.

"Know them!" cried his friend; "why, the Prince is the finest gentleman in Europe, the only living creature who looks like a king; and as for Jack Vandeleur, if you can imagine Ulysses at seventy years of age, and with a sabre-cut across his face, you have the man before you! Know them, indeed! Why, you could pick either of them out of a Derby day!"

Rolles eagerly hurried to the dining-room. It was as his friend had asserted; it was impossible to mistake the pair in question. Old John Vandeleur was of a remarkable force of body, and obviously broken to the most difficult exercises. He had neither the carriage of a swordsman, nor of a sailor, nor yet of one much inured to the saddle; but something made up of all these, and the result and expression of many different habits and dexterities. His features were bold and aquiline; his expression arrogant and predatory; his whole appearance that of a swift, violent, unscrupulous man of action; and his copious white hair and the deep sabre-cut that traversed his nose and temple added a note of savagery to a head already remarkable and menacing in itself.

In his companion, the Prince of Bohemia, Mr. Rolles was astonished to recognise the gentleman who had recommended him the study of Gaboriau. Doubtless Prince Florizel, who rarely visited the club, of which, as of most others, he was an honorary member, had been waiting for John Vandeleur when Simon accosted him on the previous evening.

The other diners had modestly retired into the angles of the room, and left the distinguished pair in a certain isolation, but the young clergyman was unrestrained by any sentiment of awe, and, marching boldly up, took his place at the nearest table.

The conversation was, indeed, new to the student's ears. The ex-Dictator of Paraguay stated many extraordinary experiences in different quarters of the world; and the Prince supplied a commentary which, to a man of thought, was even more interesting than the events themselves. Two forms of experience were thus brought together and laid before the young clergyman; and he did not know which to admire the most—the desperate actor or the skilled expert in life; the man who spoke boldly of his own deeds and perils, or the man who seemed, like a god, to know all things and to have suffered nothing. The manner of each aptly fitted with his part in the discourse. The Dictator indulged in brutalities alike of speech and gesture; his hand opened and shut and fell roughly on the table; and his voice was loud and heavy. The Prince, on the other hand, seemed the very type of urbane docility and quiet; the least movement, the least inflection, had with him a weightier significance than all the shouts and pantomime of his companion; and if ever, as must frequently have been the case, he described some experience personal to himself, it was so aptly dissimulated as to pass unnoticed with the rest.

At length the talk wandered on to the late robberies and the Rajah's Diamond.

"That diamond would be better in the sea," observed Prince Florizel.

"As a Vandeleur," replied the Dictator, "your Highness may imagine my dissent."

"I speak on grounds of public policy," pursued the Prince. "Jewels so valuable should be reserved for the collection of a Prince or the treasury of a great nation. To hand them about among the common sort of men is to set a price on Virtue's head; and if the Rajah of Kashgar—a Prince, I understand, of great enlightenment—desired vengeance upon the men of Europe, he could hardly have gone more efficaciously about his purpose than by sending us this apple of discord. There is no honesty too robust for such a trial. I myself, who have many duties and many privileges of my own—I myself, Mr. Vandeleur, could scarce handle the intoxicating crystal and be safe. As for you, who are a diamond hunter by taste and profession, I do not believe there is a crime in the calendar you would not perpetrate—I do not believe you have a friend in the world whom you would not eagerly betray—I do not know if you have a family, but if you have I declare you would sacrifice your children—and all this for what? Not to be richer, nor to have more comforts or more respect, but simply to call this diamond yours for a year or two until you die, and now and again to open a safe and look at it as one looks at a picture."

"It is true," replied Vandeleur. "I have hunted most things, from men and women down to mosquitos; I have dived for coral; I have followed both whales and tigers; and a diamond is the tallest quarry of the lot. It has beauty and worth; it alone can properly reward the ardours of the chase. At this moment, as your Highness may fancy, I am upon the trail; I have a sure knack, a wide experience; I know every stone of price in my brother's collection as a shepherd knows his sheep; and I wish I may die if I do not recover them every one!"

"Sir Thomas Vandeleur will have great cause to thank you," said the Prince.

"I am not so sure," returned the Dictator, with a laugh. "One of the Vandeleurs will. Thomas or John—Peter or Paul—we are all apostles."

"I did not catch your observation," said the Prince with some disgust.

And at the same moment the waiter informed Mr. Vandeleur that his cab was at the door.

Mr. Rolles glanced at the clock, and saw that he also must be moving; and the coincidence struck him sharply and unpleasantly, for he desired to see no more of the diamond hunter.

Much study having somewhat shaken the young man's nerves, he was in the habit of travelling in the most luxurious manner; and for the present journey he had taken a sofa in the sleeping carriage.

"You will be very comfortable," said the guard; "there is no one in your compartment, and only one old gentleman in the other end."

It was close upon the hour, and the tickets were being examined, when Mr. Rolles beheld this other fellow-passenger ushered by several porters into his place; certainly, there was not another man in the world whom he would not have preferred—for it was old John Vandeleur, the ex-Dictator.

The sleeping carriages on the Great Northern line were divided into three compartments—one at each end for travellers, and one in the centre fitted with the conveniences of a lavatory. A door running in grooves separated each of the others from the lavatory; but as there were neither bolts nor locks, the whole suite was practically common ground.

When Mr. Rolles had studied his position, he perceived himself without defence. If the Dictator chose to pay him a visit in the course of the night, he could do no less than receive it; he had no means of fortification, and lay open to attack as if he had been lying in the fields. This situation caused him some agony of mind. He recalled with alarm the boastful statements of his fellow-traveller across the dining-table, and the professions of immorality which he had heard him offering to the disgusted Prince. Some persons, he remembered to have read, are endowed with a singular quickness of perception for the neighbourhood of precious metals; through walls and even at considerable distances they are said to divine the presence of gold. Might it not be the same with diamonds? he wondered; and if so, who was more likely to enjoy this transcendental sense than the person who gloried in the appellation of the Diamond Hunter? From such a man he recognised that he had everything to fear, and longed eagerly for the arrival of the day.

In the meantime he neglected no precaution, concealed his diamond in the most internal pocket of a system of great-coats, and devoutly recommended himself to the care of Providence.

The train pursued its usual even and rapid course; and nearly half the journey had been accomplished before slumber began to triumph over uneasiness in the breast of Mr. Rolles. For some time he resisted its influence; but it grew upon him more and more, and a little before York he was fain to stretch himself upon one of the couches and suffer his eyes to close; and almost at the same instant consciousness deserted the young clergyman. His last thought was of his terrifying neighbour.

When he awoke it was still pitch dark, except for the flicker of the veiled lamp; and the continual roaring and oscillation testified to the unrelaxed velocity of the train. He sat upright in a panic, for he had been tormented by the most uneasy dreams; it was some seconds before he recovered his self-command; and even after he had resumed a recumbent attitude sleep continued to flee him, and he lay awake with his brain in a state of violent agitation, and his eyes fixed upon the lavatory door. He pulled his clerical felt hat over his brow still farther to shield him from the light; and he adopted the usual expedients, such as counting a thousand or banishing thought, by which experienced invalids are accustomed to woo the approach of sleep. In the case of Mr. Rolles they proved one and all vain; he was harassed by a dozen different anxieties—the old man in the other end of the carriage haunted him in the most alarming shapes; and in whatever attitude he chose to lie the diamond in his pocket occasioned him a sensible physical distress. It burned, it was too large, it bruised his ribs; and there were infinitesimal fractions of a second in which he had half a mind to throw it from the window.

While he was thus lying, a strange incident took place.

The sliding-door into the lavatory stirred a little, and then a little more, and was finally drawn back for the space of about twenty inches. The lamp in the lavatory was unshaded, and in the lighted aperture thus disclosed, Mr. Rolles could see the head of Mr. Vandeleur in an attitude of deep attention. He was conscious that the gaze of the Dictator rested intently on his own face; and the instinct of self-preservation moved him to hold his breath, to refrain from the least movement, and keeping his eyes lowered, to watch his visitor from underneath the lashes. After about a moment, the head was withdrawn and the door of the lavatory replaced.

The Dictator had not come to attack, but to observe; his action was not that of a man threatening another, but that of a man who was himself threatened; if Mr. Rolles was afraid of him, it appeared that he, in his turn, was not quite easy on the score of Mr. Rolles. He had come, it would seem, to make sure that his only fellow-traveller was asleep; and, when satisfied on that point, he had at once withdrawn.

The clergyman leaped to his feet. The extreme of terror had given place to a reaction of foolhardy daring. He reflected that the rattle of the flying train concealed all other sounds, and determined, come what might, to return the visit he had just received. Divesting himself of his cloak, which might have interfered with the freedom of his action, he entered the lavatory and paused to listen. As he had expected, there was nothing to be heard above the roar of the train's progress; and laying his hand on the door at the farther side, he proceeded cautiously to draw it back for about six inches. Then he stopped, and could not contain an ejaculation of surprise.

John Vandeleur wore a fur travelling cap with lappets to protect his ears; and this may have combined with the sound of the express to keep him in ignorance of what was going forward. It is certain, at least, that he did not raise his head, but continued without interruption to pursue his strange employment. Between his feet stood an open hat-box; in one hand he held the sleeve of his sealskin great-coat; in the other a formidable knife, with which he had just slit up the lining of the sleeve. Mr. Rolles had read of persons carrying money in a belt; and as he had no acquaintance with any but cricket-belts, he had never been able rightly to conceive how this was managed. But here was a stranger thing before his eyes; for John Vandeleur, it appeared, carried diamonds in the lining of his sleeve; and even as the young clergyman gazed, he could see one glittering brilliant drop after another into the hat-box.

He stood riveted to the spot, following this unusual business with his eyes. The diamonds were, for the most part, small, and not easily distinguishable either in shape or fire. Suddenly the Dictator appeared to find a difficulty; he employed both hands and stooped over his task; but it was not until after considerable manoeuvring that he extricated a large tiara of diamonds from the lining, and held it up for some seconds' examination before he placed it with the others in the hat-box. The tiara was a ray of light to Mr. Rolles; he immediately recognised it for a part of the treasure stolen from Harry Hartley by the loiterer. There was no room for mistake; it was exactly as the detective had described it; there were the ruby stars, with a great emerald in the centre; there were the interlacing crescents; and there were the pear-shaped pendants, each a single stone, which gave a special value to Lady Vandeleur's tiara.

Mr. Rolles was hugely relieved. The Dictator was as deeply in the affair as he was; neither could tell tales upon the other. In the first glow of happiness, the clergyman suffered a deep sigh to escape him; and as his bosom had become choked and his throat dry during his previous suspense, the sigh was followed by a cough.

Mr. Vandeleur looked up; his face contracted with the blackest and most deadly passion; his eyes opened widely, and his under jaw dropped in an astonishment that was upon the brink of fury. By an instinctive movement he had covered the hat-box with the coat. For half a minute the two men stared upon each other in silence. It was not a long interval, but it sufficed for Mr. Rolles; he was one of those who think swiftly on dangerous occasions; he decided on a course of action of a singularly daring nature; and although he felt he was setting his life upon the hazard, he was the first to break silence.

"I beg your pardon," said he.

The Dictator shivered slightly, and when he spoke his voice was hoarse.

"What do you want here?" he asked.

"I take a particular interest in diamonds," replied Mr. Rolles, with an air of perfect self-possession. "Two connoisseurs should be acquainted. I have here a trifle of my own which may perhaps serve for an introduction."

And so saying, he quietly took the case from his pocket, showed the Rajah's Diamond to the Dictator for an instant, and replaced it in security.

"It was once your brother's," he added.

John Vandeleur continued to regard him with a look of almost painful amazement; but he neither spoke nor moved.

"I was pleased to observe," resumed the young man, "that we have gems from the same collection."

The Dictator's surprise overpowered him.

"I beg your pardon," he said; "I begin to perceive that I am growing old! I am positively not prepared for little incidents like this. But set my mind at rest upon one point: do my eyes deceive me, or are you indeed a parson?"

"I am in holy orders," answered Mr. Rolles.

"Well," cried the other, "as long as I live I will never hear another word against the cloth!"

"You flatter me," said Mr. Rolles.

"Pardon me," replied Vandeleur; "pardon me, young man. You are no coward, but it still remains to be seen whether you are not the worst of fools. Perhaps," he continued, leaning back upon his seat, "perhaps you would oblige me with a few particulars. I must suppose you had some object in the stupefying impudence of your proceedings, and I confess I have a curiosity to know it."

"It is very simple," replied the clergyman; "it proceeds from my great inexperience of life."

"I shall be glad to be persuaded," answered Vandeleur.

Whereupon Mr. Rolles told him the whole story of his connection with the Rajah's Diamond, from the time he found it in Raeburn's garden to the time when he left London in the Flying Scotchman. He added a brief sketch of his feelings and thoughts during the journey, and concluded in these words:—

"When I recognised the tiara I knew we were in the same attitude towards Society, and this inspired me with a hope, which I trust you will say was not ill-founded, that you might become in some sense my partner in the difficulties and, of course, the profits of my situation. To one of your special knowledge and obviously great experience the negotiation of the diamond would give but little trouble, while to me it was a matter of impossibility. On the other part, I judged that I might lose nearly as much by cutting the diamond, and that not improbably with an unskilful hand, as might enable me to pay you with proper generosity for your assistance. The subject was a delicate one to broach; and perhaps I fell short in delicacy. But I must ask you to remember that for me the situation was a new one, and I was entirely unacquainted with the etiquette in use. I believe without vanity that I could have married or baptized you in a very acceptable manner; but every man has his own aptitudes, and this sort of bargain was not among the list of my accomplishments."

"I do not wish to flatter you," replied Vandeleur; "but upon my word, you have an unusual disposition for a life of crime. You have more accomplishments than you imagine; and though I have encountered a number of rogues in different quarters of the world, I never met with one so unblushing as yourself. Cheer up, Mr. Rolles, you are in the right profession at last! As for helping you, you may command me as you will. I have only a day's business in Edinburgh on a little matter for my brother; and once that is concluded, I return to Paris, where I usually reside. If you please, you may accompany me thither. And before the end of a month I believe I shall have brought your little business to a satisfactory conclusion."

3

STORY OF THE HOUSE WITH THE GREEN BLINDS

FRANCIS SCRYMGEOUR, a clerk in the Bank of Scotland at Edinburgh, had attained the age of twenty-five in a sphere of quiet, creditable, and domestic life. His mother died while he was young; but his father, a man of sense and probity, had given him an excellent education at school, and brought him up at home to orderly and frugal habits. Francis, who was of a docile and affectionate disposition, profited by these advantages with zeal, and devoted himself heart and soul to his employment. A walk upon Saturday afternoon, an occasional dinner with members of his family, and a yearly tour of a fortnight in the Highlands or even on the continent of Europe, were his principal distractions, and, he grew rapidly in favour with his superiors, and enjoyed already a salary of nearly two hundred pounds a year, with the prospect of an ultimate advance to almost double that amount. Few young men were more contented, few more willing and laborious than Francis Scrymgeour. Sometimes at night, when he had read the daily paper, he would play upon the flute to amuse his father, for whose qualities he entertained a great respect.

One day he received a note from a well-known firm of Writers to the Signet, requesting the favour of an immediate interview with him. The letter was marked "Private and Confidential," and had been addressed to him at the bank, instead of at home—two unusual circumstances which made him obey the summons with the more alacrity. The senior member of the firm, a man of much austerity of manner, made him gravely welcome, requested him to take a seat, and proceeded to explain the matter in hand in the picked expressions of a veteran man of business. A person, who must remain nameless, but of whom the lawyer had every reason to think well—a man, in short, of some station in the country—desired to make Francis an annual allowance of five hundred pounds. The capital was to be placed under the control of the lawyer's firm and two trustees who must also remain anonymous. There were conditions annexed to this liberality, but he was of opinion that his new client would find nothing either excessive or dishonourable in the terms; and he repeated these two words with emphasis, as though he desired to commit himself to nothing more.

Francis asked their nature.

"The conditions," said the Writer to the Signet, "are, as I have twice remarked, neither dishonourable nor excessive. At the same time I cannot conceal from you that they are most unusual. Indeed, the whole case is very much out of our way; and I should certainly have refused it had it not been for the reputation of the gentleman who entrusted it to my care, and, let me add, Mr. Scrymgeour, the interest I have been led to take in yourself by many complimentary and, I have no doubt, well-deserved reports."

Francis entreated him to be more specific.

"You cannot picture my uneasiness as to these conditions," he said.

"They are two," replied the lawyer, "only two; and the sum, as you will remember, is five hundred a-year—and unburdened, I forgot to add, unburdened."

And the lawyer raised his eyebrows at him with solemn gusto.

"The first," he resumed, "is of remarkable simplicity. You must be in Paris by the afternoon of Sunday, the 15th; there you will find, at the box-office of the Comédie Française, a ticket for admission taken in your name and waiting you. You are requested to sit out the whole performance in the seat provided, and that is all."

"I should certainly have preferred a week-day," replied Francis. " But, after all, once in a way—"

"And in Paris, my dear sir," added the lawyer soothingly. "I believe I am something of a precisian myself, but upon such a consideration, and in Paris, I should not hesitate an instant."

And the pair laughed pleasantly together.

"The other is of more importance," continued the Writer to the Signet. "It regards your marriage. My client, taking a deep interest in your welfare, desires to advise you absolutely in the choice of a wife. Absolutely, you understand," he repeated.

"Let us be more explicit, if you please," returned Francis. "Am I to marry any one, maid or widow, black or white, whom this invisible person chooses to propose?"

"I was to assure you that suitability of age and position should be a principle with your benefactor," replied the lawyer. "As to race, I confess the difficulty had not occurred to me, and I failed to inquire; but if you like I will make a note of it at once, and advise you on the earliest opportunity."

"Sir," said Francis, "it remains to be seen whether this whole affair is not a most unworthy fraud. The circumstances are inexplicable—I had almost said incredible; and until I see a little more daylight, and some plausible motive, I confess I should be very sorry to put a hand to the transaction. I appeal to you in this difficulty for information. I must learn what is at the bottom of it all. If you do not know, cannot guess, or are not at liberty to tell me, I shall take my hat and go back to my bank as came."

"I do not know," answered the lawyer, "but I have an excellent guess. Your father, and no one else, is at the root of this apparently unnatural business."

"My father!" cried Francis, in extreme disdain. "Worthy man, I know every thought of his mind, every penny of his fortune!"

"You misinterpret my words," said the lawyer. "I do not refer to Mr. Scrymgeour, senior; for he is not your father. When he and his wife came to Edinburgh, you were already nearly one year old, and you had not yet been three months in their care. The secret has been well kept; but such is the fact. Your father is unknown, and I say again that I believe him to be the original of the offers I am charged at present to transmit to you."

It would be impossible to exaggerate the astonishment of Francis Scrymgeour at this unexpected information. He pled this confusion to the lawyer.

"Sir," said he, "after a piece of news so startling, you must grant me some hours for thought. You shall know this evening what conclusion I have reached."

The lawyer commended his prudence; and Francis, excusing himself upon some pretext at the bank, took a long walk into the country, and fully considered the different steps and aspects of the case. A pleasant sense of his own importance rendered him the more deliberate: but the issue was from the first not doubtful. His whole carnal man leaned irresistibly towards the five hundred a year, and the strange conditions with which it was burdened; he discovered in his heart an invincible repugnance to the name of Scrymgeour, which he had never hitherto disliked; he began to despise the narrow and unromantic interests of his former life; and when once his mind was fairly made up, he walked with a new feeling of strength and freedom, and nourished himself with the gayest anticipations.

He said but a word to the lawyer, and immediately received a cheque for two quarters' arrears; for the allowance was ante-dated from the first of January. With this in his pocket, he walked home. The flat in Scotland Street looked mean in his eyes; his nostrils, for the first time, rebelled against the odour of broth; and he observed little defects of manner in his adoptive father which filled him with surprise and almost with disgust. The next day, he determined, should see him on his way to Paris.

In that city, where he arrived long before the appointed date, he put up at a modest hotel frequented by English and Italians, and devoted himself to improvement in the French tongue; for this purpose he had a master twice a week, entered into conversation with loiterers in the Champs Elysées, and nightly frequented the theatre. He had his whole toilette fashionably renewed; and was shaved and had his hair dressed every morning by a barber in a neighbouring street. This gave him something of a foreign air, and seemed to wipe off the reproach of his past years.

At length, on the Saturday afternoon, he betook himself to the box-office of the theatre in the Rue Richelieu. No sooner had he mentioned his name than the clerk produced the order in an envelope of which the address was scarcely dry.

"It has been taken this moment," said the clerk.

"Indeed!" said Francis. "May I ask what the gentleman was like?"

"Your friend is easy to describe," replied the official. "He is old and strong and beautiful, with white hair and a sabre-cut across his face. You cannot fail to recognise so marked a person."

"No, indeed," returned Francis; "and I thank you for your politeness."

"He cannot yet be far distant," added the clerk. "If you make haste you might still overtake him."

Francis did not wait to be twice told; he ran precipitately from the theatre into the middle of the street and looked in all directions. More than one white-haired man was within sight; but though he overtook each of them in succession, all wanted the sabre-cut. For nearly half-an-hour he tried one street after another in the neighbourhood, until at length, recognising the folly of continued search, he started on a walk to compose his agitated feelings; for this proximity of an encounter with him to whom he could not doubt he owed the day had profoundly moved the young man.

It chanced that his way lay up the Rue Drouot and thence up the Rue des Martyrs; and chance, in this case, served him better than all the forethought in the world. For on the outer boulevard he saw two men in earnest colloquy upon a seat. One was dark, young, and handsome, secularly dressed, but with an indelible clerical stamp; the other answered in every particular to the description given him by the clerk. Francis felt his heart beat high in his bosom; he knew he was now about to hear the voice of his father; and making a wide circuit, he noiselessly took his place behind the couple in question, who were too much interested in their talk to observe much else. As Francis had expected, the conversation was conducted in the English language.

"Your suspicions begin to annoy me, Rolles," said the older man. "I tell you I am doing my utmost; a man cannot lay his hand on millions in a moment. Have I not taken you up, a mere stranger, out of pure good-will? Are you not living largely on my bounty?"

"On your advances, Mr. Vandeleur," corrected the other.

"Advances, if you choose; and interest instead of goodwill, if you prefer it," returned Vandeleur angrily. "I am not here to pick expressions. Business is business; and your business, let me remind you, is too muddy for such airs. Trust me, or leave me alone and find some one else; but let us have an end, for God's sake, of your jeremiads."

"I am beginning to learn the world," replied the other, "and I see that you have every reason to play me false, and not one to deal honestly. I am not here to pick expressions either; you wish the diamond for yourself; you know you do—you dare not deny it. Have you not already forged my name, and searched my lodging in my absence? I understand the cause of your delays; you are lying in wait; you are the diamond hunter, forsooth; and sooner or later, by fair means or foul, you'll lay your hands upon it. I tell you, it must stop; push me much further and I promise you a surprise."

"It does not become you to use threats," returned Vandeleur. "Two can play at that. My brother is here in Paris; the police are on the alert; and if you persist in wearying me with your caterwauling, I will arrange a little astonishment for you, Mr. Rolles. But mine shall be once and for all. Do you understand, or would you prefer me to tell it you in Hebrew? There is an end to all things, and you have come to the end of my patience. Tuesday, at seven; not a day, not an hour sooner, not the least part of a second, if it were to save your life. And if you do not choose to wait, you may go to the bottomless pit for me, and welcome."

And so saying, the Dictator arose from the bench, and marched off in the direction of Montmartre, shaking his head and swinging his cane with a most furious air; while his companion remained where he was, in an attitude of great dejection.

Francis was at the pitch of surprise and horror; his sentiments had been shocked to the last degree; the hopeful tenderness with which he had taken his place upon the bench was transformed into repulsion and despair; old Mr. Scrymgeour, he reflected, was a far more kindly and creditable parent than this dangerous and violent intriguer; but he retained his presence of mind, and suffered not a moment to elapse before he was on the trail of the Dictator.

That gentleman's fury carried him forward at a brisk pace, and he was so completely occupied in his angry thoughts that he never so much as cast a look behind him till he reached his own door.

His house stood high up in the Rue Lepic, commanding a view of all Paris and enjoying the pure air of the heights. It was two storeys high, with green blinds and shutters; and all the windows looking on the street were hermetically closed. Tops of trees showed over the high garden wall, and the wall was protected by *chevaux-de-frise*. The Dictator paused a moment while he searched his pocket for a key; and then, opening a gate, disappeared within the enclosure.

Francis looked about him; the neighbourhood was very lonely, the house isolated in its garden. It seemed as if his observation must here come to an abrupt end. A second glance, however, showed him a tall house next door presenting a gable to the garden, and in this gable a single window. He passed to the front and saw a ticket offering unfurnished lodgings by the month; and, on inquiry, the room which commanded the Dictator's garden proved to be one of those to let. Francis did not hesitate a moment; he took the room, paid an advance upon the rent, and returned to his hotel to seek his baggage.

The old man with the sabre-cut might or might not be his father; he might or he might not be upon the true scent; but he was certainly on the edge of an exciting mystery, and he promised himself that he would not relax his observation until he had got to the bottom of the secret.

From the window of his new apartment Francis Scrymgeour commanded a complete view into the garden of the house with the green blinds. Immediately below him a very comely chestnut with wide boughs sheltered a pair of rustic tables where people might dine in the height of summer. On all sides save one a dense vegetation concealed the soil; but there, between the tables and the house, he saw a patch of gravel walk leading from the verandah to the garden-gate. Studying the place from between the boards of the Venetian shutters, which he durst not open for fear of attracting attention, Francis observed but little to indicate the manners of the inhabitants, and that little argued no more than a close reserve and a taste for solitude. The garden was conventual, the house had the air of a prison. The green blinds were all drawn down upon the outside; the door into the verandah was closed; the garden, as far as he could see it, was left entirely to itself in the evening sunshine. A modest curl of smoke from a single chimney alone testified to the presence of living people.

In order that he might not be entirely idle, and to give a certain colour to his way of life, Francis had purchased Euclid's Geometry in French, which he set himself to copy and translate on the top of his portmanteau and seated on the floor against the wall; for he was equally without chair or table. From time to time he would rise and cast a glance into the enclosure of the house with the green blinds; but the windows remained obstinately closed and the garden empty.

Only late in the evening did anything occur to reward his continued attention. Between nine and ten the sharp tinkle of a bell aroused him from a fit of dozing; and he sprang to his observatory in time to hear an important noise of locks being opened and bars removed, and to see Mr. Vandeleur, carrying a lantern and clothed in a flowing robe of black velvet with a skull-cap to match, issue from under the verandah and proceed leisurely towards the garden gate. The sound of bolts and bars was then repeated; and a moment after Francis perceived the Dictator escorting into the house, in the mobile light of the lantern, an individual of the lowest and most despicable appearance.

Half-an-hour afterwards the visitor was reconducted to the street; and Mr. Vandeleur, setting his light upon one of the rustic tables, finished a cigar with great deliberation under the foliage of the chestnut. Francis, peering through a clear space among the leaves, was able to follow his gestures as he threw away the ash or enjoyed a copious inhalation; and beheld a cloud upon the old man's brow and a forcible action of the lips, which testified to some deep and probably painful train of thought. The cigar was already almost at an end, when the voice of a young girl was heard suddenly crying the hour from the interior of the house.

"In a moment," replied John Vandeleur.

And, with that, he threw away the stump and, taking up the lantern, sailed away under the verandah for the night. As soon as the door was closed, absolute darkness fell upon the house; Francis might try his eyesight as much as he pleased, he could not detect so much as a single chink of light below a blind; and he concluded, with great good sense, that the bed-chambers were all upon the other side.

Early the next morning (for he was early awake after an uncomfortable night upon the floor), he saw cause to adopt a different explanation. The blinds rose, one after another, by means of a spring in the interior, and disclosed steel shutters such as we see on the front of shops; these in their turn were rolled up by a similar contrivance; and for the space of about an hour, the chambers were left open to the morning air. At the end of that time Mr. Vandeleur, with his own hand, once more closed the shutters and replaced the blinds from within.

While Francis was still marvelling at these precautions, the door opened and a young girl came forth to look about her in the garden. It was not two minutes before she re-entered the house, but even in that short time he saw enough to convince him that she possessed the most unusual attractions. His curiosity was not only highly excited by this incident, but his spirits were improved to a still more notable degree. The alarming manners and more than equivocal life of his father ceased from that moment to prey upon his mind; from that moment he embraced his new family with ardour; and whether the young lady should prove his sister or his wife, he felt convinced she was an angel in disguise. So much was this the case that he was seized with a sudden horror when he reflected how little he really knew, and how possible it was that he had followed the wrong person when he followed Mr. Vandeleur.

The porter, whom he consulted, could afford him little information; but, such as it was, it had a mysterious and questionable sound. The person next door was an English gentleman of extraordinary wealth, and proportionately eccentric in his tastes and habits. He possessed great collections, which he kept in the house beside him; and it was to protect these that he had fitted the place with steel shutters, elaborate fastenings, and *chevaux-de-frise* along the garden wall. He lived much alone, in spite of some strange visitors with whom, it seemed, he had business to transact; and there was no one else in the house, except Mademoiselle and an old woman servant.

"Is Mademoiselle his daughter?" inquired Francis.

"Certainly," replied the porter. "Mademoiselle is the daughter of the house; and strange it is to see how she is made to work. For all his riches, it is she who goes to market; and every day in the week you may see her going by with a basket on her arm."

"And the collections?" asked the other.

"Sir," said the man, "they are immensely valuable. More I cannot tell you. Since M. de Vandeleur's arrival no one in the quarter has so much as passed the door."

"Suppose not," returned Francis, "you must surely have some notion what these famous galleries contain. Is it pictures, silks, statues, jewels, or what?"

"My faith, sir," said the fellow with a shrug, "it might be carrots, and still I could not tell you. How should I know? The house is kept like a garrison, as you perceive."

And then as Francis was returning disappointed to his room, the porter called him back.

"I have just remembered, sir," said he. "M. de Vandeleur has been in all parts of the world, and I once heard the old woman declare that he had brought many diamonds back with him. If that be the truth, there must be a fine show behind those shutters."

By an early hour on Sunday Francis was in his place at the theatre. The seat which had been taken for him was only two or three numbers from the left-hand side, and directly opposite one of the lower boxes. As the seat had been specially chosen there was doubtless something to be learned from its position; and he judged by an instinct that the box upon his right was, in some way or other, to be connected with the drama in which he ignorantly played a part. Indeed, it was so situated that its occupants could safely observe him from beginning to end of the piece, if they were so minded; while, profiting by the depth, they could screen themselves sufficiently well from any counter-examination on his side. He promised himself not to leave it for a moment out of sight; and whilst he scanned the rest of the theatre, or made a show of attending to the business of the stage, he always kept a corner of an eye upon the empty box.

The second act had been some time in progress, and was even drawing towards a close, when the door opened and two persons entered and ensconced themselves in the darkest of the shade. Francis could hardly control his emotion. It was Mr. Vandeleur and his daughter. The blood came and went in his arteries and veins with stunning activity; his ears sang; his head turned. He dared not look lest he should awake suspicion; his play-bill, which he kept reading from end to end and over and over again, turned from white to red before his eyes; and when he cast a glance upon the stage, it seemed incalculably far away, and he found the voices and gestures of the actors to the last degree impertinent and absurd.

From time to time he risked a momentary look in the direction which principally interested him; and once at least he felt certain that his eyes encountered those of the young girl. A shock passed over his body, and he saw all the colours of the rainbow. What would he not have given to overhear what passed between the Vandeleurs? What would he not have given for the courage to take up his opera-glass and steadily inspect their attitude and expression? There, for aught he knew, his whole life was being decided—and he not able to interfere, not able even to follow the debate, but condemned to sit and suffer where he was, in impotent anxiety.

At last the act came to an end. The curtain fell, and the people around him began to leave their places, for the interval. It was only natural that he should follow their example; and if he did so, it was not only natural but necessary that he should pass immediately in front of the box in question. Summoning all his courage, but keeping his eyes lowered, Francis drew near the spot. His progress was slow, for the old gentleman before him moved with incredible deliberation, wheezing as he went. What was he to do? Should he address the Vandeleurs by name as he went by? Should he take the flower from his button-hole and throw it into the box? Should he raise his face and direct one long and affectionate look upon the lady who was either his sister or his betrothed? As he found himself thus struggling among so many alternatives, he had a vision of his old equable existence in the bank, and was assailed by a thought of regret for the past.

By this time he had arrived directly opposite the box; and although he was still undetermined what to do or whether to do anything, he turned his head and lifted his eyes. No sooner had he done so than he uttered a cry of disappointment and remained rooted to the spot. The box was empty. During his slow advance Mr. Vandeleur and his daughter had quietly slipped away.

A polite person in his rear reminded him that he was stopping the path; and he moved on again with mechanical footsteps, and suffered the crowd to carry him unresisting out of the theatre. Once in the street, the pressure ceasing, he came to a halt, and the cool night air speedily restored him to the possession of his faculties. He was surprised to find that his head ached violently, and that he remembered not one word of the two acts which he had witnessed. As the excitement wore away, it was succeeded by an overweening appetite for sleep, and he hailed a cab and drove to his lodging in a state of extreme exhaustion and some disgust of life.

Next morning he lay in wait for Miss Vandeleur on her road to market, and by eight o'clock beheld her stepping down a lane. She was simply, and even poorly, attired; but in the carriage of her head and body there was something flexible and noble that would have lent distinction to the meanest toilette. Even her basket, so aptly did she carry it, became her like an ornament. It seemed to Francis, as he slipped into a doorway, that the sunshine followed and the shadows fled before her as she walked; and he was conscious, for the first time, of a bird singing in a cage above the lane.

He suffered her to pass the doorway, and then, coming forth once more, addressed her by name from behind. "Miss Vandeleur," said he.

She turned and, when she saw who he was, became deadly pale.

"Pardon me," he continued; "Heaven knows I had no will to startle you; and, indeed, there should be nothing startling in the presence of one who wishes you so well as I do. And, believe me, I am acting rather from necessity than choice. We have many things in common, and I am sadly in the dark. There is much that I should be doing, and my hands are tied. I do not know even what to feel, nor who are my friends and enemies."

She found her voice with an effort.

"I do not know who you are," she said.

"Ah, yes! Miss Vandeleur, you do," returned Francis "better than I do myself. Indeed, it is on that, above all, that I seek light. Tell me what you know," he pleaded. "Tell me who I am, who you are, and how our destinies are intermixed. Give me a little help with my life, Miss Vandeleur—only a word or two to guide me, only the name of my father, if you will—and I shall be grateful and content."

"I will not attempt to deceive you," she replied. "I know who you are, but I am not at liberty to say."

"Tell me, at least, that you have forgiven my presumption, and I shall wait with all the patience I have," he said. "If I am not to know, I must do without. It is cruel, but I can bear more upon a push. Only do not add to my troubles the thought that I have made an enemy of you."

"You did only what was natural," she said, "and I have nothing to forgive you. Farewell."

"Is it to be *farewell*?" he asked.

"Nay, that I do not know myself," she answered. "Farewell for the present, if you like."

And with these words she was gone.

Francis returned to his lodging in a state of considerable commotion of mind. He made the most trifling progress with his Euclid for that forenoon, and was more often at the window than at his improvised writing-table. But beyond seeing the return of Miss Vandeleur, and the meeting between her and her father, who was smoking a Trichinopoli cigar in the verandah, there was nothing notable in the neighbourhood of the house with the green blinds before the time of the mid-day meal. The young man hastily allayed his appetite in a neighbouring restaurant, and returned with the speed of unallayed curiosity to the house in the Rue Lepic. A mounted servant was leading a saddle-horse to and fro before the garden wall; and the porter of Francis's lodging was smoking a pipe against the door-post, absorbed in contemplation of the livery and the steeds.

"Look!" he cried to the young man, "what fine cattle! what an elegant costume! They belong to the brother of M. de Vandeleur, who is now within upon a visit. He is a great man, a general, in your country; and you doubtless know him well by reputation."

"I confess," returned Francis, "that I have never heard of General Vandeleur before. We have many officers of that grade, and my pursuits have been exclusively civil."

"It is he," replied the porter, "who lost the great diamond of the Indies. Of that at least you must have read often in the papers."

As soon as Francis could disengage himself from the porter he ran upstairs and hurried to the window. Immediately below the clear space in the chestnut leaves, the two gentlemen were seated in conversation over a cigar. The General, a red, military-looking man, offered some traces of a family resemblance to his brother; he had something of the same features, something, although very little, of the same free and powerful carriage; but he was older, smaller, and more common in air; his likeness was that of a caricature, and he seemed altogether a poor and debile being by the side of the Dictator.

They spoke in tones so low, leaning over the table with every appearance of interest, that Francis could catch no more than a word or two on an occasion. For as little as he heard, he was convinced that the conversation turned upon himself and his own career; several times the name of Scrymgeour reached his ear, for it was easy to distinguish, and still more frequently he fancied he could distinguish the name Francis.

At length the General, as if in a hot anger, broke forth into several violent exclamations.

"Francis Vandeleur!" he cried, accentuating the last word. "Francis Vandeleur, I tell you."

The Dictator made a movement of his whole body, half affirmative, half contemptuous, but his answer was inaudible to the young man.

Was he the Francis Vandeleur in question? he wondered. Were they discussing the name under which he was to be married? Or was the whole affair a dream and a delusion of his own conceit and self-absorption?

After another interval of inaudible talk, dissension seemed again to arise between the couple underneath the chestnut, and again the General raised his voice angrily so as to be audible to Francis.

"My wife?" he cried. "I have done with my wife for good. I will not hear her name. I am sick of her very name."

And he swore aloud and beat the table with his fist.

The Dictator appeared, by his gestures, to pacify him after a paternal fashion; and a little after he conducted him to the garden-gate. The pair shook hands affectionately enough; but as soon as the door had closed behind his visitor, John Vandeleur fell into a fit of laughter which sounded unkindly and even devilish in the ears of Francis Scrymgeour.

So another day had passed, and little more learnt. But the young man remembered that the morrow was Tuesday, and promised himself some curious discoveries; all might be well, or all might be ill; he was sure, at least, to glean some curious information, and, perhaps, by good luck, get at the heart of the mystery which surrounded his father and his family.

As the hour of the dinner drew near many preparations were made in the garden of the house with the green blinds. That table which was partly visible to Francis through the chestnut leaves was destined to serve as a sideboard, and carried relays of plates and the materials for salad: the other, which was almost entirely concealed, had been set apart for the diners, and Francis could catch glimpses of white cloth and silver plate.

Mr. Rolles arrived, punctual to the minute; he looked like a man upon his guard, and spoke low and sparingly. The Dictator, on the other hand, appeared to enjoy an unusual flow of spirits; his laugh, which was youthful and pleasant to hear, sounded frequently from the garden; by the modulation and the changes of his voice it was obvious that he told many droll stories and imitated the accents of a variety of different nations; and before he and the young clergyman had finished their vermouth all feeling of distrust was at an end, and they were talking together like a pair of school companions.

At length Miss Vandeleur made her appearance, carrying the soup-tureen. Mr. Rolles ran to offer her assistance which she laughingly refused; and there was an interchange of pleasantries among the trio which seemed to have reference to this primitive manner of waiting by one of the company.

"One is more at one's ease," Mr. Vandeleur was heard to declare.

Next moment they were all three in their places, and Francis could see as little as he could hear of what passed. But the dinner seemed to go merrily; there was a perpetual babble of voices and sound of knives and forks below the chestnut; and Francis, who had no more than a roll to gnaw, was affected with envy by the comfort and deliberation of the meal. The party lingered over one dish after another, and then over a delicate dessert, with a bottle of old wine carefully uncorked by the hand of the Dictator himself. As it began to grow dark a lamp was set upon the table and a couple of candles on the sideboard; for the night was perfectly pure, starry, and windless. Light overflowed besides from the door and window in the verandah, so that the garden was fairly illuminated and the leaves twinkled in the darkness.

For perhaps the tenth time Miss Vandeleur entered the house; and on this occasion she returned with the coffee-tray, which she placed upon the sideboard. At the same moment her father rose from his seat.

"The coffee is my province," Francis heard him say.

And next moment he saw his supposed father standing by the sideboard in the light of the candles.

Talking over his shoulder all the while, Mr. Vandeleur poured out two cups of the brown stimulant, and then, by a rapid act of prestidigitation, emptied the contents of a tiny phial into the smaller of the two. The thing was so swiftly done that even Francis, who looked straight into his face, had hardly time to perceive the movement before it was completed. And next instant, and still laughing, Mr. Vandeleur had turned again towards the table with a cup in either hand.

"Ere we have done with this," said he, "we may expect our famous Hebrew."

It would be impossible to depict the confusion and distress of Francis Scrymgeour. He saw foul play going forward before his eyes, and he felt bound to interfere, but knew not how. It might be a mere pleasantry, and then how should he look if he were to offer an unnecessary warning? Or again, if it were serious, the criminal might be his own father, and then how should he not lament if he were to bring ruin on the author of his days? For the first time he became conscious of his own position as a spy. To wait inactive at such a juncture and with such a conflict of sentiments in his bosom was to suffer the most acute torture; he clung to the bars of the shutters, his heart beat fast and with irregularity, and he felt a strong sweat break forth upon his body.

Several minutes passed.

He seemed to perceive the conversation die away and grow less and less in vivacity and volume; but still no sign of any alarming or even notable event.

Suddenly the ring of a glass breaking was followed by a faint and dull sound, as of a person who should have fallen forward with his head upon the table. At the same moment a piercing scream rose from the garden.

"What have you done?" cried Miss Vandeleur. "He is dead!"

The Dictator replied in a violent whisper, so strong and sibilant that every word was audible to the watcher at the window.

"Silence!" said Mr. Vandeleur; "the man is as well as I am. Take him by the heels whilst I carry him by the shoulders."

Francis heard Miss Vandeleur break forth into a passion of tears.

"Do you hear what I say?" resumed the Dictator, in the same tones. "Or do you wish to quarrel with me? I give you your choice, Miss Vandeleur."

There was another pause, and the Dictator spoke again.

"Take that man by the heels," he said. "I must have him brought into the house. If I were a little younger, I could help myself against the world. But now that years and dangers are upon me and my hands are weakened, I must turn to you for aid."

"It is a crime," replied the girl.

"I am your father," said Mr. Vandeleur.

This appeal seemed to produce its effect. A scuffling noise followed upon the gravel, a chair was overset, and then Francis saw the father and daughter stagger across the walk and disappear under the verandah, bearing the inanimate body of Mr. Rolles embraced about the knees and shoulders. The young clergyman was limp and pallid, and his head rolled upon his shoulders at every step.

Was he alive or dead? Francis, in spite of the Dictator's declaration, inclined to the latter view. A great crime had been committed; a great calamity had fallen upon the inhabitants of the house with the green blinds. To his surprise, Francis found all horror for the deed swallowed up in sorrow for a girl and an old man whom he judged to be in the height of peril.

A tide of generous feeling swept into his heart; he, too, would help his father against man and mankind, against fate and justice; and casting open the shutters he closed his eyes and threw himself with out-stretched arms into the foliage of the chestnut.

Branch after branch slipped from his grasp or broke under his weight; then he caught a stalwart bough under his armpit, and hung suspended for a second; and then he let himself drop and fell heavily against the table. A cry of alarm from the house warned him that his entrance had not been effected unobserved. He recovered himself with a stagger, and in three bounds crossed the intervening space and stood before the door in the verandah.

In a small apartment, carpeted with matting and surrounded by glazed cabinets full of rare and costly curios, Mr. Vandeleur was stooping over the body of Mr. Rolles. He raised himself as Francis entered, and there was an instantaneous passage of hands. It was the business of a second; as fast as an eye can wink the thing was done; the young man had not the time to be sure, but it seemed to him as if the Dictator had taken something from the curate's breast, looked at it for the least fraction of time as it lay in his hand, and then suddenly and swiftly passed it to his daughter.

All this was over while Francis had still one foot upon the threshold, and the other raised in air. The next instant he was on his knees to Mr. Vandeleur.

"Father!" he cried. "Let me too help you. I will do what you wish and ask no questions; I will obey you with my life; treat me as a son, and you will find I have a son's devotion."

A deplorable explosion of oaths was the Dictator's first reply.

"Son and father?" he cried. "Father and son? What d—d unnatural comedy is all this? How do you come in my garden? What do you want? And who, in God's name, are you?"

Francis, with a stunned and shamefaced aspect, got upon his feet again, and stood in silence.

Then a light seemed to break upon Mr. Vandeleur, and he laughed aloud

"I see," cried he. "It is the Scrymgeour. Very well, Mr. Scrymgeour. Let me tell you in a few words how you stand. You have entered my private residence by force, or perhaps by fraud, but certainly with no encouragement from me; and you come at a moment of some annoyance, a guest having fainted at my table, to besiege me with your protestations. You are no son of mine. You are my brother's bastard by a fishwife, if you want to know. I regard you with an indifference closely bordering on aversion; and from what I now see of your conduct, I judge your mind to be exactly suitable to your exterior. I recommend you these mortifying reflections for your leisure; and, in the meantime, let me beseech you to rid us of your presence. If I were not occupied," added the Dictator, with a terrifying oath, "I should give you the unholiest drubbing ere you went!"

Francis listened in profound humiliation. He would have fled had it been possible; but as he had no means of leaving the residence into which he had so unfortunately penetrated, he could do no more than stand foolishly where he was.

It was Miss Vandeleur who broke the silence.

"Father," she said, "you speak in anger. Mr. Scrymgeour may have been mistaken, but he meant well and kindly."

"Thank you for speaking," returned the Dictator. "You remind me of some other observations which I hold it a point of honour to make to Mr. Scrymgeour. My brother," he continued, addressing the young man, "has been foolish enough to give you an allowance; he was foolish enough and presumptuous enough to propose a match between you and this young lady. You were exhibited to her two nights ago; and I rejoice to tell you that she rejected the idea with disgust. Let me add that I have considerable influence with your father; and it shall not be my fault if you are not beggared of your allowance and sent back to your scrivening ere the week be out."

The tones of the old man's voice were, if possible, more wounding than his language; Francis felt himself exposed to the most cruel, blighting, and unbearable contempt; his head turned, and he covered his face with his hands, uttering at the same time a tearless sob of agony. But Miss Vandeleur once again interfered in his behalf.

"Mr. Scrymgeour," she said, speaking in clear and even tones, "you must not be concerned at my father's harsh expressions. I felt no disgust for you; on the contrary, I asked an opportunity to make your better acquaintance. As for what has passed to-night, believe me it has filled my mind with both pity and esteem."

Just then Mr. Rolles made a convulsive movement with his arm, which convinced Francis that he was only drugged, and was beginning to throw off the influence of the opiate. Mr. Vandeleur stooped over him and examined his face for an instant.

"Come, come!" cried he, raising his head. "Let there be an end of this. And since you are so pleased with his conduct, Miss Vandeleur, take a candle and show the bastard out."

The young lady hastened to obey.

"Thank you," said Francis, as soon as he was alone with her in the garden. "I thank you from my soul. This has been the bitterest evening of my life, but it will have always one pleasant recollection."

"I spoke as I felt," she replied, "and in justice to you. It made my heart sorry that you should be so unkindly used."

By this time they had reached the garden gate; and Miss Vandeleur, having set the candle on the ground, was already unfastening the bolts.

"One word more," said Francis. "This is not for the last time—I shall see you again, shall I not?"

"Alas!" she answered. "You have heard my father. What can I do but obey?"

"Tell me at least that it is not with your consent," returned Francis; "tell me that you have no wish to see the last of me."

"Indeed," replied she, "I have none. You seem to me both brave and honest."

"Then," said Francis, "give me a keepsake."

She paused for a moment, with her hand upon the key; for the various bars and bolts were all undone, and there was nothing left but to open the lock.

"If I agree," she said, "will you promise to do as I tell you from point to point?"

"Can you ask?" replied Francis. "I would do so willingly on your bare word."

She turned the key and threw open the door.

"Be it so," said she. "You do not know what you ask, but be it so. Whatever you hear," she continued, "whatever happens, do not return to this house; hurry fast until you reach the lighted and populous quarters of the city; even there be upon your guard. You are in a greater danger than you fancy. Promise me you will not so much as look at my keepsake until you are in a place of safety."

"I promise," replied Francis.

She put something loosely wrapped in a handkerchief into the young man's hand; and at the same time, with more strength than he could have anticipated, she pushed him into the street.

"Now, run!" she cried.

He heard the door close behind him, and the noise of the bolts being replaced.

"My faith," said he, "since I have promised!"

And he took to his heels down the lane that leads into the Rue Ravignan.

He was not fifty paces from the house with the green blinds when the most diabolical outcry suddenly arose out of the stillness of the night. Mechanically he stood still; another passenger followed his example; in the neighbouring floors he saw people crowding to the windows; a conflagration could not have produced more disturbance in this empty quarter. And yet it seemed to be all the work of a single man, roaring between grief and rage, like a lioness robbed of her whelps; and Francis was surprised and alarmed to hear his own name shouted with English imprecations to the wind.

His first movement was to return to the house; his second, as he remembered Miss Vandeleur's advice, to continue his flight with greater expedition than before; and he was in the act of turning to put his thought in action, when the Dictator, bareheaded, bawling aloud, his white hair blowing about his head, shot past him like a ball out of the cannon's mouth, and went careering down the street.

"That was a close shave," thought Francis to himself. "What he wants with me, and why he should be so disturbed, I cannot think; but he is plainly not good company for the moment, and I cannot do better than follow Miss Vandeleur's advice."

So saying, he turned to retrace his steps, thinking to double and descend by the Rue Lepic itself while his pursuer should continue to follow after him on the other line of street. The plan was ill-devised: as a matter of fact, he should have taken his seat in the nearest café, and waited there until the first heat of the pursuit was over. But besides that Francis had no experience and little natural aptitude for the small war of private life, he was so unconscious of any evil on his part, that he saw nothing to fear beyond a disagreeable interview. And to disagreeable interviews he felt he had already served his apprenticeship that evening; nor could he suppose that Miss Vandeleur had left anything unsaid. Indeed, the young man was sore both in body and mind—the one was all bruised, the other was full of smarting arrows; and he owned to himself that Mr. Vandeleur was master of a very deadly tongue.

The thought of his bruises reminded him that he had not only come without a hat, but that his clothes had considerably suffered in his descent through the chestnut. At the first magazine he purchased a cheap wideawake, and had the disorder of his toilet summarily repaired. The keepsake, still rolled in the handkerchief, he thrust in the meanwhile into his trousers pocket.

Not many steps beyond the shop he was conscious of a sudden shock, a hand upon his throat, an infuriated face close to his own, and an open mouth bawling curses in his ear. The Dictator, having found no trace of his quarry, was returning by the other way. Francis was a stalwart young fellow; but he was no match for his adversary whether in strength or skill; and after a few ineffectual struggles he resigned himself entirely to his captor.

"What do you want with me?" said he.

"We will talk of that at home," returned the Dictator grimly.

And he continued to march the young man up hill in the direction of the house with the green blinds.

But Francis, although he no longer struggled, was only waiting an opportunity to make a bold push for freedom. With a sudden jerk he left the collar of his coat in the hands of Mr. Vandeleur, and once more made off at his best speed in the direction of the Boulevards.

The tables were now turned. If the Dictator was the stronger, Francis, in the top of his youth, was the more fleet of foot, and he had soon effected his escape among the crowds. Relieved for a moment, but with a growing sentiment of alarm and wonder in his mind, be walked briskly until he debouched upon the Place de l'Opéra, lit up like day with electric lamps.

"This, at least," thought he, "should satisfy Miss Vandeleur."

And turning to his right along the Boulevards, he entered the Café Américain and ordered some beer. It was both late and early for the majority of the frequenters of the establishment. Only two or three persons, all men, were dotted here and there at separate tables in the hall; and Francis was too much occupied by his own thoughts to observe their presence.

He drew the handkerchief from his pocket. The object wrapped in it proved to be a morocco case, clasped and ornamented in gilt, which opened by means of a spring, and disclosed to the horrified young man a diamond of monstrous bigness and extraordinary brilliancy. The circumstance was so inexplicable, the value of the stone was plainly so enormous, that Francis sat staring into the open casket without movement, without conscious thought, like a man stricken suddenly with idiocy.

A hand was laid upon his shoulder, lightly but firmly, and a quiet voice, which yet had in it the ring of command, uttered these words in his ear—

"Close the casket, and compose your face."

Looking up, he beheld a man, still young, of an urbane and tranquil presence, and dressed with rich simplicity. This personage had risen from a neighbouring table, and, bringing his glass with him, had taken a seat beside Francis.

"Close the casket," repeated the stranger, "and put it quietly back into your pocket, where I feel persuaded it should never have been. Try, if you please, to throw off your bewildered air, and act as though I were one of your acquaintances whom you had met by chance. So! Touch glasses with me. That is better. I fear, sir, you must be an amateur."

And the stranger pronounced these last words with a smile of peculiar meaning, leaned back in his seat and enjoyed a deep inhalation of tobacco.

"For God's sake," said Francis, "tell me who you are and what this means? Why I should obey your most unusual suggestions I am sure I know not; but the truth is, I have fallen this evening into so many perplexing adventures, and all I meet conduct themselves so strangely, that I think I must either have gone mad or wandered into another planet. Your face inspires me with confidence; you seem wise, good, and experienced; tell me, for heaven's sake, why you accost me in so odd a fashion?"

"All in due time," replied the stranger. "But I have the first hand, and you must begin by telling me how the Rajah's Diamond is in your possession."

"The Rajah's Diamond!" echoed Francis.

"I would not speak so loud, if I were you," returned the other. "But most certainly you have the Rajah's Diamond in your pocket. I have seen and handled it a score of times in Sir Thomas Vandeleur's collection."

"Sir Thomas Vandeleur! The General! My father!" cried Francis.

"Your father?" repeated the stranger. "I was not aware the General had any family."

"I am illegitimate, sir," replied Francis, with a flush.

The other bowed with gravity. It was a respectful bow, as of a man silently apologising to his equal; and Francis felt relieved and comforted, he scarce knew why. The society of this person did him good; he seemed to touch firm ground; a strong feeling of respect grew up in his bosom, and mechanically he removed his wideawake as though in the presence of a superior.

"I perceive," said the stranger, "that your adventures have not all been peaceful. Your collar is torn, your face is scratched, you have a cut upon your temple; you will, perhaps, pardon my curiosity when I ask you to explain how you came by these injuries, and how you happen to have stolen property to an enormous value in your pocket."

"I must differ from you!" returned Francis hotly. "I possess no stolen property. And if you refer to the diamond, it was given to me not an hour ago by Miss Vandeleur in the Rue Lepic."

"By Miss Vandeleur of the Rue Lepic!" repeated the other. "You interest me more than you suppose. Pray continue."

"Heavens!" cried Francis.

His memory had made a sudden bound. He had seen Mr. Vandeleur take an article from the breast of his drugged visitor, and that article, he was now persuaded, was a morocco case.

"You have a light?" inquired the stranger.

"Listen," replied Francis. "I know not who you are, but I believe you to be worthy of confidence and helpful; I find myself in strange waters; I must have counsel and support, and since you invite me I shall tell you all."

And he briefly recounted his experiences since the day when he was summoned from the bank by his lawyer.

"Yours is indeed a remarkable history," said the stranger, after the young man had made an end of his narrative; "and your position is full of difficulty and peril. Many would counsel you to seek out your father, and give the diamond to him; but I have other views. Waiter!" he cried.

The waiter drew near.

"Will you ask the manager to speak with me a moment?" said he; and Francis observed once more, both in his tone and manner, the evidence of a habit of command.

The waiter withdrew, and returned in a moment with manager, who bowed with obsequious respect.

"What," said he, "can I do to serve you?"

"Have the goodness," replied the stranger, indicating Francis, "to tell this gentleman my name."

"You have the honour, sir," said the functionary, addressing young Scrymgeour, "to occupy the same table with His Highness Prince Florizel of Bohemia."

Francis rose with precipitation, and made a grateful reverence to the Prince, who bade him resume his seat.

"I thank you," said Florizel, once more addressing the functionary; "I am sorry to have deranged you for so small a matter."

And he dismissed him with a movement of his hand.

"And now," added the Prince, turning to Francis, "give me the diamond."

Without a word the casket was handed over.

"You have done right," said Florizel, "your sentiments have properly inspired you, and you will live to be grateful for the misfortunes of to-night. A man, Mr. Scrymgeour, may fall into a thousand perplexities, but if his heart be upright and his intelligence unclouded, he will issue from them all without dishonour. Let your mind be at rest; your affairs are in my hand; and with the aid of heaven I am strong enough to bring them to a good end. Follow me, if you please, to my carriage."

So saying the Prince arose and, having left a piece of gold for the waiter, conducted the young man from the café and along the Boulevard to where an unpretentious brougham and a couple of servants out of livery awaited his arrival.

"This carriage," said he, "is at your disposal; collect your baggage as rapidly as you can make it convenient, and my servants will conduct you to a villa in the neighbourhood of Paris where you can wait in some degree of comfort until I have had time to arrange your situation. You will find there a pleasant garden, a library of good authors, a cook, a cellar, and some good cigars, which I recommend to your attention. Jérome," he added, turning to one of the servants, "you have heard what I say; I leave Mr. Scrymgeour in your charge; you will, I know, be careful of my friend."

Francis uttered some broken phrases of gratitude.

"It will be time enough to thank me," said the Prince, "when you are acknowledged by your father and married to Miss Vandeleur."

And with that the Prince turned away and strolled leisurely in the direction of Montmartre. He hailed the first passing cab, gave an address, and a quarter of an hour afterwards, having discharged the driver some distance lower, he was knocking at Mr. Vandeleur's garden gate.

It was opened with singular precautions by the Dictator in person.

"Who are you?" he demanded.

"You must pardon me this late visit, Mr. Vandeleur," replied the Prince.

"Your Highness is always welcome," returned Mr. Vandeleur, stepping back.

The Prince profited by the open space, and without waiting for his host walked right into the house and opened the door of the *salon*. Two people were seated there; one was Miss Vandeleur, who bore the marks of weeping about her eyes, and was still shaken from time to time by a sob; in the other the Prince recognised the young man who had consulted him on literary matters about a month before, in a club smoking-room.

"Good evening, Miss Vandeleur," said Florizel; "you look fatigued. Mr. Rolles, I believe? I hope you have profited by the study of Gaboriau, Mr. Rolles."

But the young clergyman's temper was too much embittered for speech; and he contented himself with bowing stiffly, and continued to gnaw his lip.

"To what good wind," said Mr. Vandeleur, following his guest, "am I to attribute the honour of your Highness's presence?"

"I am come on business," returned the Prince; "on business with you; as soon as that is settled I shall request Mr. Rolles to accompany me for a walk. Mr. Rolles," he added with severity, "let me remind you that I have not yet sat down."

The clergyman sprang to his feet with an apology; whereupon the Prince took an armchair beside the table, handed his hat to Mr. Vandeleur, his cane to Mr. Rolles, and, leaving them standing and thus menially employed upon his service, spoke as follows:—

"I have come here, as I said, upon business; but, had I come looking for pleasure, I could not have been more displeased with my reception nor more dissatisfied with my company. You, sir," addressing Mr. Rolles, "you have treated your superior in station with discourtesy; you, Vandeleur, receive me with a smile, but you know right well that your hands are not yet cleansed from misconduct. I do not desire to be interrupted, sir," he added imperiously; "I am here to speak, and not to listen; and I have to ask you to hear me with respect, and to obey punctiliously. At the earliest possible date your daughter shall be married at the Embassy to my friend, Francis Scrymgeour, your brother's acknowledged son. You will oblige me by offering not less than ten thousand pounds dowry. For yourself, I will indicate to you in writing a mission of some importance in Siam which I destine to your care. And now, sir, you will answer me in two words whether or not you agree to these conditions."

"Your Highness will pardon me," said Mr. Vandeleur, "and permit me, with all respect, to submit to him two queries?"

"The permission is granted," replied the Prince.

"Your Highness," resumed the Dictator, "has called Mr. Scrymgeour his friend. Believe me, had I known he was thus honoured, I should have treated him with proportional respect."

"You interrogate adroitly," said the Prince; "but it will not serve your turn. You have my commands; if I had never seen that gentleman before to-night, it would not render them less absolute."

"Your Highness interprets my meaning with his usual subtlety," returned Vandeleur. "Once more: I have, unfortunately, put the police upon the track of Mr. Scrymgeour on a charge of theft; am I to withdraw or to uphold the accusation?"

"You will please yourself," replied Florizel. "The question is one between your conscience and the laws of this land. Give me my hat; and you, Mr. Rolles, give me my cane and follow me. Miss Vandeleur, I wish you good evening. I judge," he added to Vandeleur, "that your silence means unqualified assent."

"If I can do no better," replied the old man, "I shall submit; but I warn you openly it shall not be without a struggle."

"You are old," said the Prince; "but years are disgraceful to the wicked. Your age is more unwise than the youth of others. Do not provoke me, or you may find me harder than you dream. This is the first time that I have fallen across your path in anger; take care that it be the last."

With these words, motioning the clergyman to follow, Florizel left the apartment and directed his steps towards the garden gate; and the Dictator, following with a candle, gave them light, and once more undid the elaborate fastenings with which he sought to protect himself from intrusion.

"Your daughter is no longer present," said the Prince, turning on the threshold. "Let me tell you that I understand your threats; and you have only to lift your hand to bring upon yourself sudden and irremediable ruin."

The Dictator made no reply; but as the Prince turned his back upon him in the lamplight he made a gesture full of menace and insane fury; and the next moment, slipping round a corner, he was running at full speed for the nearest cab-stand.

(*Here,* says my Arabian, *the thread of events is finally diverted from* The House with the Green Blinds. *One more adventure,* he adds, *and we have done with* The Rajah's Diamond. *That last link in the chain is known among the inhabitants of Bagdad by the name of* The Adventure of Prince Florizel and a Detective.)

p. 168**THE ADVENTURE OF PRINCE FLORIZEL AND A DETECTIVE**

Prince Florizel walked with Mr. Rolles to the door of a small hotel where the latter resided. They spoke much together, and the clergyman was more than once affected to tears by the mingled severity and tenderness of Florizel's reproaches.

"I have made ruin of my life," he said at last. "Help me; tell me what I am to do; I have, alas! neither the virtues of a priest nor the dexterity of a rogue."

"Now that you are humbled," said the Prince, "I command no longer; the repentant have to do with God and not with princes. But if you will let me advise you, go to Australia as a colonist, seek menial labour in the open air, and try to forget that you have ever been a clergyman, or that you ever set eyes on that accursed stone."

"Accurst indeed!" replied Mr. Rolles. "Where is it now? What further hurt is it not working for mankind?"

"It will do no more evil," returned the Prince. "It is here in my pocket. And this," he added kindly, "will show that I place some faith in your penitence, young as it is."

"Suffer me to touch your hand," pleaded Mr. Rolles.

"No," replied Prince Florizel, "not yet."

The tone in which he uttered these last words was eloquent in the ears of the young clergyman; and for some minutes after the Prince had turned away he stood on the threshold following with his eyes the retreating figure and invoking the blessing of heaven upon a man so excellent in counsel.

For several hours the Prince walked alone in unfrequented streets. His mind was full of concern; what to do with the diamond, whether to return it to its owner, whom he judged unworthy of this rare possession, or to take some sweeping and courageous measure and put it out of the reach of all mankind at once and for ever, was a problem too grave to be decided in a moment. The manner in which it had come into his hands appeared manifestly providential; and as he took out the jewel and looked at it under the street lamps, its size and surprising brilliancy inclined him more and more to think of it as of an unmixed and dangerous evil for the world.

"God help me!" he thought; "if I look at it much oftener, I shall begin to grow covetous myself."

At last, though still uncertain in his mind, he turned his steps towards the small but elegant mansion on the river-side which had belonged for centuries to his royal family. The arms of Bohemia are deeply graved over the door and upon the tall chimneys; passengers have a look into a green court set with the most costly flowers, and a stork, the only one in Paris, perches on the gable all day long and keeps a crowd before the house. Grave servants are seen passing to and fro within; and from time to time the great gate is thrown open and a carriage rolls below the arch. For many reasons this residence was especially dear to the heart of Prince Florizel; he never drew near to it without enjoying that sentiment of home-coming so rare in the lives of the great; and on the present evening he beheld its tall roof and mildly illuminated windows with unfeigned relief and satisfaction.

As he was approaching the postern door by which he always entered when alone, a man stepped forth from the shadow and presented himself with an obeisance in the Prince's path.

"I have the honour of addressing Prince Florizel of Bohemia?" said he.

"Such is my title," replied the Prince. "What do you want with me?"

"I am," said the man, "a detective, and I have to present your Highness with this billet from the Prefect of Police."

The Prince took the letter and glanced it through by the light of the street lamp. It was highly apologetic, but requested him to follow the bearer to the Prefecture without delay.

"In short," said Florizel, "I am arrested."

"Your Highness," replied the officer, "nothing, I am certain, could be further from the intention of the Prefect. You will observe that he has not granted a warrant. It is mere formality, or call it, if you prefer, an obligation that your Highness lays on the authorities."

"At the same time," asked the Prince, "if I were to refuse to follow you?"

"I will not conceal from your Highness that a considerable discretion has been granted me," replied the detective with a bow.

"Upon my word," cried Florizel, "your effrontery astounds me! Yourself, as an agent, I must pardon; but your superiors shall dearly smart for their misconduct. What, have you any idea, is the cause of this impolitic and unconstitutional act? You will observe that I have as yet neither refused nor consented, and much may depend on your prompt and ingenuous answer. Let me remind you, officer, that this is an affair of some gravity."

"Your Highness," said the detective humbly, "General Vandeleur and his brother have had the incredible presumption to accuse you of theft. The famous diamond, they declare, is in your hands. A word from you in denial will most amply satisfy the Prefect; nay, I go farther: if your Highness would so far honour a subaltern as to declare his ignorance of the matter even to myself, I should ask permission to retire upon the spot."

Florizel, up to the last moment, had regarded his adventure in the light of a trifle, only serious upon international considerations. At the name of Vandeleur the horrible truth broke upon him in a moment; he was not only arrested, but he was guilty. This was not only an annoying incident—it was a peril to his honour. What was he to say? What was he to do? The Rajah's Diamond was indeed an accursed stone; and it seemed as if he were to be the last victim to its influence.

One thing was certain. He could not give the required assurance to the detective. He must gain time.

His hesitation had not lasted a second.

"Be it so," said he, "let us walk together to the Prefecture."

The man once more bowed, and proceeded to follow Florizel at a respectful distance in the rear.

"Approach," said the Prince. "I am in a humour to talk, and, if I mistake not, now I look at you again, this is not the first time that we have met."

"I count it an honour," replied the officer, "that your Highness should recollect my face. It is eight years since I had the pleasure of an interview."

"To remember faces," returned Florizel, "is as much a part of my profession as it is of yours. Indeed, rightly looked upon, a Prince and a detective serve in the same corps. We are both combatants against crime; only mine is the more lucrative and yours the more dangerous rank, and there is a sense in which both may be made equally honourable to a good man. I had rather, strange as you may think it, be a detective of character and parts than a weak and ignoble sovereign."

The officer was overwhelmed.

"Your Highness returns good for evil," said he. "To an act of presumption he replies by the most amiable condescension."

"How do you know," replied Florizel, "that I am not seeking to corrupt you?"

"Heaven preserve me from the temptation!" cried the detective.

"I applaud your answer," returned the Prince. "It is that of a wise and honest man. The world is a great place and stocked with wealth and beauty, and there is no limit to the rewards that may be offered. Such an one who would refuse a million of money may sell his honour for an empire or the love of a woman; and I myself, who speak to you, have seen occasions so tempting, provocations so irresistible to the strength of human virtue, that I have been glad to tread in your steps and recommend myself to the grace of God. It is thus, thanks to that modest and becoming habit alone," he added, "that you and I can walk this town together with untarnished hearts."

"I had always heard that you were brave," replied the officer, "but I was not aware that you were wise and pious. You speak the truth, and you speak it with an accent that moves me to the heart. This world is indeed a place of trial."

"We are now," said Florizel, "in the middle of the bridge. Lean your elbows on the parapet and look over. As the water rushing below, so the passions and complications of life carry away the honesty of weak men. Let me tell you a story."

"I receive your Highness's commands," replied the man.

And, imitating the Prince, he leaned against the parapet, and disposed himself to listen. The city was already sunk in slumber; had it not been for the infinity of lights and the outline of buildings on the starry sky, they might have been alone beside some country river.

"An officer," began Prince Florizel, "a man of courage and conduct, who had already risen by merit to an eminent rank, and won not only admiration but respect, visited, in an unfortunate hour for his peace of mind, the collections of an Indian Prince. Here he beheld a diamond so extraordinary for size and beauty that from that instant he had only one desire in life: honour, reputation, friendship, the love of country, he was ready to sacrifice all for this lump of sparkling crystal. For three years he served this semi-barbarian potentate as Jacob served Laban; he falsified frontiers, he connived at murders, he unjustly condemned and executed a brother-officer who had the misfortune to displease the Rajah by some honest freedoms; lastly, at a time of great danger to his native land, he betrayed a body of his fellow-soldiers, and suffered them to be defeated and massacred by thousands. In the end, he had amassed a magnificent fortune, and brought home with him the coveted diamond.

"Years passed," continued the Prince, "and at length the diamond is accidentally lost. It falls into the hands of a simple and laborious youth, a student, a minister of God, just entering on a career of usefulness and even distinction. Upon him also the spell is cast; he deserts everything, his holy calling, his studies, and flees with the gem into a foreign country. The officer has a brother, an astute, daring, unscrupulous man, who learns the clergyman's secret. What does he do? Tell his brother, inform the police? No; upon this man also the Satanic charm has fallen; he must have the stone for himself. At the risk of murder, he drugs the young priest and seizes the prey. And now, by an accident which is not important to my moral, the jewel passes out of his custody into that of another, who, terrified at what he sees, gives it into the keeping of a man in high station and above reproach.

"The officer's name is Thomas Vandeleur," continued Florizel. "The stone is called the Rajah's Diamond. And"—suddenly opening his hand—"you behold it here before your eyes."

The officer started back with a cry.

"We have spoken of corruption," said the Prince. "To me this nugget of bright crystal is as loathsome as though it were crawling with the worms of death; it is as shocking as though it were compacted out of innocent blood. I see it here in my hand, and I know it is shining with hell-fire. I have told you but a hundredth part of its story; what passed in former ages, to what crimes and treacheries it incited men of yore, the imagination trembles to conceive; for years and years it has faithfully served the powers of hell; enough, I say, of blood, enough of disgrace, enough of broken lives and friendships; all things come to an end, the evil like the good; pestilence as well as beautiful music; and as for this diamond, God forgive me if I do wrong, but its empire ends to-night."

The Prince made a sudden movement with his hand, and the jewel, describing an arc of light, dived with a splash into the flowing river.

"Amen," said Florizel with gravity. "I have slain a cockatrice!"

"God pardon me!" cried the detective. "What have you done? I am a ruined man."

"I think," returned the Prince with a smile, "that many well-to-do people in this city might envy you your ruin."

"Alas! your Highness!" said the officer, "and you corrupt me after all?"

"It seems there was no help for it," replied Florizel. "And now let us go forward to the Prefecture."

Not long after, the marriage of Francis Scrymgeour and Miss Vandeleur was celebrated in great privacy; and the Prince acted on that occasion as groomsman. The two Vandeleurs surprised some rumour of what had happened to the diamond; and their vast diving operations on the River Seine are the wonder and amusement of the idle. It is true that through some miscalculation they have chosen the wrong branch of the river. As for the Prince, that sublime person, having now served his turn, may go, along with the *Arabian Author*, topsy-turvy into space. But if the reader insists on more specific information, I am happy to say that a recent revolution hurled him from the throne of Bohemia, in consequence of his continued absence and edifying neglect of public business; and that his Highness now keeps a cigar store in Rupert Street, much frequented by other foreign refugees. I go there from time to time to smoke and have a chat, and find him as great a creature as in the days of his prosperity; he has an Olympian air behind the counter; and although a sedentary life is beginning to tell upon his waistcoat, he is probably, take him for all in all, the handsomest tobacconist in London.

THE BOTTLE IMP

THE BOTTLE IMP

THERE WAS a man of the Island of Hawaii, whom I shall call Keawe; for the truth is, he still lives, and his name must be kept secret; but the place of his birth was not far from Honaunau, where the bones of Keawe the Great lie hidden in a cave. This man was poor, brave, and active; he could read and write like a schoolmaster; he was a first-rate mariner besides, sailed for some time in the island steamers, and steered a whaleboat on the Hamakua coast. At length it came in Keawe's mind to have a sight of the great world and foreign cities, and he shipped on a vessel bound to San Francisco.

This is a fine town, with a fine harbour, and rich people uncountable; and, in particular, there is one hill which is covered with palaces. Upon this hill Keawe was one day taking a walk with his pocket full of money, viewing the great houses upon either hand with pleasure, "What fine houses these are!" he was thinking, "and how happy must those people be who dwell in them, and take no care for the morrow!" The thought was in his mind when he came abreast of a house that was smaller than some others, but all finished and beautified like a toy; the steps of that house shone like silver, and the borders of the garden bloomed like garlands, and the windows were bright like diamond; and Keawe stopped and wondered at the excellence of all he saw. So stopping, he was aware of a man that looked forth upon him through a window so clear that Keawe could see him as you see a fish in a pool upon the reef. The man was elderly, with a bald head and a black beard; and his face was heavy with sorrow, and he bitterly sighed. And the truth of it is, that as Keawe looked in upon the man, and the man looked out upon Keawe, each envied the other.

All of a sudden, the man smiled and nodded, and beckoned Keawe to enter, and met him at the door of the house.

"This is a fine house of mine," said the man, and bitterly sighed. "Would you not care to view the chambers?"

So he led Keawe all over it, from the cellar to the roof, and there was nothing there that was not perfect of its kind, and Keawe was astonished.

"Truly," said Keawe, "this is a beautiful house; if I lived in the like of it, I should be laughing all day long. How comes it, then, that you should be sighing?"

"There is no reason," said the man, "why you should not have a house in all points similar to this, and finer, if you wish. You have some money, I suppose?"

"I have fifty dollars," said Keawe; "but a house like this will cost more than fifty dollars."

The man made a computation. "I am sorry you have no more," said he, "for it may raise you trouble in the future; but it shall be yours at fifty dollars."

"The house?" asked Keawe.

"No, not the house," replied the man; "but the bottle. For, I must tell you, although I appear to you so rich and fortunate, all my fortune, and this house itself and its garden, came out of a bottle not much bigger than a pint. This is it."

And he opened a lockfast place, and took out a round-bellied bottle with a long neck; the glass of it was white like milk, with changing rainbow colours in the grain. Withinsides something obscurely moved, like a shadow and a fire.

"This is the bottle," said the man; and, when Keawe laughed, "You do not believe me?" he added. "Try, then, for yourself. See if you can break it."

So Keawe took the bottle up and dashed it on the floor till he was weary; but it jumped on the floor like a child's ball, and was not injured.

"This is a strange thing," said Keawe. "For by the touch of it, as well as by the look, the bottle should be of glass."

"Of glass it is," replied the man, sighing more heavily than ever; "but the glass of it was tempered in the flames of hell. An imp lives in it, and that is the shadow we behold there moving: or so I suppose. If any man buy this bottle the imp is at his command; all that he desires—love, fame, money, houses like this house, ay, or a city like this city—all are his at the word uttered. Napoleon had this bottle, and by it he grew to be the king of the world; but he sold it at the last, and fell. Captain Cook had this bottle, and by it he found his way to so many islands; but he, too, sold it, and was slain upon Hawaii. For, once it is sold, the power goes and the protection; and unless a man remain content with what he has, ill will befall him."

"And yet you talk of selling it yourself?" Keawe said.

"I have all I wish, and I am growing elderly," replied the man. "There is one thing the imp cannot do—he cannot prolong life; and, it would not be fair to conceal from you, there is a drawback to the bottle; for if a man die before he sells it, he must burn in hell forever."

"To be sure, that is a drawback and no mistake," cried Keawe. "I would not meddle with the thing. I can do without a house, thank God; but there is one thing I could not be doing with one particle, and that is to be damned."

"Dear me, you must not run away with things," returned the man. "All you have to do is to use the power of the imp in moderation, and then sell it to someone else, as I do to you, and finish your life in comfort."

"Well, I observe two things," said Keawe. "All the time you keep sighing like a maid in love, that is one; and, for the other, you sell this bottle very cheap."

"I have told you already why I sigh," said the man. "It is because I fear my health is breaking up; and, as you said yourself, to die and go to the devil is a pity for anyone. As for why I sell so cheap, I must explain to you there is a peculiarity about the bottle. Long ago, when the devil brought it first upon earth, it was extremely expensive, and was sold first of all to Prester John for many millions of dollars; but it cannot be sold at all, unless sold at a loss. If you sell it for as much as you paid for it, back it comes to you again like a homing pigeon. It follows that the price has kept falling in these centuries, and the bottle is now remarkably cheap. I bought it myself from one of my great neighbours on this hill, and the price I paid was only ninety dollars. I could sell it for as high as eighty-nine dollars and ninety-nine cents, but not a penny dearer, or back the thing must come to me. Now, about this there are two bothers. First, when you offer a bottle so singular for eighty odd dollars, people suppose you to be jesting. And second—but there is no hurry about that—and I need not go into it. Only remember it must be coined money that you sell it for."

"How am I to know that this is all true?" asked Keawe.

"Some of it you can try at once," replied the man. "Give me your fifty dollars, take the bottle, and wish your fifty dollars back into your pocket. If that does not happen, I pledge you my honour I will cry off the bargain and restore your money."

"You are not deceiving me?" said Keawe.

The man bound himself with a great oath.

"Well, I will risk that much," said Keawe, "for that can do no harm." And he paid over his money to the man, and the man handed him the bottle.

"Imp of the bottle," said Keawe, "I want my fifty dollars back." And sure enough he had scarce said the word before his pocket was as heavy as ever.

"To be sure this is a wonderful bottle," said Keawe.

"And now good-morning to you, my fine fellow, and the devil go with you for me!" said the man.

"Hold on," said Keawe, "I don't want any more of this fun. Here, take your bottle back."

"You have bought it for less than I paid for it," replied the man, rubbing his hands. "It is yours now; and, for my part, I am only concerned to see the back of you." And with that he rang for his Chinese servant, and had Keawe shown out of the house.

Now, when Keawe was in the street, with the bottle under his arm, he began to think. "If all is true about this bottle, I may have made a losing bargain," thinks he. "But perhaps the man was only fooling me." The first thing he did was to count his money; the sum was exact—forty-nine dollars American money, and one Chili piece. "That looks like the truth," said Keawe. "Now I will try another part."

The streets in that part of the city were as clean as a ship's decks, and though it was noon, there were no passengers. Keawe set the bottle in the gutter and walked away. Twice he looked back, and there was the milky, round-bellied bottle where he left it. A third time he looked back, and turned a corner; but he had scarce done so, when something knocked upon his elbow, and behold! it was the long neck sticking up; and as for the round belly, it was jammed into the pocket of his pilot-coat.

"And that looks like the truth," said Keawe.

The next thing he did was to buy a cork-screw in a shop, and go apart into a secret place in the fields. And there he tried to draw the cork, but as often as he put the screw in, out it came again, and the cork as whole as ever.

"This is some new sort of cork," said Keawe, and all at once he began to shake and sweat, for he was afraid of that bottle.

On his way back to the port-side, he saw a shop where a man sold shells and clubs from the wild islands, old heathen deities, old coined money, pictures from China and Japan, and all manner of things that sailors bring in their sea-chests. And here he had an idea. So he went in and offered the bottle for a hundred dollars. The man of the shop laughed at him at the first, and offered him five; but, indeed, it was a curious bottle—such glass was never blown in any human glassworks, so prettily the colours shone under the milky white, and so strangely the shadow hovered in the midst; so, after he had disputed awhile after the manner of his kind, the shop-man gave Keawe sixty silver dollars for the thing, and set it on a shelf in the midst of his window.

"Now," said Keawe, "I have sold that for sixty which I bought for fifty—or, to say truth, a little less, because one of my dollars was from Chili. Now I shall know the truth upon another point."

So he went back on board his ship, and, when he opened his chest, there was the bottle, and had come more quickly than himself. Now Keawe had a mate on board whose name was Lopaka.

"What ails you?" said Lopaka, "that you stare in your chest?"

They were alone in the ship's forecastle, and Keawe bound him to secrecy, and told all.

"This is a very strange affair," said Lopaka; "and I fear you will be in trouble about this bottle. But there is one point very clear—that you are sure of the trouble, and you had better have the profit in the bargain. Make up your mind what you want with it; give the order, and if it is done as you desire, I will buy the bottle myself; for I have an idea of my own to get a schooner, and go trading through the islands."

"That is not my idea," said Keawe; "but to have a beautiful house and garden on the Kona Coast, where I was born, the sun shining in at the door, flowers in the garden, glass in the windows, pictures on the walls, and toys and fine carpets on the tables, for all the world like the house I was in this day—only a storey higher, and with balconies all about like the King's palace; and to live there without care and make merry with my friends and relatives."

"Well," said Lopaka, "let us carry it back with us to Hawaii; and if all comes true, as you suppose, I will buy the bottle, as I said, and ask a schooner."

Upon that they were agreed, and it was not long before the ship returned to Honolulu, carrying Keawe and Lopaka, and the bottle. They were scarce come ashore when they met a friend upon the beach, who began at once to condole with Keawe.

"I do not know what I am to be condoled about," said Keawe.

"Is it possible you have not heard," said the friend, "your uncle—that good old man—is dead, and your cousin—that beautiful boy—was drowned at sea?"

Keawe was filled with sorrow, and, beginning to weep and to lament, he forgot about the bottle. But Lopaka was thinking to himself, and presently, when Keawe's grief was a little abated, "I have been thinking," said Lopaka. "Had not your uncle lands in Hawaii, in the district of Kau?"

"No," said Keawe, "not in Kau; they are on the mountain-side—a little way south of Hookena."

"These lands will now be yours?" asked Lopaka.

"And so they will," says Keawe, and began again to lament for his relatives.

"No," said Lopaka, "do not lament at present. I have a thought in my mind. How if this should be the doing of the bottle? For here is the place ready for your house."

"If this be so," cried Keawe, "it is a very ill way to serve me by killing my relatives. But it may be, indeed; for it was in just such a station that I saw the house with my mind's eye."

"The house, however, is not yet built," said Lopaka.

"No, nor like to be!" said Keawe; "for though my uncle has some coffee and ava and bananas, it will not be more than will keep me in comfort; and the rest of that land is the black lava."

"Let us go to the lawyer," said Lopaka; "I have still this idea in my mind."

Now, when they came to the lawyer's, it appeared Keawe's uncle had grown monstrous rich in the last days, and there was a fund of money.

"And here is the money for the house!" cried Lopaka.

"If you are thinking of a new house," said the lawyer, "here is the card of a new architect, of whom they tell me great things."

"Better and better!" cried Lopaka. "Here is all made plain for us. Let us continue to obey orders."

So they went to the architect, and he had drawings of houses on his table.

"You want something out of the way," said the architect. "How do you like this?" and he handed a drawing to Keawe.

Now, when Keawe set eyes on the drawing, he cried out aloud, for it was the picture of his thought exactly drawn.

"I am in for this house," thought he. "Little as I like the way it comes to me, I am in for it now, and I may as well take the good along with the evil."

So he told the architect all that he wished, and how he would have that house furnished, and about the pictures on the wall and the knick-knacks on the tables; and he asked the man plainly for how much he would undertake the whole affair.

The architect put many questions, and took his pen and made a computation; and when he had done he named the very sum that Keawe had inherited.

Lopaka and Keawe looked at one another and nodded.

"It is quite clear," thought Keawe, "that I am to have this house, whether or no. It comes from the devil, and I fear I will get little good by that; and of one thing I am sure, I will make no more wishes as long as I have this bottle. But with the house I am saddled, and I may as well take the good along with the evil."

So he made his terms with the architect, and they signed a paper; and Keawe and Lopaka took ship again and sailed to Australia; for it was concluded between them they should not interfere at all, but leave the architect and the bottle imp to build and to adorn that house at their own pleasure.

The voyage was a good voyage, only all the time Keawe was holding in his breath, for he had sworn he would utter no more wishes, and take no more favours from the devil. The time was up when they got back. The architect told them that the house was ready, and Keawe and Lopaka took a passage in the *Hall*, and went down Kona way to view the house, and see if all had been done fitly according to the thought that was in Keawe's mind.

Now the house stood on the mountain side, visible to ships. Above, the forest ran up into the clouds of rain; below, the black lava fell in cliffs, where the kings of old lay buried. A garden bloomed about that house with every hue of flowers; and there was an orchard of papaia on the one hand and an orchard of breadfruit on the other, and right in front, toward the sea, a ship's mast had been rigged up and bore a flag. As for the house, it was three storeys high, with great chambers and broad balconies on each. The windows were of glass, so excellent that it was as clear as water and as bright as day. All manner of furniture adorned the chambers. Pictures hung upon the wall in golden frames: pictures of ships, and men fighting, and of the most beautiful women, and of singular places; nowhere in the world are there pictures of so bright a colour as those Keawe found hanging in his house. As for the knick-knacks, they were extraordinary fine; chiming clocks and musical boxes, little men with nodding heads, books filled with pictures, weapons of price from all quarters of the world, and the most elegant puzzles to entertain the leisure of a solitary man. And as no one would care to live in such chambers, only to walk through and view them, the balconies were made so broad that a whole town might have lived upon them in delight; and Keawe knew not which to prefer, whether the back porch, where you got the land breeze, and looked upon the orchards and the flowers, or the front balcony, where you could drink the wind of the sea, and look down the steep wall of the mountain and see the *Hall* going by once a week or so between Hookena and the hills of Pele, or the schooners plying up the coast for wood and ava and bananas.

When they had viewed all, Keawe and Lopaka sat on the porch.

"Well," asked Lopaka, "is it all as you designed?"

"Words cannot utter it," said Keawe. "It is better than I dreamed, and I am sick with satisfaction."

"There is but one thing to consider," said Lopaka; "all this may be quite natural, and the bottle imp have nothing whatever to say to it. If I were to buy the bottle, and got no schooner after all, I should have put my hand in the fire for nothing. I gave you my word, I know; but yet I think you would not grudge me one more proof."

"I have sworn I would take no more favours," said Keawe. "I have gone already deep enough."

"This is no favour I am thinking of," replied Lopaka. "It is only to see the imp himself. There is nothing to be gained by that, and so nothing to be ashamed of; and yet, if I once saw him, I should be sure of the whole matter. So indulge me so far, and let me see the imp; and, after that, here is the money in my hand, and I will buy it."

"There is only one thing I am afraid of," said Keawe. "The imp may be very ugly to view; and if you once set eyes upon him you might be very undesirous of the bottle."

"I am a man of my word," said Lopaka. "And here is the money betwixt us."

"Very well," replied Keawe. "I have a curiosity myself. So come, let us have one look at you, Mr. Imp."

Now as soon as that was said, the imp looked out of the bottle, and in again, swift as a lizard; and there sat Keawe and Lopaka turned to stone. The night had quite come, before either found a thought to say or voice to say it with; and then Lopaka pushed the money over and took the bottle.

"I am a man of my word," said he, "and had need to be so, or I would not touch this bottle with my foot. Well, I shall get my schooner and a dollar or two for my pocket; and then I will be rid of this devil as fast as I can. For to tell you the plain truth, the look of him has cast me down."

"Lopaka," said Keawe, "do not you think any worse of me than you can help; I know it is night, and the roads bad, and the pass by the tombs an ill place to go by so late, but I declare since I have seen that little face, I cannot eat or sleep or pray till it is gone from me. I will give you a lantern and a basket to put the bottle in, and any picture or fine thing in all my house that takes your fancy;—and be gone at once, and go sleep at Hookena with Nahinu."

"Keawe," said Lopaka, "many a man would take this ill; above all, when I am doing you a turn so friendly, as to keep my word and buy the bottle; and for that matter, the night and the dark, and the way by the tombs, must be all tenfold more dangerous to a man with such a sin upon his conscience, and such a bottle under his arm. But for my part, I am so extremely terrified myself, I have not the heart to blame you. Here I go then; and I pray God you may be happy in your house, and I fortunate with my schooner, and both get to heaven in the end in spite of the devil and his bottle."

So Lopaka went down the mountain; and Keawe stood in his front balcony, and listened to the clink of the horse's shoes, and watched the lantern go shining down the path, and along the cliff of caves where the old dead are buried; and all the time he trembled and clasped his hands, and prayed for his friend, and gave glory to God that he himself was escaped out of that trouble.

But the next day came very brightly, and that new house of his was so delightful to behold that he forgot his terrors. One day followed another, and Keawe dwelt there in perpetual joy. He had his place on the back porch; it was there he ate and lived, and read the stories in the Honolulu newspapers; but when anyone came by they would go in and view the chambers and the pictures. And the fame of the house went far and wide; it was called *Ka-Hale Nui*—the Great House—in all Kona; and sometimes the Bright House, for Keawe kept a Chinaman, who was all day dusting and furbishing; and the glass, and the gilt, and the fine stuffs, and the pictures, shone as bright as the morning. As for Keawe himself, he could not walk in the chambers without singing, his heart was so enlarged; and when ships sailed by upon the sea, he would fly his colours on the mast.

So time went by, until one day Keawe went upon a visit as far as Kailua to certain of his friends. There he was well feasted; and left as soon as he could the next morning, and rode hard, for he was impatient to behold his beautiful house; and, besides, the night then coming on was the night in which the dead of old days go abroad in the sides of Kona; and having already meddled with the devil, he was the more chary of meeting with the dead. A little beyond Honaunau, looking far ahead, he was aware of a woman bathing in the edge of the sea; and she seemed a well-grown girl, but he thought no more of it. Then he saw her white shift flutter as she put it on, and then her red holoku; and by the time he came abreast of her she was done with her toilet, and had come up from the sea, and stood by the track-side in her red holoku, and she was all freshened with the bath, and her eyes shone and were kind. Now Keawe no sooner beheld her than he drew rein.

"I thought I knew everyone in this country," said he. "How comes it that I do not know you?"

"I am Kokua, daughter of Kiano," said the girl, "and I have just returned from Oahu. Who are you?"

"I will tell you who I am in a little," said Keawe, dismounting from his horse, "but not now. For I have a thought in my mind, and if you knew who I was, you might have heard of me, and would not give me a true answer. But tell me, first of all, one thing: Are you married?"

At this Kokua laughed out aloud. "It is you who ask questions," she said. "Are you married yourself?"

"Indeed, Kokua, I am not," replied Keawe, "and never thought to be until this hour. But here is the plain truth. I have met you here at the roadside, and I saw your eyes, which are like the stars, and my heart went to you as swift as a bird. And so now, if you want none of me, say so, and I will go on to my own place; but if you think me no worse than any other young man, say so, too, and I will turn aside to your father's for the night, and to-morrow I will talk with the good man."

Kokua said never a word, but she looked at the sea and laughed.

"Kokua," said Keawe, "if you say nothing, I will take that for the good answer; so let us be stepping to your father's door."

She went on ahead of him, still without speech; only sometimes she glanced back and glanced away again, and she kept the strings of her hat in her mouth.

Now, when they had come to the door, Kiano came out on his verandah, and cried out and welcomed Keawe by name. At that the girl looked over, for the fame of the great house had come to her ears; and, to be sure, it was a great temptation. All that evening they were very merry together; and the girl was as bold as brass under the eyes of her parents, and made a mock of Keawe, for she had a quick wit. The next day he had a word with Kiano, and found the girl alone.

"Kokua," said he, "you made a mock of me all the evening; and it is still time to bid me go. I would not tell you who I was, because I have so fine a house, and I feared you would think too much of that house and too little of the man that loves you. Now you know all, and if you wish to have seen the last of me, say so at once."

"No," said Kokua; but this time she did not laugh, nor did Keawe ask for more.

This was the wooing of Keawe; things had gone quickly; but so an arrow goes, and the ball of a rifle swifter still, and yet both may strike the target. Things had gone fast, but they had gone far also, and the thought of Keawe rang in the maiden's head; she heard his voice in the breach of the surf upon the lava, and for this young man that she had seen but twice she would have left father and mother and her native islands. As for Keawe himself, his horse flew up the path of the mountain under the cliff of tombs, and the sound of the hoofs, and the sound of Keawe singing to himself for pleasure, echoed in the caverns of the dead. He came to the Bright House, and still he was singing. He sat and ate in the broad balcony, and the Chinaman wondered at his master, to hear how he sang between the mouthfuls. The sun went down into the sea, and the night came; and Keawe walked the balconies by lamplight, high on the mountains, and the voice of his singing startled men on ships.

"Here am I now upon my high place," he said to himself. "Life may be no better; this is the mountain top; and all shelves about me toward the worse. For the first time I will light up the chambers, and bathe in my fine bath with the hot water and the cold, and sleep alone in the bed of my bridal chamber."

So the Chinaman had word, and he must rise from sleep and light the furnaces; and as he wrought below, beside the boilers, he heard his master singing and rejoicing above him in the lighted chambers. When the water began to be hot the Chinaman cried to his master; and Keawe went into the bathroom; and the Chinaman heard him sing as he filled the marble basin; and heard him sing, and the singing broken, as he undressed; until of a sudden, the song ceased. The Chinaman listened, and listened; he called up the house to Keawe to ask if all were well, and Keawe answered him "Yes," and bade him go to bed; but there was no more singing in the Bright House; and all night long, the Chinaman heard his master's feet go round and round the balconies without repose.

Now the truth of it was this: as Keawe undressed for his bath, he spied upon his flesh a patch like a patch of lichen on a rock, and it was then that he stopped singing. For he knew the likeness of that patch, and knew that he was fallen in the Chinese Evil.[1]

Now, it is a sad thing for any man to fall into this sickness. And it would be a sad thing for anyone to leave a house so beautiful and so commodious, and depart from all his friends to the north coast of Molokai between the mighty cliff and the sea-breakers. But what was that to the case of the man Keawe, he who had met his love but yesterday, and won her but that morning, and now saw all his hopes break, in a moment, like a piece of glass?

Awhile he sat upon the edge of the bath; then sprang, with a cry, and ran outside; and to and fro, to and fro, along the balcony, like one despairing.

"Very willingly could I leave Hawaii, the home of my fathers," Keawe was thinking. "Very lightly could I leave my house, the high-placed, the many-windowed, here upon the mountains. Very bravely could I go to Molokai, to Kalaupapa by the cliffs, to live with the smitten and to sleep there, far from my fathers. But what wrong have I done, what sin lies upon my soul, that I should have encountered Kokua coming cool from the sea-water in the evening? Kokua, the soul ensnarer! Kokua, the light of my life! Her may I never wed, her may I look upon no longer, her may I no more handle with my loving hand; and it is for this, it is for you, O Kokua! that I pour my lamentations!"

Now you are to observe what sort of a man Keawe was, for he might have dwelt there in the Bright House for years, and no one been the wiser of his sickness; but he reckoned nothing of that, if he must lose Kokua. And again, he might have wed Kokua even as he was; and so many would have done, because they have the souls of pigs; but Keawe loved the maid manfully, and he would do her no hurt and bring her in no danger.

A little beyond the midst of the night, there came in his mind the recollection of that bottle.

He went round to the back porch, and called to memory the day when the devil had looked forth; and at the thought ice ran in his veins.

"A dreadful thing is the bottle," thought Keawe, "and dreadful is the imp, and it is a dreadful thing to risk the flames of hell. But what other hope have I to cure my sickness or to wed Kokua? What!" he thought, "would I beard the devil once, only to get me a house, and not face him again to win Kokua?"

Thereupon he called to mind it was the next day the *Hall* went by on her return to Honolulu. "There must I go first," he thought, "and see Lopaka. For the best hope that I have now is to find that same bottle I was so pleased to be rid of."

Never a wink could he sleep; the food stuck in his throat; but he sent a letter to Kiano, and about the time when the steamer would be coming, rode down beside the cliff of the tombs. It rained; his horse went heavily; he looked up at the black mouths of the caves, and he envied the dead that slept there and were done with trouble; and called to mind how he had galloped by the day before, and was astonished. So he came down to Hookena, and there was all the country gathered for the steamer as usual. In the shed before the store they sat and jested and passed the news; but there was no matter of speech in Keawe's bosom, and he sat in their midst and looked without on the rain falling on the houses, and the surf beating among the rocks, and the sighs arose in his throat.

"Keawe of the Bright House is out of spirits," said one to another. Indeed, and so he was, and little wonder.

Then the *Hall* came, and the whaleboat carried him on board. The after-part of the ship was full of Haoles[2] who had been to visit the volcano, as their custom is; and the midst was crowded with Kanakas, and the forepart with wild bulls from Hilo and horses from Kau; but Keawe sat apart from all in his sorrow, and watched for the house of Kiano. There it sat, low upon the shore in the black rocks, and shaded by the cocoa palms, and there by the door was a red holoku, no greater than a fly, and going to and fro with a fly's busyness. "Ah, queen of my heart," he cried, "I'll venture my dear soul to win you!"

Soon after, darkness fell, and the cabins were lit up, and the Haoles sat and played at the cards and drank whiskey as their custom is; but Keawe walked the deck all night; and all the next day, as they steamed under the lee of Maui or of Molokai, he was still pacing to and fro like a wild animal in a menagerie.

Towards evening they passed Diamond Head, and came to the pier of Honolulu. Keawe stepped out among the crowd and began to ask for Lopaka. It seemed he had become the owner of a schooner—none better in the islands—and was gone upon an adventure as far as Pola-Pola or Kahiki; so there was no help to be looked for from Lopaka. Keawe called to mind a friend of his, a lawyer in the town (I must not tell his name), and inquired of him. They said he was grown suddenly rich, and had a fine new house upon Waikiki shore; and this put a thought in Keawe's head, and he called a hack and drove to the lawyer's house.

The house was all brand new, and the trees in the garden no greater than walking-sticks, and the lawyer, when he came, had the air of a man well pleased.

"What can I do to serve you?" said the lawyer.

"You are a friend of Lopaka's," replied Keawe, "and Lopaka purchased from me a certain piece of goods that I thought you might enable me to trace."

The lawyer's face became very dark. "I do not profess to misunderstand you, Mr. Keawe," said he, "though this is an ugly business to be stirring in. You may be sure I know nothing, but yet I have a guess, and if you would apply in a certain quarter I think you might have news."

And he named the name of a man, which, again, I had better not repeat. So it was for days, and Keawe went from one to another, finding everywhere new clothes and carriages, and fine new houses and men everywhere in great contentment, although, to be sure, when he hinted at his business their faces would cloud over.

"No doubt I am upon the track," thought Keawe. "These new clothes and carriages are all the gifts of the little imp, and these glad faces are the faces of men who have taken their profit and got rid of the accursed thing in safety. When I see pale cheeks and hear sighing, I shall know that I am near the bottle."

So it befell at last that he was recommended to a Haole in Beritania Street. When he came to the door, about the hour of the evening meal, there were the usual marks of the new house, and the young garden, and the electric light shining in the windows; but when the owner came, a shock of hope and fear ran through Keawe; for here was a young man, white as a corpse, and black about the eyes, the hair shedding from his head, and such a look in his countenance as a man may have when he is waiting for the gallows.

"Here it is, to be sure," thought Keawe, and so with this man he noways veiled his errand. "I am come to buy the bottle," said he.

At the word, the young Haole of Beritania Street reeled against the wall.

"The bottle!" he gasped. "To buy the bottle!" Then he seemed to choke, and seizing Keawe by the arm carried him into a room and poured out wine in two glasses.

"Here is my respects," said Keawe, who had been much about with Haoles in his time. "Yes," he added, "I am come to buy the bottle. What is the price by now?"

At that word the young man let his glass slip through his fingers, and looked upon Keawe like a ghost.

"The price," says he; "the price! You do not know the price?"

"It is for that I am asking you," returned Keawe. "But why are you so much concerned? Is there anything wrong about the price?"

"It has dropped a great deal in value since your time, Mr. Keawe," said the young man stammering.

"Well, well, I shall have the less to pay for it," says Keawe. "How much did it cost you?"

The young man was as white as a sheet. "Two cents," said he.

"What?" cried Keawe, "two cents? Why, then, you can only sell it for one. And he who buys it—" The words died upon Keawe's tongue; he who bought it could never sell it again, the bottle and the bottle imp must abide with him until he died, and when he died must carry him to the red end of hell.

The young man of Beritania Street fell upon his knees. "For God's sake buy it!" he cried. "You can have all my fortune in the bargain. I was mad when I bought it at that price. I had embezzled money at my store; I was lost else; I must have gone to jail."

"Poor creature," said Keawe, "you would risk your soul upon so desperate an adventure, and to avoid the proper punishment of your own disgrace; and you think I could hesitate with love in front of me. Give me the bottle, and the change which I make sure you have all ready. Here is a five-cent piece."

It was as Keawe supposed; the young man had the change ready in a drawer; the bottle changed hands, and Keawe's fingers were no sooner clasped upon the stalk than he had breathed his wish to be a clean man. And, sure enough, when he got home to his room, and stripped himself before a glass, his flesh was whole like an infant's. And here was the strange thing: he had no sooner seen this miracle, than his mind was changed within him, and he cared naught for the Chinese Evil, and little enough for Kokua; and had but the one thought, that here he was bound to the bottle imp for time and for eternity, and had no better hope but to be a cinder for ever in the flames of hell. Away ahead of him he saw them blaze with his mind's eye, and his soul shrank, and darkness fell upon the light.

When Keawe came to himself a little, he was aware it was the night when the band played at the hotel. Thither he went, because he feared to be alone; and there, among happy faces, walked to and fro, and heard the tunes go up and down, and saw Berger beat the measure, and all the while he heard the flames crackle, and saw the red fire burning in the bottomless pit. Of a sudden the band played *Hiki-ao-ao*; that was a song that he had sung with Kokua, and at the strain courage returned to him.

"It is done now," he thought, "and once more let me take the good along with the evil."

So it befell that he returned to Hawaii by the first steamer, and as soon as it could be managed he was wedded to Kokua, and carried her up the mountain side to the Bright House.

Now it was so with these two, that when they were together, Keawe's heart was stilled; but so soon as he was alone he fell into a brooding horror, and heard the flames crackle, and saw the red fire burn in the bottomless pit. The girl, indeed, had come to him wholly; her heart leapt in her side at sight of him, her hand clung to his; and she was so fashioned from the hair upon her head to the nails upon her toes that none could see her without joy. She was pleasant in her nature. She had the good word always. Full of song she was, and went to and fro in the Bright House, the brightest thing in its three storeys, carolling like the birds. And Keawe beheld and heard her with delight, and then must shrink upon one side, and weep and groan to think upon the price that he had paid for her; and then he must dry his eyes, and wash his face, and go and sit with her on the broad balconies, joining in her songs, and, with a sick spirit, answering her smiles.

There came a day when her feet began to be heavy and her songs more rare; and now it was not Keawe only that would weep apart, but each would sunder from the other and sit in opposite balconies with the whole width of the Bright House betwixt. Keawe was so sunk in his despair, he scarce observed the change, and was only glad he had more hours to sit alone and brood upon his destiny, and was not so frequently condemned to pull a smiling face on a sick heart. But one day, coming softly through the house, he heard the sound of a child sobbing, and there was Kokua rolling her face upon the balcony floor, and weeping like the lost.

"You do well to weep in this house, Kokua," he said. "And yet I would give the head off my body that you (at least) might have been happy."

"Happy!" she cried. "Keawe, when you lived alone in your Bright House, you were the word of the island for a happy man; laughter and song were in your mouth, and your face was as bright as the sunrise. Then you wedded poor Kokua; and the good God knows what is amiss in her—but from that day you have not smiled. Oh!" she cried, "what ails me? I thought I was pretty, and I knew I loved him. What ails me that I throw this cloud upon my husband?"

"Poor Kokua," said Keawe. He sat down by her side, and sought to take her hand; but that she plucked away. "Poor Kokua," he said, again. "My poor child—my pretty. And I had thought all this while to spare you! Well, you shall know all. Then, at least, you will pity poor Keawe; then you will understand how much he loved you in the past—that he dared hell for your possession—and how much he loves you still (the poor condemned one), that he can yet call up a smile when he beholds you."

With that, he told her all, even from the beginning.

"You have done this for me?" she cried "Ah, well, then what do I care!"—and she clasped and wept upon him.

"Ah, child!" said Keawe, "and yet, when I consider of the fire of hell, I care a good deal!"

"Never tell me," said she; "no man can be lost because he loved Kokua, and no other fault. I tell you, Keawe, I shall save you with these hands, or perish in your company. What! you loved me, and gave your soul, and you think I will not die to save you in return?"

"Ah, my dear! you might die a hundred times, and what difference would that make?" he cried, "except to leave me lonely till the time comes of my damnation?"

"You know nothing," said she. "I was educated in a school in Honolulu; I am no common girl. And I tell you, I shall save my lover. What is this you say about a cent? But all the world is not American. In England they have a piece they call a farthing, which is about half a cent. Ah! sorrow!" she cried, "that makes it scarcely better, for the buyer must be lost, and we shall find none so brave as my Keawe! But, then, there is France; they have a small coin there which they call a centime, and these go five to the cent or there-about. We could not do better. Come, Keawe, let us go to the French islands; let us go to Tahiti, as fast as ships can bear us. There we have four centimes, three centimes, two centimes, one centime; four possible sales to come and go on; and two of us to push the bargain. Come, my Keawe! kiss me, and banish care. Kokua will defend you."

"Gift of God!" he cried. "I cannot think that God will punish me for desiring aught so good! Be it as you will, then; take me where you please: I put my life and my salvation in your hands."

Early the next day Kokua was about her preparations. She took Keawe's chest that he went with sailoring; and first she put the bottle in a corner; and then packed it with the richest of their clothes and the bravest of the knick-knacks in the house. "For," said she, "we must seem to be rich folks, or who will believe in the bottle?" All the time of her preparation she was as gay as a bird; only when she looked upon Keawe, the tears would spring in her eye, and she must run and kiss him. As for Keawe, a weight was off his soul; now that he had his secret shared, and some hope in front of him, he seemed like a new man, his feet went lightly on the earth, and his breath was good to him again. Yet was terror still at his elbow; and ever and again, as the wind blows out a taper, hope died in him, and he saw the flames toss and the red fire burn in hell.

It was given out in the country they were gone pleasuring to the States, which was thought a strange thing, and yet not so strange as the truth, if any could have guessed it. So they went to Honolulu in the *Hall*, and thence in the *Umatilla* to San Francisco with a crowd of Haoles, and at San Francisco took their passage by the mail brigantine, the *Tropic Bird*, for Papeete, the chief place of the French in the south islands. Thither they came, after a pleasant voyage, on a fair day of the Trade Wind, and saw the reef with the surf breaking, and Motuiti with its palms, and the schooner riding within-side, and the white houses of the town low down along the shore among green trees, and overhead the mountains and the clouds of Tahiti, the wise island.

It was judged the most wise to hire a house, which they did accordingly, opposite the British Consul's, to make a great parade of money, and themselves conspicuous with carriages and horses. This it was very easy to do, so long as they had the bottle in their possession; for Kokua was more bold than Keawe, and, whenever she had a mind, called on the imp for twenty or a hundred dollars. At this rate they soon grew to be remarked in the town; and the strangers from Hawaii, their riding and their driving, the fine holokus and the rich lace of Kokua, became the matter of much talk.

They got on well after the first with the Tahitian language, which is indeed like to the Hawaiian, with a change of certain letters; and as soon as they had any freedom of speech, began to push the bottle. You are to consider it was not an easy subject to introduce; it was not easy to persuade people you were in earnest, when you offered to sell them for four centimes the spring of health and riches inexhaustible. It was necessary besides to explain the dangers of the bottle; and either people disbelieved the whole thing and laughed, or they thought the more of the darker part, became overcast with gravity, and drew away from Keawe and Kokua, as from persons who had dealings with the devil. So far from gaining ground, these two began to find they were avoided in the town; the children ran away from them screaming, a thing intolerable to Kokua; Catholics crossed themselves as they went by; and all persons began with one accord to disengage themselves from their advances.

Depression fell upon their spirits. They would sit at night in their new house, after a day's weariness, and not exchange one word, or the silence would be broken by Kokua bursting suddenly into sobs. Sometimes they would pray together; sometimes they would have the bottle out upon the floor, and sit all evening watching how the shadow hovered in the midst. At such times they would be afraid to go to rest. It was long ere slumber came to them, and, if either dozed off, it would be to wake and find the other silently weeping in the dark, or, perhaps, to wake alone, the other having fled from the house and the neighbourhood of that bottle, to pace under the bananas in the little garden, or to wander on the beach by moonlight.

One night it was so when Kokua awoke. Keawe was gone. She felt in the bed and his place was cold. Then fear fell upon her, and she sat up in bed. A little moonshine filtered through the shutters. The room was bright, and she could spy the bottle on the floor. Outside it blew high, the great trees of the avenue cried aloud, and the fallen leaves rattled in the verandah. In the midst of this Kokua was aware of another sound; whether of a beast or of a man she could scarce tell, but it was as sad as death, and cut her to the soul. Softly she arose, set the door ajar, and looked forth into the moonlit yard. There, under the bananas, lay Keawe, his mouth in the dust, and as he lay he moaned.

It was Kokua's first thought to run forward and console him; her second potently withheld her. Keawe had borne himself before his wife like a brave man; it became her little in the hour of weakness to intrude upon his shame. With the thought she drew back into the house.

"Heaven!" she thought, "how careless have I been—how weak! It is he, not I, that stands in this eternal peril; it was he, not I, that took the curse upon his soul. It is for my sake, and for the love of a creature of so little worth and such poor help, that he now beholds so close to him the flames of hell—ay, and smells the smoke of it, lying without there in the wind and moonlight. Am I so dull of spirit that never till now I have surmised my duty, or have I seen it before and turned aside? But now, at least, I take up my soul in both the hands of my affection; now I say farewell to the white steps of heaven and the waiting faces of my friends. A love for a love, and let mine be equalled with Keawe's! A soul for a soul, and be it mine to perish!"

She was a deft woman with her hands, and was soon apparelled. She took in her hands the change—the precious centimes they kept ever at their side; for this coin is little used, and they had made provision at a Government office. When she was forth in the avenue clouds came on the wind, and the moon was blackened. The town slept, and she knew not whither to turn till she heard one coughing in the shadow of the trees.

"Old man," said Kokua, "what do you here abroad in the cold night?"

The old man could scarce express himself for coughing, but she made out that he was old and poor, and a stranger in the island.

"Will you do me a service?" said Kokua. "As one stranger to another, and as an old man to a young woman, will you help a daughter of Hawaii?"

"Ah," said the old man. "So you are the witch from the eight islands, and even my old soul you seek to entangle. But I have heard of you, and defy your wickedness."

"Sit down here," said Kokua, "and let me tell you a tale." And she told him the story of Keawe from the beginning to the end.

"And now," said she, "I am his wife, whom he bought with his soul's welfare. And what should I do? If I went to him myself and offered to buy it, he would refuse. But if you go, he will sell it eagerly; I will await you here; you will buy it for four centimes, and I will buy it again for three. And the Lord strengthen a poor girl!"

"If you meant falsely," said the old man, "I think God would strike you dead."

"He would!" cried Kokua. "Be sure he would. I could not be so treacherous—God would not suffer it."

"Give me the four centimes and await me here," said the old man.

Now, when Kokua stood alone in the street, her spirit died. The wind roared in the trees, and it seemed to her the rushing of the flames of hell; the shadows tossed in the light of the street lamp, and they seemed to her the snatching hands of evil ones. If she had had the strength, she must have run away, and if she had had the breath she must have screamed aloud; but, in truth, she could do neither, and stood and trembled in the avenue, like an affrighted child.

Then she saw the old man returning, and he had the bottle in his hand.

"I have done your bidding," said he. "I left your husband weeping like a child; to-night he will sleep easy." And he held the bottle forth.

"Before you give it me," Kokua panted, "take the good with the evil—ask to be delivered from your cough."

"I am an old man," replied the other, "and too near the gate of the grave to take a favour from the devil. But what is this? Why do you not take the bottle? Do you hesitate?"

"Not hesitate!" cried Kokua. "I am only weak. Give me a moment. It is my hand resists, my flesh shrinks back from the accursed thing. One moment only!"

The old man looked upon Kokua kindly. "Poor child!" said he, "you fear; your soul misgives you. Well, let me keep it. I am old, and can never more be happy in this world, and as for the next—"

"Give it me!" gasped Kokua. "There is your money. Do you think I am so base as that? Give me the bottle."

"God bless you, child," said the old man.

Kokua concealed the bottle under her holoku, said farewell to the old man, and walked off along the avenue, she cared not whither. For all roads were now the same to her, and led equally to hell. Sometimes she walked, and sometimes ran; sometimes she screamed out loud in the night, and sometimes lay by the wayside in the dust and wept. All that she had heard of hell came back to her; she saw the flames blaze, and she smelt the smoke, and her flesh withered on the coals.

Near day she came to her mind again, and returned to the house. It was even as the old man said—Keawe slumbered like a child. Kokua stood and gazed upon his face.

"Now, my husband," said she, "it is your turn to sleep. When you wake it will be your turn to sing and laugh. But for poor Kokua, alas! that meant no evil—for poor Kokua no more sleep, no more singing, no more delight, whether in earth or heaven."

With that she lay down in the bed by his side, and her misery was so extreme that she fell in a deep slumber instantly.

Late in the morning her husband woke her and gave her the good news. It seemed he was silly with delight, for he paid no heed to her distress, ill though she dissembled it. The words stuck in her mouth, it mattered not; Keawe did the speaking. She ate not a bite, but who was to observe it? for Keawe cleared the dish. Kokua saw and heard him, like some strange thing in a dream; there were times when she forgot or doubted, and put her hands to her brow; to know herself doomed and hear her husband babble, seemed so monstrous.

All the while Keawe was eating and talking, and planning the time of their return, and thanking her for saving him, and fondling her, and calling her the true helper after all. He laughed at the old man that was fool enough to buy that bottle.

"A worthy old man he seemed," Keawe said. "But no one can judge by appearances. For why did the old reprobate require the bottle?"

"My husband," said Kokua, humbly, "his purpose may have been good."

Keawe laughed like an angry man.

"Fiddle-de-dee!" cried Keawe. "An old rogue, I tell you; and an old ass to boot. For the bottle was hard enough to sell at four centimes; and at three it will be quite impossible. The margin is not broad enough, the thing begins to smell of scorching—brrr!" said he, and shuddered. "It is true I bought it myself at a cent, when I knew not there were smaller coins. I was a fool for my pains; there will never be found another: and whoever has that bottle now will carry it to the pit."

"O my husband!" said Kokua. "Is it not a terrible thing to save oneself by the eternal ruin of another? It seems to me I could not laugh. I would be humbled. I would be filled with melancholy. I would pray for the poor holder."

Then Keawe, because he felt the truth of what she said, grew the more angry. "Heighty-teighty!" cried he. "You may be filled with melancholy if you please. It is not the mind of a good wife. If you thought at all of me, you would sit shamed."

Thereupon he went out, and Kokua was alone.

What chance had she to sell that bottle at two centimes? None, she perceived. And if she had any, here was her husband hurrying her away to a country where there was nothing lower than a cent. And here—on the morrow of her sacrifice—was her husband leaving her and blaming her.

She would not even try to profit by what time she had, but sat in the house, and now had the bottle out and viewed it with unutterable fear, and now, with loathing, hid it out of sight.

By-and-by, Keawe came back, and would have her take a drive.

"My husband, I am ill," she said. "I am out of heart. Excuse me, I can take no pleasure."

Then was Keawe more wroth than ever. With her, because he thought she was brooding over the case of the old man; and with himself, because he thought she was right, and was ashamed to be so happy.

"This is your truth," cried he, "and this your affection! Your husband is just saved from eternal ruin, which he encountered for the love of you—and you can take no pleasure! Kokua, you have a disloyal heart."

He went forth again furious, and wandered in the town all day. He met friends, and drank with them; they hired a carriage and drove into the country, and there drank again. All the time Keawe was ill at ease, because he was taking this pastime while his wife was sad, and because he knew in his heart that she was more right than he; and the knowledge made him drink the deeper.

Now there was an old brutal Haole drinking with him, one that had been a boatswain of a whaler, a runaway, a digger in gold mines, a convict in prisons. He had a low mind and a foul mouth; he loved to drink and to see others drunken; and he pressed the glass upon Keawe. Soon there was no more money in the company.

"Here, you!" says the boatswain, "you are rich, you have been always saying. You have a bottle or some foolishness."

"Yes," says Keawe, "I am rich; I will go back and get some money from my wife, who keeps it."

"That's a bad idea, mate," said the boatswain. "Never you trust a petticoat with dollars. They're all as false as water; you keep an eye on her."

Now, this word struck in Keawe's mind; for he was muddled with what he had been drinking.

"I should not wonder but she was false, indeed," thought he. "Why else should she be so cast down at my release? But I will show her I am not the man to be fooled. I will catch her in the act."

Accordingly, when they were back in town, Keawe bade the boatswain wait for him at the corner, by the old calaboose, and went forward up the avenue alone to the door of his house. The night had come again; there was a light within, but never a sound; and Keawe crept about the corner, opened the back door softly, and looked in.

There was Kokua on the floor, the lamp at her side; before her was a milk-white bottle, with a round belly and a long neck; and as she viewed it, Kokua wrung her hands.

A long time Keawe stood and looked in the doorway. At first he was struck stupid; and then fear fell upon him that the bargain had been made amiss, and the bottle had come back to him as it came at San Francisco; and at that his knees were loosened, and the fumes of the wine departed from his head like mists off a river in the morning. And then he had another thought; and it was a strange one, that made his cheeks to burn.

"I must make sure of this," thought he.

So he closed the door, and went softly round the corner again, and then came noisily in, as though he were but now returned. And, lo! by the time he opened the front door no bottle was to be seen; and Kokua sat in a chair and started up like one awakened out of sleep.

"I have been drinking all day and making merry," said Keawe. "I have been with good companions, and now I only come back for money, and return to drink and carouse with them again."

Both his face and voice were as stern as judgment, but Kokua was too troubled to observe.

"You do well to use your own, my husband," said she, and her words trembled.

"O, I do well in all things," said Keawe, and he went straight to the chest and took out money. But he looked besides in the corner where they kept the bottle, and there was no bottle there.

At that the chest heaved upon the floor like a sea-billow, and the house span about him like a wreath of smoke, for he saw he was lost now, and there was no escape. "It is what I feared," he thought. "It is she who has bought it."

And then he came to himself a little and rose up; but the sweat streamed on his face as thick as the rain and as cold as the well-water.

"Kokua," said he, "I said to you to-day what ill became me. Now I return to carouse with my jolly companions," and at that he laughed a little quietly. "I will take more pleasure in the cup if you forgive me."

She clasped his knees in a moment; she kissed his knees with flowing tears.

"O," she cried, "I asked but a kind word!"

"Let us never one think hardly of the other," said Keawe, and was gone out of the house.

Now, the money that Keawe had taken was only some of that store of centime pieces they had laid in at their arrival. It was very sure he had no mind to be drinking. His wife had given her soul for him, now he must give his for hers; no other thought was in the world with him.

At the corner, by the old calaboose, there was the boatswain waiting.

"My wife has the bottle," said Keawe, "and, unless you help me to recover it, there can be no more money and no more liquor to-night."

"You do not mean to say you are serious about that bottle?" cried the boatswain.

"There is the lamp," said Keawe. "Do I look as if I was jesting?"

"That is so," said the boatswain. "You look as serious as a ghost."

"Well, then," said Keawe, "here are two centimes; you must go to my wife in the house, and offer her these for the bottle, which (if I am not much mistaken) she will give you instantly.

Bring it to me here, and I will buy it back from you for one; for that is the law with this bottle, that it still must be sold for a less sum. But whatever you do, never breathe a word to her that you have come from me."

"Mate, I wonder are you making a fool of me?" asked the boatswain.

"It will do you no harm if I am," returned Keawe.

"That is so, mate," said the boatswain.

"And if you doubt me," added Keawe, "you can try. As soon as you are clear of the house, wish to have your pocket full of money, or a bottle of the best rum, or what you please, and you will see the virtue of the thing."

"Very well, Kanaka," says the boatswain. "I will try; but if you are having your fun out of me, I will take my fun out of you with a belaying pin."

So the whaler-man went off up the avenue; and Keawe stood and waited. It was near the same spot where Kokua had waited the night before; but Keawe was more resolved, and never faltered in his purpose; only his soul was bitter with despair.

It seemed a long time he had to wait before he heard a voice singing in the darkness of the avenue. He knew the voice to be the boatswain's; but it was strange how drunken it appeared upon a sudden.

Next, the man himself came stumbling into the light of the lamp. He had the devil's bottle buttoned in his coat; another bottle was in his hand; and even as he came in view he raised it to his mouth and drank.

"You have it," said Keawe. "I see that."

"Hands off!" cried the boatswain, jumping back. "Take a step near me, and I'll smash your mouth. You thought you could make a cat's-paw of me, did you?"

"What do you mean?" cried Keawe.

"Mean?" cried the boatswain. "This is a pretty good bottle, this is; that's what I mean. How I got it for two centimes I can't make out; but I'm sure you shan't have it for one."

"You mean you won't sell?" gasped Keawe.

"No, *sir*!" cried the boatswain. "But I'll give you a drink of the rum, if you like."

"I tell you," said Keawe, "the man who has that bottle goes to hell."

"I reckon I'm going anyway," returned the sailor; "and this bottle's the best thing to go with I've struck yet. No, sir!" he cried again, "this is my bottle now, and you can go and fish for another."

"Can this be true?" Keawe cried. "For your own sake, I beseech you, sell it me!"

"I don't value any of your talk," replied the boatswain. "You thought I was a flat; now you see I'm not; and there's an end. If you won't have a swallow of the rum, I'll have one myself. Here's your health, and good-night to you!"

So off he went down the avenue towards town, and there goes the bottle out of the story.

But Keawe ran to Kokua light as the wind; and great was their joy that night; and great, since then, has been the peace of all their days in the Bright House.

---

1. Leprosy.
2. Whites.

THE STORY OF A LIE

❧ I ❧

INTRODUCES THE ADMIRAL

WHEN DICK NASEBY was in Paris he made some odd acquaintances; for he was one of those who have ears to hear, and can use their eyes no less than their intelligence. He made as many thoughts as Stuart Mill; but his philosophy concerned flesh and blood, and was experimental as to its method. He was a type-hunter among mankind. He despised small game and insignificant personalities, whether in the shape of dukes or bagmen, letting them go by like sea-weed; but show him a refined or powerful face, let him hear a plangent or a penetrating voice, fish for him with a living look in some one's eye, a passionate gesture, a meaning and ambiguous smile, and his mind was instantaneously awakened. 'There was a man, there was a woman,' he seemed to say, and he stood up to the task of comprehension with the delight of an artist in his art.

And indeed, rightly considered, this interest of his was an artistic interest. There is no science in the personal study of human nature. All comprehension is creation; the woman I love is somewhat of my handiwork; and the great lover, like the great painter, is he that can so embellish his subject as to make her more than human, whilst yet by a cunning art he has so based his apotheosis on the nature of the case that the woman can go on being a true woman, and give her character free play, and show littleness, or cherish spite, or be greedy of common pleasures, and he continue to worship without a thought of incongruity. To love a character is only the heroic way of understanding it. When we love, by some noble method of our own or some nobility of mien or nature in the other, we apprehend the loved one by what is noblest in ourselves. When we are merely studying an eccentricity, the method of our study is but a series of allowances. To begin to understand is to begin to sympathise; for comprehension comes only when we have stated another's faults and virtues in terms of our own. Hence the proverbial toleration of artists for their own evil creations. Hence, too, it came about that Dick Naseby, a high-minded creature, and as scrupulous and brave a gentleman as you would want to meet, held in a sort of affection the various human creeping things whom he had met and studied.

One of these was Mr. Peter Van Tromp, an English-speaking, two-legged animal of the international genus, and by profession of general and more than equivocal utility. Years before he had been a painter of some standing in a colony, and portraits signed 'Van Tromp' had celebrated the greatness of colonial governors and judges. In those days he had been married, and driven his wife and infant daughter in a pony trap. What were the steps of his declension? No one exactly knew. Here he was at least, and had been any time these past ten years, a sort of dismal parasite upon the foreigner in Paris.

It would be hazardous to specify his exact industry. Coarsely followed, it would have merited a name grown somewhat unfamiliar to our ears. Followed as he followed it, with a skilful reticence, in a kind of social chiaroscuro, it was still possible for the polite to call him a professional painter. His lair was in the Grand Hotel and the gaudiest cafés. There he might be seen jotting off a sketch with an air of some inspiration; and he was always affable, and one of the easiest of men to fall in talk withal. A conversation usually ripened into a peculiar sort of intimacy, and it was extraordinary how many little services Van Tromp contrived to render in the course of six-and-thirty hours. He occupied a position between a friend and a courier, which made him worse than embarrassing to repay. But those whom he obliged could always buy one of his villainous little pictures, or, where the favours had been prolonged and more than usually delicate, might order and pay for a large canvas, with perfect certainty that they would hear no more of the transaction.

Among resident artists he enjoyed celebrity of a non-professional sort. He had spent more money—no less than three individual fortunes, it was whispered—than any of his associates could ever hope to gain. Apart from his colonial career, he had been to Greece in a brigantine with four brass carronades; he had travelled Europe in a chaise and four, drawing bridle at the palace-doors of German princes; queens of song and dance had followed him like sheep and paid his tailor's bills. And to behold him now, seeking small loans with plaintive condescension, sponging for breakfast on an art-student of nineteen, a fallen Don Juan who had neglected to die at the propitious hour, had a colour of romance for young imaginations. His name and his bright past, seen through the prism of whispered gossip, had gained him the nickname of *The Admiral.*

Dick found him one day at the receipt of custom, rapidly painting a pair of hens and a cock in a little water-colour sketching box, and now and then glancing at the ceiling like a man who should seek inspiration from the muse. Dick thought it remarkable that a painter should choose to work over an absinthe in a public café, and looked the man over. The aged rakishness of his appearance was set off by a youthful costume; he had disreputable grey hair and a disreputable sore, red nose; but the coat and the gesture, the outworks of the man, were still designed for show. Dick came up to his table and inquired if he might look at what the gentleman was doing. No one was so delighted as the Admiral.

'A bit of a thing,' said he. 'I just dash them off like that. I—I dash them off,' he added with a gesture.

'Quite so,' said Dick, who was appalled by the feebleness of the production.

'Understand me,' continued Van Tromp; 'I am a man of the world. And yet—once an artist always an artist. All of a sudden a thought takes me in the street; I become its prey: it's like a pretty woman; no use to struggle; I must—dash it off.'

'I see,' said Dick.

'Yes,' pursued the painter; 'it all comes easily, easily to me; it is not my business; it's a pleasure. Life is my business—life—this great city, Paris—Paris after dark—its lights, its gardens, its odd corners. Aha!' he cried, 'to be young again! The heart is young, but the heels are leaden. A poor, mean business, to grow old! Nothing remains but the *coup d'œil*, the contemplative man's enjoyment, Mr. —,' and he paused for the name.

'Naseby,' returned Dick.

The other treated him at once to an exciting beverage, and expatiated on the pleasure of meeting a compatriot in a foreign land; to hear him, you would have thought they had encountered in Central Africa. Dick had never found any one take a fancy to him so readily, nor show it in an easier or less offensive manner. He seemed tickled with him as an elderly fellow about town might be tickled by a pleasant and witty lad; he indicated that he was no precision, but in his wildest times had never been such a blade as he thought Dick. Dick protested, but in vain. This manner of carrying an intimacy at the bayonet's point was Van Tromp's stock-in-trade. With an older man he insinuated himself; with youth he imposed himself, and in the same breath imposed an ideal on his victim, who saw that he must work up to it or lose the esteem of this old and vicious patron. And what young man can bear to lose a character for vice?

At last, as it grew towards dinner-time, 'Do you know Paris?' asked Van Tromp.

'Not so well as you, I am convinced,' said Dick.

'And so am I,' returned Van Tromp gaily. 'Paris! My young friend—you will allow me?—when you know Paris as I do, you will have seen Strange Things. I say no more; all I say is, Strange Things. We are men of the world, you and I, and in Paris, in the heart of civilised existence. This is an opportunity, Mr. Naseby. Let us dine. Let me show you where to dine.'

Dick consented. On the way to dinner the Admiral showed him where to buy gloves, and made him buy them; where to buy cigars, and made him buy a vast store, some of which he obligingly accepted. At the restaurant he showed him what to order, with surprising consequences in the bill. What he made that night by his percentages it would be hard to estimate. And all the while Dick smilingly consented, understanding well that he was being done, but taking his losses in the pursuit of character as a hunter sacrifices his dogs. As for the Strange Things, the reader will be relieved to hear that they were no stranger than might have been expected, and he may find things quite as strange without the expense of a Van Tromp for guide. Yet he was a guide of no mean order, who made up for the poverty of what he had to show by a copious, imaginative commentary.

'And such,' said he, with a hiccup, 'such is Paris.'

'Pooh!' said Dick, who was tired of the performance.

The Admiral hung an ear, and looked up sidelong with a glimmer of suspicion.

'Good night,' said Dick; 'I'm tired.'

'So English!' cried Van Tromp, clutching him by the hand. 'So English! So *blasé*! Such a charming companion! Let me see you home.'

'Look here,' returned Dick, 'I have said good night, and now I'm going. You're an amusing old boy: I like you, in a sense; but here's an end of it for to-night. Not another cigar, not another grog, not another percentage out of me.'

'I beg your pardon!' cried the Admiral with dignity.

'Tut, man!' said Dick; 'you're not offended; you're a man of the world, I thought. I've been studying you, and it's over. Have I not paid for the lesson? *Au revoir*.'

Van Tromp laughed gaily, shook hands up to the elbows, hoped cordially they would meet again and that often, but looked after Dick as he departed with a tremor of indignation. After that they two not unfrequently fell in each other's way, and Dick would often treat the old boy to breakfast on a moderate scale and in a restaurant of his own selection. Often, too, he would lend Van Tromp the matter of a pound, in view of that gentleman's contemplated departure for Australia; there would be a scene of farewell almost touching in character, and a week or a month later they would meet on the same boulevard without surprise or embarrassment. And in the meantime Dick learned more about his acquaintance on all sides: heard of his yacht, his chaise and four, his brief season of celebrity amid a more confiding population, his daughter, of whom he loved to whimper in his cups, his sponging, parasitical, nameless way of life; and with each new detail something that was not merely interest nor yet altogether affection grew up in his mind towards this disreputable stepson of the arts. Ere he left Paris Van Tromp was one of those whom he entertained to a farewell supper; and the old gentleman made the speech of the evening, and then fell below the table, weeping, smiling, paralysed.

2

A LETTER TO THE PAPERS

OLD MR. NASEBY had the sturdy, untutored nature of the upper middle class. The universe seemed plain to him. 'The thing's right,' he would say, or 'the thing's wrong'; and there was an end of it. There was a contained, prophetic energy in his utterances, even on the slightest affairs; he *saw* the damned thing; if you did not, it must be from perversity of will; and this sent the blood to his head. Apart from this, which made him an exacting companion, he was one of the most upright, hot-tempered, hot-headed old gentlemen in England. Florid, with white hair, the face of an old Jupiter, and the figure of an old fox-hunter, he enlivened the vale of Thyme from end to end on his big, cantering chestnut.

He had a hearty respect for Dick as a lad of parts. Dick had a respect for his father as the best of men, tempered by the politic revolt of a youth who has to see to his own independence. Whenever the pair argued, they came to an open rupture; and arguments were frequent, for they were both positive, and both loved the work of the intelligence. It was a treat to hear Mr. Naseby defending the Church of England in a volley of oaths, or supporting ascetic morals with an enthusiasm not entirely innocent of port wine. Dick used to wax indignant, and none the less so because, as his father was a skilful disputant, he found himself not seldom in the wrong. On these occasions, he would redouble in energy, and declare that black was white, and blue yellow, with much conviction and heat of manner; but in the morning such a licence of debate weighed upon him like a crime, and he would seek out his father, where he walked before breakfast on a terrace overlooking all the vale of Thyme.

'I have to apologise, sir, for last night—' he would begin.

'Of course you have,' the old gentleman would cut in cheerfully. 'You spoke like a fool. Say no more about it.'

'You do not understand me, sir. I refer to a particular point. I confess there is much force in your argument from the doctrine of possibilities.'

'Of course there is,' returned his father. 'Come down and look at the stables. Only,' he would add, 'bear this in mind, and do remember that a man of my age and experience knows more about what he is saying than a raw boy.'

He would utter the word 'boy' even more offensively than the average of fathers, and the light way in which he accepted these apologies cut Richard to the heart. The latter drew slighting comparisons, and remembered that he was the only one who ever apologised. This gave him a high station in his own esteem, and thus contributed indirectly to his better behaviour; for he was scrupulous as well as high-spirited, and prided himself on nothing more than on a just submission.

So things went on until the famous occasion when Mr. Naseby, becoming engrossed in securing the election of a sound party candidate to Parliament, wrote a flaming letter to the papers. The letter had about every demerit of party letters in general; it was expressed with the energy of a believer; it was personal; it was a little more than half unfair, and about a quarter untrue. The old man did not mean to say what was untrue, you may be sure; but he had rashly picked up gossip, as his prejudice suggested, and now rashly launched it on the public with the sanction of his name.

'The Liberal candidate,' he concluded, 'is thus a public turncoat. Is that the sort of man we want? He has been given the lie, and has swallowed the insult. Is that the sort of man we want? I answer No! With all the force of my conviction, I answer, *No*!'

And then he signed and dated the letter with an amateur's pride, and looked to be famous by the morrow.

Dick, who had heard nothing of the matter, was up first on that inauspicious day, and took the journal to an arbour in the garden. He found his father's manifesto in one column; and in another a leading article. 'No one that we are aware of,' ran the article, 'had consulted Mr. Naseby on the subject, but if he had been appealed to by the whole body of electors, his letter would be none the less ungenerous and unjust to Mr. Dalton. We do not choose to give the lie to Mr. Naseby, for we are too well aware of the consequences; but we shall venture instead to print the facts of both cases referred to by this red-hot partisan in another portion of our issue. Mr. Naseby is of course a large proprietor in our neighbourhood; but fidelity to facts, decent feeling, and English grammar, are all of them qualities more important than the possession of land. Mr. — is doubtless a great man; in his large gardens and that half-mile of greenhouses, where he has probably ripened his intellect and temper, he may say what he will to his hired vassals, but (as the Scotch say)—

here
He mauna think to domineer.

'Liberalism,' continued the anonymous journalist, 'is of too free and sound a growth,' etc.

Richard Naseby read the whole thing from beginning to end; and a crushing shame fell upon his spirit. His father had played the fool; he had gone out noisily to war, and come back with confusion. The moment that his trumpets sounded, he had been disgracefully unhorsed. There was no question as to the facts; they were one and all against the Squire. Richard would have given his ears to have suppressed the issue; but as that could not be done, he had his horse saddled, and furnishing himself with a convenient staff, rode off at once to Thymebury.

The editor was at breakfast in a large, sad apartment. The absence of furniture, the extreme meanness of the meal, and the haggard, bright-eyed, consumptive look of the culprit, unmanned our hero; but he clung to his stick, and was stout and warlike.

'You wrote the article in this morning's paper?' he demanded.

'You are young Mr. Naseby? I *published* it,' replied the editor, rising.

'My father is an old man,' said Richard; and then with an outburst, 'And a damned sight finer fellow than either you or Dalton!' He stopped and swallowed; he was determined that all should go with regularity. 'I have but one question to put to you, sir,' he resumed. 'Granted that my father was misinformed, would it not have been more decent to withhold the letter and communicate with him in private?'

'Believe me,' returned the editor, 'that alternative was not open to me. Mr. Naseby told me in a note that he had sent his letter to three other journals, and in fact threatened me with what he called exposure if I kept it back from mine. I am really concerned at what has happened; I sympathise and approve of your emotion, young gentleman; but the attack on Mr. Dalton was gross, very gross, and I had no choice but to offer him my columns to reply. Party has its duties, sir,' added the scribe, kindling, as one who should propose a sentiment; 'and the attack was gross.'

Richard stood for half a minute digesting the answer; and then the god of fair play came upper-most in his heart, and murmuring 'Good morning,' he made his escape into the street.

His horse was not hurried on the way home, and he was late for breakfast. The Squire was standing with his back to the fire in a state bordering on apoplexy, his fingers violently knitted under his coat tails. As Richard came in, he opened and shut his mouth like a cod-fish, and his eyes protruded.

'Have you seen that, sir?' he cried, nodding towards the paper.

'Yes, sir,' said Richard.

'Oh, you've read it, have you?'

'Yes, I have read it,' replied Richard, looking at his foot.

'Well,' demanded the old gentleman, 'and what have you to say to it, sir?'

'You seem to have been misinformed,' said Dick.

'Well? What then? Is your mind so sterile, sir? Have you not a word of comment? no proposal?'

'I fear, sir, you must apologise to Mr. Dalton. It would be more handsome, indeed it would be only just, and a free acknowledgment would go far—' Richard paused, no language appearing delicate enough to suit the case.

'That is a suggestion which should have come from me, sir,' roared the father. 'It is out of place upon your lips. It is not the thought of a loyal son. Why, sir, if my father had been plunged in such deplorable circumstances, I should have thrashed the editor of that vile sheet within an inch of his life. I should have thrashed the man, sir. It would have been the action of an ass; but it would have shown that I had the blood and the natural affections of a man. Son? You are no son, no son of mine, sir!'

'Sir!' said Dick.

'I'll tell you what you are, sir,' pursued the Squire. 'You're a Benthamite. I disown you. Your mother would have died for shame; there was no modern cant about your mother; she thought—she said to me, sir—I'm glad she's in her grave, Dick Naseby. Misinformed! Misinformed, sir? Have you no loyalty, no spring, no natural affections? Are you clockwork, hey? Away! This is no place for you. Away!' (waving his hands in the air). 'Go away! Leave me!'

At this moment Dick beat a retreat in a disarray of nerves, a whistling and clamour of his own arteries, and in short in such a final bodily disorder as made him alike incapable of speech or hearing. And in the midst of all this turmoil, a sense of unpardonable injustice remained graven in his memory.

3

IN THE ADMIRAL'S NAME

THERE WAS no return to the subject. Dick and his father were henceforth on terms of coldness. The upright old gentleman grew more upright when he met his son, buckrammed with immortal anger; he asked after Dick's health, and discussed the weather and the crops with an appalling courtesy; his pronunciation was *point-de-vice,* his voice was distant, distinct, and sometimes almost trembling with suppressed indignation.

As for Dick, it seemed to him as if his life had come abruptly to an end. He came out of his theories and clevernesses; his premature man-of-the-worldness, on which he had prided himself on his travels, 'shrank like a thing ashamed' before this real sorrow. Pride, wounded honour, pity and respect tussled together daily in his heart; and now he was within an ace of throwing himself upon his father's mercy, and now of slipping forth at night and coming back no more to Naseby House. He suffered from the sight of his father, nay, even from the neighbourhood of this familiar valley, where every corner had its legend, and he was besieged with memories of childhood. If he fled into a new land, and among none but strangers, he might escape his destiny, who knew? and begin again light-heartedly. From that chief peak of the hills, that now and then, like an uplifted finger, shone in an arrow of sunlight through the broken clouds, the shepherd in clear weather might perceive the shining of the sea. There, he thought, was hope. But his heart failed him when he saw the Squire; and he remained. His fate was not that of the voyager by sea and land; he was to travel in the spirit, and begin his journey sooner than he supposed.

For it chanced one day that his walk led him into a portion of the uplands which was almost unknown to him. Scrambling through some rough woods, he came out upon a moorland reaching towards the hills. A few lofty Scotch firs grew hard by upon a knoll; a clear fountain near the foot of the knoll sent up a miniature streamlet which meandered in the heather. A shower had just skimmed by, but now the sun shone brightly, and the air smelt of the pines and the grass. On a stone under the trees sat a young lady sketching. We have learned to think of women in a sort of symbolic transfiguration, based on clothes; and one of the readiest ways in which we conceive our mistress is as a composite thing, principally petticoats. But humanity has triumphed over clothes; the look, the touch of a dress has become alive; and the woman who stitched herself into these material integuments has now permeated right through and gone out to the tip of her skirt. It was only a black dress that caught Dick Naseby's eye; but it took possession of his mind, and all other thoughts departed. He drew near, and the girl turned round. Her face startled him; it was a face he wanted; and he took it in at once like breathing air.

'I beg your pardon,' he said, taking off his hat, 'you are sketching.'

'Oh!' she exclaimed, 'for my own amusement. I despise the thing.'

'Ten to one, you do yourself injustice,' returned Dick. 'Besides, it's a freemasonry. I sketch myself, and you know what that implies.'

'No. What?' she asked.

'Two things,' he answered. 'First, that I am no very difficult critic; and second, that I have a right to see your picture.'

She covered the block with both her hands. 'Oh no,' she said; 'I am ashamed.'

'Indeed, I might give you a hint,' said Dick. 'Although no artist myself, I have known many; in Paris I had many for friends, and used to prowl among studios.'

'In Paris?' she cried, with a leap of light into her eyes. 'Did you ever meet Mr. Van Tromp?'

'I? Yes. Why, you're not the Admiral's daughter, are you?'

'The Admiral? Do they call him that?' she cried. 'Oh, how nice, how nice of them! It is the younger men who call him so, is it not?'

'Yes,' said Dick, somewhat heavily.

'You can understand now,' she said, with an unspeakable accent of contented noble-minded pride, 'why it is I do not choose to show my sketch. Van Tromp's daughter! The Admiral's daughter! I delight in that name. The Admiral! And so you know my father?'

'Well,' said Dick, 'I met him often; we were even intimate. He may have mentioned my name—Naseby.'

'He writes so little. He is so busy, so devoted to his art! I have had a half wish,' she added laughing, 'that my father was a plainer man, whom I could help—to whom I could be a credit; but only sometimes, you know, and with only half my heart. For a great painter! You have seen his works?'

'I have seen some of them,' returned Dick; 'they—they are very nice.'

She laughed aloud. 'Nice?' she repeated. 'I see you don't care much for art.'

'Not much,' he admitted; 'but I know that many people are glad to buy Mr. Van Tromp's pictures.'

'Call him the Admiral!' she cried. 'It sounds kindly and familiar; and I like to think that he is appreciated and looked up to by young painters. He has not always been appreciated; he had a cruel life for many years; and when I think'—there were tears in her eyes—'when I think of that, I feel incline to be a fool,' she broke off. 'And now I shall go home. You have filled me full of happiness; for think, Mr. Naseby, I have not seen my father since I was six years old; and yet he is in my thoughts all day! You must come and call on me; my aunt will be delighted, I am sure; and then you will tell me all—all about my father, will you not?'

Dick helped her to get her sketching traps together; and when all was ready, she gave Dick her hand and a frank return of pressure.

'You are my father's friend,' she said; 'we shall be great friends too. You must come and see me soon.'

Then she was gone down the hillside at a run; and Dick stood by himself in a state of some bewilderment and even distress. There were elements of laughter in the business; but the black dress, and the face that belonged to it, and the hand that he had held in his, inclined him to a serious view. What was he, under the circumstances, called upon to do? Perhaps to avoid the girl? Well, he would think about that. Perhaps to break the truth to her? Why, ten to one, such was her infatuation, he would fail. Perhaps to keep up the illusion, to colour the raw facts; to help her to false ideas, while yet not plainly stating falsehoods? Well, he would see about that; he would also see about avoiding the girl. He saw about this last so well, that the next afternoon beheld him on his way to visit her.

In the meantime the girl had gone straight home, light as a bird, tremulous with joy, to the little cottage where she lived alone with a maiden aunt; and to that lady, a grim, sixty years old Scotchwoman, with a nodding head, communicated news of her encounter and invitation.

'A friend of his?' cried the aunt. 'What like is he? What did ye say was his name?'

She was dead silent, and stared at the old woman darkling. Then very slowly, 'I said he was my father's friend; I have invited him to my house, and come he shall,' she said; and with that she walked off to her room, where she sat staring at the wall all the evening. Miss M'Glashan, for that was the aunt's name, read a large bible in the kitchen with some of the joys of martyrdom.

It was perhaps half-past three when Dick presented himself, rather scrupulously dressed, before the cottage door; he knocked, and a voice bade him enter. The kitchen, which opened directly off the garden, was somewhat darkened by foliage; but he could see her as she approached from the far end to meet him. This second sight of her surprised him. Her strong black brows spoke of temper easily aroused and hard to quiet; her mouth was small, nervous and weak; there was something dangerous and sulky underlying, in her nature, much that was honest, compassionate, and even noble.

'My father's name,' she said, 'has made you very welcome.'

And she gave him her hand, with a sort of curtsy. It was a pretty greeting, although somewhat mannered; and Dick felt himself among the gods. She led him through the kitchen to a parlour, and presented him to Miss M'Glashan.

'Esther,' said the aunt, 'see and make Mr. Naseby his tea.'

And as soon as the girl was gone upon this hospitable intent, the old woman crossed the room and came quite near to Dick as if in menace.

'Ye know that man?' she asked in an imperious whisper.

'Mr. Van Tromp?' said Dick. 'Yes, I know him.'

'Well, and what brings ye here?' she said. 'I couldn't save the mother—her that's dead—but the bairn!' She had a note in her voice that filled poor Dick with consternation. 'Man,' she went on, 'what is it now? Is it money?'

'My dear lady,' said Dick, 'I think you misinterpret my position. I am young Mr. Naseby of Naseby House. My acquaintance with Mr. Van Tromp is really very slender; I am only afraid that Miss Van Tromp has exaggerated our intimacy in her own imagination. I know positively nothing of his private affairs, and do not care to know. I met him casually in Paris—that is all.'

Miss M'Glashan drew along breath. 'In Paris?' she said. 'Well, and what do you think of him?—what do ye think of him?' she repeated, with a different scansion, as Richard, who had not much taste for such a question, kept her waiting for an answer.

'I found him a very agreeable companion,' he said.

'Ay,' said she, 'did ye! And how does he win his bread?'

'I fancy,' he gasped, 'that Mr. Van Tromp has many generous friends.'

'I'll warrant!' she sneered; and before Dick could find more to say, she was gone from the room.

Esther returned with the tea-things, and sat down.

'Now,' she said cosily, 'tell me all about my father.'

'He'—stammered Dick, 'he is a very agreeable companion.'

'I shall begin to think it is more than you are, Mr. Naseby,' she said, with a laugh. 'I am his daughter, you forget. Begin at the beginning, and tell me all you have seen of him, all he said and all you answered. You must have met somewhere; begin with that.'

So with that he began: how he had found the Admiral painting in a café; how his art so possessed him that he could not wait till he got home to—well, to dash off his idea; how (this in reply to a question) his idea consisted of a cock crowing and two hens eating corn; how he was fond of cocks and hens; how this did not lead him to neglect more ambitious forms of art; how he had a picture in his studio of a Greek subject which was said to be remarkable from several points of view; how no one had seen it nor knew the precise site of the studio in which it was being vigorously though secretly confected; how (in answer to a suggestion) this shyness was common to the Admiral, Michelangelo, and others; how they (Dick and Van Tromp) had struck up an acquaintance at once, and dined together that same night; how he (the Admiral) had once given money to a beggar; how he spoke with effusion of his little daughter; how he had once borrowed money to send her a doll—a trait worthy of Newton, she being then in her nineteenth year at least; how, if the doll never arrived (which it appeared it never did), the trait was only more characteristic of the highest order of creative intellect; how he was—no, not beautiful—striking, yes, Dick would go so far, decidedly striking in appearance; how his boots were made to lace and his coat was black, not cut-away, a frock; and so on, and so on by the yard. It was astonishing how few lies were necessary. After all, people exaggerated the difficulty of life. A little steering, just a touch of the rudder now and then, and with a willing listener there is no limit to the domain of equivocal speech. Sometimes Miss M'Glashan made a freezing sojourn in the parlour; and then the task seemed unaccountably more difficult; but to Esther, who was all eyes and ears, her face alight with interest, his stream of language flowed without break or stumble, and his mind was ever fertile in ingenious evasions and—

What an afternoon it was for Esther!

'Ah!' she said at last, 'it's good to hear all this! My aunt, you should know, is narrow and too religious; she cannot understand an artist's life. It does not frighten me,' she added grandly; 'I am an artist's daughter.'

With that speech, Dick consoled himself for his imposture; she was not deceived so grossly after all; and then if a fraud, was not the fraud piety itself?—and what could be more obligatory than to keep alive in the heart of a daughter that filial trust and honour which, even although misplaced, became her like a jewel of the mind? There might be another thought, a shade of cowardice, a selfish desire to please; poor Dick was merely human; and what would you have had him do?

4

ESTHER ON THE FILIAL RELATION

A MONTH later Dick and Esther met at the stile beside the cross roads; had there been any one to see them but the birds and summer insects, it would have been remarked that they met after a different fashion from the day before. Dick took her in his arms, and their lips were set together for a long while. Then he held her at arm's-length, and they looked straight into each other's eyes.

'Esther!' he said; you should have heard his voice!

'Dick!' said she.

'My darling!'

It was some time before they started for their walk; he kept an arm about her, and their sides were close together as they walked; the sun, the birds, the west wind running among the trees, a pressure, a look, the grasp tightening round a single finger, these things stood them in lieu of thought and filled their hearts with joy. The path they were following led them through a wood of pine-trees carpeted with heather and blue-berry, and upon this pleasant carpet, Dick, not without some seriousness, made her sit down.

'Esther!' he began, 'there is something you ought to know. You know my father is a rich man, and you would think, now that we love each other, we might marry when we pleased. But I fear, darling, we may have long to wait, and shall want all our courage.'

'I have courage for anything,' she said, 'I have all I want; with you and my father, I am so well off, and waiting is made so happy, that I could wait a lifetime and not weary.'

He had a sharp pang at the mention of the Admiral. 'Hear me out,' he continued. 'I ought to have told you this before; but it is a thought I shrink from; if it were possible, I should not tell you even now. My poor father and I are scarce on speaking terms.'

'Your father,' she repeated, turning pale.

'It must sound strange to you; but yet I cannot think I am to blame,' he said. 'I will tell you how it happened.'

'Oh Dick!' she said, when she had heard him to an end, 'how brave you are, and how proud. Yet I would not be proud with a father. I would tell him all.'

'What!' cried Dick, 'go in months after, and brag that I had meant to thrash the man, and then didn't. And why? Because my father had made a bigger ass of himself than I supposed. My dear, that's nonsense.'

She winced at his words and drew away. 'But when that is all he asks,' she pleaded. 'If he only knew that you had felt that impulse, it would make him so proud and happy. He would see you were his own son after all, and had the same thoughts and the same chivalry of spirit. And then you did yourself injustice when you spoke just now. It was because the editor was weak and poor and excused himself, that you repented your first determination. Had he been a big red man, with whiskers, you would have beaten him—you know you would—if Mr. Naseby had been ten times more committed. Do you think, if you can tell it to me, and I understand at once, that it would be more difficult to tell it to your own father, or that he would not be more ready to sympathise with you than I am? And I love you, Dick; but then he is your father.'

'My dear,' said Dick, desperately, 'you do not understand; you do not know what it is to be treated with daily want of comprehension and daily small injustices, through childhood and boyhood and manhood, until you despair of a hearing, until the thing rides you like a nightmare, until you almost hate the sight of the man you love, and who's your father after all. In short, Esther, you don't know what it is to have a father, and that's what blinds you.'

'I see,' she said musingly, 'you mean that I am fortunate in my father. But I am not so fortunate after all; you forget, I do not know him; it is you who know him; he is already more your father than mine.' And here she took his hand. Dick's heart had grown as cold as ice. 'But I am sorry for you, too,' she continued, 'it must be very sad and lonely.'

'You misunderstand me,' said Dick, chokingly. 'My father is the best man I know in all this world; he is worth a hundred of me, only he doesn't understand me, and he can't be made to.'

There was a silence for a while. 'Dick,' she began again, 'I am going to ask a favour, it's the first since you said you loved me. May I see your father—see him pass, I mean, where he will not observe me?'

'Why?' asked Dick.

'It is a fancy; you forget, I am romantic about fathers.'

The hint was enough for Dick; he consented with haste, and full of hang-dog penitence and disgust, took her down by a backway and planted her in the shrubbery, whence she might see the Squire ride by to dinner. There they both sat silent, but holding hands, for nearly half an hour. At last the trotting of a horse sounded in the distance, the park gates opened with a clang, and then Mr. Naseby appeared, with stooping shoulders and a heavy, bilious countenance, languidly rising to the trot. Esther recognised him at once; she had often seen him before, though with her huge indifference for all that lay outside the circle of her love, she had never so much as wondered who he was; but now she recognised him, and found him ten years older, leaden and springless, and stamped by an abiding sorrow.

'Oh Dick, Dick!' she said, and the tears began to shine upon her face as she hid it in his bosom; his own fell thickly too. They had a sad walk home, and that night, full of love and good counsel, Dick exerted every art to please his father, to convince him of his respect and affection, to heal up this breach of kindness, and reunite two hearts. But alas! the Squire was sick and peevish; he had been all day glooming over Dick's estrangement—for so he put it to himself, and now with growls, cold words, and the cold shoulder, he beat off all advances, and entrenched himself in a just resentment.

5

THE PRODIGAL FATHER MAKES HIS DEBUT AT HOME

THAT TOOK PLACE UPON A TUESDAY. On the Thursday following, as Dick was walking by appointment, earlier than usual, in the direction of the cottage, he was appalled to meet in the lane a fly from Thymebury, containing the human form of Miss M'Glashan. The lady did not deign to remark him in her passage; her face was suffused with tears, and expressed much concern for the packages by which she was surrounded. He stood still, and asked himself what this circumstance might portend. It was so beautiful a day that he was loth to forecast evil, yet something must perforce have happened at the cottage, and that of a decisive nature; for here was Miss M'Glashan on her travels, with a small patrimony in brown paper parcels, and the old lady's bearing implied hot battle and unqualified defeat. Was the house to be closed against him? Was Esther left alone, or had some new protector made his appearance from among the millions of Europe? It is the character of love to loathe the near relatives of the loved one; chapters in the history of the human race have justified this feeling, and the conduct of uncles, in particular, has frequently met with censure from the independent novelist. Miss M'Glashan was now seen in the rosy colours of regret; whoever succeeded her, Dick felt the change would be for the worse. He hurried forward in this spirit; his anxiety grew upon him with every step; as he entered the garden a voice fell upon his ear, and he was once more arrested, not this time by doubt, but by indubitable certainty of ill.

The thunderbolt had fallen; the Admiral was here.

Dick would have retreated, in the panic terror of the moment; but Esther kept a bright look-out when her lover was expected. In a twinkling she was by his side, brimful of news and pleasure, too glad to notice his embarrassment, and in one of those golden transports of exultation which transcend not only words but caresses. She took him by the end of the fingers (reaching forward to take them, for her great preoccupation was to save time), she drew him towards her, pushed him past her in the door, and planted him face to face with Mr. Van Tromp, in a suit of French country velveteens and with a remarkable carbuncle on his nose. Then, as though this was the end of what she could endure in the way of joy, Esther turned and ran out of the room.

The two men remained looking at each other with some confusion on both sides. Van Tromp was naturally the first to recover; he put out his hand with a fine gesture.

'And you know my little lass, my Esther?' he said. 'This is pleasant; this is what I have conceived of home. A strange word for the old rover; but we all have a taste for home and the home-like, disguise it how we may. It has brought me here, Mr. Naseby,' he concluded, with an intonation that would have made his fortune on the stage, so just, so sad, so dignified, so like a man of the world and a philosopher, 'and you see a man who is content.'

'I see,' said Dick.

'Sit down,' continued the parasite, setting the example. 'Fortune has gone against me. (I am just sirrupping a little brandy—after my journey.) I was going down, Mr. Naseby; between you and me, I was *décavé*; I borrowed fifty francs, smuggled my valise past the concierge—a work of considerable tact—and here I am!'

'Yes,' said Dick; 'and here you are.' He was quite idiotic.

Esther, at this moment, re-entered the room.

'Are you glad to see him?' she whispered in his ear, the pleasure in her voice almost bursting through the whisper into song.

'Oh yes,' said Dick, 'very.'

'I knew you would be,' she replied; 'I told him how you loved him.'

'Help yourself,' said the Admiral, 'help yourself; and let us drink to a new existence.'

'To a new existence,' repeated Dick; and he raised the tumbler to his lips, but set it down untasted. He had had enough of novelties for one day.

Esther was sitting on a stool beside her father's feet, holding her knees in her arms, and looking with pride from one to the other of her two visitors. Her eyes were so bright that you were never sure if there were tears in them or not; little voluptuous shivers ran about her body; sometimes she nestled her chin into her throat, sometimes threw back her head, with ecstasy; in a word, she was in that state when it is said of people that they cannot contain themselves for happiness. It would be hard to exaggerate the agony of Richard.

And, in the meantime, Van Tromp ran on interminably.

'I never forget a friend,' said he, 'nor yet an enemy: of the latter, I never had but two—myself and the public; and I fancy I have had my vengeance pretty freely out of both.' He chuckled. 'But those days are done. Van Tromp is no more. He was a man who had successes; I believe you knew I had successes—to which we shall refer no farther,' pulling down his neckcloth with a smile. 'That man exists no more: by an exercise of will I have destroyed him. There is something like it in the poets. First, a brilliant and conspicuous career—the observed, I may say, of all observers, including the bum-bailie: and then, presto! a quiet, sly, old, rustic *bonhomme*, cultivating roses. In Paris, Mr. Naseby—'

'Call him Richard, father,' said Esther.

'Richard, if he will allow me. Indeed, we are old friends, and now near neighbours; and, *à propos*, how are we off for neighbours, Richard? The cottage stands, I think, upon your father's land—a family which I respect—and the wood, I understand, is Lord Trevanion's. Not that I care; I am an old Bohemian. I have cut society with a cut direct; I cut it when I was prosperous, and now I reap my reward, and can cut it with dignity in my declension. These are our little *amours propres*, my daughter: your father must respect himself. Thank you, yes; just a leetle, leetle, tiny—thanks, thanks; you spoil me. But, as I was saying, Richard, or was about to say, my daughter has been allowed to rust; her aunt was a mere duenna; hence, in parenthesis, Richard, her distrust of me; my nature and that of the duenna are poles asunder—poles! But, now that I am here, now that I have given up the fight, and live henceforth for one only of my works—I have the modesty to say it is my best—my daughter—well, we shall put all that to rights. The neighbours, Richard?'

Dick was understood to say that there were many good families in the Vale of Thyme.

'You shall introduce us,' said the Admiral.

Dick's shirt was wet; he made a lumbering excuse to go; which Esther explained to herself by a fear of intrusion, and so set down to the merit side of Dick's account, while she proceeded to detain him.

'Before our walk?' she cried. 'Never! I must have my walk.'

'Let us all go,' said the Admiral, rising.

'You do not know that you are wanted,' she cried, leaning on his shoulder with a caress. 'I might wish to speak to my old friend about my new father. But you shall come to-day, you shall do all you want; I have set my heart on spoiling you.'

'I will just take *one* drop more,' said the Admiral, stooping to help himself to brandy. 'It is surprising how this journey has fatigued me. But I am growing old, I am growing old, I am growing old, and—I regret to add—bald.'

He cocked a white wide-awake coquettishly upon his head—the habit of the lady-killer clung to him; and Esther had already thrown on her hat, and was ready, while he was still studying the result in a mirror: the carbuncle had somewhat painfully arrested his attention.

'We are papa now; we must be respectable,' he said to Dick, in explanation of his dandyism: and then he went to a bundle and chose himself a staff. Where were the elegant canes of his Parisian epoch? This was a support for age, and designed for rustic scenes. Dick began to see and appreciate the man's enjoyment in a new part, when he saw how carefully he had 'made it up.' He had invented a gait for this first country stroll with his daughter, which was admirably in key. He walked with fatigue, he leaned upon the staff; he looked round him with a sad, smiling sympathy on all that he beheld; he even asked the name of a plant, and rallied himself gently for an old town bird, ignorant of nature. 'This country life will make me young again,' he sighed. They reached the top of the hill towards the first hour of evening; the sun was descending heaven, the colour had all drawn into the west; the hills were modelled in their least contour by the soft, slanting shine; and the wide moorlands, veined with glens and hazelwoods, ran west and north in a hazy glory of light. Then the painter wakened in Van Tromp.

'Gad, Dick,' he cried, 'what value!'

An ode in four hundred lines would not have seemed so touching to Esther; her eyes filled with happy tears; yes, here was the father of whom she had dreamed, whom Dick had described; simple, enthusiastic, unworldly, kind, a painter at heart, and a fine gentleman in manner.

And just then the Admiral perceived a house by the wayside, and something depending over the house door which might be construed as a sign by the hopeful and thirsty.

'Is that,' he asked, pointing with his stick, 'an inn?'

There was a marked change in his voice, as though he attached importance to the inquiry: Esther listened, hoping she should hear wit or wisdom.

Dick said it was.

'You know it?' inquired the Admiral.

'I have passed it a hundred times, but that is all,' replied Dick.

'Ah,' said Van Tromp, with a smile, and shaking his head; 'you are not an old campaigner; you have the world to learn. Now I, you see, find an inn so very near my own home, and my first thought is my neighbours. I shall go forward and make my neighbours' acquaintance; no, you needn't come; I shall not be a moment.'

And he walked off briskly towards the inn, leaving Dick alone with Esther on the road.

'Dick,' she exclaimed, 'I am so glad to get a word with you; I am so happy, I have such a thousand things to say; and I want you to do me a favour. Imagine, he has come without a paint-box, without an easel; and I want him to have all. I want you to get them for me in Thymebury. You saw, this moment, how his heart turned to painting. They can't live without it,' she added; meaning perhaps Van Tromp and Michel Angelo.

Up to that moment, she had observed nothing amiss in Dick's behaviour. She was too happy to be curious; and his silence, in presence of the great and good being whom she called her father, had seemed both natural and praiseworthy. But now that they were alone, she became conscious of a barrier between her lover and herself, and alarm sprang up in her heart.

'Dick,' she cried, 'you don't love me.'

'I do that,' he said heartily.

'But you are unhappy; you are strange; you—you are not glad to see my father,' she concluded, with a break in her voice.

'Esther,' he said, 'I tell you that I love you; if you love me, you know what that means, and that all I wish is to see you happy. Do you think I cannot enjoy your pleasures? Esther, I do. If I am uneasy, if I am alarmed, if—. Oh, believe me, try and believe in me,' he cried, giving up argument with perhaps a happy inspiration.

But the girl's suspicions were aroused; and though she pressed the matter no farther (indeed, her father was already seen returning), it by no means left her thoughts. At one moment she simply resented the selfishness of a man who had obtruded his dark looks and passionate language on her joy; for there is nothing that a woman can less easily forgive than the language of a passion which, even if only for the moment, she does not share. At another, she suspected him of jealousy against her father; and for that, although she could see excuses for it, she yet despised him. And at least, in one way or the other, here was the dangerous beginning of a separation between two hearts. Esther found herself at variance with her sweetest friend; she could no longer look into his heart and find it written with the same language as her own; she could no longer think of him as the sun which radiated happiness upon her life, for she had turned to him once, and he had breathed upon her black and chilly, radiated blackness and frost. To put the whole matter in a word, she was beginning, although ever so slightly, to fall out of love.

6

THE PRODIGAL FATHER GOES ON FROM STRENGTH TO STRENGTH

We will not follow all the steps of the Admiral's return and installation, but hurry forward towards the catastrophe, merely chronicling by the way a few salient incidents, wherein we must rely entirely upon the evidence of Richard, for Esther to this day has never opened her mouth upon this trying passage of her life, and as for the Admiral—well, that naval officer, although still alive, and now more suitably installed in a seaport town where he has a telescope and a flag in his front garden, is incapable of throwing the slightest gleam of light upon the affair. Often and often has he remarked to the present writer: 'If I know what it was all about, sir, I'll be—' in short, be what I hope he will not. And then he will look across at his daughter's portrait, a photograph, shake his head with an amused appearance, and mix himself another grog by way of consolation. Once I heard him go farther, and express his feelings with regard to Esther in a single but eloquent word. 'A minx, sir,' he said, not in anger, rather in amusement: and he cordially drank her health upon the back of it. His worst enemy must admit him to be a man without malice; he never bore a grudge in his life, lacking the necessary taste and industry of attention.

Yet it was during this obscure period that the drama was really performed; and its scene was in the heart of Esther, shut away from all eyes. Had this warm, upright, sullen girl been differently used by destiny, had events come upon her even in a different succession, for some things lead easily to others, the whole course of this tale would have been changed, and Esther never would have run away. As it was, through a series of acts and words of which we know but few, and a series of thoughts which any one may imagine for himself, she was awakened in four days from the dream of a life.

The first tangible cause of disenchantment was when Dick brought home a painter's arsenal on Friday evening. The Admiral was in the chimney-corner, once more 'sirrupping' some brandy and water, and Esther sat at the table at work. They both came forward to greet the new arrival; and the girl, relieving him of his monstrous burthen, proceeded to display her offerings to her father. Van Tromp's countenance fell several degrees; he became quite querulous.

'God bless me,' he said; and then, 'I must really ask you not to interfere, child,' in a tone of undisguised hostility.

'Father,' she said, 'forgive me; I knew you had given up your art—'

'Oh yes!' cried the Admiral; 'I've done with it to the judgment-day!'

'Pardon me again,' she said firmly, 'but I do not, I cannot think that you are right in this. Suppose the world is unjust, suppose that no one understands you, you have still a duty to yourself. And, oh, don't spoil the pleasure of your coming home to me; show me that you can be my father and yet not neglect your destiny. I am not like some daughters; I will not be jealous of your art, and I will try to understand it.'

The situation was odiously farcical. Richard groaned under it; he longed to leap forward and denounce the humbug. And the humbug himself? Do you fancy he was easier in his mind? I am sure, on the other hand, that he was acutely miserable; and he betrayed his sufferings by a perfectly silly and undignified access of temper, during which he broke his pipe in several pieces, threw his brandy and water in the fire, and employed words which were very plain although the drift of them was somewhat vague. It was of very brief duration. Van Tromp was himself again, and in a most delightful humour within three minutes of the first explosion.

'I am an old fool,' he said frankly. 'I was spoiled when a child. As for you, Esther, you take after your mother; you have a morbid sense of duty, particularly for others; strive against it, my dear—strive against it. And as for the pigments, well, I'll use them, some of these days; and to show that I'm in earnest, I'll get Dick here to prepare a canvas.'

Dick was put to this menial task forthwith, the Admiral not even watching how he did, but quite occupied with another grog and a pleasant vein of talk.

A little after Esther arose, and making some pretext, good or bad, went off to bed. Dick was left hobbled by the canvas, and was subjected to Van Tromp for about an hour.

The next day, Saturday, it is believed that little intercourse took place between Esther and her father; but towards the afternoon Dick met the latter returning from the direction of the inn, where he had struck up quite a friendship with the landlord. Dick wondered who paid for these excursions, and at the thought that the reprobate must get his pocket money where he got his board and lodging, from poor Esther's generosity, he had it almost in his heart to knock the old gentleman down. He, on his part, was full of airs and graces and geniality.

'Dear Dick,' he said, taking his arm, 'this is neighbourly of you; it shows your tact to meet me when I had a wish for you. I am in pleasant spirits; and it is then that I desire a friend.'

'I am glad to hear you are so happy,' retorted Dick bitterly. 'There's certainly not much to trouble *you*.'

'No,' assented the Admiral, 'not much. I got out of it in time; and here—well, here everything pleases me. I am plain in my tastes. '*A propos*, you have never asked me how I liked my daughter?'

'No,' said Dick roundly; 'I certainly have not.'

'Meaning you will not. And why, Dick? She is my daughter, of course; but then I am a man of the world and a man of taste, and perfectly qualified to give an opinion with impartiality—yes, Dick, with impartiality. Frankly, I am not disappointed in her. She has good looks; she has them from her mother. So I may say I *chose* her looks. She is devoted, quite devoted to me—'

'She is the best woman in the world!' broke out Dick.

'Dick,' cried the Admiral, stopping short; 'I have been expecting this. Let us—let us go back to the "Trevanion Arms" and talk this matter out over a bottle.'

'Certainly not,' went Dick. 'You have had far too much already.'

The parasite was on the point of resenting this; but a look at Dick's face, and some recollection of the terms on which they had stood in Paris, came to the aid of his wisdom and restrained him.

'As you please,' he said; 'although I don't know what you mean—nor care. But let us walk, if you prefer it. You are still a young man; when you are my age— But, however, to continue. You please me, Dick; you have pleased me from the first; and to say truth, Esther is a trifle fantastic, and will be better when she is married. She has means of her own, as of course you are aware. They come, like the looks, from her poor, dear, good creature of a mother. She was blessed in her mother. I mean she shall be blessed in her husband, and you are the man, Dick, you and not another. This very night I will sound her affections.'

Dick stood aghast.

'Mr. Van Tromp, I implore you,' he said; 'do what you please with yourself, but, for God's sake, let your daughter alone.'

'It is my duty,' replied the Admiral, 'and between ourselves, you rogue, my inclination too. I am as matchmaking as a dowager. It will be more discreet for you to stay away to-night. Farewell. You leave your case in good hands; I have the tact of these little matters by heart; it is not my first attempt.'

All arguments were in vain; the old rascal stuck to his point; nor did Richard conceal from himself how seriously this might injure his prospects, and he fought hard. Once there came a glimmer of hope. The Admiral again proposed an adjournment to the 'Trevanion Arms,' and when Dick had once more refused, it hung for a moment in the balance whether or not the old toper would return there by himself. Had he done so, of course Dick could have taken to his heels, and warned Esther of what was coming, and of how it had begun. But the Admiral, after a pause, decided for the brandy at home, and made off in that direction.

We have no details of the sounding.

Next day the Admiral was observed in the parish church, very properly dressed. He found the places, and joined in response and hymn, as to the manner born; and his appearance, as he intended it should, attracted some attention among the worshippers. Old Naseby, for instance, had observed him.

'There was a drunken-looking blackguard opposite us in church,' he said to his son as they drove home; 'do you know who he was?'

'Some fellow—Van Tromp, I believe,' said Dick.

'A foreigner, too!' observed the Squire.

Dick could not sufficiently congratulate himself on the escape he had effected. Had the Admiral met him with his father, what would have been the result? And could such a catastrophe be long postponed? It seemed to him as if the storm were nearly ripe; and it was so more nearly than he thought.

He did not go to the cottage in the afternoon, withheld by fear and shame; but when dinner was over at Naseby House, and the Squire had gone off into a comfortable doze, Dick slipped out of the room, and ran across country, in part to save time, in part to save his own courage from growing cold; for he now hated the notion of the cottage or the Admiral, and if he did not hate, at least feared to think of Esther. He had no clue to her reflections; but he could not conceal from his own heart that he must have sunk in her esteem, and the spectacle of her infatuation galled him like an insult.

He knocked and was admitted. The room looked very much as on his last visit, with Esther at the table and Van Tromp beside the fire; but the expression of the two faces told a very different story. The girl was paler than usual; her eyes were dark, the colour seemed to have faded from round about them, and her swiftest glance was as intent as a stare. The appearance of the Admiral, on the other hand, was rosy, and flabby, and moist; his jowl hung over his shirt collar, his smile was loose and wandering, and he had so far relaxed the natural control of his eyes, that one of them was aimed inward, as if to watch the growth of the carbuncle. We are warned against bad judgments; but the Admiral was certainly not sober. He made no attempt to rise when Richard entered, but waved his pipe flightily in the air, and gave a leer of welcome. Esther took as little notice of him as might be.

'Aha! Dick!' cried the painter. 'I've been to church; I have, upon my word. And I saw you there, though you didn't see me. And I saw a devilish pretty woman, by Gad. If it were not for this baldness, and a kind of crapulous air I can't disguise from myself—if it weren't for this and that and t'other thing—I—I've forgot what I was saying. Not that that matters, I've heaps of things to say. I'm in a communicative vein to-night. I'll let out all my cats, even unto seventy times seven. I'm in what I call *the* stage, and all I desire is a listener, although he were deaf, to be as happy as Nebuchadnezzar.'

Of the two hours which followed upon this it is unnecessary to give more than a sketch. The Admiral was extremely silly, now and then amusing, and never really offensive. It was plain that he kept in view the presence of his daughter, and chose subjects and a character of language that should not offend a lady. On almost any other occasion Dick would have enjoyed the scene. Van Tromp's egotism, flown with drink, struck a pitch above mere vanity. He became candid and explanatory; sought to take his auditors entirely into his confidence, and tell them his inmost conviction about himself. Between his self-knowledge, which was considerable, and his vanity, which was immense, he had created a strange hybrid animal, and called it by his own name. How he would plume his feathers over virtues which would have gladdened the heart of Cæsar or St. Paul; and anon, complete his own portrait with one of those touches of pitiless realism which the satirist so often seeks in vain.

'Now, there's Dick,' he said, 'he's shrewd; he saw through me the first time we met, and told me so—told me so to my face, which I had the virtue to keep. I bear you no malice for it, Dick; you were right; I am a humbug.'

You may fancy how Esther quailed at this new feature of the meeting between her two idols.

And then, again, in a parenthesis:—

'That,' said Van Tromp, 'was when I had to paint those dirty daubs of mine.'

And a little further on, laughingly said perhaps, but yet with an air of truth:—

'I never had the slightest hesitation in sponging upon any human creature.'

Thereupon Dick got up.

'I think perhaps,' he said, 'we had better all be thinking of going to bed.' And he smiled with a feeble and deprecatory smile.

'Not at all,' cried the Admiral, 'I know a trick worth two of that. Puss here,' indicating his daughter, 'shall go to bed; and you and I will keep it up till all's blue.'

Thereupon Esther arose in sullen glory. She had sat and listened for two mortal hours while her idol defiled himself and sneered away his godhead. One by one, her illusions had departed. And now he wished to order her to bed in her own house! now he called her Puss! now, even as he uttered the words, toppling on his chair, he broke the stem of his tobacco-pipe in three! Never did the sheep turn upon her shearer with a more commanding front. Her voice was calm, her enunciation a little slow, but perfectly distinct, and she stood before him as she spoke, in the simplest and most maidenly attitude.

'No,' she said, 'Mr. Naseby will have the goodness to go home at once, and you will go to bed.'

The broken fragments of pipe fell from the Admiral's fingers; he seemed by his countenance to have lived too long in a world unworthy of him; but it is an odd circumstance, he attempted no reply, and sat thunderstruck, with open mouth.

Dick she motioned sharply towards the door, and he could only obey her. In the porch, finding she was close behind him, he ventured to pause and whisper, 'You have done right.'

'I have done as I pleased,' she said. 'Can he paint?'

'Many people like his paintings,' returned Dick, in stifled tones; 'I never did; I never said I did,' he added, fiercely defending himself before he was attacked.

'I ask you if he can paint. I will not be put off. *Can* he paint?' she repeated.

'No,' said Dick.

'Does he even like it?'

'Not now, I believe.'

'And he is drunk?'—she leaned upon the word with hatred.

'He has been drinking.'

'Go,' she said, and was turning to re-enter the house when another thought arrested her. 'Meet me to-morrow morning at the stile,' she said.

'I will,' replied Dick.

And then the door closed behind her, and Dick was alone in the darkness. There was still a chink of light above the sill, a warm, mild glow behind the window; the roof of the cottage and some of the banks and hazels were defined in denser darkness against the sky; but all else was formless, breathless, and noiseless like the pit. Dick remained as she had left him, standing squarely upon one foot and resting only on the toe of the other, and as he stood he listened with his soul. The sound of a chair pushed sharply over the floor startled his heart into his mouth; but the silence which had thus been disturbed settled back again at once upon the cottage and its vicinity. What took place during this interval is a secret from the world of men; but when it was over the voice of Esther spoke evenly and without interruption for perhaps half a minute, and as soon as that ceased heavy and uncertain footfalls crossed the parlour and mounted lurching up the stairs. The girl had tamed her father, Van Tromp had gone obediently to bed: so much was obvious to the watcher in the road. And yet he still waited, straining his ears, and with terror and sickness at his heart; for if Esther had followed her father, if she had even made one movement in this great conspiracy of men and nature to be still, Dick must have had instant knowledge of it from his station before the door; and if she had not moved, must she not have fainted? or might she not be dead?

He could hear the cottage clock deliberately measure out the seconds; time stood still with him; an almost superstitious terror took command of his faculties; at last, he could bear no more, and, springing through the little garden in two bounds, he put his face against the window. The blind, which had not been drawn fully down, left an open chink about an inch in height along the bottom of the glass, and the whole parlour was thus exposed to Dick's investigation. Esther sat upright at the table, her head resting on her hand, her eyes fixed upon the candle. Her brows were slightly bent, her mouth slightly open; her whole attitude so still and settled that Dick could hardly fancy that she breathed. She had not stirred at the sound of Dick's arrival. Soon after, making a considerable disturbance amid the vast silence of the night, the clock lifted up its voice, whined for a while like a partridge, and then eleven times hooted like a cuckoo. Still Esther continued immovable and gazed upon the candle. Midnight followed, and then one of the morning; and still she had not stirred, nor had Richard Naseby dared to quit the window. And then, about half-past one, the candle she had been thus intently watching flared up into a last blaze of paper, and she leaped to her feet with an ejaculation, looked about her once, blew out the light, turned round, and was heard rapidly mounting the staircase in the dark.

Dick was left once more alone to darkness and to that dulled and dogged state of mind when a man thinks that Misery must now have done her worst, and is almost glad to think so.

He turned and walked slowly towards the stile; she had told him no hour, and he was determined, whenever she came, that she should find him waiting. As he got there the day began to dawn, and he leaned over a hurdle and beheld the shadows flee away. Up went the sun at last out of a bank of clouds that were already disbanding in the east; a herald wind had already sprung up to sweep the leafy earth and scatter the congregated dewdrops. 'Alas!' thought Dick Naseby, 'how can any other day come so distastefully to me?' He still wanted his experience of the morrow.

7
THE ELOPEMENT

It was probably on the stroke of ten, and Dick had been half asleep for some time against the bank, when Esther came up the road carrying a bundle. Some kind of instinct, or perhaps the distant light footfalls, recalled him, while she was still a good way off, to the possession of his faculties, and he half raised himself and blinked upon the world. It took him some time to recollect his thoughts. He had awakened with a certain blank and childish sense of pleasure, like a man who had received a legacy overnight; but this feeling gradually died away, and was then suddenly and stunningly succeeded by a conviction of the truth. The whole story of the past night sprang into his mind with every detail, as by an exercise of the direct and speedy sense of sight, and he arose from the ditch and, with rueful courage, went to meet his love.

She came up to him walking steady and fast, her face still pale, but to all appearance perfectly composed; and she showed neither surprise, relief, nor pleasure at finding her lover on the spot. Nor did she offer him her hand.

'Here I am,' said he.

'Yes,' she replied; and then, without a pause or any change of voice, 'I want you to take me away,' she added.

'Away?' he repeated. 'How? Where?'

'To-day,' she said. 'I do not care where it is, but I want you to take me away.'

'For how long? I do not understand,' gasped Dick.

'I shall never come back here any more,' was all she answered.

Wild words uttered, as these were, with perfect quiet of manner and voice, exercise a double influence on the hearer's mind. Dick was confounded; he recovered from astonishment only to fall into doubt and alarm. He looked upon her frozen attitude, so discouraging for a lover to behold, and recoiled from the thoughts which it suggested.

'To me?' he asked. 'Are you coming to me, Esther?'

'I want you to take me away,' she repeated with weary impatience. 'Take me away—take me away from here.'

The situation was not sufficiently defined. Dick asked himself with concern whether she were altogether in her right wits. To take her away, to marry her, to work off his hands for her support, Dick was content to do all this; yet he required some show of love upon her part. He was not one of those tough-hided and small-hearted males who would marry their love at the point of the bayonet rather than not marry her at all. He desired that a woman should come to his arms with an attractive willingness, if not with ardour. And Esther's bearing was more that of despair than that of love. It chilled him and taught him wisdom.

'Dearest,' he urged, 'tell me what you wish, and you shall have it; tell me your thoughts, and then I can advise you. But to go from here without a plan, without forethought, in the heat of a moment, is madder than madness, and can help nothing. I am not speaking like a man, but I speak the truth; and I tell you again, the thing's absurd, and wrong, and hurtful.'

She looked at him with a lowering, languid look of wrath.

'So you will not take me?' she said. 'Well, I will go alone.'

And she began to step forward on her way. But he threw himself before her.

'Esther, Esther!' he cried.

'Let me go—don't touch me—what right have you to interfere? Who are you, to touch me?' she flashed out, shrill with anger.

Then, being made bold by her violence, he took her firmly, almost roughly, by the arm, and held her while he spoke.

'You know well who I am, and what I am, and that I love you. You say I will not help you; but your heart knows the contrary. It is you who will not help me; for you will not tell me what you want. You see—or you could see, if you took the pains to look—how I have waited here all night to be ready at your service. I only asked information; I only urged you to consider; and I still urge and beg you to think better of your fancies. But if your mind is made up, so be it; I will beg no longer; I give you my orders; and I will not allow—not allow you to go hence alone.'

She looked at him for awhile with cold, unkind scrutiny like one who tries the temper of a tool.

'Well, take me away, then,' she said with a sigh.

'Good,' said Dick. 'Come with me to the stables; there we shall get the pony-trap and drive to the junction. To-night you shall be in London. I am yours so wholly that no words can make me more so; and, besides, you know it, and the words are needless. May God help me to be good to you, Esther—may God help me! for I see that you will not.'

So, without more speech, they set out together, and were already got some distance from the spot, ere he observed that she was still carrying the hand-bag. She gave it up to him, passively, but when he offered her his arm, merely shook her head and pursed up her lips. The sun shone clearly and pleasantly; the wind was fresh and brisk upon their faces, and smelt racily of woods and meadows. As they went down into the valley of the Thyme, the babble of the stream rose into the air like a perennial laughter. On the far-away hills, sun-burst and shadow raced along the slopes and leaped from peak to peak. Earth, air and water, each seemed in better health and had more of the shrewd salt of life in them than upon ordinary mornings; and from east to west, from the lowest glen to the height of heaven, from every look and touch and scent, a human creature could gather the most encouraging intelligence as to the durability and spirit of the universe.

Through all this walked Esther, picking her small steps like a bird, but silent and with a cloud under her thick eyebrows. She seemed insensible, not only of nature, but of the presence of her companion. She was altogether engrossed in herself, and looked neither to right nor to left, but straight before her on the road. When they came to the bridge, however, she halted, leaned on the parapet, and stared for a moment at the clear, brown pool, and swift, transient snowdrift of the rapids.

'I am going to drink,' she said; and descended the winding footpath to the margin.

There she drank greedily in her hands and washed her temples with water. The coolness seemed to break, for an instant, the spell that lay upon her; for, instead of hastening forward again in her dull, indefatigable tramp, she stood still where she was, for near a minute, looking straight before her. And Dick, from above on the bridge where he stood to watch her, saw a strange, equivocal smile dawn slowly on her face and pass away again at once and suddenly, leaving her as grave as ever; and the sense of distance, which it is so cruel for a lover to endure, pressed with every moment more heavily on her companion. Her thoughts were all secret; her heart was locked and bolted; and he stood without, vainly wooing her with his eves.

'Do you feel better?' asked Dick, as she at last rejoined him; and after the constraint of so long a silence, his voice sounded foreign to his own ears.

She looked at him for an appreciable fraction of a minute ere she answered, and when she did, it was in the monosyllable—'Yes.'

Dick's solicitude was nipped and frosted. His words died away on his tongue. Even his eyes, despairing of encouragement, ceased to attend on hers. And they went on in silence through Kirton hamlet, where an old man followed them with his eyes, and perhaps envied them their youth and love; and across the Ivy beck where the mill was splashing and grumbling low thunder to itself in the chequered shadow of the dell, and the miller before the door was beating flour from his hands as he whistled a modulation; and up by the high spinney, whence they saw the mountains upon either hand; and down the hill again to the back courts and offices of Naseby House. Esther had kept ahead all the way, and Dick plodded obediently in her wake; but as they neared the stables, he pushed on and took the lead. He would have preferred her to await him in the road while he went on and brought the carriage back, but after so many repulses and rebuffs he lacked courage to offer the suggestion. Perhaps, too, he felt it wiser to keep his convoy within sight. So they entered the yard in Indian file, like a tramp and his wife.

The grooms eyebrows rose as he received the order for the pony-phaeton, and kept rising during all his preparations. Esther stood bolt upright and looked steadily at some chickens in the corner of the yard. Master Richard himself, thought the groom, was not in his ordinary; for in truth, he carried the hand-bag like a talisman, and either stood listless, or set off suddenly walking in one direction after another with brisk, decisive footsteps. Moreover he had apparently neglected to wash his hands, and bore the air of one returning from a prolonged nutting ramble. Upon the groom's countenance there began to grow up an expression as of one about to whistle. And hardly had the carriage turned the corner and rattled into the high road with this inexplicable pair, than the whistle broke forth—prolonged, and low and tremulous; and the groom, already so far relieved, vented the rest of his surprise in one simple English word, friendly to the mouth of Jack-tar and the sooty pitman, and hurried to spread the news round the servants' hall of Naseby House. Luncheon would be on the table in little beyond an hour; and the Squire, on sitting down, would hardly fail to ask for Master Richard. Hence, as the intelligent reader can foresee, this groom has a part to play in the imbroglio.

Meantime, Dick had been thinking deeply and bitterly. It seemed to him as if his love had gone from him, indeed, yet gone but a little way; as if he needed but to find the right touch or intonation, and her heart would recognise him and be melted. Yet he durst not open his mouth, and drove in silence till they had passed the main park-gates and turned into the cross-cut lane along the wall. Then it seemed to him as if it must be now, or never.

'Can't you see you are killing me?' he cried. 'Speak to me, look at me, treat me like a human man.'

She turned slowly and looked him in the face with eyes that seemed kinder. He dropped the reins and caught her hand, and she made no resistance, although her touch was unresponsive. But when, throwing one arm round her waist, he sought to kiss her lips, not like a lover indeed, not because he wanted to do so, but as a desperate man who puts his fortunes to the touch, she drew away from him, with a knot in her forehead, backed and shied about fiercely with her head, and pushed him from her with her hand. Then there was no room left for doubt, and Dick saw, as clear as sunlight, that she had a distaste or nourished a grudge against him.

'Then you don't love me?' he said, drawing back from her, he also, as though her touch had burnt him; and then, as she made no answer, he repeated with another intonation, imperious and yet still pathetic, 'You don't love me, *do* you, *do* you?'

'I don't know,' she replied. 'Why do you ask me? Oh, how should I know? It has all been lies together—lies, and lies, and lies!'

He cried her name sharply, like a man who has taken a physical hurt, and that was the last word that either of them spoke until they reached Thymebury Junction.

This was a station isolated in the midst of moorlands, yet lying on the great up line to London. The nearest town, Thymebury itself, was seven miles distant along the branch they call the Vale of Thyme Railway. It was now nearly half an hour past noon, the down train had just gone by, and there would be no more traffic at the junction until half-past three, when the local train comes in to meet the up express at a quarter before four. The stationmaster had already gone off to his garden, which was half a mile away in a hollow of the moor; a porter, who was just leaving, took charge of the phaeton, and promised to return it before night to Naseby House; only a deaf, snuffy, and stern old man remained to play propriety for Dick and Esther.

Before the phaeton had driven off, the girl had entered the station and seated herself upon a bench. The endless, empty moorlands stretched before her, entirely unenclosed, and with no boundary but the horizon. Two lines of rails, a waggon shed, and a few telegraph posts, alone diversified the outlook. As for sounds, the silence was unbroken save by the chant of the telegraph wires and the crying of the plovers on the waste. With the approach of midday the wind had more and more fallen, it was now sweltering hot and the air trembled in the sunshine.

Dick paused for an instant on the threshold of the platform. Then, in two steps, he was by her side and speaking almost with a sob.

'Esther,' he said, 'have pity on me. What have I done? Can you not forgive me? Esther, you loved me once—can you not love me still?'

'How can I tell you? How am I to know?' she answered. 'You are all a lie to me—all a lie from first to last. You were laughing at my folly, playing with me like a child, at the very time when you declared you loved me. Which was true? was any of it true? or was it all, all a mockery? I am weary trying to find out. And you say I loved you; I loved my father's friend. I never loved, I never heard of, you, until that man came home and I began to find myself deceived. Give me back my father, be what you were before, and you may talk of love indeed!'

'Then you cannot forgive me—cannot?' he asked.

'I have nothing to forgive,' she answered. 'You do not understand.'

'Is that your last word, Esther?' said he, very white, and biting his lip to keep it still.

'Yes, that is my last word,' replied she.

'Then we are here on false pretences, and we stay here no longer,' he said. 'Had you still loved me, right or wrong, I should have taken you away, because then I could have made you happy. But as it is—I must speak plainly—what you propose is degrading to you, and an insult to me, and a rank unkindness to your father. Your father may be this or that, but you should use him like a fellow-creature.'

'What do you mean?' she flashed. 'I leave him my house and all my money; it is more than he deserves. I wonder you dare speak to me about that man. And besides, it is all he cares for; let him take it, and let me never hear from him again.'

'I thought you romantic about fathers,' he said.

'Is that a taunt?' she demanded.

'No,' he replied, 'it is an argument. No one can make you like him, but don't disgrace him in his own eyes. He is old, Esther, old and broken down. Even I am sorry for him, and he has been the loss of all I cared for. Write to your aunt; when I see her answer you can leave quietly and naturally, and I will take you to your aunt's door. But in the meantime you must go home. You have no money, and so you are helpless, and must do as I tell you; and believe me, Esther, I do all for your good, and your good only, so God help me.'

She had put her hand into her pocket and withdrawn it empty.

'I counted upon you,' she wailed.

'You counted rightly then,' he retorted. 'I will not, to please you for a moment, make both of us unhappy for our lives; and since I cannot marry you, we have only been too long away, and must go home at once.'

'Dick,' she cried suddenly, 'perhaps I might—perhaps in time—perhaps—'

'There is no perhaps about the matter,' interrupted Dick. 'I must go and bring the phaeton.' And with that he strode from the station, all in a glow of passion and virtue. Esther, whose eyes had come alive and her cheeks flushed during these last words, relapsed in a second into a state of petrifaction. She remained without motion during his absence, and when he returned suffered herself to be put back into the phaeton, and driven off on the return journey like an idiot or a tired child. Compared with what she was now, her condition of the morning seemed positively natural. She sat white and cold and silent, and there was no speculation in her eyes. Poor Dick flailed and flailed at the pony, and once tried to whistle, but his courage was going down; huge clouds of despair gathered together in his soul, and from time to time their darkness was divided by a piercing flash of longing and regret. He had lost his love—he had lost his love for good.

The pony was tired, and the hills very long and steep, and the air sultrier than ever, for now the breeze began to fail entirely. It seemed as if this miserable drive would never be done, as if poor Dick would never be able to go away and be comfortably wretched by himself; for all his desire was to escape from her presence and the reproach of her averted looks. He had lost his love, he thought—he had lost his love for good.

They were already not far from the cottage, when his heart again faltered and he appealed to her once more, speaking low and eagerly in broken phrases.

'I cannot live without your love,' he concluded.

'I do not understand what you mean,' she replied, and I believe with perfect truth.

'Then,' said he, wounded to the quick, 'your aunt might come and fetch you herself. Of course you can command me as you please. But I think it would be better so.'

'Oh yes,' she said wearily, 'better so.'

This was the only exchange of words between them till about four o'clock; the phaeton, mounting the lane, 'opened out' the cottage between the leafy banks. Thin smoke went straight up from the chimney; the flowers in the garden, the hawthorn in the lane, hung down their heads in the heat; the stillness was broken only by the sound of hoofs. For right before the gate a livery servant rode slowly up and down, leading a saddle horse. And in this last Dick shuddered to identify his father's chestnut.

Alas! poor Richard, what should this portend?

The servant, as in duty bound, dismounted and took the phaeton into his keeping; yet Dick thought he touched his hat to him with something of a grin. Esther, passive as ever, was helped out and crossed the garden with a slow and mechanical gait; and Dick, following close behind her, heard from within the cottage his father's voice upraised in an anathema, and the shriller tones of the Admiral responding in the key of war.

8

BATTLE ROYAL

SQUIRE NASEBY, on sitting down to lunch, had inquired for Dick, whom he had not seen since the day before at dinner; and the servant answering awkwardly that Master Richard had come back but had gone out again with the pony phaeton, his suspicions became aroused, and he cross-questioned the man until the whole was out. It appeared from this report that Dick had been going about for nearly a month with a girl in the Vale—a Miss Van Tromp; that she lived near Lord Trevanion's upper wood; that recently Miss Van Tromp's papa had returned home from foreign parts after a prolonged absence; that this papa was an old gentleman, very chatty and free with his money in the public-house—whereupon Mr. Naseby's face became encrimsoned; that the papa, furthermore, was said to be an admiral—whereupon Mr. Naseby spat out a whistle brief and fierce as an oath; that Master Dick seemed very friendly with the papa—'God help him!' said Mr. Naseby; that last night Master Dick had not come in, and to-day he had driven away in the phaeton with the young lady—

'Young woman,' corrected Mr. Naseby.

'Yes, sir,' said the man, who had been unwilling enough to gossip from the first, and was now cowed by the effect of his communications on the master. 'Young woman, sir!'

'Had they luggage?' demanded the Squire.

'Yes, sir.'

Mr. Naseby was silent for a moment, struggling to keep down his emotion, and he mastered it so far as to mount into the sarcastic vein, when he was in the nearest danger of melting into the sorrowful.

'And was this—this Van Dunk with them?' he asked, dwelling scornfully upon the name.

The servant believed not, and being eager to shift the responsibility of speech to other shoulders, suggested that perhaps the master had better inquire further from George the stableman in person.

'Tell him to saddle the chestnut and come with me. He can take the gray gelding; for we may ride fast. And then you can take away this trash,' added Mr. Naseby, pointing to the luncheon; and he arose, lordly in his anger, and marched forth upon the terrace to await his horse.

There Dick's old nurse shrunk up to him, for the news went like wildfire over Naseby House, and timidly expressed a hope that there was nothing much amiss with the young master.

'I'll pull him through,' the Squire said grimly, as though he meant to pull him through a threshing-mill; 'I'll save him from this gang; God help him with the next! He has a taste for low company, and no natural affections to steady him. His father was no society for him; he must go fuddling with a Dutchman, Nance, and now he's caught. Let us pray he'll take the lesson,' he added more gravely, 'but youth is here to make troubles, and age to pull them out again.'

Nance whimpered and recalled several episodes of Dick's childhood, which moved Mr. Naseby to blow his nose and shake her hard by the hand; and then, the horse arriving opportunely, to get himself without delay into the saddle and canter off.

He rode straight, hot spur, to Thymebury, where, as was to be expected, he could glean no tidings of the runaways. They had not been seen at the George; they had not been seen at the station. The shadow darkened on Mr. Naseby's face; the junction did not occur to him; his last hope was for Van Tromp's cottage; thither he bade George guide him, and thither he followed, nursing grief, anxiety, and indignation in his heart.

'Here it is, sir,' said George stopping.

'What! on my own land!' he cried. 'How's this? I let this place to somebody—M'Whirter or M'Glashan.'

'Miss M'Glashan was the young lady's aunt, sir, I believe,' returned George.

'Ay—dummies,' said the Squire. 'I shall whistle for my rent too. Here, take my horse.'

The Admiral, this hot afternoon, was sitting by the window with a long glass. He already knew the Squire by sight, and now, seeing him dismount before the cottage and come striding through the garden, concluded without doubt he was there to ask for Esther's hand.

'This is why the girl is not yet home,' he thought: 'a very suitable delicacy on young Naseby's part.'

And he composed himself with some pomp, answered the loud rattle of the riding-whip upon the door with a dulcet invitation to enter, and coming forward with a bow and a smile, 'Mr. Naseby, I believe,' said he.

The Squire came armed for battle; took in his man from top to toe in one rapid and scornful glance, and decided on a course at once. He must let the fellow see that he understood him.

'You are Mr. Van Tromp?' he returned roughly, and without taking any notice of the proffered hand.

'The same, sir,' replied the Admiral. 'Pray be seated.'

'No sir,' said the Squire, point-blank, 'I will not be seated. I am told that you are an admiral,' he added.

'No sir, I am not an admiral,' returned Van Tromp, who now began to grow nettled and enter into the spirit of the interview.

'Then why do you call yourself one, sir?'

'I have to ask your pardon, I do not,' says Van Tromp, as grand as the Pope.

But nothing was of avail against the Squire.

'You sail under false colours from beginning to end,' he said. 'Your very house was taken under a sham name.'

'It is not my house. I am my daughter's guest,' replied the Admiral. 'If it *were* my house—'

'Well?' said the Squire, 'what then? hey?'

The Admiral looked at him nobly, but was silent.

'Look here,' said Mr. Naseby, 'this intimidation is a waste of time; it is thrown away on me, sir; it will not succeed with me. I will not permit you even to gain time by your fencing. Now, sir, I presume you understand what brings me here.'

'I am entirely at a loss to account for your intrusion,' bows and waves Van Tromp.

'I will try to tell you then. I come here as a father'—down came the riding-whip upon the table—'I have right and justice upon my side. I understand your calculations, but you calculated without me. I am a man of the world, and I see through you and your manœuvres. I am dealing now with a conspiracy—I stigmatise it as such, and I will expose it and crush it. And now I order you to tell me how far things have gone, and whither you have smuggled my unhappy son.'

'My God, sir!' Van Tromp broke out, 'I have had about enough of this. Your son? God knows where he is for me! What the devil have I to do with your son? My daughter is out, for the matter of that; I might ask you where she was, and what would you say to that? But this is all midsummer madness. Name your business distinctly, and be off.'

'How often am I to tell you?' cried the Squire. 'Where did your daughter take my son to-day in that cursed pony carriage?'

'In a pony carriage?' repeated Van Tromp.

'Yes, sir—with luggage.'

'Luggage?'—Van Tromp had turned a little pale.

'Luggage, I said—luggage!' shouted Naseby. 'You may spare me this dissimulation. Where's my son. You are speaking to a father, sir, a father.'

'But, sir, if this be true,' out came Van Tromp in a new key, 'it is I who have an explanation to demand?'

'Precisely. There is the conspiracy,' retorted Naseby. 'Oh!' he added, 'I am a man of the world. I can see through and through you.'

Van Tromp began to understand.

'You speak a great deal about being a father, Mr. Naseby,' said he; 'I believe you forget that the appellation is common to both of us. I am at a loss to figure to myself, however dimly, how any man—I have not said any gentleman—could so brazenly insult another as you have been insulting me since you entered this house. For the first time I appreciate your base insinuations, and I despise them and you. You were, I am told, a manufacturer; I am an artist; I have seen better days; I have moved in societies where you would not be received, and dined where you would be glad to pay a pound to see me dining. The so-called aristocracy of wealth, sir, I despise. I refuse to help you; I refuse to be helped by you. There lies the door.'

And the Admiral stood forth in a halo.

It was then that Dick entered. He had been waiting in the porch for some time back, and Esther had been listlessly standing by his side. He had put out his hand to bar her entrance, and she had submitted without surprise; and though she seemed to listen, she scarcely appeared to comprehend. Dick, on his part, was as white as a sheet; his eyes burned and his lips trembled with anger as he thrust the door suddenly open, introduced Esther with ceremonious gallantry, and stood forward and knocked his hat firmer on his head like a man about to leap.

'What is all this?' he demanded.

'Is this your father, Mr. Naseby?' inquired the Admiral.

'It is,' said the young man.

'I make you my compliments,' returned Van Tromp.

'Dick!' cried his father, suddenly breaking forth, 'it is not too late, is it? I have come here in time to save you. Come, come away with me—come away from this place.'

And he fawned upon Dick with his hands.

'Keep your hands off me,' cried Dick, not meaning unkindness, but because his nerves were shattered by so many successive miseries.

'No, no,' said the old man, 'don't repulse your father, Dick, when he has come here to save you. Don't repulse me, my boy. Perhaps I have not been kind to you, not quite considerate, too harsh; my boy, it was not for want of love. Think of old times. I was kind to you then, was I not? When you were a child, and your mother was with us.' Mr. Naseby was interrupted by a sort of sob. Dick stood looking at him in a maze. 'Come away,' pursued the father in a whisper; 'you need not be afraid of any consequences. I am a man of the world, Dick; and she can have no claim on you—no claim, I tell you; and we'll be handsome too, Dick—we'll give them a good round figure, father and daughter, and there's an end.'

He had been trying to get Dick towards the door, but the latter stood off.

'You had better take care, sir, how you insult that lady,' said the son, as black as night.

'You would not choose between your father and your mistress?' said the father.

'What do you call her, sir?' cried Dick, high and clear.

Forbearance and patience were not among Mr. Naseby's qualities.

'I called her your mistress,' he shouted, 'and I might have called her a—'

'That is an unmanly lie,' replied Dick, slowly.

'Dick!' cried the father, 'Dick!'

'I do not care,' said the son, strengthening himself against his own heart; 'I—I have said it, and it is the truth.'

There was a pause.

'Dick,' said the old man at last, in a voice that was shaken as by a gale of wind, 'I am going. I leave you with your friends, sir—with your friends. I came to serve you, and now I go away a broken man. For years I have seen this coming, and now it has come. You never loved me. Now you have been the death of me. You may boast of that. Now I leave you. God pardon you.'

With that he was gone; and the three who remained together heard his horse's hoofs descend the lane. Esther had not made a sign throughout the interview, and still kept silence now that it was over; but the Admiral, who had once or twice moved forward and drawn back again, now advanced for good.

'You are a man of spirit, sir,' said he to Dick; 'but though I am no friend to parental interference, I will say that you were heavy on the governor.' Then he added with a chuckle: 'You began, Richard, with a silver spoon, and here you are in the water like the rest. Work, work, nothing like work. You have parts, you have manners; why, with application you may die a millionaire!' Dick shook himself. He took Esther by the hand, looking at her mournfully.

'Then this is farewell,' he said.

'Yes,' she answered. There was no tone in her voice, and she did not return his gaze.

'For ever,' added Dick.

'For ever,' she repeated mechanically.

'I have had hard measure,' he continued. 'In time I believe I could have shown you I was worthy, and there was no time long enough to show how much I loved you. But it was not to be. I have lost all.'

He relinquished her hand, still looking at her, and she turned to leave the room.

'Why, what in fortune's name is the meaning of all this?' cried Van Tromp. 'Esther come back!'

'Let her go,' said Dick, and he watched her disappear with strangely mingled feelings. For he had fallen into that stage when men have the vertigo of misfortune, court the strokes of destiny, and rush towards anything decisive, that it may free them from suspense though at the cost of ruin. It is one of the many minor forms of suicide.

'She did not love me,' he said, turning to her father.

'I feared as much,' said he, 'when I sounded her. Poor Dick, poor Dick. And yet I believe I am as much cut up as you are. I was born to see others happy.'

'You forget,' returned Dick, with something like a sneer, 'that I am now a pauper.'

Van Tromp snapped his fingers.

'Tut!' said he; 'Esther has plenty for us all.'

Dick looked at him with some wonder. It had never dawned upon him that this shiftless, thriftless, worthless, sponging parasite was yet, after and in spite of all, not mercenary in the issue of his thoughts; yet so it was.

'Now,' said Dick, 'I must go.'

'Go?' cried Van Tromp. 'Where? Not one foot, Mr. Richard Naseby. Here you shall stay in the meantime! and—well, and do something practical—advertise for a situation as private secretary—and when you have it, go and welcome. But in the meantime, sir, no false pride; we must stay with our friends; we must sponge a while on Papa Van Tromp, who has sponged so often upon us.'

'By God,' cried Dick, 'I believe you are the best of the lot.'

'Dick, my boy,' replied the Admiral, winking, 'you mark me, I am not the worst.'

'Then why,' began Dick, and then paused. 'But Esther,' he began again, once more to interrupt himself. 'The fact is, Admiral,' he came out with it roundly now, 'your daughter wished to run away from you to-day, and I only brought her back with difficulty.'

'In the pony carriage?' asked the Admiral, with the silliness of extreme surprise.

'Yes,' Dick answered.

'Why, what the devil was she running away from?'

Dick found the question unusually hard to answer.

'Why,' said he, 'you know, you're a bit of a rip.'

'I behave to that girl, sir, like an archdeacon,' replied Van Tromp warmly.

'Well—excuse me—but you know you drink,' insisted Dick.

'I know that I was a sheet in the wind's eye, sir, once—once only, since I reached this place,' retorted the Admiral. 'And even then I was fit for any drawing-room. I should like you to tell me how many fathers, lay and clerical, go upstairs every day with a face like a lobster and cod's eyes—and are dull, upon the back of it—not even mirth for the money! No, if that's what she runs for, all I say is, let her run.'

'You see,' Dick tried it again, 'she has fancies—'

'Confound her fancies!' cried Van Tromp. 'I used her kindly; she had her own way; I was her father. Besides I had taken quite a liking to the girl, and meant to stay with her for good. But I tell you what it is, Dick, since she has trifled with you—Oh, yes, she did though!—and since her old papa's not good enough for her—the devil take her, say I.'

'You will be kind to her at least?' said Dick.

'I never was unkind to a living soul,' replied the Admiral. 'Firm I can be, but not unkind.'

'Well,' said Dick, offering his hand, 'God bless you, and farewell.'

The Admiral swore by all his gods he should not go. 'Dick,' he said, 'You are a selfish dog; you forget your old Admiral. You wouldn't leave him alone, would you?'

It was useless to remind him that the house was not his to dispose of, that being a class of considerations to which his intelligence was closed; so Dick tore himself off by force, and, shouting a good-bye, made off along the lane to Thymebury.

9

IN WHICH THE LIBERAL EDITOR RE-APPEARS AS 'DEUS EX MACHINA'

IT WAS PERHAPS A WEEK LATER, as old Mr. Naseby sat brooding in his study, that there was shown in upon him, on urgent business, a little hectic gentleman shabbily attired.

'I have to ask pardon for this intrusion, Mr. Naseby,' he said; 'but I come here to perform a duty. My card has been sent in, but perhaps you may not know, what it does not tell you, that I am the editor of the *Thymebury Star*.'

Mr. Naseby looked up, indignant.

'I cannot fancy,' he said, 'that we have much in common to discuss.'

'I have only a word to say—one piece of information to communicate. Some months ago, we had—you will pardon my referring to it, it is absolutely necessary—but we had an unfortunate difference as to facts.'

'Have you come to apologise?' asked the Squire, sternly.

'No, sir; to mention a circumstance. On the morning in question, your son, Mr. Richard Naseby—'

'I do not permit his name to be mentioned.'

'You will, however, permit me,' replied the Editor.

'You are cruel,' said the Squire. He was right, he was a broken man.

Then the Editor described Dick's warning visit; and how he had seen in the lad's eye that there was a thrashing in the wind, and had escaped through pity only—so the Editor put it—'through pity only sir. And oh, sir,' he went on, 'if you had seen him speaking up for you, I am sure you would have been proud of your son. I know I admired the lad myself, and indeed that's what brings me here.'

'I have misjudged him,' said the Squire. 'Do you know where he is?'

'Yes, sir, he lies sick at Thymebury.'

'You can take me to him?'

'I can.'

'I pray God he may forgive me,' said the father.

And he and the Editor made post-haste for the country town.

Next day the report went abroad that Mr. Richard was reconciled to his father and had been taken home to Naseby House. He was still ailing, it was said, and the Squire nursed him like the proverbial woman. Rumour, in this instance, did no more than justice to the truth; and over the sickbed many confidences were exchanged, and clouds that had been growing for years passed away in a few hours, and as fond mankind loves to hope, for ever. Many long talks had been fruitless in external action, though fruitful for the understanding of the pair; but at last, one showery Tuesday, the Squire might have been observed upon his way to the cottage in the lane.

The old gentleman had arranged his features with a view to self-command, rather than external cheerfulness; and he entered the cottage on his visit of conciliation with the bearing of a clergyman come to announce a death.

The Admiral and his daughter were both within, and both looked upon their visitor with more surprise than favour.

'Sir,' said he to Van Tromp, 'I am told I have done you much injustice.'

There came a little sound in Esther's throat, and she put her hand suddenly to her heart.

'You have, sir; and the acknowledgment suffices,' replied the Admiral. 'I am prepared, sir, to be easy with you, since I hear you have made it up with my friend Dick. But let me remind you that you owe some apologies to this young lady also.'

'I shall have the temerity to ask for more than her forgiveness,' said the Squire. 'Miss Van Tromp,' he continued, 'once I was in great distress, and knew nothing of you or your character; but I believe you will pardon a few rough words to an old man who asks forgiveness from his heart. I have heard much of you since then; for you have a fervent advocate in my house. I believe you will understand that I speak of my son. He is, I regret to say, very far from well; he does not pick up as the doctors had expected; he has a great deal upon his mind, and, to tell you the truth, my girl, if you won't help us, I am afraid I shall lose him. Come now, forgive him! I was angry with him once myself, and I found I was in the wrong. This is only a misunderstanding, like the other, believe me; and with one kind movement, you may give happiness to him, and to me, and to yourself.'

Esther made a movement towards the door, but long before she reached it she had broken forth sobbing.

'It is all right,' said the Admiral; 'I understand the sex. Let me make you my compliments, Mr. Naseby.'

The Squire was too much relieved to be angry.

'My dear,' said he to Esther, 'you must not agitate yourself.'

'She had better go up and see him right away,' suggested Van Tromp.

'I had not ventured to propose it,' replied the Squire. '*Les convenances,* I believe—'

'*Je m'en fiche,*' cried the Admiral, snapping his fingers. 'She shall go and see my friend Dick. Run and get ready, Esther.'

Esther obeyed.

'She has not—has not run away again?' inquired Mr. Naseby, as soon as she was gone.

'No,' said Van Tromp, 'not again. She is a devilish odd girl though, mind you that.'

'But I cannot stomach the man with the carbuncles,' thought the Squire.

And this is why there is a new household and a brand-new baby in Naseby Dower House; and why the great Van Tromp lives in pleasant style upon the shores of England; and why twenty-six individual copies of the *Thymebury Star* are received daily at the door of Naseby House.

THE BODY SNATCHER

THE BODY SNATCHER

EVERY NIGHT IN THE YEAR, four of us sat in the small parlour of the George at Debenham—the undertaker, and the landlord, and Fettes, and myself. Sometimes there would be more; but blow high, blow low, come rain or snow or frost, we four would be each planted in his own particular arm-chair. Fettes was an old drunken Scotchman, a man of education obviously, and a man of some property, since he lived in idleness. He had come to Debenham years ago, while still young, and by a mere continuance of living had grown to be an adopted townsman. His blue camlet cloak was a local antiquity, like the church-spire. His place in the parlour at the George, his absence from church, his old, crapulous, disreputable vices, were all things of course in Debenham. He had some vague Radical opinions and some fleeting infidelities, which he would now and again set forth and emphasise with tottering slaps upon the table. He drank rum—five glasses regularly every evening; and for the greater portion of his nightly visit to the George sat, with his glass in his right hand, in a state of melancholy alcoholic saturation. We called him the Doctor, for he was supposed to have some special knowledge of medicine, and had been known, upon a pinch, to set a fracture or reduce a dislocation; but beyond these slight particulars, we had no knowledge of his character and antecedents.

One dark winter night—it had struck nine some time before the landlord joined us—there was a sick man in the George, a great neighbouring proprietor suddenly struck down with apoplexy on his way to Parliament; and the great man's still greater London doctor had been telegraphed to his bedside. It was the first time that such a thing had happened in Debenham, for the railway was but newly open, and we were all proportionately moved by the occurrence.

'He's come,' said the landlord, after he had filled and lighted his pipe.

'He?' said I. 'Who?—not the doctor?'

'Himself,' replied our host.

'What is his name?'

'Doctor Macfarlane,' said the landlord.

Fettes was far through his third tumbler, stupidly fuddled, now nodding over, now staring mazily around him; but at the last word he seemed to awaken, and repeated the name 'Macfarlane' twice, quietly enough the first time, but with sudden emotion at the second.

'Yes,' said the landlord, 'that's his name, Doctor Wolfe Macfarlane.'

Fettes became instantly sober; his eyes awoke, his voice became clear, loud, and steady, his language forcible and earnest. We were all startled by the transformation, as if a man had risen from the dead.

'I beg your pardon,' he said, 'I am afraid I have not been paying much attention to your talk. Who is this Wolfe Macfarlane?' And then, when he had heard the landlord out, 'It cannot be, it cannot be,' he added; 'and yet I would like well to see him face to face.'

'Do you know him, Doctor?' asked the undertaker, with a gasp.

'God forbid!' was the reply. 'And yet the name is a strange one; it were too much to fancy two. Tell me, landlord, is he old?'

'Well,' said the host, 'he's not a young man, to be sure, and his hair is white; but he looks younger than you.'

'He is older, though; years older. But,' with a slap upon the table, 'it's the rum you see in my face—rum and sin. This man, perhaps, may have an easy conscience and a good digestion. Conscience! Hear me speak. You would think I was some good, old, decent Christian, would you not? But no, not I; I never canted. Voltaire might have canted if he'd stood in my shoes; but the brains'—with a rattling fillip on his bald head—'the brains were clear and active, and I saw and made no deductions.'

'If you know this doctor,' I ventured to remark, after a somewhat awful pause, 'I should gather that you do not share the landlord's good opinion.'

Fettes paid no regard to me.

'Yes,' he said, with sudden decision, 'I must see him face to face.'

There was another pause, and then a door was closed rather sharply on the first floor, and a step was heard upon the stair.

'That's the doctor,' cried the landlord. 'Look sharp, and you can catch him.'

It was but two steps from the small parlour to the door of the old George Inn; the wide oak staircase landed almost in the street; there was room for a Turkey rug and nothing more between the threshold and the last round of the descent; but this little space was every evening brilliantly lit up, not only by the light upon the stair and the great signal-lamp below the sign, but by the warm radiance of the bar-room window. The George thus brightly advertised itself to passers-by in the cold street. Fettes walked steadily to the spot, and we, who were hanging behind, beheld the two men meet, as one of them had phrased it, face to face. Dr. Macfarlane was alert and vigorous. His white hair set off his pale and placid, although energetic, countenance. He was richly dressed in the finest of broadcloth and the whitest of linen, with a great gold watch-chain, and studs and spectacles of the same precious material. He wore a broad-folded tie, white and speckled with lilac, and he carried on his arm a comfortable driving-coat of fur. There was no doubt but he became his years, breathing, as he did, of wealth and consideration; and it was a surprising contrast to see our parlour sot—bald, dirty, pimpled, and robed in his old camlet cloak—confront him at the bottom of the stairs.

'Macfarlane!' he said somewhat loudly, more like a herald than a friend.

The great doctor pulled up short on the fourth step, as though the familiarity of the address surprised and somewhat shocked his dignity.

'Toddy Macfarlane!' repeated Fettes.

The London man almost staggered. He stared for the swiftest of seconds at the man before him, glanced behind him with a sort of scare, and then in a startled whisper, 'Fettes!' he said, 'You!'

'Ay,' said the other, 'me! Did you think I was dead too? We are not so easy shut of our acquaintance.'

'Hush, hush!' exclaimed the doctor. 'Hush, hush! this meeting is so unexpected—I can see you are unmanned. I hardly knew you, I confess, at first; but I am overjoyed—overjoyed to have this opportunity. For the present it must be how-d'ye-do and good-bye in one, for my fly is waiting, and I must not fail the train; but you shall—let me see—yes—you shall give me your address, and you can count on early news of me. We must do something for you, Fettes. I fear you are out at elbows; but we must see to that for auld lang syne, as once we sang at suppers.'

'Money!' cried Fettes; 'money from you! The money that I had from you is lying where I cast it in the rain.'

Dr. Macfarlane had talked himself into some measure of superiority and confidence, but the uncommon energy of this refusal cast him back into his first confusion.

A horrible, ugly look came and went across his almost venerable countenance. 'My dear fellow,' he said, 'be it as you please; my last thought is to offend you. I would intrude on none. I will leave you my address, however—'

'I do not wish it—I do not wish to know the roof that shelters you,' interrupted the other. 'I heard your name; I feared it might be you; I wished to know if, after all, there were a God; I know now that there is none. Begone!'

He still stood in the middle of the rug, between the stair and doorway; and the great London physician, in order to escape, would be forced to step to one side. It was plain that he hesitated before the thought of this humiliation. White as he was, there was a dangerous glitter in his spectacles; but while he still paused uncertain, he became aware that the driver of his fly was peering in from the street at this unusual scene and caught a glimpse at the same time of our little body from the parlour, huddled by the corner of the bar. The presence of so many witnesses decided him at once to flee. He crouched together, brushing on the wainscot, and made a dart like a serpent, striking for the door. But his tribulation was not yet entirely at an end, for even as he was passing Fettes clutched him by the arm and these words came in a whisper, and yet painfully distinct, 'Have you seen it again?'

The great rich London doctor cried out aloud with a sharp, throttling cry; he dashed his questioner across the open space, and, with his hands over his head, fled out of the door like a detected thief. Before it had occurred to one of us to make a movement the fly was already rattling toward the station. The scene was over like a dream, but the dream had left proofs and traces of its passage. Next day the servant found the fine gold spectacles broken on the threshold, and that very night we were all standing breathless by the bar-room window, and Fettes at our side, sober, pale, and resolute in look.

'God protect us, Mr. Fettes!' said the landlord, coming first into possession of his customary senses. 'What in the universe is all this? These are strange things you have been saying.'

Fettes turned toward us; he looked us each in succession in the face. 'See if you can hold your tongues,' said he. 'That man Macfarlane is not safe to cross; those that have done so already have repented it too late.'

And then, without so much as finishing his third glass, far less waiting for the other two, he bade us good-bye and went forth, under the lamp of the hotel, into the black night.

We three turned to our places in the parlour, with the big red fire and four clear candles; and as we recapitulated what had passed, the first chill of our surprise soon changed into a glow of curiosity. We sat late; it was the latest session I have known in the old George. Each man, before we parted, had his theory that he was bound to prove; and none of us had any nearer business in this world than to track out the past of our condemned companion, and surprise the secret that he shared with the great London doctor. It is no great boast, but I believe I was a better hand at worming out a story than either of my fellows at the George; and perhaps there is now no other man alive who could narrate to you the following foul and unnatural events.

In his young days Fettes studied medicine in the schools of Edinburgh. He had talent of a kind, the talent that picks up swiftly what it hears and readily retails it for its own. He worked little at home; but he was civil, attentive, and intelligent in the presence of his masters. They soon picked him out as a lad who listened closely and remembered well; nay, strange as it seemed to me when I first heard it, he was in those days well favoured, and pleased by his exterior. There was, at that period, a certain extramural teacher of anatomy, whom I shall here designate by the letter K. His name was subsequently too well known. The man who bore it skulked through the streets of Edinburgh in disguise, while the mob that applauded at the execution of Burke called loudly for the blood of his employer. But Mr. K— was then at the top of his vogue; he enjoyed a popularity due partly to his own talent and address, partly to the incapacity of his rival, the university professor. The students, at least, swore by his name, and Fettes believed himself, and was believed by others, to have laid the foundations of success when he had acquired the favour of this meteorically famous man. Mr. K— was a *bon vivant* as well as an accomplished teacher; he liked a sly illusion no less than a careful preparation. In both capacities Fettes enjoyed and deserved his notice, and by the second year of his attendance he held the half-regular position of second demonstrator or sub-assistant in his class.

In this capacity the charge of the theatre and lecture-room devolved in particular upon his shoulders. He had to answer for the cleanliness of the premises and the conduct of the other students, and it was a part of his duty to supply, receive, and divide the various subjects. It was with a view to this last—at that time very delicate—affair that he was lodged by Mr. K— in the same wynd, and at last in the same building, with the dissecting-rooms. Here, after a night of turbulent pleasures, his hand still tottering, his sight still misty and confused, he would be called out of bed in the black hours before the winter dawn by the unclean and desperate interlopers who supplied the table. He would open the door to these men, since infamous throughout the land. He would help them with their tragic burden, pay them their sordid price, and remain alone, when they were gone, with the unfriendly relics of humanity. From such a scene he would return to snatch another hour or two of slumber, to repair the abuses of the night, and refresh himself for the labours of the day.

Few lads could have been more insensible to the impressions of a life thus passed among the ensigns of mortality. His mind was closed against all general considerations. He was incapable of interest in the fate and fortunes of another, the slave of his own desires and low ambitions. Cold, light, and selfish in the last resort, he had that modicum of prudence, miscalled morality, which keeps a man from inconvenient drunkenness or punishable theft. He coveted, besides, a measure of consideration from his masters and his fellow-pupils, and he had no desire to fail conspicuously in the external parts of life. Thus he made it his pleasure to gain some distinction in his studies, and day after day rendered unimpeachable eye-service to his employer, Mr. K—. For his day of work he indemnified himself by nights of roaring, blackguardly enjoyment; and when that balance had been struck, the organ that he called his conscience declared itself content.

The supply of subjects was a continual trouble to him as well as to his master. In that large and busy class, the raw material of the anatomists kept perpetually running out; and the business thus rendered necessary was not only unpleasant in itself, but threatened dangerous consequences to all who were concerned. It was the policy of Mr. K— to ask no questions in his dealings with the trade. 'They bring the body, and we pay the price,' he used to say, dwelling on the alliteration—'*quid pro quo*.' And, again, and somewhat profanely, 'Ask no questions,' he would tell his assistants, 'for conscience' sake.' There was no understanding that the subjects were provided by the crime of murder. Had that idea been broached to him in words, he would have recoiled in horror; but the lightness of his speech upon so grave a matter was, in itself, an offence against good manners, and a temptation to the men with whom he dealt. Fettes, for instance, had often remarked to himself upon the singular freshness of the bodies. He had been struck again and again by the hang-dog, abominable looks of the ruffians who came to him before the dawn; and putting things together clearly in his private thoughts, he perhaps attributed a meaning too immoral and too categorical to the unguarded counsels of his master. He understood his duty, in short, to have three branches: to take what was brought, to pay the price, and to avert the eye from any evidence of crime.

One November morning this policy of silence was put sharply to the test. He had been awake all night with a racking toothache—pacing his room like a caged beast or throwing himself in fury on his bed—and had fallen at last into that profound, uneasy slumber that so often follows on a night of pain, when he was awakened by the third or fourth angry repetition of the concerted signal. There was a thin, bright moonshine; it was bitter cold, windy, and frosty; the town had not yet awakened, but an indefinable stir already preluded the noise and business of the day. The ghouls had come later than usual, and they seemed more than usually eager to be gone. Fettes, sick with sleep, lighted them upstairs. He heard their grumbling Irish voices through a dream; and as they stripped the sack from their sad merchandise he leaned dozing, with his shoulder propped against the wall; he had to shake himself to find the men their money. As he did so his eyes lighted on the dead face. He started; he took two steps nearer, with the candle raised.

'God Almighty!' he cried. 'That is Jane Galbraith!'

The men answered nothing, but they shuffled nearer the door.

'I know her, I tell you,' he continued. 'She was alive and hearty yesterday. It's impossible she can be dead; it's impossible you should have got this body fairly.'

'Sure, sir, you're mistaken entirely,' said one of the men.

But the other looked Fettes darkly in the eyes, and demanded the money on the spot.

It was impossible to misconceive the threat or to exaggerate the danger. The lad's heart failed him. He stammered some excuses, counted out the sum, and saw his hateful visitors depart. No sooner were they gone than he hastened to confirm his doubts. By a dozen unquestionable marks he identified the girl he had jested with the day before. He saw, with horror, marks upon her body that might well betoken violence. A panic seized him, and he took refuge in his room. There he reflected at length over the discovery that he had made; considered soberly the bearing of Mr. K—'s instructions and the danger to himself of interference in so serious a business, and at last, in sore perplexity, determined to wait for the advice of his immediate superior, the class assistant.

This was a young doctor, Wolfe Macfarlane, a high favourite among all the reckless students, clever, dissipated, and unscrupulous to the last degree. He had travelled and studied abroad. His manners were agreeable and a little forward. He was an authority on the stage, skilful on the ice or the links with skate or golf-club; he dressed with nice audacity, and, to put the finishing touch upon his glory, he kept a gig and a strong trotting-horse. With Fettes he was on terms of intimacy; indeed, their relative positions called for some community of life; and when subjects were scarce the pair would drive far into the country in Macfarlane's gig, visit and desecrate some lonely graveyard, and return before dawn with their booty to the door of the dissecting-room.

On that particular morning Macfarlane arrived somewhat earlier than his wont. Fettes heard him, and met him on the stairs, told him his story, and showed him the cause of his alarm. Macfarlane examined the marks on her body.

'Yes,' he said with a nod, 'it looks fishy.'

'Well, what should I do?' asked Fettes.

'Do?' repeated the other. 'Do you want to do anything? Least said soonest mended, I should say.'

'Some one else might recognise her,' objected Fettes. 'She was as well known as the Castle Rock.'

'We'll hope not,' said Macfarlane, 'and if anybody does—well, you didn't, don't you see, and there's an end. The fact is, this has been going on too long. Stir up the mud, and you'll get K— into the most unholy trouble; you'll be in a shocking box yourself. So will I, if you come to that. I should like to know how any one of us would look, or what the devil we should have to say for ourselves, in any Christian witness-box. For me, you know there's one thing certain—that, practically speaking, all our subjects have been murdered.'

'Macfarlane!' cried Fettes.

'Come now!' sneered the other. 'As if you hadn't suspected it yourself!'

'Suspecting is one thing—'

'And proof another. Yes, I know; and I'm as sorry as you are this should have come here,' tapping the body with his cane. 'The next best thing for me is not to recognise it; and,' he added coolly, 'I don't. You may, if you please. I don't dictate, but I think a man of the world would do as I do; and I may add, I fancy that is what K— would look for at our hands. The question is, Why did he choose us two for his assistants? And I answer, because he didn't want old wives.'

This was the tone of all others to affect the mind of a lad like Fettes. He agreed to imitate Macfarlane. The body of the unfortunate girl was duly dissected, and no one remarked or appeared to recognise her.

One afternoon, when his day's work was over, Fettes dropped into a popular tavern and found Macfarlane sitting with a stranger. This was a small man, very pale and dark, with coal-black eyes. The cut of his features gave a promise of intellect and refinement which was but feebly realised in his manners, for he proved, upon a nearer acquaintance, coarse, vulgar, and stupid. He exercised, however, a very remarkable control over Macfarlane; issued orders like the Great Bashaw; became inflamed at the least discussion or delay, and commented rudely on the servility with which he was obeyed. This most offensive person took a fancy to Fettes on the spot, plied him with drinks, and honoured him with unusual confidences on his past career. If a tenth part of what he confessed were true, he was a very loathsome rogue; and the lad's vanity was tickled by the attention of so experienced a man.

'I'm a pretty bad fellow myself,' the stranger remarked, 'but Macfarlane is the boy—Toddy Macfarlane I call him. Toddy, order your friend another glass.' Or it might be, 'Toddy, you jump up and shut the door.' 'Toddy hates me,' he said again. 'Oh yes, Toddy, you do!'

'Don't you call me that confounded name,' growled Macfarlane.

'Hear him! Did you ever see the lads play knife? He would like to do that all over my body,' remarked the stranger.

'We medicals have a better way than that,' said Fettes. 'When we dislike a dead friend of ours, we dissect him.'

Macfarlane looked up sharply, as though this jest were scarcely to his mind.

The afternoon passed. Gray, for that was the stranger's name, invited Fettes to join them at dinner, ordered a feast so sumptuous that the tavern was thrown into commotion, and when all was done commanded Macfarlane to settle the bill. It was late before they separated; the man Gray was incapably drunk. Macfarlane, sobered by his fury, chewed the cud of the money he had been forced to squander and the slights he had been obliged to swallow. Fettes, with various liquors singing in his head, returned home with devious footsteps and a mind entirely in abeyance. Next day Macfarlane was absent from the class, and Fettes smiled to himself as he imagined him still squiring the intolerable Gray from tavern to tavern. As soon as the hour of liberty had struck he posted from place to place in quest of his last night's companions. He could find them, however, nowhere; so returned early to his rooms, went early to bed, and slept the sleep of the just.

At four in the morning he was awakened by the well-known signal. Descending to the door, he was filled with astonishment to find Macfarlane with his gig, and in the gig one of those long and ghastly packages with which he was so well acquainted.

'What?' he cried. 'Have you been out alone? How did you manage?'

But Macfarlane silenced him roughly, bidding him turn to business. When they had got the body upstairs and laid it on the table, Macfarlane made at first as if he were going away. Then he paused and seemed to hesitate; and then, 'You had better look at the face,' said he, in tones of some constraint. 'You had better,' he repeated, as Fettes only stared at him in wonder.

'But where, and how, and when did you come by it?' cried the other.

'Look at the face,' was the only answer.

Fettes was staggered; strange doubts assailed him. He looked from the young doctor to the body, and then back again. At last, with a start, he did as he was bidden. He had almost expected the sight that met his eyes, and yet the shock was cruel. To see, fixed in the rigidity of death and naked on that coarse layer of sackcloth, the man whom he had left well clad and full of meat and sin upon the threshold of a tavern, awoke, even in the thoughtless Fettes, some of the terrors of the conscience. It was a *cras tibi* which re-echoed in his soul, that two whom he had known should have come to lie upon these icy tables. Yet these were only secondary thoughts. His first concern regarded Wolfe. Unprepared for a challenge so momentous, he knew not how to look his comrade in the face. He durst not meet his eye, and he had neither words nor voice at his command.

It was Macfarlane himself who made the first advance. He came up quietly behind and laid his hand gently but firmly on the other's shoulder.

'Richardson,' said he, 'may have the head.'

Now Richardson was a student who had long been anxious for that portion of the human subject to dissect. There was no answer, and the murderer resumed: 'Talking of business, you must pay me; your accounts, you see, must tally.'

Fettes found a voice, the ghost of his own: 'Pay you!' he cried. 'Pay you for that?'

'Why, yes, of course you must. By all means and on every possible account, you must,' returned the other. 'I dare not give it for nothing, you dare not take it for nothing; it would compromise us both. This is another case like Jane Galbraith's. The more things are wrong the more we must act as if all were right. Where does old K— keep his money?'

'There,' answered Fettes hoarsely, pointing to a cupboard in the corner.

'Give me the key, then,' said the other, calmly, holding out his hand.

There was an instant's hesitation, and the die was cast. Macfarlane could not suppress a nervous twitch, the infinitesimal mark of an immense relief, as he felt the key between his fingers. He opened the cupboard, brought out pen and ink and a paper-book that stood in one compartment, and separated from the funds in a drawer a sum suitable to the occasion.

'Now, look here,' he said, 'there is the payment made—first proof of your good faith: first step to your security. You have now to clinch it by a second. Enter the payment in your book, and then you for your part may defy the devil.'

The next few seconds were for Fettes an agony of thought; but in balancing his terrors it was the most immediate that triumphed. Any future difficulty seemed almost welcome if he could avoid a present quarrel with Macfarlane. He set down the candle which he had been carrying all this time, and with a steady hand entered the date, the nature, and the amount of the transaction.

'And now,' said Macfarlane, 'it's only fair that you should pocket the lucre. I've had my share already. By the bye, when a man of the world falls into a bit of luck, has a few shillings extra in his pocket—I'm ashamed to speak of it, but there's a rule of conduct in the case. No treating, no purchase of expensive class-books, no squaring of old debts; borrow, don't lend.'

'Macfarlane,' began Fettes, still somewhat hoarsely, 'I have put my neck in a halter to oblige you.'

'To oblige me?' cried Wolfe. 'Oh, come! You did, as near as I can see the matter, what you downright had to do in self-defence. Suppose I got into trouble, where would you be? This second little matter flows clearly from the first. Mr. Gray is the continuation of Miss Galbraith. You can't begin and then stop. If you begin, you must keep on beginning; that's the truth. No rest for the wicked.'

A horrible sense of blackness and the treachery of fate seized hold upon the soul of the unhappy student.

'My God!' he cried, 'but what have I done? and when did I begin? To be made a class assistant—in the name of reason, where's the harm in that? Service wanted the position; Service might have got it. Would *he* have been where *I* am now?'

'My dear fellow,' said Macfarlane, 'what a boy you are! What harm *has* come to you? What harm *can* come to you if you hold your tongue? Why, man, do you know what this life is? There are two squads of us—the lions and the lambs. If you're a lamb, you'll come to lie upon these tables like Gray or Jane Galbraith; if you're a lion, you'll live and drive a horse like me, like K—, like all the world with any wit or courage. You're staggered at the first. But look at K—! My dear fellow, you're clever, you have pluck. I like you, and K— likes you. You were born to lead the hunt; and I tell you, on my honour and my experience of life, three days from now you'll laugh at all these scarecrows like a High School boy at a farce.'

And with that Macfarlane took his departure and drove off up the wynd in his gig to get under cover before daylight. Fettes was thus left alone with his regrets. He saw the miserable peril in which he stood involved. He saw, with inexpressible dismay, that there was no limit to his weakness, and that, from concession to concession, he had fallen from the arbiter of Macfarlane's destiny to his paid and helpless accomplice. He would have given the world to have been a little braver at the time, but it did not occur to him that he might still be brave. The secret of Jane Galbraith and the cursed entry in the day-book closed his mouth.

Hours passed; the class began to arrive; the members of the unhappy Gray were dealt out to one and to another, and received without remark. Richardson was made happy with the head; and before the hour of freedom rang Fettes trembled with exultation to perceive how far they had already gone toward safety.

For two days he continued to watch, with increasing joy, the dreadful process of disguise.

On the third day Macfarlane made his appearance. He had been ill, he said; but he made up for lost time by the energy with which he directed the students. To Richardson in particular he extended the most valuable assistance and advice, and that student, encouraged by the praise of the demonstrator, burned high with ambitious hopes, and saw the medal already in his grasp.

Before the week was out Macfarlane's prophecy had been fulfilled. Fettes had outlived his terrors and had forgotten his baseness. He began to plume himself upon his courage, and had so arranged the story in his mind that he could look back on these events with an unhealthy pride. Of his accomplice he saw but little. They met, of course, in the business of the class; they received their orders together from Mr. K—. At times they had a word or two in private, and

Macfarlane was from first to last particularly kind and jovial. But it was plain that he avoided any reference to their common secret; and even when Fettes whispered to him that he had cast in his lot with the lions and foresworn the lambs, he only signed to him smilingly to hold his peace.

At length an occasion arose which threw the pair once more into a closer union. Mr. K— was again short of subjects; pupils were eager, and it was a part of this teacher's pretensions to be always well supplied. At the same time there came the news of a burial in the rustic graveyard of Glencorse. Time has little changed the place in question. It stood then, as now, upon a cross road, out of call of human habitations, and buried fathom deep in the foliage of six cedar trees. The cries of the sheep upon the neighbouring hills, the streamlets upon either hand, one loudly singing among pebbles, the other dripping furtively from pond to pond, the stir of the wind in mountainous old flowering chestnuts, and once in seven days the voice of the bell and the old tunes of the precentor, were the only sounds that disturbed the silence around the rural church. The Resurrection Man—to use a byname of the period—was not to be deterred by any of the sanctities of customary piety. It was part of his trade to despise and desecrate the scrolls and trumpets of old tombs, the paths worn by the feet of worshippers and mourners, and the offerings and the inscriptions of bereaved affection. To rustic neighbourhoods, where love is more than commonly tenacious, and where some bonds of blood or fellowship unite the entire society of a parish, the body-snatcher, far from being repelled by natural respect, was attracted by the ease and safety of the task. To bodies that had been laid in earth, in joyful expectation of a far different awakening, there came that hasty, lamp-lit, terror-haunted resurrection of the spade and mattock. The coffin was forced, the cerements torn, and the melancholy relics, clad in sackcloth, after being rattled for hours on moonless byways, were at length exposed to uttermost indignities before a class of gaping boys.

Somewhat as two vultures may swoop upon a dying lamb, Fettes and Macfarlane were to be let loose upon a grave in that green and quiet resting-place. The wife of a farmer, a woman who had lived for sixty years, and been known for nothing but good butter and a godly conversation, was to be rooted from her grave at midnight and carried, dead and naked, to that far-away city that she had always honoured with her Sunday's best; the place beside her family was to be empty till the crack of doom; her innocent and almost venerable members to be exposed to that last curiosity of the anatomist.

Late one afternoon the pair set forth, well wrapped in cloaks and furnished with a formidable bottle. It rained without remission—a cold, dense, lashing rain. Now and again there blew a puff of wind, but these sheets of falling water kept it down. Bottle and all, it was a sad and silent drive as far as Penicuik, where they were to spend the evening. They stopped once, to hide their implements in a thick bush not far from the churchyard, and once again at the Fisher's Tryst, to have a toast before the kitchen fire and vary their nips of whisky with a glass of ale. When they reached their journey's end the gig was housed, the horse was fed and comforted, and the two young doctors in a private room sat down to the best dinner and the best wine the house afforded. The lights, the fire, the beating rain upon the window, the cold, incongruous work that lay before them, added zest to their enjoyment of the meal. With every glass their cordiality increased. Soon Macfarlane handed a little pile of gold to his companion.

'A compliment,' he said. 'Between friends these little d-d accommodations ought to fly like pipe-lights.'

Fettes pocketed the money, and applauded the sentiment to the echo. 'You are a philosopher,' he cried. 'I was an ass till I knew you. You and K— between you, by the Lord Harry! but you'll make a man of me.'

'Of course we shall,' applauded Macfarlane. 'A man? I tell you, it required a man to back me up the other morning. There are some big, brawling, forty-year-old cowards who would have turned sick at the look of the d-d thing; but not you—you kept your head. I watched you.'

'Well, and why not?' Fettes thus vaunted himself. 'It was no affair of mine. There was nothing to gain on the one side but disturbance, and on the other I could count on your gratitude, don't you see?' And he slapped his pocket till the gold pieces rang.

Macfarlane somehow felt a certain touch of alarm at these unpleasant words. He may have regretted that he had taught his young companion so successfully, but he had no time to interfere, for the other noisily continued in this boastful strain:—

'The great thing is not to be afraid. Now, between you and me, I don't want to hang—that's practical; but for all cant, Macfarlane, I was born with a contempt. Hell, God, Devil, right, wrong, sin, crime, and all the old gallery of curiosities—they may frighten boys, but men of the world, like you and me, despise them. Here's to the memory of Gray!'

It was by this time growing somewhat late. The gig, according to order, was brought round to the door with both lamps brightly shining, and the young men had to pay their bill and take the road. They announced that they were bound for Peebles, and drove in that direction till they were clear of the last houses of the town; then, extinguishing the lamps, returned upon their course, and followed a by-road toward Glencorse. There was no sound but that of their own passage, and the incessant, strident pouring of the rain. It was pitch dark; here and there a white gate or a white stone in the wall guided them for a short space across the night; but for the most part it was at a foot pace, and almost groping, that they picked their way through that resonant blackness to their solemn and isolated destination. In the sunken woods that traverse the neighbourhood of the burying-ground the last glimmer failed them, and it became necessary to kindle a match and re-illumine one of the lanterns of the gig. Thus, under the dripping trees, and environed by huge and moving shadows, they reached the scene of their unhallowed labours.

They were both experienced in such affairs, and powerful with the spade; and they had scarce been twenty minutes at their task before they were rewarded by a dull rattle on the coffin lid. At the same moment Macfarlane, having hurt his hand upon a stone, flung it carelessly above his head. The grave, in which they now stood almost to the shoulders, was close to the edge of the plateau of the graveyard; and the gig lamp had been propped, the better to illuminate their labours, against a tree, and on the immediate verge of the steep bank descending to the stream. Chance had taken a sure aim with the stone. Then came a clang of broken glass; night fell upon them; sounds alternately dull and ringing announced the bounding of the lantern down the bank, and its occasional collision with the trees. A stone or two, which it had dislodged in its descent, rattled behind it into the profundities of the glen; and then silence, like night, resumed its sway; and they might bend their hearing to its utmost pitch, but naught was to be heard except the rain, now marching to the wind, now steadily falling over miles of open country.

They were so nearly at an end of their abhorred task that they judged it wisest to complete it in the dark. The coffin was exhumed and broken open; the body inserted in the dripping sack and carried between them to the gig; one mounted to keep it in its place, and the other, taking the horse by the mouth, groped along by wall and bush until they reached the wider road by the Fisher's Tryst. Here was a faint, diffused radiancy, which they hailed like daylight; by that they pushed the horse to a good pace and began to rattle along merrily in the direction of the town.

They had both been wetted to the skin during their operations, and now, as the gig jumped among the deep ruts, the thing that stood propped between them fell now upon one and now upon the other. At every repetition of the horrid contact each instinctively repelled it with the greater haste; and the process, natural although it was, began to tell upon the nerves of the companions. Macfarlane made some ill-favoured jest about the farmer's wife, but it came hollowly from his lips, and was allowed to drop in silence. Still their unnatural burden bumped from side to side; and now the head would be laid, as if in confidence, upon their shoulders, and now the drenching sack-cloth would flap icily about their faces. A creeping chill began to possess the soul of Fettes. He peered at the bundle, and it seemed somehow larger than at first. All over the country-side, and from every degree of distance, the farm dogs accompanied their passage with tragic ululations; and it grew and grew upon his mind that some unnatural miracle had been accomplished, that some nameless change had befallen the dead body, and that it was in fear of their unholy burden that the dogs were howling.

'For God's sake,' said he, making a great effort to arrive at speech, 'for God's sake, let's have a light!'

Seemingly Macfarlane was affected in the same direction; for, though he made no reply, he stopped the horse, passed the reins to his companion, got down, and proceeded to kindle the remaining lamp. They had by that time got no farther than the cross-road down to Auchenclinny. The rain still poured as though the deluge were returning, and it was no easy matter to make a light in such a world of wet and darkness. When at last the flickering blue flame had been transferred to the wick and began to expand and clarify, and shed a wide circle of misty brightness round the gig, it became possible for the two young men to see each other and the thing they had along with them. The rain had moulded the rough sacking to the outlines of the body underneath; the head was distinct from the trunk, the shoulders plainly modelled; something at once spectral and human riveted their eyes upon the ghastly comrade of their drive.

For some time Macfarlane stood motionless, holding up the lamp. A nameless dread was swathed, like a wet sheet, about the body, and tightened the white skin upon the face of Fettes; a fear that was meaningless, a horror of what could not be, kept mounting to his brain. Another beat of the watch, and he had spoken. But his comrade forestalled him.

'That is not a woman,' said Macfarlane, in a hushed voice.

'It was a woman when we put her in,' whispered Fettes.

'Hold that lamp,' said the other. 'I must see her face.'

And as Fettes took the lamp his companion untied the fastenings of the sack and drew down the cover from the head. The light fell very clear upon the dark, well-moulded features and smooth-shaven cheeks of a too familiar countenance, often beheld in dreams of both of these young men. A wild yell rang up into the night; each leaped from his own side into the roadway: the lamp fell, broke, and was extinguished; and the horse, terrified by this unusual commotion, bounded and went off toward Edinburgh at a gallop, bearing along with it, sole occupant of the gig, the body of the dead and long-dissected Gray.

Printed in Great Britain
by Amazon

52997495R00206